Bonds
of
Vengeance

A TOM DOHERTY ASSOCIATES BOOK
NEW YORK

Bonds
of
Vengeance

DAVID B. COE

BOOK THREE

OF

Winds of the Forelands

BONDS OF VENGEANCE: BOOK THREE OF WINDS OF THE FORELANDS

Copyright © 2005 by David B. Coe

This book is printed on acid-free paper.

Edited by James Frenkel

Maps by Ellisa Mitchell

A Tor Book
Published by Tom Doherty Associates, LLC
175 Fifth Avenue
New York, NY 10010

www.tor.com

Tor® is a registered trademark of Tom Doherty Associates, LLC.

ISBN 0-312-87809-5
EAN 978-0312-87809-2

First Edition: February 2005

Printed in the United States of America

0 9 8 7 6 5 4 3 2 1

For Bill and Joan Berner

Acknowledgments

✦

Many thanks as always to my wonderful agent, Lucienne Diver; my publisher, Tom Doherty; the great people at Tor Books, in particular Scott Gould and Peter Lutjen; Carol Russo and her staff; my terrific editor and good friend, Jim Frenkel; his editorial assistant in New York, Liz Gorinsky; his assistant in Wisconsin, Derek Tiefenthaler; and his interns, in particular Michael Manteuffel and Kellen O'Brien.

As with all my books, and everything else I do, I'm most grateful to Nancy, Alex, and Erin. With their love, their support, and their laughter, they make my world a wondrous, magical place.

—D. B. C.

The Forelands

Ocean

THAR

Galdasten
of Eibithar

City of
Kings

Glyndwr

Thorald

North

Eardley

Thorald Wood

Thorald River

Lothar's Wash

Lake
Glendr

Glyndwr
Highlands

Jetaya
Uplands

Jetaya
Kett River

Brugaosa

CAERISSE

Cabrissan

Central Basin of
Caerisse

Lake Ilias

Red
Forest

Enharfe

Uniri
Wild

Steppe

The Narrows

Enwyl Island

Gulf of
Kreanna

Helke

Wethy
Crown

Duvenry

Duvenry
Wood

Jistingham

Aylsan Strait

Avatamme

WETHYRN

Grey Hills

Dark Wood of
Sanbira

Adamma's River

SANBIRA

Orlagh's River

Shyssir's
Wood

Lake
Yserne

Yserne

Sanbiri
Hills

Curlinte

Curlinte
Moor

Mornas
Plain

Great
Sanctuary

Kebb's Wood

Elined's Forest

Qusar's Mountains

AYLSA

Sea
of
Stars

Trescari
Frintae

Highlands

Trescari

Kinsarta

Range

Bonds
of
Vengeance

Chapter One

Glyndwr Highlands, Eibithar, year 880, Eilidh's Moon waning

n icy wind whipped across the road, screaming in the spokes of the cart like a demon from Bian's realm and tearing at Cresenne's wrap and clothes like a taloned hand. A heavy snow rode the gale, shards of ice stinging her cheeks and forcing her to shield her eyes.

The two great geldings pulling the cart plodded through the storm, their heads held low, the slow rhythm of their steps muffled by the thick snow blanketing the highlands. Occasionally the cart swayed, jostling Cresenne and ripping a gasp from her chest, but for the most part the snow had smoothed the lane, a small grace on a day more miserable than any she could remember.

Pain had settled at the base of her back, unlike any she had known before. It was both sharp and dull; she felt as if she had been impaled on the blunt end of a battle pike. Every movement seemed to make it worse, and more than once as the cart rocked, she had to fight to keep from being ill. She lay curled on her side—the one position in which she could bear each new wave of agony—cushioned by the merchant's cloth. She propped her head on the satchel in which she carried what few belongings she had taken with her from Kett: a change of clothes, a bound travel journal that had once belonged to her mother, a Sanbiri dagger, and the leather pouch that held the gold she had earned as a festival gleaner and chancellor in the Weaver's movement.

It was too cold to sleep, and even had it not been, the pain would have kept her awake. That, and her fear for the baby inside her.

"Are ye sure ye don' want t' stop, child?" the merchant called to her from his perch atop the cart, turning slightly so that she could see his red cheeks and squinting dark eyes. "There's plenty o' villages a'tween here an' Glyndwr. One's bound t' have a midwife for ye. Maybe even a healer, one o' yer kind."

I'm a healer myself, she wanted to say. *If this pain could be healed, don't you think I'd have done so by now?* "No," she said, wincing with the effort. "It has to be Glyndwr."

"If it's a matter o' gold, I can help ye."

She would have smiled had she been able. The man had been kinder than she deserved, sharing his food willingly, though the twenty qinde she paid him for passage up the steppe and into Eibithar hardly covered the expense of half her meals. The gloves she wore were his; an extra pair, to be sure, but still, no Eandi had ever treated her so well.

"Thank you," she said, trying to sound grateful. "But it's not the gold. I just need to get to Glyndwr; I need to have my baby there."

Even through the snow, she could see him frowning.

"I don' know how much farther the beasts can go," he said at last. "I'll do my best for ye, but I won' kill them jes' so ye can get t' Glyndwr."

She nodded and the man faced forward again. Then she closed her eyes, her hands resting on her belly, and tried to feel the child, even as she weathered another surge of pain. She remembered hearing once that a baby's movements decreased as the time of birth approached. It made sense. The larger it grew, the less room it had. Where once it had turned somersaults like a festival tumbler, it could now only wriggle and kick.

But with the onset of her labor, the baby's movements had ceased altogether, and panic had seized her heart.

"Just a bit longer, little one," she whispered in the wind. "We're in the highlands. It won't be long now."

Cresenne had known for some time now that she would have a daughter. At first she had assumed that such knowledge came to all gleaners who were with child. But speaking with the other Qirsi of Aneira's Eastern Festival, she learned this wasn't so. Yet this did nothing to diminish her certainty. There had been no dream, no vision to confirm the affinity she already felt for her child; she had wondered briefly if she might have been mistaken. She quickly dismissed the idea. It *was* a girl. The more she thought about it, the more confident she grew. Perhaps, she thought, her powers as a gleaner ran even deeper than she had known.

No sooner had she thought this, however, than she dismissed this notion as well. If her powers were so great, wouldn't she have realized sooner that Grinsa, the child's father, was a Weaver rather than a mere Revel gleaner? Wouldn't she have realized that this man she was supposed to seduce so that she might turn him to the purposes of the Qirsi conspiracy could not be used so easily? No, hers was an ordinary magic. Her powers had served her well over the years, and because she wielded three magics—fire, in addition to healing and gleaning—she had drawn the attention of the other Weaver, the one who led the Qirsi movement. But the power to know that her child would be a girl? That lay beyond her.

Instead, she was forced to consider a most remarkable possibility. What if she knew she would have a daughter because this child, begotten by her reluctant love for Grinsa jal Arriet, had communicated as much to her? What if the baby she carried already possessed enough magic to tell her so? She had never heard of such a thing. Most Qirsi did not begin to show evidence of their powers until they approached Determining age. Then again, most Qirsi women never carried the child of a Weaver.

Cresenne hadn't told anyone that her baby would be a girl—she hadn't even revealed it to the Weaver when he entered her dreams to give her orders or hurt her, though by defying him in this way, even over such a trifle, she invited death. It was her secret, hers and the baby's. Perhaps when she found Grinsa, she would tell him. Perhaps.

She would name the girl Bryntelle, after her mother. Even the child's father would not have any say in that. Bryntelle ja Grinsa. A strong name for a strong girl, who would grow to become a powerful woman, maybe even a Weaver. For if she could already tell her mother so much about herself, wasn't she destined for greatness?

"You won't have to fear anyone," Cresenne said, whispering the words breathlessly in the chill air. "Not even another Weaver." *Provided you survive this day.*

The cart lurched to the side forcing Cresenne to grip the nearest pile of cloth. The effort brought another wave of nausea. An instant later, they stopped, and the merchant climbed down from his seat to examine the geldings.

"What happened?" Cresenne called through clenched teeth.

"One o' the beasts stepped in a hole," the man said, squatting to rub the back leg of the horse on the left. "He's lucky he didn' break a bone." The man stood again and walked back to the cart. "It's no good, child. We have t' stop, a' least until the worst o' this storm is past."

She shook her head. "We can't."

"We've no choice. The beasts can't keep on this way."

"How far are we from Glyndwr?"

He stared past the horses as if he could see the road before them winding through the highlands. "Another league. Maybe two."

"We can be there before prior's bells."

"We won' ge' there at all if the beasts come up lame!"

"My baby—"

"Yer baby can be born in a village jes as easily as in Glyndwr."

"No, listen to me. There's something wrong." She swallowed the bile rising in her throat. "There's so much pain."

He smiled sympathetically. "I saw six o' my own born, child. It's never easy."

"This is different. I feel it in my back. And the baby hasn't moved for a long time."

His smile vanished, chilling her as if from a new gust of wind. "Yer back, ye say?"

Cresenne nodded, wiping tears from her cheeks with a snow-crusted glove.

The merchant muttered something under his breath and glanced at the geldings. Then he forced another smile and laid a hand gently on her shoulder.

"All right, child. Glyndwr i' 'tis."

He started to walk back to the front of the cart, then stopped and bent close to her again. "Yer too young t' be doin' this alone. Where's the father?"

"Glyndwr," she managed. "He's in Glyndwr."

The man nodded and returned to his seat atop the cart. In a moment they were on their way again, the jolt of the horses' first steps knifing through her like a poorly honed blade. Her stomach heaved and she scrambled to the edge of the cart and vomited into the snow until her throat ached. She sensed the merchant eyeing her, but he had the good sense not to say anything.

When her retching ceased, she crawled back to her frigid bed of cloth and lay down once more, hoping that what she had told the old man would prove true.

After the murder of Lady Brienne in Kentigern, and Tavis of Curgh's escape from the dungeon of the great castle, Kearney, then duke of Glyndwr, granted the young lord asylum. Kearney had since become king, and Tavis had traveled through Aneira with Grinsa, no doubt searching for the assassin responsible for Brienne's death. But if Grinsa and the Curgh boy had returned to Eibithar—and Cresenne had good reason to believe that they had—they would have to stop first in Glyndwr and ask the king's leave to venture farther into the realm. Getting word to the City of Kings and waiting for Kearney's reply would take time, especially during the snows. Even with all the time it had taken her to find a merchant who was headed north from Kett, Cresenne thought there might be a chance they were still in Glyndwr Castle. And if they weren't, at least she'd be able to find healers.

Gods, let her live.

The ocean of pain within her began to crest again, like a storm tide in the Aylsan Strait. There had been no jarring of the cart, no movement on her part. Her time was approaching. This baby was coming, whether or not they reached the castle. She let out a low cry, squeezing her eyes shut and gripping the cloth beneath her.

"Steady, child. We've still a ways t' go."

"Faster," she gasped. "Can't you go any faster?"

"I can, but it'll be a rougher ride."

"I don't care!" She cried out again, feeling her stomach rise, though there was nothing left in it.

The merchant called to his beasts and snapped the reins. The cart leaped forward, jouncing her mercilessly. Cresenne clung to the cart, trying to keep herself still and whimpering with each breath. The tide had her now. Agony was all around her; she was drowning in it.

She heard the merchant speaking to her again, but she had no idea what he was saying. Snow and wind still stung her face and she fixed her mind on that, for cold and miserable as it was, it was better by far than the appalling pain in her back.

"It's the promise of that baby that keeps you going," someone had once told her, speaking of childbirth. Had it been her mother? "All the pain in the world can't match the joy of that moment when your child is born."

All the pain in the world. Yes.

Except that she still didn't feel her daughter. Not at all. Bryntelle. Somewhere in this ocean she had to find Bryntelle. Before her babe was lost to the tide as well.

Grinsa stood at the open window, the biting wind off Lake Glyndwr making his white hair dance around his face like a frenzied child. Snow drifted into the chamber and a candle on the table near the window sputtered and was extinguished. It was a fine chamber, larger and more comfortable than one they might have expected had Kearney the Elder and his wife still lived in Glyndwr. But with the old duke now king, and so many of his advisors with him in Audun's Castle, Glyndwr Castle had a preponderance of empty chambers. This one, they were told, had once belonged to Gershon Trasker and his wife. No doubt they would not have been pleased to see snow covering the woven mat on the stone floor.

"Close the shutters," Tavis said, standing before the hearth. "The fire's barely warming the room as it is."

The gleaner watched the snow for another moment, then pulled the shutters in and locked them.

"I suppose we can wait another day," he said, facing the young lord. "Though if you're willing to brave the storm, I'm happy to go."

A messenger from the City of Kings had arrived at last just after the ringing of the midday bells. They had leave from the king to journey north to Curgh, though Kearney had warned that they would be safer if they remained in Glyndwr. He even went so far as to recommend that, if they chose to leave the highlands despite his misgivings, they take a small contingent of guards. "I have sent separate word to my son, Kearney the Younger," the king wrote, in a message addressed to Tavis, "instructing him to make available to you as many of his soldiers as you deem appropriate. I urge you to accept their protection."

Kearney wrote nothing of recent events in his realm; he didn't have to. His offer of an armed escort told Grinsa and Tavis all they needed to know about the state of the king's relations with Aindreas of Kentigern.

Tavis rubbed his hands together. "Let's wait another day. It's late now to be setting out. We'll make our preparations today and be ready to go with first light, regardless of the weather."

"All right. And the king's offer of guards?"

The young lord appeared to weigh this briefly. Then he shook his head. "We'll draw more attention with an escort than we will alone. And I don't want reach the gates of my father's castle with Glyndwr's men in tow." He smiled sadly. To those who hadn't grown used to the lattice of scars that covered his face, he might have looked bitter. "He'll think I don't trust him to protect me."

Grinsa smiled as well and shook his head. "I doubt that. But I understand."

The smile lingered on Tavis's face, but he kept his dark eyes fixed on the flames crackling in the stone hearth. "Do you think we're safe here for another night?"

There would have been no sense in lying to the boy. Ever since the day Kearney first granted Tavis asylum, when the armies of Kentigern, Glyndwr, and Curgh marched from the battle plain at the Heneagh River to Kentigern, where the duke of Mertesse had laid siege to Aindreas's castle, it had been clear to all of them that Glyndwr's men thought Tavis a butcher. Most of Eibithar believed that he had murdered Lady Brienne, and though it would have been an act of brazen defiance, many of Kearney's men would have thought themselves justified in killing him. Grinsa had little doubt that if Tavis had chosen to remain here in exile, rather than journeying south into Aneira, the young lord would be dead by now.

"We're safe here, yes," he said.

"But only because you're powerful enough to protect me."

Grinsa shrugged. "I don't think Glyndwr's men would act against you in the castle. To be honest, the real danger lies in our departure, after we leave the castle and city, but before we're out of the highlands."

Taking a long breath, Tavis nodded.

"We'll be all right," the gleaner told him. "It shouldn't be any worse than Aneira."

"That's a fine thing to say about my own kingdom."

"Do you want me to tell the duke that we won't need an escort?"

For a moment Tavis didn't respond. Then he shook his head, like a dog rousing itself from slumber. "No," he said, glancing at the gleaner. "I should speak with him, courtesy of the courts and all. There may come a day when we're both dukes under his father, or when I have to pay tithe to his throne. My father would tell me that this is a friendship to be cultivated."

"Your father is probably right." Grinsa stepped to the door. "I'll see if I can convince the kitchenmaster to give us a bit of food for the journey north."

The gleaner left the chamber and made his way to the kitchens. Before he reached them however, he nearly collided with an older man turning a corner in the dim corridor below the chambers. It took Grinsa a moment to recognize the castle's herbmaster.

"Forgive me, herbmaster," he said, stepping out of the man's path.

The man frowned at him and continued on his way. After just a few strides, however, he stopped.

"Say there," he called, narrowing his pale eyes. "Are you a healer?"

Grinsa hesitated, but only for an instant. Eibithar was his home, but he could ill afford to reveal too much about his powers, even here. "No, I'm not. Doesn't the castle have a Qirsi healer?"

"It does, but I haven't been able to find him."

"Is the need urgent?" Preserving his secret was one thing, letting an innocent die to preserve it was quite another.

"Not terribly," the herbmaster said, turning to walk away. "A woman at the gate in a difficult labor. I'll see to it."

"If I see the healer, I'll send him to you."

The older man raised a hand, but did not look back again. Grinsa watched him briefly, then resumed his search for the kitchenmaster.

The head of Glyndwr's kitchen, like most men in his profession, proved rather reluctant to part with any of the food in his realm. Grinsa had anticipated this, however, and had brought with him the message from Kearney. Though the king's words had no direct bearing on Tavis's need for food, they had the desired effect on the kitchenmaster, who, upon reading the letter, began barking orders at the servants around him. Suddenly, there wasn't a man or woman in Glyndwr who could give the gleaner what he wanted fast enough. Within a short while, Grinsa had two satchels packed full with dried meats, cheeses, hard bread, dried fruits, and even some wineskins, filled from the duke's private cellar.

He carried the satchels back to the chamber he shared with Tavis, intending to talk next with the stablemaster. The journey to Curgh would be easier and faster if they had mounts. Reaching the room, however, he found the door ajar and a pair of guards speaking with the young lord. Fearing for the boy's safety, he shoved the door open.

"What's all this?" he demanded, eyeing the soldiers warily and resting his hand on the hilt of his blade.

"This is the man you're looking for," Tavis said evenly, nodding in the gleaner's direction as the guards turned.

"What do you want with me?"

"There's a woman come to the south gate, sir. She's with child."

"Yes, I'd heard. I've already told your herbmaster that I'm not a healer."

"Begging your pardon, sir, but that's not why we've come. She was asking for you."

Grinsa narrowed his eyes. "What? By name?"

"Yes, sir. She even knew you was with Lord Curgh."

For some time, the gleaner didn't move. It hadn't been too long since he traveled with Bohdan's Revel, Eibithar's great festival. Certainly he knew a few people in the highlands, but none he could think of who had a daughter of age to bear children. Could it be a deception of some sort, an attempt by Tavis's enemies to leave the boy unprotected? Or had the Weaver found him already and sent this woman to kill him?

"Did she give her name?"

"No, sir. She came with a merchant, but he's gone now. We don't know who she is.

He didn't like the sound of this at all.

"All right," he said at last, gesturing toward the door. "Lead the way."

The soldiers stepped from the room and Grinsa started to follow.

"Do you want me to come?" Tavis asked.

The gleaner hesitated. "Yes." The boy would be safer if they were together.

"You have no idea who it could be?" Tavis asked.

He shook his head.

"Guess he's been busy," one of the men whispered, drawing a snicker from his companion.

Even as Grinsa felt his face redden, realization crashed over him, cold as Amon's Ocean in the snows. He faltered in midstride. It had been Elined's turn when he left her in Galdasten, and they had been together for nearly a full turn before that. Certainly it was possible . . .

"Grinsa?" Tavis asked, stepping closer to him. "Are you all right?"

"Is the woman Qirsi?" he asked the guards.

"Yes, sir."

"You know who—?" The boy stopped, staring at him. They had spoken of Cresenne only a few times. The pain of her betrayal still scored his heart and though he had cursed her name a thousand times since their last night together, the very thought of her still made his breath catch. Tavis had asked few questions about her, but for all his faults, the boy was observant and uncommonly clever.

"It's the woman from the Revel, isn't it? That would have been about the right time."

"It would have."

They started walking again, then broke into a run.

"Does your duke know of the woman's arrival?" Tavis asked the men, his voice carrying over the beat of their footsteps.

"Yes, my lord."

"Good. Tell him that Lord Tavis suggests he post guards outside her room at all times. She may be a member of the Qirsi conspiracy."

Grinsa looked at the boy sharply, but then gave a reluctant nod. Tavis was right. If this was Cresenne she needed to be watched, no matter her condition. He had loved her—perhaps he still did—but that did nothing to change the fact that she was a traitor, that her gold had bought Brienne's death.

They reached the herbmaster's chambers a few moments later and were greeted by a breathless scream from within. Grinsa reached for the door handle, only to draw back his trembling hand. His heart was a smith's sledge hammering in his chest. He tried to take a breath and nearly retched.

"Stay out here," he managed through gritted teeth.

"Of course," Tavis said.

Another scream made them both wince.

Grinsa gripped the door handle and entered the chamber. It was far too warm within, and the air smelled of sweat, vomit, and an oversweet blend of healing herbs. The gleaner gagged.

The herbmaster looked up at him, his face pale, a sheen of sweat on his brow glowing in the candlelight. "Are you the one she's been asking for?"

Grinsa nodded, unable to tear his eyes from the figure propped up in the bed next to the man. Her eyes were squeezed shut, her damp face a mask of pain, her white, sweat-soaked hair clinging to her brow. Her breath came in great gasps and she rocked her head from side to side as if trying to break free of some great evil.

Yet through it all, Grinsa could see the exquisite woman with whom he had fallen in love ten turns before. Silently he cursed Adriel, goddess of love, for smiting him so.

"Well, come on, then, and help me," the herbmaster said, laying a wet cloth on her forehead. "She's worsening, and the child may be lost already."

At that the gleaner hurried to the bed.

"What do you mean, it may be lost?"

"The baby is blocked somehow. I'm not a healer, and it turns out the duke's healer is gone from the castle. There may be an outbreak of Murnia's pox in one of the baronies and he's gone to check on it."

"So there's no one here at all?"

"I'm doing the best I can. I've given her dewcup and groundsel to stanch the bleeding, and dittany and maiden's weed for the blockage." He handed Grinsa a cup of pungent, steaming liquid.

"What's this?"

"A brew of a bit more dittany, as well as some common wort to calm her and ease the pain. She barely kept any of the first cup down. See if you can get her to take more."

The gleaner knelt beside the bed and carefully raised the cup to Cresenne's cracked lips.

"Drink," he whispered.

She took a small sip, choked on it, and turned her head away. An instant later, though, as if his voice had finally reached her, she turned to him, opening her eyes. Pale yellow they were, the color of a candle's flame, the color of passion and love and, ultimately, deepest pain. Unable to hold her gaze, he looked away, though he raised the cup again.

"You need to drink this," he said.

"You came." Her voice was scraped raw from her ordeal, and even as she spoke, her body convulsed.

"Yes. Drink. It will ease the pain."

"Save our baby, Grinsa. Please. She's dying. I know she is, and I'm not strong enough to help her."

"The herbmaster—"

She reached up and grabbed his arm, her slender fingers like a vise. "He can't save her," she said in a fierce whisper, forcing him to look into those pale eyes again. "He knows it, and so do you. But you can. We both know that as well. Whatever you may think of me—however much you hate me now—you must save our daughter."

"What does she mean?" the herbmaster demanded, leaning closer. "I thought you said you couldn't heal her."

A moment before Grinsa had been unwilling to meet her glance. Now he felt powerless to look away. "I told you I wasn't a healer," he answered, his eyes never straying from hers. "And I'm not. I'm a gleaner by trade." *And a Weaver by birth.* No doubt Cresenne knew this by now. She might have reasoned it out for herself, or she might have been told by the other Weaver, the one who led the conspiracy. The one for whom she had betrayed him. "But I do have some healing power."

"So you can help her?"

"Perhaps." He cupped her cheek with his hand. Her skin felt cold. "Perhaps together we can save the baby. You have healing magic as well. I remember from . . . from before."

Cresenne nodded slowly, her eyes widening at what he was proposing.

"How can you both help the baby?"

First, though, Grinsa knew, the Eandi had to leave the chamber, at least briefly. Grinsa looked up at the man. "This may take some time, herbmaster. Lord Tavis of Curgh is in the corridor just outside this chamber. Please tell him that we won't be leaving in the morning as we had planned."

The herbmaster frowned. "But—"

"I assure you, herbmaster, she'll be fine. Your brew has seen to that."

The man straightened, and, after a moment's hesitation, turned toward the door.

"Give me your hand," Grinsa whispered, looking at Cresenne once more.

She slid her hand into his, their fingers intertwining like lovers. Closing his eyes, Grinsa reached for her power with his own, entering her mind as he might have stepped into her dreams had she been sleeping. Instantly, the pain hit him, excruciating and consuming, as if Cresenne had struck at him with her fire magic. He couldn't imagine how she bore it. As he struggled to keep from succumbing to it himself, the gleaner followed her anguish to its source at the base of her back . . . and doing so, he encountered something utterly unexpected.

His eyes flew open. "I sense her!"

"She's alive?"

"Yes." He could feel the baby's pain as well. It wasn't nearly as severe as her mother's, but it was real nevertheless and growing worse by the moment.

"I'm going to try to stop the pain," he said. "I need you to help me, and then I need for you to relax all your muscles."

"Do you know what's wrong?"

"Yes." He lifted his head and called for the herbmaster, who returned immediately. "The blood cord is around the baby's neck," he told the man. "You'll have to slip it back over the baby's head before she can be born."

"How can you know this?"

"I just do." He exhaled, sensing that the man wasn't ready to accept such a poor explanation. "In trying to heal the mother's pain, I sensed the child's as well. Now please, as you told me before, there isn't much time."

"I've never done such a thing before."

"You have to try, herbmaster. She needs my healing magic. There is no one else." The man stared at him for several seconds, then nodded reluctantly.

Grinsa looked at Cresenne again. "Are you ready?"

She nodded, and together, their hands still clasped, they turned their powers toward her pain, so that magic flowed over the tender muscles and bone like cool water from the steppe. After a time, he began to feel her muscles slackening.

"Now, herbmaster. Quickly."

For several moments the room was silent, save for Cresenne's breathing and the low conversation of the soldiers in the hallway beyond the oak door.

Finally, the herbmaster exhaled loudly and nodded to Grinsa. "It's done."

"Thank you. You should be all right now," he told Cresenne, releasing her hand. He tried to stand, but she reached for his arm once more, her grasp more gentle this time, but no less insistent.

"Don't leave me." She faltered, her eyes holding his. "If . . . if something goes wrong again, I may need you."

He didn't want to stay. He still loved her. As much as he wanted to hate her, he couldn't. And now they were bound to each other by this child she carried, the daughter whose mind he had touched just a moment before. He knew that he should run, that he and Tavis should leave Glyndwr this night and drive their mounts northward heedless of the wind and snow.

But all he could do was nod and smile, taking her hand once again.

"All right," he said, the words rending his heart. "I'll stay."

Chapter
Two

Glyndwr, Eibithar

avis had thought that when Grinsa called the herbmaster back into the chamber, the woman's labor was near its end. But though she no longer screamed out with such desperate anguish, she continued to moan and cry, as if pushed beyond endurance. The soldiers who stood with him in the corridor had long since stopped talking among themselves. Mostly they kept their eyes lowered, exchanging looks occasionally, when the Qirsi woman sounded particularly wretched.

After a time, the duke of Glyndwr entered the hallway and the men straightened. He nodded to them as he walked past, but he didn't stop until he reached Tavis.

In most respects, Kearney the Younger was the image of his father. He had the king's bright green eyes and fine features, but his hair was a soft brown, perhaps like Kearney the Elder's had been before it turned silver. Though still two years shy of his Fating, the boy was already nearly as tall as Tavis. He was thin as a blade, however, and awkward. He wore the silver, red, and black baldric on his back, as did all Glyndwr's dukes. But the baldric and the sword it held appeared far too large for him. His father had chosen to give him the dukedom rather than appointing a regent to oversee the realm until Kearney the Younger's Fating. As Tavis looked at the young duke now, he couldn't help but wonder if the elder Kearney had placed too great a burden on the boy.

The Qirsi woman groaned again and Kearney glanced at the door, the color draining from his face.

"She labors still?"

Tavis nodded. "She doesn't cry out as she did earlier, but I've heard no babe yet."

Kearney faced him. "I've posted guards as you suggested, but I'd like to know more of this woman. You say she's part of the conspiracy?"

"We believe so, yes. My companion, the gleaner, knew her in the Revel. When he left for Kentigern, intending to win my freedom, she sent an assassin for him."

"So after her child is born, I should imprison her?"

One of the guards glanced at Tavis, then quickly looked away, his face twisting sourly. Kearney had seemed afraid of him a few turns before, when they met at Kearney the Elder's investiture. He since seemed to have accepted that Tavis was innocent of Brienne's murder, treating the Curgh lord as he would any noble from a rival house. Glyndwr's soldiers might consider Tavis a murderer, but their duke did not, and the young lord vowed silently to remember the boy's courtesy when he finally reclaimed his rightful place in the Curgh court.

"To be honest, Lord Glyndwr, I'm not certain what you should do. I felt you should know who the woman was before extending to her the hospitality of your house. But as to her future, I would have to defer to Grinsa's judgment."

"The Qirsi? He's but a gleaner."

"He's as wise as any of my father's ministers," Tavis said. "And the woman bears his child as we speak. I would ask you to consider his counsel before you do anything with the woman."

Kearney appeared to weigh this briefly before nodding once. "Very well. Still, we'd be wise to guard against any possible dangers. Aside from your friend, I intend to keep all Qirsi out of her chamber. My father and I don't suspect any of the white-hairs who serve Glyndwr, but we'd be fools to ignore all we've heard from other courts across the Forelands."

"It seems a most sensible precaution, Lord Glyndwr," Tavis said, and meant it. Kearney might look callow and ungainly, but there was more to this young duke than Tavis had thought. It seemed the king's faith had been justified.

"I trust you've been treated well since your arrival, Lord Curgh," the young duke said after a brief silence. Tavis noted that Kearney's eyes were fixed on the nearest of the guards.

"I have, Lord Glyndwr. Your castle is all it was reputed to be, and more, as are those who serve in your name."

"Thank you."

Tavis expected the duke to leave then, but Kearney surprised him again, leaning against the opposite wall, as if intending to take up Tavis's vigil as his own.

"You said she bears his child," the boy began, meeting the young lord's glance for just an instant. "Yet she sent an assassin for him?"

"Yes."

The duke pursed his lips. "What does a man do after such a thing?"

Tavis gave a small, sad smile and shook his head. "I hope never to find out, Lord Glyndwr."

Kearney grinned, but quickly grew serious again. "You also said that the woman hoped to stop your friend from reaching Kentigern. Do you believe she had something to do with . . . with the events there?"

"We believe the conspiracy did. We suspect that they wanted to make me appear her killer in order to drive a wedge between my father and Aindreas of Kentigern."

"It seems they succeeded."

Tavis felt his throat constrict. They had indeed. True, with Grinsa's help, and the timely intervention of Kearney's father, the kingdom had managed to avoid a civil war. But Tavis's father had been forced to relinquish his place in the Order of Ascension and Tavis had become an exile, cast out of his own court until he could prove his innocence, something he had not yet been able to do, though he'd confronted Brienne's killer in a tavern in Mertesse. From all Tavis had heard, Aindreas still threatened war against Curgh and had even gone so far as to challenge the legitimacy of Kearney the Elder's reign.

"Yes," he murmured. "I suppose they did."

"Forgive me, Lord Curgh, but my point is this: if this woman was involved with Lady Brienne's murder, then she can help prove your innocence."

Tavis stared at the boy as if he had just conjured mists and winds like a Qirsi.

"I'm not certain anyone would listen to her," he said, hoping the duke would gainsay him. So many times already in the turns since Brienne's murder, Tavis had thought that his redemption was at hand. The discovery of blood on the window shutter outside his chamber in Kentigern Castle; his encounter with Brienne's spirit in the Sanctuary of Bian; his struggle with the assassin in Mertesse. Yet each time, his hopes had been dashed. "She's a Qirsi traitor. Some will claim that she'd say anything to escape execution."

"Perhaps. But others may listen."

He had denied himself the luxury of hope for so long that he couldn't bring himself to embrace it now.

"Not the ones who matter. Not Galdasten or Eardley or Rennach. Certainly not Kentigern."

"Perhaps not at first. But you have to try. Surely you don't mean to ignore the possibility."

Tavis would have smiled had it not been rude to do so. He remembered what it was to be this young. Not very long ago he would have argued much as Kearney did now. But Aindreas's prison had aged him. Every cut of Kentigern's blade, every searing touch of his damned torches had struck at Tavis's faith in justice, or even in the mercy of the gods.

"No, Lord Glyndwr. I won't ignore the possibility. But neither will I celebrate my absolution prematurely. I've done that before, to my rue."

The boy nodded, seeming to sense that there was more at work here than he could fathom.

A lengthy silence ensued, to be pierced at last by a long wail from within the chamber that trailed off into gentle sobs. A moment later came a different sound, unexpected after so much anguish, and welcome as rain after drought: the cry of a babe.

For just a few seconds it was easy to forget that this was the child of a Qirsi traitor. Even the guards grinned.

"I should tell the prelate," the duke said, pushing away from the wall. Then his face reddened. "Though I suppose the child's mother will prefer that the prior come from Morna's Sanctuary."

This time Tavis did smile. "I would think so, yes."

Kearney started leave. "I'll send a message."

"Don't you want to see the child?"

The boy shook his head. "I still remember when my brother was born, and my sister as well. I'm not very fond of babies."

Tavis watched Kearney walk away, deciding that he liked this boy-duke. Finding himself alone once more with the guards, the young lord allowed himself a quick glance at the men positioned around him. Still, none looked at him. Even their duke's acceptance was not enough to overcome their suspicions.

The baby soon stopped crying, to suckle, or perhaps to sleep, but still Grinsa did not emerge from the chamber. After some time Tavis began to wonder if he should return to their room rather than wait any longer. Abruptly he realized that his journeying with the Qirsi was about to change drastically. Perhaps it had even come to an end. Grinsa was a father now and regardless of whether or not the woman was to be punished, Grinsa's first responsibility had to be to their child. For all he knew, the gleaner had forgotten that he was in the corridor and had no intention of leaving the woman's side until morning. Tavis could hardly blame him, and yet neither could he deny that he felt angry, even betrayed.

Just as he was ready make his way back to the chamber, however, the door opened, and the gleaner stepped out into the hallway, his skin flushed deep red, and his hair damp with sweat. In the past nine turns, he and Grinsa had been pursued by the king's guard in Aneira and the soldiers of Kentigern. Yet Tavis had never seen the gleaner look so weary.

"Is she all right?" the young lord asked.

"Yes. They both are, though we almost lost each of them in turn." A smile touched his lips and was gone. "I have a daughter. Cresenne tells me she's to be called Bryntelle."

"This was her decision? You have nothing to do with naming your own child?"

"You forget. My daughter is Qirsi. She'll always bear my name. Bryntelle ja Grinsa. I couldn't have chosen any better."

Tavis nodded. "Well, I'm . . . I'm happy for you."

"Thank you. I'm not sure that I am."

"What do you mean?"

Grinsa eyed the guards for a moment. "Walk with me." They started toward the nearest of the towers, descended the stairs, and stepped out into the castle's upper ward. The wind had died down, but snow still fell, the flakes soft and cold on Tavis's face.

For a short while, the two of them merely walked, following a meandering path through the Glyndwr gardens.

"What have I told you about her?" Grinsa finally asked, his voice low.

"Very little. I gather that you thought her a gleaner, just as she did you. I believe you loved her and that you only learned she was with the conspiracy after you left her."

"I should have known earlier." He shook his head. "She kept asking me about your Fating, about what I saw in the stone. The night I left she pretended to be hurt that I was leaving her, but I could tell there was more to it than that. I just chose not to see it for what it was."

"You were in love."

"That's a poor excuse."

Tavis started to argue, but quickly thought better of it. Grinsa expected a great deal of himself, more than was fair, it sometimes seemed to the young lord. If the gleaner had decided to blame himself for the woman's betrayal, there was little Tavis could do to talk him out of it. And since he had never been in love, Tavis could hardly claim to be knowledgeable on the subject. Instead he walked and waited for Grinsa to continue.

"I'd always known that I would have to find Cresenne eventually. She serves the conspiracy and she may know something about the Weaver who leads it. But I had hoped to put this off as long as possible. I wanted to find Shurik first, and since his death I've hoped that my sister could find out what I might otherwise have to learn from Cresenne. I didn't expect to see her this soon, and certainly not under these circumstances."

He didn't want to ask, but there seemed little choice. "Now that she's here, what are you going to do?"

The gleaner shrugged. "I don't know."

"Do you still love her?"

"I'd be a fool if I did."

Tavis grinned. "That does nothing to answer my question."

Grinsa actually laughed. "I don't suppose it does." His smile gave way to a grimace that told Tavis all he needed to know. "I don't know if I can love her after what she's done. But I am still . . . drawn to her."

"Does she know that you're—?" He stopped himself, searching the ward for Kearney's guards.

"Does she know the extent of my powers?"

"Yes."

"I never told her, but I think she's reasoned it out by now. It's one of the reasons she called for me today, maybe the only reason. She needed my healing magic."

"I expect that she called for you because you're the child's father. Whatever else lies between you, nothing can change that."

The gleaner smiled and put his hand on Tavis's shoulder. "Thank you. You may be right. But still your question raises an interesting point. If she knows I'm a Weaver, she's a danger to me, to Keziah, and to our hopes of defeating the conspiracy."

"Maybe now she can be turned from their cause."

"You mean because of the baby."

"I'm sorry, Grinsa," Tavis said, retreating quickly. "I wasn't implying that we should use your daughter as—"

"It's all right, Tavis. Before this is over, we may have to think in such terms. For now, though—for tonight—I'd just like to think of Bryntelle as my babe, and nothing more."

"Of course."

They both fell silent, though Grinsa gave no indication that he was ready to return to the herbmaster's chamber.

"There's more on your mind," the gleaner said at last. "I can always tell."

Tavis was eager to tell him of his conversation with Kearney, but this didn't seem to be the time.

"It's nothing."

The Qirsi halted, forcing Tavis to face him. "I don't believe you. Just speak and be done with it."

"All right." He took a breath. "The duke came to the chamber during Cresenne's childbirth. We spoke briefly, and he suggested that if she is or once was a part of the conspiracy, and if she had anything to do with arranging Brienne's murder, she might be able to prove my innocence."

Tavis saw the gleaner's jaw tighten, but his expression remained the same, and when he finally replied, his voice was even and low. "The duke makes an interesting point. What is it you'd have me do?"

"I don't know. First, we need to learn all she knows about what happened in Kentigern."

"I already intended to ask her about that, along with a host of other matters. What then?"

He shrugged. "If it turns out she knows something of the plans to kill Brienne and of the assassin, I suppose we'll need to bring her before the other dukes, perhaps even the king."

Grinsa looked away, his lip pressed in a tight line. "I don't want her journeying with us."

"It wouldn't be for long."

"Any time at all will be too much. She's dangerous, Tavis. For you, and especially for me."

"Even now? Even after what you two have shared this night?"

"She lied to me!" Grinsa said, his voice rising. "She tried to have me killed!"

"Perhaps she can change." It seemed to Tavis that he and the gleaner had reversed roles for just a moment. How often had Grinsa urged him to use reason, to move beyond his anger and resentment?

"Just because of the child?" The Qirsi shook his head. "That's a great burden to put upon such tiny shoulders."

"It's not just the child. You said yourself that you almost lost both mother and daughter tonight. If it weren't for you, Cresenne might be dead, or she might be mourning the babe rather than nursing her. Whatever happened between you before tonight, it's all different now. You saved her despite her betrayal, and together you share responsibility for another life." He chanced a smile. "Even I know enough to see the significance of that."

"We're not a family, Tavis. I don't think we ever can be. We're adversaries in a war. That's more powerful than any bond that ties us to each other." He rubbed a hand over his face, looking haggard and worn. "I'll consider what you're asking of me. Truly I will. And I'll speak with her tomorrow. But I make you no promises."

"I wouldn't ask you to." Tavis gestured toward the tower entrance. "You should sleep. It's been a long night."

Grinsa smiled wearily. "Are you ministering to me, Lord Curgh?"

"It seems someone needs to."

They turned and started back the way they had come. It was snowing harder now and already it was difficult to see their footprints in the dim light of the castle torches.

"I do think you're mistaken, though," the young lord said after a few moments. "Whatever else you and Cresenne may have been, you are a family now. Not even this war can change that."

She would have liked to sleep for days, uninterrupted. But Bryntelle woke her several times during the course of the night, the first few times to suckle, and the fourth time, Cresenne finally realized, because she had soiled her swaddling. When Bryntelle did sleep, Cresenne managed to as well, but as dawn broke, and the baby drifted into slumber during yet another feeding, Cresenne remained awake, lighting a nearby candle with her magic and staring at her daughter in the firelight.

She had promised herself that she would not be one of those mothers who saw her child through ensorcelled eyes. If the babe was ugly, so be it. She would admit as much to herself and to the world. And seeing Bryntelle for the first time, she had to concede that her baby did not look as she had hoped. Her skin was too red, her eyes swollen from the trauma of her birth, her head somewhat misshapen.

With every hour that passed, however, these flaws seemed to diminish, leaving Cresenne with a child she could describe only as beautiful. Overnight, her skin had lightened to a pale shade of pink, the swelling around her eyes had lessened. Her lips were perfectly shaped, as was her tiny nose. Her fingers and toes, wrinkled like the skin of some ancient Eandi, were smaller than Cresenne had ever imagined possible. Wisps of fine hair covered her head and the back of her neck, softer than Uulranni silk and as white as the new snow covering the highlands. Sitting in her bed, she felt helpless to do anything more than gaze upon her baby and weep, not for fear, or exhaustion, but for a joy unlike any she had known before.

Eventually, Bryntelle awoke again, her yellow eyes opening slowly. They were the color of fire, not quite as pale as Cresenne's but not so bright as those of her father.

"Are you hungry again, little one?" Cresenne whispered, placing a finger on the child's lips to see if she wanted to nurse. Immediately, Bryntelle took the finger in her mouth and began sucking on it. Cresenne laughed. "Very well."

She sat up straighter, wincing at the dull ache in her back and hips. She pulled off her shift and raised Bryntelle to her breast. The babe began to suckle greedily.

"You'd think I hadn't fed you all night."

She heard a knock at the door and felt her body tense.

"Come in."

She had expected Grinsa, but instead the herbmaster bustled in, crossing hurriedly to the shelf near her bed where he kept his herbs and stoppered vials of various extracts.

He glanced at her. "How are you feeling?"

"I'm sore. But other than that I feel all right, thank you."

"Some pain is normal, particularly after a difficult labor. And the child?"

"I think she's fine."

"Good." He stepped to the bed and looked at Bryntelle a moment. "She's nursing quite well, and her color seems right for a Qirsi child." He turned and started for the door. "I'd stay longer, but one of the guards was wounded in training this morning. I'll try to return later." He hesitated at the door, facing her again. "The gleaner is here to see you. Shall I send him in?"

She didn't answer. As much as Cresenne wanted to refuse him, to avoid this encounter for as long as possible, she knew that she couldn't, not after what Grinsa had done for her the night before. "Yes," she said at last, the word coming out as a sigh. "Thank you."

He nodded and let himself out of the room, leaving the door ajar. A moment later Grinsa walked in.

Cresenne, though very much aware of his presence the night before, hadn't really looked at him until now. She hadn't remembered his face being so thin, and though he had always been an imposing man, he appeared taller and broader in the shoulders than he had in Curgh. She silently cursed the racing of her pulse.

His bright eyes fell on her as soon as he entered the room, but he quickly averted his gaze, his face coloring, as if embarrassed to see her nursing the baby.

She should have found a way to use this against him, but instead she felt herself growing discomfited as well. With her free arm, she draped her shift over her shoulders and breast so that only Bryntelle's face could be seen.

Grinsa paced the room briefly, like a restless dog, finally stopping before the hearth.

"How do you feel?"

She shrugged, glancing down at Bryntelle. The baby's eyes were beginning to droop again. "Not too bad."

"And Bryntelle?"

She smiled in spite of herself. It was the first time someone else had used her—their—daughter's name.

"She's hungry all the time."

"Isn't she supposed to be?"

"I think so, yes."

He nodded, resuming his pacing.

"I believe she looks a little bit like you."

"Don't!" he said, halting near the door and glaring at her.

"Don't what?"

"Don't talk to me like we're husband and wife! Don't pretend that this child changes who you are and what you've done!"

"What do you know about who I am, Grinsa?"

"I know you're a traitor."

"A traitor to whom? The kingdom of Eibithar? I was born in Braedon and raised in Wethyrn. How can I betray a kingdom that's not my own?" She forced a thin smile. "From where I sit, you're the one who's guilty of treason. You've forsaken your people for the Eandi courts. You, of all people."

He narrowed his eyes. "What does that mean?"

"I think you know. We live in a land where you risk your life simply by admitting the extent of your powers, yet you willingly serve those who would be your executioners."

She thought he would deny it. Until this moment none in the movement, not even the Weaver himself, knew for certain that Grinsa was a Weaver as well. They suspected, of course, and Cresenne had been fairly confident of it for some time. But only now, watching him wrestle with the implications of what she had said, did she know beyond doubt.

"Do you really want Bryntelle to grow up in a world where her father fears for his life every day?" she went on. "And what if she inherits more from you than just her name and the shape of her face? What if she carries your power in her blood? Do you want her to live in fear as well?"

The Weaver had said much the same thing to her several turns before, walking in her dreams as he often did. At the time it had been mere speculation, one possibility among many. Yet still, it frightened her, as if the Weaver had already claimed her child for his movement. Yet here she was echoing his words to Grinsa, the one man in the Forelands whose claim to Bryntelle rivaled her own. As she searched Aneira for the gleaner, carrying his child, dreading her next dream of the Weaver, Cresenne had wondered if she could turn Grinsa to her cause and thus trade one Weaver for another. She had thought to control him then, so that rather than serving a Weaver she feared, she might wield this man as a weapon. Gazing at him now, though, seeing how he regarded her, with loathing in his yellow eyes, she wondered if that had been folly.

"Of course I don't want her to grow up as I did," he said, "bearing the burden of that secret and that fear."

"Then why do you fight us?"

"Because I've seen what your Weaver can do."

She felt the blood drain from her cheeks. "What?"

"Yes, I know about him. I know that he's capable of great cruelty, that he wields his power as a weapon, not just against the Eandi but against Qirsi as well."

"How is this possible?" she asked. "Has he seen you? Does he know where you are?"

"If I didn't know better, I'd think you were concerned for my safety."

"I am."

He let out a bitter laugh, though not before Cresenne saw something else flash in his eyes. "Of course you are. That's why you sent that assassin for me."

Actually, I've sent two. She hadn't intended to give Grinsa's name to the second man, Cadel, the partner of the one Grinsa killed. But Cadel asked upon learning that Jedrek was dead, and to have denied him the name would have raised his suspicions. "That was before. . . ."

"Before what? The baby? I've already told you, this child changes nothing."

She met his glare as long as she could, seeing once again all the hurt and hatred in his eyes, and knowing this time what lay at the root of it all. He had loved her so deeply. Twisted as it was now, that love still resided within him, waiting to be rekindled. Waiting to be used again. Yes, she loved him, too, though he would never believe that. But she loved Bryntelle more. Her love for this child was already the most powerful force in her life, more so even than her fear of the Weaver. No doubt he would sense this the next time he walked in her dreams. Only Grinsa could protect her now, if he could be convinced to do so. Folly or not, she had little choice but to try.

"She changes everything, Grinsa, and you know it. Not long ago I expect you thirsted for my death. You planned to capture me and have me executed as a traitor." She looked down at Bryntelle, who had fallen asleep at her breast. "You won't do that now. How would you explain such a thing to your daughter?"

"So much for a mother's love."

She looked up. "What does that mean?"

"You don't see a child lying in your arms. You see a tool, a weapon, perhaps even a shield."

"That's not true!"

"You think that I'll spare your life for her sake. You probably even think that you can use my concern for her to turn me to your purposes."

"I love her more than you could ever know!"

"Good. Because this blade cuts both ways."

Cresenne shivered. "I don't understand."

"I need you to do certain things. You sent the assassin for me, which tells me that you sent his partner—the singer?—to Kentigern. You paid him to kill Brienne and make it look like Tavis's crime."

She should have denied it, just as he should have denied being a Weaver. And like Grinsa, she couldn't bring herself to speak the words. "What is it you want?"

"As soon as you're able, you're going to come with us to the City of Kings, where you'll tell the king just what you've done."

"You can't be serious!"

He gave a thin smile, his reply.

"Why? So that I can restore the Curgh boy's good name. Don't you understand that I hate the Eandi, that I'd sooner bring ruin to the Forelands than help even one of their nobles?"

"Yes, I understand. But you should understand that if you don't do as I ask, I'll have Bryntelle taken from you, and I'll instruct the duke of Glyndwr to place you in his dungeon."

She searched his face for some sign that he was dissembling. Seeing none, she began to tremble, as if he had doused the fire and thrown open the shutters to the icy wind. "She needs me," she said in a small voice, holding Bryntelle so tightly to her breast that the baby awoke and began to cry.

"I know she does." He spoke gently now, stepping closer to the bed. "And if you do as I ask, she'll remain with you. I'll do what I can to make certain of that. But you have to begin to make right all that you did in the service of your Weaver."

"He'll kill me."

"I'll protect you."

She made herself smile, though abruptly there were tears on her cheeks. "If you really wanted to kill someone, is there a person in all the world who could stop you?"

"I don't know. I've never been so desperate to kill someone."

"Not even me?"

"I never wanted to kill you, Cresenne. And I never wanted to see you executed. To be honest, there was a part of me that hoped I'd never have to see you again at all. It would have been far easier that way."

She nodded, looking at Bryntelle again. A tear fell on the bridge of the girl's nose and she wrinkled her brow. Cresenne laughed, wiping the tear away.

He sat in the chair beside her bed. "What do you know about this Weaver?"

She stared at the fire. She had expected this, though she had hoped that she might be able to avoid his questions for a few more days, at least until she had time to decide whether or not to lie to him. For now, however, she realized that the truth would serve her as well as any lie. The fact was, she couldn't tell him much. "Very little," she said. "He makes certain of that."

"Is he in one of the courts?"

"Possibly."

"He seems to have a lot of gold. Do you know where he gets it?"

"No."

He exhaled through his teeth. "You have to give me more than this, Cresenne."

"I don't know more. I've never seen his face, he's never told me his name, or anything about his life beyond the conspiracy."

"How does he contact you?"

"He enters my dreams." She glanced at him for just an instant. "Isn't that how all Weavers do it?"

"How does he pay you?"

"He seems to have a network of couriers. I imagine he uses merchants to get the gold from one place to another."

"Are all of them Qirsi?"

"So far."

Grinsa looked down at his hands. "Has he ever hurt you?"

She felt her stomach clench. "What do you mean?"

35

"You know exactly what I mean. Has he hurt you?"

"Sometimes he needs to demonstrate the extent of his powers. It's not like he hurts me every time we speak."

He just stared at her, saying nothing.

"I suppose Eandi nobles never use the threat of pain to maintain discipline among those who serve them."

"An interesting comparison. If your Weaver is so much like an Eandi noble, what's the point of this movement he leads?"

"That's not what I meant!"

"No, I don't suppose it was."

"I didn't say he was like the Eandi," she said, her face growing hot. "I just meant that a leader—any leader—sometimes has to use force to keep order among those who follow him."

"I see."

She swiped at a strand of hair falling into her eyes. "Look, I'm still tired and sore from last night. Can we talk about this another time?"

Grinsa regarded her for a moment before giving a small nod and standing. "Of course. Do you need anything? Can I bring you some food, perhaps?"

"No, thank you."

He turned from the bed and started toward the door.

"Do you want to hold her?" she called after him.

He stopped, facing her again. "What?"

"Do you want to hold her? She's your daughter, too, and you haven't held her yet. I thought maybe you'd like to."

He stood motionless, as if held by some unseen hand.

Cresenne laughed aloud. Strange how this powerful man, who spoke of defeating the conspiracy and protecting her from the Weaver, could suddenly look so frightened at the notion of holding his own child.

"She's not going to hurt you. You're the Weaver, not she."

"I—I don't know how."

"To hold a baby?"

He approached the bed, his steps uncertain. "I've never held one before."

She lifted Bryntelle, holding her out to him. "Just be certain to support her head. Her neck isn't strong enough yet."

Grinsa swallowed, nodded. Taking her in his slender hands, he cradled her awkwardly against his chest. Immediately, Bryntelle began to cry.

"See?" he said, trying to give her back to Cresenne. "I told you I didn't know how."

"You're holding her like she's a crate of pipeweed. Have you ever held an animal in your arms?"

"Well, yes. A cat."

"Good. Hold her as you would a cat."

"By the scruff of her neck?"

Cresenne arched an eyebrow.

"Please take her," he said. "I'll try again another time. I think she senses that you and I are at odds right now."

She shrugged, taking Bryntelle to her breast again. The baby fretted a moment longer, then began to nurse again.

"Do you think there'll ever be a time when we're not at odds?" Cresenne asked, her eyes fixed on the baby.

"I hope so, for Bryntelle's sake."

"So do I." She looked up, meeting his gaze. "Truly I do."

"I'll check on the two of you later." He crossed to the door. "Consider what I've told you, Cresenne," he said, pausing with his hand on the door handle. "Whatever affections I still harbor for you, whatever I may feel for our child, I won't let sentiment be my guide in this. I can't. Too many people are depending on me."

She eyed him for a moment, then nodded, though she kept her silence. At least until he was gone.

"Don't worry," she whispered to the baby, once the door had closed. "He won't really take you away from me. He can't. We're all he has in the world, unless he actually thinks of that Curgh boy as family."

Brave words. But her hands still trembled as they had when he first threatened to take Bryntelle. A voice in her head screamed for her to take the baby and flee, but her body wasn't ready for a walk through the corridors, much less flight through the highlands. Which actually worked to her advantage. It would be several days before the herbmaster would let her leave for the City of Kings, and the journey would have to be a slow one. That gave her time.

Grinsa might have been allied with the Eandi now, but he was a Weaver. And who had more to gain from the Qirsi movement than a Weaver?

A Weaver with a child.

Chapter
Three

Curlinte, Sanbira

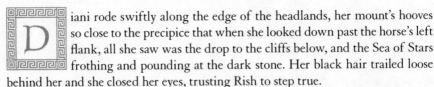iani rode swiftly along the edge of the headlands, her mount's hooves so close to the precipice that when she looked down past the horse's left flank, all she saw was the drop to the cliffs below, and the Sea of Stars frothing and pounding at the dark stone. Her black hair trailed loose behind her and she closed her eyes, trusting Rish to step true.

There was still snow in the northern highlands and even atop the highest ridges of the Sanbiri Hills a mere two days' ride to the south and west. But here in Curlinte, where the wind blew warm off the sea and the sun shone upon the headland moors, it seemed that the planting had come early. She wore a cloak yet, and a heavy blouse below that. Nonetheless, there could be no mistaking the sweet hint of the coming thaw carried by the mild breeze, or the exuberant singing of the sealarks that darted overhead and alighted to sun themselves on the boulders strewn across the grasslands.

Her father had not approved of her decision to ride today. Her mother had been dead but a turn and a day, and though the castle banners flew high again, and those living in the duchy were permitted once more to open the shutters on their windows, it was, he told her, still too soon for Curlinte's new duchess to be taking frivolous rides across the headlands.

"The people will look to you now," he had said, appearing weary and old, as if grieving for his wife had cost him years. "You lead them. You must help them through this time of loss."

"I understand," she answered, knowing that he would think her childish and irresponsible. "And this is the way I see through. Mother was ill for more than a year. Curlinte has had her shutters closed for too long. I ride to end the mourning." She stepped forward then and kissed his cheek. "It's what Mother would have done."

His eyes blazed, and she thought for just an instant that he would berate her. Instead, he turned away. She could see from his expression that he recognized the truth of what she had said. He would be angry with her for a time, but he would forgive her.

Her father had been right about one thing. The people of the duchy needed her now. Diani was two years past her Fating, old enough to assume command of the castle and Curlinte's army. But she had yet to prove herself. Her grandmother had lived to be nearly eighty, so that when her mother became duchess, much of the duchy already knew her. Dalvia had been mediating disputes and joining the planting and harvesting celebrations for many years. Diani had started to do the same when her mother became ill, but there hadn't been time to visit all the baronies, not with the more mundane tasks of accounting the tribute and paying tithe to the queen intruding as well.

Normally her father would have helped her, but as duke, it was his duty to train the soldiers, and as husband, his place was by Dalvia's bed, watching as she wasted away.

If this weather held, Diani decided, she would spend the early turns of the planting visiting all the baronies to oversee the sowing of crops. It was important that she be seen, particularly now, and not just in the courts but in the villages and farming communities of the Curlinte countryside as well. Even her father could not find fault with such a plan.

Diani reined Rish to a halt at the promontory, swinging herself off the beast so that she might walk out to the edge. There she sat on the stone and closed her eyes once more, feeling the sun on her face. There would be less time for these rides in the turns to come—the demands of the duchy would tether her to the castle, or force her to ride away from the sea. Either way, these rides to the headlands were about to become a rare luxury. She knew it was foolish, but she begrudged the loss.

It was here that she and her father had scattered her mother's ashes just a turn before. Dalvia had loved this spot as much as Diani did. Often, before her mother grew ill, the two of them, mother and daughter, duchess and lady, had ridden out together to discuss matters of state, or just to escape the burdens of the castle.

Their last ride together had come on a cold, clear day near the end of Kebb's turn more than a year before. Her mother had been more talkative than usual that day, perhaps sensing that her health was beginning to fail, and she had offered a good deal of counsel.

"A duchess must marry well," she had said. "Your father will want you to marry for an alliance—one of the brothers Trescarri I would imagine, or perhaps Lord Prentarlo."

"I prefer one of the twins to Prentarlo," Diani said, smiling.

Her mother had glanced at her, a smile tugging at her lips and her dark eyes dancing. "As would I. But my point is this. A marriage based on military might is as fraught with peril as one based solely on your mate's good looks or skill with a blade. With luck you'll lead Curlinte long after his hair thins and his muscles begin to fail him." She stared out at the sea, brilliant blue that day, like a gem. "Marry a man you trust, a man with whom you can share your fears and doubts as well as your triumphs. Your father is still a fine swordsman." The smile returned briefly. "And I still think him handsome. But I value his friendship above all else. You would do well to marry as fine a man."

Diani glanced sidelong at her mother. "Choosing a husband seems more complicated than I realized," she said lightly. "Perhaps I'd be wise to claim both the Trescarris as my own."

Her mother laughed long and hard. At times it seemed to Diani that this was the last she had ever heard of her mother's strong, deep laughter. She knew it wasn't—in the turns that followed they managed to share small precious moments that shone like gold and then vanished, as if illusions conjured by festival Qirsi. But it might as well have been the last. Grief had consumed Castle Curlinte ever since. And as much as she wanted to order an end to their sorrow, to banish her mother's ghost with some sweeping ducal decree, she knew that her father clung to the pain, as if he thought it better to mourn than to live without his love.

She would ride to the baronies to reassure her people. But she couldn't deny that she rode also to seek refuge from Sertio's despair.

She heard a falcon cry out, and opening her eyes, saw a saker soar past her, following the contour of the cliff. It was the color of rust, of the rich soil in the hills. Its wings remained utterly still, its tail twisting to direct its flight. The Curlinte crest bore an image of a saker—seeing one, it was said among her people, was a portent of good tidings. Diani watched the bird as it glided up the coast, until she lost sight of it among the angles of the rock face.

From behind her, Rish snorted and stomped.

"I know," she said, climbing to her feet. "Father will be expecting us." She stepped to her mount and tightened his saddle before starting to swing herself onto his back.

The first arrow embedded itself just above her breast on the left side, knocking her to the ground. No warning, no sense of where the archer had concealed himself, though she guessed that he must be in the jumble of hulking grey stones just off the promontory.

A second arrow skipped harmlessly off the stone and past her head before diving into the sea below. A third struck her thigh, making her cry out.

She grabbed at the shaft of the arrow in her chest to pull it out, then thought better of it, remembering instructions her father had given her many years before.

"You'll do more damage pulling the thing out than it did going in," he had told her. "If you have to break off the shaft, do. But don't remove it. You'll bleed to death."

Right.

"Down, Rish!" she said through clenched teeth, as another arrow struck the stone and clattered over the edge.

She crawled back a bit toward the cliff, flattening herself against the stone, her chest and thigh screaming. The pain wasn't spreading, though—no poison on the points.

Rish lowered himself to the ground. Diani scrambled over to him, took hold of his mane and the pommel of his saddle, and kicked at his flanks with her good leg.

"Ride, Rish! Now!"

A third dart buried itself in the back of her shoulder and yet another whistled past her ear. But by now she was speeding away from the promontory, clinging desperately to Rish's neck and steering him from side to side to present a more difficult target. She wasn't certain she could hold on if she was struck again; if Rish was hit her life would be forfeit. Even as she rode, though, she glanced over her bloodied shoulder toward the stones. She saw her attackers immediately. They weren't bothering to conceal themselves anymore.

Two men, both with heads shaved, both tall and wearing dun cloaks. They loosed their bows again in unison, but the arrows fell short. She was too far.

Diani shifted her gaze to the shaft jutting from her chest. There were two rings just below the fletching—yellow and blue, the colors of Brugaosa. Of course. The Brugaosans had long been Curlinte's sworn enemies. They were a patriarchal dukedom within the Sanbiri matriarchy, and had long chafed at the Yserne Supremacy. Unwilling to oppose the Crown openly, however, they had instead sought to undermine Yserne's strongest allies: Curlinte, Prentarlo, and Listaal. The Brugaosans often boasted that theirs was the finest ducal army in the realm, second in skill and strength only to the queen's own. Their archers were renowned throughout all the southern Forelands.

Except that even through the pain, even dazed and weak, Diani knew that the Brugaosans wouldn't make an attempt on her life. Yes, Brugaosa and Curlinte were rivals. There had even been a time within the last hundred years when the two houses had spoken brazenly of going to war. Many, including her father, still blamed Brugaosa for the murder, a bit more than three years ago, of Cyro, Diani's brother. But Diani saw a darker, more sinister purpose behind Cyro's assassination, and she felt certain that the same shadowy hand had given gold to the archers whose arrows had pierced her flesh.

An assassination attempt at the promontory implied intimate knowledge of her habits, and such knowledge had to have come from within the court.

"The conspiracy," she murmured into Rish's mane.

Which meant that danger awaited her within the walls of Castle Curlinte looming before her.

She whispered a word to her mount, and he slowed. Glancing behind her again, Diani saw no sign of the assassins. She didn't remember seeing horses with them, and even if they had been riding, they wouldn't have followed her so close to the castle. If she rode to the west gate or the sea gate, too many people would see her. Word of the attack would spread through the city and castle like the pestilence, and the traitor, whoever it was, would have time to prepare for her arrival.

She urged Rish onward again, steering him toward the south gate, which she could reach without having to ride through the city. She was starting to feel dizzy and cold—she couldn't imagine that she had ever thought this day warm enough for a ride to the promontory.

Four soldiers stood at the gate watching her approach. They knew her horse, and so it was not until she was quite close to the castle that they realized something was wrong. Two of the men started forward while the other two ran toward the inner barbican.

"Don't raise the alarm!" she called to them, the effort nearly toppling her from her saddle.

The first of the guards reached her and eased her from atop the mount. There were tears in his eyes. Was she dying, then?

"My lady! Who did this?"

"Assassins, at the promontory."

"We should send men there. Those are Brugaosan arrows."

"No, it's not them." It was getting very difficult to keep her thoughts clear. "Get me to my father's chamber. And find a healer, a Qirsi. But be quiet about it. No one but the healer should know I'm here."

"But, my lady—"

"Just do as I say. And hide my mount. No one should know I've returned."

She made herself stare at the man, his face swimming before her eyes. "Do you understand?"

He nodded. "Yes, my lady. It shall be done."

Diani closed her eyes, feeling consciousness slip away. "My father's chamber," she managed to say again. Then blackness.

She awoke to the sound of bells. Distant, tolling in the city. Her vision was blurred and she didn't recognize the room. She tried to sit up, but was held to the bed by strong hands.

"What is the time?" she rasped.

"Those are the prior's bells." Her father's voice.

"What day?"

"The same day you rode. The tenth of the waning."

She took a breath, allowing herself to relax. Slowly, as her eyes adjusted to the candlelight, she recognized the familiar shapes of her father's quarters. She was lying on her back, so at least one of the arrows had been removed. She put a hand to her chest and then her thigh. All of them were gone.

A pallid face loomed above her, framed by white hair. A healer, one she didn't know.

"You were fortunate, my lady. The injury to your leg was a small matter, but less than half a span's difference with either of the other two arrows, and you would have died on the moors."

Diani exhaled slowly, nodded. "Thank you."

"She needs rest," the white-hair said, facing her father. "Have some soup brought from the kitchens and keep her still for a few days. I've mended the wounds, but her body needs time to heal. She bled a great deal."

Her father stepped to her bed and took her hand. "All right."

The man started to go.

"Wait," Diani said, making herself sit up. The room spun like a child's top, and she nearly passed out.

The healer frowned. "Didn't you hear what I just said?"

"You can't leave," she said, ignoring the question.

"What?"

"I'm sorry, but you'll have to remain here until I know who's responsible for what happened today."

"But I live in the city. I have family there."

She glanced at her father. "How many people know he's here?"

"Only the two of us, and the two guards who brought you to me. After they told me what you'd said, I thought it best to find a healer from outside the castle. They took him out of the city through the sea gate and then around to the south to enter the castle. As long as he's escorted back the same way, I don't think there's any danger in letting him go."

She looked briefly at the healer. "Forgive me."

"Of course, my lady." He started toward the door again.

"I take it you know nothing of the conspiracy?" she said, before he could leave.

"Nothing beyond what I've heard, my lady."

"You know what I'll do to you if I learn that you're lying?"

He gave a thin smile. "I have some idea, yes."

She gave a single nod. "Go, then. Don't speak of this to anyone, not even your wife."

"Yes, my lady."

He opened the door. The same two guards who met her at the gate stood in the corridor, just outside the chamber.

When the healer was gone, Diani lay back down again, closing her eyes and waiting for the dizziness to pass.

"I already have a hundred soldiers searching the moor," her father said. "But they have little idea of what they're looking for other than archers. I told them that I'd received word from one of the baronies that thieves with bows had been seen on the roads." He paused, gazing down at her hand, which he still held. "Did you see the men who did this?"

"Briefly. Tall, shaved heads, wearing riding cloaks."

"Did they have horses?"

"Not that I saw." She touched her shoulder gingerly—it was still tender. "You saw the arrows?"

"Yes. Brugaosans?"

"That's what someone wants us to think."

"But you don't believe it."

"Why would Edamo so such a thing, Father?" she asked, her eyes still closed. "He has no reason. With me dead, power would fall to you, a man with nothing to live for but vengeance. It makes no sense."

"Maybe he wants war."

"To what end? His army may be greater than ours, but he must know that under such circumstances, the queen would come to our aid. Even Trescarri might fight on our behalf." She shook her head. "No, this wasn't Brugaosa."

"Then who?"

At that, she did open her eyes. "You have to ask?"

He twisted his mouth sourly and returned to the chair by his writing table. "We have no evidence that the conspiracy has been active here in Curlinte."

"No, we don't. But Cyro's murder has never been explained to my satisfaction, and we've heard enough from Aneira and Eibithar to convince me that the Qirsi are sowing discontent across the Forelands."

"Cyro was killed by the Brugaosans," he said, looking away. "We know that." She saw the pained expression on his face and felt an aching in her chest. Three years since her brother's death and still his loss was a raw wound on their hearts.

"Why?" she said, her voice thick. "Because of the garrote? Because Edamo had threatened him after their encounter in the Dark Wood?"

"Isn't that enough?"

She sat up again, her head feeling a bit clearer. "He's denied it, Father. If he was going to make such a show of killing him—using the garrote rather than poison, or a dagger—why would he bother denying it?"

"He's Brugaosan! He needs a reason to lie?"

"You know what I mean."

Her father said nothing and Diani knew that no good would come of arguing the point further.

"Those men who attacked me today were not Brugaosans," she said again. "I'm certain of it. It was the conspiracy."

To her relief, Sertio didn't ask her for proof. "Which one do you think is the traitor?"

"That I don't know. But I think we should assume the worst."

Sertio winced. "Kreazur?"

Kreazur jal Sylbe had served as Curlinte's first minister for six years, and as second minister for three years before that. In truth, though Diani had never cared for the man, she didn't want to believe it either. He had been her mother's favorite among all the Qirsi in the castle, and while others, Diani's father among them, had urged her to look outside the castle for a new minister when Kreazur's predecessor died, she had insisted on promoting the underminister. Just considering that he might have betrayed Dalvia's trust in this way made Diani tremble with rage.

"Perhaps it's not him," she said weakly. "In which case we'll try the underministers."

"But we start with Kreazur," her father said. It was hard to tell if he was acquiescing to her wishes or acknowledging his own doubts.

"I think so."

"What do you want me to do?"

"Summon him. When he gets here, tell him that you expected me back hours ago and that you're concerned for my safety."

"Where will you be?"

She scanned the chamber briefly. She had been in this room thousands of times, but it had been years since she and the other court children played find-the-wraith. There was a small space beside her father's wardrobe in the far corner of the room. During the warmer turns, when the windows were open, it would have been a poor place to hide. But today, in the cold of the snows, with the shutters locked, the space was only dimly lit.

"There," she said pointing. "By the wardrobe."

Her father nodded. "All right. What do you expect him to say?"

"I'm not certain," she said, shrugging. "I suppose I'll know when I hear it."

"Wouldn't it be easier to wait until we find the archers?"

"We may not find them."

Sertio nodded, still looking uncertain.

She stood and walked stiffly back to the wardrobe. Her entire left side ached still and her thigh was throbbing. It would be days before she could ride again.

Sertio crossed to the door and spoke quietly to the soldiers in the corridor. Then he returned to his table and sat, holding his head in his hands. Diani hadn't given much thought to him since waking from her ordeal. Seeing her bloodied, with arrows jutting from her body in all directions, must have struck at his heart. They had just recently lost her mother, and for at least a moment he probably thought that he was about to lose his daughter as well.

The knock at his door came sooner than Diani had expected. Her father glanced quickly in her direction, then faced the door again. He looked frightened and she could see his hands trembling.

"Enter," he called.

She heard the door open, but couldn't see it from where she stood.

"You summoned me, my lord?" The first minister's smooth voice.

"Yes, Kreazur. I'm wondering if you've seen the duchess since midmorning. I expected her to return from her ride long before now. I'm . . . I fear for her."

"I haven't seen her, my lord. But I doubt there's cause for concern. She's an accomplished rider, and she handles a sword well." A brief pause. "She learned from the best."

Her father gave a thin smile. "Thank you, Kreazur. Just the same, I wonder if we shouldn't send out a party of soldiers."

"I don't think that's necessary, my lord. I'm sure she'll be returning shortly. You know how the duchess loves her rides. No doubt she's simply enjoying the last few hours of daylight."

Sertio looked down at his hands, his eyes flicking in her direction for just an instant. Diani wasn't certain what to do. Even if Kreazur had betrayed them, she realized too late, he would have been expecting to have such a conversation with her father. If they wished to surprise him, they would have to let him see her.

Her father glanced at her again and she shook her head.

"You're probably right, First Minister," Sertio said, standing. "Thank you."

The Qirsi stood as well. "Of course, my lord." He walked toward the door. "If you need me, I'll be in my quarters."

"Very good, Kreazur. Again, my thanks."

She heard the door open and close, but still Diani waited a few moments before stepping out of the shadows.

"Perhaps it's not him," her father said, sounding relieved.

"I'm not convinced of that. We're going to wait a short while and then summon him again. And this time when he comes, I'll be sitting right out in the open."

"Let him see a wraith, eh?"

She grinned.

They waited until the tolling of the twilight bells. Once more Sertio sent the soldiers for Kreazur, and once more they hadn't long to wait. His knock came just a few minutes later.

Diani had seated herself just beside her father's table, facing the door, so that she would have a clear view of his face when he saw her.

"Yes, my lor—"

He hesitated at the sight of her, his eyes widening slightly. "Duchess," he said, mild surprise in his voice. It was the first time he had called her that; she had rarely heard him address her mother that way. Always "my lady."

"You didn't expect to see me, Kreazur?"

"Not here, my lady. The guard who summoned me said only that the duke wished to speak with me. To be honest, I feared that you still hadn't returned. Your father has been worried."

"Perhaps you thought your assassins killed me on the moor."

"Assassins? On the moor?" He glanced at the duke. "Are you saying there was an attempt on your life?"

"You knew nothing of this?" Sertio asked.

"Of course I didn't, my lord." He looked at Diani again. "Were you wounded, my lady?"

She raised an eyebrow. "I'm touched by your concern."

The Qirsi narrowed his eyes, bright yellow in the candlelight. "My lady, I don't understand. Are you accusing me of being in league with these men?"

"Does it surprise you that I should have figured it out?"

"There is nothing to figure out! I didn't have anything to do with this!"

He appeared genuinely alarmed, which only served to make his deception that much more galling.

"You deny being party to this conspiracy wreaking havoc across the Forelands? You deny paying these men to kill me?"

"I do! My lady, I have served your house since you were but a child, years from your Determining. I never gave your mother cause to doubt my loyalty. What cause have I given you?"

"Today's attempt was cause enough."

"You're certain it was the conspiracy?"

"Of course it was!" She propelled herself from the chair angrily, gasping at the pain in her shoulder and thigh.

"You were wounded."

She said nothing, refusing to look at him.

"She was struck by three arrows," her father said. "Two near her shoulder and one in the leg. The healer who attended her says she's lucky to be alive."

Kreazur exhaled through his teeth. "I'm sorry, my lady. Truly. And I swear to you, this is the first I've heard of it."

She faced him, schooling her features. "What if I told you that we've captured the men, that they've already confessed to working on behalf of the Qirsi, and that they named you as the man who paid them?"

"I'd say they're lying." His voice didn't waver, nor did his gaze. Not that she should have been surprised. He would have had to be an accomplished liar to have managed to fool her mother all these years. Or perhaps he just knew that she was lying.

"You expect us to believe you over them?"

"Yes, my lady, I do," he said, pride and anger in his tone. "These men have just tried to murder you, while I have served House Curlinte faithfully for nearly ten years. How is it that they've earned your trust and I haven't?"

Because they're Eandi and you're Qirsi. She couldn't say it, of course. She couldn't even believe she was thinking it. But there it was. With the conspiracy killing nobles throughout the seven realms, she realized that she would have been more willing to trust Eandi assassins than her mother's first minister.

Kreazur seemed to sense the truth that lay behind her silence. He turned to Sertio.

"And you, my lord. Do you believe me a traitor as well?"

"I don't want to, First Minister. Please believe that. But the men who attacked Diani used Brugaosan arrows and had their heads shaved like—"

"Father!"

He stared at her briefly, until Diani finally lowered her gaze.

"They had their heads shaved as Brugaosan warriors do."

Kreazur shook his head. "The Brugaosans wouldn't risk a war by killing the duchess. They have too much to lose."

"Precisely," the duke said. "Which leaves us with the conspiracy."

"I see. But there are other Qirsi in Castle Curlinte. Why assume that I'm the traitor?"

"Because no other Qirsi in Curlinte wields as much influence," she said, rounding on him. "Because no one else knows as much about my habits. Because no other Qirsi is paid so well, or is more likely to have allies throughout the Fore-lands."

"So it's precisely because I'm first minister. My reward for serving your mother so well is to be the most suspect in your eyes?" He shook his head. "That makes no sense at all!"

"Perhaps not to you. It seems perfectly reasonable to me. To whom else would the leaders of this conspiracy turn?"

"Even if they had turned to me, my lady, I would have refused them. If you can't see that, then you're far less wise than your mother believed."

She felt her face color. "How dare you!"

"First Minister," her father broke in, "perhaps you should leave us for a time so that I might speak with the duchess alone. We'll summon you again shortly."

"No!" Diani said, her wounds throbbing. Had that healer done anything more than close her skin? "He's not to leave, at least not alone."

"Diani!"

"I'm duchess now, Father—such matters fall to my discretion. Under Sanbiri law an attempt on my life is tantamount to an assault on our castle; it is, in essence, a declaration of war, and I intend to treat it as such."

"A declaration by whom?" the minister asked.

"By the conspiracy. You yourself said that the Brugaosans wouldn't have done this—and I came to the same conclusion while their arrows were still in my flesh." She turned toward the door. "Guards!" she called.

An instant later the door opened and two guards entered the chamber.

"Yes, my lady?"

"I want the first minister taken to the prison tower."

The Qirsi gaped at her. *"What?"*

She ignored him, keeping her gaze on the guards, who were eyeing the minister with manifest unease. As large and powerful as these men appeared, she knew that they feared Qirsi magic. She also knew, however, that Kreazur posed no real danger to them. Like most Qirsi, he was weak, and though he wielded powerful magics—gleaning, mists and winds, language of beasts—they were not of a type to harm the soldiers.

"He can't hurt you," she said. "He wears a dagger on his belt, but I doubt you'll have any trouble taking it from him."

"You can't do this!" the minister said, a plea in his golden eyes.

Her father took a step toward her. "He's right, Diani. You mustn't go through with this. We don't know for certain that any Qirsi was involved. Imprisoning Kreazur won't accomplish anything. Indeed, for all we know, you're punishing an innocent man. That isn't the Curlinte way."

"What am I supposed to do, Father? Pretend that nothing happened today? Wait for them to try again?"

"The men who attacked you are lying, my lady," Kreazur said. "I had nothing to do with this. Don't you see? They're trying to weaken House Curlinte by sowing distrust between us."

Diani and her father exchanged a look.

"You should at least tell him the truth," Sertio said, his voice flat.

She cast a quick look at the Qirsi.

His entire body appeared to sag. "You were lying. You haven't captured the men. You're acting on your mistrust and nothing more."

She stepped to the hearth, her back to the soldiers and her minister. "Take him to the tower. He's to be treated well. Fresh food from the kitchens, as many blankets as he needs, and whatever else he requests, within reason."

"Yes, my lady."

"You're making a terrible mistake, Duchess. Even if these men were paid with Qirsi gold, it didn't come from me. Imprisoning me will only deny you a faithful servant and make you that much more vulnerable when they make their next attempt on your life. I could help you find the traitor in your castle, if only you'd let me. But like a willful child you heed no counsel but your own. I fear for you, my lady. But mostly, I fear for Curlinte."

"Take him now!" she said, steel in her voice.

"Yes, my lady."

She heard the minister turn, the rustling of his robes like dried leaves in a chill wind. A moment later the door closed, and she and her father were alone once more.

Diani turned to him, allowing her anger to show on her features. "You shouldn't contradict me like that, Father. Certainly not in front of my men. Mother is gone and I'm duchess now."

"No one knows that better than I, Diani. And I'll show you as much deference as I did her. But when your mother acted the fool, I was always the first person to tell her so. And I'll do no less with you."

"Kreazur is a traitor."

"You don't know that! You don't know anything for certain!"

"I know that I nearly died today!"

He grimaced. "Yes. And I know how frightened you are. To be honest, I am as well."

She wanted to deny it, to tell him that she wasn't afraid, that she truly believed this the best way to meet the Qirsi threat. But the words wouldn't come, and he probably wouldn't have believed them anyway.

"But fear doesn't justify this," he went on. "A leader who acts out of fear and suspicion is far more likely to make mistakes. Kreazur is right: there may be a traitor in the castle. And who better to find the real renegade among your Qirsi than the first minister?"

Listening to her father, she suddenly knew what she would do to fight her enemies. She wouldn't have considered such a thing before today, but as long as she lived she would remember the sensation of that first arrow piercing her flesh. She was not the same woman she had been yesterday.

"I don't need Kreazur's help," she said.

Sertio raised an eyebrow. "No?"

"Are there any shapers among the healers and other ministers?"

Her father hesitated. "I don't believe so. Why?"

"Because I intend to confine all the Qirsi to the prison tower until I find the traitor, and I don't want any of them shattering the walls that hold them."

Sertio stared at her for so long without responding that Diani began to wonder if he had even heard her. At last, though, he shook his head and looked away, his brow creased.

"I had wondered when it would come to this, when Eandi nobles would begin imprisoning Qirsi for no more reason than the color of their eyes. But I never believed that Curlinte would be first. I certainly never thought it would be you who started it."

Chapter

Four

ven after he walked Diani back to her own chamber, urging her to sleep and silently hoping that a night's rest would clear her mind, so that she might recognize the danger of what she had done, Sertio did not return to his bed. There would be no sleeping this night, certainly not until he had received word from the soldiers searching Curlinte Moor.

First Cyro, then Dalvia. And today someone—the Brugaosans, or the Qirsi, or some enemy they didn't know—had tried to take Diani from him as well. He should have been enraged, but all he felt was afraid. Losing his son had scored his heart. Losing his wife had left him empty and joyless. Sometimes he wondered if he would ever find a way to laugh again. But losing Diani . . . He shook his head as if to rid himself of the very notion. Losing his daughter would kill him.

His was an odd position, one few dukes in the other realms of the Forelands would have understood. As husband to the duchess in a matriarchal duchy, he had no claim to the Curlinte seat. He was master of arms because Dalvia had chosen him to take that post and Diani had asked him to continue to serve after his wife's death. But he had no real power. Had Cyro still been alive, he, as the son of the late duchess, would have been next in line after Diani to lead the house. As matters stood now, were something to happen to Diani, Dalvia's younger sister, the marchioness of Invelsa, would take her place. Once Diani married and had children, they would take their place in the line of succession ahead of the marchioness, who, though well-intentioned, possessed neither the wisdom nor the strength of will to govern one of Sanbira's leading houses. Until then, however, Curlinte's stability and continued influence with the royal house depended entirely upon Diani's survival. Not that he needed more incentive to keep her alive.

He had sent nearly two hundred men into the countryside to search for the assassins, double what he had told Diani. She wouldn't have approved, despite her fears. She would say that sending so many after only two men made them appear weak. Her mother had been the same way, and so Sertio would tell Diani the same thing he had told Dalvia. There was no sense in having a powerful army if you didn't use it. Perhaps one hundred men would have been sufficient to find the archers, but two hundred would be more likely to succeed and would probably do so sooner. And they still had more than a thousand men remaining to guard the city and castle in the unlikely event of an attack.

He left his chamber and descended the nearest of the towers to the upper ward. Panya, the white moon, hung low, a narrow crescent in the eastern sky. Red Ilias had yet to rise. It would soon be Pitch Night, and then the new turn would begin. To the north, the beginning of Elhir's waning meant only more snows, but in the southern realms, particularly along the eastern shores, Elhir's turn usually brought storms and fierce winds. If someone wished to start a war with House Curlinte, this was a strange time to do it.

The click of a boot on stone echoed through the ward. Turning toward the sound, Sertio saw one of his captains approaching.

"What news?" the duke asked as the man halted before him.

"We've found nothing yet, my lord."

"Nothing at all?"

"We found blood where the duchess was wounded, and crushed grass near some of the stones where the assassins must have hidden. But they left no trail to or from that spot."

"Any sign of horses?"

"None, my lord."

"Well, they didn't fly to the moor. They must have left some other sign that they were there."

The man stared at his shoes. "Perhaps they had a boat, my lord."

He'd thought of that. The climb from the sea up to the moor and then back down again would have been difficult, but not impossible. If they had a boat, they were gone by now. Sertio and his men would never find them.

"Yes, that's possible. Have some of the men search the shoreline when morning breaks. And I want the moor searched again as well, just in case they missed something."

"Yes, my lord."

"You have someone looking in the villages and inns?"

The soldier nodded. "Of course, my lord."

"Good. Widen your search southward to the north boundary of Kretsaal barony and tell all you meet that there's a bounty on these men. Five hundred qinde, guaranteed by the duchess herself."

The soldier's eyes widened. "That's certain to help, my lord."

"I hope so."

A lone cloud, thin and grey, drifted in front of Panya, darkening the castle for a moment.

"That's all, Captain," Sertio said. "Keep me apprised."

"I will, my lord."

The man spun away, and hurried back toward the west gate.

There was a part of Sertio that wanted to believe that the archers had come and gone by boat. He would gladly have traded their freedom for the knowledge that they were far from Curlinte and no longer posed any threat to Diani. But he knew better. Whoever hired them wanted her dead, and these men had seen her ride away from the headlands, very much alive.

On the thought, Sertio started across the ward toward the prison tower. It was quite late, and even confined to one of the small, sparse chambers, Kreazur was probably asleep. Still, the man would speak with him. What choice did he have?

Climbing the winding stairs, he saw that nearly all the tower chambers were occupied by ministers and healers, white-hairs all. Some slept. Others stared out of their chambers through the narrow barred windows in the steel doors, their yellow eyes luminous in the torch fire.

Kreazur was on the top floor, in a chamber by himself. A guard in the corridor stood as Sertio emerged from the stairway, but the Qirsi's cell remained silent.

"I believe he's sleeping, my lord."

Now that he was in the tower, faced with the prospect of waking the minister from a sound sleep, Sertio found his resolve wavering. He couldn't even say what he had come to ask the man, much less why his questions couldn't wait for morning.

"Perhaps I'll return with the morning bells," he said quietly, turning to leave.

Before he reached the stairs, however, he heard the rustling of blankets and the scrape of a boot on the stone floor.

"My lord?" the minister said, his pale features appearing at the small window. His hair looked wild in the fire glow and his cheeks and eyes were swollen with sleep. "Has something happened?"

"No, nothing. I'm sorry to have disturbed you, First Minister. I'll speak with you during the day."

"It makes no difference, my lord. I have nothing to do come morning, unless you're here to release me. I can sleep anytime."

Sertio nodded, feeling awkward and still not knowing why he had wanted to speak with the man.

"I take it the duchess is resting?" the Qirsi asked.

"Yes. The herbmaster gave her a tonic of comfrey and common wort to aid healing and ease her pain. I expect she'll sleep through much of the morning."

"Good."

They stood for several moments, saying nothing.

"You have more questions for me, my lord?"

Sertio glanced at the guard. "Open the door. I wish to speak with the minister in his chamber."

"Yes, my lord," the man said, crossing to the door and fitting a large iron key in the lock.

"You can go," the duke said, stepping past the man and pulling the door closed behind him. "I'll call for you when I'm done."

The guard eyed the minister, looking uneasy. "Yes, my lord."

The cell was dark, save for the dim light of the torches seeping through the grate of the door. Sertio wished he'd remembered to take a torch from the wall outside the chamber, but he saw no sense in calling the guard back just for that.

Kreazur sat on the floor opposite his small bed, his back against the stone wall. With an open hand he indicated the bed, inviting the duke to sit. Sertio shook his head, and began instead to pace about the room.

The minister watched him briefly, then cleared his throat. "The guards tell me that the duchess has imprisoned all the Qirsi in Castle Curlinte."

"Yes. She decided to do that soon after she had you taken from my chamber. She wasn't certain enough of your guilt to let the others remain free."

The man gave a wan smile. "I suppose I should be pleased."

"We both know better, Minister."

The smile fled from the Qirsi's lips. "I'm glad to hear you say so, my lord. There are great perils in what the duchess has done, not only for my people but also for herself, for you, for every court in the Forelands."

"I know."

"Have you told her as much?"

Sertio faltered briefly.

"I see," the minister said quietly.

"My daughter is a proud, difficult woman, First Minister. Being so new to the throne, she isn't likely to accept counsel that runs counter to her own ideas."

"That doesn't speak well of her as a ruler, my lord."

"It says only that she's young, First Minister," the duke said, an edge to his voice. "Her mother was much the same way when she first claimed the duchy as her own, and I think you'll agree that she turned out to be a fine leader."

Kreazur looked away. "Of course, my lord."

"I do intend to speak with her," Sertio went on, his voice softening once more. "I see the dangers as well. I find myself convinced of your innocence in this matter, Kreazur. I'd be far less concerned for Diani's safety knowing that you were at her side. And like you, I have no desire to see Qirsi imprisoned and persecuted here, or anywhere in the Forelands."

"With all respect, my lord, I'm not certain that you do see the danger. This is about far more than your daughter's safety or the mistreatment of my people."

Sertio felt his stomach tightening. "You think this could lead to a civil war? A conflict between the races?"

The Qirsi let out a high, harsh laugh. "My lord, we're on our way to such a war already! Don't you understand? That's what the leaders of the conspiracy want. They believe my people can prevail in such a war, perhaps not yet, but someday, sooner rather than later."

"You know this?"

"Not from any reliable source, but the other ministers and I have spoken of the conspiracy, wondering where these killings and machinations may be leading. On the one hand it seems quite clear: the leaders of the conspiracy wish to divide the seven realms, both against one another and against themselves. But more than that, I believe they wish to destroy the trust between Eandi nobles and their ministers, indeed, between all Eandi and all Qirsi. By imprisoning us, by indicating so clearly that she distrusts us, and, in turn, by nurturing our resentment against the arbitrary exercise of her power, the duchess is doing more to help the conspiracy's leaders than any Qirsi traitor in the seven realms."

Sertio had halted in front of the minister and was staring down at him as if he had never seen the man before. The duke should have thought of all this long ago. For that matter, Diani should have as well. But clearly neither of them had. By considering it for them, Kreazur was merely doing his job, proving himself to be a loyal servant of House Curlinte and an enemy of the renegade Qirsi. Yet, the mere fact that he could think in such a way, that he could anticipate the desires of the conspiracy with such chilling certitude, made him more suspect in Sertio's eyes, not less. Did all the white-hairs think this way? Were they born with a propensity toward treachery, or was it a product of their service in the Eandi courts?

"You disagree with me," the minister said, misreading his expression.

"Not at all. It just never occurred to me to think . . . in such terms."

The man actually smiled, shaking his head. He was heavier than most Qirsi, with a fuller face, and in the dim light, looking both hurt and amused, he resembled an overindulged child. "So now you think me a traitor, just as your daughter does."

Sertio resumed his pacing. "Not at all."

"Please don't dissemble with me, my lord. It does both of us a disservice."

"I don't think you've betrayed us, Kreazur. If you had, you wouldn't have been so honest a moment ago in your assessment of the danger facing the courts." He faltered briefly. "I merely find myself thinking that the Eandi mind and the Qirsi mind work differently. No Eandi could have devised such an ingenious plot."

"I think you give your people too little credit, my lord," the minister said, his voice thick with irony.

They both fell silent once more, Sertio wishing he hadn't come at all. He feared for his daughter more now than when he had come, and though convinced of Kreazur's innocence, he doubted that he could ever rely on the minister's counsel again. It wouldn't come as a surprise if the Qirsi and his fellow ministers left House Curlinte permanently upon winning their freedom from the prison tower. If Kreazur had accurately gauged the intent of the conspiracy's leaders, the duke and his daughter had been all too quick to further their plans.

"I take it you haven't found the assassins yet," Kreazur said at last.

"No. I have men searching the countryside, but I fear they may have come to Curlinte by sea. They may be impossible to find."

"Perhaps not impossible. More difficult certainly. But our house has good relations with most of the merchant captains between here and the Crown, even those sailing under the Wethy flag. They may be able to help us."

"Yes, that's a good thought. I'll send messages to the ports later today, provided there's no word from the moor. Thank you, First Minister." It was sound advice. Perhaps Kreazur could still serve House Curlinte after all.

"Of course, my lord."

They slipped into another uncomfortable silence, until Sertio finally decided that he had best leave. He stepped to the door and called for the guard.

"I'll leave you to sleep, First Minister. Please forgive the disturbance."

"There's nothing to forgive, my lord. Were I in my chambers neither of us would think twice about such an interruption. Despite this unpleasantness I still serve you and your house."

Sertio nodded as the soldier appeared in the corridor and unlocked the steel door.

"I will speak with.the duchess about gaining your release. You have my word."

"I'd be most grateful, my lord."

Sertio nodded and walked out of the chamber as soon as the soldier pulled open the door. He was eager to leave the prison tower and the company of this man. No doubt Kreazur had been wronged, by Diani as well as by the duke himself. But though he would keep his word and attempt to prevail upon his daughter to free Kreazur and his fellow ministers, he had no desire to prolong their conversation.

It was still dark when he stepped into the ward once more and began to make his way back to his chamber. Dawn couldn't have been far off, but the stars still shone brilliantly against the black sky, even in the east. Panya glowed directly overhead and red Ilias hung just above the eastern wall of the castle like some curved, bloodied blade.

"My lord!"

He turned at the sound of the voice and saw two soldiers approaching from the lower ward.

"You've found something?"

"Possibly, my lord," answered the older of the two men. "An innkeeper to the south remembers seeing two men with shaved heads and bows just before dusk. They were on foot and claimed to have been hunting. They inquired about staying at his inn, but didn't like his price and so continued south."

"Where?" the duke asked eagerly, striding to the stable. "Show me. I'll ride with you."

"It's almost all the way to Kretsaal barony, my lord. It's an hour's ride from the castle, at least."

"I don't care. If they were heading south and looking for a place to stay, they probably chose Kretsaal. If we ride now, we may find them before they leave whatever inn they settled on for the night."

The soldier and his companion exchanged a look and the second man shrugged.

"If you insist, my lord," the first man said. "But we can just as easily bring them to you."

Riding to Kretsaal himself made little sense. They couldn't even be certain that these were the same men, though Sertio had little doubt that they were—no one hunted the moors this time of year. But after sitting by helplessly while Dalvia died, and watching in idle frustration as Diani struggled to learn the rudiments of leadership, Sertio needed to do something. Anything. The ride would do him good, and he wanted to interrogate these men himself, before Diani had a chance to vent her rage at them through torture or summary execution.

The stableboy saddled his mount quickly and within moments the duke was leading the two soldiers through the west gate and onto Curlinte Moor. They road south toward Kretsaal by the dim glow of the moons, drumming past the jumbled boulders and the still, tall grasses of the headlands and then past small farmhouses that already smelled of cooking fires lit in the cold hours before first light.

Before they were halfway to the barony, the sky over the Sea of Stars began to brighten, silver at first, then blending to soft shades of rose and purple, and finally, as they came within sight of the walls of Kretsaal, to pale gold.

They reached the village gate just as the sun emerged from the shining waters and began its long, slow climb from sea to sky. One of Sertio's soldiers and several of Kretsaal's guards met them inside the walls. Sertio's man looked weary but pleased.

"Good morrow, my lord."

Sertio swung himself off his mount, tossing the reins to one of the baroness's men. "Have you found them?"

"We believe so, my lord. The two men we've been following took a room at an inn on the south edge of the village. We've men posted in front of the house and behind it. We were waiting for word from Curlinte before taking them. We had no idea that you'd be coming yourself."

They hurried through the village, Sertio laying a hand on the hilt of his sword. Already there were men and women in the narrow, muddy lanes, leading small herds of goats to the gate or casting a critical eye at the wares of one of the few peddlers in the small marketplace. All of them stopped to stare at Sertio, looking wary, even frightened. House Curlinte ruled its lesser courts with a gentle hand, but the appearance of the duke or duchess in the barony usually meant trouble of some sort.

Upon reaching the southern end of the village, Sertio found several of his men standing a short distance from the inn, speaking to a gray-haired woman with clear brown eyes and a toothless grin.

"This is the innkeeper, my lord," the guard said, as he and the duke stepped into the circle.

"The men are still in their room?" Sertio asked her.

"Must be. Haven't seen them since they paid me. They didn't even come down for their supper, though they paid for it." She grinned again, but when Sertio remained grave, her smile faded.

"What did they look like?"

"Like I told these others, they was bald, both of them fairly tall. They wore riding cloaks and carried bows. They said they'd been hunting."

"They paid you in silver or gold?"

"Gold, my lord."

"Did you see anyone with them? A white-hair perhaps?"

"No one, my lord. And it was a slow night. Just the one other fellow who took a room was all. And he ate his supper like a gentleman and went upstairs."

"Where is he now?"

"He left before dawn. I didn't even see him go. That's why I have them pay when they get here. If I didn't, I'd be chasing all over the realm trying to collect."

Sertio looked toward the inn, feeling vaguely uneasy. Whether they intended to flee or make another attempt on Diani's life, they should have been up and moving by now. "Which room?"

"Last one on the left."

He was walking before she finished, several of his men falling in step around him.

"Get them!" he called to the captain standing by the entrance to the inn. "We've waited long enough."

"Yes, my lord," the man said. He shouted a command to the men standing with him and immediately they filed into the inn.

Sertio drew his sword, but he remained in the lane, awaiting word from the men inside. For several moments there was silence. Then the captain appeared in the doorway once more, a sour expression on his face. Even before he spoke, Sertio felt certain that the assassins had managed somehow to escape.

"What is it?" he demanded, ice in his voice.

"You'd better come look, my lord."

The duke eyed him a moment before following him into the house. Inside, the inn smelled of roasting meat and stale wine. The captain and Sertio climbed the steps swiftly, taking them two at a time. A knot of soldiers stood in the upstairs corridor just outside the last room, but they parted to let Sertio pass, most of them lowering their gazes.

The two men lay in the center of the room, their throats slit, dark blood pooling around their heads.

"Demons and fire," the duke muttered.

He squatted beside them to take a closer look, noting that the blood on their necks was already dry. They'd been dead for some time.

"I guess they got what was coming to them," the captain said. "Question is, from who?" He glanced at Sertio. "I suppose the duchess will want to know. Shall I—?"

Instantly Sertio was up and striding to the door, his heart battering his breastbone like a siege engine. The duchess. "Bring your men, Captain! We have to get back to the castle!"

He ran down the corridor and nearly fell rushing down the stairs. Bursting through the door, he crossed to the innkeeper and gripped her arm.

"The other man who stayed the night! What did he look like?"

She blinked, looking confused.

"Quickly, woman!" he said, shaking her.

"Tall, like the others. Yellow hair, pleasant face."

"What else? A mustache? A beard?"

"No." She shook her head, as if groping for an image of the man. "He had a small scar by the side of his mouth, like from a fight."

"Good." He released her and started running toward the village gate, heedless of the stares that followed him. "See to it that she's paid for her trouble," he called over his shoulder to the captain, who had emerged from the inn. "Leave a few men to clean up the mess and bring the rest with me!"

He was too old for this. He should never have left his mount with the baroness's men.

He heard footsteps, and looking back once more, saw the captain just behind him. "Where are we going, my lord?"

"Back to the castle, you fool! The man who killed those archers will be after the duchess next!"

Diani awoke to the sound of knocking at her door. She felt light-headed and confused for several moments until she moved, wincing at the pain in her shoulder and leg. Of course. The herbmaster's tonic. Damn his potions.

The knock came again.

She rose carefully from her bed and crossed on unsteady legs to where her robe hung. She shivered slightly as she shrugged it onto her shoulders. There was warm water in her basin and a bright fire in her hearth. It seemed she had slept through a good deal.

Whoever had come rapped on her door a third time.

"Yes, enter!" she called, belatedly passing a hand through her tangled hair.

The door swung open revealing a guard, who looked uncertain and just a bit frightened. He glanced first at her bed before seeing her at the wardrobe.

"What is it? Why do you disturb me?"

"Forgive me, my lady. But a soldier has come from Kretsaal bearing news from the barony. He says it pertains to the attempt on your life."

"Have him speak with my father. The duke is looking into this matter."

"The duke rode southward during the night, my lady. He received word that the men had been seen near the barony."

Diani frowned and shook her head, still trying to clear her mind. "Father rode to the barony?"

"Yes, my lady."

"And yet this man comes from Kretsaal?"

"He does, my lady. He bears the barony's colors. He and your father must have passed each other in the darkness without either of them knowing it."

She nodded, though she found all of it rather puzzling. Why would her father leave, without telling her, particularly with assassins abroad? And what news could a man of Kretsaal have that her own soldiers did not?

"Tell this soldier that I'll speak with him shortly. I want my breakfast served first, in here. And I want the herbmaster told that I'm awake."

"Of course, my lady," the man said, bowing and withdrawing from the chamber.

Diani splashed some water on her face and then sat at her writing table, staring at the fire. The next thing she knew, yet another knock had pulled her from her dazed musings.

"Come." She pulled her robe tighter around her shoulders.

The herbmaster entered the chamber, bearing a tray that held a full breakfast and a pot of some steaming broth.

"I didn't know you were working in the kitchens now, herbmaster. It seems a waste of your talents."

He smiled. "Some would say it's the best use of them anyone's found yet."

"None who had tasted your brews."

He placed the tray on her table and regarded her closely, his brow creased. "You don't look well."

"It's your bloody tonic. It's left my mind fogged."

"Don't blame the tonic. You were supposed to rest. Had you slept as late as I wanted, your mind would be clear. How are your wounds?"

"They hurt still." She allowed him to examine her shoulder and then her leg.

"I expected that," he said absently, looking closely at her injuries. They were still discolored, though less so than they had been the night before. After some time he straightened and nodded. "They appear to be healing nicely."

"Good."

"But you still need rest. I don't want you doing anything today beyond sleeping, eating, and drinking more of my brew."

"You should have told my father that. He's ridden south, and there's a soldier come from Kretsaal with news of the assassins. I have no choice but to speak with him."

The herbmaster twisted his mouth sourly. "Fine, then. Nothing more after you've seen him."

"Yes, herbmaster. Thank you."

He sketched a quick bow and left her. Diani glanced at her breakfast. Bread and butter, smoked meat, stewed sour fruit from Macharzo, and, of course, the herbmaster's sweet-smelling brew. Her head had started to clear, but her appetite had not yet returned and she decided to speak with the baroness's man before eating.

"Guard!" she called.

One of her men opened the door.

"Have the soldier from Kretsaal brought to me at once."

He had made his way out of the village as soon as the inn grew quiet, leaving by way of the gate nearest the tavern shortly before the ringing of the midnight bells and the closing of the village gates. He circled quickly to the north gate and waited within sight of it, just off the road, until the bells tolled. He stayed low in the grasses, so as not to be seen in the dim moonlight. If Kretsaal barony was like nearly every other court in the Forelands, the guards would change at midnight.

It was, and they did. No sooner had the last echo of the bells died away than the replacements appeared in the lane that led from the modest castle to the gate.

Immediately, before the replacements could get too close, he stood, calling out, "Hold the gate!" and then, "My wares are a bit heavy. Can one of you help me with these sacks? It'll get me into the city faster."

Two of the guards had already begun to close the gate and now they stopped, peering out into the darkness. He heard one spit a curse and the other begin to laugh. This second man turned and started walking toward the center of the village, but the first man stepped beyond the walls, still trying to spot him. He noticed that the guard unsheathed his sword.

"Where are you?" the guard called, walking slowly along the worn lane that led into the city.

"Over here." He made his voice sound strained, as if he were struggling with heavy satchels. He had chosen a place near a cluster of stones, and he bent over them now, as if they were his sacks.

"Don't you have a horse and cart?" The soldier had adjusted his approach at the sound of his voice and was coming directly toward him.

"The cart threw a wheel back on the moor. Snapped the rim. I left the horse and most of my wares there, but needed to bring some with me. I'll have to sell most of this tomorrow to be able to pay a wheelwright to come with me and fix it."

He could hear the soldier's footsteps in the soft grasses now, and he drew the garrote from within his cloak, pulling the wire taut and wrapping it twice around each fist. He remained bent over the stones until the soldier reached him.

"What do you want me? ..." The guard trailed off, taking a step back. "Where are your satchels?"

The one satchel he did have—the one he always carried—was already in his hand and he straightened now, in the same motion swinging it at the soldier with all his strength and hitting the man full in the temple. The soldier fell to the ground, but managed somehow to keep hold of his sword. Not that it mattered. He was on the guard instantly, wrapping the garrote around his throat and pulling it taut. The soldier struggled, but to no avail. He'd used this same garrote against men far larger and stronger than this one.

Sitting back on his haunches and taking a long breath, he looked toward the gate. It still stood ajar, but none of the men was looking out at the moor. The guard's friend was nowhere to be seen, and the men who had replaced them probably didn't even know enough to be looking for him.

As if to prove his point, two of the new guards pulled the gate shut. The man wouldn't be missed until morning.

He stripped the guard's uniform from the limp body and began to put it on himself. It wasn't a perfect fit, but it would do. He put his clothes on the soldier, thus perhaps delaying for a bit longer the discovery of just what he had done. Then he started westward, away from the castle and the sea, to the place where his horse was tethered.

He rode swiftly, hoping to reach Curlinte well before sunrise. At one point he heard riders in the distance approaching from the ducal city. Reining his mount to a halt, he made the beast lie down on the grasses, ducked down himself, and peered over the horse's flanks, watching the riders. They didn't slow, nor did they give any indication that they had seen him. He waited until he could no longer hear them and they were but dim, distant figures in the moonlight. Then he coaxed his mount back onto its feet and rode on. Even with the delay, he thought that he could reach the walls of Curlinte before daybreak. He might even have time to rest before seeking an audience with the duchess.

Diani didn't have to wait long before her guards returned with the soldier from Kretsaal. Straightening in her chair, she beckoned the men into her chamber.

The duchess noticed his hair first. It was yellow and fine, more like that of a man from northern Aneira or even Eibithar than that of a Sanbiri. His eyes, too, seemed wrong. They were pale blue, almost grey, not at all as they should have been. He wore the grey and red of Kretsaal, but the uniform fit him poorly. Sanla, the baroness, never would have allowed such a thing.

Could he be an assassin?

The thought never would have occurred to her before the attack at the headlands the day before, and Diani wondered if she were allowing her lingering fears to cloud her judgment. The guard had a kindly face, hardly that of a killer. Though he did bear a small scar near the corner of his mouth.

"You bring tidings for me?" she asked. But even as she spoke, she rose from the chair and returned to her writing table, as if she might draw comfort from having something substantial between herself and the soldier.

"I do, my lady." No accent, at least none that Diani could discern. He glanced at the two soldiers behind him before facing her again. "I was told by my baroness to speak only with you."

Strange, and presumptuous. If he turned out to be just a soldier, she would have to speak of this with Sanla.

"The soldiers who serve me know that I expect not only their loyalty but also their discretion. They'll remain here."

"But, my lady, I have my instructions."

Strange indeed. She allowed her eyes to wander to her table, searching for something to use as a weapon. Her dagger and sword were near the wardrobe, too far if he struck at her quickly.

"And now you have different instructions from your duchess. Do you really believe the baroness would have you argue the point?"

He stared at her, not appearing cowed as he should have, but rather seeming to search her face for some sign that she was growing suspicious.

"Your tidings?" she prompted again.

"Of course, my lady." Something in the voice, the icy intensity that suddenly appeared in those pale eyes.

Diani took a step back, expecting an attack, but the man surprised her. Seizing the pot of hot brew from her tray, he whirled on the two guards, throwing the pot at one and pulling his sword free to run the other through.

The two guards were caught completely unaware. The pot hit one of them in the chest, splattering hot liquid on his face and staggering him. By the time the other man had his sword free, the killer had already driven the point of his sword into his chest. The guard could only drop his weapon to the floor, blood staining the front of his uniform as he fell to his knees and then toppled over. The first man had recovered enough to draw his blade, but the assassin was on him too quickly. The soldier parried one blow and then another, but even with the skills he had learned from Diani's father, he was no match for the yellow-haired man.

For a moment, Diani couldn't move. She had seen dead men before—soldiers killed in the hills by brigands and carried by their comrades back to the castle—but that was a far cry from actually watching a man die.

As the assassin drove the second soldier back toward the far corner of the chamber, she forced herself into motion. The pot of hot tonic, the one possible weapon she had spotted on her writing table, was gone. She thought about trying to make it to the corridor to call for help, but the two men were closer to the door than she. Instead she sprinted to where her own blade hung and pulled it free. As an afterthought, she grabbed her dagger as well. By the time she turned around, the second of her guards was dead as well, his head nearly severed from his body. The assassin, only slightly out of breath, a faint sheen of sweat on his face, was advancing on her.

"You truly think to succeed where your soldiers have failed?" he asked, grinning. This time the accent was unmistakable. Wethyrn, though she doubted he was here on behalf of the archduke. Assassins, it seemed, came from all realms of the Forelands.

He was bigger than she, stronger as well. And she had seen that he moved quickly for his size. Still, at almost any other time, speed would have been her one advantage. But she was conscious of the throbbing in her leg and shoulder, and she knew that she could not fight as she might have usually.

He closed the distance between them swiftly, trapping her near her wardrobe and leveling a powerful blow at her head. Rather than trying to parry it and being knocked off balance, she dropped into a crouch allowing the man's blade to whistle harmlessly over her head. Anticipating her counter he swept his blade downward, to block her own sword. But Diani struck with the dagger instead, slashing him across the side of his knee. She gasped at the pain in her shoulder, but seeing blood soak into his trouser leg, allowed herself a small smile. Perhaps he wouldn't be quite so quick now.

The assassin offered no response at all, but launched himself at her again, chopping downward at her so that she couldn't avoid the attack by ducking. She raised her sword and was nearly hammered to the floor by the force of his blow. Her arm felt numb and as he raised his blade to strike once more she wondered if she could absorb another assault.

She stepped back and cried out for help, but she knew it would do her no good. There were always two men positioned just outside her chambers, but those two men lay dead on the floor, and with her guest wearing the colors of loyal Kretsaal, the captain of the guard would never have thought to send more men.

The assassin merely grinned and hacked at her again and then a third time. She blocked his sword with her own each time, but she fell to her knees after the third attack and had to drop her dagger in order to hold her blade with both hands.

He backed off for just an instant, lowered his hands and brought back his sword to deliver what would be the killing stroke. Desperate, she did the only thing she could. With all the strength in her frame, she swung both arms around, throwing her sword at the man. It hit him in the chest, hilt first, and clattered to the floor. But it stopped him for just an instant, long enough for Diani to retrieve her dagger and dive past him into the middle of the chamber. He came after her, lunging for her once with his sword and missing, then closing the distance between himself and the door so that she couldn't escape.

She started toward the window, thinking to open the shutters and call for help, but he advanced on her, and she didn't dare turn her back on him. Then she thought to reclaim her sword, but he cut her off from that as well.

In the end she could only back away from him, trying to keep her writing table between them. She started to cry for help, but was cut off when he leaped at her again, his blade just barely missing her breast.

"You must stop doing that, my lady," he said, throwing the table aside as he spoke.

He had her trapped again, in the back corner of her room. She held her dagger before her, but she knew it would not be enough to stop him.

"Diani?" Her father's voice, from out in the corridor.

"Father!" she yelled.

The door burst open revealing the duke and several of his men, all with swords drawn.

The assassin froze, looking frightened for the first time since entering Diani's chamber. His pale eyes flicked about the room, as if searching for some path to freedom. He still held his sword before him and as his gaze fell upon the duchess he appeared to consider killing her, even though it would have meant his death.

Sertio seemed to see this as well, for he quickly placed himself between Diani and the killer. His soldiers followed him into the chamber, surrounding the yellow-haired man.

"I don't want him killed!" Diani said, her voice unsteady as she lowered her dagger. Her pulse raced and her hands were shaking so violently she could barely maintain her grip on the hilt of her blade.

"Drop your weapon," Sertio said, his dark eyes never leaving the man's face.

The assassin did nothing, but he continued to glance around the chamber, perhaps trying to decide who among his captors would be easiest to kill.

"Drop your sword and you won't be hurt," the duke said again, his voice harder this time.

Still the man did not move, though a slight smile touched his lips. "You're lying," he said softly. "You'll torture me until I tell you whose gold paid for my blade."

Her father opened his mouth, perhaps to deny it, though everyone in the chamber knew it to be the truth. He never got the chance. The assassin raised his sword as to cleave the duke in two, roaring like a cornered beast.

Sertio, stepped to the side to avoid the strike, aiming a thrust of his own at the man's shoulder, to spare his life, but disarm him. Had it been just the two of them fighting it might have worked. But the other men, seeing their duke threatened, closed on the assassin as well, pounding at him with their blades. In a matter of seconds the man lay on the floor of Diani's chamber, blood flowing from several deep wounds.

Diani took a step forward. "Call for a healer! I want him alive!"

"The Qirsi who healed you would never get here in time," her father said, staring down at the man, his voice low.

"One of the castle's healers, then!"

Sertio glanced at her, his face as grim as it had been the day her mother finally died. "They're all in the prison tower."

She swallowed. "We could free one of them, just for this."

But a guard who had bent to feel the man's pulse shook his head. "He dies as we speak, my lady. The tower is too far."

Diani dropped to her knees beside the man. "Who paid you? Was it the Qirsi? The Brugaosans? Who?"

But he merely lay there, the same inscrutable smile on his lips, his eyes open but utterly lifeless.

Chapter
Five

Dantrielle, Aneira, Elhir's Moon waxing

ost years, the beginning of Elhir's turn brought warm days and clear nights to the southern Forelands. Usually the snows maintained their icy grip on the northern kingdoms through at least the waxing of the god's turn, but in the south, frigid winds gave way to temperate breezes and the hard blizzards of the cold turns were replaced by gentle rains that presaged the coming of the planting.

Not this year. There had been a pleasant day or two at the end of Eilidh's turn, but with the first days of the new waxing, the snows returned like a vengeful army, battering at the castle gates and shuttered windows with howling winds, and burying the wards and surrounding city under mounds of drifting snow. Neither the tapestries that hung on Evanthya's walls nor the bright blaze in her hearth that the servants fed constantly could keep the chill from her chamber. She had never paid much heed to the passing of the seasons. Living in Dantrielle, where the turns of the snows were mild and even the hottest days of the growing turns were cooled by the soft breezes that drifted among the shadows of Aneira's Great Forest, she never had cause. This year, however, the snows had seemed interminable, the wait for a true thaw excruciating.

Perhaps it had been too long since she last held Fetnalla. Perhaps she just longed to leave Dantrielle for a time, to escape the suspicions of her duke and the pall that had settled over the castle since the death of King Carden the Third and the selection of Numar of Renbrere as regent for the late king's daughter. Or maybe, now that she had purchased the death of the traitorous minister from Kentigern, thus striking a blow at the Qirsi conspiracy, she so thirsted for more blood that she could not wait for the warmth of the growing.

Beginning the very day she received the assassin's cryptic message telling her that the traitor in Mertesse had been killed, Evanthya had been of two minds about what she and Fetnalla had done. From the moment she paid the assassin at the Red Boar Inn in Dantrielle city, the minister had wondered if they had been justified in killing the man, if indeed such an act could ever be forgiven, no matter the justness of their cause. She knew the dead man's name now. Shurik jal Marcine. She had learned it soon after the arrival of the assassin's note, as word spread southward of the man's mysterious death, and it served only to deepen her doubts.

But even as she wrestled with her guilt, Evanthya also found herself wanting desperately to continue her private war with the conspiracy, to open a new front somewhere in the Forelands. Like a battle-crazed warrior, she was suddenly avid for more violence. A part of her, deep in the dark recesses of her mind, wondered if she might even take up a weapon herself. According to what she had heard whispered in the marketplace among traveling merchants, the traitor died at the hands of a drunken lutenist who also was killed in their struggle. Evanthya knew better of course, but though she shuddered just to think about it, she could not help being curious as to how the singer had made it appear so. How did one kill two men and escape blame for both murders? What kind of person devoted his life to mastering such a dark art?

Upon hearing from the assassin, Evanthya sent a missive to Fetnalla in Orvinti, informing her of their success. Her love's gold had paid for the assassination and Shurik's murder had been as much Fetnalla's idea as her own. Truth be told, Fetnalla had been more eager than she for the man's death. But would she be satisfied at having purchased Shurik's death, or would she, like Evanthya, see this as but an opening salvo in a far longer struggle? Evanthya had yet to receive any response, and with each day that passed she grew more impatient. In the last day or two, she had come to a startling decision: no matter what Fetnalla wrote in her reply, Evanthya intended to proceed with her war on the conspiracy. She didn't know where she would find the gold to pay another assassin, or how she would choose her next target, but she could not sit by idly and allow the conspiracy to destroy the Forelands, not after having tasted success.

There was an irony here, and bitter though it was, she still managed to find some humor in it. Despite the role she had played in Shurik's death, and notwithstanding her resolve to send other conspirators to the Underrealm, her duke still suspected her of being a part of the conspiracy. Tebeo's doubts about her loyalty were not nearly so deep as those the duke of Orvinti openly expressed about Fetnalla, but they rankled nevertheless. And she knew—a deeper irony—that as she plotted her next assault on the Qirsi traitors, she would only fuel her duke's fears.

He hadn't yet turned from her entirely—nor, to his credit, had Brall of Orvinti turned from Fetnalla—but across the Forelands Eandi nobles who had lost faith in their Qirsi ministers were barring the advisors from their chambers or banishing them from their castles entirely. It seemed only a matter of time before Tebeo and Brall did the same.

On this morning, though, her duke had summoned her to his chambers as he always did, just as the midmorning bells rang in the city, their echoes softened by the winds and snow. When Evanthya entered the duke's room, she found him pacing, which he often did when agitated. In the past few turns he had been agitated nearly all the time.

"Good day, my lord," she said, trying to keep her voice bright.

He looked up at her briefly and grunted a greeting. She could see his jaw clenching, and his short, round frame moved jerkily from one end of the chamber to the other. Tebeo was prone to worry, but she hadn't seen him this unnerved since Bohdan's turn when Carden died, beginning the chain of events that led to the poisoning in Solkara, the execution of Grigor of Renbrere, and the selection of Numar as regent.

"Has something happened, my lord?"

"There's a message," he said, nodding toward his writing table without breaking stride. "You're welcome to read it." Evanthya crossed to the table and unrolled the scroll. "There's not much to it," he went on as she read. "Numar is on his way here. He should be arriving by midday, although I wouldn't be surprised if this weather slowed his company a bit."

Evanthya frowned as she read the curt message. This day at least, she understood her duke's concern. These were unsettling tidings.

"Strange that he would have been abroad for Pitch Night."

The duke nodded. "I agree. To say nothing of his decision to leave Solkara before the snows ended."

Few nobles chose to travel during the snows, and fewer still left their castles just before Pitch Night, the last night of the turn, when neither moon shone in the sky. Each Pitch Night carried with it a dark curse or omen—legend held that on Pitch Night in the turn of Eilidh, the goddess of fire, which had been just two nights before, a blaze that was allowed to burn out could not be relit until morning. Even if Numar dismissed the moon legends as mere superstition, as some men did, most commoners did not. The soldiers in his company would be reluctant to leave the safety of their homes for Pitch Night. Apparently, whatever had drawn the regent from Castle Solkara could not wait.

"Perhaps he was fooled by the warm days at the end of the last turn."

"I'd thought of that," the duke said. "But still, to leave before the new moon . . ."

"You think he intends to ask for more men?"

Tebeo shrugged, then nodded, his mouth twisting with disapproval. "I'd be surprised if he didn't." Since Numar's investiture, Tebeo and his allies in Orvinti and Kett had been alarmed by overtures made to the regent by Harel the Fourth, emperor of Braedon. Harel seemed to be preparing the empire for a naval war with Eibithar, and they feared that Numar would allow Aneira to be drawn into the conflict.

"It might be something else," Evanthya said. *It might be something more.* "He could have ordered you to send more men without even leaving his chamber in Solkara. Carden did it all the time."

"I'd considered that as well. It may be that war is even more imminent than we'd thought." He rubbed a hand over his face and shook his head, looking like a parent who worries over a wayward child. "In any case, First Minister, I want you to prepare the castle for his arrival. He may be regent in name, but in all ways that matter he is Aneira's king. We must welcome him appropriately."

"Of course, my lord."

The regent had given them little notice, and for the next few hours, Castle Dantrielle bustled with activity. Servants scrubbed the walls and floors of every corridor and prepared the castle's great hall for a feast. Soldiers polished their swords and helms under the watchful eye of the master of arms before gathering in the snowy ward to rehearse their formal reception of the regent. Men and women ran to and from the kitchens as the smell of roasting meat and baked bread drifted through the wards and hallways. Other laborers cleared snow from the stone paths in the castle courtyards. Like her duke, Evanthya had hoped that the weather might keep the regent from arriving when his message said he would—she would have liked another hour or two to ready the castle. As it happened, however, Numar reached Dantrielle just when his message had said he would, despite the wind and snow. The midday bells began to ring as the final touches were put on the great hall, and they continued to toll long after they should have stopped, announcing Numar's approach to the gates of Dantrielle city.

Immediately the duke and duchess rode toward the main gate, with Evanthya just behind them. The introductions in the city would take some time, giving the underministers time enough to see to the completion of preparations.

Tebeo's worries still obviously weighed heavily on his mind, but the duke did seem pleased by the work his servants had done during the morning. As they rode to the gate, he favored Evanthya with a rare smile.

"Well done, First Minister. I wouldn't have believed we could be ready in time."

"Thank you, my lord. All who serve you worked quite hard this morning. I had only to direct them."

The duchess turned at that, smiling as well, snow clinging to her black hair. "I, of all people, know what it is to direct them, First Minister. You're to be commended for what you accomplished today."

Evanthya inclined her head, accepting the praise. "You're too kind, my lady."

Word of the regent's visit had spread through the city and in spite of the wind and cold, the people of Dantrielle had already begun to line the city lanes to greet him. Seeing their duke and duchess now, the people cheered. Just as they crossed through the marketplace in the center of the city, Evanthya heard horns blowing from the gate. Numar had reached the city walls. The three of them spurred their mounts to a gallop and came to the gate just as the heralds concluded their flourish.

Numar sat atop a white horse, his cloak—red and gold, lined with black fur—caked with snow at the shoulders. He had thrown back his hood so that his wheat-colored hair was stirred by the icy wind. He wasn't as broad as Carden had been, or even Grigor, and his face was too kind and youthful to make him appear truly formidable. But there was a simple elegance to his every move, a grace that his older brothers lacked, the two who had died as well as the one who remained. He looked like a king, and something in his manner told Evanthya that he thought of himself as such. That could be a dangerous thing in a regent.

"Lord Renbrere," Tebeo said, swinging himself off his mount and taking a step forward. He bowed to the man. "Be welcome in Dantrielle. Our city, and our castle, are offered for your comfort for as long as you choose to honor us with your presence."

Tebeo had often told Evanthya that he depended upon her memory for names when it came to greeting nobles from other courts, but in this case she would have failed him; she had been ready to call the regent 'Lord Solkara.' That title, however, belonged to Numar's lone surviving brother, Henthas, who, as the older of the two, inherited the dukedom from Grigor. Because of Henthas's reputation for ruthlessness, however, the other dukes of Aneira had not trusted him with the regency and had turned to Numar instead. When Carden, the oldest of the brothers Renbrere, was still alive, Grigor and Henthas had been known as the Jackals, Numar as the Fool. In the turns since, Numar had proven himself a thoughtful, intelligent man. But Henthas, the new duke, still appeared to be every bit the Jackal.

"Lord Dantrielle," the regent answered, dismounting in turn. "It is you who do me the honor with this most gracious greeting."

He stepped to where Tebeo stood and the two men embraced.

Glancing up at the rest of the regent's small company, Evanthya saw that Pronjed jal Drenthe had come as well. This surprised her, thought she couldn't say why. Pronjed had served as archminister under Carden and continued to serve the kingdom in that capacity. It wouldn't have been at all unusual for a king to bring his minister on such a journey, but at least nominally the archminister served Kalyi, the young queen. Evanthya couldn't help thinking that the minister belonged with her rather than with Numar, and once more she was struck by the degree to which the regent seemed to consider himself Aneira's rightful leader. In point of fact, Tebeo enjoyed greater status in Aneira's courts than Numar. He was a duke, while the regent, by grace of his birth and his position in House Solkara, was only the marquess of Renbrere. But Numar's appointment as regent changed everything, bestowing upon him power and rank that had nothing to do with bloodlines. He was, in essence, a creation of Aneira's Council of Dukes, one who now controlled a vast army and great riches, the like of which even the realm's most powerful dukes could only dream.

The archminister was watching her and she nodded to him, feeling vaguely uncomfortable even as she made herself smile. It remained to be seen if Numar controlled this man as well. Fetnalla trusted Pronjed and had built something of a rapport with him during the days just before and after Carden's funeral. Evanthya, however, thought him dangerous, perhaps even a traitor. At each of their previous encounters Pronjed had given every indication of disliking her and now he nodded to her in return, but his expression did not change. A moment later he returned his gaze to Numar and Tebeo.

The formal introductions went quickly, both men hurrying through them to escape the storm. In a short while they were riding back through the city to the castle, acknowledging the cheers of the men and women who lined the city streets.

After the horses of the regent's party had been left in the able hands of Dantrielle's stablemaster, and the small contingent of Solkaran guards was housed with Dantrielle's men, Numar and Pronjed accompanied the duke and Evanthya back to Tebeo's chamber. The wood in the fire had been replenished, and the room glowed with a bright, warming blaze. Numar and Tebeo took the two large chairs by the hearth, while Evanthya and the archminister remained standing, Pronjed near the duke's writing table, she closer to the fire. Pronjed was watching her again and Evanthya, uncomfortable under his gaze, tried to keep from glancing his way.

Two servants were placing food and hot tea on the low table before the two nobles, and a strangely expectant silence enveloped the room. Once the servants were gone, Numar leaned forward and took a sip of his tea. Then he sat back, smiling at the duke.

"You're wondering why I've come."

"Yes, my lord. Given the weather and how early it is in the new turn, I've feared the worst."

"War, you mean?" the regent said with a small laugh. "No, it's nothing that dire. At least not yet. Actually, Lord Dantrielle, I've been abroad for some time now. I've just come from Orvinti, and Bistari before that."

"My lord?"

"After all that happened following Carden's death, in particular the poisoning and the decision of the dukes to pass over Henthas in my favor, I thought it best to speak privately with all of Aneira's dukes. To reassure them. I may only be regent, but for the next several years, I'll be leading this kingdom, commanding her armies and protecting her people. With your help, of course. I thought it best that we take the time to become better acquainted."

Tebeo eyed the man with unconcealed surprise. "A most noble endeavor, my lord. I never . . ." He hesitated, as if uncertain as to how he should continue. "All leaders should think as you do."

Numar smiled. "You never thought a Renbrere would do such a thing. Is that what you were going to say?"

Tebeo's round face shaded to crimson.

"It's all right, Lord Dantrielle. Your friend Lord Orvinti was as astounded as you are. And the new duke of Bistari nearly choked when I told him why I had come."

Tebeo laughed. House Bistari and House Solkara had been bitter rivals for centuries. Any gesture of friendship between them would have been cause for astonishment.

"You intend to go to all the dukedoms, my lord?"

"In time, yes. I'll return to Solkara from here. When the planting begins I'll ride north to Mertesse. The lesser houses can wait, but I wanted to visit·our most powerful houses as soon as possible."

Tebeo gave a modest smile. "Again, my lord, you honor us."

"I merely point out what we both know to be true, Lord Dantrielle." The regent paused. "May I call you Tebeo?"

"Of course, my lord."

"One of the things my eldest brother never understood, Tebeo, is that in order to rule Aneira, a king must seek to unite its most powerful houses. As it happens, my father, as great a ruler as he was, never understood this either. Both of them remained so committed to Solkara's foolish feud with Bistari that they never allowed our kingdom to realize its true promise."

Tebeo shifted in his chair, looking uncomfortable. "Its true promise, my lord?"

"Yes. Right now Aneira is considered a secondary realm in the Forelands. Oh, most would say that we've a more formidable army than Caerisse or Wethyrn, but when compared to Braedon or Eibithar, or even Sanbira, we're seen as a lesser power."

"Forgive me for saying so, my lord, but I'm not certain that I agree with you."

Numar raised an eyebrow. "Really."

"No one doubts that the Eibitharians hate us as much as we hate them. Yet they've done nothing to provoke a war. In fact, it seems to me that they've tried their best to avoid any conflict with us in recent years. Why would they do this if they thought us weak?"

The regent gave a brittle smile. "You don't like to speak of war, do you, Tebeo?"

The duke's gaze remained steady, though his face appeared to pale slightly. "No, my lord, I don't. Regardless of how strong we are, Aneira is surrounded by hostile realms. I fear that any war with Eibithar would be harmful to our kingdom."

"What if we had the support of the empire? What if we could prevail upon the king of Caerisse to join our cause? We wouldn't be surrounded then."

Evanthya glanced at Pronjed, who was gazing at the fire, his face impassive. After a moment, as if sensing her eyes upon him, he looked her way, but she could gauge nothing from his expression.

"It seems you've given this a good deal of thought, my lord," the duke said, his voice low.

"As leader of the kingdom, I have little choice but to think in such terms."

"Does the emperor of Braedon continue to make overtures regarding an attack on Eibithar?"

"Harel has made it clear to me," Numar began, seeming to choose his words with care, "as he did to my brother before me, that the empire views a conflict with Eibithar as inevitable. The two realms are party to so many disputes that a negotiated peace is out of the question. I suppose we could simply stand by and await the outcome. But if Eibithar manages to prevail, then our most bitter enemy in all the land will also be the preeminent power in all the land. Or we could join with Braedon, ensuring her success, and sharing in the spoils of that victory." The regent shrugged. "It seems an easy choice to me."

Tebeo looked deeply troubled, but he nodded and murmured, "Yes, my lord."

"Brall agreed with me, Tebeo. And even Bistari's new duke admitted to seeing the logic in this approach, though he reserved his judgment for now."

"What of the queen, my lord? Does she agree as well?"

Numar seemed genuinely surprised by the question. "The girl? You expect me to consult with her on such matters? She's but a child."

"Forgive me, my lord. I meant the queen mother. Chofya."

Carden's widow, the daughter of a lesser noble whose beauty had attracted the eye of the young lord, much to the chagrin of his father, who had intended to marry Carden to the daughter of a more powerful house.

"Chofya," Numar repeated, his expression darkening. "To be honest with you, Tebeo, I saw no need to discuss the matter with her either. She cares for the girl and she manages many of the social affairs of the dukedom, for which my brother Henthas has neither patience nor aptitude. But she is no statesman."

"Of course not, my lord."

The regent smiled, and again it looked forced. "Perhaps I should retire to my quarters for a time. My ride has left me weary, and I sense that our discussion is not going as either one of us might have hoped."

Numar stood, as did Tebeo, who bowed to the regent as he had at the city gate. "I hope my lord finds his quarters satisfactory."

"I'm sure I will. The hospitality of House Dantrielle is legendary throughout the realm."

"Thank you, my lord. We will feast in the great hall this evening, at your convenience, of course."

Numar was already striding to the door. "I'll look forward to it." He stopped, with his hand resting lightly on the door handle and turned to face the duke again. "Would Chofya's opinion truly have mattered to you, Tebeo?" he asked. "Would you trust her judgment more than you would mine?"

Evanthya held her breath, her eyes flitting from the regent to her duke and back again. She sensed that their conversation had taken a most perilous turn. Tebeo seemed to understand this as well, for he cleared his throat, his gaze straying to her face for just an instant.

"No, my lord, I wouldn't," he said, facing the regent again. "As you observed before, I'm discomfited by discussions of war. Given the choice between going to war and maintaining the peace, I would invariably choose the latter. No doubt this makes me a poor leader, one who is far better suited to running a dukedom than an entire kingdom. I merely asked about the queen mother because I wished to know if any others in the realm share my concerns. I meant no offense."

Numar smiled again, and this time it appeared genuine. "Then I'll take none and will look forward to dining with you and the duchess this evening."

He pulled open the door and left the chamber, his footsteps echoing in the corridor. Pronjed started to follow, then hesitated, turning once more to face Evanthya.

"May I have a word with you, First Minister?" He glanced at the duke. "With your permission, of course, my lord."

"What?" Tebeo said, obviously distracted. "Oh, yes. That would be fine." He waved a hand vaguely toward the door. "You may accompany him back to his chamber, First Minister."

I'd rather not. "Yes, my lord." She followed the archminister into the hallway, pulling the duke's door closed behind her.

They began to walk toward the west end of the castle, where the guest chambers were located, neither of them speaking.

"Why don't we walk in the ward?" Pronjed said at last.

Evanthya nodded and led him down the winding stairway of the cloister tower and out into the swirling snow. She pulled her cloak tighter around her shoulders and lowered her head against the storm.

"Your duke took a great chance just now," the archminister said, raising his voice so that it would carry over the wind that keened like a demon among the castle walls. "The men of Solkara have little patience with those who would question their decisions. I don't know whether to ascribe your duke's actions to courage or folly." She glanced at him and he grinned, looking gaunt as a cadaver. "Perhaps we should call it both."

"Perhaps we should call it honesty, Archminister. My duke is a man who is not afraid to speak his mind, even to those who might be disturbed by what he has to say."

"A trait he shares with his first minister."

"I'm not certain I know what you mean," she said, the lie coming to her easily. In the days after Carden's death, Evanthya had argued forcefully against accepting Grigor, the eldest of the king's surviving brothers, as Aneira's new ruler, though she knew that defying him might lead to civil war. Pronjed never said anything to her, but she had seen the venom in his yellow eyes when he looked at her, and she knew that he had spoken to Fetnalla, hoping to convince her that Evanthya's approach would lead Aneira to ruin.

"Of course you do. You were willing to oppose Grigor no matter the consequences for yourself or your duke. And as it turns out, you were right. A man who could resort to poisoning the queen and her Council of Dukes would have been capable of even greater atrocities once on the throne. We owe you a great debt, First Minister."

"Thank you, Archminister." It was the last thing she would have expected him to say. This was part of what made him so dangerous. He could be charming when he wished to be. Walking with him now, Evanthya had to remind herself that Fetnalla believed Pronjed might possess delusion magic—a powerful Qirsi magic that allowed him to bend the minds of Eandi to his purposes and to lie without fear of detection to other Qirsi. Fetnalla and her duke had even surmised that the archminister had used this power to make Carden take his own life. *If he's flattering you he must want something.* The warning echoed in her mind, as if Fetnalla were shouting the words to her all the way from Orvinti.

"What is it you want of me, Archminister?"

"Want of you?"

Evanthya actually smiled. Delusion magic or not, he could be rather transparent at times.

"Never mind that you asked me to speak with you, the fact is that you've never cared for me, nor I for you, your compliments notwithstanding. So I ask you again, what do you want?"

He smiled in return, a cold, thin smile that actually struck her as being more guileless than any other expression she had seen on his bony features that day.

"Very well, First Minister. I want to know how far your duke will go in opposing the regent's plans for war."

Evanthya felt her stomach tighten. "Is a war imminent?"

"What do you think? Would a Solkaran leader travel this far in the midst of the snows merely in the interest of building good relations with his dukes?"

She said nothing, her silence an admission that he must be right.

"Would Lord Dantrielle withhold men from the royal army?"

"You know I can't answer that," she said quietly. "Even if I knew the duke's mind, which I don't, I couldn't tell you. You're the regent's man."

"No," he said. "I'm not."

Evanthya looked at him sharply.

"I was Carden's archminister," he told her, "and Chofya's after that. But I've never seen myself as belonging to the Solkarans. I'm Qirsi, First Minister, as are you."

"But you're here with the regent."

"Yes, and I still don't know why."

Evanthya hadn't expected him to be so blunt, and she found herself wondering if he was deceiving her. Did delusion magic work on other Qirsi if they were aware of its use?

"I don't think the regent trusts me," Pronjed went on. "If I had to guess, I'd say that he brought me along because he felt safer knowing where I was and what I was doing. I don't believe he trusts the queen mother either—that's why he responded as he did to your duke's question about her. He knows that I supported her against Grigor, and he fears that she and I will plot against him as well."

"Then do you ask about my duke's intentions on her behalf?"

"No. As I told you, I'm Qirsi before I'm anything else. I ask you, Qirsi to Qirsi, because I want to be prepared for all contingencies."

Qirsi to Qirsi. She had heard it said that members of the conspiracy spoke to each other in this way, placing their devotion to the Qirsi people above all else. Was that what he had in mind? To turn her to the Qirsi conspiracy?

"Can't you tell me anything?" he prodded again.

"As I've already explained, Archminister, the duke has told me nothing. I have no knowledge of his plans."

"But you know him. Even without knowing his mind, you know his tendencies, what he's capable of doing. I'm not asking you to betray Tebeo's confidence. I merely wish to know if you think that his desire for peace is more powerful than his fear of defying the regent."

She stopped, turning to face him as a gust of wind whipped her white hair about her face. "Forgive me for saying so, Archminister, but I believe you are asking me to betray Tebeo's confidence. You would never think to ask me such questions in front of the duke, nor would you tolerate such questions from me as they pertained to the regent or the queen mother."

"Actually, you're wrong about that. As a servant of House Solkara I couldn't tell you anything. But speaking with you in private, Qirsi to Qirsi, I'll answer any question you ask me." He grinned, adding, "Within reason, of course."

Evanthya just stared at the man, uncertain as to whether to believe him.

"How soon will this war be starting?" she finally asked.

"Very soon. Perhaps within half a year. The regent awaits word from the emperor, but already he's making plans to expand the army so that it's half again as great as it is now."

"Doesn't the regent understand that by attacking Eibithar, we risk drawing every realm in the Forelands into the conflict?"

"I believe he does. Despite what others have said about him in the past, he's no fool, and even Harel, who may well be a fool, must realize where their attack on Eibithar will lead."

"And yet they make their plans anyway?"

The archminister raised an eyebrow. "That should tell you something."

Evanthya nodded. "They're that confident."

"Yes. Whether they have cause to be is open to debate, but there's no doubt that they expect to prevail, no matter the scope of the conflict." He paused, eyeing her closely. "So, First Minister, in light of what you know of your duke, faced with the prospect of this war, will he defy the regent, or will he commit Dantrielle's men to the effort?"

Evanthya looked away, taking a long breath. She could hardly refuse to answer him now, not after he had answered her questions so directly. It seemed to the minister that Pronjed had led her here, knowing all along that he could compel her to reply, and once more she wondered if he had been using magic to cloud her perception of the truth.

"I can't answer with any certainty," she said at last, feeling as she spoke that she was betraying the duke's trust. "But if forced to guess, I'd say that he'll send men as the regent asks. My duke values peace, but he is Aneiran above all else. He won't allow men from the other houses to fight and die without adding Dantrielle's army to their cause."

Pronjed appeared to weigh this. "And if any of Dantrielle's allies considered defying House Solkara—the new dukes in Tounstrel or Noltierre, for instance— would Tebeo be able to prevail upon them to commit their armies as well?"

It struck her as an odd question. "Do you expect the southern houses to oppose you?"

"I expect nothing, First Minister. But as I told you already, I must prepare myself for every possibility."

"Well, I'm afraid I can't help you with this, Archminister. I know little about the dukes in question. As you must know, Tebeo was quite close to Bertin of

Noltierre and Vidor of Tounstrel. But he only met their sons on a few occasions, and the younger men keep their own counsel. Even if Tebeo tried to sway them one way or another—and I'm not certain that he would—I don't believe they would be moved."

Evanthya frowned slightly, realizing that she had answered his question after all. She hadn't sensed him using his powers on her, but the effect had been much the same. She couldn't decide which notion she found more disturbing, that he might be able to use his magic against her without her knowledge or that he could turn her to his purposes so easily without using any magic at all.

Another gust of wind swept through the ward, making the snow whirl and dance like tiny, frenzied wraiths.

Pronjed cast a look back toward the great hall and the tower from which they had come. "Perhaps we should return. The storm seems to be worsening."

"Yes. And you've learned all that you had hoped from our conversation."

Pronjed faced her again, his eyes, the color of sand on the Wethy shores, locking on hers. "Do you feel used, First Minister? You shouldn't. This was a profitable exchange for both of us. You probably know more about the regent's intentions than any other first minister in Aneira." A thin smile touched his lips and was gone. "I do hope that you use the knowledge wisely."

He turned again and started back the way they had come, leaving Evanthya little choice but to follow.

I intend to use it wisely, you bastard. I'll tell Fetnalla and every other first minister who'll listen to me. Maybe my duke and I can stop this war after all.

The rest of their visit to Dantrielle went just as Pronjed had anticipated. Or rather, just as the Weaver had said it would. The archminister had ideas of his own as to how they ought to proceed from here, but after nearly destroying the Weaver's plans with his decision to kill Carden a few turns before, and nearly getting himself killed in the process, Pronjed kept such thoughts to himself. For now at least, he would follow the Weaver's instructions without deviation. There had been a time when Pronjed believed himself essential to the movement. He knew better now. One day he would assert his influence again—when the Weaver's plans bore fruit, he would need trusted servants to run the various realms of the new Qirsi empire, and Pronjed had every intention of being one of those fortunate few. But during the next few turns he needed to repair the damage he had done to the Weaver's trust.

On the third morning since their arrival in Dantrielle, Numar, his small company of soldiers, and the archminister gathered in the castle's lower ward, mounted their horses, and, accompanied by the duke, duchess, and first minister, began to wend their way through the city streets.

He still sensed a residue of the tension that had clouded much of their stay in Tebeo's castle, but he could see as well that both Eandi men were trying to end their encounter cordially, Tebeo, no doubt, out of fear of the Solkaran temper, Numar out of his desire to appear reasonable until he had gathered enough power to let his true nature show.

The evening before, after avoiding any discussion of the coming war for more than a day, the regent had returned to the subject once again, asking the duke if he could foresee any circumstances under which Dantrielle might allow its army to join with those of the other houses to wage war against the Eibitharians.

Tebeo's first minister glanced at Pronjed, looking uncomfortable, as if the question itself had revealed to all the substance of their discussion in the ward. The duke, however, did not appear to notice. He had been sipping from his wine goblet and now he placed it carefully on the table and glared at the regent, firelight reflected in his dark brown eyes.

"With all respect, Lord Renbrere," the duke said, his voice shaking with anger. "I find your question insulting. It presumes that I would keep my house from fulfilling its duty to the realm and the Crown."

"I meant no offense, Tebeo, but after our conversation the day I arrived—"

"The men of Dantrielle have fought and died in every war ever waged by this realm," the duke broke in, leaning forward, his hands resting on the table. "We have acquitted ourselves nobly over the course of Aneira's history. I would even say admirably, and while I am not a boastful man, my lord, I assure you that I would willingly compare Dantrielle's performance in this regard with that of any house in the kingdom, including Solkara. For I have every confidence that Dantrielle would not suffer for the comparison."

At last the duchess laid a hand on Tebeo's arm. Glancing at her, the duke's face colored and he sat back, lowering his gaze.

"Forgive me, my lord. I've said too much."

"Not at all, Tebeo. I admire a man of passion. I only wished to know if we could count on you. Obviously, we can."

The duke continued to stare at his hands. "I must add, my lord, though I risk angering you by doing so, that even as the soldiers of Dantrielle have shown their valor in defense of Aneira, when her dukes have seen the land being led toward a foolish and destructive war, they have never shied from saying so."

Numar bristled. "Is that what you think I'm doing?"

"Yes, my lord, it is."

Abruptly the regent was on his feet. "How dare you speak to me so!"

"You forget, Lord Renbrere, that while you may be regent, I am a duke and you but a marquess. Further, sir, you are in my castle. If you speak to me thus, I will not hesitate to respond in kind."

The regent straightened, the corner of his mouth turning up in a bitter smirk. "I may be but a marquess, Lord Dantrielle, but I speak for the queen and for House Solkara. I assure you that my words carry as much force as Carden's ever did."

The two men stared at each other for some time, and at last it was Tebeo who looked away. "I don't doubt that they do, my lord. Forgive me if I spoke rashly."

Numar smiled benignly, but Pronjed saw the satisfaction in his eyes. "As I said, I admire passion, misguided though it might be."

The meal had almost ended and though both men seemed intent on not allowing the evening to end in anger, it was but a few moments before Numar excused himself from the great hall and returned to his chamber.

He said little to Pronjed as they walked through the corridors and he did not ask the archminister to join him in his quarters before retiring for the night. Pronjed hadn't been entirely honest with the first minister when they spoke in the ward, but he had meant what he said about Numar's mistrust of all he did. As far as he could tell, the regent viewed him as Chofya's man. No doubt he always would.

Numar had the archminister awakened early in the morning, and the regent did not linger long in the castle before departing. The duke and duchess offered to serve them a formal breakfast, but Numar asked only that they be given provisions for their ride back to Solkara.

Tebeo and Numar did not speak as they rode through the streets of Dantrielle. When they reached the gate and dismounted to say their farewells, however, the duke bowed to Numar, then straightened, clearing his throat.

"I hope the good relations Dantrielle has enjoyed with House Solkara will not suffer for my reckless words. I know little of what you and the emperor have discussed, my lord. It was not my place to make judgments."

"Don't trouble your mind with it further, Tebeo," the regent said, though his voice was tight. "Our houses have worked together for centuries, making Aneira great. Surely a friendship as old as that can weather a storm or two."

The duke smiled. "My lord is too kind. May your journey home be swift and safe."

Numar smiled, though it appeared forced, and began to leave the city. Pronjed bowed to the duke, murmuring a quick, "My lord." Then, glancing at Evanthya, he nodded, and steered his mount through the gate.

For the balance of the morning the company from Solkara made its way through the Great Forest in silence, Pronjed riding just behind the regent. Around midday, however, as the sun finally burned through the dark clouds that had hung over the land for so long, Numar slowed his mount so that the archminister could ride beside him.

"A most interesting visit."

"Indeed, my lord."

"Did you learn anything of value from the first minister?"

"Very little."

"Would you tell me if you had?"

Pronjed glanced at the regent, who was gazing at the road ahead.

"Of course, my lord. I serve House Solkara, and though your brother may be called duke, only a fool would fail to see that you lead us."

A grin flashed across the regent's face and was gone. "An interesting choice of words, Archminister."

"Yes, my lord."

"Tell me about the woman."

Pronjed shrugged. "She's protective of her duke and wary of Dantrielle's rivals."

Numar laughed. "Solkara and Dantrielle are hardly rivals. The Solkaran Supremacy is well over four centuries old. We haven't truly been rivals since the earliest days of the kingdom."

"Perhaps not to the Solkaran mind, my lord. But with all that's happened in the royal city over the past few turns, some of the other houses perceive weakness in the throne."

"You can't honestly think that Dantrielle has designs on the crown. He'd be a fool to challenge us."

It had to be done carefully. There were soldiers all around them and though they rode at a respectful distance, they would notice anything unusual.

"And yet, I believe that in questioning the wisdom of the coming war, Tebeo has, in effect, declared his intention to defy you." As he spoke the words, Pronjed reached out with his magic to touch the regent's mind. He didn't push hard, as he had when he forced Carden to plunge the dagger into his own chest. Rather, this touch was as light and gentle as a warm breeze in the growing turns. It was so soft that Numar never realized what had happened. He simply heard Pronjed's words and believed them as if he himself had spoken them.

"I fear you're right," he said, nodding sagely.

Pronjed nearly laughed aloud. He had convinced Evanthya to oppose the war, and to counsel her duke to do the same. He hadn't even drawn upon his magic for that. He had wounded her pride and then made her believe that he wanted Dantrielle to support the war. She would do all she could to oppose him.

And now, with what he had just done to Numar, he had ensured that Tebeo's reluctance to send his men into battle would be seen as treason in Solkara. He still had to win back the Weaver's trust, but if all in Aneira went as he thought it would, that would prove easy enough. He had long been one of the Weaver's most valued chancellors and in time he would be again. In the end, the Weaver would see fit to give him charge of whatever realm he wanted.

Chapter
Six

Curtell, Braedon

I t is the wrong decision!" the older Qirsi said again, gesturing sharply for emphasis. "You know this is so, High Chancellor. You have to tell the emperor he's made a terrible mistake!"

Dusaan shook his head, his frustration mounting by the moment. Didn't the man know that it wouldn't matter what he said to the emperor? Didn't he understand how this emperor's mind worked?

"I've spoken to him, Chancellor," he said, struggling to keep his voice even. "I've told him several times that his decision is likely to disturb several of the southern lords."

"Then tell him again!"

That nearly ended the discussion. True, none of them knew that he was a Weaver, that he led a great movement. But still, even in his capacity as high chancellor of the Braedon Empire, Dusaan could only tolerate so much. Before he could say anything, however, one of the young ministers broke in, and the debate began anew.

For much of the morning Dusaan had watched and listened as the same arguments chased one another around his ministerial chamber again and again. Only a turn before, his suspicions of the Qirsi growing, Emperor Harel the Fourth had decided to reclaim from his ministers and chancellors responsibility for mediating disputes among his nobles. At the time, fearing that the emperor would take from him responsibility for the treasury, Dusaan had welcomed the decision. The high chancellor depended upon the Braedon treasury for funds to pay the cost of running his conspiracy. Had the emperor forced him to relinquish control of the fee accountings, it might have dealt the movement a crippling blow. The mediation of disputes, on the other hand, had seemed a harmless enough duty to hand back to the Eandi fool. Little had he known.

"The lords of Grensyn, have always laid claim to the moors west of the Grensyn River," the old chancellor said. "Indeed, all the southern lordships, from Finkirk across to Muelry have traditionally controlled the lands to their west. All, that is, except the coastal houses. Muelry's new claims fly in the face of eight centuries of practice."

"We've been over this, Stavel," Dusaan said, his eyes closed.

"Yes, we have. But someone needs to explain all this to the emperor."

"Why?" Nitara. Among all the Qirsi serving in Harel's palace the Weaver thought her and one other the most likely to join his movement.

The older man blinked, and in spite of his annoyance, Dusaan had to stifle a chuckle. "What?" Stavel asked.

The woman shrugged. "Why does this need to be explained to the emperor? Yes, it's been done this way for hundreds of years. But people in Muelry are starving. It's been common knowledge for years that the land between the Rimerock and Muelry Rivers is poor land for farming. The land between the Rimerock and Rawsyn's Wash isn't much better." She glanced around the room as if to see who was listening to her. They all were. "It must be something in the waters of the Rimerock." She faced Stavel again. "In any case, Grensyn Moor has far better land, and it's more than broad enough to accommodate some of Muelry's people."

"That's not the point!"

"But it should be." Kayiv. The other one Dusaan hoped to turn. "Should we continue to let the people of Muelry suffer, just because a group of Eandi lords decided eight hundred years ago that the entire moor belonged to Grensyn?"

It was a sound argument, yet one that also struck Dusaan as quite illuminating. More than any other Qirsi he had ever met, Kayiv reminded the Weaver of himself as a younger man. Proud, keenly intelligent, willing—some might say even eager—to challenge custom, and fiercely devoted to the Qirsi people. When the time came, he would be a valuable member of the movement. Yet, Dusaan's aim in leading this cause had always been the betterment of his own people. It had never occurred to him that centuries of Eandi rule had taken their toll on Eandi commoners as well, that the destruction of the Eandi courts and the establishment of a Qirsi nobility might be hailed by Ean's children as well as by Qirsar's.

The young man's reasoning in this discussion, like Dusaan's own, seemed odd for another reason as well. It placed them both in the position of supporting the emperor. Dusaan would have little choice but to take Harel's part no matter his personal opinion on the matter. As high chancellor, this was his duty. But he found himself forced to admit that Harel's decision in this one instance was absolutely correct. The mere notion of it made him uncomfortable.

"Surely, High Chancellor," the older Qirsi began once again, "you see the importance of preserving custom in matters pertaining to the lordships. If we can take part of the moor from Grensyn, then what's to stop Pinthrel from laying claim to the rest of Braedon Wood, or Refte from challenging Oerdd's claim to the northern half of the hills?" He opened his hands, as if in supplication. "This path leads to turmoil. You must not be blind to this."

Dusaan had to smile at the old man's fear. Some Qirsi, he knew, were sorely ill prepared for the changes that were coming to the Forelands.

"I assure you, Chancellor, the emperor's decision will do no such thing. It may anger a few of the lords, but it will not lead to the downfall of the empire." Several of the ministers laughed at this, though Stavel only appeared to grow more distraught. "Circumstances in the south are especially difficult right now," Dusaan went on, trying to sound reasonable. "Muelry is still recovering from the pestilence that struck there during the last growing. And as Nitara has pointed out, her lands are poorly suited to growing anything more than grasses and thistle. Pinthral and Refte have no need of more land, and would not be granted such if they requested it."

Stavel started to protest, but Dusaan raised his hand, silencing him. "The matter is decided. The emperor has spoken, and I believe that a majority of those in this chamber agree with his solution." This might have been a stretch, but none of the others would question him, not on this. "Word of the emperor's decision will be sent south in the morning." He glanced around the chamber. The older chancellor and his small group of allies appeared disheartened, but Nitara, Kayiv, and several of the younger ministers looked far more pleased than they usually did at these discussions. "Is there anything else?"

He knew there would be—he had heard several of the ministers speaking of it in the corridor earlier that day—but it was not for him to broach the subject.

That task fell to Kayiv. Naturally.

"You've heard of the death of Lord Lachmas?" There seemed to be a gleam in the young Qirsi's bright golden eyes.

"Yes, I have. A tragedy for all of Braedon. The emperor was rather distraught."

"I don't doubt it."

Dusaan held the man's gaze until at last Kayiv looked away.

"If there's something on your mind, Minister, you should speak and be done with it."

"Isn't it obvious, High Chancellor?" Nitara asked, answering for the young man. As he had before on several occasions, Dusaan found himself thinking that she and Kayiv might very well be lovers. "Nobles have been dying throughout the other realms over the past year, all of their deaths attributed to the Qirsi conspiracy. Now it seems that this conspiracy has finally reached Braedon."

Actually it hadn't. The Weaver had not ordered Lord Lachmas's death and he had no reason to believe that any of his underlings in the movement had acted without his consent. Indeed, he had no underlings in Braedon. He needed to be able to walk in the dreams of those who served him, and his renown in Braedon would have made it too dangerous for him to do so. This was, until just a few days before, one of the great weaknesses in his plan. He could not afford to have Qirsi in the Braedon courts serving him, but the longer Braedon remained immune to the movement's attacks, the more the realm's lack of strife would draw the attention of others in the Forelands, Eandi and Qirsi. With Lord Lachmas's death, that was no longer a concern.

As far as Dusaan could tell, the man had truly died as the result of a hunting accident. According to the message from Lachmas, a stray arrow, apparently from the bow of his younger son, struck the lord in the back. The arrow itself might not have killed him, but the fall from his mount snapped his neck. A tragic accident that aided Dusaan's cause as much as any planned assassination could have. The emperor was terrified. He had ordered the doubling of the number of guards positioned at every gate in Curtell city, and had taken even more drastic precautions with the palace walls and barbicans. It seemed the emperor's Qirsi were frightened as well, or at least curious.

"We have no evidence that the conspiracy had anything to do with this," he said calmly. "The message the emperor received from Lachmas made it sound like an accident. Tragic to be sure, but completely innocent."

Kayiv smirked. "Of course it did. Lachmas dies in a hunting accident. Filib of Thorald is killed by common road thieves. Carden of Aneira takes his own life. Grigor, his brother, is hanged for poisoning the queen and her dukes. And we're just to accept that all of these deaths have nothing to do with the conspiracy, that Eandi nobles are dying in great number by sheer coincidence." He shook his head. "I, for one, don't believe it."

"I see." Dusaan glanced at the others. "And the rest of you?"

"It does seem odd," Stavel said. Others nodded. "You say that the emperor was distraught. Was there more to it than that? Is it true that he trebled the palace guard?"

Dusaan hesitated, as they would expect. "Yes," he admitted. "It's true."

"Is there reason to believe that an attack on the emperor is imminent?"

The high chancellor had to smile. "There is no reason to believe that there has been any attack, or that any is forthcoming."

"It wouldn't matter if there was," Kayiv said, and Dusaan thought he heard a hint of pride in the young man's voice. "If the conspiracy decides that our emperor is next on their list of Eandi nobles to be killed, all the guards in Curtell won't be able to stop them."

Stavel eyed him warily. "You speak as would one of these renegades, Minister. You'd best take care you're not branded a traitor."

Kayiv glared at the man. "Branded by whom, Chancellor? Traitors come in many forms."

"That's enough! Both of you," Dusaan added, glowering at Kayiv and Stavel in turn. He could foresee a day when having Harel's ministers and chancellors questioning each others' loyalty might serve his purposes, but that time had not yet come. The emperor was frightened enough already. Any whisperings among his Qirsi to the effect that one or more of them might be disloyal would convince the emperor that no white-hair could be trusted, not even Dusaan. "I will not have the Qirsi of this palace casting accusations at one another like quarrelsome children! For the last time, Lord Lachmas died as a result of a hunting accident, and until we have proof to the contrary, we shall not discuss the matter further. Those of you who can't accept that should leave the palace at once." He allowed his gaze to travel the chamber, as if waiting for any number of them to walk out of the room. "Good," he said at last, lowering his voice. "The emperor is imagining Qirsi traitors in every corner. The last thing he needs right now is to have his most trusted advisors fueling his suspicions."

Kayiv gave a small mirthless laugh. "He hasn't trusted us for some time now. Lachmas's death is probably just the excuse he's been looking for to have us all hanged."

For all the promise the Weaver saw in this young man, he also found him thoroughly exasperating, in no small part because of comments like these. The minister seemed to assume that Dusaan was just another fawning Qirsi advisor who had turned his back on their people to devote himself to the Eandi courts. Well, the time had come to banish that notion from his mind.

"This discussion is over," he said. "We'll meet again tomorrow."

He watched as the underministers stood and began to leave his chamber, some of them whispering among themselves, but most of them silent and withdrawn.

Dusaan did not usually allow himself to grow anxious about anything—in his position, how could he? But waiting for the ministers to go, he felt his pulse racing like that of a war stallion driven beyond endurance. There was a risk here. Not much of one, to be sure. He had studied these two for some time, and he felt fairly confident of how they would respond. But there was danger nonetheless, far more than he had ever entertained before.

"Minister, would you stay a moment?" he called, just as Kayiv reached the door. His voice sounded even, calm.

The woman remained as well. They had to be lovers. Normally he would not have tolerated her presence, but in this case he had expected it, even hoped for it. The promise that had drawn him to the one could be found in both.

He wouldn't tell all. Not even his most trusted servants knew that much. But all wouldn't be necessary.

"Close the door."

Kayiv and Nitara exchanged a look. Then he pushed the door closed and they returned to their seats. They made a fine pair, he slender and muscular for a Qirsi, she lean as well, but with a round, attractive face, and full lips. Just the kind of young nobility that the Weaver would need to lead the Forelands when the Eandi courts finally fell.

"You need to learn when to speak your mind and when to remain silent," the Weaver said, taking a seat near theirs. "You've nearly got old Stavel convinced that you're a traitor."

Kayiv looked away. "We're all Qirsi here," he said, a bitter note in his voice. "We should be able to say what we wish without worrying that others will go running to the emperor spouting tales of the conspiracy."

"Come now. You can't really be that simple."

The younger man glared at him, but Dusaan was watching Nitara. All this time he had been planning to turn Kayiv, with the hope that the woman would follow. But it suddenly occurred to him that she was the more reasonable of the two, the one who could control the other.

"What do you mean by that?" she asked, clearly understanding already.

"Just what you think I do. To say that we're all Qirsi is to ignore the lessons of our people's history. No doubt the Weavers who led the Qirsi invasion nine centuries ago thought much as Kayiv does, just before Carthach betrayed them to the armies of the north."

She sat forward, light yellow eyes wide and eager. "Lachmas was killed by the conspiracy, wasn't he?"

Dusaan smiled. He wasn't ready to answer her just yet. "Why would the conspiracy want him dead?"

Kayiv shrugged. "Because he's Eandi."

"You think that's reason enough?"

Nitara shook her head. "No, it wouldn't be. They have to see some gain in it, some way in which it would weaken the empire."

"Good," Dusaan said, nodding. "Can you think of any?"

She sat still for several moments, her eyes trained on the floor, as if she were looking for answers in the patterned carpet. "Lachmas and Curtell were rivals in the earliest days of the empire," she said at last. "But for the past several centuries, the lords of Lachmas have been among Curtell's more reliable allies." She looked up. "Is it possible that they wanted to make it seem the act of one of the other houses, say Qestryd or Hanyck? Houses that have been more vocal in their dissatisfaction with the Curtell Dynasty."

Dusaan pressed his fingertips together, watching her reason it out. She really was quite lovely. "Perhaps. To what end?"

Nitara frowned, looking to Kayiv for help. "Could they be trying to start a civil war? That's been their aim elsewhere. At least that's how it seems."

Kayiv shook his head. "It wouldn't work here. The ruling houses in the other realms need at least a few allies among the rest of the houses. Without it they could be overthrown. But here . . ." He shrugged. "House Curtell is really the only power in Braedon. The emperor could crush any dissent before it became a threat to his hold on the throne."

Dusaan nodded. "Good," he said again. "Very good."

"So then why was Lachmas murdered?" Nitara asked, her brow creased.

The Weaver regarded her placidly. "Actually he wasn't."

Kayiv narrowed his eyes. "You know this for certain?"

"Yes, as it happens, I do."

"How?"

Dusaan could hear it in the man's voice. He knew already, just as she had before. They both would serve him well.

"Because if he had been, I would have been the one paying the assassins."

They shared a glance again, and Nitara grinned as if to say, *You see, I told you.*

"You're with the conspiracy?" Kayiv asked, sounding doubtful.

"We prefer to call it 'the movement,' but yes, I am."

Nitara started to speak, but the minister stopped her, placing a hand on her shoulder. "Why should we believe you?" He gave that same small laugh again, his eyes darting about the chamber as if he expected the imperial army to appear at any moment. "Why shouldn't we just go to the emperor right now and reveal you as a traitor?"

"You're welcome to, if that's what you wish to do. I'll deny it, of course. I'll tell the emperor that I was testing you, that after your strange comments in our discussion today, I feared that you had betrayed the empire. Your decision to inform the emperor will have established your innocence, and so life in the palace will continue on as if nothing happened at all. Except that the three of us will know the truth, and eventually, when the opportunity presents itself, I'll have you both killed, or imprisoned as traitors, which I suppose is the same thing."

The blood drained from Nitara's face and even Kayiv looked unnerved, although he managed to hold the Weaver's gaze. Dusaan continued to stare at them for a few moments, his expression grave. Then at last he smiled, though neither of them looked relieved when he did.

"But I don't think that will be necessary, because I don't think either of you is going to repeat any of this to the emperor."

Kayiv took Nitara's hand, his eyes never straying from the Weaver's face. "You sound so certain."

"I've been watching you both for some time now."

"Watching us?"

"All of you, really—the emperor's ministers and chancellors—trying to decide which of you might be prepared to join the movement."

"And you chose us."

"Does that surprise you?"

Kayiv didn't answer, but Nitara released his hand, shifting in her chair. Her color had returned and she was eyeing the Weaver with interest.

"What would we have to do?"

"Not much at first. Mostly you'd act as though nothing at all had happened. The three of us would meet from time to time so that I might inform you of how our plans are progressing. And you'd probably receive some gold."

To their credit, neither of them asked the obvious question.

"How long have you been with the movement?" she asked instead.

Forever. I am the movement. "A long time. Since its inception."

"Are you one of its leaders."

"The movement is led by a Weaver. None of those who serve him know his name or where he can be found. But all instructions come from him."

"A Weaver," she repeated breathlessly. "I thought they were all gone."

Dusaan had to smile at the irony. Somewhere in the Forelands, another Weaver, a man named Grinsa, searched for him, even as he hunted the man in turn. "I believe you'll find that there are more of them than any have imagined. With the Eandi ruling the Forelands, they keep themselves hidden, fearing for their lives. But when this war is over and the Forelands belong to the Qirsi, they'll be free to reveal themselves." *And then the Eandi will see how powerful our people truly can be.*

"A Weaver," she whispered again, as if the word itself were new to her. "How does he—"

"He walks in the dreams of those who serve his cause."

Kayiv nodded. "Of course. How else could the consp—?" He stopped himself. "How else could the movement strike at so many courts at once?"

"The realms of the Eandi are weakened already. It won't be long until the Weaver reveals himself and asserts his power over all the Forelands. When that happens, the men and women who serve him will take their place in a new pantheon of Qirsi nobility. Those who oppose him—Eandi and Qirsi—will perish."

"What if his movement fails?" the younger man asked.

"It won't."

"The invasion," Nitara whispered. "The invasion is part of his plan, isn't it? First he weakens the kingdoms, and then, when the Eandi go to war, further weakening themselves, he strikes at them." She stared at Dusaan, as if seeing him for the first time. "You've been pushing the emperor toward this invasion all along, haven't you? That's your role in this."

"That's part of my role, yes, although in truth, I haven't had to push very hard. Harel wants this war, or at least he thinks he does. That's something you should always remember about the Eandi. Given the opportunity to destroy themselves, they will usually take it. We need only be patient and await a time when we can use their foolishness to our advantage."

"It sounds as though the movement can't fail," Kayiv said, a familiar note of defiance in his tone. It almost seemed that the man couldn't speak without challenging someone to a fight. "All the work's been done already. Why would you need us?"

"Our work won't be done for many years. Surely you must understand that. The Eandi may be fools but they're not cowards, and they don't take defeat lightly. We need to know which Qirsi will support us when the time comes, and we need to know that we can count on those Qirsi when the Eandi realize their error and turn their weapons on us." He paused, smiling at both of them. "And of course, when victory is ours, we'll need those young Qirsi nobles of whom I spoke just a moment ago."

Bells began to toll in Curtell city and all of them paused. Midday. The emperor would be expecting him shortly, and he still had to attend to the treasury accounting.

"I'm afraid I need your answer now," Dusaan said. "I've told you what the movement can offer you, and I've told you as well what will happen to you both should you refuse us. Now the two of you must decide."

Kayiv opened his hands. "You haven't given us much of a choice, High Chancellor. Riches and power on the one hand, or death on the other. Do you really expect us to say no?"

"Of course not. But I do expect you to follow all of my instructions. The first time one of you defies me in any way, either by refusing a command, or by doing or saying anything that endangers the movement, I'll kill you both. I won't have you joining our cause merely to acquire wealth or ensure your survival. We're offering you and every Qirsi in the land a wondrous future, but you'll have to earn your right to see that future, just as you'll have to earn your gold. Do you understand?"

Nitara nodded. "Yes." She actually smiled, though the color had fled her cheeks again. "I've hoped for this for some time now. Truly I have. I just never imagined that my path to the movement was so close at hand."

"I know that you'll serve us well." He turned his gaze to Kayiv. "And you, Minister? Are you ready to serve the Weaver as well?"

The young man looked away, his mouth twisting sourly.

Nitara, slipped from her chair and knelt before him, taking both his hands in hers and looking up into his bright eyes. "We've spoken of this. We've dreamed of it. Why do you fight it now?"

Kayiv gave a small shake of his head. "I don't know," he said quietly.

"He fights it because he dislikes me," Dusaan said, knowing as he spoke the words that it was true. "Isn't that right, Minister?"

The man faced him, though reluctantly. "I don't know you well enough to dislike you, High Chancellor. But I can't say that I trust you, at least not enough to place our lives in your hands."

"I'm afraid you're too late, Kayiv. Your lives are in my hands. You need to make your peace with that. Serve the movement well and I assure you, you have nothing to fear from me."

Kayiv looked down at Nitara again. After several moments, he nodded, all the time gazing into her eyes. "Very well."

"Good. Leave me now. I must see the emperor. You'll receive your gold shortly and we'll speak again after our daily discussion two days hence." Dusaan paused briefly, thinking. "Kayiv, during that discussion you'll say something to Stavel that will anger me, that will force me to ask you to remain here again after the others have gone. I don't know what we'll be speaking of, so you'll have to think of it on your own." He grinned. "You seem quite adept at saying the inappropriate thing, however. I don't expect you'll have much trouble finding the right words."

That, of all things, brought a smile to the young minister's lips. "No, I don't suppose I will."

The two of them rose and started toward the door.

"Neither of you has asked me how much gold you'll be receiving," he said, stopping them once more. "That pleases me."

Kayiv turned. "I had wondered."

"I don't doubt it. It should be approximately one hundred qinde, imperial, of course."

Kayiv raised an eyebrow at this, but Dusaan merely smiled.

"I'm paid in imperials, as well," he said, the first direct falsehood he had told them. "If we were to start spending common currency in the markets in Curtell it would draw unwanted attention."

Actually, Dusaan usually paid those who served him in the common currency used by the other realms. Imperial qinde were held to have less value than the qinde used by the six; his underlings would prefer the common currency. More to the point, he feared that paying imperial qinde to his servants in Sanbira or Aneira or any of the other realms might reveal his identity. Few Qirsi in Braedon had access to so much gold and it wouldn't take the more clever ones much time to realize that he was the mysterious Weaver who entered their dreams at night. By the same token, he feared that paying the more valuable currency to these two would raise their suspicions. Why would the high chancellor of Braedon have access to so much common currency if he were merely another soldier in the Weaver's army?

"That's a good deal of gold," Kayiv said.

"One hundred is a guess. It may be a bit more, it may be less. Either way, you're right, it's more than you make in an entire year. Don't spend it like a drunken Eandi. You'll only draw the emperor's attention."

"How is it that the Qirsi we now serve have become so wealthy?"

The Weaver gave a thin smile. "You'll find, Minister, that the movement's leaders have little tolerance for such questions. The Weaver has resources that you can't even fathom, and power to match. Leave it at that, and be grateful that he's asked you to be his ally in this fight."

Kayiv nodded, and a moment later he and Nitara stepped into the corridor, pulling Dusaan's door closed behind them.

Dusaan returned to his writing table and pulled the imperial treasury accounting from the shelf beside it. Arranging for the ministers' gold would be easy. The wages of all the emperor's ministers and chancellors were paid at the end of the waxing, as were those of his soldiers and laborers. Finding two hundred qinde for these two would be no more difficult than it had been appropriating gold for his other servants.

He had no doubt that Nitara would serve him well, as long as she listened more to him than to her lover. Kayiv, however, was another matter. He possessed three magics, two of which—shaping and language of beasts—were among the more potent Qirsi powers. He had a keen intellect and great confidence in his own abilities, qualities that Dusaan looked for in his most trusted servants. But he was contentious and too quick to question his superiors. Since the young man's arrival in the palace several years before, Dusaan had attributed his difficult manner to dissatisfaction with Eandi rule in general and Harel's ineptitude in particular, sentiments the Weaver shared. After this day's conversation, however, he was forced to wonder if it was something inherent in Kayiv himself.

Dusaan had long been reluctant to turn any of Harel's Qirsi to his cause, fearing that working so closely with those who served him might make it impossible to maintain the secrecy on which his very life depended. But in this instance, he drew some comfort from the fact that he would be able to keep watch on Kayiv himself. The man struck him as a most dangerous addition to the movement.

They didn't dare say a word until they were back in her chamber, and even with her door closed, Nitara was afraid to speak in anything more than a whisper. Despite her fear of what the high chancellor had suddenly become, seemingly before their eyes, she could barely contain the mixture of exhilaration and apprehension that gripped her now. For nearly a year, she and Kayiv had spoken of joining the conspiracy, sharing their dreams of a new Qirsi Supremacy in hushed tones as they lay together in her bed, still breathless, their passion sated. It had never occurred to either of them that others in the palace shared this dream. Certainly they had never guessed that Dusaan might be anything less than completely loyal to the emperor.

Learning that he had joined the movement years ago, that he had guessed that they would be open to doing the same simply by observing them in their daily discussions, both thrilled her and frightened her. Had they really been so obvious? Or was the high chancellor simply far more formidable than they had ever believed? In either case she could not help but wonder at her own carelessness.

Kayiv dropped himself into the chair by her hearth and Nitara sat on the bed, watching him. He had surprised her with his reluctance to join the movement, and even now, alone with her, he appeared uncertain, as if he feared they had made a terrible mistake.

"What is it?" she asked, her voice low. "What's bothering you so?"

He gave a small shake of his head. "I honestly don't know. I sense that Dusaan isn't telling us everything. I suppose I'm still not convinced that he's really with the conspiracy. What if he goes to the emperor? We've just committed treason against the empire, and though we've spoken of doing so for some time, I feel that we were coerced into pledging ourselves to the movement. It almost seemed that the high chancellor had a blade pointed at my heart."

"Well, he did threaten us. But I don't see that he had much choice. He confessed to being a traitor, too. He needed to be certain that we wouldn't betray him to Harel."

"No, he didn't." Kayiv stood, walking to the tapestry that hung on her wall and pushing it to the side so that he could gaze out the narrow window onto the palace courtyard. Cold air swirled through the room. "He said it himself. If we tried to betray him, he'd claim that it had been a deception, a test of our loyalty to the throne."

"I'm not certain that would have saved him. A turn or two ago it might have, but with Lachmas's death the emperor sees traitors everywhere. He might not have believed such a story, even hearing it from Dusaan. And I think the chancellor knew that as well."

"Maybe," he said, sounding unconvinced.

"It's getting cold in here."

Kayiv glanced at her, then let the tapestry fall over the window once more. He returned to his chair and sat again, rubbing his hands together, his jaw clenched.

"I sensed the same thing you did," she told him. "He wasn't telling us everything. But I don't think he was lying to us about where his loyalties lie. He's with the conspiracy. And now we are as well. Isn't that what you want?"

"I thought it was."

"What's changed?"

"Nothing. Nothing will change. Maybe that's what bothers me. I'm not certain that replacing the Eandi courts with Qirsi courts is going to do much good, especially if the Qirsi nobles all answer to this Weaver Dusaan mentioned. How long do you think the Eandi will tolerate that before they rebel?"

"We'll control the armies by then. We'll control them with our magic."

"There aren't enough of us, Nitara. Think about it for a moment. There are ten Eandi for every Qirsi in the Forelands. Unless the Weaver intends to execute ten of thousands of them and imprison the rest, there's no way we can hold the realms once we have them."

"Maybe they won't rebel."

He frowned. "You can't really believe that's a possibility."

"Of course I can. They might resist at first. But what if Qirsi rule brings better times for the Eandi as well? Not for the nobles, mind you, but for the commoners. What if the Qirsi end the kind of foolishness we were discussing today—the dispute in Grensyn? Don't you think that might win their loyalty?"

"I think you're asking an awful lot of Eandi commoners. And I don't think you truly understand how much our people are hated throughout the land." Kayiv shook his head, a look of despair in his golden eyes. "Our power would be based on fear—fear of our magic, fear of the Weaver, fear created by more executions than I care to imagine. That's really the only way it would work."

"So then you admit that it could work."

He stared at her, as if unable to believe what he had just heard her say. "Yes, but at what cost?"

Nitara felt her anger rising, and when next she spoke it was with a passion she hadn't known she possessed. "After the invasion failed, the Eandi killed all the Qirsi commanders, and all the Weavers as well! To this day, they've continued to kill every Weaver they could find! And you believe we should feel sorry for those who'll have to die so that we can win our freedom?"

He actually looked afraid—afraid of her, she realized, a twisting pain in her chest. "It probably won't come to that," she went on a moment later, trying to sound more reasonable. "The high chancellor said there might be more Weavers than we thought. With a Weaver leading each realm, there'll be little need for executions."

She swung herself off the bed, stepping to his chair so that she could stand behind him and rub his shoulders. "Come now, love. We've spoken of this for too long for you to back away from it now. Besides, we've given Dusaan our word, and I certainly didn't sense any deception in his voice when he spoke of killing us if we defied him." She bent over and kissed the side of his neck. "We're led by a Weaver," she whispered in his ear. "We're going to win this war. We can be nobles, rich, powerful. We can rule together. Surely you want that."

He took hold of her hands, drawing one to his lips and then the other. "Yes," he said quietly. "I do want that."

She circled the chair, stopping in front of him. "Then quit your brooding," she said, removing her ministerial robe and unbuttoning the dress she wore beneath it. "We're going to change the world together. We should be celebrating."

She let the dress fall to the floor and, stepping out of it, took Kayiv's hand and led him to her bed.

"It feels strange to celebrate a war," he said.

Nitara smiled and kissed him lightly on the lips, as she began to remove his clothes. "We're not. We're celebrating victory."

Chapter
Seven

t was several days before Cresenne felt well enough to undertake any sort of journey, and several more before she admitted as much to Grinsa and the herbmaster. Grinsa came to see her and Bryntelle each day, and, after two more unsuccessful attempts to hold their baby, actually managed to have her fall asleep in his arms. The look of joy on his face as he carefully returned his daughter to Cresenne's arms left no doubt in her mind that his love for the child was quickly becoming the most important consideration in his life.

Just as it was in hers.

She hadn't slept for more than a few hours at a time since Bryntelle's birth. The baby still was hungry almost all the time, her swaddling wet or soiled nearly as often. Never in her life had Cresenne worked so hard and had so little to show for the effort. Yet it was all she could do to remember to eat her own meals during the course of a day, so enamored was she of the girl, so willing, even eager, to pass her hours just staring at Bryntelle's face and hands. She should have been thinking of ways to use Grinsa's love of the girl to her advantage, but instead she was consumed with fear at the thought that he might do the same to her.

If you don't do as I ask, I'll have Bryntelle taken from you. He had threatened to have her placed in Glyndwr's dungeon as well, but he needn't have bothered. Cresenne's fear of losing her daughter overmastered all other concerns. And she sensed that Grinsa knew this.

She and the gleaner were swordsmen in a duel that had proven all too evenly matched. Each had a blade at the other's throat and a second pressed against the other's heart. A word from her and he would be executed as were all Weavers. A single thought conveyed to the Weaver who led the conspiracy and assassins would descend upon them like locusts on a ripe crop. A word from him and the baby would be torn from her arms and she would be executed as a traitor, leaving Bryntelle without a mother. Fear of the other stayed their hands. Fear, and love, though neither of them would have admitted it.

Watching Grinsa as he held Bryntelle, Cresenne wondered if he could really follow through on his threats, just as she questioned whether she could bring herself to have him killed. How could she ever explain such a thing to Bryntelle? How could she justify lying to the child about her father's death?

Still, though Cresenne doubted that Grinsa could harm her, she hadn't the courage to test his resolve. She claimed as long as she could to be too weary and sore to journey, but when at last both Glyndwr's healer and herbmaster pronounced her fit to leave the castle, she did not resist Grinsa's demand that she travel north off the steppe to Eibithar's City of Kings. She still had no intention of revealing to the king all she had done on the Weaver's behalf. She may well have loved Grinsa. She may even have harbored hopes of reconciling with him, of finding some way to rediscover their love so that the three of them could be a family. But she owed nothing to Tavis of Curgh. She wasn't about to risk the Weaver's wrath merely to prove his innocence.

The journey, which was only twelve leagues, went slowly, mostly because Cresenne insisted on resting each time Bryntelle needed to nurse. Still, this did not delay them as much as she had hoped it would. It seemed the baby found the rocking motion of the mount comforting. She slept far more and ate far less than usual as they rode.

Grinsa spent most of the journey beside them, straight backed and alert atop his mount, as if expecting an assault at any moment. As his father had instructed, Kearney the Younger had given them leave to take as many soldiers as they desired. In the end, fearing that too large an escort might draw unwanted attention, Grinsa and Tavis asked for only eight, a small number given how many people in Eibithar wanted the Curgh boy dead. It only took Cresenne half a day to understand that the young noble feared Glyndwr's men as much as he did road brigands or assassins from Kentigern. He rode alone much of the time, in front of Grinsa and Cresenne, but behind the first line of guards. He spoke to no one, and eyed the soldiers as one might rivals on the first day of a battle tournament. Cresenne could see the boy measuring himself against them, trying to determine if he could protect himself should they turn on him.

Though a short journey, the terrain proved difficult. For the first few days, as they steered their mounts through the highlands, the wind blew hard and cold from the west, howling in the boulders strewn across the land and making the tall brown grasses bow and quiver like frightened supplicants in Bian's Sanctuary. On the third day, they began the slow descent off the Caerissan Steppe, following a winding path that had been worn by years and years of use. At times the path grew so narrow that they had to ride in a single line. The wind continued to blow, and though Cresenne had hoped to keep them from reaching the royal city too quickly, she longed for this portion of their journey to end.

"What is it you see in the boy?" she finally asked Grinsa on that third morning, as they made their way down the slope of the steppe. The path was wider here, and Grinsa was just beside her.

She kept her voice low, but still the gleaner immediately looked at Tavis to see if he had heard. When the boy gave no indication that he had, Grinsa slowed his mount slightly, to put more distance between himself and Tavis. Cresenne did the same.

"I see what you see," he said softly. "An arrogant, spoiled boy, embittered by his dark fate, and more concerned with his own welfare than that of those around him."

She raised an eyebrow. "My, what a special friend you're found."

"I also see much promise in him, and many fine qualities that already distinguish him from other nobles. He's fiercely loyal to his realm and his house. He has more courage than you might expect—the scars he bears are testimony to his strength as well as his pride. And he's uncommonly clever. I believe, in time, he'll make a fine ruler, either for his dukedom or his kingdom."

"I see. Has he offered to make you his first minister?"

Grinsa laughed. "If you're trying to goad me, it won't work. Tavis would never think to do so, and I have no ambitions of that kind." He glanced at her, his expression turning grim. "But you should know this as well. He knows as much about my powers as you do, and he has never once tried to use that knowledge against me, nor has he shown any fear of my abilities. And of the two of you, I worry far less about him betraying me than I do about you."

He kicked at the flanks of his horse and sped forward until he had caught up to the boy. And for the rest of that day, Cresenne and Bryntelle rode alone.

They reached the royal city on the sixth day after their departure from Glyndwr. They had been able to see the city from the slope of the steppe for several days, and even from leagues away, Cresenne could not help but be impressed by the size of the city and its great castle. Both were square in shape, the fortress centered within the stone walls of the city. There was a sanctuary in each corner, one each, she knew, for the four ancient ones, Elined and Amon, Morna and Bian. But until their small company came to the city gates, she did not appreciate the true immensity of Eibithar's City of Kings. Neither the castle nor the city could be called beautiful. There was something ponderous and unimaginative in the design of both. She saw here none of the grace of the castles of southern Caerisse or Aneira, nor even the more subtle beauty of the older Eibitharian cities. What she did see was power, raw and unassailable. A royal city was supposed to be the realm's last defense against any invader, and more than all the other royal seats in the Forelands, except perhaps for the Imperial Palace in Curtell, the City of Kings met that need. She could not imagine any army, or combination of armies, defeating these walls and gates. Staring at the white stone and the formidable soldiers standing before them, Cresenne found herself wondering if the Weaver had ever seen this castle.

She had been curious to see if Tavis would be welcomed as a noble, but other than an ordinary complement of guards, no one awaited them at the city gate. If the Curgh boy was surprised by this, he gave no indication of it. But though Tavis wasn't met at the gate by the king or those who served him, he certainly was recognized. Guards glared at him, as did commoners in the streets and the city marketplace. Many of them pointed openly at the boy and a few brave souls shouted obscenities at him. The soldiers of Glyndwr offered no response, though one or two of them smirked at their companions. Tavis, to his credit, kept his eyes trained on the lane before him. Clearly he heard what was said—even riding behind him Cresenne could see his ears and neck reddening—but he didn't say anything or change the gait of his mount.

After a few moments, Grinsa looked over at Cresenne, and said simply, "I should ride with him," before leaving her to join Tavis.

She couldn't say for certain whether he did this to offer comfort to the boy or out of concern for his safety, but he remained by the noble's side until they were within the castle's inner walls.

The king met them at the interior gate. He was dressed simply in soldier's garb, and aside from the silver, red, and black baldric he wore on his back, there was little about him to indicate that he was a noble at all. At least, this was Cresenne's initial impression, watching him from a distance as he offered a solemn greeting to Tavis and Grinsa. The three men spoke quietly for several moments, or rather, Grinsa did a good deal of talking while the king and Tavis listened. At last, Kearney nodded and led the three of them to where Cresenne still waited on her mount. She was holding Bryntelle, of course, and as the king approached, she pulled her baby closer to her chest.

"You know who I am," he said, stopping just beside her.

Seeing him up close, she realized that he was younger than he had appeared. Though his hair was silver, his face was smooth and boyish, his eyes a bright, clear green. She would have liked to say something cutting, something that would make him realize that she owed no allegiance to him or his realm. But all she could manage was a simple, "Yes, Your Majesty."

"You should know as well that no matter what those leading your movement have told you, I'm neither a tyrant nor a fool. If you answer my questions honestly, you'll be treated fairly. If you refuse me, or try to deceive me in any way, your child will be taken from you and you'll be imprisoned. Do you understand?"

Her heart pounded in her chest like ocean breakers and she was shivering despite the sun. She looked past the king to Grinsa, who stood just behind him, his gaze lowered. She wanted to rail at him, to ask him how he could choose this man and his court over Bryntelle, but once more the words wouldn't come. After a moment's pause, she merely nodded.

"Good," the king said. "Lord Curgh and the gleaner tell me that you're part of the conspiracy we've heard so much about, and I have no reason to doubt their word. They also tell me that you're unlikely to flee or try something foolish. They say that you love your daughter too much to risk harming her or yourself. On their recommendation, you'll be given a chamber near theirs and food, and you'll be allowed to come and go as you please. Don't do anything to make me regret the faith I'm placing in your good sense." He turned to Grinsa and Tavis. "Eat, rest. We'll speak later in the day."

Both men bowed to Kearney.

"My thanks, Your Majesty," Tavis said. "We'll await your summons."

The king nodded and walked back into the nearest of the tower entrances. An instant later one of the king's soldiers stepped forward and gestured toward a different doorway.

"This way, my lord," he said to Tavis, and even Cresenne heard the ice in his voice. The king's men, it seemed, were no more convinced of the young lord's innocence than were the soldiers of Glyndwr.

Grinsa helped Cresenne from her mount, and all of them followed the guard up a winding stairway and into the castle corridors. They were given three rooms on an otherwise empty hallway. Grinsa took the room between Cresenne's and Tavis's, telling them both to await word from him before going anywhere.

"Surely I'm safe within Audun's Castle," the boy said, frowning. "I'm not a child to be kept in my chamber while you wander freely about the place."

For once, Cresenne agreed with him. But a sharp look from the gleaner made it clear to both of them that he would not discuss the point.

Cresenne's room was ample for guest quarters, though rather spare and chill. Aside from a bed, a wardrobe, and a single chair by the dark hearth, it was empty. She gently laid Bryntelle on the bed and watched her for a moment. The child slept still, though her mouth moved as though she were suckling.

Almost immediately someone knocked at the door. Pulling it open, she saw a young servant, burdened with a large load of wood and kindling. He bowed shyly to her and hurried to the hearth, where he began to build her a fire. She nearly stopped him—she could have started the flame with a single thought—but before she could speak, Grinsa appeared in the doorway.

He cast a quick look at the servant, then cleared his throat.

"How is she?" he asked, nodding toward Bryntelle.

"She's fine."

He nodded, his eyes wandering to the servant again. The boy had piled several logs in the hearth, placing the rest beside it.

"That will do," Grinsa told him. "We can take care of the rest."

The boy stared up at them, looking frightened. Certainly he had seen Qirsi before, living and laboring in a castle, but from the expression on his face, one might have thought that they were the first sorcerers he had ever met.

"Yes, sir," he murmured. He bowed and quickly left the room.

Grinsa closed the door.

Cresenne turned away from him. "It didn't take you long to tell the king all about me, did it?"

"You work for the conspiracy. Do you honestly think I'd allow him to make you a guest in his castle without telling him that first?"

She shrugged.

"I also told him I didn't think you were a threat to him or anyone else."

"That might have been a mistake."

"I don't think so."

She gave a small laugh, facing him again. "You're just like them. You think nothing of using our baby as a weapon against me."

"We're both guilty of that, Cresenne. She deserves better from both of us."

"I won't tell the king anything. I won't betray the movement and I won't risk my life to save the Curgh boy."

He gazed at her for some time, offering no response, until she began to grow uncomfortable. She crossed her arms over her chest, her eyes wandering the room.

"What are you looking at?" she finally asked.

"Did you ever love me?"

"I did what I did for the movement. You must know that by now." Her hands were shaking and she rubbed her arms, trying to get warm.

Grinsa glanced back at the hearth and an instant later flames leaped from the wood.

"That should warm you."

"Thank you."

"I did love you," he said, stepping past her and sitting on the bed beside their baby. He looked down at Bryntelle for a long time, running a gentle finger along her cheek. *Hands more gentle than any I've ever known . . .*

"I loved you more than I've loved anyone since my wife died," he went on, his voice low now. "When I realized you were the one who sent that assassin, it nearly killed me."

"Why are you telling me this?"

"I'm not sure. I suppose I've been wanting to for some time now. I never thought I'd get the chance."

"So is this the reason you brought me to the City of Kings? Are you trying to exact some measure of revenge for what I did to you?"

He shook his head, though he still gazed a the child. "I'm doing it because I have to, just as I had to leave you in Galdasten."

"To protect the boy."

"It's more than that." He looked back at her. "Your movement will bring ruin to the Forelands, Cresenne. You may think that you're building a new realm for the Qirsi, but all you're doing is destroying the land, destroying Bryntelle's home."

"She has no home so long as the Eandi rule." Cresenne said the words with all the force she could muster, but even she could hear how hollow they sounded.

"I'm going to defeat your Weaver." He spoke with such certainty that she didn't dare argue. "I may not live to see the end of the war, but neither will he. So you need to choose. Are you going to devote yourself to a doomed cause, or are you going to help me, and make certain that your daughter grows up knowing her father?" He stood, crossing to the door. "The king will want to speak with Tavis and me before questioning you. I doubt he'll summon you before tomorrow morning, so you have some time to think about it." He pulled the door open and started to leave. Then he stopped himself, facing her once more. "You never answered my question."

She held his gaze as best she could, balling her hands into fists so that he wouldn't see how she trembled. "Of course I did."

"You told me that you seduced me for the movement. But you didn't say whether or not you loved me."

Cresenne tossed her hair and smiled coldly. "I didn't love you. I could never love a man like you."

He nodded, his eyebrows going up. She could see the hurt in his eyes. "I see," he said quietly. "Well, thank you for being so candid."

"Of course."

She waited even after he closed the door, listening as his footsteps faded away. Only when she couldn't hear them anymore did she collapse onto the bed beside her baby, sobs racking her body.

Grinsa walked for some time, prowling the castle corridors in search of Keziah, his sister, who was now archminister to Eibithar's king. At least that was his excuse. As it happened he was just as happy not to find her right away.

He had hoped to begin the process of winning Cresenne's trust, perhaps even her affection, though he wouldn't have admitted that to anyone. But rather than accepting his honesty as a gesture of trust, the woman had seen in it only an opportunity to hurt him again. Her denials notwithstanding, Grinsa knew that she had loved him, or at the very least had cared for him. He still remembered, with a clarity that made his chest ache, their last night together in Galdasten, when he left her to win Tavis's freedom from Kentigern's dungeon. Her anger at his decision had been genuine and far too fervent to be dismissed as the ire of a frustrated conspirator. She had been hurt and bitter, as only a spurned lover could be. In the turn that followed, as he learned of her betrayal and battled to the death the assassin she sent to kill him, he came to question his perceptions, not only of that last night but of all the passion-filled nights that had come before it.

He had railed at himself for his stupidity and the ease with which she had deluded him. He was a Weaver, the most powerful of Qirsi sorcerers, and though even a Weaver did not possess the power to recognize a false heart, Grinsa felt that he should have known. Only with the passage of time did he begin to forgive himself, to see that perhaps he hadn't realized she was deceiving him because she hadn't been, not completely. It was true that she asked repeatedly about Tavis's Fating, but it was equally true that he never revealed to her what the Qiran showed the boy. And still she remained with him until he left the Revel.

He wasn't a fool. He knew why she had taken to his bed in the first place. But he had loved and been loved before, and he knew as well that no matter her talents for trickery, Cresenne couldn't have been lying about everything. Passion such as they had shared could not be feigned.

What does it matter? asked a voice within his head, as he turned yet another corner in the castle corridors. *Why do this to yourself?*

"I do it for Bryntelle," he said aloud. "We're her parents. Even with what we've both become, shouldn't there have been love between us once?"

To which the voice replied, *You do it for pride. You do it to soothe the pain that lingers in your heart like infection in an old wound.*

Grinsa rubbed a hand over his face. "I do it because I'm a fool."

"Did you say something?"

Startled, he spun around to see two soldiers standing by a door he had just passed.

"No, I . . ." He shook his head. "Whose chamber is this?"

"The queen's. She doesn't wish to be disturbed."

"Do you know where I can find the king's archminister?"

The two men exchanged a look. "What do you want her for?" one of them asked.

Grinsa felt the hairs on his neck prickle. He didn't like the sound of this at all. "She's an old friend," he said, keeping his tone as casual as possible.

The man frowned as if not believing him.

"Is she all right?"

"She's well enough. You might find her in her chambers, or maybe walking the gardens."

The gleaner nodded. "My thanks."

He started to walk past them, but the soldier held out a hand, forcing him to halt.

"I'm not sure how you got through the gates, but we keep a close watch on white-hairs in this castle. You remember that."

Perhaps he should have held his tongue, but the man had pushed him too far.

"I got through the gate because the men there knew that I had been asked here by the king, along with Lord Tavis of Curgh. If you'd like, I can accompany you to the king's chambers, and you can express your reservations to him. Otherwise I'd suggest you let me pass."

The man's face reddened, but he didn't look away. "Forgive me, sir. I would have addressed you differently had I known."

"What's your name?"

The guard's mouth twitched. "Cullum Minfeld, sir."

"Well, Cullum, I'll say nothing of this to your king or the swordmaster, provided it doesn't happen again."

"It won't, sir." His tone was insolent, but there was little Grinsa could do about that.

"You say the archminister could be in the gardens or in her chambers. I checked her chambers not long ago. Is there somewhere else I might look before walking all the way to the gardens?"

Cullum glanced at his companion. "She spends a good deal of time alone on the ramparts, sir. You'll probably find her there."

"Thank you." He nodded to both men, then walked on without looking back. Grinsa had no doubt that soldiers throughout the realm, indeed, throughout the Forelands, felt as much contempt for the Qirsi as did those two. But it was unusual for men as disciplined as those serving the king of Eibithar to be so obvious about it. He walked to the nearest of the towers and climbed the steps to the ramparts. Stepping out into the sunlight, he spotted Keziah immediately. She stood on the wall opposite his, her back to him, leaning on the stone and staring up at Raven Falls, a thin white ribbon in the distance.

He walked to where his sister stood, passing several guards along the way, all of whom watched him warily. Keziah glanced at him as he approached. A light breeze stirred her fine white hair, but otherwise she didn't move. There were lines around her mouth and eyes, and she looked like she hadn't slept in days.

"I'd greet you properly," she said, her voice low, "but I don't think it would be wise with the soldiers watching us."

He was a Weaver, and for centuries, Weavers had been executed simply because the Eandi feared their powers. But more than that, a Weaver's family usually suffered the same fate, and so for years now, since his Fating, Grinsa and Keziah had concealed the fact that they were brother and sister.

"I understand. Are you well?"

She shrugged. A single tear rolled down her cheek. "Not really."

He would have liked to take her in his arms, to let her cry against his chest until the tears finally stopped. Instead he surveyed the ramparts as unobtrusively as he could. None of the soldiers was close enough to hear their conversation.

"Have you spoken to the Weaver again?"

Against his better judgment, and unbeknownst to her king, Keziah had made an effort to join the conspiracy, believing it the best way to learn of the Weaver's plans and tactics. As far as Grinsa knew, her last conversation with the leader of the conspiracy had been the one he overheard, having sought to enter her dreams himself so that they could speak.

"Twice, the first time a few nights after you were there as well, and a second time two nights ago."

Two nights. No wonder she looked so weary. "And?"

"I think he's starting to trust me. He asked a lot of questions about Kearney's intentions regarding Aindreas of Kentigern and those who seem willing to follow him."

"What did you tell him?"

"The truth. That Kearney is concerned, but he has no intention of abdicating, and that if he believes any of his dukes are guilty of treason, he'll take their castles by force and install new dukes who are loyal to the throne."

Grinsa eyed her closely, searching for some sign that she found this talk of a civil war disturbing. Seeing none, he felt his own apprehension growing.

"I take it the Weaver was pleased by this."

"Yes. I have no proof of this, but I think he must have someone else working on Aindreas's end, and perhaps in Galdasten as well. I expect he plans to push both sides away from any thought of reconciliation, hoping that this time we can bring about a civil war that involves all the major houses."

It seemed to Grinsa that the Deceiver himself ran an icy finger down his spine. "We?"

"What?"

"You said he hoped that 'we' could bring about a civil war."

"Yes, the conspiracy."

"So you count yourself as one of them now?"

"What choice do I have?" She brushed a wisp of hair from her brow. "I'm trying to convince Kearney that I've turned against him, and I'm trying to convince the Weaver that I've joined his cause. Day and night, awake and asleep, I'm acting the part of a traitor. If I'm to play the role properly, I have to give myself over to it. My life depends upon it."

Again, he would have liked to find some way to ease her burden, or at least express his sympathy. But he didn't know how. Throughout their lives, he had been the older sibling, the Weaver, the one who faced dangers and took risks in order to protect her. Now, for the first time, he found himself overwhelmed by the sacrifice Keziah was making, not only for him but for all the Forelands. It felt strange to him, and just a bit frightening.

"You weren't with Kearney when he met us in the ward. Have you lost his trust?"

She gave a wan smile. "Not entirely, not yet. The Weaver wants me to repair the damage I've done to our rapport. He says that if Kearney no longer trusts me, or worse, if he banishes me from the castle, I'm of little value to the conspiracy. I've assumed that to mean that the Weaver would then have me killed."

"Is it working? Is Kearney starting to turn to you again?"

She straightened, folding her arms over her chest. "As you say, I wasn't with him when he greeted you. I've tried apologizing for my behavior. I've explained to him that I was embittered by the end of our love affair and desperate to hurt him, but that I still wish to serve him as archminister."

"And what does he say?"

"Very little. He hasn't ordered me from the castle yet, for which I suppose I should be grateful, but neither has he begun to confide in me again."

Grinsa looked at the nearest of the guards. "It seems the king's men have a rather low opinion of all Qirsi. One of them tried to keep me from finding you until I told him that I was here as a guest of the king."

"They take their cue from Gershon."

"The swordmaster? I thought he knew you were attempting to join the conspiracy and approved."

"He does. But he's always hated our people, and me most of all. We both felt that it would be dangerous for him to grow tolerant of me too abruptly. He continues to speak against me to the king, questioning my loyalty even as I try to regain Kearney's favor."

"Doesn't he realize that he's putting your life in peril by doing so?"

Keziah shrugged again, a haunted look in her eyes. "There's peril in everything we do right now. This seemed the safest course."

The gleaner shook his head. He didn't like any of this, least of all his own sense of powerlessness.

"Tell me why you've come here," she said, after a lengthy silence. "Did you find Brienne's assassin?"

"Actually, yes."

Her eyes widened. "Is he here with you?"

"No. We let him go."

"What?"

As briefly as he could, Grinsa told her of Tavis's encounter with the assassin, how the boy surprised the singer in the corridor of a tavern in Mertesse and nearly managed to kill him. And he explained as well, why, in the end, Grinsa insisted that the young noble let him go, so that the man could kill the traitor Shurik, as he had been hired to do. For Shurik knew that Grinsa was a Weaver, and so long as he lived, he was a threat not only to the gleaner himself but also to Keziah.

"So he's still free?"

"I'm afraid so. It was the price we had to pay for Shurik's death."

"Did you learn anything from him? Can you prove Tavis's innocence?"

"We can, but not because of anything the assassin told us."

She narrowed her eyes. "I don't understand."

Grinsa took a long breath. It was still difficult even to talk about all this. He was forced to wonder if he could carry through on his threats if Cresenne refused to help them.

"Tavis and I are here with Cresenne."

Keziah looked puzzled. "Cresenne?"

"The woman from the Revel."

Comprehension flashed in her eyes like lightning. "The traitor? The one you loved?"

He nodded.

"Are you all right?"

It was his turn to shrug. "What choice do I have?"

"Poor Grinsa," she said, a sad smile on her face. "Always the strong one."

"There's more, Kezi." He paused, searching for the right words. Realizing there weren't any, he just told her. "I'm a father. Cresenne and I have a daughter."

She stared at him a moment, as if she didn't understand what he had said. Then a dazzling smile lit her face and tears began to flow freely from her eyes. "Oh, Grinsa! That's wonderful! That's the happiest thing I've heard in so long. What's her name?"

"Bryntelle."

"Bryntelle," she repeated. "I like that."

He frowned. "You know what this woman has done. You know how she hurt me."

"Yes, of course I do. But you have a child. In the midst of all this madness—the betrayals and the fear and the killing—you've become a father." A small breathless laugh escaped her. "I'm an aunt!"

"I suppose you are."

"Don't you see how wondrous that is?"

"It doesn't feel wondrous to me," he said grimly. "Cresenne is the one who hired the assassin in the first place. She had Lady Brienne killed. And merely by admitting this to Kearney, she can put to rest for good all doubts as to Tavis's innocence. Yet she refuses, and I find myself forced to use our child as a cudgel to compel her to speak the truth. I've told her that unless she tells all to the king, I'll have Bryntelle taken from her."

"And still she resists?"

"Thus far, yes. But the true test comes tomorrow, when I take her before Kearney."

"You believe she remains that devoted to the movement?"

He shook his head. "I believe she's that afraid of the Weaver."

Keziah shuddered. "She should be. If she betrays him in any way, he'll kill her."

He raised an eyebrow. "Perhaps you should speak with her."

"To what end? I can't risk telling her what I'm doing."

"I know that. But you know the Weaver. You understand her fear far better than I do. It may be that you can find a way to convince her. If you succeed, it may help you regain a measure of the king's goodwill."

"It may also cost the woman her life."

"If she doesn't help us, she'll spend the rest of her life in Kearney's dungeon, bereft of her child and branded a traitor. Her only hope lies in working with us and allowing me to protect her."

Keziah looked up at the falls again. "I'll try," she said at last. "But I doubt that even you can protect her, Grinsa. Your powers are formidable, they may be a match for those of the Weaver. But he can reach her in her sleep. How do you protect her from a man who can do that?"

"I don't know. But there was a time when I would have given my life for her. I suppose I still would. Not because I love her, though it's possible that I do, but because of Bryntelle. What kind of a father would I be if I allowed something to happen to her mother?"

Chapter
Eight

The following morning, Cresenne ja Terba, Qirsi traitor, and the mother of Grinsa's daughter, was brought before King Kearney of Eibithar. Keziah had wondered if the king would even ask her to attend his questioning of the woman. Such was the state of their relations at this point that the archminister wouldn't have been surprised if he had asked Wenda or one of the other ministers to join the discussion in her stead. But perhaps remembering that she knew Grinsa—she hadn't told Kearney that they were brother and sister—he had sent word late the previous evening that she was to be in the king's chambers by midmorning bells.

Keziah couldn't help but be curious about this woman who had scored her brother's heart and borne him a child. She had known Pheba, Grinsa's Eandi wife who died of the Pestilence several years before, but not well. Though she loved her brother, and in the midst of her own affair with Kearney had no right to judge him for falling in love with an Eandi, she had thought Pheba the wrong woman for him. It was not just that she was Eandi, nor that as a Weaver he had much to fear from tying himself so closely to Ean's race. Pheba had seemed too strong-willed, or perhaps Grinsa had just been too young.

Whatever the reason, Keziah never felt close to her brother's wife. She mourned Pheba's death, or rather Grinsa's loss, but she always hoped that he would find a way to love again, and that this time he would choose a Qirsi woman.

There was an old Qirsi saying: a wish realized is a most dangerous thing.

Reaching Kearney's door, she knocked, waited for his reply, then entered. Only when she was in the chamber did she realize that she was the first to arrive; even Gershon Trasker, Kearney's swordmaster, wasn't there yet. As part of her effort to repair the damage she had done to her rapport with the king, Keziah had arrived promptly for all their recent discussions. But this was the first time in well over a turn that she had found herself alone with him.

He was at his writing table, poring over several scrolls of parchment. He stood when she stepped into the room, but remained where he was, his eyes widening slightly, as if he were afraid to be alone with her.

"I'm sorry, Your Majesty," she said. "I seem to be early. Have I mistaken the time of our meeting?"

He shook his head, his jaw set. "No. I expect the bells will be ringing shortly."

"Shall I leave you until they do?"

He glanced down at his scrolls again. "Not unless you wish to."

There was a correct reply to this. She felt sure of it. But she had no idea what it might be. After a moment's silence, she walked to a chair near his table and sat.

For some time, he continued to stare at his papers, rustling them noisily. At last he cast a quick look her way, and forced a smile. "You must have been . . . pleased to see the gleaner again."

"Yes, Your Majesty." Even now, after all that had passed between them, he still could not speak to her of Grinsa without sounding like a jealous lover.

"He's the reason I asked you here, you know."

"I thought so."

"Knowing him as you do, I thought it best that you be present. This promises to be a most delicate discussion."

"Yes, Your Majesty."

"I hope I can trust you not to say anything . . . inappropriate, either to me or to Lord Tavis."

Keziah grimaced. When she was still trying to attract the attention of the conspiracy, and trying as well to make herself suspect in the king's eyes, she had been insolent and insulting, not only to Kearney but also to several of his noble guests. During one feast given in honor of the dukes of Rouvin and Grinnyd, she had so offended the Wethy noble that Wenda had felt compelled to apologize on Keziah's behalf. No doubt, word of her transgression had found its way back to the king.

"Of course, Your Majesty. As I've already told you, I wasn't myself in the days immediately following Paegar's death. But I'm better now. You needn't worry about me anymore."

"I'd like to believe you, Keziah. But I'm not yet ready to surrender all to trust."

She nodded, her eyes stinging. "I understand, Your Majesty."

This was all of her own doing. She had chosen to alienate her king, to draw the eye of the Weaver so that she might learn more of his movement. But still, it grieved her to think that Kearney, who she had loved more than any other man in her life, should now find it so hard to trust her.

They sat in uncomfortable silence for several moments. Keziah stared at her hands, but she sensed that Kearney was watching her, perhaps waiting for her to say more. When she finally gathered the courage to meet his gaze, however, she found that he had turned his attention back to the scrolls on his table.

The bells began to toll in the city, and before they had finished there came a knock on the king's door.

"At last," he murmured. Then, in a louder voice, "Enter!"

The door opened revealing Gershon and two soldiers. The swordmaster walked into the room, eying the minister and the king with interest. At the same time, the guards stepped to the side. Behind them stood Grinsa, Lord Tavis, and a Qirsi woman.

Kearney stepped out from behind his table and beckoned them into the chamber with a wave of his hand.

Seeing Keziah, Grinsa gave a tight smile, but he remained by the woman, as if guarding her. It took Keziah a moment to realize that she was carrying a baby.

She almost stood then, to get a better look at her niece, but to have done so would have raised too many questions. Instead, she studied the girl's mother. She shouldn't have been surprised that the woman was beautiful—Pheba had been as well. But Keziah had to admit that she had never met any woman so attractive. She had long, fine hair that she wore pulled back loosely from her oval face. Her eyes were quite pale, no deeper in color than the parchment on Kearney's table, and her lips were full and wide. She glanced around the room warily, her eyes lingering briefly on Keziah before flitting away once more. She clutched her baby to her breast, as if expecting one of them to rip the child from her arms at any moment, and she kept herself as close to Grinsa as he did to her. If Keziah hadn't known that she had hurt him, that she had gone so far as to send an assassin to kill him, she might have thought them very much in love.

"Please sit," the king said, crossing to the hearth and turning so that he faced all of them.

Cresenne looked to Grinsa, who led her to one of the chairs near the hearth, taking the other one himself. Tavis sat near Keziah, nodding to her once as he lowered himself into the chair. He appeared just as she remembered him. Straight hair the color of wheat, dark, intelligent eyes, the refined features of an Eandi noble. He would have been handsome had it not been for the lattice of dark, angry scars that covered his face, remembrances from his stay in the dungeon of Kentigern Castle.

Kearney pulled a chair just in front of Cresenne's and sat as well, facing her. "I know you won't believe this," he said, "at least not at first. But you have nothing to fear from me. Answer our questions honestly, and no harm will come to you or your child."

"And if I refuse?" she asked, her voice barely carrying to where Keziah sat.

Kearney smiled. "Let's not talk about that for now. Listen first to what I have to say. Consider what I ask of you."

She hesitated, then nodded.

The king indicated Gershon with a nod of his head. "That's Gershon Trasker, captain of the King's Guard and my swordmaster since I first became duke of Glyndwr. I asked him here so that he might assess the risk posed by the . . . by your movement."

She stared at the swordmaster, who offered no response at all. No doubt he thought the woman should be imprisoned immediately for her betrayal, the king's questions saved for the dungeonmaster and his instruments of torture. Keziah knew that Gershon had little tolerance for traitors, and even less when their eyes were yellow.

"The woman sitting beside Lord Tavis is Keziah ja Dafydd, my archminister."

Cresenne looked at her again, but quickly turned her attention back to the king.

Kearney started to say more, then stopped himself, his eyes meeting Keziah's for just an instant. Then he faced Grinsa. "Gleaner, I believe you know better than I what questions she might be able to answer. Would you?"

"Of course, Your Majesty."

"Pardon, Your Majesty," Gershon broke in, standing as he spoke, a hand resting on the hilt of his sword. "But before we continue, I'd like to know what powers this woman possesses."

Cresenne smiled coldly. "Gleaning, healing, and fire, swordmaster. I'm hardly a threat to your king. I'd imagine you have more to fear from his archminister." She eyed Grinsa, the smile lingering. "Or perhaps the gleaner."

It was a curious comment, and a dangerous one. Clearly she knew of Grinsa's powers, but did she know as well that Keziah had spoken with the Weaver who led her movement?

Whatever she meant to imply, Gershon did not seem mollified. "Fire, eh?"

She rolled her eyes. "Think for a moment, swordmaster. Not like a warrior but like a man and a father. Do you honestly think I'd do anything so foolish with my child in my arms?"

That seemed to reach him. His mouth twisted sourly, but after another few seconds he nodded, returning to his seat.

"Gleaner?" the king prompted once more.

Grinsa sat forward. "How long have you been with the conspiracy, Cresenne?"

She furrowed her brow. "Conspiracy? I'm not certain I know what you mean."

"Would you prefer I called it the Qirsi movement?"

"I still wouldn't know what you were—"

"Stop it!" The gleaner glared at her. "You think this is a game. You think that I'll be stayed by pity and love of our child. You're wrong. Archminister," he said, not taking his eyes off the woman. "Please take my daughter from the chamber. I have no doubt that you can find someone in the castle who'll care for her until I'm finished here."

Keziah glanced at Kearney, who nodded his approval. She stood and started walking to where Cresenne sat. She could see the baby now, eyes closed, lips slightly pursed. She had not spent much time with babies. She knew little about how to care for them; she wasn't even certain she could hold her niece properly. But even she could see how beautiful the child was, her face a perfect blending of Cresenne's features and Grinsa's.

As she approached, Cresenne shrank back against her chair, tightening her grip on the baby. Her eyes, wild and afraid, flew to Grinsa's face. "You can't do this."

"If you resist," he said calmly, "if you make us take Bryntelle by force, she's more likely to be hurt."

"You bastard! She's your daughter!"

"And as I've told you already, I won't allow myself to be swayed by that. This is your doing, Cresenne, not mine."

"I won't hurt her," Keziah said softly, holding out her arms for the child. "You have my word."

Still Cresenne clung to her. "She'll be hungry soon. She'll need me."

Grinsa looked away. "I've no doubt we can find a wet nurse in the city."

Cresenne glared at him. "I despise you," she whispered. "I don't care that you are her father. I wish you were dead."

"Yes, I know. You made that clear when you sent the assassin for me." His face wore a bitter smile, but Keziah could see how this was hurting him. "Take the child, Archminister."

Reluctantly, her hands shaking as if from a palsy, Cresenne placed Bryntelle in Keziah's arms. She was crying now, and she fussed over the child a moment, tucking in her swaddling until it was snug and smoothing the wisps of snowy hair on the baby's head.

"Her name is Bryntelle," she said, meeting Keziah's gaze.

"I know. Neither of you has anything to fear from me."

The woman gave a hesitant nod. Keziah straightened and started toward the door. Before she was halfway across the chamber, however, Cresenne, cried out, "Wait!"

Keziah halted, turned.

"I'll tell you what you want to know," she said. "Just don't leave with her."

"It's too late for that," Grinsa said.

The archminister shook her head. "It doesn't have to be."

Her brother shot her a baleful look, but once more the king nodded. "Let me remain here," she went on. "I'll hold Bryntelle. So long as Cresenne answers your questions, I'll stay. But if she refuses you again, I'll leave immediately, taking the child with me."

A frown creased Grinsa's forehead, but he looked to Cresenne, as if gauging her response.

"Very well," the woman said.

Grinsa exhaled heavily. "Let's begin again. How long have you been with the conspiracy?"

The woman stared at her hands. "Nearly three years."

"Why did you join?"

"They offered me gold."

"Is that the only reason?"

Her gaze met Grinsa's for just an instant, then dropped again. "No. It offered me a way to strike at the Eandi courts. The movement seeks to end Eandi rule in the Forelands."

Kearney turned to Gershon, his face grim. He didn't look surprised—no doubt he had expected something like this. Her words would have served only to confirm his darkest fears.

"How does your movement intend to do this?"

"I don't know. I know that's our goal, and I know that much of what we've done has sought to bring turmoil and instability to the seven realms. But beyond that, I've been told nothing."

"You've told me already that you're paid by couriers and Qirsi merchants. Do you know where the gold comes from?"

She shook her head.

"Are you paid in common currency or imperials?" the king asked.

"Common currency."

Kearney looked disappointed. "Forgive me, gleaner. Please go on."

"What do you know about the movement's leaders?"

Cresenne started to reply, then stopped herself. She stared at Grinsa, her eyes narrowing slightly. "What?"

"What can you tell us about the movement's leaders?"

There was something strange in the way Cresenne was looking at him, as if she abruptly knew that she had the advantage. It took Keziah only a moment to understand why. Apparently Grinsa had made clear to her that he knew of the Weaver, only to find himself unable to use that knowledge now for fear of bringing harm to Keziah. She felt certain that Cresenne didn't know all of this, only that he knew more about the movement than he was willing to allow the others to hear, and that this provided her with a refuge of sorts.

"Very little," she said.

Gershon narrowed his eyes.

"As I told you a moment ago, they pay me through couriers, and they give me instructions the same way. I believe they prefer not to be known, even by those who support their cause."

"I think you're lying," Gershon said.

Grinsa nodded. "I believe she is as well, swordmaster."

Cresenne said nothing. She merely watched Grinsa, as if daring him to challenger her.

"But perhaps we should return to this later," the gleaner went on smoothly. "Tell us about the murder of Lady Brienne of Kentigern."

Keziah sensed Tavis's anticipation, though he didn't move or change his expression

"I know only what I've heard."

"Now I know you're lying," Grinsa said. "The assassin you sent for me said that you didn't want me helping Tavis, that you didn't want me reaching Kentigern at all. Now, why would he have thought that?"

"I sent no assassin."

Grinsa looked up at Keziah. "Go. Take Bryntelle and go."

Keziah started to leave the room, though she didn't care for the idea. Before she could go, however, the baby woke and began to cry. It was almost as if she felt her mother's distress and cried out in answer.

"She needs to eat," Cresenne said quickly.

"We'll find a wet nurse." Keziah had never known Grinsa could sound so cold.

"Not soon enough. She's just a babe. She can't wait while you search the city for a woman to nurse her."

"It's all right, gleaner," the king said. "We'll have a brief respite while Cresenne nurses her child. Then we'll continue."

Grinsa looked displeased, but he knew better than to argue with Kearney.

"Go with her, Archminister," Kearney said. "Take her to my private quarters."

"Yes, Your Majesty." Keziah glanced at Grinsa as she waited for Cresenne by the door. Her brother eyed her briefly, then gave a small nod, one none of the others would have noticed.

The two women left the chamber, walked down the corridor to the nearest of the castle's spiral stairways, and climbed to the next floor. From there, it was but a short walk to the king's private quarters. Cresenne said nothing as they walked. Keziah assumed that she was too angry with Grinsa, or just unwilling to show any courtesy to a servant of the king. But only when they reached the door and it occurred to the minister that she was still carrying Bryntelle did she realize that the woman was too distracted to speak. Keziah could guess as to why.

"Why don't you hold her," she said, holding Bryntelle out to the woman.

"What?" Cresenne looked at her briefly, then blushed deeply, taking the baby from her. "Of course. Thank you."

Keziah pushed open the door, motioning the woman inside.

Cresenne took the chair closest to the hearth, loosened her shirt and placed the child so that she could reach her breast. Bryntelle began to suckle immediately.

Keziah had to smile at the sounds the child made as she fed. It was hard to believe that such a small person could make so much noise.

"She's a beautiful child."

Cresenne smiled, though she didn't look up. "Thank you."

"It's hard for me to think of Grinsa as a father."

That did draw the woman's gaze. Keziah wished instantly that she had kept that thought to herself. She wanted to win the woman's trust. Making it clear from the outset that she was Grinsa's friend wasn't likely to make matters easier for her.

"You know him?"

"We grew up together." Hiding the truth about Grinsa had become habit by now. She didn't even have to think about it anymore.

"You know him well, then."

"To the extent that anyone does."

Cresenne seemed to weigh this, looking down at the baby again. For a time she seemed to wrestle with something—Keziah guessed that Cresenne wanted to ask if she knew of Grinsa's powers. In the end, she seemed to decide against it.

"Were you ever his lover?" she asked instead.

Keziah smiled. "No."

"But you care for him."

"Very much."

"I wish I'd never met him." This she said quietly, as if to herself.

"If you'd never met him, you wouldn't have Bryntelle."

"Will he really take her from me?"

"I believe he will. He'll grieve at doing so, but he's stubborn and when he decides he wants something, he won't be deterred. You can establish Tavis's innocence, and you can tell us a great deal about the conspiracy. That's what he wants, and if you refuse him, he'll take her."

"His own child."

"Don't be too quick to judge him," Keziah said, her anger growing. "She's your child as well, and yet you risk losing her to save yourself."

Cresenne glowered at her for a moment, then looked away.

"You don't understand."

"Understand what? That you're frightened. That you fear betraying the conspiracy lest word of what you've done gets back to the Weaver?"

Her gaze snapped up once more, her mouth dropping open.

"Yes," Keziah said. "I know about your Weaver."

"You're the one who told Grinsa about him," Cresenne whispered.

It was close enough to the truth. "Yes."

"So he was protecting you in there."

"I suppose."

"But how did you learn of the Weaver?"

"That's not important."

"It would be to him."

Keziah felt the color drain from her face.

"I expect it would be to your king as well, since he obviously knows nothing of the Weaver yet."

Keziah started to deny this, but Cresenne stopped her with a shake of her head. "Don't bother lying to me. If your king knew, Grinsa would have spoken of the Weaver openly a few moments ago." She stared at Keziah for some time, looking thoughtful. "Have you betrayed him? Is that it?"

"No."

"That's the only explanation that makes sense."

She wanted to protest her innocence. It was one thing to play the traitor in her conversations with the Weaver, who walked in her dreams and never revealed his identity; it was quite another to have this woman thinking she had betrayed her king and her land. But as she continued to think about it, she realized that having Cresenne believe she was a traitor would help her continue her deception. The Weaver had access to Cresenne's thoughts just as he did to Keziah's. If the minister could make this woman believe that she was with the conspiracy, it might help her allay whatever doubts remained in the Weaver's mind.

"If I was with the conspiracy, why would I be trying to convince you to tell them what they want to know?" She wouldn't lie to the woman. Better to let Cresenne provide her own answers.

"To deflect the king's suspicions, and Grinsa's for that matter."

"That makes no sense."

"Doesn't it? For all I know, the Weaver wants me to betray the movement. He doesn't trust me as he once did. He'd probably like an excuse to kill me. So he gets you to befriend me, to wheedle information from me."

He doesn't trust me as he once did. Perhaps there was another way. Perhaps this woman could be trusted with the truth after all.

"From what I've seen of your Weaver, he doesn't need an excuse to kill those who serve him, particularly if he loses faith in them. Besides, the answers I seek from you will hurt your conspiracy, not help it. You had an assassin kill Brienne. If you'll admit that, it may allow us to win back Kentigern's loyalty and avoid the civil war your Weaver wants so desperately."

"Now I know you're with the conspiracy. You know too much about the Weaver and his wishes."

"You say he doesn't trust you anymore. Does he know whose child you carry? Does he know who and what Grinsa is?"

Cresenne swallowed, nodded.

"What will he think when he learns that the two of you are together?"

"If you're threatening me it won't work. The Weaver has told me to find Grinsa. He'll be pleased."

"I'm not threatening you, Cresenne, and I'm not with the conspiracy. But I know the Weaver well enough to realize that if he's had doubts about you already, your presence here with Grinsa and the child you share will only serve to deepen them." She knelt before Cresenne, looking up at her. "Your time with the movement is over," she said softly. "Surely you see that."

There were tears on the woman's face, and she brushed them away quickly, as if annoyed. "It's not that easy. He can find me anytime he wants. If I try to leave the movement, he'll kill me. I know it. I don't get to decide when my time is over. Only he has that power."

"He's not as strong as you think he is."

"Perhaps I've been wrong about you. If you were with the movement you'd know how foolish you sound. Of course he's strong. He's a Weaver."

"So is Grinsa. And if you'd stop pretending that you feel nothing for him anymore, you'd understand that he wants to protect you. Both of you."

"He can't protect me. No one can."

Keziah shrugged. "Perhaps you're right. But you have two choices, Cresenne. You can remain with the movement, protecting its secrets and its leader. That path leads to Kearney's dungeon and it leaves your daughter without a mother. Or you can trust Grinsa and me, and try to make right some of the damage you've done over the past few years. I don't know where that path leads—none of us does—but at least you'll get to find out with Bryntelle in your arms and her father by your side."

Cresenne didn't respond, and after several moments Keziah climbed to her feet again, intending to leave.

"I'll let you think about it. If you need me I'll be just outside the door."

"Why did you say that before?"

"Say what?"

"That the Weaver isn't as strong as he thinks he is. If you're not with the conspiracy, how can you know all that you do?"

Keziah hesitated. There was so much peril in what she was about to do. "Were I to tell you, I'd be placing my life in your hands. You wouldn't be able to tell anyone, not even the Weaver. Especially the Weaver."

"It's very difficult to keep things from the Weaver."

"But it can be done."

Cresenne's eyes widened. "You are with the conspiracy," she whispered. "But as an agent of the king."

She nodded. "In a sense, yes. Although Kearney doesn't know. He . . . wouldn't approve."

"How long?"

"Not very. Just over a turn."

"If the Weaver finds out—"

Keziah shuddered, but managed a wan smile. "I know. But I've found a way to conceal my loyalties while making him believe that I've opened myself to him fully. That's what you must do, Cresenne, not only for yourself and Bryntelle but for me as well. And for Grinsa."

"Why would you trust me with this?" the woman asked, shaking her head.

"Because I've seen how you look at that baby. Anyone who can love one child so much is capable of doing good, no matter what she's done in the past."

"There are those who'd say you're a fool to trust me, Grinsa foremost among them."

"I know. And I'll tell Grinsa what I've done. If you betray me to the Weaver, and I die because of it, I assure you Grinsa will avenge me. Our bond goes deep."

Cresenne held her gaze. "I understand."

I doubt that. "Good. I'll wait for you in the corridor."

She let herself out of the chamber, her hands trembling and her mind filled with doubts. Perhaps she was a fool. But after confiding in no one but the swordmaster for so long, it felt good to have placed her faith in another, no matter the risks.

For a long time after the two women left the chamber, none of the men spoke. Grinsa gazed at the door, as if he longed to follow them. His sister, his lover, his daughter. The three most important people in his life. For more than half a year, Tavis had seen the lengths to which the gleaner had gone to protect him. He could only imagine what the man would do to keep these three safe.

The king still sat by the hearth, his elbows resting on his knees, his hands folded together. There was a troubled look in his eyes and Tavis could see the muscles in his jaw clenching.

"Can they be trusted together?" Gershon Trasker asked at last, staring after the women much as Grinsa was. The swordmaster reminded Tavis a good deal of Hagan MarCullet, his father's swordmaster, whose son, Xaver, remained Tavis's pledged liegeman to this day. Like Gershon—maybe like all Eandi warriors—Hagan was suspicious of Qirsi, and quickly grew impatient with talk. Gershon's hand rested on the grip of his sword. It almost seemed that he was waiting for Kearney to give him leave to draw his blade and bring the women back.

"Give them some time," the king said softly. "Perhaps Keziah can convince her to talk to us."

Grinsa turned at last to face Kearney. "I'm sorry that I couldn't, Your Majesty."

"It's not your fault, gleaner, but rather mine for asking you to question her. It seems clear that she wanted to do whatever she could to hurt you."

"She had cause."

"She had cause?" Tavis repeated, barely able to believe what he had heard. "She betrayed you, sent an assassin for you, gave gold to the men who killed Brienne! And you're blaming yourself?"

"The lad's right," Gershon said. "You've done nothing to her that she didn't deserve. In my opinion, you've shown her too much kindness."

The king shook his head. "It's not as easy as all that, Gershon, and you know it. She's had his child." He glanced at Grinsa. "And if I'm not mistaken, before her betrayal you loved her very much."

"Yes, Your Majesty."

"Love . . . complicates matters."

Something in the king's tone told Tavis that he was speaking as much of himself as of Grinsa. He knew that the king and his archminister, Grinsa's sister, had once been lovers, and it seemed from what he had observed since their arrival in the City of Kings the day before, that their love had ended since last he saw them.

"It does, Your Majesty."

"Do you think she'll actually risk losing her child just to spite you? Does her thirst for vengeance run so deep?"

"No," Grinsa said. "Her love of the child is more powerful than her rage at me."

"But were it not for the child, how far do you think her anger would take her?"

"Your Majesty?"

Kearney looked away. "It's a foolish question. Forget I asked it."

"I believe, Your Majesty, that love doesn't merely vanish to be replaced by hatred. Cresenne tried to have me killed, and though I cursed her name a thousand times for doing so, I've never stopped loving her. I wish I could. I would have been happy never to see her again. But not because I don't still want her. And child or none, I would do anything to keep her safe. As you say, love complicates matters. Just as I still love her, I believe in some small way she still loves me, though she denies that she ever did. We're tied to each other, and I expect we always will be. Such is the nature of Adriel's gift."

The Qirsi talked only of his love for Cresenne, yet it was clear to Tavis that he was speaking to the king's pain at losing Keziah.

Perhaps Kearney recognized this as well, for he stared at Grinsa for some time before finally nodding, and saying, "You may well be right, gleaner." He paused briefly, looking uneasily at Tavis and Gershon. "You've known her longer than any of us. Do you believe she's capable of betraying the land?"

"Of whom do you speak, Your Majesty?"

Kearney's face shaded scarlet. "Forgive me. I speak of Keziah, my archminister."

The king couldn't have known how difficult a question he had asked. Grinsa and Tavis knew of the archminister's attempt to join the conspiracy—the gleaner had told Tavis something of what she had done to convince those in the king's court that her loyalties to Kearney had grown tenuous. Indeed, Tavis gathered that the only other person who knew her true intentions was the swordmaster, meaning that in this chamber, Kearney was the one person who didn't understand that Keziah was risking her life to defeat the conspiracy. Grinsa would never have called his sister a traitor, even though she might have wanted Kearney to believe she was capable of such treachery. But neither could he defend her as fervently as he probably would have liked.

"Your Majesty," Gershon said quickly. "I don't believe it's wise to speak of such things in the presence of men from another house."

"It's all right, Gershon. Under the law, Tavis is of Glyndwr still, and will be until he no longer requires the protection we've offered him. And the gleaner has known the archminister since she was a child."

The swordmaster frowned, casting a quick look at Grinsa. To Tavis's amazement, the gleaner winked at the man in such a way that the king couldn't see. Gershon's mouth dropped open for just an instant. Then he recovered, looking sidelong at the king.

"I've known Keziah for many years, Your Majesty," the gleaner said slowly. "And though we seldom see each other anymore, we still understand each other quite well. But I'm afraid I can't speak to her feelings about the conspiracy. Even those of us who would give our lives fighting against it have sympathy for the cause. There are those among our people who have suffered greatly under Eandi rule. Do I think Keziah will betray you? No, I don't. Am I certain of this? No, I'm afraid I'm not."

The king eyed him a moment longer, tight-lipped and pale. "Thank you, gleaner. I'm grateful for your honesty."

"Of course, Your Majesty."

Kearney stood and walked back to his writing table. As he did, Gershon looked at the gleaner again and nodded once.

"You've been quiet through all of this, Lord Tavis," the king said. "What do you think of this woman who holds your life in her hands?"

Tavis shrugged, abruptly feeling uncomfortable under the gazes of these three men. "I think she's fortunate that Grinsa is as wise and forgiving as he is, Your Majesty. And I fear that even the threat of having her child taken from her won't persuade a woman with such a black heart to tell the truth."

Kearney frowned. "I certainly hope you're wrong."

"As do I, Your Majesty. But since this ordeal began, I've thought on several occasions that my salvation was at hand, only to have my hopes dashed. I find that hope doesn't come easily anymore."

"You're terribly young to have such a grim view of the world."

I haven't been young since Aindreas threw me in his dungeon. "Yes, Your Majesty."

"Perhaps this woman will surprise you, Lord Tavis. The love of a mother for her child can be quite powerful. I believe that's a lesson your own mother taught Aindreas at the Battle of the Heneagh just a few turns ago."

Tavis had to smile, remembering the sight of his mother in full battle garb, riding toward him as the armies of Curgh and Kentigern did battle on the broad plain west of the Heneagh River. "I pray that you're right, Your Majesty."

There was a knock at the door, and all of them turned at the sound.

"Come," the king called.

The door opened, revealing the two Qirsi women standing side by side. Cresenne looked small, though she was nearly the same height as the archminister. She still held her baby close, and her face was so white that Tavis wondered for a moment if she was ill.

But Keziah was smiling, a hand resting lightly on the other woman's shoulder, and she whispered something to her.

Cresenne stepped into the chamber, the archminister following.

"We're sorry to have kept you waiting, Your Majesty," Keziah said. "Please sit, all of you. Cresenne has much to tell you."

Chapter
Nine

he arguments with Evanthya began almost as soon as Numar left his castle, forcing Tebeo to wonder what had passed between his first minister and the regent's Qirsi during their conversation in the gardens of Castle Dantrielle. He asked the minister about it, but of course she told him nothing, saying only that she and the archminister had spoken of the coming war. Tebeo didn't believe her. He had long been opposed to engaging the Eibitharians in battle; without going so far as to advocate war, Evanthya had often made clear her belief that a war, properly fought, could benefit the kingdom.

But abruptly they had reversed roles. After his disastrous encounter with the regent, Tebeo felt that he had little choice but to support Numar in whatever course the regent followed. He had come dangerously close to making an enemy of the man during the Solkaran's visit. He risked being hanged as a traitor if he even spoke against the war again, much less withheld Dantrielle's army from the effort as Evanthya now counseled.

Back and forth they went for the entire day after Numar's departure and into the night. Their debate took them nowhere, and when Evanthya finally left him as the midnight bells tolled in the city, Tebeo was exhausted, but too frustrated to sleep. He avoided her the next day, even going so far as to deny her entry to his chamber when she came to speak with him.

During the course of that morning it occurred to him that Pronjed may have prevailed upon her to argue as she now did. At the time of Carden's death, Brall and his first minister had speculated that the archminister was a traitor who had the power to control people's minds. Tebeo knew far less of Qirsi magic than he should have, since he relied on Qirsi ministers for counsel nearly every day, but he knew enough to suspect that the first minister had fallen victim to one of her own. That was the only explanation that made any sense to him.

He said as much to her the following day when they resumed their dialogue. Naturally she denied it, and the more she made her case, the more the duke wavered. It didn't help that he continued to question the wisdom of this war, or that he disliked Braedon's emperor, or even that he was, at heart, a man of peace. But there was one other factor that he could not ignore, one that lent great strength to Evanthya's argument.

Numar frightened him, perhaps not as much as Carden had or Grigor would have had he lived, but enough. He had the full force of the royal army behind him and if he chose to turn its might on Dantrielle the dukedom would be crushed in a matter of days. But it wasn't just the power of Solkara's army that frightened the duke. Numar, it seemed, was both more and less than he had appeared to be when Aneira's dukes chose him as regent for Kalyi, the young queen. Tebeo, Brall, and many of the others had thought him a benign alternative to his older brother, intelligent enough to lead the kingdom until Kalyi was of Fating age, but lacking his brother's ambition. Having faced his wrath, however, having heard him speak of war and the growing alliance with Braedon, Tebeo realized that he and his fellow dukes had seen only what they wanted to see. The regent was keenly intelligent, far more so even than Carden had been, and the duke feared that Numar harbored dark ambitions for Aneira and for himself.

The more Tebeo and his first minister spoke of the regent and his war, the more uncertain the duke grew, until he found himself advocating points of view with which he did not agree.

Evanthya, who knew him too well, seemed to sense her advantage, for after a time, she began to smile. When Tebeo stated that Aneira's alliance with Braedon outweighed all other concerns, even his desire for peace, she actually laughed.

"Forgive me, my lord," she said, shaking her head. "But I know that you don't truly believe that, not unless you received word during the night that Harel has died and been replaced by a new emperor."

He winced. "You shouldn't jest about such things, First Minister."

"My apologies, my lord. But the fact remains that you think Harel a poor leader and a dangerous ally for the kingdom. You've said as much to me several times in the past."

"You're right, I have. And I suppose I still feel that way."

"Then why do you argue as you do?"

"Because I have no desire to stand alone against Numar. As it is, after what I said to him while he was here, I'm fortunate that he's a generous man. He could easily have taken offense and he might still decide to punish Dantrielle for my impudence. I can't risk angering him further."

The minister regarded him in silence briefly, her brow furrowed, as if she were struggling with something. Then, appearing to come to a decision, she asked, "What if you didn't have to stand against him alone?"

"What?"

She licked her lips. "When I spoke with the archminister, he asked me if I thought you could prevail upon the southern houses to support the war if they proved reluctant."

He gaped at her, not quite believing that Pronjed would think to ask her such a question. "Why didn't you tell me this before?"

She lowered her gaze. "I was afraid to, my lord. Just as you fear Numar, I fear the archminister. Fetnalla and Lord Orvinti suspect that he may be a traitor, that he may even have used mind-bending magic to kill the king. If he learned that I had revealed to you anything of our conversation, he . . . he might seek to do me harm."

"How?" Tebeo asked, eyes narrowing. "Do you think he'd try to kill you?"

"Not directly, my lord. But he might accuse me of treason. These are difficult days for Qirsi and Eandi alike. It requires only a well-placed word to destroy the reputation of a minister."

The duke nodded. That much at least he could understand. "Do you think he expects the southern houses to resist the war?"

"He told me he was merely preparing himself for all possibilities. But I don't think he would have asked the question unless he thought it likely." She hesitated, her bright gaze dropping once more. "He asked as well if I thought you would resist."

"That doesn't surprise me at all, not after my conversation with Numar."

"Yes, my lord."

"What did you tell him?"

"I told him that I thought you would send however many men Numar requested, that you were Aneiran before all else."

It was the only proper response she could have given, but still he was relieved. "Thank you. And what about his other question? How did you answer that?"

"I wasn't certain what to say, my lord. I told him that you were not as close to the new dukes in Tounstrel and Noltierre as you had been to their fathers, and that you didn't have as much influence with them as the question implied."

Tebeo frowned. "Frankly, First Minister, that's more of an answer than such a question deserved."

"Yes, my lord."

"Still, it's close enough to the truth, and it doesn't give Numar much hope that I can act on his behalf if Vistaan and Bertin the Younger refuse to comply. Under the circumstances, things could be far worse."

"Thank you, my lord." She opened her mouth to say more, then stopped herself, taking a breath and playing absently with the satin edge of her robe.

"Out with it, Evanthya. If there's more to your conversation with Pronjed I'd best know it now."

Still she paused, seeming to search for the correct words. "I'm not entirely certain that he was asking these questions on the regent's behalf, my lord."

He had thought that nothing more could surprise him, that between Numar's unexpected visit and the archminister's blunt questioning of his first minister he had been inured to shock. But this was too much. "Explain."

"He told me that he didn't think the regent trusted him and that Numar only brought him to Dantrielle and the other dukedoms because he didn't trust the minister enough to leave him alone in Solkara."

"Do you think the regent fears for the queen?"

She shook her head, playing now with a strand of white hair. "No, I think he fears Chofya and Pronjed's ties to her."

At that the duke felt a surge of hope. "Did Pronjed indicate that he still remained loyal to her?"

"Not really, my lord. He told me that he was asking me these other questions on no one's behalf, but rather as one Qirsi to another."

Just as quickly, the duke's hope vanished to be replaced by a feeling of coldest, deepest dread. "What does that mean? Do you think he's with the conspiracy?"

"I think it's possible. It's also possible that he thinks I am, and that he hoped to determine this for certain."

"Why would he think you were a traitor?" He tried to keep his tone neutral, but he could see from the way she regarded him that he had failed.

"You of all people should know the answer to that, my lord." She gave a sad smile. "With all that's happened in Aneira and throughout the Forelands, all Qirsi are suspect. Traitors seem to lurk in every corner, be it in Solkara, or Orvinti, or here, in Dantrielle."

Tebeo nodded again, but said nothing.

"I've told you this before, my lord, and I'll say it again. I have not betrayed you, nor do I intend to. But I believe this war must be stopped before it begins. It will bring ruin to the realm, perhaps to all the Forelands."

"Do you know this? Have you gleaned something?"

Evanthya shook her head. "No, my lord. This is my opinion, it's not prophecy."

He almost wished it had been a vision. A part of him felt just as his first minister did. But Dantrielle would fare no better if her duke was labeled a traitor and her castle besieged by the royal army. At least in this war, his people might have a chance to prove their mettle or die loyal subjects of the kingdom. The alternative was unthinkable.

"I share your fears, Evanthya. You know I do. But you're asking me to exchange one war for another. If I defy House Solkara it will put us on a path to civil war, a hopeless war at that, and one that will be no less ruinous for the kingdom than this alliance with the empire." He shook his head. "I can't do it."

"You could at least speak with Lord Orvinti, my lord."

"To what end? The regent told us that Brall supports this war."

"Of course he did, my lord. What else would he say? But what if Lord Orvinti feels as we do, and only said what he did to avoid angering Numar? What if Bertin the Younger and Vistaan of Tounstrel do the same? The dukes chose Numar over Henthas because they didn't want a kingdom governed by fear and the threat of violence. Yet isn't that what we have?"

"Numar isn't Henthas!" the duke said, flinging the words at her like a blade.

Evanthya looked away. "No, my lord."

She didn't deserve his anger. As with so many things, she was right about this. He feared the coming war, but had been compelled to pledge his support by a regent he feared even more. And Dantrielle was one of Aneira's stronger houses. If Numar could force his compliance, couldn't he do the same to the dukes of Kett and Noltierre, Rassor and Tounstrel?

"Have you received word from Fetnalla since the regent's visit?" he asked. "Do you have any reason to believe that she and Brall have similar doubts?"

"I've heard nothing, my lord. For all I know, the regent was correct in saying that he had Lord Orvinti's support. But if I may be so bold, even if Lord Orvinti is in favor of this war, as you seem to be, it strikes me that you would benefit from such assurances right now."

"I probably would. But assurances can be conveyed by messenger. If we're to discuss defying the regent, we'd best do so in Orvinti."

Evanthya met his gaze again, her bright yellow eyes dancing like torch fire. It took the duke a moment to remember that she and Brall's first minister were lovers. A journey to Orvinti meant more to her than just an opportunity to press her argument again.

"Then we're going?" she asked.

"Yes. But hear this, First Minister: if Brall truly supports the war, this is over. There will be no correspondence with Noltierre or Tounstrel on the matter."

"Of course, my lord. Without Orvinti we can't stand against House Solkara."

They held each other's gaze for another moment before Tebeo sent her off to prepare for the journey. But long after she had left him, he continued to shake his head at the memory of this last comment. Notwithstanding her kind manner and reasoned thinking on matters of state, there were times when Evanthya spoke of war and rebellion with chilling indifference.

They rode at dawn the following day, steering their mounts into the teeth of yet another icy storm. Tebeo could not remember the snows lasting this long in past years. It almost seemed that the gods themselves were trying to keep the land's armies from marching to war. The duke kept his company small, much as Numar had. Evanthya rode with him of course, as did eight of his finest soldiers, four swordsmen and four archers. Brigands tended to move south during the colder turns and though some of them might have come north again, fooled by the brief warm spell that had come at the end of Eilidh's waning, most would not be haunting the roads again for another turn or two. Eight men would be more than enough.

He had sent a message ahead, informing Brall of his impending visit and telling the duke to expect him within the first five days of the waning. He hadn't waited for a response, nor did he expect the messenger to find him again in the forest. Such was the nature of his friendship with Brall that no reply was necessary. Both the duke and Pazice, his wife, would have welcomed them even without such a courtesy, just as he and Pelgia would have opened their home to Brall. But in this case Tebeo reasoned that the nature of his visit would be enough of a surprise. There was no need to compound the matter by arriving unannounced.

They traveled swiftly despite the weather—or perhaps because of it. No one in the company had any desire to linger on the road. By midmorning on the sixth day, they had come within sight of the Hills of Shanae, rising above the Plain of the Stallions and gleaming with fresh snow. It would be another day before they reached Lake Orvinti and Brall's magnificent castle, but seeing the hills, the duke felt his spirits rise. Even faced with the prospect of war, he looked forward to speaking with his friend. Brall had his faults. He could be arrogant at times, and he was even more likely than Tebeo to take a position in the Council of Dukes based not on what he believed but rather on what he thought the majority of dukes wanted. But he could also be thoughtful and uncommonly clever. And Tebeo knew that when the two of them spoke privately, he could depend upon Brall to be entirely honest with him. With Bertin and Chago dead, he could not say the same about any other noble in the realm.

The Plain of the Stallions remained a wild stretch of land, mostly devoid of towns and villages. A few farms could be found on the expanse, particularly in the regions just south and west of Lake Orvinti and just north and west of the Tall Grass River, but except for falcons and ptarmigans, wild dogs and, of course, the herds of horses for which the plain was named, there was little to be found between Dantrielle and Brall's castle. For this reason, and despite the fact that it added several leagues to their journey, Tebeo and his company followed the Rassor along its south bank. Even on the river, there weren't many towns. But there were a few, and every night of their journey they were able to find shelter.

On this night, because they were so close to the ducal city, the village was larger and the inn more comfortable than any they had encountered since leaving Dantrielle. Their meal, a spicy mutton stew and the black bread and light wine for which western Aneira was renowned, reminded Tebeo of nights spent in Bistari when Chago used to regale the other dukes with tales of his father's blood feud with Farrad the Sixth of Solkara. Long after his soldiers had gone off to bed, Tebeo remained in the tavern's hall, sipping wine and filling himself with fine food. Evanthya, who had long since stopped eating, stayed dutifully by his side, playing idly with her goblet. They had spoken little on this journey, and Tebeo wondered if she were merely anticipating her reunion with Fetnalla or distracted by weightier matters.

"It seems in recent turns that we don't often speak unless we're arguing," the duke said at last, draining his goblet and motioning to the serving girl for more.

"Yes, my lord. I've noticed that as well."

"I suppose I'm to blame."

"No more than I am, my lord."

Tebeo gave a small, dry laugh and shook his head. "Your courtesy is admirable, First Minister, but we both know better. You believe that I don't trust you, that my fear of the conspiracy has made me wary of all Qirsi, even those who serve me well."

Evanthya started to respond, no doubt to deny that this was true, as a good minister should, but the duke stopped her with a raised hand.

"Please don't, Evanthya. The truth is, I don't trust you, at least not as I did. I don't really think that you've betrayed me or my house, at least not in the customary sense. I'm not even certain that you're capable of such a thing. But I find myself wondering now about matters that never concerned me before. Do you serve House Dantrielle out of loyalty or because doing so brings you gold? Is the courtesy you show me genuine or is it a mask you wear to conceal your contempt for me?" The serving girl returned with more wine, which the duke accepted with a quick smile.

He watched her as she returned to the bar, then took a small sip from his goblet. Turning his gaze back to the minister, he felt a sudden ache in his chest.

She was crying, silent tears coursing down her pale cheeks.

He hadn't thought to wound her with his words. On the contrary, he had hoped to begin to bridge the rift that had grown between them. Only now, seeing the pain written on her thin face and thinking of what he had said, did it occur to him that his admission might hurt her. He wished he hadn't drunk so much wine.

"First Minister, please. I—"

She shook her head so that tears flew from her face, staining the wooden table like raindrops on castle stone. "I've known you felt this way for some time," she said. "I merely chose not to think about it. Perhaps it would be best—" She stopped, stifling a sob. "Perhaps I should leave your service now, before we reach Orvinti."

Tebeo closed his eyes, wincing. What a fool he was. "I don't want that," he told her. "I rely on your counsel, Evanthya. I need you now more than I ever have."

"How can you accept my counsel when you imagine me hating you, when you look for lies in my every word and gesture?"

"That's not what I said."

She swiped at the tears on her face. "It's close; close enough, anyway."

"Then I misspoke."

"Did you, my lord?" She sounded angry, as if her pain had suddenly given way to rage. "It seems to me those were the most honest words you've spoken to me since the king's death. You, Lord Orvinti, the regent—all of you see white hair and think 'traitor.'"

"You liken me to Numar?"

"Yes, my lord. Just as you liken me to the archminister."

"We have cause to be frightened, Evanthya. You yourself have spoken many times of the dangers of the conspiracy."

"Yes, I have. But I should not be branded a traitor because other Qirsi have betrayed their lords. Would you expect me to accuse you of poisoning my wine tonight simply because Grigor poisoned the Council of Dukes in Solkara?"

He rubbed a hand over his brow. "Of course not."

"My people have had to endure accusations of this sort for centuries, simply because the Qirsi wars ended with Carthach's betrayal. The Eandi see us as a race of traitors, and no matter what we do, no matter how ably we serve in your courts, you'll always see us that way."

"Is it any wonder, First Minister? When Brall and I speak of ourselves, it's always as Aneirans, or as men of our houses. But the Qirsi speak always of themselves as a race first. You're Qirsi before you're anything else. You may serve Dantrielle, you may live in Aneira, but you think of yourself as Qirsi."

"That's only because you won't allow me to be anything else! I am Aneiran, and I would give my life for House Dantrielle, whether you believe it or not. But when you look at me, you don't see an Aneiran. You see white hair and yellow eyes. You see me raising mists or whispering magic words to my mount. We're a race of sorcerers. All of the Qirsi share that, just as we share the physical traits that make us so strange in your eyes. So yes, in some small way we may feel a bond to other Qirsi, regardless of what house or realm they serve. But what choice do we have when you won't truly accept us as one of your own?" She shook her head, raking a rigid hand through her fine hair. "Still, it's one thing to feel such a kinship, it's another entirely to band with a handful of traitors simply because they happen to wield magic like mine. I hate the conspiracy, not only for what it's done to the Eandi but also for what it's done to me."

"And what is that?"

She opened her arms, as if it should have been obvious. "This argument, your distrust, the ache in my heart every time I have to take care choosing a word for fear of raising your suspicions again. I hate all of it! And I hate them for doing this to me! If you only knew—"

She broke off, looking away as tears poured from her golden eyes once more.

He hadn't been fair with her, not for several turns. He could see that now, though he didn't know how to win back her friendship. "If I only knew what?" he asked, his voice as gentle as a caress.

"Nothing."

"Please, Evanthya."

Their eyes met for but a moment before she looked away again. "If you only knew how much I want to defeat them," she whispered.

"We have that in common, don't we?"

She shrugged, still not looking at him "I suppose we do," she said, sounding unconvinced.

"I know it's not much, but perhaps it's a place to start. I don't want you to leave Dantrielle, Evanthya, not only because I depend upon you for counsel but also because I've grown quite fond of you over the years. Pelgia and I both have." He reached across the table and placed his hand on hers. Her fingers were slender and small, almost like those of a child. *These hands can raise a gale that would topple oaks.* She didn't take hold of his hand in return, but neither did she pull hers away. "I'm sorry I hurt you," he went on. "You're right about us, the Eandi, I mean. We do see you as different, as not sharing our devotion to the kingdom. We should know better by now, but we don't. That's what makes this conspiracy so insidious and also so cunning. It strikes at our weakness, our inability to see beyond the differences between us, our inability to think of you and your people as anything more than failed invaders who were undone by treachery. We've made it too easy for them."

Evanthya grimaced slightly. "You're not alone in that. For every Eandi lord who assumes that his minister has betrayed him, there are three ministers who think the same of their colleagues." She looked up. "The conspiracy has brought out the worst in all of us, my lord. As you say, that's what it makes it so dangerous."

"All the more reason to defeat it, then, First Minister. I'd be honored to fight this battle beside you."

The woman actually smiled, wiping away her tears again.

"Forgive me for what I said, Evanthya. I'm frightened by the conspiracy—I prefer an enemy I can see. But I didn't wish to hurt you, nor do I want to drive you away."

She took a long breath, her eyes meeting his for just an instant before flitting away again. After some time she nodded.

They returned to their rooms a short time later and rose the next morning to complete their ride to Orvinti. The air had grown warmer overnight, but it rained on the company throughout the day. When finally they followed the road around the south end of Lake Orvinti and into the castle, all of them were soaked and shivering.

The duke of Orvinti was not a man to waste time on formalities, and he soon had all of them taken to their quarters, where they could change clothes and warm themselves before being fed. Orvinti's duchess joined the two dukes and their ministers for the meal, but left them after the final course was served, claiming to be weary. Tebeo knew better. Unlike his own wife, Pazice had little interest in matters of state, but she knew enough of such things to understand that Tebeo's visit was unusual, and that the two men wished to discuss whatever had brought him to her home.

Once the duchess was gone, Brall stood, glancing first at Tebeo and then at the first ministers. He looked just as he always did, tall and hale, youthful for his age despite the shock of thick silver hair that hung over his brow. If he still suffered any lingering effects from the poisoning in Solkara, he showed no sign of it. His broad face may have had a few more lines than Tebeo remembered, but his eyes were still clear and as blue as the sky in the harvest turns.

"Shall we return to my chambers and talk there?" he asked, gesturing with a meaty hand toward the door of the hall in which they were sitting.

"Why don't we speak alone tonight, and allow our ministers to renew their friendship? The four of us can meet tomorrow."

Evanthya favored him with a smile of such profound gratitude that the duke felt his cheeks coloring. Brall, on the other hand, did not look at all pleased. When Fetnalla looked at him, however, a question in her yellow eyes, he nodded his assent.

When the ministers had gone, and the two dukes began to wind their way back through the dim corridors to Brall's quarters, the tall duke cast a dark look at Tebeo. "Why did you do that?"

"Do what?"

"Give Fetnalla and Evanthya leave to go."

Tebeo gave a small shrug. "I wished to speak with you in private, and I saw no harm in allowing them to have their privacy as well." He didn't think that Brall knew of the ministers' love affair, but apparently he had given offense where none was intended and he didn't wish to compound his error with lies.

"There is harm in it," Brall said harshly. "You might as well give them leave to plot against us."

"You'd rather they were party to our conversation?"

"At least then we could watch them, make certain we know what they're doing."

Tebeo gave a small laugh. "And would you also have us stay up through the night, so that our slumber doesn't give them opportunity to weave their conspiracies?"

Brall just stared at him, his expression unchanged. "Make your jokes, my friend. But I assure you, in this castle, my sleep does not afford the Qirsi any opportunities."

It took him a moment. "You have her watched?"

"Of course I do. You should do the same with Evanthya. These times require no less of us."

"You can't be serious!"

"But I am. Haven't you been paying heed to all that's happened in this kingdom since the harvest? Haven't you been listening to the tidings brought to your city by merchants and the festivals? The conspiracy is real, Tebeo. It's not just rumors anymore. Nobles are dying, not just here but all through the Forelands."

"But to have her watched, as if she were already a known traitor . . ." He shook his head. "I couldn't do such a thing."

"So instead you wait until their treachery is revealed. That's the fool's way, Tebeo. That's what Chago did, and Carden, and who knows how many others who are already in Bian's realm."

They came to Brall's chamber and stopped before the door. Guards stood on either side of the door, both dressed in Orvinti colors, blue and green. Brall pulled a key from within his ducal robe, unlocked the door, and indicated with an open hand that Tebeo should enter. In all his years as duke of Dantrielle, Tebeo had never locked his chambers.

Tebeo and Brall sat in the large chairs in the center of the chamber while a servant threw a pair of logs into the hearth and squatted to stir the glowing embers.

"I suppose you have guards watching her?" Tebeo asked.

"Guards, servants. Occasionally I use some of Pazice's ladies." He glanced at the servant. When he began again, he had lowered his voice to a whisper. "Pazice knows nothing of this, and I'd be grateful if you didn't tell her."

"Of course." He sat still a moment, watching as the servant tried to rekindle the fire. "So, has Fetnalla done anything . . . unusual? Have you any reason to believe that she's betrayed you?"

"Not yet. But she may have some idea that I've been keeping watch on her. It may be that I'm keeping her from joining the conspiracy."

I think it more likely that you're driving her to it. He didn't say this, though he wanted to. Theirs was a strong friendship, but still Brall would have taken offense. Tebeo had never seen him so suspicious of anyone, not even the Eibitharians. Moreover, it occurred to him that if Fetnalla was under constant observation, Brall was about to receive tidings of a different sort. Best he hear it first from Tebeo.

"There's something I should tell you, Brall. If your watchers are doing their jobs properly, you'll learn of it soon enough, but since I've known for some time now, I ought to be the one to tell you."

Brall narrowed his eyes. "Tell me what?"

Tebeo took a breath, watching as the servant finally lit the blaze and left the chamber. The Brall he knew a year ago would have been surprised, by what he was about to say. He might even have disapproved, though he would have had the good sense to keep his thoughts to himself. But Tebeo wasn't certain how the man before him would respond. Distrustful as he was of his own minister, and frightened as he seemed to be of all Qirsi, there was no way to know for certain.

"What is it, Tebeo? You're scaring me."

"It's nothing really. Fetnalla and Evanthya are . . . they're in love."

The man's brow creased. "What?"

"Our first ministers—"

"Do you mean in love with each other?"

He nodded. "That's exactly what I mean."

"Are you certain it's not a trick, a story they've told you to hide something else?"

"Brall, please! Stop imagining traitors at every turn and think for a moment! If our ministers wanted to plot against us, and wished to find time alone to do so, they would simply claim friendship and have done with it. They certainly wouldn't go to this length, not when it's bound to draw more attention to them rather than less."

Orvinti eyed him a moment, looking angry. Then he gave a small nod and glanced at the fire.

"So they're lovers," he said, a look of distaste twisting his features.

Tebeo smiled. "Yes."

"How long have you known?"

"Since around the time of Carden's funeral."

"She told you?"

"I guessed."

Brall raised an eyebrow. "You guessed?"

"I could tell from the way Evanthya spoke of your minister, from the way she behaved when they were together." He grinned. "I may be old, but I still remember what it is to be in love."

The silver-haired duke shook his head. "If I had your eyes, I'd never wonder again about Fetnalla's loyalty." He paused briefly, watching the blaze. "Do you approve of this love?"

"I'm not certain it's my place to approve or disapprove. If Fetnalla served another duke I might be uncomfortable with it, and I did tell Evanthya that if ever you and I had a falling-out, their affair would have to end or she would have to leave my service. But as matters stand now, I see nothing wrong with it."

"The prelates would tell us that it's . . . unnatural."

"Probably. In certain respects I remain a man of the Old Faith. Besides, they're Qirsi. They worship in the sanctuaries, not the cloisters. They should be governed by the old teachings."

Brall shrugged. "You may be right. Just the same, I'd prefer you didn't mention this to Pazice either."

"Careful, Brall. You're accumulating secrets in your old age. You know the saying: a man who keeps his own counsel is doomed to suffer from bad advice."

For the first time since Tebeo's arrival in Orvinti, Brall smiled. "My old age? You've got nerve calling me old, Dantrielle. What are you, three years younger than I am?"

"Actually, it's four."

Brall gave an exaggerated nod. "Ah, four years, then." He laughed, as did Tebeo. After a few moments their laughter subsided, and Brall fixed his gaze on the duke, his expression growing grim once more. "Why are you here, Tebeo? What's happened?"

"The same thing that happened here. Numar's visit."

"I should have guessed. You're concerned about the alliance with Braedon."

"Of course," Tebeo said. "Shouldn't we all be? This war could be a disaster for Aneira and all the Forelands."

"It could also be our greatest triumph."

Tebeo felt a dull ache in his chest. He had expected Brall to balk at the notion of defying the regent, but he never imagined that his friend might actually be eager for battle. Not that he could fault the man for what he said. Tebeo had argued much the same point with Evanthya in the wake of Numar's visit.

"Is that really what you believe?" he asked.

Brall exhaled through his teeth. "I certainly wish it was. I don't think much of Harel and I've no appetite for war. We've just lost Chago, Bertin, and Vidor. I've had enough of funerals for a lifetime." He gave Tebeo a long look. "But surely you didn't come all this way merely to exchange opinions on an ill-advised war."

"No," Tebeo said, shaking his head. He told Brall briefly of his unpleasant encounter with the regent and his lengthy discussions with Evanthya. "I came at the minister's urging," he concluded. "She believes that I should try to convince you, Bertin the Younger, and Vistaan to defy the regent when he asks for men for the war."

Brall's eyes widened. "We'd be trading one war for another."

"I know."

"Yet you came anyway."

"Not to convince you but rather to ask your opinion."

"My opinion? She's mad. Or she's a traitor."

Tebeo gave a small smile and shook his head again. "She's neither. She may be young, perhaps a bit reckless, but she's loyal, and I fear she's right about this."

"No, Tebeo, she's not! The royal army would crush us in no time. It would be a futile gesture, one that would bring disaster to all of our houses."

"Perhaps not. I've been thinking of this since I left Dantrielle. The four of us might not be able to withstand Numar's assault, but if Bistari were to join us, and Ansis of Kett, we'd have a chance."

Brall appeared to consider this. "Have you spoken with Silbron?"

"No. I won't mention it to any of the others unless you agree to join me."

Brall grinned again. "Afraid to swing alone, eh?"

"Chago would have agreed to this in an instant, but no one hated the Solkarans more than he did. Silbron isn't like his father. He's more ambitious, and more sensible. I believe he wants Bistari to reclaim it's place as one of Aneira's leading houses and the only way to do that is to end Bistari's feud with House Solkara."

"Then he'll be reluctant to stand with us."

"That's why we need Ansis. If we have Kett and Bistari, there will be no war. Numar would have to lead the royal army against six houses. He'd only have Rassor and Mertesse by his side, and Mertesse is still recovering from its failed assault on Kentigern Tor. We could actually stop the attack on Eibithar without plunging the land into civil war."

Brall put a finger to his lips, looking thoughtful. "That might actually weaken the Solkarans."

"Exactly. Silbron doesn't want to anger Numar so long as the regency remains powerful. But if he sees this as a way to weaken the Solkaran Supremacy, I think he'll leap at the chance."

"Then we're still talking about leading the realm to civil war. Perhaps not immediately, but that's where this is headed."

Tebeo faltered, though only for an instant. "I suppose it is. I'm willing to risk that. This is no time for the Eandi realms to be weakening themselves by fighting foolish wars. That's exactly what the conspiracy wants us to do."

"Are you sure?" Brall asked. "It seems to me that the conspiracy has been fomenting dissent within the realms, not between them. Chago's death increased the likelihood of civil war here in Aneira, as did Carden's. We can't say for certain that either of them was killed by the Qirsi, but the fact remains that their deaths weakened the kingdom. And the houses of Curgh and Kentigern actually fought a battle on the Moors of Eibithar before riding back to Kentigern to fight off Rouel's siege. Isn't it just as possible that this civil war you're willing to risk is precisely what the Qirsi want?"

"Yes, it's possible. But as you said yourself, the risk of civil war isn't immediate." Tebeo gave a wan smile. "We're dancing with wraiths, my friend. We have no choice but to evade them one at a time."

Chapter

Ten

T hey had so much to discuss, so many plans to make. And her time here in Orvinti was short. Yet all Evanthya wanted to do was take Fetnalla's hand in her own and lead her back to her chambers. She wanted to taste her love's skin, to feel Fetnalla's lips on her own, to hear her cry out with pleasure and longing fulfilled. It was all she had dreamed of for more nights than she cared to count.

Instead they walked the corridors, speaking in hushed tones of nothing at all: the snows; the festivals, one of which would be arriving in Orvinti later in the turn; Evanthya's journey to the castle. They hadn't even discussed the message Evanthya sent the previous turn, informing Fetnalla of Shurik's death, a death they had paid for with their own gold. Evanthya tried to bring the matter up, only to have Fetnalla change the subject with some trifling question about the plantings in Dantrielle.

She did manage to draw from Orvinti's first minister that she was feeling well, that she had recovered fully from the poisoning. But she did not look well, and despite her assurances, Evanthya felt fear balling itself into a fist around her heart. Fetnalla had always been thin, as were most Qirsi, and her height exaggerated this, making her appear long legged and graceful like a pale heron. Yet, never before had she looked so frail. Her thin face had a pinched look, and there were dark purple lines beneath her eyes, as if it had been days since last she slept. Even her voice sounded weak, and Evanthya had not heard her laugh or seen her smile even once since her arrival. She wanted to ask Fetnalla what was wrong. Again. She knew, though, that her love would insist all was well, just as she had three times already that evening.

When they turned yet another corner, however, and started down the same corridor they had walked an hour before, Evanthya could stand it no longer. She stopped, taking hold of Fetnalla's arm so that the woman was forced to face her. Fetnalla had been speaking of the festival again, as if Evanthya had never seen one before. She fell silent now, looking off to the side, seeming to wait for Evanthya to question her again, or perhaps berate her.

Evanthya wanted to do both. But instead she stepped forward and placing a hand lightly on Fetnalla's cheek so that the woman had to look at her, stood on her toes and kissed her lips. Fetnalla returned the kiss for just a moment before pulling away, her eyes scanning the corridor in both directions. The ghost of a smile touched her face and was gone. "We shouldn't," she whispered.

Evanthya smiled, kissing her again. "Perhaps not here . . ." She raised an eyebrow, leaving the thought unfinished.

Fetnalla shook her head and began to walk again. "No. We can't."

"Why not?" Evanthya demanded, striding after the minister and pulling her to a halt again.

Fetnalla jerked her arm away. "We just can't. Someone might find out."

"That's never stopped us before. What is this, Fetnalla? Why won't you talk to me?"

Fetnalla stared at her until Evanthya thought the woman might cry. But for a long time, she said nothing.

"Walk with me," she finally said.

Evanthya shook her head. "I won't. Not until—"

"In the gardens." She looked down the corridor again. It almost seemed to Evanthya that she expected to see soldiers coming for them at any moment. "We can talk in the gardens."

Fetnalla started to walk again, leaving Evanthya little choice but to follow. Neither of them spoke while they were in the hallways and even when they stepped into the cold night air, Fetnalla said nothing. The skies had cleared and Panya shone upon the castle, silver-white and bright enough to cast dark shadows across the ward.

They made their way past grey hedgerows and the small, lifeless trees of the orchard. In another turn, all of them would be in bud, but for now it felt to Evanthya that they were walking among wraiths.

Still, Fetnalla did not speak. Evanthya stopped and waited for the other woman to face her. When she didn't, Evanthya folded her arms over her aching chest and swallowed.

"Tell me what this is about," she said. "Tell me now, or I'm going back to my chamber."

Fetnalla turned at that, her lips pressed thin. "I wish you wouldn't."

"I don't want to." Evanthya took a step toward her, taking hold of her slender hands. "But you have to talk to me." She wanted to put her arms around her, but even here, alone in the night, Fetnalla seemed reluctant to have her come close.

"They're watching me," Fetnalla whispered, her eyes darting back toward the nearest of the towers.

Evanthya shivered as from an icy wind, though the air was still. "Who?"

"The duke, his men, maybe even some of the other ministers. I'm not certain."

"Have you seen them?"

She shook her head. "No, but I've heard them outside my door at night. And I can . . . I can feel them."

Evanthya's first thought was that her love had gone mad, that she was gripped by some senseless fear. She thrust the notion away almost as quickly as it came, forcing herself to believe that Brall's men were indeed keeping watch on her, or at least to accept that Fetnalla believed it.

"Why would they be watching you?"

Fetnalla frowned. "You think I'm imagining it."

"I only asked—"

"I know what you asked, and I heard the doubt in your voice. You don't believe me."

"I believe that you're frightened and that—"

"Is it so hard to believe that Brall would want to have me watched? He's been accusing me of every kind of treachery for several turns. My denials mean nothing to him. You know that. You saw how he was in Solkara."

She had a point. The duke of Orvinti had been suspicious of Fetnalla since before Carden's death, and subsequent events had served only to deepen his doubts. But for her own duke to spy on her . . .

"Could it be someone else? The conspiracy perhaps. Maybe they hope to turn you, and so they're watching for signs of a rift between you and Brall."

Fetnalla shook her head. "Not unless their spies wear swords and soldiers' boots." She exhaled, closing her eyes briefly. "I know how this sounds. If you were telling all this to me, I'd probably think you were crazed. But I swear to you, he's having me watched. Brall is so afraid of the conspiracy and so convinced that I've betrayed him that he'll go to any length to protect himself, even though I pose no threat to him."

Evanthya had no choice but to believe her. Hadn't her own duke, a far more reasonable man than Lord Orvinti, expressed similar suspicions?

"So we can't be together," she said, her voice flat.

"I'm afraid we can't, not until this passes, or my duke banishes me from the castle."

"He's a fool." She sounded bitter and small, but she couldn't help herself.

Fetnalla allowed herself a grim smile. "He's merely the first of what will soon be a large group of Eandi nobles taking similar steps against their ministers. We have to do something, Evanthya."

"I know. I've wanted to speak of it all night." She glanced about the ward, abruptly feeling that she was being watched as well. She shivered again and pulled her robes tight around her shoulders. "You received my message."

Fetnalla arched an eyebrow. "Yes," she said drily. "You should have heard me trying to explain that to Brall."

"I'm sorry. I thought you'd want to know."

"It's all right. I was . . . relieved to learn that we'd succeeded."

Evanthya glanced up at white Panya. "Only 'relieved'? I was elated. I wanted nothing more than to find another assassin and start again."

"And yet you cried for Shurik."

She looked sharply at Fetnalla. "How did you know that?"

"I know you."

"Yes," she admitted. "I cried for him. I cried for what the Forelands have become and for what the conspiracy has done to us all, that it might drive me to such a killing. But that won't stop me from striking at them again."

"Of course it won't."

"The question is, what do we do next?"

"I don't know." Fetnalla glanced back toward the castle. "I don't have enough gold to hire another assassin, and I can't imagine that either of us is willing to wield a blade ourselves."

"So what are you saying? That we can't do any more?"

"I'm merely pointing out that we may have done all that we can, at least for now."

"No, we can't stop now. We can at least try to upset their plans."

Fetnalla shrugged. "We'd need to know their plans first."

Evanthya nodded, considering this briefly. "Tell me about Numar's visit."

"There's really not much to tell. He spoke with my duke in only the vaguest terms about a possible alliance with Braedon." Her mouth twitched. "At least that's all they said in front of me. They spoke for some time in private, and Brall's told me nothing of what they discussed."

"What about Pronjed?"

"He and I spoke briefly." Her brow furrowed. "Actually, now that you ask, we spoke about you."

"About me?"

"Yes. He wanted to know if you were likely to counsel Tebeo to support a war with Eibithar, should it come to that."

All the rage Evanthya felt during her own conversation with the archminister returned in a rush, until her hands began to tremble. "What did you tell him?"

Fetnalla smiled. "I told him that I had as much chance of predicting your actions as I did of predicting storms in the planting turns."

"Good. I had an interesting conversation with him as well." Once more, as she had for her duke several days before, Evanthya described her discussion with Pronjed, relating to Fetnalla not only his questions about Tounstrel and Noltierre but also his comments about the regent and their mutual distrust.

"You think he's a traitor," Fetnalla said when Evanthya had finished.

"I think it's possible. You thought so after Carden's death. You even guessed that he had mind-bending magic."

"I remember."

"What if you were right? I found myself telling him things that I hadn't intended, as if he were forcing me to reveal more than I wanted. Perhaps he did kill Carden."

"What are you suggesting?"

She opened her arms wide. "Isn't it obvious? I believe Pronjed is a traitor, and I think he's pushing the regent toward this war with Eibithar as a way of further weakening the Eandi courts."

"You don't know this for certain."

"I'm certain enough. Think about the questions he asked us. He's trying to make certain that all of Aneira's dukes support the alliance, yet he's clearly concerned that they won't. Why? Because if they give it any thought at all, they'll see that a war with Eibithar would be disastrous, even if we join with the empire."

"Listen to yourself, Evanthya! That's not proof that he's a traitor. Isn't it possible that he's merely using poor judgment, that both he and Numar have been seduced by this notion of an alliance with Harel?"

"I don't think so," Evanthya said. "Not after what he said about the regent."

"Maybe he was lying about that."

"To what end? If he only wished to win Tebeo's support for the war he would have spoken as the regent's man. But he didn't, in fact he made a point of telling me that Numar didn't trust him, that he was speaking to me without the regent's knowledge. I believe he was testing my loyalty. He might even have hoped to turn me to his cause."

Fetnalla turned away again, the look of barely controlled panic returning to her face. "Pronjed scares me. If he really does have delusion magic, he's too dangerous a foe, at least for us alone."

Evanthya smiled, touching Fetnalla's soft cheek so that the woman would meet her gaze again. "That's the beauty of what I'm proposing. We won't be standing against him alone. I'm merely suggesting that we serve our dukes as we would anyway. We have to tell them that this war is a mistake and should be opposed. I've already said as much to Tebeo. No doubt he and Brall are discussing the matter as we speak."

"I don't know that Brall will listen to me."

"Of course he will, especially because his closest ally will be telling him just what you are. Don't you see, Fetnalla? If we do this right, we can deal the conspiracy another blow and prove our loyalty at the same time."

A tear appeared on Fetnalla's cheek, shimmering in the moonlight as it rolled over her white skin. "You make it sound so easy."

"It can be."

"No, it can't, not anymore, not with what Brall has done to me." She dabbed her cheek with the edge of her sleeve. "It almost doesn't matter what I tell him anymore. If I advise him to withhold his men from Solkara's army, he won't do it. He'll be convinced that this is what the conspiracy wants me to say. It won't matter that Tebeo agrees with me, because he'll know that you offered the same counsel, and since you're Qirsi, you're suspect in his eyes as well."

Evanthya felt her patience waning. It wasn't like Fetnalla to surrender so easily, and though she didn't doubt that Brall's suspicions and his spies had taken their toll, she knew as well that she couldn't do this alone.

"Then what do you propose we do?" she asked.

"I told you before, I don't know. What you're suggesting makes sense. I just . . ." She exhaled, shaking her head again.

"You're frightened."

"Very. More than I've ever been."

"I'll do everything I can to protect you, from Brall and from the conspiracy." She kissed her once more. "You know that I'd give my life if it meant saving yours."

"Yes, I do. I just don't want it to come to that."

Evanthya took her hands again. They were shaking. She raised Fetnalla's fingers to her lips, kissing them gently. It was strange. For so long, Fetnalla had been the brave one, leading Evanthya into this battle, helping her overcome fears and doubts much like those to which she was giving voice now.

"It won't," she said, trying to sound strong and certain. "Do as I tell you, and we'll be fine. I promise."

Fetnalla's shivering seemed only to grow more violent. Evanthya frowned.

"Let's get you to your chamber," she said. "You're cold, and you look like you haven't been sleeping."

Fetnalla nodded. "Yes. I need to sleep." She regarded Evanthya for a moment, tilting her head to the side as she often did when she grinned. Her expression remained grim, however, and there was an apology in her eyes. "I'm sorry you can't join me, but with Brall's spies about . . ."

"I understand. Perhaps we'll find time to steal away before the duke and I return to Dantrielle."

Fetnalla nodded, though she looked doubtful. "I'd like that."

They walked back to the castle and wound their way through the corridors to Fetnalla's chamber. Evanthya saw no soldiers, but several times she heard boots scraping on the stone floors just ahead of them, only to turn a corner and find the hallway empty. By the time she had said goodnight to Fetnalla and walked hurriedly back to her own chamber on the other side of the ward, Evanthya no longer doubted that Fetnalla was being watched, as were those who consorted with her.

Weary from her journey, lonely for her love, Evanthya fell quickly into a fitful slumber, only to awaken what seemed a short time later to the sound of knocking at her door. Rising and wrapping herself in her robe, she crossed to the door.

"Who's there?" she called.

"Your duke," came the reply. "It's past midmorning, First Minister. Lord Orvinti and I are about to meet in his chambers and we'd like you and Fetnalla to be there."

Evanthya pulled the door open, smoothing her white hair. "I'll be along shortly, my lord, but I'm afraid Fetnalla isn't with me."

His eyes widened slightly. "Do you know where she is?"

"I haven't seen her since I left her last night. Isn't she in her quarters?"

"No. That's why I came here."

She felt herself blanch. "Does Lord Orvinti know that you've come to me?"

Tebeo took a breath, wincing slightly. "Yes, he does. I told him about the two of you last night."

She had to resist an urge to rail at him. What right did he have to share her secret with Brall? An instant later she realized that he wouldn't see it that way. Fetnalla was Orvinti's minister, just as she was his. Certainly Brall had as much right to know of their love as Tebeo did. The Qirsi were not chattel, but as ministers in the Eandi courts they did sacrifice certain freedoms, such as the right to share a bed with the ministers of rival nobles. It would have been within Tebeo's authority to demand that she end her affair with Fetnalla as soon as he learned of it. Allowing it to continue had been an act of kindness. Evanthya doubted that Brall would be so generous.

"You're angry with me," the duke said, his eyes meeting hers.

It would have been useless to deny it. "I have no right to be, my lord."

"Brall was displeased with me last night when I sent the two of you away. He was convinced that you would be plotting behind our backs. I thought it better that he know the truth."

"I think you're probably right, my lord."

"Unfortunately, this brings us no closer to finding Fetnalla." He rubbed a hand across his brow, as he often did when concerned. "Would she have gone to the city for any reason?"

"It's certainly possible, my lord. We didn't speak of her plans for the day, nor did we know that you and Lord Orvinti wished to speak with us this morning. She might have gone to the marketplace without realizing that her duke would be looking for her." She hesitated. "I take it Lord Orvinti is scouring the castle for her."

He gave a wan smile. "I'm afraid he is. I tried to assure him last night that Fetnalla serves him loyally, but he's even more disturbed by what he hears of the conspiracy than I am. This will do nothing to put his fears to rest. The sooner we find her, the better for all concerned."

Evanthya nodded, trying to think of where Fetnalla might have gone. She thought it strange that the minister would leave the castle at all. It was true that they hadn't known when the dukes would wish to speak with them, but Evanthya had assumed it would be this morning. Indeed, she had intended to be awake far earlier than this, expecting that they would all meet with the ringing of the mid-morning bells. Fetnalla should have expected the same. She also should have known better than to leave the castle when her duke had guests, particularly in light of Brall's suspicions. This was not like her at all.

She was about to say as much to Tebeo, when she heard a voice calling for him. A moment later a guard stepped into the corridor, breathless and flushed.

"They found her, my lord," the man said. "She was walking the gardens. She's with the duke now." His eyes flicked toward Evanthya. "They're waiting for you both."

Evanthya closed her eyes for an instant, surprised by how relieved she felt, or rather, how frightened she had been.

"Thank you," Tebeo said to the man. "Tell Lord Orvinti we'll be joining them shortly."

"Yes, my lord." The man bowed once and left them.

"I'll dress as quickly as I can, my lord."

"Very well. I'll wait."

Evanthya started to close the door, but Tebeo spoke her name, stopping her.

"For what it's worth, Brall took the news of your ... of you and Fetnalla rather well. He agreed with me that so long as he and I remain allies, and the two of you continue to serve us well, your private lives are none of our concern."

She nodded. That was a relief as well, though a part of her couldn't help feeling that they shouldn't have needed permission from their dukes to be in love. "Thank you, my lord. I'm glad to hear that."

It took Evanthya but a few moments to dress and soon she and her duke were making their way through Orvinti's corridors to Brall's chambers.

The door was open when they arrived. Brall sat at his writing table, looking at a large ledger by the light of several candles. Fetnalla stood at the hearth, her back to the duke, her color high.

Brall looked up as Tebeo and Evanthya stepped into the room and immediately closed the volume.

"Our apologies for keeping you waiting," Tebeo said, smiling first at the other duke and then at Fetnalla, who didn't appear to notice.

"And my apologies as well for sleeping so late," Evanthya added, hoping to deflect some of Brall's anger away from Fetnalla. "I must have been more weary from our travels than I knew."

"No apology is necessary," Brall said, a sour smile on his lips. He indicated the chairs near where Fetnalla was standing. "Please sit. First Minister, can I offer you something to eat?"

Evanthya shook her head as she lowered herself into the nearest chair. "No thank you, my lord."

"Some tea perhaps?"

She forced a smile, sensing that his courtesy was merely a mask for other sentiments. Suspicion, distaste, anger. There had been a time when Evanthya actually liked Fetnalla's duke, seeing him as a man much like her own duke; honorable, kind, though perhaps gruffer than Tebeo and not quite so wise. But it seemed that his fine qualities had been overwhelmed by his growing distrust of the Qirsi.

"Tea would be fine, my lord."

He rang a bell on his table, and almost immediately a door on the side wall of the chamber opened, revealing a young servant.

"Some tea, and some pastries as well."

The boy bowed, pulling the door closed once more.

"Lord Dantrielle has told me of your counsel, First Minister," Brall said, sitting across from her. "He tells me as well that you fear this coming war with Eibithar."

"I do, my lord."

"The prospect of a civil war doesn't frighten you more?"

"These are difficult times, my lord. Every possible path presents unique risks, and unique opportunities as well."

He wrinkled his brow, looking puzzled. "Opportunities," he repeated. "What an interesting choice of words. Opportunities for whom, First Minister?"

She heard the insinuation in his question and glanced for a moment at Fetnalla, who continued to stand before the fire, as if ignoring their conversation.

"I believe," Tebeo broke in, "that Evanthya sees an opportunity in this course of action for all who feel as we do, that Numar's alliance with the empire will lead Aneira to ruin."

Brall frowned at the duke, as if annoyed by the interruption. He opened his mouth, no doubt to question her further, only to be stopped by the return of his servant with the tea. By the time the boy had finished pouring out cups for all of them, which took several moments, Brall's face had turned a mild shade of purple.

Finishing with the tea, the boy faced his duke once more. "Will there be anything else, my—?"

"No! Leave us!"

The servant bowed again and hurried from the room.

The duke of Orvinti exhaled heavily and looked at Tebeo. "Where were we?" he asked.

Evanthya picked up her teacup, pleased to see that her hands remained steady. "You were asking me about my counsel to Lord Dantrielle, my lord. I believe you were trying to determine where my loyalties lie."

"Evanthya!" Tebeo said, glaring at her.

Fetnalla eyed her as well, her expression unreadable.

"Forgive me, my lord," Evanthya said, facing Tebeo, so that all in the room would know for whom the apology was intended. "But Lord Orvinti's intent was clear enough to compel an answer from you in my defense. I feel I have little choice but to respond."

"You're offended easily, First Minister," Brall said.

"Not at all, my lord. But you think me a traitor, as you do all Qirsi. I merely wish to assure you that I serve my duke and my house faithfully and that I offered this counsel to Lord Dantrielle believing fully that this was the correct course of action. If you choose to reject my counsel, you should do so knowing that."

She chanced a quick glance at Tebeo, and though the duke sat tight-lipped, still appearing angry, he nodded once, as if to tell her that he understood. Fetnalla still had not said a word, nor did she now.

"I don't think that all Qirsi are traitors," Brall said, sounding sullen.

"But you treat those who serve you as if they are."

The duke leveled a rigid finger at her as he would a blade. "It's not your place to tell me how to treat my ministers! I don't care whose bed you share!"

Fetnalla stiffened, all color draining from her cheeks.

Tebeo closed his eyes briefly, giving a weary shake of his head. "That's enough from both of you." He looked up at Fetnalla. "I'm sorry, First Minister. I told your duke last night. I meant to assure him that there was no harm in allowing you and Evanthya to leave us. I hope you can forgive me for doing so."

She nodded, keeping her silence.

"As for the two of you," he continued, fixing his glare on Brall and then Evanthya, "this bickering must stop. We have plenty of enemies throughout the realm without imagining more in this chamber. Now, Evanthya has suggested that we oppose Solkara's call to arms when it comes, and I trust that she has the best interests of my house at heart. I've told her that Dantrielle won't defy the regent unless Orvinti does the same. So we can discuss this matter for as long as necessary, Brall, but before I leave Orvinti, I need to know what you intend to do."

The duke had not taken his eyes off Evanthya, and even now, giving a small mirthless laugh, he continued to stare at her. "So it comes down to me, does it? She steers us toward civil war, but I'm the one who'll be branded a traitor."

Evanthya shuddered at what she saw in the man's light blue eyes. Despite what her duke had said about imagining enemies, she knew that this was no trick of her mind. She had made an enemy today. *One more among many,* she thought.

"As I told you last night," Tebeo said, "it may not come to that."

Brall nodded, finally looking away from her. "Yes, I remember. If we can convince the other houses to join this rebellion, we may keep Numar from destroying us. And who's to say that none of the other dukes will reveal our treachery to Numar, winning the regent's favor for himself and dooming us to hangings?" He stood abruptly, stepping past Fetnalla and returning to his writing table. "I don't like this. Lies and betrayal are not our way. That's not how Eandi nobles ought to conduct themselves."

It's the Qirsi way.

He didn't have to say it. Everyone in the chamber knew what he was thinking.

Tebeo gave a small shake of his head. "Forgive me, Brall, but that may be the most foolish thing I've ever heard you say. Eandi nobles have been lying to each other for centuries, and with all we know of the clan wars before the Qirsi invasion, I feel confident in saying that we didn't learn this from our ministers."

Evanthya expected Brall to grow angry again, but he surprised her.

"You're right," he admitted. "But I still don't like it."

"None of us does, my lord," Evanthya said, careful to keep her tone respectful. "I didn't give this counsel lightly or without regret. But this is a time for Aneira and the other realms to join together and fight as one to defeat the conspiracy. I grew up hating the Eibitharians, and at another time, under different circumstances, I would support this war with all my heart. But not now, not while there are traitors among us."

Brall seemed to weigh this for some time. Then, clearing his throat, he turned to Fetnalla. "What do you think of this, First Minister?"

She narrowed her eyes, as if looking for some sign that he was mocking her.

"I truly would like to hear your thoughts on this, Fetnalla. I know it's been some time since I sought your counsel on any matter of importance, but I'm asking you now."

The minister shrugged, appearing uncomfortable. "I fear this war, just as Evanthya does," she said at last. "But I'm no less frightened by the prospect of a civil war. Numar will try to crush those who oppose him, no matter how many houses stand with us."

"So you don't think we should oppose him?"

She hesitated again, looking like an innocent caught between advancing armies. It seemed to Evanthya that Fetnalla was unwilling to state an opinion, for fear of giving her duke more cause to doubt her.

"I believe we should be prepared to go to battle in either case. This alliance with Braedon is a grave mistake, but Orvinti and Dantrielle aren't powerful enough to stop Solkara. If we intend to fight the regent we'll need to have the southern houses with us, and perhaps Bistari and Kett as well."

"I said much the same thing last night," Tebeo told her. "I believe the others can be convinced to join us."

Fetnalla raised an eyebrow. "If they can, this just might work."

"Does that mean you'd advise me to defy the regent?"

The minister took a long breath. "Yes, my lord. I suppose it does."

"We can compose messages to the other houses immediately," Tebeo said. "Even Bertin would receive his before the end of the turn."

Brall shook his head. "No. This is too dangerous to trust to messengers. You and I should make the journeys ourselves."

Tebeo grinned. "You're with me, then?"

"I must be mad, but yes, I am."

"You're not mad, my friend. War with Eibithar would be madness. This is an act of courage."

That she should be so eager to leave Brall's chamber and the company of the two dukes didn't surprise her at all. Brall had long since poisoned their relationship with his spies and the silent accusations she read in every glance, every question about her activities. And whatever kindnesses Tebeo had shown Evanthya over the years did not change the fact that he was Eandi and a noble, and therefore no different from her own duke.

But as she hurried down the corridor after their discussion had ended, desperately hoping that she could turn the nearest corner before Evanthya emerged into the hallway, she scarcely recognized herself.

"Fetnalla!"

She briefly considered walking on, as if she hadn't heard, but she knew that Evanthya would not give up so easily. She halted and turned, not bothering to mask her impatience.

"You were just going to leave without me?"

"I thought your duke would want to speak with you. I intended to find you later."

Evanthya came closer, wary and ashen. "Then why are you acting like you can't wait to get away from me?"

"You're being ridiculous."

"Am I? Where were you this morning?"

"Walking the gardens."

"I don't believe that for a moment."

"You think I'm lying to you?" She spoke with as much conviction as she could muster, but her hands had begun to tremble again, and she feel a muscle in her cheek jumping, as if her body itself were rebelling against her.

"I'm not certain what to think, Fetnalla. You won't speak to me, you very nearly run away from me, you claim to be walking in the castle gardens when you ought to have been in your duke's chambers." She swallowed. "And I know that you're lying to me now. I can always tell."

She shivered. "When else have I ever lied to you?"

Evanthya looked around, then took Fetnalla's arm and led her out of the castle and into the bright sun of the ward. "During the last planting," she said, once they were a good distance from the nearest of Brall's guards, "when you told you me you'd had a vision of Shurik, that you knew for certain he was with the conspiracy. There was no vision, was there?"

Fetnalla opened her mouth, closed it again. It had seemed such a trifle at the time. She was certain that Shurik was a traitor, though she hadn't even known his name. It made sense that he was. Why else would he have betrayed Kentigern when he did, so soon after Lady Brienne's murder, with Eibithar on the cusp of civil war? But even seeing the logic of it, Evanthya wouldn't have agreed to have him killed, at least not then. The Evanthya standing before her now—emboldened by their success, confident enough to stand up to Fetnalla's duke—she might have. But a year ago, Evanthya had been timid and not yet prepared to compromise her morality for the exigencies of this private war they had begun. So yes, Fetnalla had lied, telling her of a vision she never really had. With all the lies she had told in recent turns, this one had slipped her mind.

"How long have you known?" she finally asked.

"I think I always did. I just wanted to believe it so much that I accepted your word at the time. Only after the assassin's message telling me of Shurik's death did it occur to me that you had lied." She gave a small smile, though it vanished as quickly as it had come. "In a way I'm glad you did. I never would have gone through with it otherwise."

"That's why I did it."

"So then why are you lying to me now?"

She faltered, feeling trapped. "Habit, I suppose. I lie to Brall all the time now, because even the most innocent truth makes him suspicious. I went to the city this morning." She pulled from within her robe the necklace she had bought. It was a chain of finely worked silver with an oval pendant bearing a brilliant sapphire.

Evanthya examined it briefly, though she never took it from Fetnalla's hand. "It's beautiful."

"It's for you."

The other woman's face reddened, and she smiled, meeting Fetnalla's gaze. "Thank you."

Fetnalla stepped around her, putting the necklace around Evanthya's neck and closing the clasp. Evanthya held the pendant before her so that the sun caught the facets, making it glitter like Lake Orvinti on a harvest morning.

"Put it down," Fetnalla said, standing in front of her again. "Let me see it on you."

Evanthya let the pendant drop again, her color deepening.

"It's perfect."

Evanthya's smile lingered a moment longer, then gave way to a frown. "How could you afford it?" she asked. "You spent all your gold on . . . on the man we hired."

"Brall's paid my wage since then."

"But still, not enough for something like this."

Fetnalla threw up her hands. "Now you sound like Brall. This is why I lied about going to the city in the first place. If he learned that I'd spent money on a necklace, he'd start wondering where I got the gold, and what I had to do to earn it."

Evanthya started to say something, then faltered.

"I got it from a Caerissan merchant, Evanthya, and the price was quite good. It's not Wethy silver. If you insist, I can tell you just what I paid for it, but I'd rather not."

"No," she said, shaking her head. "I'm sorry." She smiled, falsely bright. "As I said, it's beautiful. I love it." She took Fetnalla's hand and gave it a squeeze, glancing about for guards as she did. "I love you."

"And I love you."

"Does that mean we can be together tonight?"

Fetnalla looked away. "You know we can't."

"Why not? Your duke knows about us now. Tebeo told me that he even accepts that it's none of his concern."

"It doesn't matter what Tebeo says. We just can't, not with Brall's spies about."

"But—"

Fetnalla started away. "I can't talk about this now." She took several steps before stopping and facing Evanthya again. Her love looked dazed, her color high, as if Fetnalla had slapped her cheeks. Fetnalla thought she might cry. Walking back to her, Fetnalla kissed her lightly on the lips. "I'm sorry, but having him know is one thing. Having all the guards in Orvinti talking about it is quite another."

Evanthya nodded, saying nothing.

"I'll see you later." She made herself smile, then walked away again, forcing herself not to look back.

They saw each other again at the evening meal. Fetnalla had no doubt that Evanthya had looked for her throughout the day, but she kept herself hidden, first in her chamber, and then later in the smaller gardens of the lower ward. She wanted desperately to take comfort and shelter in the warmth of Evanthya's bed. Though the nights were no longer theirs to share, they could easily have found a way to be together during the day. But Fetnalla couldn't bring herself to accept even that solace.

They were seated together in the great hall—a small grace from her duke, no doubt. They said little, but Fetnalla did see that Evanthya was wearing her necklace. She wore it under her robe, so that no one would notice, but Fetnalla caught a glimpse of the silver chain along the side of her neck. In spite of everything, she was pleased.

When the meal ended, they bade each other a quiet good night. Fetnalla tried to smile, but there was a reproachful look in Evanthya's golden eyes, as if she knew the real reason they couldn't be together.

Fetnalla had done little all day, yet she returned to her chamber weary and eager for sleep. Climbing into bed, she fell asleep almost immediately, and began to dream just as quickly.

She recognized the plain at once, the black sky, the grasses swaying in a cool breeze, and she began to walk. Soon she reached the incline and without hesitating, started to climb. It was the dream she had been expecting, and even as she felt her heart pounding in her chest and fear settling like a stone in her stomach, she managed a single thought that brought a smile to her lips. *At least tomorrow we can share her bed.*

The light appeared as she crested the hill. It was even more brilliant than she had remembered from the first time and she had to shield her eyes. When she looked again, the Weaver was there.

"You received the gold?" His voice was like a smith's hammer on glowing steel, clear and powerful.

"Yes, Weaver."

"Good. Has Dantrielle arrived yet?"

"Yesterday."

"And what have he and your duke decided to do?"

"They will oppose the war, Weaver. They intend to speak with several of the other dukes—Tounstrel, Noltierre, Bistari, Kett. If they can convince them to defy the regent as well, they believe they can keep Aneira from the alliance and still avoid a civil war."

"We shall see about that."

She sensed that he was smiling, and she knew that the dukes' plan would fail. It occurred to her that her duke might be killed in the coming conflict. She couldn't say for certain if the thought frightened her or pleased her.

"You've done well," he said.

"Thank you, Weaver. Actually, it was Dantrielle's first minister who convinced them. I did little more than agree with her."

"I see. Do you think she can be turned as well?"

Fear gripped her heart. Evanthya would die before she betrayed the land. "No, Weaver. I don't."

"You care for her." A pause, and then, "You're lovers."

It shouldn't have surprised her. He had entered her mind, he was walking in her dreams. Still, she was disturbed by the ease with which he had divined her thoughts. It suddenly seemed that all of her secrets had been laid bare for the world to see. Now, when she could least afford this to be so.

"Yes, Weav—"

Suddenly there was a hand at her throat, unseen but with a grip like steel, as if some black demon from the Underrealm had taken hold of her.

"You continue to close your mind to me," the Weaver said, his voice even. "You shouldn't. I've paid you well, and I've promised you freedom from your duke." He paused, though only briefly. "You fear for this other minister. You think I'll hurt her."

She nodded, clawing uselessly at the skin of her neck.

"Why would I?"

Still he held her, so that she couldn't answer, and she realized that he was still probing her mind.

Finally the hand released her and she fell to the ground, gasping for breath.

"Why would I?" he demanded again.

"Because she'll refuse you if you go to her. She still serves her duke—she'd see any other choice as a betrayal. I fear that if you reveal yourself to her, you'll have to kill her." *And because of what we did to Shurik.*

"I see. You understand that if she remains so until the end, I'll put her to death anyway."

"Yes, Weaver. In time, I may convince her to join us. But she's not ready yet."

"Very well. Do what you can."

"Yes, Weaver."

She was awake almost before the words crossed her lips. The chamber was dark, save for the deep orange embers of her fire. She had no idea how much of the night remained. Closing her eyes once more, she lay back on the sweat-soaked pillow, trying to slow her racing pulse.

Not long ago, before she knew that there was a Weaver leading the movement, she would have thought it impossible that she could be lured into what Evanthya still called the conspiracy. Even after Brall first started to spy on her she remained loyal to House Orvinti, despite the pain her duke's distrust had caused her. But his decision to have her watched was only the beginning. She hadn't told Evanthya about the rest. She still found it all so humiliating that she couldn't bring herself to speak the words.

Soon after she first heard the soldiers in the corridor outside her door and noticed servants skulking about near her chamber, she was summoned to the duke's hall for a conversation with Brall. They spoke of the soldiers' training and of the duke's plans to visit the outlying baronies when the thaw began, trifles that hardly warranted discussion. Yet, he kept her in the hall for some time, even going so far as to eat his midday meal with her, something he hadn't done in nearly a year.

When at last Fetnalla returned to her chamber, she found several of her belongings out of place. It didn't take her long to realize that her chamber had been searched, that her audience with the duke had been a pretense intended to keep her occupied while his soldiers went through her possessions, no doubt searching for evidence of her treachery.

She was furious, but still she did not contemplate joining the renegades. Rather, she wished only to leave the castle, to put as much distance as possible between herself and Brall. She didn't mean to leave for good—she merely wished to sit astride her horse, her beloved Zetya, and ride out past Lake Orvinti into the Great Forest. The day was cold and grey, but she didn't care. She wanted only to ride. Upon reaching the stables, however, she was told that she could not. Her horse was fine. The stablemaster was taking good care of her. But by order of the duke, the minister was not allowed to ride her beyond the castle walls.

Fetnalla wandered away from the stables, unsure of where to go. She was too dumbfounded to speak, too enraged to cry. "I'm a prisoner," she muttered to herself, the truth of this making her chest ache, as if Brall had struck at her with his sword. She wore no shackles; there were no bars on her door or her window. But the duke had robbed her of her privacy, her freedom, her joy, all in the name of preventing her betrayal.

Instead, he drove her to the conspiracy.

The first time the Weaver walked in her dreams, she knew that she would follow him to the brilliant future he described for her, that she would do whatever he demanded of her. There had been no warning prior to that first night—the gold came later. Fetnalla didn't even know how the Weaver had known to come to her. Clearly, though, someone with the conspiracy had heard of her duke's suspicions and had gauged accurately her growing resentment of his distrust. For she was drawn to the movement by far more than just fear of the Weaver and her certainty that he would kill her if she refused him. Dangerous as it was, she found that she wanted to join, to strike a blow against Brall. *He already believes I'm a traitor,* she thought upon awaking from that first dream. *He's earned my betrayal.*

She had done little for the movement since then. The Weaver had come to her two other times before this night, and she had told him what she could of Brall's intentions regarding the coming war with Eibithar. Soon he would ask more of her. Others had killed for the movement, she knew, and perhaps she would as well.

She also knew that eventually the Weaver would learn of her role in Shurik's death. By then, she hoped to have proven her worth to him, so that he might spare her. But it had never occurred to her until tonight that she would lead him to Evanthya. And Fetnalla knew that unless she managed to turn her love to the cause before that happened, the Weaver might well kill them both.

Chapter
Eleven

Yserne, Sanbira

I t was said throughout Sanbira, and even in the other kingdoms by those who had journeyed to the southern realm and found it impossible to deny the truth, that Castle Yserne, seat of the Sanbiri matriarchy, was the most beautiful fortress in all the Forelands. Rising from the base of the Sanbiri Hills, and built of the russet stone mined from their depths, its soaring rounded towers, elaborately detailed ramparts, and gently curving walls seemed more a work of art than a castle. And on days like this one, when the sun shone and the air was still so that the castle's image was perfectly reflected in the brilliant blue waters of Lake Yserne, it seemed a creation of the gods, as much a part of the landscape as the hills themselves and Shyssir's Wood to the west. Yet, as history had shown time and again, marked by the failure of sieges launched by the Brugaosans, the Trescarris, and even, centuries before, by the Curlintes, its battlements and the red walls surrounding Yserne city sacrificed nothing for their grace.

Olesya of Sanbira, the fourth queen of that name to rule Sanbira from Castle Yserne, the Lioness of the Hills, as she was known throughout the southern Forelands, had lived in the fortress all her life, nearly half a century now. To this day, she had found no finer structure anywhere, not even in Curtell, where she had gone years before to visit the renowned Imperial Palace of Braedon. Despite its glazed windows and interior fountains, or perhaps because of them, there was something garish about Harel's palace. Those who built Castle Yserne had both the good sense and good taste to err on the side of simplicity rather than excess.

In recent turns, the queen had found herself looking at the castle through different eyes. Where once she had taken it for granted, accepting Yserne's beauty and strength with little thought for its creators, she now couldn't go anywhere in her demesne without admiring the craft that had yielded such a place. Tanqel the First, the second man of Yserne to rule Sanbira, oversaw construction of the castle more than five and a half centuries before, and though he was remembered for his violent temper and bloody reign, Olesya had decided not long ago that if he could build a castle like this one, there had to be more to the man than cruelty and a quick blade.

Which, she was wise enough to understand, brought her to the core of the matter. How would she be remembered? She had ruled well for twenty-nine years, enjoying one of the longest reigns of any ruler in Sanbiri history, king or queen. She had been wise and fair, tolerating far more from the northern dukes than most reasonable women would have, and striving to maintain peaceful relations with Wethyrn to the north and Caerisse to the west. During her reign, Sanbira had weathered droughts and floods, outbreaks of the pestilence and once, in the earliest days of her rule, a land tremor that devastated the cities of Trescarri, Listaal, and Kinsarta. But in all, hers had been a prosperous reign, and mercifully uneventful.

"Is that how I'm to be remembered, then?" she asked herself aloud, standing before an open window in her chambers. "As the queen who ruled when nothing happened?" She gave a rueful smile. A fine legacy for the Lioness of the Hills.

She had never thought in such terms before Dalvia's illness. But watching from afar as her dearest friend wasted away, like a wild beast caged against its will, Olesya had been forced to accept that even queens didn't live forever. She was young yet—merely in her forty-ninth year—but her own mother had died at fifty-one, her father at fifty-three. She felt fine, but so had Dalvia only a turn or two before the illness struck her.

She shuddered, turning away from the window but leaving it open. Diani's message had made her think this way. She had tried to put Dalvia out of her mind since the funeral. Naturally she had no intention of ending Yserne's ties to House Curlinte. The alliance between the two families was nearly as old as the Yserne Dynasty, and the army of House Curlinte had fought to protect the matriarchy on many occasions. Olesya was fond of Sertio and loved Diani almost as she did her own children. She merely wished for some time to mourn her friend, to heal the wound Dalvia's death had left on her heart.

It seemed, however, that Diani needed her, and who was Olesya to deny the girl the comfort or guidance she sought.

The message from Curlinte had been quite vague and brief, nearly to the point of impropriety. It merely stated that she had already left Curlinte and expected to reach the royal city by the twelfth day of the waxing—today. There was no mention of what she wished to discuss, no request for an audience with the queen, a familiarity even Dalvia would not have allowed herself. Perhaps Olesya should have expected this. Diani was still quite young, and she had always been an impetuous child, though no more so than Olesya's own daughters. Boys, the queen had decided long ago, were easier to raise than girls. She laughed at the thought, wondering if that were as true in patriarchies.

Notwithstanding her desire to have no dealings with House Curlinte for a time, and the inappropriate tone of Diani's message, Olesya had spared no effort in preparing the castle for the girl's arrival. It was to be Diani's first visit to the royal city as duchess in her own right, and custom dictated that she be received as befitted her new title. She would be met at the city gates by a hundred of Yserne's soldiers, including men bearing the colors of both houses. Heralds would greet her with the Sanbiri anthem and, of course, the queen herself would welcome her to the city, declaring her guestfriend of all the people of Yserne. There would be a feast this night and a sword tournament among the soldiers of the royal army and whatever men Diani brought with her from Curlinte. Musicians would perform at the feast and in the streets of the city, as would tumblers and Qirsi fire conjurers. To the people of the city, it would almost seem that the Festival had arrived early. Diani, the queen was quite certain, would remember this visit for the rest of her days.

No sooner had she formed the thought than Olesya heard bells ringing from the east gate of the city. Diani's company was approaching the city walls.

The queen wrapped herself in the royal mantle—blue and red, the colors of Yserne—and placed on her brow the silver circlet worn by Yserne's queens for more than five centuries. Glancing briefly at her image in the large mirror on her sleeping chamber's far wall, she stepped to the door and pulled it open, only to find Abeni ja Krenta, her archminister, standing in the corridor, her hand poised to knock.

The Qirsi woman raised an eyebrow and smiled. "Some would say you have gleaning power, Your Highness. You anticipate my knock before you hear it."

Olesya gave an indulgent smile. "I merely heard the same bells you did, Abeni."

The archminister's eyebrows went up in feigned innocence. "Were there bells? I didn't hear them."

"Come along," the queen said, still smiling as she started down the corridor. Abeni quickly fell in step beside her, smoothing her ministerial robes with a white hand. "I take it all is ready for Diani's arrival."

"Yes, Your Highness. The kitchenmaster is complaining that the cellarmaster has chosen the wrong wine for the feast tonight, but I've spoken with them both and made it clear that they're to have the matter settled before the duchess sets foot in the castle."

"I imagine they have their swords drawn as we speak."

Abeni gave a small laugh. "No doubt, Your Highness."

They emerged from the castle at the base of the queen's tower and crossed through the vast network of gates and wards that guarded the fortress from would-be invaders. At the outermost gate, they were joined by eight soldiers who arrayed themselves around the queen, the silver hilts of their blades gleaming in the sunlight. From the castle gate, the queen and her escort followed a winding lane down toward the city. It was lined with people who had set aside their chores and business to greet Curlinte's duchess, and seeing the queen, they cheered loudly.

Before they reached the entrance to the city, Olesya heard the first strains of Sanbiri's anthem echo off the castle walls. Diani's company had reached the city gate, and the queen would do the same just as the anthem ended.

Olesya glanced at Abeni and favored her with a smile. "You planned this well, Archminister. You're to be commended."

"Thank you, Your Highness. It was nothing."

As the last strains of the anthem died away, Olesya stepped through the city gate with Abeni just behind her. The soldiers of Yserne stood to the side of the road, their blades raised in salute, their blue-and-red uniforms as bright as new blooms. But Olesya could not take her eyes off the duchess. Diani sat on her great bay, her face white and covered with sweat, though the day was cool. Sertio, her father, was beside her atop a grey stallion, his hand holding her reins. Behind them, all mounted, a company of soldiers waited in silence, twenty strong, a surprisingly large contingent of guards for such a journey. The queen felt her stomach tighten.

"We'll dispense with the formalities, Archminister," Olesya said in a low voice.

Abeni nodded. "Of course, Your Highness."

The queen stepped forward, opening her arms in greeting. "Diani, duchess of Curlinte, we welcome you to Yserne. I name you guestfriend of this house so that all will know that you are under my protection. So long as you remain in this city, the soldiers of Yserne will guard your life as they would my own."

Diani swung herself off her mount stiffly, and knelt before her. A moment later, Sertio and the Curlinte guards did the same.

"My thanks, Your Highness," the duchess said, her voice strained. "You do us great honor by welcoming us so."

"Rise, child. Let me look at you."

Diani and the men in her company stood and the duchess kept herself utterly still, suffering the queen's gaze as if she were ashamed of her appearance.

"What's happened?" Olesya asked. She cast a look at Sertio, whose concern was as obvious as Diani's weariness. "Is she ill?"

"I'll tell you everything when we're safely in the castle," the duchess said. And as she spoke, her eyes wandered not to the soldiers or the mob of people visible through the gate but rather to Abeni.

Only then did the queen realize that Diani had come to Yserne without her first minister.

"Of course." Olesya faced the Qirsi woman. "Perhaps you should return to the castle ahead of us, Archminister. Make certain that our guests' quarters are ready."

Abeni was eying the duchess, her expression grim, her cheeks even more pallid than usual. "Yes, Your Highness." She bowed to Diani. "Welcome to Yserne, my lady."

Diani said nothing, though she did nod once.

Clearly the duchess was in a good deal of pain, but she walked with the queen back up to the castle, even managing a smile and an occasional wave to the men and women cheering her arrival. She was her mother's daughter.

Once inside the castle, Diani and Sertio followed the queen back to her chambers, none of them speaking. Only when the door was closed and they were alone did Olesya turn and look at the duchess again.

"Now tell me," she said. "What's happened?"

Diani dropped herself into a chair, her eyes closed. She should have waited for leave from the queen to sit, but Olesya was not about to remark on it now.

"There was an attempt on my life."

"There were two," her father corrected.

"During your journey here?"

The young woman shook her head. "Near the end of the waning. This is why we came to see you."

"You were wounded?"

"Yes, but the wounds have healed."

"They're not bleeding anymore," Sertio broke in. "That doesn't mean that you're whole again. Three arrows," he said to the queen. "One in the leg, one in the chest, one in the back. The healer told her to rest." This last came out as a plea, as if he wanted Olesya to tell Diani to get herself to bed.

"I did rest, Father."

"Not nearly enough. We shouldn't have ridden so soon."

"Her Highness had to know, and we agreed that sending a messenger presented too many risks."

"Who did this?" the queen asked.

Diani opened her eyes, her gaze clear. "It was made to seem that Edamo ordered the assassination. The archers had their heads shaved, and their arrows were marked blue and yellow."

"But you don't believe this."

"Edamo isn't that bold."

"Have you captured the assassins? Have you questioned them?"

"They were murdered themselves," Sertio said, "by another man who made the second attempt on Diani's life the following day. He's dead as well."

They didn't believe the Brugaosans were responsible, which left only one other choice. A lioness wasn't supposed to show fear, but Olesya had to struggle to keep her voice steady as she said, "Your first minister isn't with you. Is he responsible?"

Diani nodded. "We believe it's possible."

"We know nothing for certain." There could be no mistaking the anger in Sertio's voice. There was far more to this than they had told her.

"But you suspect the conspiracy."

"Yes," Sertio said, though even this he offered with some reluctance.

"It had to have been the conspiracy," Diani said, more to her father than to the queen.

"Do you have any evidence of Qirsi involvement?" Olesya asked.

Diani twisted her mouth, looking like a child caught in a lie. "No, Your Highness. Not yet."

The queen nodded. "I agree that it makes little sense for the Brugaosans to have done this. They'd have little to gain, and for all his bluster, Edamo is not ready to test his army against mine." She nearly said something about Cyro's murder, but quickly thought better of it. Neither the duchess nor her father had raised the matter, and there seemed little point in doing so herself. "Still," she said instead, "I can't do much without proof that the conspiracy has come to Sanbira." She pressed her fingertips together, fearing their answer to her next question. "Where is your first minister now?"

Olesya sensed that Sertio wanted to respond, but was holding his tongue. It seemed this was Diani's tale to tell.

"He's in the prison tower of Castle Curlinte, Your Highness. Even without the evidence of which you speak, I have little doubt of his complicity in this matter. I felt it most prudent to confine him to the tower. He won't be able to strike at me again from there."

She couldn't believe what she was hearing. Nobles of the other realms imprisoned men without cause as a matter of course. Perhaps the dukes of Brugaosa and Norinde did as well. But the duchesses of Sanbira did not do such things. It was not their way. "And what if he's innocent?" she demanded. "Kreazur served your mother loyally for years. If he had betrayed House Curlinte, she would have known."

"She was ill for a long time, Your Highness. She wasn't the same woman at the end. She might not have known."

"Nevertheless, child. To treat a trusted advisor in such a way . . ." She shook her head. "What if one of your other Qirsi is the traitor? Don't you think that Kreazur could help you discover the truth?"

Diani shifted uncomfortably in her chair, her eyes darting toward Sertio.

"Go on," he said. "Tell her the rest."

The duchess took a breath, as if gathering herself for a fight. "I've imprisoned all the Qirsi who serve our house."

"*What?*" Olesya felt as if she'd been kicked in the stomach. "Diani, how could you do this?"

"Until I know which of them have betrayed me, I feel safest with them in the tower."

"You allowed her to do this?" she asked of Sertio.

"It wasn't my father's place to give or deny me permission, Your Highness. You know that as well as anyone."

The queen shook her head again. "This is wrong." She stepped to her window. *I've imprisoned all the Qirsi. . . .* "How long have they been held?"

"A bit more than half a turn." Sertio. Clearly he didn't approve of this either. Diani had done it all on her own.

"You must release them at once," Olesya said, turning to face them both. "This can't be allowed to continue."

"But, Your Highness—"

"Release them, Diani. Send a message to Curlinte instructing whoever you left in charge to free them all."

The young woman stood. "You would dictate to one of your nobles how she must govern her duchy?"

"If she acts the fool, yes."

Diani's cheeks burned crimson and Olesya had to remind herself that despite the ducal robes, this was still but a girl standing before her, new to her power, still grieving for Dalvia, and still recovering from an assassination attempt. It was so easy to forget with Diani, for she had always been wise beyond her years and so like her mother in many ways. Dalvia and Olesya had often spoken of how the girl seemed to have been born to rule, but really this wasn't true of anyone, not even a queen. Statecraft couldn't be bred into a child. It had to be taught, and Diani had lost her tutor at far too tender an age. Too late, the queen realized that she had approached this matter in the wrong way.

"Surely you see the danger in what you've done," she began again, her tone far more gentle than it had been a moment before. "To imprison people solely because they're Qirsi is to make yourself no different from those in the conspiracy who kill nobles simply because they're Eandi. It's not our way, Diani."

"With all respect, Your Highness, I don't know what our way is. Sanbira has never before faced a threat like the conspiracy. No realm in the Forelands has. All of us are journeying in unknown lands. I don't know what nobles elsewhere are doing, but clearly it's not working."

"And this is your answer?"

"It's an imperfect solution, Your Highness. I realize that. But it's not without merits. This traitor, whoever he or she may be, can't plot against us from the prison, nor can he flee before we learn his identity." She faltered, though only for an instant. "And he can't find another assassin either. I know you think I've done wrong, but you don't know what it's like to feel afraid in your own castle."

"You don't even know if there is a traitor," Olesya said, trying to keep her voice even. "If you had proof even of that I might understand—"

"There is a traitor. Of that much, I'm certain. These men knew just where to find me though I was on the headlands, at a place my mother had shared with me and Father and few others."

Olesya couldn't help but smile. Dalvia's promontory. She and the old duchess had visited the headlands together several times. One only needed to go once, to hear the roar of the breakers and watch the tide advance and ebb, to understand the allure of the place. "I was one of the fortunate few," she murmured.

"Then you know how difficult it would be to find without knowledge of the lands surrounding Castle Curlinte. The assassins were hired by someone close to me, and then they were made to resemble Brugaosan archers. Who but the Qirsi would do such a thing?"

In spite of herself, Olesya found herself swayed somewhat by the young woman's logic. It was easy to see how Diani had come to take this action, though that only made the course she had chosen that much more perilous.

"Are your Qirsi being mistreated?" the queen asked.

Sertio bristled. "You mean aside from being thrown in prison without cause?"

Olesya eyed him briefly, before facing the duchess again. "Are they?"

"No, Your Highness. They're in the tower, not the dungeon. They receive three meals a day and as many blankets as they need. There are no more than four in any given chamber."

She nodded. Intolerable though it was, the situation could have been far worse.

"Is this why you came?" the queen asked, stepping to the chair across from Diani's and sitting. "To tell me of the assassination attempt?"

"Wait a moment!" Sertio said. "That's all you have to say about the Qirsi? It's wrong, but if they're not being mistreated I'll allow it?"

"I don't like this any more than you do, Sertio. But it's hard to deny the reasoning behind what she's done."

"Reasoning? There is no reason here! There's fear and injustice, and not much else! Diani is young and still shaken by what's been done to her. But you should know better."

Olesya glared at him. "In my castle you will address me as Your Highness or Queen Olesya, and you will speak to me with respect. Do you understand, Lord Curlinte?"

Sertio looked to the side and nodded, his face reddening. "Forgive me, Your Highness."

She said nothing, her eyes fixed on him for several moments more. At last, she turned to Diani again. "Why did you come, Diani?"

"To tell you of the assassins. To warn you that the conspiracy has come to Sanbira."

"We knew that it would. We couldn't remain immune forever while the other realms suffered."

"No, Your Highness."

"What do you propose we do about it?"

Diani blinked. "I—I'm not certain, Your Highness."

"Well, you've placed your Qirsi in Curlinte's prison tower. Should we do the same in all the courts? Should we end the Festival until the threat has passed? If no Qirsi can be trusted, then doesn't it make sense for us to keep watch on all the Qirsi in Sanbira?"

The duchess seemed to weigh this for some time. "You still want me to release them, don't you?" she finally said.

"You see where your actions lead," Olesya said, ignoring the young woman's question for the moment. "If what you've done is the answer in Curlinte, then it must be in the other duchies as well. If we were all to think as you do, then even a single Qirsi who is allowed to remain free represents a threat to us all. Soon, every Qirsi in the Forelands would be imprisoned. You must see the injustice in that." She leaned forward. "I don't like saying this, child, but if the conspiracy is determined to make another attempt on your life, they will find a way to do it. We must be vigilant. We must warn Sanbira's other nobles of the danger. But we must never forget who and what we are."

Diani gazed back at her, looking terribly young and so frightened that for a moment Olesya thought she might cry. "They almost succeeded," she whispered. "The healer said that the arrows came within a halfspan of killing me. And the other man . . ." She stopped, shaking her head.

The queen shuddered, but forced a smile. "It seems the gods were with you."

"Or maybe I was just fortunate."

"Perhaps you were. But from this day on, you'll be more wary. They're not apt to surprise you a second time. That's to your advantage."

The duchess nodded. "Yes, Your Highness. I'll send the message at once." She started to stand, but Olesya stopped her with an outstretched hand.

"Sit for a time, child. You can send your message shortly. First, I'd like you to answer the question I asked you earlier. What should we do about this? I do agree with you that the conspiracy may have been behind these attacks. But how do we combat an enemy that smiles at us, even as he slips a blade between our ribs? Imprisoning all the Qirsi is no solution, but there must be others."

"I can think of none, Your Highness. As I said before, other realms have been faced with attacks from the Qirsi far longer than we have, and they've thought of nothing."

"What is it that the Qirsi want?" Sertio asked, drawing the gaze of both women. "Assuming for a moment that the conspiracy did try to have Diani killed, what would her death bring them?"

"My wrath," the queen said immediately.

"You forget the colors on their arrows," Diani said. "They wanted your wrath to be directed at the Brugaosans."

"So it's civil war they want." Sertio was looking from one of them to the other.

Diani shrugged. "That would follow from all we've heard of their activities in the other realms."

"I agree," the queen said. "But it seems to me that the more they rely on this tactic the less effective it becomes. After a time, all the Eandi courts are bound to stop blaming each other and start looking to the Qirsi."

"Then perhaps that's what we need to do," Diani said, her voice brightening. "I believe you should call together the other nobles, Your Highness. Tell them what's happened in Curlinte and see if we can all agree to band together against the conspiracy."

"You mean a treaty, within the realm?"

She nodded, actually smiling now. "In a sense, yes, that's just what I mean. The conspiracy seeks to weaken us. What if we find a way to keep that from happening, to use the attack on me against them?"

Olesya glanced at Sertio, who was fairly beaming with pride. "It's a fine idea, Lady Curlinte."

Diani blushed, a small smile on her lips. "My thanks, Your Highness."

"Indeed," the queen went on, her mind suddenly racing, "we may want to take it a step further. I believe we should make overtures not only to the other houses in Sanbira but also to the other realms of the Forelands."

"The other realms will resist, Your Highness," Sertio said. "You may convince the Caerissans, and I hear that Kearney, Eibithar's new king, is a reasonable man. But the emperor won't listen, and neither will the Aneirans. And of course the Wethys have little regard for anything that comes from the Matriarchy."

"I know it won't be easy, Sertio, but to be honest, neither will getting our own nobles to agree. Edamo may see in the turmoil created by the conspiracy an opportunity to end the Yserne Dynasty, and if Brugaosa opposes us, Norinde is certain to do so as well. But still we have to try. We don't know where or when the Qirsi will strike next, and it seems to me that Diani has given voice to our only hope of defeating them."

There was a knock at the door.

"Enter," the queen called, rising from her chair.

The door opened and Abeni stepped into the chamber.

"Yes, Archminister. What is it?"

"There is food for our guests in the great hall, Your Highness. I thought they might be hungry after their journey."

"You're right, of course. I should have thought of it." She indicated the door with an open hand, looking first at Diani and then at Sertio. "Eat, and then rest. We'll speak again later."

"I'll dispatch a messenger at once, Your Highness."

"After you eat, Diani. I'll have my archminister make the arrangements so that a rider will be ready as soon as you've composed your message."

Abeni looked at her, a question in her yellow eyes, but the queen gave a quick shake of her head. She would explain later.

"My soldiers will escort you to the hall. I'll be along shortly."

"Yes, Your Highness."

Diani and Sertio both bowed to her and started toward the door. After only a step of two, however, the duke stopped, facing her again.

"I apologize for my behavior before, Your Highness. I didn't understand."

"Think no more of it, Sertio. You're a wise and honorable man, and you wish only to guide your child through this most difficult time. It's no wonder Dalvia loved you as she did."

The man's eyes welled and he swallowed. "Thank you, Your Highness," he said softly.

Bowing a second time, he left her chamber, his footsteps echoing in the corridor.

"A messenger, Your Highness?"

The queen glanced at Abeni, then walked to her writing table. "Yes, we'll actually need quite a few before the day is out."

"Will they be going far?"

"Some of them will. I intend to summon the leaders of all Sanbira's houses to Yserne to discuss the Qirsi conspiracy. I also wish to speak of this matter with the rulers of the other realms, though I realize that will be a bit more difficult."

Abeni said nothing and after several moments the queen looked up from the papers before her. "No response, Archminister? Don't tell me I've finally silenced you."

The Qirsi woman smiled, though only for an instant. "I'm merely surprised, Your Highness. What's happened to bring this about?"

The queen briefly recounted her conversation with the duchess and her father, describing for Abeni the attempts on Diani's life. "It seems," the queen said, "that the conspiracy has finally come to Sanbira."

The minister raised her eyebrows. "I see. I'll find riders right away, Your Highness."

"Yes, and use the usual merchants to get the messages to the other realms."

"Of course, Your Highness." She hesitated. "Seven riders, Your Highness? One for each of the houses other than Yserne and Curlinte?"

"Actually eight. Lady Curlinte needs to send a message to her castle."

"Ah, yes, so you said."

Olesya couldn't help but grin. Abeni hadn't forgotten this, of course. She merely wanted an explanation.

"In the wake of the assassination attempts, the duchess has imprisoned all the Qirsi who live and work in Castle Curlinte."

The woman's eyes widened. "All of them? Even her first minister?"

"Yes. I've prevailed upon her to have them freed at once."

"Why?"

The queen stared at her a moment, wondering if she had heard correctly. "What?"

"Why would you have the duchess free them? It seems a logical precaution to me. Until she knows which of them is the traitor, none of them should be free to roam the castle and city. To do less is to invite additional mischief."

"You can't be serious."

Abeni shrugged. "I realize it's a bit extreme—"

"Extreme? It's unconscionable! Surely you of all people can see that!"

The minister smiled, albeit sadly. "I'm a Qirsi who serves loyally in the royal house of Sanbira, Your Highness. I have as much cause as any Eandi noble to hate the Qirsi conspiracy. In many ways more. I understand your concerns, but I have great sympathy for what the duchess has done. Respectfully, I believe you should reconsider your request that she have the Qirsi released, at least until we learn the identity of Curlinte's traitor."

The queen exhaled heavily. "Well, Archminister, I can't say that I expected this. I'll consider what you've said, but in the meantime I still want you to find eight riders."

Abeni bowed. "Yes, Your Highness. Is that all?"

Olesya didn't respond for several moments. She merely stared at the woman, grappling with an overwhelming sense of sadness and, even more, utter confusion. As a young girl, the queen had been taught by her mother to see beyond race and realm, profession and status. "There is as much nobility in those who till fields and pound steel to earn their gold as there is in any woman or man of the courts," her mother often said. "There is as much goodness and inhumanity in Sanbira as there is in Wethyrn or Aneira, and there is as much capacity for both fealty and treachery in the Eandi heart as in the Qirsi heart. A queen sees people as they are, not as she assumes them to be." Olesya had tried to live and rule by these words, to meet her mother's expectations even after the old queen's death. Yet now her archminister stood before her, suggesting that she treat men and women of her own race as criminals simply because their hair was white and their eyes yellow. And what frightened her most was that her world had become a place in which this counsel seemed perfectly reasonable.

"You understand, Abeni, that were I to apply Diani's logic to my own court, I would have to imprison you, as well as the others?"

That same sad smile lingered on the archminister's face. "Of course, Your Highness. To do less would make no sense at all."

"And still you counsel me to allow her action to stand?"

"I do so with a heavy heart, Your Highness, but yes, I do. The conspiracy threatens all. From what I understand, its leaders have as much contempt for court Qirsi as they do for the nobles we serve. If they prevail in this fight, I imagine I'll be tortured and executed. Next to that, your prison seems rather inviting."

The queen gave a wry smile and nodded. "I see. Thank you, Archminister. That will be all."

Abeni bowed again and left her.

Glancing down at the scrolls before her, Olesya picked up her quill and began trying to compose a message she could send to her duchesses and dukes. Edamo would be looking for signs of fear or weakness, anything he could use to Brugaosa's advantage. Hence, she would offer none. This would be a challenge to her writing skills, for she *was* afraid, and she felt powerless to halt the conspiracy's advance across the southern Forelands.

Chapter
Twelve

e had pushed himself hard after leaving Mertesse, driven in equal measure by his fear of being captured and imprisoned for the murder of Dario Henfuerta, his last partner, and by his desire to begin a new life for himself, free of the Qirsi and their insatiable demand for his deadly talents. If all went as he hoped, he would never again be known as Cadel Nistaad, assassin. Instead, he would simply be Corbin, a traveling singer with an uncommonly fine voice.

In many ways, Wethyrn was a dangerous place to begin his pursuit of this new profession. Even the largest of the realm's festivals did not rival those of Sanbira, Eibithar, or even Aneira. A musician of his ability might easily draw too much attention to himself, particularly if he spent a good deal of time searching for others with whom to perform. As a lone singer he would be a curiosity, prompting difficult questions. Where are you from? How could a man of your talents have no partners? What happened to the people with whom you used to perform?

The safest course of action, Cadel decided, as he crossed the Caerissan Steppe, skirting the southern edge of the Glyndwr Highlands on his way to the Wethy border, was to visit several of Wethyrn's major cities until he found a group in need of a male singer. Best to answer the inevitable questions only once.

He reached the Wethy border with the beginning of the new turn, entering the walled city of Grinnyd on the third morning of the waxing. He took a room at a small inn and spent several nights wandering the city streets, stopping in tavern after tavern in his search for other musicians. By the end of his fourth night in the city, Cadel's spirits had fallen. He had expected to face risks, but he hadn't expected to have so much trouble finding any musicians at all. Surely there were singers somewhere in Wethyrn. Clearly, however, they weren't in Grinnyd.

He left the city the next morning, continuing on to Ailwyck. Located on the Ailwyck River, in the center of lower Wethyrn, just north of the Grey Hills, the city of Ailwyck was the third largest in the realm. Only the royal city of Duvenry, and Jistingham on the eastern shore, were larger, and together the three great cities formed what the people of Wethyrn called the Granite Triangle. Wethyrn was generally regarded as the weakest of the seven realms of the Forelands, though Cadel thought it more likely that his native Caerisse deserved that dubious distinction. The Wethy army was smaller than those of its rivals, and its weaponry of only middling quality. But Wethyrn's men were well trained, and the Wethy fleet was renowned for its fine ships and skilled crews. She was no rival for Braedon or Aneira, Sanbira or Eibithar, but Wethyrn would be a valuable ally in any conflict. Anyone who thought otherwise had only to look at the mighty of walls of Ailwyck to understand the undeniable strength of the Wethy people. The cities of the Granite Triangle had never once been occupied by a hostile force. No other realm in the Forelands could say that about its three greatest cities.

Once in Ailwyck, Cadel's fortunes quickly changed. His very first night in the city, he found a group of musicians of great ability who were desperately in need of a male singer. He was wandering the narrow byways west of the city marketplace when he heard strains of music coming from a small tavern. He recognized the piece immediately. "Panya's Devotion" from *The Paean to the Moons*. The *Paean* had long been one of his favorite pieces both to sing and to hear. It was also one of the most difficult to play, much less to play well. And even from a distance, he could tell that these musicians were playing it beautifully.

He entered the tavern, more out of curiosity than anything else. Musicians accomplished enough to play the *Paean* like this probably would not be looking to add to their group. The tavern, though on a small street and tucked away in a remote corner of the city, was filled near to bursting. Seeing no place to sit, Cadel remained by the door, listening and watching. There were four musicians in all. Two men, one playing the lute, the other the pipes, and two women, one of them singing at that moment, the other standing beside her. Since this second woman held no instrument, Cadel assumed she was a singer as well.

The men played their instruments deftly. There was an art to accompaniment, a demand for subtlety that few players could master. These two had. Their music lent texture to the piece and complemented the singer's voice without overpowering it. They were playing the counterpoint, which, in the *Paean*, was usually done by other singers, and they were doing so quite well.

But it was the woman who drew Cadel's ear and eye. She sang the "Devotion" exquisitely, but more than that, she looked familiar to him. It was several moments before he realized why. Her name was Anesse, and the woman beside her was her sister, Kalida. The two of them had sung this same piece with Cadel and Jedrek several years before. They had been in Thorald at the time, traveling with Bohdan's Revel; he and Jed were there to murder Filib the Younger, heir to the throne of Eibithar. As they made their preparations for the assassination, they were fortunate enough to meet the two women, accomplished singers both, and gain some small measure of notoriety for their magnificent performances of the *Paean*. Jedrek and Kalida spent at least one night in each other's arms, and though Cadel and Anesse did not, they both made it clear that they were attracted to each other. "Perhaps

Adriel will bring us together again," he had said at the time, speaking of the goddess of love. To which Anesse had replied, "She will if she has an ear for music."

She looked just as he remembered her. She still wore her dark hair short, so that it framed her round face. Her eyes were a soft green, and though she appeared somewhat leaner than the last time he saw her, she was still a bit on the heavy side, which he found quite attractive.

Cadel was already thinking that finding her here in Ailwyck had been a stroke of enormous good fortune, when the "Devotion" ended and the music wound its way toward the beginning of "Ilias's Lament." Only when the *Paean*'s second movement began did he understand fully the extent to which the gods smiled upon him.

He had expected one of the men to sing "Ilias's Lament." It had been written for a man's voice and it had always been his part. But instead, Kalida sang it, an octave above where he would have. She did so competently, blending her voice with the counterpoint of the lutenist and piper, and turning what could have been a disastrous performance into a satisfying one.

Still, when the musicians finished and the tavern began to empty, Cadel knew that he had found a job. He waited until most of the patrons had left and the players were waiting for their payment from the barkeep. Then he approached Anesse and the others. It occurred to him to wonder if she would remember him as he remembered her, but he needn't have worried.

"That was an enjoyable performance," he said, drawing their gazes. It had been more than that, of course, but he needed to convince them that they needed another singer. Too much praise would undermine his efforts to that end. "I've never seen the *Paean* performed so."

The man with the lute smiled. "Thank you, friend."

But Cadel was watching Anesse.

"Corbin?" she said, her eyes widening.

"You remember."

She colored slightly, her eyes flicking toward the lutenist. "Of course I do. Yours is a voice few could forget."

"The two of you know each other?" the lutenist asked, stepping forward so that he stood beside her and laying a hand on her shoulder.

"Yes. Kalida and I sang with Corbin and a friend of his a few years back. In Thorald. Isn't that right?"

Cadel nodded. "It is."

"What was you friend's name again?"

"Honok," her sister answered, coming closer as well. "Is he with you?"

"I'm afraid not," he said, forcing a smile. "He and I parted ways about a year ago."

"I'm sorry to hear that," Kalida said, with genuine regret. She resembled her sister more than Cadel recalled. Her eyes were blue rather than green, and she wore her hair long, but their features were similar and the coloring nearly identical.

"Perhaps you should introduce us," the lute player said, eyeing Anesse.

"Yes, of course. Corbin..." She trailed off. "I never did learn your family name."

"Ortan," he said, extending a hand to the lutenist. Actually, that was Jedrek's family name, but under the circumstances, his friend wouldn't mind.

The lute player took his hand in a firm grip as Anesse said, "This is Jaan Pelsor. Jaan is my husband as well as my accompanist."

By now Cadel had expected this, and he smiled warmly at the man. "My congratulations. How long has it been since your joining?"

"Nearly eight turns now," Jaan said. He was as tall as Cadel and solidly built. He had black hair, flecked extensively with silver, and pale grey eyes. He must have been at least ten years older than Anesse, perhaps more.

"I'm very happy for both of you."

The man nodded, then indicated the piper with an open hand. "And this is Dunstan MarClen. Dunstan and I grew up together."

Cadel shook hands with the piper as well. "You play beautifully," he said.

Dunstan merely grinned.

"All of you do," Cadel went on a moment later. "It's rare to find musicians of such talent."

"Thank you," Jaan said. "I gather from what Anesse said a moment ago that you're rather a fine singer yourself."

"I believe I am." Cadel answered, knowing how brazen he sounded. "I'll get right to the point, Jaan." He wasn't certain whether this man spoke for the rest of them or not. But he sensed that Jaan was wary of Cadel's past friendship with Anesse, perhaps even jealous. If he could overcome Jaan's objections, he could deal with the rest. "I enjoyed your performance today, but it seems clear to me that you need a male voice in your company. Anesse and Kalida both know that I can sing. If they remember anything of Thorald, they also know that I take my music seriously and that I can be trusted with gold."

The lutenist looked doubtful. He glanced briefly at the two sisters, then looked back at Dunstan, who was regarding Cadel warily.

"I won't deny that we could use another singer," Jaan said at last. "But I'm not certain we can afford one. In another two or three turns, as the winds change and trade along the coast improves, we may be able to ask for a better wage, but for now we're barely making enough for four. To add a fifth..." He shrugged, then gave a small shake of his head.

"This tavern was packed tonight," Cadel said. "The innkeeper should be paying you plenty."

Kalida nodded. "I've been saying much the same thing for more than a turn now. We draw enough people to this place to deserve twice what the old goat pays us."

"Perhaps. But I'm not willing to risk steady work by demanding more."

Cadel regarded the man for a moment. "Can we speak in private?" he asked.

"All right."

They walked together to the back of the tavern.

"Let me offer you a compromise," Cadel said. "I still have a bit of gold left from previous jobs." In reality, he had a great deal, enough to keep him comfortable for years. But nearly all musicians were concerned foremost with their wage, and he could ill afford to appear indifferent to money. "Let me sing with you for half a turn. If at the end of that time the company is making no more gold than it is now, I'll move on. You don't have to pay me a single silver. But if your wage goes up enough to pay me what each of you is making now, we remain together."

Still the man hesitated, just as Cadel had thought he would.

"Let me add this," he went on. "Were I newly joined to a woman as lovely as Anesse, I'd be wary of any old friend of hers, just as you are of me. I assure you, Jaan—I swear to you on the memory of my dearest friend—I have no designs on your wife. I need work. I want to sing with musicians who are as good as I am. I'm not going to do anything foolish."

Jaan gave a grudging smile. "You don't lack for confidence, do you, Corbin?"

"Allow me to practice with you tomorrow. You can see for yourself why."

"Let me make certain I understand this. You sing with us for a half turn, and if we're not making more gold by the end of that time, you leave without being paid anything at all?"

"That's right. We'll consider it an apprenticeship of sorts."

"Even apprentices get paid."

"So will I."

Jaan laughed. "You're that sure."

"I've heard you play, and I have a sense of what we'll sound like together."

The man put out his hand, which Cadel took.

"Very well. We'll give this a try." He looked back at the others. "Let me go explain it to them. Dunstan will object until he hears that it's not to cost him anything."

"Of course. Tell me where you practice and I'll be on my way."

"We have three rooms upstairs. We generally practice up there. I'd recommend that you take a room here as well. The food isn't bad, and the innkeeper doesn't charge us for the rooms or our meals. I think we can at least convince him to offer the same to you."

"All right. If he refuses, I can pay my way for a time."

Jaan walked back to where the others were waiting and spoke with them for a time. Cadel saw Dunstan shaking his head at one point, but their discussion never grew heated, and finally they approached him, all of them but the piper with smiles on their faces.

"It's agreed," Jaan said. "We'll begin rehearsals tomorrow." Each of them shook his hand in turn, Dunstan last.

"Don't worry, piper," Cadel said quietly, gripping the man's hand. "I'm going to make you more money than you ever thought a musician could have."

Dunstan grinned at him.

The others retired for the night and Cadel went to speak with the innkeeper. The tavern's owner was reluctant to give away another free room, so Cadel paid him, after extracting a promise from the man that the room would be free if Cadel remained with the musicians for at least a turn. That night, for the first time since before Jedrek's death, Cadel lay down to sleep feeling that he actually was where he belonged.

Their first rehearsal the following morning went just as Cadel had hoped it would. They began with the *Paean*, and Cadel sang "Ilias's Lament." It had been some time since last he sang the piece, but it came to him as if he had sung it just the day before.

When they finished the third movement, "The Lover's Round," a four-part canon in which Anesse and Kalida sang the women's parts, Cadel sang the first male part, and Dunstan played the second on the pipes, a stunned silence fell over the room. All the others were watching him as if he had summoned flames like a Qirsi sorcerer.

"I told you he was good," Anesse said at last.

Jaan shook his head. "I've never heard the 'Lament' sung that well. I've certainly never played with anyone who could sing it like that."

"Thank you." Cadel smiled. "I thought it sounded quite good, though I have a suggestion or two as to how we might make it sound even better."

At this point he could have suggested that they sing it backwards to the tune of "The Elegy for Shanae" and they would have done so willingly, but he had nothing so extreme in mind. He merely wished to have Kalida and Dunstan change the rhythm of their counterpoint slightly, while Anesse slowed the "Devotion" a bit; subtle changes that his new partners accommodated with ease. Working with them throughout the morning, he realized that they were even finer musicians than he had thought the previous night. Jaan especially was a rare talent on the lute. He didn't use the intricate picking patterns Dario had, though Cadel had no doubt that he could have had he only chosen to. But his rhythms were as steady as the tide, every note he hit as clear as Morna's stars on a cold night. With Dario, Cadel had struggled to match his cadence to the sound of the instrument. He had no such troubles with Jaan, whose playing seemed to wrap itself around each voice like a blanket, warm and comforting, effortlessly matching the contour of the lyrics and notes being sung. Certainly Anesse had chosen well in a playing partner.

Over the next few days, Cadel began to see that she had chosen well in a husband as well. Clearly he loved her, doting on her at every opportunity. But he was more than just a love-struck old man entranced by his young wife. He had a fine humor and good business sense. He agreed with much of what Cadel suggested by way of changes in the way they performed various pieces, but when he disagreed, he held his ground, and on more than one occasion Cadel relented, seeing the merits of the man's arguments.

Kalida and Anesse could be strong-willed as well, and their musical instincts were every bit as good as Cadel's and Jaan's. Even Dunstan, who said little most of the time, suggested slowing their performance of "Tanith's Threnody," which improved the piece immeasurably.

After having heard Cadel sing, the piper began to warm to him. He was a kind man, if rather simple, but there could be no mistaking his skill with the pipes. There could also be no doubt of his feelings for Kalida. Whenever he wasn't playing, he watched her, looking unsure of himself, as if hoping that she would declare her love for him and save him the ordeal of speaking first. For her part, Kalida appeared to have no interest in him. He had a kindly face and a quick smile, but beside Jaan, whom he clearly admired, he looked plain and soft, with a round body and slightly stooped shoulders. Add to that the fact that he was so terribly shy around her, and Cadel could see why she didn't return his affections. This, after all, was a woman who had been drawn to Jedrek, with his lean wiry frame, wild black hair, and jaunty manner.

On only the third day after their first practice together, the five musicians gave their first performance. The tavern was packed, as it had been every night since Cadel's arrival in Ailwyck, and though he had sung before dukes and thanes, and placed himself in gravest danger to earn gold in his other profession, he could not remember being as nervous as he was this night. Not that he needed to be. They sang and played flawlessly. Their performance of the *Paean* drew cheers and applause so loud that Cadel actually feared that the tavern roof might collapse. Even the innkeeper, a dour man who had shown little interest in their music the previous nights, whistled and smiled.

The following night, the tavern began to fill before the ringing of the prior's bells, hours before the musicians were to begin their performance. By the time the company stepped onto the small wooden stage, the entire courtyard outside the tavern entrance was full, and many of those both inside and outside were drunk. The innkeeper had to promise a second performance to those beyond the door in order to prevent a riot. Cadel and his friends didn't mind, for they were paid double their usual wage, and the others agreed without dissent that Cadel should receive an equal share of the extra gold.

It was a late night, which became a sleepless one when Kalida let herself into his room after the others had gone to sleep. Cadel had already climbed into bed, but was still awake. He sat up, lighting the candle beside his bed with a flint. She closed the door behind her, then stood there, as if awaiting an invitation to join him.

She was wearing a simple shift, and her hair hung loose to the small of her back.

"You don't seem surprised to see me," she said.

"Actually, I am. Won't Dunstan be disappointed?"

She shrugged, a small smile tugging at the corners of her mouth. She was quite lovely, really. And it had been a long time since he last passed a night with a woman. "All three of them will be."

"They will?"

"Dunstan is Jaan's oldest friend," she said, beginning to wander about the small room. "They're like brothers. And so when Jaan was joined to Anesse, they all assumed that I'd be a dutiful girl and promise myself to him."

"A woman could do worse."

She paused by the wardrobe, regarding him, an eyebrow arched. "She could do better, too."

"I'm not certain that I'm the joining kind," Cadel said.

Kalida laughed. "I don't want to be joined to you, Corbin. To be honest, I don't think of myself as the joining kind either. If I did, I'd still be with your friend, Honok. As I recall, when we were in Thorald together, I spent Lovers' Night in his bed. Where Anesse and I come from that's the same as a betrothal."

"In other words, you wish to share my bed so as to make it clear to the others that you have no intention of being joined to Dunstan."

She walked to the bed and sat beside him, running a finger down the center of his chest. "That's not the only reason."

He felt a stirring in his groin, saw Kalida glance down at the sheets covering him and grin. Pulling the shift off over her head, she slid under the sheets beside him and kissed the side of his neck.

"Your sister may object," he said, closing his eyes as her lips began to travel his body.

"How can she? She's married to Jaan."

With all of them sleeping under the same roof, it took only a day or two for the others to realize that Cadel and Kalida were sharing a bed. Despite his fears, Cadel saw no evidence that Dunstan was angry with him. The piper was downcast for a short while, but it seemed to Cadel that whatever sadness he felt was tempered by a profound sense of relief. Indeed, the only one of the other three who did show any sign of being angry was Anesse, who said nothing to either Cadel or Kalida for a full day after seeing them emerge together from Cadel's room. Jaan, on the other hand, seemed genuinely pleased, perhaps seeing in their affair proof that he needn't be jealous of the singer any longer.

Within six nights of their first performance, the innkeeper more than doubled the musicians' wages, in part because they were now doing two performances each night, and in part because he was unwilling to risk having Cadel leave. He also gave Cadel his room for free, though it quickly became a wasted expense. Cadel and Kalida spent nearly every night together, either in her bed or his. She was a skilled lover, far more so than he, and the singer found himself anticipating their lovemaking even more than he did the company's performances.

His one concern in the midst of all his newfound success was that word of the company's performances would travel beyond Ailwyck, drawing the attention of the Qirsi conspiracy or Lord Tavis of Curgh. In Mertesse, Cadel had allowed the fame he and Dario enjoyed to lull him into carelessness. As a result, Tavis surprised him in the upstairs corridor of their inn, and nearly succeeded in exacting his revenge for Lady Brienne's murder. And over the past several years, the conspiracy had managed to find him no matter where he went, giving him gold he could not refuse and demanding that he kill for them yet again. Upon leaving Mertesse, Cadel had decided that his days as an assassin were over, and now, having found a company with which to sing, a city in which their music was appreciated, and a lover with whom he could share his nights, he was ever more determined to embrace this new life.

Midway through the waning of Elhir's turn, however, it became clear that indeed their fame had started to travel the land. Late in the morning, as they practiced a new piece that Jaan had written, a messenger arrived at the inn from the marquessate of Fanshyre in the Ailwyck countryside. The marquess, it seemed, had heard tales of their extraordinary talent and requested a private concert. He offered to host a feast in their honor two days hence and to pay them ten qinde each for a single performance.

As an assassin Cadel had spent little time in Wethyrn, and so he had little fear of being recognized. Still, he was certain the marquess had at least one Qirsi minister, and there was always the danger that this person might be a traitor who would have heard whisperings of the singer-assassin. More to the point, such a performance would only serve to widen their renown, increasing the danger that he would be found.

Unfortunately, none of the others shared his concerns. Nor could he voice them himself. Invitations like this one were exceedingly rare for all but the most talented performers. Any musician in the Forelands would have been delighted to receive one and deeply envious of others who did. Cadel could no more object to making the journey than he could admit outright that he was a hired blade.

They accepted the invitation immediately, sending the marquess's messenger back to Fanshyre with word that they would be at his castle on the appointed day. The others were far too excited to continue with their rehearsal and Cadel did his best to make it seem that he shared their enthusiasm. That night, however, as he and Kalida lay in bed, she made it all too clear that he had failed.

"Why are you reluctant to go to Fanshyre?" she asked, staring up at him, her legs still wrapped around his hips.

He forced a smile. "I'm not."

"Don't lie to me, Corbin. You tried to seem as pleased as the rest of us, but it took an effort. I could tell."

He exhaled, leaving the warm comfort between her legs and sitting on the bed beside her. How many lies were too many between lovers?

"It has nothing to do with Fanshyre. I've never even been there. I simply don't like the courts."

"Why not?"

"My father served in one when I was young. I hated the way he was treated."

The lie just came to him, and it struck him as a strange twisting of the truth of his childhood. He had grown up in the court of his father, a viscount in southern Caerisse, and what he had hated most about it was the viscount himself.

Kalida seemed to ponder what he had said for several moments, absently playing with his hair. Then she shrugged, and said, "Well, then enjoy taking his money. It's not like we're going to live there. It's one day, and nearly as much gold as we'll make here during the rest of the waning."

"You're right. I should be grateful for the invitation. I'll try to be."

"You're humoring me. There's more to it than what you've said."

Cadel smiled, looking away. "Yes, there is. But leave it at that, Kalida. Please."

"Is this about Honok?"

He looked at her again. She hadn't mentioned Jed since their first night together.

"Why would you think that?"

"I don't know. He once told me that his father didn't think much of the courts either. And I know the two of you were good friends before whatever made you part ways."

He pushed the hair back from her brow. "We're still good friends, he and I. And no, this has nothing to do with him."

"I'm sorry. I won't ask you anything more."

"Thank you. I promise you that I'll sing my best. Whatever my feelings about the courts, they won't hurt our performance."

"They'd better not," she said, pulling him down to her again. "You may not have an appetite for gold, but I do."

Two mornings hence, they set out southward for the marquess's castle. It was a bright, mild morning, a fine day for a journey. It seemed the planting winds had come to Wethyrn at last. The innkeeper had given them leave to miss their early performance in the tavern, but had made it clear that he expected them back in Ailwyck for the later one. From what he told them, it seemed a simple journey. Fanshyre Castle stood less than two leagues away, nestled in the northern reaches of the Grey Hills near the source of the Ailwyck River.

"If you leave early enough, you can be there before midday," the innkeeper said. "And if you leave Fanshyre with the prior's bells, you should have plenty of time to get back here, change your clothes, and earn your keep."

He wasn't a subtle man, but he knew the countryside. The company reached Fanshyre just as the midday bells tolled from the gates of the small village. They were greeted by the marquess himself, a short, rotund man with a broad grin and round face. His wife might well have been his sister, so alike did they look, and she welcomed them heartily before leading them to the castle's hall. There, true to his word, the marquess made them honored guests at a simple but ample feast. Afterward, they sang for him, performing every song they knew, and, at the marquess's request, repeating several pieces, including the *Paean* and, much to Jaan's delight, the new piece the lutenist had just written. Usually Cadel did not like to perform the same piece more than once for the same audience, but Fanshyre had been kind enough to feed them, and, as Kalida reminded him once again on their walk to the castle, he was paying them handsomely for their music.

They left Fanshyre just after the ringing of the prior's bells, gold jingling in their pockets, their spirits high. There had been only one Qirsi in the castle, the marquess's lone minister, a frail old woman who appeared to nod off in the middle of their performance. Cadel felt confident in assuming that she wasn't with the conspiracy and that his fears of this journey had been unfounded. As they made their way through the hills, he found himself joking with the others and singing along with Jaan to the bawdy Mettai folk songs the lutenist was playing.

He didn't even notice the three men in the road ahead of them until the company had almost reached them. And by then it was too late.

They were still in the hills, though they couldn't have been more than a hundred strides from more open land. Just here, however, the road narrowed and the rocky hills formed a steep canyon. The company halted and Cadel glanced behind them. Already there were two more men there, leering at them.

"I could hear the coins in your pockets from up there," one of the thieves said, pointing toward the top of the nearest hill.

Jaan stepped in front of Anesse and Cadel did the same with Kalida. He had a dagger on his belt—Jaan and Dunstan did as well—and a second strapped to his calf inside his boot.

The thieves all carried blades, and the one who had spoken, their leader no doubt, carried a short sword as well, stolen from a noble by the look of it. He nodded at the others and they began to advance on the company.

Jaan reached for his belt, but Cadel held out a hand, stopping him.

"Don't, Jaan. They'll kill us." Actually Cadel felt fairly certain that he could fight them off with just a bit of help from the others. But he was a musician now, not a killer, and he was willing to trade a bit of gold to keep all of them alive and preserve the secret of his past.

"We can't just let them take the gold," the lutenist said.

"Better the gold than our lives. We can always earn more."

The leader stopped in front of Jaan, a smirk on his begrimed face. He was about Cadel's size and he walked with the swagger of a man who had killed before and would do so again without hesitation. One of the others appeared far younger than he, and a bit unsure of himself, but the other three seemed just as confident as their leader. Two of them planted themselves in front of Cadel, their daggers drawn, and another stood beside Dunstan.

"Yer gold, old man," the leader said to Jaan. "An' that o' yer friends."

"Shouldn' we take their blades?" asked one of the men by Cadel.

The leader shrugged laconically. "Sure, take 'em. They migh' be worth something."

The man who had spoken laid his blade against Cadel's throat with one hand, and took the weapon from his belt with the other. In a moment they also had Jaan and Dunstan's blades.

"Now, give us yer gold."

Cadel, Dunstan, and the two women handed over their money, but Jaan, who carried his in a small leather pouch, took out his gold rounds and threw them over the man's head into the brush on the slope of the hill.

"You want it, you bastard?" he said. "Get it yourself."

The leader gave a short harsh laugh, glancing at his friends, but making no move to retrieve the coins. "Did ye see tha'?" he asked. "Th' old man has some darin'." He faced Jaan again. "No brains, though."

And with a motion so swift that his hand was but a blur, the thief hammered the hilt of his sword into Jaan's face.

The lutenist crumpled to the ground, blood pouring from his nose and mouth. Anesse screamed out his name, but before she could even drop to her knees beside him, the man kicked him in the stomach.

Cadel made a motion toward the leader, but the two thieves beside him brandished their daggers, forcing him to stop.

Seeing this, the leader walked to where the singer stood, the same cruel grin on his lips. "Ye want t' try too?" he asked, as if daring Cadel to hit him. "Ye want t' end up like yer friend?"

"Just take the gold and go," Cadel said, holding the man's gaze.

"Well, ye know, I would ha'. But now I don' think so." He looked at the women, and with a quick glance back at Cadel, stepped back to where Anesse now knelt. She was sobbing and cradling Jaan's head in her lap, trying to stanch the blood with a kerchief. The thief sheathed his sword, pushed Jaan away from her with his foot, and forced her to stand, stepping around behind her, one hand gripping her by the hair and the other grasping her breast. "How 'bout it, boys?" he called to the others. "Feel like a bit o' mutton?"

One of the men guarding Cadel walked over to Kalida, grabbing her by the arm, and tearing the front of her dress.

The man who remained with Cadel was looking past him at what his friends were doing, grinning with amusement. Cadel threw the punch so quickly, with such force, that the man never even had time to look at him. He merely dropped to the ground, his larynx shattered by the blow. The man by Dunstan cried out and bounded toward Cadel, but by that time the singer had his second blade in hand. The man swung at him wildly with his own weapon, but Cadel ducked under the attack and plunged his dagger into the man's chest.

Shoving the thief off his blade, he spun toward the two who had Anesse and Kalida. The one with Kalida, pushed her to the ground, and held his weapon ready, dropping into a fighter's crouch. Cadel didn't falter. Striding toward the man, he lifted his weapon as if to attack. The thief lunged at him, just as Cadel knew he would. His kick caught the man just under the chin. The thief fell, rolled, tried to stand, but Cadel was on him too quickly, slashing at the brigand's throat.

"Corbin!"

He just had time to dive away from the leader's sword as it whistled past his head. He rolled as the other man had, and came up in his crouch, his dagger ready.

The leader advanced on him warily, the grin gone from his face, though his teeth were still bared.

"Watch behind you!" Dunstan called.

The young one had finally thrown off his fear and joined the fray. He was approaching slowly as well, dagger drawn. But Cadel had no doubt that the leader was the dangerous one. He saw Dunstan go to retrieve a dropped blade.

"Stay where you are, Dunstan! Leave them to me!"

"Ye think ye can take us, eh?" the leader said.

Even as he spoke the words though, he was already launching his next assault. He leaped at Cadel, lashing out with the short sword and holding his dagger ready. The singer danced away, seeing no opening for a counter.

"Fight, ye coward!" the leader roared at the other brigand. "Or when I'm done with 'im, ye'll be next!"

It would be a clumsy attack, born of fear and desperation. Under most circumstances, Cadel would have had no trouble defending himself. But he didn't dare turn his back on the leader. The singer opened his stance slightly, so that he could look as easily to the rear as to the front, and he held his dagger ready.

He heard a footfall behind him, close. Dunstan cried out again.

Glancing quickly at the younger man, Cadel saw that he had already raised his weapon to strike. The leader was moving as well, closing the distance between them with a quick lunge and chopping down with his sword. Ducking wouldn't work this time.

Instead, he swung himself down and backwards, swinging his blade arm at the younger man's leg as he went down. He felt his blade embed itself in flesh, heard the man cry out. But rather than rolling as he had intended, he landed awkwardly, his wrist buckling under his weight.

Pain shot up his arm, white hot, like lightning in the heat of the planting turns.

The leader, who had missed with his first blow, pounced a second time, hammering down with his sword.

Cadel kicked out blindly—his only chance—and his boot glanced off the man's forearm, deflecting the blow just enough to save him. For the moment.

The man struck at him again. Cadel rolled away and scrambled to his feet, only to find the leader leveling yet another blow at him. But this time he didn't chop down at the singer. Instead he swung the blade, as if to take off Cadel's head.

Cadel spun away from him, avoiding the sword. And allowing the momentum of his turn to carry him all the way around, switching his grip on his own dagger in midmotion, he tried to slam his blade into the man's back. He misjudged the distance, however, slicing through the leader's shirt and drawing blood from his shoulder, but doing no real damage.

Both of them backed away for just an instant, breathing hard. Cadel chanced a quick look at the other man. He was on the ground still, clutching his leg, which was bloodied just below his crotch. The leader put a hand to his shoulder, looked at the blood on his fingers, and gave a fierce grin.

"Yer no musician," he said, his voice low.

Before Cadel could think of anything to say, the man rushed him again, raising his sword.

It was a clumsy attack. Too clumsy. At the last moment, Cadel looked not at the short sword but at the dagger, nearly forgotten, in the man's other hand. It was swinging at his side in a wide, powerful arc, the steel glinting in the sun's dying light.

Rather than ducking or retreating, Cadel stepped toward the attack, raising his injured arm to block the man's dagger hand, and with the other arm pounding his own blade into the man's stomach.

The leader let out a short, harsh gasp, his eyes widening. His dagger dropped to the ground and he grasped the hilt of his sword with both hands. But he was trembling, his legs failing him. Cadel pulled his blade from the man's gut and thrust it into his chest. The thief sagged to his knees, blood spouting from his mouth. A moment later he toppled sideways to the dirt.

Cadel retrieved his dagger and advanced on the last man, who still lay on the ground, whimpering like a child.

"Corbin, no!" Kalida's voice. "It's enough!"

He halted, glaring at her. After a moment he nodded.

"Can you walk?" he asked the young thief.

"I—I don't know."

"Well, you're going to have to. It'll be dark soon, and the nights get cold here this time of year, even on a warm day."

Dunstan began to reclaim their gold, including the coins Jaan had thrown. Cadel wanted to tell him to forget the money, but he didn't. Instead he walked to where Anesse and Kalida were tending to Jaan. The bleeding had slowed from his nose and mouth, though his face looked a mess. His breathing seemed labored.

"I think he has a broken rib," Anesse said, her voice tight.

"Can we get him back to Ailwyck?"

She shook her head. "I think we'd be better off returning to Fanshyre."

"The distance is roughly the same. And the terrain's easier to the north."

"Ailwyck," Jaan said weakly. "I don't want to go back to Fanshyre like this."

Dunstan joined them. "I found most of it. Not all."

"It doesn't matter," Cadel said. "We need to get Jaan back to the tavern. Can you help me carry him?"

"Of course."

"Are you all right?" Kalida asked him, looking closely at his face.

"I'm fine."

"It looked like you hurt—"

"I'm fine," he said again, his voice rising.

Her face colored and she looked away.

"Let's get him on his feet," he said to the piper.

Dunstan nodded toward the injured man. "What about him?"

"Leave him. He's no threat, and he's not worth helping." He turned to Anesse. "Find our daggers," he said. "And theirs as well."

"What about the sword?"

He stared at the body of the leader. "That, too."

His wrist was screaming, and he wondered if he had broken the bone. Not that it would slow him. He'd been injured before, far worse than this. Back when he was an assassin. He nearly laughed aloud. *You'll always be an assassin.* His father's voice. He would have liked to curse the old man's name aloud.

It was a slow, painful walk back to Ailwyck, and before they were done it turned dark and chill as well. The tavern was already full when they arrived—they could hear laughter and raucous singing coming from within. When they opened the door, however, and the tavern patrons saw the blood on Jaan's face, silence spread through the great room like the pestilence.

"What happened?" the innkeeper said, hurrying through the parting crowd.

"Thieves. In the Grey Hills."

"Someone get a healer!" he shouted to the men closest to the door. "Are the rest of you all right?"

"I've hurt my wrist. The bone may be broken. Otherwise we're fine."

"How much did you lose?"

Dunstan grinned. "Only a few qinde."

The innkeeper's eyes widened. "You were fortunate."

"I suppose," the piper said. "But you should have seen Corbin! He—"

"You're right," Cadel broke in. "We were fortunate. But Jaan needs healing, and a place to lie down."

Dunstan stared at him a moment, then nodded.

The innkeeper led them to his own quarters in the back of the tavern, allowing them to lay Jaan on his bed. "I'll be back with some food and tea," he said, bustling back toward the kitchen.

Dunstan and Anesse remained beside the lutenist, but Kalida pulled Cadel into the next room. Her lips were pressed in a thin line and her face was pale. Once more he was struck by how lovely she was. He was going to miss her.

"You said we were fortunate," she began at last, her eyes meeting his. "I don't think fortune had anything to do with it."

"Of course it did," he said, looking down at his wrist and flexing his hand. He could move it with only a bit of pain. Perhaps it wasn't broken after all. "Anytime you encounter thieves and escape with both your life and your gold, you've been lucky."

"That's not what I meant. The way you fought them . . ." She shook her head. "I was watching you fight. You never had any doubt that you could defeat them, did you?"

"Of course I did." He wasn't certain why he bothered lying. He couldn't stay. Dunstan was ready to write songs about his prowess with a blade, and now this from Kalida. When the shock of what had happened wore off, the others would have questions as well. They would never look at him the same way again. Still, his dream of leading a quiet life wouldn't die so easily. "There's always doubt," he told her. "When I fell today, when I hurt my wrist, that could have given him the opening he needed to kill me."

"But you fought—"

"Honok and I used to travel a good deal. We encountered many thieves, and over the years we learned to defend ourselves. That's why I fight as well as I do."

"That's not what I was going to say. You fought only when Anesse and I—" She swallowed. "When it seemed they were going to take more than just our gold. You could have fought them at any time, but you waited until then. It was almost as if you didn't want us to see you fight, as if you were afraid to let us see how good you are with a blade."

He started toward the door, intending to retrieve what few possessions he carried from his room upstairs. "I should go."

"Who are you, Corbin?"

"I'm a singer."

"And what else? A mercenary? Are you a thief yourself?"

He turned and walked to where she stood. She didn't shy from him, and when he bent to kiss her lips, she returned the kiss.

"It doesn't matter what else I am or was. I came here hoping to be a singer, and I became your lover because I thought you beautiful and kind. Never doubt that."

He crossed to the door once more and pulled it open.

"Where are you going to go?"

"It's best I don't tell you."

"What about your wrist?"

"I'll find a healer."

"What about us?"

He glanced back at her and smiled. "I'll remember . . . us for the rest of my days. Tell Anesse and the others what you will. Be well, Kalida. Gods keep you safe."

She gazed at him sadly, but there were no tears on her face, nor did he expect that there would be. Given time, he might have loved this woman.

"And you, Corbin," she said.

He slipped past the other musicians, returned briefly to his room, and then left the tavern, knowing that several of those who remained in the great room of the inn marked his departure. He knew as well that people in Ailwyck would speak for years of the singer who came to their city, bringing music such as few of them had heard before, only to leave a short time later, after single-handedly defeating five road brigands in the Grey Hills. This couldn't be helped, nor could the fact that this tale would spread through the land, eventually reaching Qirsi ears, or perhaps those of Tavis of Curgh. There was nothing he could do but journey onward. He was an assassin. He had been an assassin for more years than he could count, and he would die an assassin. This, it seemed, was his fate.

Chapter Thirteen

ou're wasting time," Henthas said, sulking in his chair.

Numar had to smile. "Perhaps. But it's my time, not yours."

There was a part of him that actually enjoyed seeing his brother so agitated. Certainly these discussions grew tiresome, but they also served a purpose, reminding Henthas that though he might have been duke of Solkara, Numar, in his capacity as regent, led their house now.

"The longer you remain regent to Carden's child, the weaker you grow. She's ten now, and with each year—"

"That's right, Henthas: she's ten. She has no claim to the throne for another six years. The fool's way is to rush matters. And as we both know, I'm no fool."

The duke's face colored, and Numar nearly laughed aloud. He was no more a fool than Henthas was a jackal. Jackals were cunning; they were dangerous. His brother was neither. Numar had reduced him to little more than a lapdog, toothless and completely dependent on Numar's goodwill.

"The dukes won't follow a regent to war. You said yourself that Dantrielle was already showing signs of defiance. What if he can convince others to stand with him?"

"Then I'll crush them, just as I intend to crush Tebeo. I don't have to be king to wield power. Indeed, I believe in most respects you're entirely wrong. As regent, I have as much sway with the dukes as I would as king, and far more goodwill. Wearing the crown, I become just another Solkaran tyrant, a man to be feared and distrusted, just as Carden was. But so long as I remain regent, I am merely the dead king's younger brother, humbly serving the land in its time of need."

Henthas snorted. "You honestly believe they see you that way?"

"Enough of them, yes. And I'm fully certain that were Kalyi to meet her untimely end anytime soon, it would mean my downfall, and Solkara's as well. Killing a noble or two is one thing. Murdering the child-queen is quite another."

He saw a quick smile touch his brother's face and vanish, and there could be no mistaking the gleam in his brother's eyes. There was just enough malice in Henthas to make the prospect of such an end to Numar's reign attractive to him.

He would never be king, and he would remain duke of Solkara regardless of the house's standing in the realm. Indeed, Henthas was the sole person in the royal house who would actually benefit from the girl's death, provided he escaped blame in the matter. With Kalyi gone, her mother, Chofya, the former queen, would no longer have any claim to the status she had first attained as Carden's wife. Numar, if he weren't hanged for killing the girl, would be relegated once more to the marquessate of Renbrere, leaving Henthas as Solkara's leader. The Solkaran riches would belong to him, and any hope the house had of reclaiming the throne would rest with Henthas and his heirs. In light of how little power Henthas had now, he would have been mad not to consider such a course.

Fortunately, Numar had considered it as well.

"I know what you're thinking, brother," he said mildly. "I give you my word, you will be blamed for any harm that comes to the girl, not I."

"How can you be so certain?"

He grinned, opening his hands as if to reveal the answer. "Which of us is the Jackal, and which is the Fool? The dukes may not yet trust me completely, but they're genuinely afraid of you. To them, you're just like Grigor. In fact, several of them are still convinced that you had as much to do with the poisoning of the queen and the Council of Dukes as our dear, late brother."

"Thanks to you, no doubt."

Numar merely shrugged.

"So what is it you want of me? You summoned me here. There must be something on your mind."

"I require nothing but your patience, my lord duke. When the time comes, I'll see to the girl. No one wants her dead more than I. But I've a war to fight as well, sooner rather than later if the missives from Curtell are to be believed. If all goes as the emperor says it will, we've much to gain from allying ourselves with Braedon. You need only to wait, and support me, and help keep the other dukes in the fold."

"And how will my patience be rewarded?"

"Our success, and the continuation of the Solkaran Supremacy should be its own reward. But if you require more, I can offer you the lands of Dantrielle."

Henthas sat forward. "Dantrielle?"

"If Tebeo opposes me, as I fully suspect he will, I'll have little choice but to lay siege to his castle and seize his lands. The dukedom itself will remain, of course— my authority only goes so far. But as provided in the Volumes of Pernandis, his lesser holdings will be forfeit. And I'll make certain that they're given to you."

"Can you do that?"

"I'll have little choice, if he's guilty of treason."

Henthas shook his head. "I think you give the other dukes too little credit. As you said a moment ago, they chose you to be regent, not tyrant. They won't stand by while you strip one of the major dukedoms of her lands. They might have allowed Father to do such a thing, but not you."

"Treason is treason, Henthas, and the volumes are quite clear on the point. The other dukes will have no choice but to accept my decision."

Henthas bared his teeth in what Numar took for a grin. "You think you've won already. Grigor was the same way, you know. He thought he'd won, and look how it turned out for him."

"You forget. I'm the one who destroyed him. Grigor would have prevailed, but he took me too lightly. You'd be wise not to make the same mistake, brother."

"You're not as smart as you think you are, Numar. Not nearly."

"Perhaps not, but I'm smarter than you."

Henthas just stared back at him with an air of calm the regent had never seen in his brother before. That look, that air of grim resolve, frightened Numar far more than anything the duke had said to him. *I know more than you think I do,* it seemed to be telling him. *I know things you don't.* Henthas had always been the least formidable of the brothers Renbrere, weaker than Grigor and Carden, with little of their intelligence. But he was still Tomaz the Ninth's son, and thus a far more dangerous foe than nearly any other man in Aneira. Could he have finally mastered the art of court politics? Could he have discovered a path to power that Numar had missed?

The regent forced a smile. "We're being foolish, brother. Father wouldn't have wanted us to work at cross-purposes."

Henthas actually laughed. "And would Father have wanted to see Grigor executed so that you could claim the regency?" He shook his head again. "This is a strange time for you to start worrying about what Father would and wouldn't have wanted."

"All right. I don't want you as an enemy."

The duke stood, still grinning. "It may be too late for that."

"I've already offered you the lands of Dantrielle. What more do you want?"

"I'm not convinced that Dantrielle is yours to offer. To be honest, I'm not certain that you're in a position to offer me anything at all."

"You're wrong," Numar said. "Long after those who oppose me have fallen, I'll still be leading this realm, as regent, or as king."

"You haven't the faintest idea who opposes you, brother, much less how to defeat them. I'll enjoy watching the battle, however. I'll enjoy watching you fail."

There was a knock at the door, but for several moments they merely held each other's gaze, neither of them moving. The knock came a second time and Henthas leered at him.

"Duty calls, brother."

"Yes, who is it?" Numar demanded.

"The archminister," came the reply. "Queen Kalyi is with me. She wishes to speak with you."

Henthas looked like he might laugh once more. "You should see yourself now, Numar. You truly believe that playing nursemaid to the girl doesn't weaken you in the eyes of your dukes? Just look in any mirror." He reached for the door handle. "When you find the time."

The duke opened the door, revealing Pronjed and the young queen. Seeing Henthas, Kalyi shied away, hiding behind the minister as if she expected the duke to make an attempt on her life right there. From the beginning of the regency, Numar had taken care in his conversations with the girl to portray Henthas as a threat, as a man who would murder her, despite their blood relation, to satisfy his ambitions. Chofya had done the same, he knew, though out of a sincere belief that her warnings were justified. Clearly, the girl had taken these admonitions to heart.

The minister stepped into the chamber, urging Kalyi to follow. "Lord Rembrere," he said nodding to the regent. Then, to Henthas, he added an icy, "My lord."

"Archminister," Numar said, mustering another strained smile and wondering if his brother was right after all. He bowed to Kalyi, who could barely bring herself to tear her eyes from Henthas. "Your Highness."

"I should be on my way," Henthas said, with an effortless smile. He eyed the girl. "Your Highness," he said, bowing as well.

Kalyi flinched, then seemed to will herself to step forward from the archminister's shadow. "Uncle," she said in a small voice.

His smile broadening, Henthas left the chamber, closing the door smartly behind him.

"Forgive the interruption, my lord," Pronjed said. "But as I say, the queen requested a word."

Numar continued to stare at the door a moment longer before facing the Qirsi. *And here, no doubt, is another enemy.* Pronjed did not appear terribly formidable, with his ghostly eyes and narrow, bony face. But Numar sensed that the minister disliked him, or, more precisely, that he saw the regent—perhaps the regency itself—as an obstacle to his own ambitions. He had often sensed that the man was hiding something from him, and had even wondered if the minister might be part of the Qirsi conspiracy, though he had no evidence to support his suspicions. Regardless of where the Qirsi's loyalties lay, whether with Chofya or with the conspiracy, Numar knew that he couldn't trust the man. Or rather, he couldn't trust him fully. For while their ambitions might have been at odds, Numar and Pronjed both needed House Solkara to remain strong in order to realize them. Thus they needed each other, at least for the time being. Of this the regent was equally certain.

"There's no need to apologize, Archminister. I'm usually glad for any reason to end a conversation with my brother." He glanced at Kalyi and gave a wink. The child grinned back at him.

"Of course, my lord," the minister said. "I'm certain we won't take but a moment of your time."

"Nonsense. I'm always happy to speak with my niece."

She smiled again.

"You can go, Archminister," the regent said, with a quick look toward the Qirsi. "Kalyi and I will be fine."

Pronjed hesitated, as if unwilling to leave the two of them alone together. "Are you certain, my lord? I'm happy to stay."

"That won't be necessary."

Kalyi turned to the white-haired man. "Good-bye, Pronjed."

She said it with such innocence—Numar felt certain she had no idea what she was doing. But it had the effect of a dismissal.

Looking displeased, the Qirsi bowed to both of them. "My lord. Your Highness."

When they were alone, Numar took a seat by the hearth, gesturing for Kalyi to do the same.

"I trust you're well, Your Highness."

"Yes, uncle," she said, sitting beside him. "Thank you."

"Good. Your tutors tell me that your studies are going quite well. Not that I'm surprised, you being such an intelligent young woman. But I am pleased."

Actually, the tutors told him little, and he asked even less. But he needed something to talk about.

Her cheeks reddened, but she smiled shyly. "Thank you, uncle."

"It's very important that you continue to learn about Aneira and her neighbors. A queen must be knowledgeable about both her allies and her enemies in order to rule wisely."

"Yes, uncle. I'm working very hard. I didn't know being queen would be so much work."

"Oh, yes. All nobles work very hard, kings and queens most of all."

She nodded, and they sat a moment in silence.

"You wished to speak with me?" Numar prompted.

"Yes." She paused, twisting her mouth, as if uncertain as to how to say what was on her mind. "Were you and my father very close?" she finally asked.

The question caught him utterly unprepared. "We were brothers," he said, hoping that would satisfy her. The truth was, none of the brothers Renbrere had ever shared anything even resembling affection. Carden and Grigor had been near enough in age to be rivals in every endeavor. Henthas had always been too full of spite and envy to be close to anyone. Even their mother had been afraid of him. And the three older ones had been so wary of each other that they barely took notice of Numar.

She frowned. "I know you were brothers. But Henthas and my father were brothers, too. And I don't think my father liked him very much."

A clever response.

"Your father and I were closer to each other than we were to Henthas."

"Did it surprise you that he killed himself?"

He narrowed his eyes. Where was she going with this? "Yes. I suppose it did."

Kalyi nodded. "Me, too. He always told me never to be afraid, that a soldier or a king learned to master his fear. I don't think my father was afraid of anything."

"Your father was a very brave man."

"I know. That's why I don't think he would kill himself."

Numar blinked. "What?"

She looked down at her hands, which she was twisting and turning in her lap. "Well, it seems to me that a person would have to be very afraid of something to want to kill himself. And you said yourself that my father was brave."

"Your father was dying, Kalyi. The surgeon had told him so. That was why—"

He was going to say, *That was why Carden had the man garroted,* but he thought better of it. There were other things he could have said to put her off, but he was forced to admit that she had a point. Numar and his brothers had given little thought to Carden's death at the time it happened. They had seen it as an opportunity to be exploited, rather than a mystery to be explored. But thinking of it now, it did seem a strange way for Carden to die.

"So you think my father was afraid of dying?"

"I'm not certain," he admitted. "But clearly you don't."

She shook her head.

"What is this about, Kalyi? Why are we speaking of your father's death?"

"Because I want to know why he did it." She looked up, meeting his gaze. "I'd like your permission to try to find out."

He couldn't help but grin. "You don't need my permission for this. You're queen. This is your castle."

Her face brightened. She so resembled her mother, with her dark hair and eyes. Even the golden circlet on the girl's brow had once belonged to Chofya. It wasn't the traditional headpiece of an Aneiran ruler, but it was far more fitting for the girl than was the great crown worn once by her father, and it became her, making her look older than she was and even prettier. She would be a beautiful woman and queen, were she to live that long.

"Really?" she said.

"Of course." Chances were there was no mystery here at all. Numar had never imagined that Carden would die by his own hand, but there was no telling what a man might do when confronted with the prospect of his own death. Carden was brave, but he was also proud to a fault. Forced to chose between a quick death and a lingering one, turn upon turn wasting away in his shuttered bedroom, he probably would have chosen the former.

But what if the girl was right? What if there was more to this than any of them had guessed? With the surgeon dead, they might never know for certain. But it couldn't hurt to have the child ask some questions. At least it would keep her busy while Numar saw to more important matters.

"If anyone refuses to help you," he said, "tell them that I've asked you to look into this."

She practically leaped to her feet, so eager was she to begin. "Thank you, uncle."

"You're welcome, my dear."

She ran to the door, then stopped, facing him again. "Can I ask you a question?"

"Of course."

"I mean about Father's death."

He paused briefly. "All right."

"They didn't let me see his . . . see him. After, I mean. Did you see him?"

"No. By the time I arrived in Solkara, he had been taken to the cloister."

"Well, everyone seemed so certain that he killed himself. I was wondering how they knew."

Numar winced. The girl might have been intelligent beyond her years, but she was still only ten. Perhaps he had been too quick to encourage her in this endeavor. If Chofya learned that he had given Kalyi permission to look into Carden's death, she'd have his head.

"I don't think it's my place to say. It's enough for you to know that it was, from all I've been told, a rather gruesome sight. But not one that could be misconstrued. There can be little doubt that your father took his own life, Kalyi. I wish I could say there was, but I'd be lying to you. Your inquiry will be best served if you limit yourself to questions of why, rather than how." He offered a sympathetic smile. "Do you understand?"

The girl nodded, looking far less hopeful than she had a moment before. "Yes, uncle. Thank you."

She let herself out of the room, leaving Numar to ponder whether he had just made a terrible mistake.

The girl hadn't been gone more than a few moments when there came yet another knock at the door. Pronjed.

"What do you want?" the regent asked as the Qirsi let himself into the chamber.

"You've had a busy morning, my lord. First the duke and now the queen."

Numar raised an eyebrow. "Are you spying on me, Archminister?"

The Qirsi gave an easy laugh. "Of course not, my lord. But if I'm to serve you and this house, I should know as much as possible about the matters that occupy you."

"I assure you, Archminister, if I determine that any of my private conversations pertain to you in any way, I'll be certain to let you know."

"You don't trust me, my lord?"

The regent allowed himself a small grin. "No, I don't. Nor do you trust me."

"And yet we have a good deal to gain from working together."

"I was thinking the same thing just a short time ago."

Pronjed smiled. "I'm glad to hear that, my lord. Perhaps we can agree at last to put aside our differences, for the good of the queen, of course."

"Of course."

The Qirsi just gazed at him, as if waiting for something.

"Is there anything else, Archminister?"

"In fact there is, my lord. I've been charged by the queen mother with the responsibility of overseeing the girl's studies."

"And so you wish to know what we discussed."

Pronjed shrugged. "If I may be so bold as to ask."

"It was nothing, Archminister. She questioned me about her father."

"Her father, my lord?" Something in the way the minister's expression changed gave the regent pause.

"Yes. She wanted to know if we had been close as children. If I remembered what Carden was like as a boy, before he became duke and king." He smiled. "It's only natural, really. Having lost him at so tender an age, she finds herself desperate to learn all she can of him. Still, I thought it touching in a way, and just a bit sad."

"Indeed." The minister pressed the tips of his fingers together. "And your conversation with the duke? What was that about?"

He would have liked to tell the man to mind his own affairs, that a regent did not answer to a mere minister. But the words wouldn't come. Instead, he told Pronjed the truth.

"He fears that I'm wasting time. That I ought to be planning for the girl's murder already."

"Why does he think this?"

"Because he thinks the dukes are more likely to follow a king than a regent."

"He sees no danger in killing the girl so soon?"

"He claims not to, but I think there's a part of him that would like to see me fail."

"Even knowing that your failure could bring an end to the Solkaran Supremacy?"

"Yes."

"How did you respond when he urged you to kill the girl?"

"I told him to be patient, that eventually I would rule Aneira as king, and when I did he would be rewarded for supporting me."

"And did he pledge his support?"

"No. He thinks I'm destined to fail. He says I have enemies close by who will destroy me."

"Did he say who they were?"

"No."

The minister said something else, though Numar couldn't say for certain what it was. Indeed, a moment later he found that he couldn't remember at all what he had just been saying.

"My lord?"

He stared at the Qirsi for a moment. "What?"

"You were telling me that you've yet to hear from the emperor as to his request for soldiers."

"Was I?"

"Yes. And so you don't know how high to set the quotas for the other houses."

"That's right, I don't. I expect it will be at least five hundred men from each."

"Some of the dukes may object. Dantrielle, for instance."

"Yes. Dantrielle, Bistari, perhaps Tounstrel. I'm aware of the problem." He frowned. The man always seemed to be prying into Numar's affairs, as if he considered himself regent. "The dukes are my concern, Archminister. I'd ask you to leave them to me."

The Qirsi inclined his head slightly and stood. "Of course, my lord. Forgive me. I'll leave you now."

"Yes, please."

He watched the minister leave, and only when the door finally closed did he feel his anger begin to sluice away. He would have to be more wary of Pronjed.

The man was probably every bit as dangerous as Henthas. Numar walked back to his writing table and began to search for the most recent message from Braedon's emperor. After a few moments he paused, however, gazing at the door once more.

Something about his conversation with the Qirsi disturbed him. If only he could remember what it was.

Pronjed strode through the castle corridors, his rage threatening to break free at any instant. It was bad enough that he had to humiliate himself before the Weaver, begging his forgiveness for actions that should have been lauded rather than punished. But to have to tolerate such treatment from the regent was almost too much. Numar might have been intelligent for an Eandi, he might even have been the canniest of the brothers Renbrere, but he was still a weak-minded oaf. Bending the man's will and mind was proving itself all too easy. Unfortunately, what he had learned from this most recent encounter had disturbed him greatly. Numar, it seemed, was but one dolt among many.

Reaching the door he sought, he rapped hard on the oak and pushed the door open in response to the summons from within.

He was careful to close the door before saying anything. But once it was shut, he whirled toward the figure standing by the open window, leveling a rigid finger at him.

"You're a fool!"

Henthas grinned, though his eyes blazed angrily. "No, Archminister. I'm a Jackal, remember. I believe you've just come from the Fool."

"This is no joke!"

" 'This is no joke, *my lord.*' Isn't that what you mean?"

"You told him he had enemies in the castle?" Pronjed said, ignoring comment. "You told him that he was destined to fail?"

Henthas eyed him keenly. "How do you know what I said to him?"

"I have my sources. I've lived in this castle, and among these people, far longer than you have."

"You had someone listening to our conversation?"

"Why would you tell him these things? Are you so childish that you just have to gloat, or is it more than that?" He took a step toward the man. "Are you planning to betray me to him? Is that it? Are you playing both sides of this?"

He knew, of course, that Henthas was doing just that, but he needed to give the duke an opportunity to deny it. Which the man did, quite convincingly.

"Calm yourself, Archminister. I'm not planning to betray you, and I've done far less damage than you seem to think. Numar has never trusted you—you've been Chofya's ally from the very beginning, at least that's how it seemed to Numar, and to Grigor as well. He's thought of you as his enemy for so long that I'd imagine he's looking elsewhere trying to decide who I meant. All I've done is confuse him."

Pronjed exhaled through his teeth and straightened. The duke was probably right, though that did little to ease the minister's frustration with the man. He shouldn't have spoken to the regent of enemies, nor should he have been encouraging the man to kill the girl-queen. Of course he could say nothing about that part of their discussion, not without making Henthas even more curious about the sources of his information.

Apparently the duke's thoughts had wandered in a similar direction.

"What else do you know about what Numar and I said to one another?"

"Very little. Perhaps you'd care to tell me more."

He shook his head. "I don't think so."

"You still think he means to do harm to the queen?"

"I believe it's possible. Numar wants to be king, and the girl stands in his path."

"You want to be king, too."

His face colored. "Yes, I do. But I know that the dukes will never allow such a thing. They'd overthrow the Supremacy before they accepted me as their ruler. That's why Numar is so dangerous for the girl. They'd believe him innocent of any crime against her. I doubt Chofya will ever believe this, but I'm far more suited to be regent than my brother."

"Because your reputation is so poor that you could never get away with murdering the child."

"Precisely."

Pronjed gave a thin smile. "Such reasoning hardly flatters you, my lord."

"No," the man said, "I don't suppose it does. But you can't deny that it makes sense."

It was hard to know just what Henthas had in mind to accomplish with all his machinations. The minister could have used magic to divine his thoughts, just as he had with Numar, but he thought it safer to employ such tactics against only one of them. And though the regent had made the mistake of taking his brother too lightly, Pronjed still considered Numar the more intelligent of the two brothers, and therefore the more dangerous. Thus he had to content himself with gleaning what he could of Henthas's intentions from his conversations with the man, and from his probing of Numar's mind.

It seemed that the duke hoped to raise Pronjed's fears of Numar, claiming that he did so out of concern for the queen, and as a secret ally of Chofya. At the same time, he plotted with the regent, urging him to kill the girl. No doubt he hoped that any attempt on Kalyi's life would confirm all he had said to Pronjed of Numar's dark ambitions. If the girl survived, Numar's disgrace would hand him the regency. If she died, Numar would be executed, and he would claim the throne.

The role he envisioned for Pronjed in all of this was even less apparent. Clearly he needed to have someone else calling Numar a murderer, since no one would trust him to tell the truth. But more than that, he had probably guessed that Numar would attempt to blame him for Kalyi's death. He needed Pronjed to protect him from his brother.

"So," Henthas began after a long silence, "do you intend to speak to Chofya of this?"

"She should probably know that the queen's life is in danger," Pronjed said. "But if you'd prefer to tell her yourself, I'll keep silent."

The duke shook his head. "That won't be necessary. I . . . I don't think she'd believe any of this coming from me. And then the danger to Kalyi would remain. You should tell her."

"What if I don't believe you?"

Henthas frowned. "Why wouldn't you?"

"Any number of reasons. Your reputation, all that you have to gain from destroying your brother, all that you could gain from killing the queen yourself and making it seem that the regent was responsible. You came to me some time ago, indicating that you would help me keep the girl alive, and telling me that Numar was my enemy. But I've seen no evidence of any of this beyond your word." He opened his hands. "And I'm afraid that doesn't count for very much."

Henthas gave that same thin smile again. "What is it you want?"

This had to be handled delicately. The Weaver wanted Solkara weakened as war with Eibithar drew nearer, but Henthas would resist any action that was too obvious. And with relations between the brothers deteriorating, there was no guarantee that Numar would listen to him anyway. Still, Pronjed had to try.

"What do you think of this war your brother is planning with the emperor?"

"If it succeeds, it will strengthen the realm and our house for generations. If it fails, it will probably mean the end of the Supremacy."

"Do you think it will fail?"

Henthas stared at him, his eyes narrowing. "Perhaps I should ask the same of you, Archminister."

"I'm not certain I know what you mean."

"Then allow me to be more explicit. For some time now I've wondered when this conspiracy of which we've heard so much might strike at House Solkara. Ours is the leading house in the realm, after all, and if the rumors reaching Aneira from throughout the Forelands are to be believed, the Qirsi have been more than willing to strike at other royal houses. I find it impossible to fathom that the conspiracy would ignore us. Which leads to a most obvious question: who is the traitor in our midst?"

Pronjed stood motionless, struggling to ease the pounding of his pulse. He had anticipated such an accusation from Numar—not because he thought the regent knew anything for certain but because it would have served the man's purposes to raise doubts about Pronjed's loyalty. But for Henthas to have reasoned it through . . . This was the last thing he had expected.

"Are you asking me if I am this traitor?"

"Would that surprise you?"

"Yes, my lord, it would. I've served House Solkara for many years, and no one has ever questioned my loyalty."

"Nevertheless, I must ask. Are you a traitor?"

The minister let out a short laugh. "How am I to answer? Would you believe me if I said I wasn't?"

"Probably not. But neither would I have you hanged if you said you were. At least not right away."

"I don't understand."

"We're both traitors, Archminister."

"I never said—"

"That you were part of the conspiracy? Of course you didn't. You don't have to. Even without such an admission, you're guilty of treason, as am I. We speak openly of defying the regent, of undermining his power. Yes, we do so to save the queen, but it's still treason. It matters little if you have compounded that betrayal by joining the conspiracy. If one of us decides to betray the other, we're both dead men."

Pronjed wasn't certain what to say. The duke's accusations left him shaken; the man's reassurances only confused him.

"You needn't look so worried, Pronjed. I don't intend to speak of this to anyone, at least not for a while. Regardless of where your loyalties lie, our interests are the same for now. We both need House Solkara to remain strong and we both need to keep Numar from growing too powerful, which means that we share a desire to keep the queen safe. At some point in the future, our interests will diverge, and I make no promises about what I will and won't do then. But for now, you have nothing to fear from me."

"You speak of treason with unsettling ease, my lord. I assure you, I am no traitor. I may speak against the regent, but only because you tell me that he threatens the queen, to whom I owe my allegiance."

Even the minister could hear how hollow his denials sounded, but he had little choice but to offer them anyway. The duke would expect no less.

"Of course, Archminister," Henthas said, sounding unconvinced. "You understand, I had to ask."

"Of course, my lord." He paused. Then, "Perhaps I should go."

"Probably."

He turned toward the door, but the duke spoke his name, stopping him.

"My lord?"

The man was grinning once more, as if he had just won a great victory, looking every bit the jackal. "I trust you'll never come in here again calling me a fool, or questioning my actions."

Pronjed had to stifle a retort. "Yes, my lord."

"Good. Now get out."

The archminister stalked from the chamber, gritting his teeth. It would be a pleasure killing the man. Killing them both, actually. The brothers Renbrere.

In good time.

Chapter Fourteen

S he still didn't want to believe that her father had killed himself. It was a violation of Ean's doctrines and it bespoke a sadness she wouldn't even have wished on her uncle, the duke. But Numar had told her that there could be little doubt about how her father died, and she remembered overhearing her mother say much the same thing at the time of her father's funeral.

Kalyi had hoped, in speaking with the regent, that she might find some proof that her father had been killed, that all of the adults in the castle had been wrong about his death. In the wake of their conversation, she lost all enthusiasm for her "inquiry," as Numar had called it. How was she to learn what her father had been thinking when he died? If there had been a way to know this, wouldn't her mother have found it by now?

But as the day wore on, and she dreamed her way through her studies, thinking more about her father than about Aneiran history and the battle tactics of Queen Amnalla the Second, her resolve began to return. She had first decided in the days just after her father's death to learn all she could about why he had died. It had been the most frightening time of her life. Her uncle Grigor had poisoned her mother and the Council of Dukes, an Eibitharian spy had been spotted in the city, and it seemed the entire land was poised to go to war over whether or not to make her queen. She was too young to defend herself or her castle, too ignorant in the ways of the court to command an army, too small even to wear the heavy golden crown that her father had left for her. But she had a quick mind—all her tutors told her so—and she had always been good at reasoning things out. So she had set herself this task. It was too late to save her father from whatever had caused him such grief, but it wasn't too late to understand.

Somewhere in the time since, she had tried to convince herself that her father had been murdered, that he couldn't have died by his own hand. She knew now that she was wrong.

But nothing else had changed. She was still intelligent enough to ask the right questions and to learn what she could from what her father had left behind. And that, she decided in the middle of her lessons, was what she would do.

It seemed only natural that she should speak first with her mother, and so when her last tutor of the day ended her lesson, asking her please to be more attentive tomorrow, she ran from the chamber to her mother's sleeping quarters, which were just beside her own.

She found her mother sitting by the open window, staring out at a clear blue sky. Her mother rarely left her chambers anymore. She took most of her meals there, only venturing beyond her walls for formal meals in the great hall and occasional walks in the castle gardens. She was still beautiful—Kalyi thought her the most beautiful woman in the realm—but there were thin strands of silver appearing in the dark hair at her temples, and her face was paler than Kalyi remembered from before her father's death.

"Good day, love," her mother said from her chair, her face brightening as Kalyi let herself into the room.

"Hello, Mother."

She crossed to where her mother sat and kissed her cheek.

"How were your studies today?"

Kalyi shrugged. "All right, I suppose."

Her mother frowned. "Is there something wrong?"

"No. I just was thinking about other things."

Chofya regarded her solemnly. "A queen must learn to discipline her mind so that 'other things' won't distract her. Do you understand?"

"Yes, Mother."

Her mother smiled. "Good. Now, why don't you tell me what you were thinking about when you should have been listening to your tutors."

"I was thinking about Father."

The smile fled her mother's face, as it always seemed to when Kalyi mentioned her father.

"What about him?"

"About how he died."

"Kalyi, you mustn't—"

"You're always telling me that I'm not a child anymore, that a queen has to be grown-up, even if other girls my age aren't. Why should this be different? He was my father—someday I'm to sit on his throne. Shouldn't I know how he died?"

Her mother looked toward the window again, taking a deep breath. "Why would you want to know such a thing?"

"Because I want to understand why he did it."

"He was dying, Kalyi. That's why he killed himself."

"I don't believe that."

Her mother looked at her once more. "Whyever not?"

"Because Father wasn't afraid of dying. He told me so. And only a man who was afraid of dying would take his own life upon learning that he was ill."

Chofya gazed at her for a long time as if trying to decide something. At last she gave a small smile and pulled Kalyi close, in a long embrace.

"It's good that you think so highly of him, that you remember him with so much love."

It seemed a strange thing to say. Why shouldn't she love her father?

"So will you tell me?"

Her mother released her, her eyes meeting Kalyi's once more. The smile had gone away again. "What do you want to know?" she asked, sounding weary.

"Well," she began slowly, abruptly questioning whether she really did want to know any more about the way he died, "everyone keeps telling me that there can be little doubt that he killed himself. How can they be so sure?"

Chofya frowned, and for a moment Kalyi thought she might refuse to answer. But her mother surprised her.

"He killed himself with a blade. He thrust it into his own chest. He was sitting at his table in the great hall at the time. There was a good deal of blood, but all of it remained right there, covering his hands and his place at the table. Had someone killed him . . . well, it would have looked different."

Kalyi swallowed. She should have been scared, she knew, and repulsed. And perhaps a small part of her was. But mostly she was so grateful for even this small bit of knowledge that she didn't mind.

Her mother eyed her closely. "Are you sorry you asked?"

"No. Who found him?"

"What?"

"Who found him?"

"One of the servants, I believe."

"When?"

"Kalyi—"

"When?"

"I don't remember. The next morning I think."

"Had he been alone all night?"

"Actually, no. The duke of Orvinti was here and the two of them spoke well into the evening. Your father killed himself sometime after the duke retired for the night."

"You're certain the duke had gone?"

"Yes, Kalyi. I'm certain. One of the servants brought wine to your father after the duke left him."

"Do you know what Father and the duke talked about?"

"No, I don't." Her mother stood. "And I don't see the point of all this. Your father died by his own hand. I'm sorry if that disturbs you, but it's the truth. He learned from the surgeon that he was dying, and rather than face a long, slow death, he chose to end his life that night. Why is it so hard for you to accept that?"

"I told you. It means that he was afraid, and I know that Father wasn't afraid of anything."

"Each of us is afraid of something, Kalyi. Anyone who claims to have no fear is either a fool or a liar. You father was no different. He might not have been afraid of death, but he was afraid of appearing weak. And rather than spend his last days weakened by an illness the healers couldn't cure, he chose to die while he was still strong and able to make such a choice. Is that so difficult to fathom?"

"Yes. All that you say may be true for other men, but not for Father. He was king, and he was brave." Kalyi felt as though she might cry, which was the last thing she wanted to do. She was queen now, and she was trying to show her mother that she was mature enough to speak of such things. But her mother seemed not to care about any of this. She should have been as eager to know the truth as Kalyi was. Yet she seemed more than happy to just accept that he was gone, without asking any questions.

"Did you love Father?"

Her mother looked away, color draining from her face. "What kind of question is that? I was his queen."

"Sometimes kings and queens don't love each other."

"Who told you that?"

"I've been learning history, Mother. I know that Aneira has seen more than its share of court bastards, and I know what that means."

"I think we've spoken of this enough for one day," her mother said.

"That's why you don't care about this. You didn't love him."

"You're talking nonsense!"

But Kalyi could see her mother trembling.

"Well, you don't have to talk about this with me if you don't want to. I'm going to find out why he died, no matter how long it takes. I'll even talk to the surgeon if I have to." She started toward the door. Then stopped turning to face her mother again. "Father wasn't a coward, and he wouldn't have violated Ean's doctrines without a good reason. That's not the kind of man he was."

She started to turn again.

"You want to know what kind of man he was?" her mother demanded. "You want to know why I'm so certain that he killed himself because he was dying?"

Kalyi didn't answer. She was afraid to.

"You're free to talk to the surgeon, child. But it won't do you any good, because this isn't the same surgeon who told your father that he was dying. That man is dead as well. Your father had him garroted before taking his own life. That's the kind of man your father was. He was proud, and vengeful, and he cared little for Ean's doctrines."

There were tears on her mother's face to match her own. For a long time they stood staring at each other, holding themselves perfectly still.

Then her mother whispered Kalyi's name and took a faltering step toward her, her arms outstretched. But Kalyi ran from the room, choking back a sob.

She nearly collided with Nurse, who called her name as well, but Kalyi didn't stop for her. Instead she darted to the nearest of the towers, and made her way up to the ramparts at the very top. To her relief, there were no soldiers atop this tower, and she sat on the stone, her back against the wall, and cried until her chest hurt and her eyes burned.

That's the kind of man your father was.... There had been no love in her mother's tone, no sense of loss, no indication of any kind that she missed Kalyi's father even a bit. Kalyi had asked Chofya if she loved the king, and she had believed when she did that she wanted a truthful answer. But she had expected reassurance from her mother that, yes, of course she had loved him. Certainly she hadn't expected this.

He was proud, and vengeful. . . .

"No," Kalyi whispered, the word lost amidst the wind and snapping of the banners flying above her.

He couldn't have been those things. He was Carden of Solkara, son of Tomaz the Ninth, heir to the Solkaran Supremacy. He was king. He was her father.

Your father had him garroted. . . .

That was how Solkarans dealt with their enemies. Garroting. Her tutors had never taught her that. Perhaps they were forbidden to tell her. But she had heard talk of it in the castle, mostly among the older children, the boys who found the idea of it exciting. Even hearing such talk, however, she had never given it much thought before now. Her house, the royal house of Aneira, had its own special way of killing. Was it that common, then? Did Eandi nobles kill with such frequency that each house had its own favorite method? How many times had her father ordered his men to murder? Had he ever pulled the killing wire taut himself? He had sent men into battle, to kill and be killed. She knew that, just as she knew that Ean's doctrines said all killing was sinful in the eyes of the God. In which case, all kings violated Ean's teachings. Someday, when she was queen, she might have to as well.

Surely her mother knew all this. Yet she condemned her father for it, using it to prove that he was a bad man. Kalyi shook her head. It made no sense. Could her mother have hated him that much? The very idea of it brought fresh tears to her eyes.

She didn't know how long she cried, or when sleep overcame her, but the next thing she knew someone was touching her shoulder gently, and speaking her name.

Kalyi opened her eyes to a darkened sky and the torch-lit face of Nurse. Her brow was furrowed with concern, her pale eyes intent on Kalyi's face. There were two soldiers standing just behind her.

"What happened?" Kalyi asked.

Nurse smiled, her relief palpable. "You fell asleep, Your Highness."

"What's the time?"

"Just past twilight bells. You gave us all quite a fright. Particularly your mother." It all came back in a rush.

"It's Mother's fault that I'm up here."

"Your mother feels terrible, Your Highness. She didn't mean to make you cry, and she certainly didn't want you running from her."

"Then she shouldn't have said what she did." She felt her cheeks suddenly burning. "She didn't tell you, did she?"

"She told me nothing, Your Highness. Only that you were dismayed when you left her, and that much I could tell for myself when I saw you in the corridor. When I told her that none of us had seen you since, she became frightened." Nurse held out a hand. "Let me take you to her."

"No," Kalyi said quickly.

"But, Your Highness, the air grows cold, and it's been hours since you last ate."

Kalyi realized she was shivering, and at the mention of food, her stomach growled loudly. "I'll go with you," she said, climbing to her feet. "But I don't want to see Mother."

"But, Your Highness—"

"I don't wish to discuss it, Nurse. I'll take my meal in my bedchamber. If Mother asks, tell her I'm too tired to eat in the hall."

Nurse frowned, brushing a wisp of silver hair off her face. "Very well." She gestured toward the tower stairs. "After you, Your Highness."

Kalyi started down the steps, pleased with how forceful she had sounded, but also frightened of what her mother might do. She had never defied her in this way before. She wondered if her mother might turn to Numar to make Kalyi speak with her. At the thought, she nearly changed her mind. But then she decided that if it came to that, she would defy Numar was well. She was queen, and if she wished to eat by herself, it was her right to do so.

This, at least, was what she told herself as she descended the stairs, readying herself for the fight with her mother she knew was coming.

But even after Nurse left her in her chamber and went to fetch the meal, Kalyi's mother didn't come. In fact, Kalyi did not see Chofya for several days following their conversation. For a time, she sought to avoid her mother, but soon it became clear to Kalyi that her mother was avoiding her as well. Maybe this should have surprised her, or saddened her, but it did neither. The pain caused by her mother's words had begun to recede, and just as a waning tide leaves shells and driftwood on the shore, so their conversation left its mark on Kalyi's mind. Her father, she now realized, might have been flawed as both man and king. No doubt that was the lesson her mother hoped to teach her, that even Carden was not without his fears and foibles. By the same token, her mother had her own faults. She could be frightened and cross, even when she did not wish to be. Just as she had been that day. That was why she avoided Kalyi now. Not because she didn't love her but rather because she felt ashamed of what she had said and how she had said it.

Kalyi had resolved to go to her mother this day, as soon as she completed her lessons. Or rather, as soon as she completed the small task that would follow her lesson. For though she had been sobered by their conversation, she had not been discouraged from pursuing her inquiry. Already she had gone to speak with the new surgeon, who, as her mother predicted, could tell her nothing about her father's condition. She had also spoken with several of the servants, including the poor boy who found her father's body. He was but a few years older than she, and had been so unnerved by her questions that he actually cried as he answered them, as if fearing that she would have him hanged for what he told her.

She learned little from him, though she did have a slightly better sense of just how ghastly her father's death had been.

"Took four of us nearly the whole day to wipe up all the blood, and even then, they had to get a new table for the hall. The wood just soaked it up like a cloth."

Much to her disappointment, though, she was no closer to understanding why her father killed himself than she had been before she began. Which was why she had decided on this day to speak with the prelate of Castle Solkara's cloister. She wasn't certain that the prelate would be able to tell her anything about what her father was thinking the day he died—even she had noticed that her father had little patience for the litanies of the cloister. But he could at least explain why a man— any man—would defy the God in this way. And perhaps he could also tell her that Bian would not judge her father by this act alone, that there could be a place of honor in the Deceiver's realm even for a man who had died by his own hand.

Her tutor dismissed her early once more, seeming more annoyed than usual by her lack of attention.

"You must mind your studies, Your Highness," he said, sounding a bit desperate. "Your uncle will be displeased if this continues. With both of us."

Kalyi nodded even as she hurried to the door. "I will, I promise."

She was in the corridor before he could answer, running toward the nearest tower. During the colder turns she would have followed the corridors in a wide turn to the cloister tower. With the return of the warmer winds, however, she could cross the inner courtyard, which is what she chose to do this day. Entering the base of the cloister tower, she started up the winding stairs.

After taking only a few steps, however, she heard men's voices coming from just above her, echoing off the curved walls. At first she thought the men were descending the stairs, but she quickly realized that they weren't moving at all. She should have kept climbing—their conversation was none of her concern. But then she caught just a fragment of their discussion.

". . . More soldiers by the end of the turn."

And for reasons she couldn't have explained, she slowed her ascent. After another moment, she stopped entirely and listened.

"How long will it take before all the houses have met the new quotas?"

"That I don't know. It could take as much as half the year. But when they've done so, we'll have more than doubled the size of our force."

"What of the challenge from Dantrielle?"

"I don't imagine it will cause the regent much trouble. Dantrielle is but one house among many, and not even the strongest."

"She could have allies."

Both voices sounded familiar, though Kalyi couldn't place them at first.

"The regent seems to believe she'll stand alone."

"The regent is wrong. The last I heard, Tebeo was speaking with Orvinti. If he can convince Brall to stand with him, that might bring Tounstrel, Bistari, and Noltierre to his cause as well."

The other man whistled softly through his teeth. "Taken together, they would make a formidable opponent."

"More than the royal army could overcome?"

"Perhaps, Archminister. Perhaps."

Pronjed, of course. And the other voice belonged to Tradden Grontalle, Solkara's master of arms.

"If this proves to be the case, what will you counsel the regent to do?" the arch-minister asked.

"I'd have to give that some thought. As you know, the king had long sought a full military alliance with the empire. It had been, in his mind, Aneira's only hope for waging a successful war against Eibithar. We're so close to realizing his dream, I'd be reluctant to abandon this opportunity."

"But?"

"But if opposition to such an alliance includes the houses you mentioned, we may have no choice. Against such a force, the Supremacy itself might be at risk. Surely the alliance isn't worth that."

"That's not the answer I wished to hear, Tradden."

"Forgive me, Archminister. I'm being as honest with you as I can be. Indeed, I'm not entirely certain that the regent would approve of this conversation were he to know of it."

"Leave that to me."

"Archminister?"

"Let me think on this a moment."

A long silence ensued. Kalyi didn't dare move, fearing that she might be pun-ished for listening to a conversation between two adults that was clearly none of her affair. But she had stopped with her feet on different steps, and her bottom leg was beginning to tire. And she couldn't help but think that she had a right to hear what they were saying, even if they wouldn't have thought so. She was queen. This was her realm, her castle, her army. The war of which they spoke would be fought in her name, regardless of who led the soldiers into battle.

"You said that if all the houses meet their quotas, it will more than double the size of Solkara's army. Isn't that right?"

"Yes, Archminister."

"If we add only the men from Rassor, Mertesse, and Kett to the army we have now, would that force be enough to stand against the other houses?"

"It would be a close thing. Too close. Mertesse is still weakened from the failed siege at Kentigern. And if the other houses band together, Kett may well stand with them."

"But our army would be greater than theirs, even without Kett."

"Greater, yes. But you must understand, Archminister, the point is not to pre-vail in a civil war but to prevent one. If the renegade houses believe that they can engage House Solkara in a war without being crushed they'll do so, and so accom-plish their aim, which is to keep us from the alliance with Braedon. We must find a way to allay their concerns about this war. We might even—"

"Enough." The archminister barely raised his voice enough for Kalyi to hear, but Tradden fell silent immediately.

"The regent listens to you, does he not?"

"Yes," the armsman answered, his voice abruptly sounding odd.

"If you tell him that we can defeat the renegade houses, even if Kett is with them, he'll believe you, won't he?"

"Yes, he will."

"Good. Then that is what you'll do. You now believe—"

She didn't think he'd hear her, not while he was speaking. But when she tried to move her leg, she scraped her foot on the stone stair. Not for long, not loudly. But still it was enough for the archminister to notice.

"Who's there?" he called softly.

Kalyi said nothing. But then she heard him say, "Remain here," to the armsman, and take a step down the stairs.

She pressed herself against the stone wall of the stairs, holding her breath and closing her eyes, as if that might help her blend into the shadows.

Pronjed took another step.

Kalyi opened her eyes again and retreated down the stairs as carefully and silently as she could. She had in mind to leave the tower entirely, but it occurred to her at the last moment that as she went through the doorway, she would cast a shadow. And the truth was, she didn't want to leave. She wanted to hear the rest of Pronjed's conversation with Tradden. So instead of leaving, she slipped around to the base of the stairs and hid in the small space there, holding herself as still as possible. The archminister took another step down the stairway, and yet another. But after what seemed an eternity, he ascended the steps again.

"You now believe that we can prevail against Dantrielle and his allies," he began again. It was harder for Kalyi to hear now. The distance was greater, and her heart was pounding so loudly in her chest that she feared it would give her away. But she strained her ears, listening to every word.

"It will take all the men the remaining dukes can spare," the Qirsi went on, "and the entire royal army. But Solkara can defeat them. Can you say that?"

"We can defeat them," the master of arms repeated dully.

"Good. You need to tell this to the regent. You need to make him see that traitors like Tebeo are not to be tolerated."

"Yes."

"The alliance with Braedon will make Aneira the greatest power among the six. Next to the empire, ours will be the preeminent realm in the Forelands. We mustn't allow the renegade houses to destroy this opportunity. Can you remember that?"

"Yes, I'll remember."

"And you'll tell the regent."

"Yes.

"When do you meet with him next?"

"In the morning, with the ringing of the bells."

"Good. In a moment, I'll speak to you of another matter, and you'll respond as you would at any other time. You'll remember nothing of what we've just discussed." There was a pause. Kalyi heard feet scuffling on the steps above her and once more she feared that the archminister was approaching.

A moment later, however, she heard Pronjed's voice again.

"Tradden? Are you well?"

"I—I'm sorry, Archminister. I seem to have lost the thread of whatever I was saying."

"You were telling me that if the houses meet their quotas, we'll more than double the size of our army."

"Yes. Yes, that's right. We should begin to see the first of the men here in Solkara by the end of the turn."

"That's fine news, Commander. I know the regent will be pleased."

"Thank you, Archminister. Good day to you."

She heard footsteps once more.

"And to you," Pronjed called from far away. Apparently he was climbing to the next floor.

A moment later someone came down the stairs and left the tower. Peering out from the shadows under the stairs, Kalyi saw the master of arms walking across the courtyard. Still she waited several moments before leaving the tower herself, in case Pronjed or someone else was watching for her.

Thinking back on what she had heard, Kalyi couldn't help but feel uneasy. She was quite certain that Pronjed had ordered Tradden to lie to her uncle Numar. Under most circumstances, she would have thought that the master of arms would refuse to do such a thing. But from all she had heard, it seemed that he had agreed. Or rather, that he had been forced to agree. She shook her head. That wasn't quite right, either. And how could the archminister expect the man simply to forget that the entire conversation had taken place? It made no sense to her. She needed to speak of it with someone. But who?

When she felt certain that it was safe, she stepped out from under the stairs and walked to her mother's chamber. Chofya was very pleased to see her, holding her close for a long time, and then kissing her forehead.

"I'm sorry I hurt you, Kalyi," she finally said. "Truly I am."

Kalyi looked down at her shoes. "I'm sorry I frightened you by hiding."

"It's all right. Nurse told me you fell asleep."

Kalyi laughed and nodded. "I did. On top of the tower."

Chofya smiled, cupping Kalyi's cheek in her hand and gazing at her for some time. "If you want to talk about your father, we can," she said. "I know I said some mean things about him before, but he had some fine qualities as well."

"Maybe later," Kalyi said, feeling uncomfortable. She really wanted to tell her mother about what she had heard in the tower stairway, but she was afraid of making her mad once more.

"All right," her mother said. "Tell me about your lessons."

They spoke for some time—longer than they had in several turns. Eventually they walked down to the great hall together to have their evening meal before returning to Chofya's chamber for a while longer.

When at last Nurse came to put Kalyi to bed, it was well past dark.

"It's good to see you and your mother laughing together again," Nurse said as

Kalyi climbed into bed. "She needs you, Your Highness. You're really all she has left now that . . . well, you know."

Kalyi nodded.

Nurse kissed her cheek. "Good night, Your Highness."

"Good night."

Nurse blew out the candle by Kalyi's bed and crossed to the door, leaving a second candle burning near the wardrobe, as she always did.

"Wait," Kalyi called to her, still sitting up.

"Yes, Your Highness?"

She hesitated, afraid now to speak of what had happened. After a few moments though, her need to speak of it overmastered her fear.

"I overheard something today."

Nurse arched an eyebrow. "Overheard?"

"I was in one of the towers, and I heard two men speaking on the stairs above me." She looked away, her mouth twisting briefly. "And I listened."

"Kalyi!"

"They were speaking of soldiers," she said quickly. "And since they're my soldiers, I thought it was all right."

"It's never all right to eavesdrop, particularly for a queen."

Kalyi kept her eyes fixed on the second flame. "I know," she said. "I'm sorry."

"Who did you hear speaking, child?"

"The archminister and the master of arms."

"And what was it you heard?"

"That's just it. I don't really understand it."

"Well, you shouldn't feel badly about that. They were probably speaking of alliances and quotas and such things. I wouldn't have understood it either."

Kalyi shook her head. "It wasn't just that. The archminister told him . . ." She trailed off, unable to find the words to describe what she had heard. "I don't know how to describe it."

"Did he sound angry?"

"No. He sounded like . . ." *He sounded like a sorcerer.* It came to her suddenly. She had heard tales of Qirsi who could control other men's thoughts and though she had always dismissed such tales as nonsense and myth, she realized that it was the only reasonable explanation for what she had heard earlier this day. Which brought to mind other tales she had heard, these about a conspiracy of sorcerers who were trying to destroy the kingdoms of the Forelands. Was Pronjed a traitor?

At last she knew who to tell about the conversation she'd heard.

"Your Highness?" Nurse said, looking worried.

Kalyi flung off her blanket and jumped from the bed.

"Where are you going?"

"I must speak with Uncle Numar."

"You can speak with him tomorrow. It's very—"

"It can't wait, Nurse."

"It will have to."

Kalyi tried to look as stern as possible. "I'm the queen of Aneira, and I wish to speak with my regent right now. You may take me to his chamber or you may remain here. But either way, I'm going."

Nurse gave a small smile. "Very well, Your Highness. I'll take you to him right away."

Numar had finished with the last of the fee accountings, a task he found tiring, but which he refused to delegate to anyone else, particularly the archminister or one of his Qirsi friends. He had yet to eat, and he had received a perfumed missive from one of Chofya's ladies earlier in the day. He had every intention of thanking her in person for the kindness of her note.

Hence, he did not welcome the knock at his door just as he was putting on his waistcoat. He strode to the door and flung it open impatiently. Finding the queen there, with her nurse in tow, did nothing to improve his mood.

"Your Highness," he said, managing with great effort to smile. "Shouldn't you be asleep at this hour?" This last he said with his eyes fixed on the nurse, who merely shrugged and looked away.

"There's something I must discuss with you, uncle."

"I'm certain it can wait for morning. I promise to seek you out first thing."

"No," she said, though he read the uncertainty in her dark eyes. "It can't wait."

"I'm afraid it—"

"It's about the archminister."

That caught his attention. Numar narrowed his eyes. "What about him?"

She glanced back at the nurse, who nodded encouragement. "I overheard him talking to the master of arms today."

By itself that didn't seem overly strange. Numar knew that the archminister didn't trust him, that if he wanted information about what the regent had in mind for Solkara's army he would be best served by asking Tradden. Still, he could learn a good deal about Pronjed's intentions by knowing what the two of them discussed.

"Would you like to tell me what they said?"

"Yes, but it's more than that. I think the archminister . . . I think he used magic on him."

Numar stared at her a moment, not quite understanding what she meant. "Magic."

"I think he used magic to make the master of arms say things, maybe even do things."

It seemed that there was a cold hand at his throat, making it impossible for him to swallow or breathe. He had heard of Qirsi who could bend the minds of others, but he had never imagined that he might know one.

"Leave us," he told the nurse. When the woman hesitated he added, "I'll see to it that she returns to her bedchamber safely."

The nurse curtsied reluctantly and withdrew, her gaze flicking repeatedly from Numar to the girl and back again.

"Please sit, Your Highness," the regent said when she was gone.

Kalyi sat in a chair by the hearth, the one she always chose when they spoke. Numar sat beside her.

"Now, tell me everything you heard."

Numar found her description of what the two men said to each other a bit clouded, though he did manage to piece together enough of it to be alarmed. It was one thing for Pronjed to seek information about Numar's plans for the Solkaran army and the men sent to him by his dukes. It was quite another to discuss the possibility of civil war and alliances among the dukedoms. It almost seemed that the archminister was looking for weaknesses that he might exploit. But Kalyi had promised him more, and had yet to deliver on that promise.

"Forgive me, Your Highness," he said, his patience beginning to fail him. "But I still don't see how the archminister's magic enters into any of this."

She twisted her hands anxiously, and for a moment Numar wondered if the girl had imagined it all.

"Well, one moment the master armsman was saying that House Solkara couldn't risk a civil war if too many of the other houses stood together against us, and the next moment he was saying that we could, and that we needed the alliance with Braedon no matter what."

"Is it possible the archminister merely convinced him of this? A man can change his mind, you know."

She shook her head. "That's not how it happened. Pronjed told him . . . what to think. At least, that's how it sounded. He said, 'You now believe that we can prevail against Dantrielle and his allies.' And then he made the master of arms say it. He told him just what to say to you."

"Do you remember what else Tradden is to say to me?" There was, it seemed, an easy way to confirm what she was telling him.

"Some of it. 'The alliance with Braedon will make Aneira the greatest power among the six.' That was some of it. And, 'We mustn't allow the renegade houses to destroy this opportunity.'" She frowned. "There was more, but I can't remember now."

"That's all right. Thank you, Kalyi. That may be very helpful."

"There's something else. The strangest part of it all."

"Tell me."

"When they were done talking about the war and the other houses, the archminister told him that he would remember nothing about their conversation."

"*What?*"

"He said, 'You'll remember nothing of what we've just discussed.' And a moment later they started talking about something else, and that's just how it seemed. The master of arms sounded confused, almost like he was sleepy. And he didn't seem to remember any of it."

Numar merely gaped at her. He couldn't imagine that she would lie about such a thing. Indeed, she wasn't the type to lie at all. But if all this were true . . .

Abruptly the regent was on his feet, pacing before the hearth. Actually, this explained a good deal. Just a few days before, he had spoken with the archminister about something—he still couldn't remember what it was—and had emerged from their conversation dazed, confused, as if he had nodded off in the middle of their discussion. Had the Qirsi bastard used magic on him as well?

"Is it all right that I told you?"

"What? Oh, yes. Of course it is. It's more than all right, Your Highness. You've done me a great service, and our house as well." He meant it. Whatever plans he had for the girl in the future, she had proven herself a most valuable ally this night.

"Do you think Pronjed is a traitor? Do you think he's with the conspiracy?"

"I don't know, Kalyi. It appears possible, doesn't it?"

She nodded, looking frightened. "What should we do?"

"I'm not certain." He didn't dare confront the man. At least not yet, not until he had a better understanding of just how deep the archminister's powers went. A sorcerer who could control a man's thoughts, his words, his actions, was capable of anything.

It hit him with the power of a land tremor, shifting his entire world. *A sorcerer with such power could make a man take his own life.* He didn't say it to the girl. She wasn't ready for that. Someday, perhaps. Someday soon, when he needed to turn her fully against the archminister. But not tonight.

"I'm not certain," he repeated. He saw the fear in her eyes, a mirror of what he felt in his heart, and he made himself smile. "Don't worry, Kalyi. We don't know yet that he's a traitor. And even if he is, I'll keep you safe. I'm your regent. That's what I'm supposed to do."

Chapter
Fifteen

House Yserne had taken hold of the throne for good nearly four centuries before, following the third war with Wethyrn and a period of bloody civil war known in Sanbiri history as the Second Barbarism. Even after Meleanna, the first Sanbiri queen, took the crown from Ticho the Fourth of Trescarri in the last violent days of the Barbarism, many of the houses continued to fight against the Yserne Dynasty, fearing that the establishment of a matriarchy would weaken Sanbira in its relations with the other realms.

As it happened, this wasn't the case. Under the queens of Yserne Sanbira had become one of the dominant powers of the Forelands, and even with the dukes of Brugaosa and Norinde continuing to challenge Yserne authority from time to time, the realm had never since been in any danger of falling to an invader.

One reason for this was the geographic position of the royal house. Located in the center of the realm, it was protected on all sides by the duchies, none of which was more than forty leagues from the royal city. In times of crisis, when the queen wished to meet with her duchesses and dukes, she could summon them, knowing that even the most remote house, Kinsarta, was no more than ten days' ride from her walls.

Thus, when Olesya sent messages to the other houses, asking the leading nobles to Yserne to discuss the attempts on Diani's life, she and the duchess had only to wait a bit more than half a turn for the others to arrive. Not surprisingly, Edamo of Brugaosa and Alao of Norinde, were the last to reach the royal city, and in fairness, though Kinsarta was farther from Yserne than the northern dukedoms, Ajy's ride across Morna's Plain was far easier than the route taken by either duke.

Still, it was nearly two days after Ajy's arrival before the dukes finally rode into the city; when they rode in together, it was clear to all that they had met to discuss matters before continuing on to the queen's castle. Meeting them at the castle gate with the duchesses and their ministers, Olesya made no effort to hide her displeasure.

"I didn't know that the journey from Brugaosa would take you so close to Norinde, Lord Brugaosa," she said to Edamo, smiling thinly.

The duke smiled as well. He looked far older than Diani remembered. He had been handsome once, with fine features and a thick shock of wheat-colored hair. But his hair was white now, and thinning, and his cheeks looked sunken, his skin sallow. His face seemed too sharp, like the jagged edge of a shattered old dish. She still thought it likely that her brother, Cyro, had been murdered by the conspiracy rather than by the Brugaosans, as her father believed. But even so, she could not help but hate this man. There had even been times, more recent than she cared to admit, when she had wished for his death.

"We met near the northeast edge of Lake Yserne, Your Highness," he said. "Surely you didn't expect me to ride across the lake."

Norinde laughed, but none of the others did.

The queen regarded Alao for a moment, long enough to silence the young duke, before facing Edamo once more. "Surely steering a mount across such a small expanse of water is nothing for a man of your many talents."

"I assure you, Your Highness," Brugaosa said, wisely choosing to ignore the gibe, "ours was a chance meeting. And it made the last portion of both our journeys far less tedious."

Her smile was a match for the duke's. "I'm so glad. Be welcome, both of you," she added, turning away, her tone brusque. "As soon as you've changed out of your riding clothes you're to join the rest of us in my presence chamber. Don't keep us waiting any longer than necessary."

Diani had thought that the dukes would use the opportunity to goad her once more, but they seemed to gauge her mood with some care. They arrived in the chamber far sooner than the duchess expected, bowing as they entered and taking seats together at the far end of the table, opposite Olesya.

Once again, Diani noticed that she was the only noble not to have brought her Qirsi minister with her. To be sure, none of them knew why the queen had summoned them; it was quite possible that once they learned of the assassination attempts they would grow more wary of their Qirsi. Nevertheless, she found herself wishing that Kreazur had come, or rather, that she had asked him to join her. The message she sent back to Curlinte merely instructed the captain of her army to free the first minister and the other Qirsi who served her. She did not invite Kreazur to join her in Yserne, and now, sitting among the other duchesses and dukes, all of whom were older and far more experienced than she, Diani regretted it.

"I thank all of you for coming," the queen began, standing at her place, sunlight from the window shining in her black-and-silver hair. "All of you journeyed far, and at a moment's notice, and I know that few of us like to be abroad this early in the year. But these are extraordinary times that will demand more of us still before we see their end."

"What's happened, Your Highness?" asked Vasyonne, duchess of Listaal. Next to Diani, she was the youngest of the duchesses, though Diani's mother had often spoken quite highly of her. She wore her black hair short, just as the queen did, and had a square, expressive face. "Why have you called us here?"

"There's been an attack on one of our own, and I believe it presages more such incidents to come."

"What kind of attack?" Edamo asked.

"An assassination attempt—two, actually—on the duchess of Curlinte."

"By whom?"

The queen glanced at Diani and gave a small nod, lowering herself into her chair.

"Archers the first time," she said. She had carried one of the arrow shafts with her from her home and she brought it forth now, tossing it onto the table. "They had shaved heads and wore the dun cloaks of northern riders."

Vasyonne leaned forward, examining the arrow. "Blue and yellow," she said, looking at Edamo. "Those are Brugaosan colors, aren't they, Lord Brugaosa?"

What?" He stood, snatching the arrow off the table to get a better look. "Brugaosa had nothing to do with this! We'd have nothing to gain from it!"

Vasyonne grinned, though there was a hard glint in her brown eyes. "I believe what you mean to say is, 'I bear my friends in Curlinte no ill will.'"

"Thank you, Lady Listaal, but I daresay I know better than you or anyone else what I meant to say."

"Agents of Brugaosa have already struck at House Curlinte once, killing the duchess's brother. Perhaps you thought—"

"Brugaosa had nothing to do with Cyro's death!"

"So you've claimed before."

Edamo leveled the arrow at Vasyonne as though it were a sword. "You dare to call me a liar?"

"Stop it!" the queen commanded. "We're here to speak of the attacks on Diani."

Rashel of Trescarri faced the queen. "You said there were two attempts, Your Highness."

"Yes."

"The second was carried out by a man dressed as a soldier of Kretsaal," Diani said. "We believe that he killed the archers, and he fought until we had no choice but to kill him as well. We never had the opportunity to question him."

Vasyonne continued to eye Edamo, as if expecting the duke to flee the castle at any moment. "Do you believe he was Brugaosan as well?"

"No," Diani said. "He spoke with a Wethy accent." She looked once more to the queen, who nodded a second time. "We don't think the archers were Brugaosan either."

Vasyonne frowned. "You don't?"

Edamo was staring at her. "You think the arrow was intended to make your death seem the work of Brugaosans."

"Yes."

"The conspiracy?"

He might have been an enemy of both the queen and House Curlinte, a man to be watched with caution, but he was clever.

"We believe so, yes."

"Do you have evidence of this?" Alao asked.

The queen shook her head. "Unfortunately, we don't."

"So this is merely a guess."

"Surely, Lord Norinde, you don't believe House Brugaosa was behind this."

"Of course not, Your Highness," he said, his tone almost insolent. He was just the opposite of Edamo in so many ways. Where the older duke was elegant and smooth, this man was blunt in both features and manner, possessing little grace. If Edamo was a Sanbiri blade, albeit a notched one, this man was a war hammer. Still, playing the part of apprentice to Lord Brugaosa, he had learned well the art of statecraft. In many ways, he was far more dangerous than Edamo, for he would be wielding power in the North long after the queen and most of her allies had died or handed power to their daughters. "But it may be," he went on, "that agents of Wethyrn were responsible, or even other houses of Sanbira who wish to sully Lord Brugaosa's good name."

Vasyonne gave a small smile. "He sullies it quite well on his own, actually."

Norinde glared at the woman. "You might want to begin your search for those responsible in Listaal. Quite often it's those who lack the strength for an overt attack who resort to the most vile treachery."

"Enough," the queen said, sounding more weary than angry. "Whoever our enemies may be, I assure you that this is just what they want: to divide us, to prey on our suspicions of each other. They seek to weaken the realm, and every poisoned word we aim at one another furthers their cause."

"His parry and thrust with Lady Listaal notwithstanding," Edamo said, "Lord Norinde does have a point. While I assure you that Brugaosa had nothing to do with the events in Curlinte, we cannot simply assume that the conspiracy is to blame."

"You were the first of us to raise the possibility." Rashel. "Now you discount it?"

"I raised it hoping that Lady Curlinte had proof to offer beyond this arrow. Without any, I'm afraid we know nothing."

"With all we've heard of the conspiracy, Lord Brugaosa," the queen said, "don't you think it likely that the Qirsi are responsible?"

"Likely, Your Highness? Yes, I suppose I do. But is that reason enough to act?"

Diani nodded, looking at the others. "I believe it is."

"I don't doubt that you do, Lady Curlinte. Had I been their target, I might well feel the same way. You want vengeance. You want to strike out at someone. We all understand." Edamo shook his head. "But that may not be the wisest course at this time."

The duchess felt her face coloring. She would have liked to fling back a retort, to deny that she was speaking out of anything more than concern for the realm. But after imprisoning Kreazur and the other Qirsi, she couldn't bring herself to speak at all. Edamo's words struck far too close to the truth.

"What do you believe we should do, Lord Brugaosa?" Olesya asked.

"I don't know. If the assassins were still alive, I'd want to question them of course. I might even be willing to use torture to learn what we need to know. But without them, without any real proof of Qirsi complicity in the attacks, I believe the prudent course would be to wait, and see what comes next."

He said it as if he usually wouldn't have considered such methods. From all that Diani had heard, however, prisoners in Brugaosa were tortured as a matter of course. Still smarting from the duke's last remarks, however, she didn't dare say this aloud.

"And the rest of you?" the queen asked. "Do you feel as Edamo does?"

"I certainly do," Alao said.

Vasyonne let out a short laugh. "How unexpected."

"And I suppose you're ready to declare war on every Qirsi in the Forelands," Norinde said, glowering at her again.

Diani stared down at the table, shame burning like a brand on her cheeks.

Vasyonne regarded him placidly. "Not at all. But if we think on this carefully, it seems quite clear that our enemy in this case has to be the Qirsi." She glanced at Yserne's archminister, who sat beside the queen. "Forgive me."

The Qirsi woman inclined her head slightly, her expression unreadable.

"I agree," Rashel said. "I'd like to believe that Brugaosa is innocent in this matter, as are the rest of us. And I don't think that the archduke is fool enough to believe that Wethyrn could prevail in a war with us. That leaves the conspiracy."

"Does it?" Edamo asked.

"Who else is there?"

The old duke gave a small shrug. "As I said before, I don't really know. That's why it would be reckless of us to take action too soon."

"So we do nothing?" Vasyonne said, her voice rising. "What if the assassins succeed next time? What if one of us dies? What if they make an attempt on the queen? The real risk lies in waiting."

Edamo started to respond, but the queen stood once more, silencing him with a glance.

"This won't be decided today," Olesya said. "Perhaps it won't be decided at all, but the more we argue the matter, the firmer our resolve to prevail, and I would rather we all remained open to compromise. We will speak of this again tomorrow, and will meet in the queen's hall this night for another feast. For now, I hope you will enjoy such comfort and hospitality as this castle and city can offer."

"But, Your Highness—"

"The discussion is at an end, Lord Brugaosa. At least for now."

The duke cast a dark look at the queen, but nodded. "Of course, Your Highness."

The duchesses and dukes stood, all of them seeming a bit uncertain as to what the queen expected of them now. Diani saw Edamo and Alao exchange a look before the younger duke swept from the presence chamber.

"This was your first meeting with other nobles as duchess of Curlinte, was it not?"

Diani turned toward the voice. Tamyra of Prentarlo was smiling at her.

"Yes, Lady Prentarlo, it was."

Tamyra nodded. Diani had always thought her severe looking, her wide mouth a dark gash on an otherwise pallid face. But when she smiled, she appeared almost kind. There was a warmth in her green eyes Diani hadn't noticed before. "I thought as much. You handled yourself quite well, Lady Curlinte."

"My thanks."

"I thought so as well," the queen said. "Your mother would have been pleased."

"Thank you, Your Highness."

She bowed to both women and started to leave the chamber in search of her father. Before she reached the doorway, however, she saw Edamo striding toward her. For just an instant, she wanted to pretend she hadn't seen him and hurry from the room. He didn't give her the chance.

"Lady Curlinte!" he called. "A word, please."

She stopped and faced him. "Of course, Lord Brugaosa."

He stopped in front of her, then cast a quick look at Olesya, who hovered nearby. "Perhaps we can speak elsewhere? Somewhere private?"

She would have liked to refuse, but as duchess she knew that she had little choice. As much as she disliked and distrusted him, she had no desire to make relations between their houses worse than they already were.

"Shall we walk, then?" she asked, indicating the door with an open hand.

"Splendid! The gardens?"

Diani nodded, and the two of them left the chamber. She felt the queen's eyes upon her, but she didn't look back.

"In the course of our discussion today, we neglected one vital question," the duke said as the two of them walked through the corridor toward the entrance to the inner courtyard. "Were you injured, and are you all right now?"

"I'm fine, thank you." She almost left it at that. But lest he take the Qirsi threat too lightly, she added, "But I was injured."

"I'm sorry to hear that. Not too seriously, I hope."

"I was struck by three arrows."

He faltered in midstride, what little color his cheeks held vanishing. "Three?"

"Yes. One in the thigh, one in the chest, and a third in the back of my shoulder."

"And yet you escaped." She heard nothing in his tone that might implicate Brugaosa. Only amazement, and more than a little admiration.

"I was fortunate that none of their darts struck my mount, or I might not have. As it was, the man who healed me said that I came within a half span of dying."

"Forgive me, my lady," the duke said. "I had no idea."

"We saw no point in telling anyone." They emerged into the sunlight and crossed the courtyard to the gardens. "But you see?" she went on after some time. "This is why I feel that we must act swiftly, to meet the Qirsi challenge."

"Were I in your position I might think so as well," the duke said with sympathy. He seemed to have recovered from his surprise at what she had told him of the attack. "Let me explain to you why I'm reluctant to do anything rash." He had been gazing at the blossoms as they continued to walk, but now he halted and faced her. "I don't want you to think for even a moment, Lady Curlinte, that I mean to diminish this abhorrent attack on you and your house. Coupled with your brother's death, I can understand why you would want to strike back at someone, and I'm grateful to you for not allowing these attempts to implicate Brugaosa to cloud your judgment. Certainly if you had evidence of the conspiracy's involvement, I would support nearly anything you proposed. And if the assassins weren't already dead, my voice would be loudest among those calling for their immediate execution. An attack on any of our houses calls for no less."

"The difference between us, Lord Brugaosa, is that where you see an attack on Curlinte and her duchess, I see an assault against all Sanbira."

"But you can't know for certain that this was anything more than what it seems: an assassination attempt against a single noble."

"Isn't it safer for all of us to assume the worst, and take appropriate actions to defend the entire realm?"

"No, I don't believe it is. You fear the conspiracy, and rightly so. But I fear tyranny just as much."

"Tyranny?"

"What steps would you expect the queen to take were the other houses to give her leave to act?"

"I should think she would raise a larger army, commit Sanbira to an alliance with the other realms, and give the houses the authority to imprison those Qirsi who were suspected of aiding the traitors."

"Good. I would add to that the likelihood that she will raise our tribute as well, but overall that's quite good. And of the three actions you named, two would serve to increase Yserne's power relative to our own."

Diani gaped at him. "You can't be serious!"

"Oh, but I am."

"Olesya is our queen! In times of war, she must have the power to lead us and protect us! And you would begrudge her such?"

"In the absence of an enemy and just cause for waging war? I certainly would, as would any duke or duchess with sufficient experience in the courts."

She felt her cheeks redden. "I have enough knowledge of our queen to know that you misjudge her, Lord Brugaosa."

"You're a woman, and her ally, and so I wouldn't expect you to understand. But Alao and I have no intention of allowing her to use the unfortunate incidents in Curlinte to tighten her grip on our houses."

"In other words, you would put the entire realm at risk in order to deny Olesya powers that she needs to fight our enemies."

"As I've said, I don't believe we know who our enemies are. Give me proof that the conspiracy was behind the attempts on your life, and I will pledge myself to defeating it, even if that means adding to Yserne's power. But without any such evidence, I will not weaken House Brugaosa."

"You're a fool."

He grinned at her, a malevolent look in his dark blue eyes. "And you're a child. I had thought to find in you a ruler worthy of House Curlinte, a woman such as your mother had been. Obviously, I was mistaken."

He spun away from her and stalked back to the tower entrance. Diani watched him vanish into the shadows of the stairway, then glanced around to see if anyone had been watching them. Seeing no one, she walked back as well, following Edamo's path toward the castle and her own chamber.

Climbing the stairs to the corridor on which her sleeping quarters were located, the duchess heard a pair of familiar voices. When she emerged into the hallway, she saw her father speaking with a white-haired man, and for a disorienting moment she thought it was Edamo again.

"Here she comes," Sertio said, looking past the man and raising a hand in greeting.

The white-haired man turned to face her, and Diani stopped where she stood. Her surprise was fleeting, giving way almost immediately to rage.

Kreazur.

Just a short time ago, sitting in the queen's presence chamber, she had wished the minister were there with her. But never had she imagined that he would presume to make the journey without leave from her.

She advanced on him, her fists clenched. "What are you doing here, First Minister?" Before he could answer she turned her glare on her father. "Was this your doing? Do you tell him to come?"

"Your father had nothing to do with this, my lady."

"Then why are you here?"

"I thought I might be of service to you, my lady. I served your mother for many years, and she and I spent a good deal of time together in Yserne."

"And if you still served my mother would you have dared journey here without her permission?"

He met her gaze, his expression grim. "Your mother never would have made the journey without me."

"I've a mind to send you back, and to have the captain of the guard imprison you once more when you reach the castle."

"That is your right, my lady. And if you order me back to Curlinte, even under such a threat, I will begin the ride back immediately."

"Don't, Diani," Sertio said. "You need him. I didn't call for him, but I should have, and I'm glad he's come. Someday you'll be a fine duchess, just as your mother was. But you're young still and there's much you don't know about the other houses, about building alliances and guarding Curlinte's reputation as well as her borders."

Diani wanted to argue the point, but she could still hear Edamo's harsh words echoing in her mind. *You're a child. . . .*

"You know those things," she said instead, sounding so young even she couldn't help but notice.

Sertio smiled. "Yes, I do. But think on it, Diani. Do you really wish to sit in the queen's chamber, among all the duchesses and dukes of the realm, with your father by your side?"

Of course she didn't. Diani knew this as well as he did. And even had she been willing to turn to her father for counsel, she would never have trusted him to sit in any chamber with Edamo. He had promised her mother that he would not seek vengeance for Cyro's murder, but Diani wondered if he had the strength to honor the oath if presented with an opportunity to strike at Brugaosa's duke.

Sertio placed a hand on her shoulder, forcing her to look him in the eye. "I understand that you're angry. To be honest, I told Kreazur that you would be, and I feel that you have cause. But next to all that's happened in the past turn, this is a trifle, a matter to be spoken of once and then forgotten. Don't allow it to weaken you and our house. That's not the way of a wise ruler."

"You have my apologies, my lady," the Qirsi said. "I shouldn't have come. But now that I'm here, I hope that you'll allow me to help you, just as your mother did."

Your mother. How many times had she heard that over the past half turn? From the queen and her father, from Edamo and Kreazur, and from so many of the duchesses as well. Most of them meant well, she knew. But she had long since grown tired of hearing it.

"Very well," she said sourly. "You may stay, First Minister. And I'll . . . I'll be grateful for whatever counsel you can offer."

He bowed to her. "Of course, my lady."

"There's to be another feast tonight," she said. "I'll expect to see both of you there. For now, I wish to rest."

Sertio nodded. "That's a fine idea." He looked like he might say more, and Diani half expected him to tell her that her mother had often done the same thing. Mercifully, though, he kept his silence.

She left them there, her anger lingering like smoke from a crop fire. It wasn't just that Kreazur had come unbidden, she realized as she returned to her chamber, though to be sure that was part of it. It was that despite all her father and the queen had said in his defense, she still didn't trust him.

Kreazur had expected the duchess to be angry with him. Had it not been of vital importance that he come to Yserne, he never would have made the journey without her permission. But though he had anticipated her reaction, and had been willing to endure her rage, he had dreaded seeing the other ministers. If even one of them had heard of his imprisonment, it would be too many, such had been his humiliation.

Arriving in the queen's hall for the feast, the minister noted with profound relief that most of the other Qirsi barely looked at him, as if they assumed he had been with the duchess all this time. Only the archminister appeared to know, and she approached him quietly, hooking her arm into his and walking him to the far end of the hall.

"How are you, cousin?" she asked in a low voice, nodding to one of the other Qirsi.

"Well enough," he said.

"I admire you for coming here at all, after what you've been through."

He shrugged. "I'm assuming you're the only one who knows."

"For now, perhaps. But word of this is bound to spread eventually. And besides, that's not really what I meant. Had she been my duchess, I would have left her service upon my release. A woman like that isn't worthy of so fine a minister."

They stopped walking and he faced her. Abeni, however, was looking over his shoulder, back toward her queen.

"I was born in Curlinte, cousin, as were my parents. I serve the house, not the woman."

She smiled, her eyes flicking to his for just an instant. "Of course you do, cousin. I was just saying that I would not be so generous, or forgiving. But each of us must find his or her way through these times." The archminister looked at him once more, the smile still fixed on her lips. "In any case, I'm glad to see you well. I hope we'll have another opportunity to speak before you leave Yserne."

He nodded. "I'd like that as well."

She started to walk away, but he held out a hand, stopping her.

"Tell me about the discussions among the dukes and duchesses."

"Actually," she said, "we had the first today." Seeing his puzzled look, she explained, "Norinde and Brugaosa were in no hurry to reach Yserne. They only arrived this morning."

"I see. And what was said when they met with the others?"

"Very little, really. The queen and your duchess have convinced many of the duchesses that the conspiracy was behind the attempt on Lady Curlinte's life, but the dukes are reluctant to take any action. I believe they fear any steps that will further strengthen the Matriarchy."

He weighed this briefly. None of it came as a surprise, though he had thought that the discussions would have progressed beyond this by now. "Thank you, Archminister."

She nodded and turned away. A moment later he followed her back to the front of the hall, where the queen and Diani were seated.

The duchess barely acknowledged the minister as he took his seat beside her father, and for the duration of the meal, she spoke not a word to him, even leaving it to Sertio to inform him of the discussion planned for the following morning in the queen's chamber.

He returned to his quarters after the feast, but only long enough to convince Diani and Sertio that he had retired for the night. After waiting for some time, he ventured from the room, following the twists and turns of the castle corridors to a tower on the far side of the courtyard. There he waited, watching.

He saw nothing that first night, and hurried back to his chamber just before dawn, taking care not to be seen.

The day's discussion among the dukes and duchesses went much as Abeni had said the first day went. Clearly the queen wished to forge an alliance between Sanbira and her neighbors to the west and north, but the dukes resisted, and Olesya seemed reluctant to push the matter too far. Diani still said little to Kreazur, though on two occasions, when one of the duchesses made reference to something that had happened before her mother's death, she looked to him for an explanation.

Together, the nobles and their ministers took a more modest evening meal in the queen's hall, before returning to their quarters for the night. Once again, Kreazur crept from his room when all was quiet, and once again he saw nothing before being forced back to his room by the coming of the dawn.

Still, he resolved to repeat his vigil until he found what he sought. His duchess had made a terrible mistake in placing the minister and the other Qirsi in Curlinte's prison tower, but Kreazur had no doubt that she was right in assuming that conspiracy gold had paid her would-be assassins. At first he had guessed, as she did, that Castle Curlinte housed a traitor. As he sat in the tower, however, awaiting his release, listening to the grumbling of the other Qirsi, a new thought entered his mind. That thought, rather than any sense of duty to the duchess, was what had drawn him to Yserne. And on the third night, his suspicions were confirmed.

He heard the door to her chamber open and close, watched as she stepped furtively to the tower stairs, and followed only when he could no longer hear her feet on the stone steps. She left the castle by way of a sally port near the north gate, one that was so well hidden he almost missed it in the dim corridors. As far as Kreazur could tell, no guards saw either of them leave.

He followed at a distance as she wound her way through the darkened streets of Yserne city to a small tavern in the northwest corner, near the Sanctuary of Elined. She didn't enter the tavern, but instead waited just outside the entrance. At the tolling of the midnight bells, a man emerged and the two of them walked a short distance down the narrow byway.

Kreazur followed cautiously, drawing only as near to them as necessary to hear their conversation.

". . . It's your gold," the man was saying. "But it seems a waste of a hundred and fifty qinde if you ask me."

"First of all," the archminister said, "it's the movement's gold, not mine. Second, it's not a waste at all. Lady Curlinte is proving far more valuable as the victim of a failed assassination than she ever would as a corpse. And third, it won't be one hundred and fifty."

"But we agreed—"

"I paid you seventy-five, with the agreement being that you would be paid the rest when the duchess was dead."

"Yes, but now—"

"Now I'm telling you not to kill her. Be grateful I haven't demanded that you return the first seventy-five."

The man swore loudly. "Suppose it serves me right for doing business with you white-hairs."

"We white-hairs will soon be the only employers you and your kind are likely to find in the Forelands." She paused, then added, "Wouldn't you agree, First Minister?" This last she called out loudly. Kreazur felt his heart begin to pound. Was she speaking to some unseen ally, or to him?

"Come now, Kreazur. You didn't really think you could follow me through my castle and my city without being detected, did you?"

Whispering an oath of his own, the minister stepped from the shadows in which he had tried to conceal himself.

Seeing him, Abeni smiled. "Does it please you to know that I've spared the life of your duchess?"

"It disappoints me greatly to know that I was right about you."

"Even now?" She tilted her head to the side, the smile lingering on her attractive face. "Do you know what the duchess did to him?" she asked the assassin. "After the first attempts on her life, she placed him in the castle prison. Her own first minister. Not only that but she imprisoned all the Qirsi in Castle Curlinte. And still he clings stubbornly to obsolete notions of loyalty and court etiquette."

The assassin, a large, dark-haired man, leered at him, but said nothing.

"She's done so much harm to her Qirsi that the movement has decided we want her alive. Doesn't that tell you something?"

"It tells me that your movement grows desperate. I think the real reason you've called off your hired blade is that the attacks of the conspiracy have grown clumsy and obvious. The attempt on the duchess fooled no one. All it's done is convince the queen that the Qirsi must be opposed with the full power of the realm. You're movement is failing even as we speak."

"Don't be a fool! We are the future of the Forelands, and our victory is far closer than you think." She paused, and when she spoke again, it was in a softer tone. "But you can be a part of that, Kreazur."

"If your movement is so strong, why do you need me?"

"We don't. I'm offering you a last chance at redemption. You can join us now, this very night. Or you can die."

The assassin looked at her, though Abeni kept her eyes on the first minister.

"You'd like to earn the rest of that gold, wouldn't you?" she asked. She didn't bother waiting for a reply. "Don't make me kill you, Kreazur. Your duchess doesn't trust you anymore. She never will again. Wouldn't it be better to join us, to cast your fate with your own people?"

"I'm not a traitor."

Her eyes narrowed at that, the smile finally vanishing. "There are those who would beg to differ. You serve an Eandi noble who treats the Qirsi in her castle like animals. I believe I speak for many of us when I say that you're the worst kind of traitor. You hide your treachery behind empty claims of fealty and honor."

"Just as you're doing now, Archminister?"

"This man will kill you. All I need to do is give the command."

"Then give it. I'll take my chances with your assassin. And I promise you, I'll prevail." Kreazur wasn't nearly as confident of this as he sounded. He could raise a mist and slip away, and given the man's size, he felt reasonably certain that he could outrun him. But his other powers—gleaning and language of beasts—were useless to him here. And he didn't know if he could make it all the way back to the castle, running the entire time, and maintaining his mists. As a younger man he might have, but he was nearly thirty-seven now, old for a Qirsi.

She took a step toward him. "I don't want to give such a command, Kreazur. Don't you see? I want your help."

"No. You want to keep me from exposing you to the queen. That's all that matters to you now. And there's little you can do about it."

"You think they'll take your word over mine?" She laughed. "Your own duchess doesn't even trust you. How can you hope to convince any of the others?"

It was a fair point. His only hope was to beat her back to the castle. He began to back away slowly, preparing to summon a mist.

The assassin pulled a large knife from his belt.

"No!" the archminister said quickly. "Not here. I have another idea."

Kreazur spun away, intending to run. But before he could take a step, pain exploded in his leg, white hot, as if the assassin had hacked through the bone with a sword. The first minister collapsed to the ground, clutching his thigh. Neither Abeni nor the man beside her had moved. Only as an afterthought did Kreazur realize that he had heard a strange noise, like the snapping of a dry tree limb.

"You didn't know that I was a shaper, did you?" the archminister asked, stepping to where he lay.

An instant later, new agony. His arm, and this time there could be no mistaking the sound of shattering bone. He cried out, clutching the mangled limb to his chest.

Abeni squatted beside him. "I gave you a chance, but you refused me. And now you're going to die, just as I promised."

"They'll learn of what you've done," he gasped through gritted teeth.

"No, they won't. They'll find you near here, dead in an alley, your neck broken along with your arm and your leg. There will be an empty coin pouch beside you and two gold rounds under your body where the men who killed you wouldn't have thought to look. It will take them a bit of time to sort it all out, but the queen's archminister will be quite helpful in that regard." She smiled, though only for a moment. "You see, this part of the city is infamous for attracting brigands and assassins. Just the sort of place a traitor would come to hire a new blade to kill his duchess. Just the sort of place a traitor might die, offering too little gold to the wrong men."

She glanced back at the assassin. "You'll take him elsewhere, to a place they won't think to look for a day or two. Make it look convincing."

"Is he . . ." The man faltered briefly. "As long as he's alive, he has his magic, doesn't he?"

Abeni looked down at him again. "Yes, but that's not a problem."

Again, the cracking of bone. Then blackness.

Chapter
Sixteen

Kentigern, Eibithar

hat does it say?"

Aindreas could scarcely hear her for the windstorm howling in his head. His hand had begun to tremble and he gripped the scroll with his other as well. But even with both hands on the parchment, he couldn't hold it steady.

"Aindreas, what does it say?"

The duke looked up. His wife was staring at him from across the table, concern creasing her brow. Her face appeared fuller than it had at any time since the previous growing season, her brown eyes clearer, less sunken. Her cheeks were pallid still, but tinged with pink, rather than the sickly, sallow hue that had suffused her skin since Brienne's death. It had taken the better part of a year, but he finally had his wife back. Earlier this very day, he had even heard her singing with Affery, their surviving daughter. He wasn't about to drive her back into her solitude and the grief bordering on madness that had consumed her mind for so long.

"Well?" Ioanna demanded again.

"It's nothing. A missive from Kearney, a waste of good parchment."

A turn ago she might have left it at that. Aindreas took it as another sign of her recovery that she didn't this day.

"What does he say?" Her expression hardened noticeably at the mention of the king's name.

"Nothing of importance."

"A message from the king, delivered to the one man in all Eibithar who has most cause to hate him. And you want me to believe that it says nothing of importance?"

"Please, wife, peace! It needn't concern you." He took a breath, knowing this wouldn't appease her. Before Brienne's murder, she had been interested in all matters of state, and truth be told, as likely to offer him sound advice as any Qirsi minister who had ever stalked the corridors of Kentigern Castle. "He seeks a parley," he added after a moment.

"A parley," she repeated. "And is it the mere thought of meeting with our king that makes your hands shake so?"

"My hands shake with rage, madam. Though whether at our king or at my meddlesome wife, I can't say just now."

Ioanna smiled at that. "What does he wish to discuss?"

Aindreas stared at the parchment again, the neat letters making him wish that he hadn't eaten any of this meal. *What have I done?* Kearney wasn't actually requesting a parley so much as ordering him to Audun's Castle. But it was the king's stated reason for doing so that had conjured this storm that roared in his heart and head. "He wishes to speak of Kentigern's grievances against the throne." He said this officiously, as if repeating it from the message.

"For how long does he propose you meet? Anything less than a full turn would be inadequate to the task." She shook her head, so that her golden curls flew. "The time for parleys is long past. You should tell him that if he wishes to address our grievances, he should simply abdicate and be done with it."

He grinned. She was indeed a splendid woman, a credit to their house. Even as he thought this, however, he felt his chest tightening, as if the Deceiver had taken hold of his heart. Looking past his wife, he saw Brienne standing in the doorway, shaking her head slowly, a sad smile on her lovely face. He squeezed his eyes shut for just an instant. When he looked again, she was gone.

"I suppose Javan will be there as well," Ioanna said. "Curgh keeps the king on a short leash."

She had been mourning for so long, lost to the world, that she couldn't have known such a thing for herself. These were his own words coming back to taunt him, those he had spoken to her in their darkened bedchamber as she lay in a stupor, too aggrieved, he had thought, even to hear him.

"No doubt," he murmured.

"What will you tell him?"

"I'll refuse, of course." *What choice do I have?*

"Refusing a king is no small matter. Are you ready to face the royal army?"

No, but there's nothing else I can do. I've led Kentigern down a path from which there are no turns. "I don't think it will come to that."

He hated lying to her, but the truth was too appalling, too humiliating.

"I always know when you're keeping the truth from me, Aindreas. You know that, and yet you still persist in these lies."

"I spent all of the harvest and the snows protecting you," he said, grateful for the opportunity to speak the truth. "I'm finding it's a habit that's not easily broken."

She nodded, even managing a smile. "So there is more to the message than you've told me."

"Yes."

He expected that she would demand to know what it was, but instead she stood, kissing him lightly on the cheek. "I hope that soon you can find it in your heart to speak to me of such things as you used to. But I won't press the matter. Do what you must, my lord duke, and guard the pride of our house." She walked to the door of the great hall, then paused, glancing back at him, the look in her dark eyes almost shy. "It's been some time since we lay together as husband and wife. But if you still desire me in that way . . ." She shrugged, the small smile still on her lips.

"I do," he said, his voice suddenly rough. In truth he had never thought to share a bed with her again, so far had she gone after Brienne's murder. Just her words had stoked a fire within him he thought had long since died.

She smiled again, deeper this time. "I'll be waiting for you in my bedchambers."

When she was gone, the duke closed his eyes, tightening his fist around the parchment as if it were Tavis of Curgh's neck.

But the boy didn't do it. Kearney's message didn't say as much. It didn't point out that Aindreas had pushed the realm to the brink of civil war for no reason at all. It didn't have to. All that and more was implied in what he had written.

The note was short and direct, the language plain, almost pungent.

> We hold in the prison tower of Audun's Castle a woman who admits complicity in the murder of your daughter. She is a member of the Qirsi conspiracy and claims that Brienne's assassination was intended to foment civil war among the houses of Eibithar.
>
> You will ride to the City of Kings at once so that you might question this woman yourself and discuss her revelations with the realm's other lords and me. Your failure to do so will be considered an act of treason and will provoke an appropriate response.

That was all, save for Kearney's signature and the royal seal.

He wanted to dismiss it as a trick, an attempt by Glyndwr and Curgh to draw him to the City of Kings so that they might imprison him, perhaps even kill him. But he knew better. If they wished to lure him to Audun's Castle, they would have done so with offers of reconciliation, promises of belated justice for Kentigern. They wouldn't have resorted to threats and such a bold claim.

No, this woman was real. She might have been lying, though for the life of him Aindreas couldn't imagine why anyone, even a Qirsi, would tell such a tale.

He felt something brush his shoulder, and looking up, saw Brienne standing beside him. Aindreas reached for her hand and smiled. Her fingers were so tiny and delicate, like a child's.

"Your mother looks well, doesn't she?" he asked.

The girl nodded, a smile lighting her face.

"When you died, I thought I'd lost her as well. But it seems she's come back to me."

"You have to tell her."

Aindreas shuddered. "It would kill her."

"She must know the truth."

He frowned. "The truth? What does this message tell us of the truth? Glyndwr and Curgh have lied to us before. They may well be lying again."

"You know better."

"You can tell me," he said, his eyes widening. "You're the only one who knows what really happened." He turned in his chair and took her other hand as well. "It was the boy, wasn't it? They're lying about this woman."

Brienne shook her head, her expression grim. She looked even more lovely than he had remembered.

"You misjudged him, Father. From the beginning."

"No!"

She nodded.

Aindreas dropped her hands and stood, spinning away from the table to pace the stone floor. "I refuse to believe any of this! The message, this woman, even you. It's all an illusion. Kearney is doing all of this to trick me. He wishes only to rule the realm. He doesn't care about honor, about truth!"

He turned to face her once more, but already the image had begun to vanish, growing thin and misshapen, the last wisps of smoke from an extinguished candle.

"Brienne!" he cried out. "I didn't mean it! I know you wouldn't deceive me! Please stay!"

But it was too late. A servant stood near the table, gaping at the duke, eyes wide with fright.

"Go to Kearney, Father!" The voice seemed to come from a great distance, as if it were the final breath of thunder from a retreating storm. "Save yourself. Save Kentigern."

Aindreas felt tears burning his cheeks. "Brienne," he said once more, a whisper. Long before now, he should have sought her wraith out at the Sanctuary of Bian. He should have asked her who had killed her. She could have told him and put all his doubts to rest. But for too long he had been so certain that he felt no need to ask. And then his doubts had begun to grow, and he had come to fear her answer. Now it was too late.

He drained his goblet of wine, then threw it against the wall so that it shattered, scattering shards of clay across the floor. The servant bent to clean the mess, joined a moment later by a second boy. Aindreas paid them little notice. He wasn't about to go to Kearney, not after all that had passed between them in recent turns. Even if Javan's boy wasn't guilty—impossible!—Glyndwr and Curgh had made it clear that they couldn't be trusted, that their contempt for him, for all of Kentigern, overrode their sense of justice.

But there was another he could find, one who could tell him how this had happened.

One of the servants straightened, facing the duke as if it took all his courage to do so. He was a yellow-haired boy whose eyes flicked nervously from the duke to his companion, who still cleaned up the broken goblet.

"A—are you well, my lord?"

"I'm fine," Aindreas said. He snatched the parchment from the table before striding toward the door. "Go to the stablemaster, boy. Tell him to have my mount saddled and ready. I ride within the hour."

"Yes, my lord."

Aindreas was in the corridor before he had finished. He walked first to his chambers, where he retrieved his sword and dagger, fastening them to his belt. He thought briefly of Ioanna and knew a moment of regret. She would be expecting him. But he was in no state to lie with her this night, and if he took the time to tell her so, she would demand an explanation, which he couldn't possibly give. Not about this.

As an afterthought, he took a pouch of gold from a drawer in his writing table. Finding the woman wouldn't be easy. It might well take a bribe or two.

He left his chamber and made his way to the inner ward. The night was clear but cold, and for just an instant he considered returning for his riding cloak. Then he thought better of it and walked on to the stables.

The stablemaster himself had come down to see to Aindreas's horse, as was appropriate.

"My lord," he said, bowing. "Your mount awaits."

"Good." Taking his reins from the man, the duke hesitated. The stablemaster was nearly as tall as Aindreas, though not nearly so large. Still . . .

"You have a cloak?" Aindreas demanded.

The man blinked. "Yes, my lord, I do."

"Give it here."

He opened his mouth, closed it again. "It's but a simple wrap, my lord. It's hardly worthy—"

"I don't give a damn what it looks like! Give it here. I'll return it to you before the night ends." Better it shouldn't look like a noble's cape. Many within the city would recognize him no matter what he wore, at least during the day. Few men in the realm were as large as Aindreas or rode as great a horse. But beyond the city walls, this plain cloak might fool a few and keep word of his late-night ride from spreading through the dukedom.

The man bowed and quickly retrieved his cloak from where it hung on a nail just inside the stable.

"You may keep it, my lord. I'd be honored if you did."

They were all so afraid of him. Had he used such a heavy hand over the years?

"As I said, I'll return it before first light. My thanks, stablemaster."

He threw the cloak over his shoulders and swung himself onto his great black mount. He snapped the reins and the beast started forward. The soldiers at the castle gates called greetings to him as he rode past, but Aindreas offered no response.

Only when he started down the winding lane toward the city did Aindreas remember that the Revel was in Kentigern. Even this late, the city streets would be choked with people, and with the dancers, musicians, and peddlers who traveled with the festival. He almost turned back, thinking to ride through the castle and use the Tarbin gate, which was still being repaired. Instead, he took the quickest route out of Kentigern, keeping his head low as he rode past the guards at the city gate. It seemed that at least one of the men recognized him, but Aindreas didn't slow his mount. Already, he was thinking of where he might find the woman he sought.

Her name was Jastanne ja Triln. She was a Qirsi merchant and the captain of a ship, the *White Erne*. Indeed, the one time they met, she told him that she was usually on her vessel. "If you need to find me," she said that night in his quarters, "just look for the *Erne*." She also told him that she expected them to communicate solely through written messages. She wouldn't be pleased to see him.

If she saw him at all. Riding away from the city walls, Aindreas realized that she could be anywhere in the Forelands, "from Rawsyn Bay to the Bronze Inlet," as she had put it. The chances of her being in the quays of the Tarbin were so remote that he actually reined his mount to a halt. After a moment, however, he rode on. He had already left Kentigern. It was but a small matter to continue on to the river. If her ship wasn't there, he would return to the castle. Perhaps it wouldn't be too late to seek out the duchess after all.

He rode westward for nearly a league and then turned south toward the river. The Tarbin was the boundary between Aneira and Eibithar and had been crossed many times by the armies of Mertesse and Kentigern. But here, west of the cities and their soldiers, the river became a place for trade, not war. Merchants from both realms traded with the sea captains who sailed up the river from the Scabbard, haggling over prices rather than borders, and counting their successes in gold rather than blood. "Kings must have their wars," it was often said, "and merchants must have their gold." Nowhere was this more true than on the banks of the Tarbin.

Long before he reached the river, Aindreas could see torches burning brightly on the quays, and as he drew nearer, he heard music and laughter. He couldn't begin to guess the time, though he thought it must be well past gate closing in Kentigern. But in the port, the night was just beginning.

Qirsi ships tended to dock near the end of the pier, although not by choice. The nearer landings were the more desirable, offering as they did easier access to the roads leading to Kentigern city and the smaller villages that lay nearby. These the rivermaster held for Eandi ships.

Aindreas halted his mount a short distance from the closest of the piers, tying the beast to a tree and covering the remaining ground on foot. The duke lowered his gaze as he walked, keeping the cloak tight about his shoulders and throwing the hood over his head. Had anyone been watching for him, they would have recognized Aindreas instantly. But he was aided by the foolishness of what he was doing. No one would have thought to look for him, and so no one noticed him.

Reaching the first quay, he passed a group of men carrying jugs of ale.

"I'm looking for the *White Erne*," he said, not bothering to stop or look at them.

"Go to the end of the third pier," one of the men answered. "I believe she arrived last night."

He could scarcely believe his good fortune. Managing a quick thank-you, he hurried on. He turned onto the third quay, the wood creaking slightly under his weight. There were three ships close to the shore—all captained by Eandi, no doubt—and a single ship at the end of the pier. The *Erne*. No one seemed to take note of him as he walked past the Eandi ships, but before he was halfway to the *Erne*, three Qirsi men blocked his path.

"What do you want, Eandi?" asked one of them, a lanky, narrow-faced man with white hair that hung loose to his shoulders and bright yellow eyes that glimmered like gold rounds in the torch fire.

"I'm going to that ship there. The *White Erne.*"

The Qirsi grinned, though the expression in those golden eyes didn't change. "I had guessed that much. It was either the *Erne,* or you fancied yourself a fish." His grin widened. "Or perhaps a whale."

The other two laughed, low and menacing. Aindreas noticed that they had unsheathed their blades.

"I see you carry a sword, Eandi," the man said, stepping closer to him. Aindreas had the distinct impression that the man had expected him, that he knew exactly who Aindreas was, and that he wasn't the least bit frightened of him. "You don't intend to use it on any of us, do you?"

The duke would have liked to pull the weapon from its scabbard and cleave this impertinent white-hair in two. Instead, he opened his hands, keeping his gaze fixed on the Qirsi.

"Not at all, friend. I merely wish a word with the *Erne*'s captain."

"Her captain," the Qirsi repeated, glancing back at his companions. "She's a busy woman, and she hasn't much patience for Eandi whales interrupting her evening meal."

Aindreas placed his hand on the hilt of his sword, no longer caring what magic this man might possess, or how far word of his visit to the *Erne* might travel. "And I haven't much patience for any man who insults me in my realm. Now tell her Aindreas, duke of Kentigern has come to speak with her, or I'll have your head on a pike before dawn."

The man didn't flinch, nor did the duke's threat wipe the grin from his face. But after a moment he nodded, and turned back toward the ship. The other two remained, blades still in hand.

Aindreas had thought she might keep him waiting, but only a minute or two later, the first man returned and with a quick gesture, beckoned Aindreas to the Qirsi vessel.

It was a larger ship than the duke had expected, with a mainmast nearly twenty fourspans tall and a wide, sturdy hull that appeared hardy enough to weather even the worst storms of the snows and early planting season. There were perhaps a dozen men on the deck and Aindreas had no doubt that the *Erne*'s crew numbered at least twice that many. All this under a captain whom he remembered looking as frail as a reed and as young as Affery.

The Qirsi men led him onto the ship and down into the hold, which was ample and clean and smelled slightly of pipeweed and brine. As they neared the bow belowdecks, they came to a small oaken door. The Qirsi knocked, and in response to the summons from within, indicated to Aindreas that he should enter.

Ducking his head to step through the doorway, Aindreas entered a small chamber, well lit by several oil lamps. It was obviously designed for a Qirsi—it seemed to the duke that his own frame took up most of the room—but it was equally clear that it offered all the comfort a sea captain could want. The walls and floors were made of a dark, polished wood, and a small bed stood in the far corner. Beside it, at a small writing table made of a lighter wood, sat Jastanne, a taunting smile on her lips. Her hair was tied back from her face, and her eyes were an even deeper gold than those of the man on the pier. She was prettier than Aindreas recalled, though no less youthful in her appearance.

"Lord Kentigern," she said, not bothering to stand. "I hadn't thought to see you again, at least not so soon."

"Really? I had the impression that your men were expecting me."

She raised an eyebrow. "You're perceptive. I dreamed three nights ago that you would come, and so, yes, my men were prepared." She held a sea chart in her lap, and now she placed it on the table so that the parchment curled up into a loose cylinder. Then she gestured toward the bed. "Please sit. I'd offer you a chair . . ." She trailed off, shrugging.

Aindreas understood. None of the chairs in the chamber was big enough to hold him. He smiled thinly and sat on the bed.

"When I said I hadn't thought to see you again," she went on, "I was referring to our conversation three turns ago, when I told you that I wished only to communicate in writing."

"I remember," he said.

"Then why have you come?"

"Because I felt it necessary. You may command the obedience of the Qirsi in your movement, Captain. But I'm a duke. I don't answer to anyone unless I so choose."

"Including your king."

"Yes, including my king."

"I see." She eyed him for a some time, her expression revealing nothing of her thoughts. "You don't look well, Lord Kentigern," she said at last. There was no concern in her tone, no sympathy. She might as well have been commenting on the prevailing winds.

"I'm well enough."

"Then perhaps you should tell me why you're here. I'm certain that you're no more eager to prolong this encounter than I am."

He faltered, unsure of how to proceed. For better or worse, he had cast his lot with the conspiracy. He had even been so foolish as to sign a pledge to that effect— a token of his good faith, the Qirsi had called it at the time. Now it was a noose around his throat. Their failure would bring with it his downfall and the disgrace of his house. But while he had little choice but to help them, he needed first to know the truth. If their deceit ran as deep as he feared, he would have to find some way to undo all that he had wrought with his own betrayal.

"Very well," he began. "I've received a message from Kearney. In it he claims to have evidence that the conspiracy was responsible for my daughter's murder."

The woman shrugged. "This is nothing new. Glyndwr and Curgh have been telling you much the same thing since Lady Brienne's death. Isn't that so?"

"Yes."

"Then what makes this message so different that you'd ride all the way here?"

"This time he says he's captured a member of your conspiracy, a woman who acknowledges her involvement in the murder."

Jastanne sat forward, the blood draining from her cheeks. For the first time since he met her, she looked truly frightened. "Did he tell you her name?"

Aindreas shook his head.

"Did you bring the message with you?"

He pulled it from his cloak and handed it to her. Watching her read the note by the light of the lamp beside her, seeing how appalled she was by these tidings, the duke found himself sifting through his memory of their previous encounter. At no time had she denied that the Qirsi ordered Brienne's death, because he never asked. No matter the truth, this woman hadn't lied to him. Aside from Shurik, whose treachery lay at the root of all that had happened since, no one had. Not Javan, not Kearney, not the white-hairs. He had done this to himself.

"Is it possible that this is a deception?" she asked at last, handing the parchment back to him.

"You tell me."

"What do you mean?"

"Was the conspiracy responsible for my daughter's murder?"

She hesitated. It was only for an instant, but that was long enough. "This seems a strange time to ask, Lord Kentigern. You're one of us now."

"I want an answer, damn you!"

"I have none to offer. I don't know who killed your daughter."

"You're lying! The first time we met you claimed to be one of the leaders of your conspiracy."

"I am. But this is a vast movement, Lord Kentigern, and its success depends in part upon secrecy. Even its leaders don't know everything. That way, if one of us is captured and tortured, he or she will not reveal enough to jeopardize the cause. Surely you can understand that."

There was a certain logic to what she said, but still he doubted her word.

"Do you think the king could be lying to you?" she asked again.

"No. Not that he's not capable of it, but this isn't how he'd go about doing it. This woman exists, and I have little choice but to believe that she had a hand in my daughter's murder."

Jastanne just stared at him, as if appraising a rival captain's ship. "That puts you in an awkward position, doesn't it? You sought an alliance with the movement believing that Tavis of Curgh was the killer, and that Kearney, in offering asylum to the boy and taking the throne with Javan's consent, was an enemy of Kentigern. Now, I would imagine, you see the Qirsi as your enemy. What do you intend to do?"

Aindreas looked away. "What can I do?"

"Very little. I suppose that's my point."

He faced her again, longing once more to draw his blade. "Meaning what?"

"You pledged yourself to this movement, Lord Kentigern. You did so in writing, on parchment bearing your mark and seal. If you turn on us now, if you seek revenge for what you believe was our complicity in Lady Brienne's murder, we'll destroy you and your family. You'll gain nothing, and lose all. You understand that?"

Of course he did. Truth be told, he had known it that first night, only moments after signing the paper and watching the Qirsi he had tortured—what was his name?—carry it from the chamber. They had defeated him, made him their slave, and he had forged the manacles himself.

"Yes," he said dully. "I understand."

"Good. I don't know who this woman is, and despite your assertions to the contrary, I still think it possible that the king intended this message as a trick, to lure you to the City of Kings." She paused, eyeing him once more. "Do you intend to go?"

"No." He had given it little thought, but he knew that he couldn't face the king and his fellow dukes. Not now, not knowing how he had betrayed them, how he would be disgraced in their eyes.

"Are you certain it's wise to defy him so soon?"

"It's what he'll expect. I'm a rebel, remember. I don't accept him as my king, and I see every effort at reconciliation as a thinly veiled attempt to force my capitulation. If I give in to him now, I'll lose the support of the other houses opposing him. Surely you don't want that."

"No, we don't."

"I'll send a message back to Kearney telling him that I remain convinced of Tavis's guilt and that I won't be lured to the City of Kings by Curgh trickery." He forced a smile, though he felt ill. "As you say, that's probably what this is."

"I'm pleased to hear you say so, Lord Kentigern. I was growing concerned."

He stood, the room seeming to pitch and roll. Was it the ship or his mind? "I should be riding back to Kentigern before I'm missed."

"Of course. If you receive further news of this woman, you'll let me know. Naturally I'll do the same."

"Naturally."

She was watching, as if waiting for him to leave, but the duke continued to stand where he was.

"I'm surprised that I found you here," he said, his gaze fixed on the floor, his hand again on the hilt of his sword. "You told me that your travels take you from one end of the Forelands to the other, and yet the one night I come looking for you on the Tarbin I'm fortunate enough to find you."

"I told you, Lord Kentigern. I dreamed three nights ago that you would come to me. I was already in the Scabbard at the time, and so I sailed to Tarbin Port. I assure you, there was nothing more to it than that."

Aindreas nodded, and let himself out of the chamber. To his surprise, there were no men waiting for him outside her door. Apparently they didn't think he posed any real danger to their captain, even armed. Once more, he thought back to their first meeting when she had used magic to shatter her wine goblet, merely by way of telling him that the Qirsi movement had no need for Kentigern's arms. That was why they didn't bother guarding her. Jastanne was a shaper. She could have broken the duke's sword with a thought. Indeed, she could have done the same with his neck.

He left the ship as swiftly as he could, retreating from the quay and returning to the small cluster of trees where his mount was tied.

As he approached the horse he realized that there was something on his saddle, glittering in the moonlight that shone through the bare limbs of the trees. Slowing, he glanced around, but saw no one. He walked cautiously to the beast and looked more closely at what lay on the saddle. It was a dagger, the blade of which had been broken in two. Instinctively he reached for his own blade, but it was still there. This one must have belonged to the Qirsi.

There was a message here, he felt certain. This, it seemed, was a day of messages. But he couldn't say what this one meant. He knew only that he wanted to be back in his castle, where, at least for this night, he would be safe.

Only when the duke was gone, his lumbering footsteps no longer echoing through her ship, did Jastanne allow herself to slump back in her chair, squeezing her eyes shut.

"Demons and fire!" she muttered, rubbing her brow with her thumb and forefinger.

There could be no doubt but that Kearney's message was genuine. She had been telling Aindreas the truth when she said that even chancellors in the Weaver's movement didn't know all that was done in his name, but she had no doubt that the Weaver's will had been behind Brienne's death. Not that he had told her so, or that she had asked. She merely understood him, as she did the sea. She could read his thoughts as she could currents, his moods like she could the sky. And she knew that in his own way the Weaver was as powerful as Amon's Ocean. She would no more defy him than she would steer her vessel into a storm. In the depths of his magic she glimpsed her own future, and a brilliant future it was. His wisdom and strength would sustain her and carry her to glory, and if he asked it of her, she would give all to him.

Right now, serving him meant learning all she could of this traitor disgracing herself in Kearney's prison tower. What kind of a woman would betray her people this way? What means had they used to compel her confession? Certainly mere torture shouldn't have been enough. True, it had been sufficient for Qerle, the cloth merchant Aindreas had used to find Jastanne. Qerle, however, was but a courier in the movement. He was no one.

But this woman, if the missive from the king was to be believed, had a hand in Lady Brienne's death. She had to be someone of importance, perhaps another of the Weaver's chancellors. In which case, she should have been willing to die for the movement. She should have been capable of withstanding all forms of torture and coercion.

Had Jastanne been there with her, she would have shattered her skull like a clay bowl. Traitors to the cause deserved no better.

She stood and began to undress. It was growing late and there was a chance the Weaver would come to her tonight, walking like a god in her dreams. Jastanne slept unclothed for him. She thought of it as an offering of sorts, a way of showing him that she was devoted to him and to his movement, a way of telling him that her mind and body were his.

And he had responded by making her a chancellor, and so much more.

For the Weaver had plans for her, important plans. Only half a turn before he had ordered Jastanne to the western waters. Again, there had been some truth in what she told the duke. She had dreamed that he would come. But her return to the Scabbard had been no coincidence.

"It is all coming together," the Weaver had told her that night, caressing her body with his mind. "Soon, very soon, we will begin the final battle with the Eandi. And you will be there when I reveal myself. You will be there to share my victory."

His caresses had grown more urgent then, more powerful, until she cried out in her sleep with pleasure and desire.

She was to be his queen. He hadn't said so, not yet. But she knew from the way he touched her. She knew him as she did the sea. He would return to her soon, to tell her how she could serve him next, and to touch her again.

It was yet another measure of the Weaver's power and of the strength of the movement he commanded that Jastanne could exact her revenge against the traitor without even leaving port. She climbed into bed, already anticipating the Weaver's caresses. Tonight, perhaps. Or tomorrow. No later than that. He would appear before her, framed against the brilliant sun, and he would speak to her again of his plans, of the future he was shaping for them all. And she would tell him then of the message from Kearney, trusting him to strike at the woman for her, for all Qirsi. He would know who this traitor was. He would know how to reach her. And he would make her pay dearly for her treachery.

Chapter
Seventeen

t was always the same dream. He was in Audun's Castle in the City of Kings, standing at the front of the fortress's magnificent great hall, with the Oaken Throne just behind him. All the dukes, thanes, earls, and barons of Eibithar sat before him, along with the queen of Sanbira, the king of Caerisse, the archduke of Wethyrn, and many nobles he didn't recognize. All had come, he knew, for his investiture. Renald of Galdasten, the first king of Eibithar to come from the house of eagles in nearly a century. Above them all flew the pennons of all the houses of the realm, led by the bronze, black, and yellow of Galdasten, and beside him, seated in a smaller version of his own great throne, sat Elspeth, looking resplendent in a red velvet gown. His three boys stood beside her, all of them dressed as young soldiers, in the colors of their house with golden hilted swords on their belts.

A prelate he didn't recognize stood with him, holding the jeweled golden circlet that was to go on Renald's brow. But before the man could give him the crown, the ceremony was interrupted by a disturbance at the rear of the hall. Everyone stood, so that Renald, standing farthest from the noise, could not see. A woman screamed, then several more, and in a moment the hall was in turmoil. The would-be king strained to get a glimpse of what was causing such panic, but though the tumult seemed to be drawing nearer, he still could see nothing.

Beside him, Elspeth stood, calmly bowed to him, and walked away, leading their sons out of the hall through a small door that had escaped Renald's notice until then. He called to her, even took a step as if to follow. But before he could, the horde before him finally parted revealing a horror beyond his imagining. A man was striding toward him, a Qirsi. The stranger's face was flushed and bathed in sweat, and his limbs were covered with swollen red welts—bites from vermin. The front of his shirt was stained with vomit and blood and in each hand he held a mouse. Renald wanted desperately to flee, to follow his wife through the doorway, but his feet would not move. And as the man stopped before him, laughing so that his foul, hot breath blasted the duke's face, he held out the rodents he carried, crushing their fur against Renald's face.

Always he woke then, gasping for air, his bedding damp with his own sweat, his stomach knotted like wet rope. He had never spoken of the dream with anyone. He hardly needed to. No one who knew the recent history of the house of Galdasten could have any doubt as to whence this vision had come. It had been but eight years since the madman brought the pestilence to Kell's Feast, killing the old duke and his family, and so many other men and women of the dukedom that it almost defied comprehension.

Before that growing season, Renald had long lamented the cruelty of his fate. He was far more clever than his older cousin. Indeed, he thought himself the most intelligent and most capable among all the grandchildren of Wistel the Eleventh. But while Kell, as the eldest son of Wistel the Twelfth, could lay claim to the house and its lofty position in the Order of Ascension, Renald, the eldest son of the second brother, was relegated to the small castle in Lynde and a thaneship that led nowhere. In the wake of the tragedy, however, if it could be called that, he began to see that the gods had far greater plans for him and his line than he had ever imagined. It was almost enough to turn him from Ean's Path, back to the Old Faith.

Yet the vision continued to haunt his dreams, as if warning him against taking too much pleasure in his good fortune. This was the fourth night in Osya's waxing alone that he had been tormented by the dream, and he had begun to suffer for lack of sleep.

For several years he had just accepted the dream as a burden he had to bear as leader of his house, the cost of his dukedom, as it were. It had never occurred to him to question it beyond that. But as word of the Qirsi conspiracy spread through the Forelands, and, in particular, after the murder of Lady Brienne of Kentigern and the subsequent defection of Aindreas's first minister, Renald had started to consider the dream anew. The commoner who brought the pestilence to Galdasten had been Eandi, not Qirsi. No one in Eibithar had ever suggested that the incident had been anything more than an act of insanity and grief—the man in question, it seemed, had lost his child to the pestilence five years before, and his wife to some other illness a few years after that. This was no mask for an assassination plot; it was not an attempt to disrupt the Order of Ascension, as Brienne's murder might have been. It was just what it seemed: the desperate, foolish act of a crazed man.

So why was the diseased man in his vision a white-hair? Was this some strange trick of his mind born of his fears of the conspiracy, fears he was certain he shared with every Eandi noble in the land? He would have liked to think so, but the vision hadn't changed at all since he first dreamed it during the harvest of 872, and he had known nothing of the conspiracy in his first years as duke. For all he knew, it hadn't even existed then.

Once more, he found himself wondering if the dream might be a warning. But of what? He had ambitions for the throne—were the gods telling him to abandon them? Or were they merely telling him that only the conspiracy could keep him from Audun's Castle, that the real threat to his desires came not from Javan and Kearney, but from the Qirsi?

In recent turns, he had settled on this interpretation, only to see the frequency of the visions increase. Again he found himself lying awake nights, questioning the meaning of this. He briefly considered making his way to the Sanctuary of Amon at the eastern end of the city to ask the priestess there what it might mean. But a duke in Eibithar didn't reveal to anyone the terrors preying on his mind, nor did he turn to the sanctuaries in times of trouble. If the prelate couldn't help him—and dreams were hardly the province of the cloisters—no man or woman of the gods could.

Instead, Renald endured his visions alone. Elspeth would have thought him a weak fool for allowing mere dreams to unman him, and there was no other person in the castle in whom the duke placed enough trust to confide such a thing. On this night, as on so many that had come before, the duke rose from his bed and threw on his clothes, though the eastern sky had yet to brighten. He knew that there was no sleeping after the vision came, and he thought it better to occupy his mind with other things rather than lie in bed seeing the Qirsi's face time and again.

Two soldiers stood just outside his bedchamber, two who were often there when the duke emerged from the room in the darkness of night. They had the good sense not to comment on his inability to sleep, silently bowing to him instead, and falling in step behind him as he led them to his ducal chambers.

The room was cold when he stepped inside, and one of the guards hurried to the hearth to light a fire.

"Leave it," the duke said.

"But, my lord—"

"Bring me some tea. That will be warmth enough."

The man bowed again. "Yes, my lord."

In a moment he was alone. The guards had left one of their torches, which cast great, shifting shadows on the chamber walls. Renald lit a lamp on his writing table and a second on the mantle above the hearth. Then he retrieved the missive from Kearney that had arrived two days before, and sat at the table.

The message was quite typical of the Glyndwr king—forthright but courteous, intelligently written and free of pretense. It seemed he had proof of Lord Tavis's innocence in the murder of Aindreas's daughter, and, perhaps more to the point, evidence as well of Qirsi involvement in the killing, which he now referred to as an assassination. Renald could only imagine how these tidings would be received in Kentigern.

The king went on to request that Renald make the journey to the City of Kings as soon as weather in the north permitted. With the snows giving way to the milder days and warmer winds of the planting, that time had already come. Still, the duke had made no plans to ride southward, nor did he expect to anytime soon.

He actually liked Kearney, and had been impressed with the king's father the one time they had occasion to meet. Galdasten and Glyndwr had long been on good terms, and why shouldn't they be? Renald's house was ranked second among the five majors in the Order of Ascension; Glyndwr was fifth. They had never truly been rivals and with one on the north shore, buffeted by winds from Amon's Ocean, and the other perched in the highlands, they had never had cause for any sort of land dispute. Renald even believed that Kearney might make a good king, given the chance to rule for several more years.

His opposition to the king had nothing to do with the man himself and everything to do with the future of his own house. Under the rules governing the Eibitharian throne, the death of Kell and his entire line in 872 removed Galdasten from the Order of Ascension for four generations. Renald had inherited the dukedom, but his house could not claim the throne until his grandson's grandson had come of age. And even then, there was no guarantee that the crown would fall to Galdasten. If Kearney's line continued to produce male heirs, Glyndrwr might still hold power, and if it did not, the crown would revert first to Thorald. Indeed, by the time a duke of Galdasten could ascend once more to the throne, any of the other four major houses might have established itself as the royal house.

Renald had sent letters to Aindreas lamenting the injustices Kentigern had suffered at the hands of Javan of Curgh and the king. He had written similar messages to Kearney, warning the king that Galdasten and its allies among the other houses of the realm would not allow Brienne's killer and those who harbored him to go unpunished. And though he had thought Tavis guilty of the crime, he wouldn't have done anything different had he not. Aindreas's opposition to the king threatened not only to topple Glyndwr from the throne but also to put an end to the Rules of Ascension themselves. And that was just what the duke wanted.

The rules had been challenged before, and the houses had turned away from them a number of times, only to see the kingdom descend into turmoil and violence. Each time, the houses eventually returned to the rules, seeing in the stability of the Thorald Supremacy an imperfect solution, but one that was preferable to civil war.

But what if Renald could convince the other houses that this time the rules themselves were the source of their troubles? Aindreas had been trying to convince anyone who would listen that Javan and Kearney had conspired to steal the throne from him. From all that the duke had heard, however, he believed that Kentigern had agreed to the arrangement. True, the decision came in the difficult hours just after the end of a siege that nearly cost Aindreas his castle, but he had given his consent nevertheless. And Renald had been reminding other dukes of this ever since. The problem lay not with any deception perpetrated by the king but rather with the Rules of Ascension. They were too easily turned to the purposes of one or two determined dukes. They were archaic and unjust. Why should the act of a madman and the assassination of a young prince be enough to remove the two preeminent houses in Eibithar from consideration for the throne? Without the rules, Tobbar of Thorald might be king now, or perhaps Renald, if the duke of Thorald was too ill to serve. In either case, there would be no talk of rebellion and civil war. Eibithar would be able to face the Qirsi challenge united and strong.

This at least is what he had been saying to the other dukes. And they were listening. Eardley, Sussyn, Domnall, and Rennach. Minor houses all, and aside from Eardley, not even the strongest of the minors. But taken together, their armies included nearly four thousand men, and combined with the soldiers of Galdasten and Kentigern, they constituted a considerable fighting force. They were not powerful enough to defeat the royal army, particularly if it was supported by the armies of Glyndwr, Curgh, Labruinn, and Tremain, as seemed likely. But unlike Aindreas, Renald didn't want a war.

The duke of Kentigern was so consumed by his grief and his need for vengeance that he would gladly have destroyed the kingdom so long as he managed to destroy Curgh and Glyndwr in the process. Everyone in the realm knew it. Certainly the other dukes did. Which was why even as he railed against the injustice of Kearney's rule, Renald never spoke of taking the kingdom by force. His was the soothing voice, the antithesis to Aindreas's cries for blood. No, he didn't need a force capable of taking Audun's Castle. He merely needed a credible army, large enough to convince a majority of the dukes that the danger of war was real, and that any peaceful settlement was preferable to the carnage such a conflict would bring.

It was a process he knew would take some time. Even those dukes who were with him still spoke of war, of the injustice done to Aindreas. Many of them believed that Thorald could be turned to their cause and that when Tobbar joined them, Kearney would be forced to surrender the throne. Renald had no such illusions. Tobbar would never be king, nor would Marston, his son. But if Kearney the Younger, the king's boy, failed to produce an heir, Marston's son or grandson could claim the throne as his own. Thorald remained the preeminent house in the land, and as such, its leaders had reason to preserve the Rules of Ascension. The lone hope for Renald and his allies was that Aindreas would lead them to the brink of war, before Kearney was forced to abdicate in order to keep the land whole.

Under any circumstances, his chances of succeeding would have been small. But Kearney's message, versions of which he had no doubt sent to every duke in the realm, made matters that much more difficult. If the king managed to convince the other nobles that Aindreas had been wrong about Tavis, that Glyndwr's offer of asylum had saved an innocent man rather than harboring a murderer, then support for the rebellion would crumble.

The guards returned to Renald's chamber a short time later bearing a pot of tea and breakfast, but from that time until just after the ringing of the midmorning bells, the duke was alone with his thoughts and the damned letter from Kearney. Even as the pealing of the bells continued to echo through the castle, a knock came at his door. Ewan Traylee and Pillad jal Krenaar, his swordmaster and first minister. They met with the duke every morning at this time. But when he called for them to enter, it was Elspeth who opened the door, not the two men.

Renald stood. "Good morrow, my lady." He stepped around the table, taking her hands in his and kissing her forehead.

She gave a quick smile, but did not return the kiss. "The guards tell me you were awake again before dawn."

He dropped her hands. "The guards should know better than to speak of their duke without leave."

"Even to his wife?"

"Even so, yes." He walked back to the table and sat once more.

"What is it that wakes you?"

Renald shook his head, looked away.

"Is it another woman? I know you've had mistresses in the past."

"No, Elspeth. There's no other woman." A lie, though strictly true for this past night.

"Then what?"

"It's nothing I wish to tell you. I spent the balance of the night here, working. That's all you need to know."

The duchess stared at him for a long time, her dark eyes holding his. She remained beautiful, even after so many years, even after three childbirths. But it was an austere beauty, as inaccessible as the high peaks of the Border Range, or the ocean just before a storm. With her brown hair up, accentuating her prominent cheekbones and wide mouth, she looked more like a prioress than a duchess. She looked very much a queen.

"Of what do you dream, my lord?"

He felt his mouth twitch, saw her smile triumphantly.

"I dream of Kell's death," he admitted.

"And that's what wakes you."

"Yes."

"It would wake me, too."

It was as much a kindness as she was likely to show him, but he didn't wish to speak of this with anyone, least of all with her. "I'm expecting the swordmaster and my minister," he said. "We have a good deal to discuss."

"Even now they stand in the corridor," she said mildly. "They said they would wait until we were through."

Damn you. "What do you want?"

"What word have you sent to the other houses?"

"Nothing yet. It's too early. The message only came two days ago—"

"Three now."

"All right, three. But that's still not enough time to compose a response."

"They'll expect one. From you. Aindreas can't say anything. I doubt he'll even accept Kearney's claims. He'd gone too far to turn back now. That leaves you to lead the others."

Where? Where do I lead them now? "I know. That's why my response must be crafted with care."

"With care, yes. But swiftly as well. It will take some time for whatever message you send to reach the others. If you wait too long, they'll think Kearney's message has settled matters and this moment will pass." She walked to where he sat and knelt beside him, placing her hand on the inside of his thigh. "Don't you want to be king? Don't you want to reclaim the glory that was once Galdasten's?"

Her hand crept up his thigh and in spite of everything he felt himself becoming aroused. Cursing his weakness, he stood and stepped away from her. She only wanted the throne for him because she wished desperately to be queen, and because she had long nurtured ambitions for their sons.

"I daresay I want the throne nearly as much as you do, Elspeth. And I plan to do all I can to get it—"

"But you don't know how."

He glared at her. "Leave me."

She smirked at him. After a moment she stood once more and walked to the door. She was nearly as tall as he and she moved with the grace of a Revel dancer.

"Are you certain you wouldn't like me to remain? I can hardly imagine Ewan or Pillad being of much help. Their minds are no more nimble than yours."

He said nothing, and she reached for the door handle.

"What would you do?" he asked, signaling his surrender.

She faced him again. If she felt she had beaten him, she hid it well. "That's why I married you, Renald. A lesser man would have allowed his pride to keep him from asking."

He already regretted not letting her leave.

"I certainly wouldn't deny the verity of Kearney's claims," she went on, after seeming to consider the question briefly. "All it takes is one duke curious enough to make the journey and you're ruined. Rather, I'd insist that the tidings from Audun's Castle have no bearing on your dispute with the Crown. In fact, they make it all the more urgent that Eibithar rid itself of this arcane method of choosing its kings. Regardless of who killed Brienne, we still have a king who rules simply because two men decided he should. The rules are too easily bent to the will of a few." She paused, as if to weigh her own words. "That's what I would say."

Renald nodded. Not surprisingly it made a good deal of sense. She was a brilliant woman. Had he loved her he might have taken pride in having made her his duchess.

"And Renald," she added, lowering her voice and glancing toward the door. "If I were you, I wouldn't speak of this with Pillad."

He frowned. "Why not?"

"Because he's Qirsi, you fool. Didn't Kearney's message teach you anything? Brienne is dead because the Qirsi wished her dead. Eibithar is poised to fall into turmoil because the Qirsi wished it so. A noble who continues to trust his whitehairs with all matters of the realm risks a similar fate."

"But Pillad—"

She raised a finger to her lips, silencing him. Her eyes flicked to the door once more. Then she walked back to where he sat.

"Please, Renald," she said, her voice low. "Don't tell me that you know him too well, that he's served your house for too long, that he couldn't possibly betray you."

The duke just stared at her, groping for a response and feeling like a chastised child.

"He's Qirsi," she said, "and therefore he's dangerous. You may be right about him, he may be as loyal as a hound. But you've come too far to take that chance."

He nodded to her a second time, knowing that she was right, hating her for it.

"We'll speak again later," she told him. "After you've spoken with the others."

She turned away from him, her gown swirling, and left the chamber, leaving the door open as she favored the two men in the corridor with a gentle smile.

"Good day, my lord," Ewan said entering the chamber.

Pillad followed him in and bowed to Renald. "My lord."

"Close the door," the duke said sourly.

The Qirsi shut the door quietly and both men sat near the hearth. Renald eyed them both for several moments. Confronted now with the need to dismiss the Qirsi from his chamber, the duke wasn't certain how to proceed. Living in a realm in which nobles gathered Qirsi ministers according to their status and rank, Renald should have been able to attract to his court the wisest and most powerful. Eandi leaders in the Forelands had been collecting Qirsi for centuries, for their magic to be sure—their ability to glean the future, to weave mists that could conceal an entire army, and to shatter swords or whisper dark words to the horses of enemy soldiers—but also because a powerful minister enhanced the reputation of the man he served. Javan of Curgh was a formidable man in his own right, but having Fotir jal Salene as his first minister served to make him seem that much more impressive.

Had he been in line for the throne, Renald might have lured such a Qirsi to his own court. Instead, he had Pillad. The man was a capable minister whose visions had proven to be of value once or twice over the years. But Pillad would have been the first to admit that the powers he possessed—gleaning, fire, and healing—were not among the deeper Qirsi magics. He would have been less likely to admit what brought him to Galdasten, though Renald knew. Under most circumstances, a Qirsi of his limited abilities could never have expected to serve the duke of a major house in one of the Forelands' most powerful realms. But when Renald became duke, he was served by an aging woman whose powers were no more impressive than Pillad's, and when she died, Pillad saw an opportunity to serve in a dukedom, despite his shortcomings. With Galdasten removed from the Order of Ascension, other Qirsi weren't exactly flocking to Renald's castle, and though one or two of the others who did come had a bit more to offer than this man, something in Pillad's manner drew the duke's attention.

He had little doubt that his minister remained loyal to the house and despite the soundness of Elspeth's reasoning, Renald was loath to exclude him from the discussion.

But can you be certain?

"How goes the training of the men?" he asked Ewan, stalling.

The swordmaster looked puzzled. "Well, my lord. As always."

"Would you trust them to prevail in a fight?"

"Against whom, my lord?"

"The army of another major house."

"Excuse me, my lord," Pillad broke in. "But are you expecting to go to war?"

"No, Minister, I'm not. But with Kentigern threatening rebellion, I feel that we should be prepared for the worst. Don't you agree?"

"Of course, my lord."

"I'd put our men up against any in the land, my lord," Ewan said, a note of pride in his voice, his black beard bristling.

"Of course, Ewan," the duke said. "Forgive the question."

In his own way, the swordmaster was as limited in his capabilities as the minister. He was a fine swordsman, nearly a match for Hagan MarCullett in Curgh. But once more, measuring the men who served him against those serving Javan, Renald found that he suffered for the comparison. Ewan was not quite as skilled with a blade as Hagan, nor could he have prevailed against Curgh's swordmaster in a battle of wits. His men loved him and would have followed him into battle against a host of demons and wraiths. But Kell's swordmaster had succumbed to the pestilence with the old duke, and replacing him with as fine a soldier had proven difficult.

Once more the duke could hear his wife mocking them all. *I can hardly imagine Ewan or Pillad being of much help. Their minds are no more nimble than yours.* And though it galled him to think it, he had to concede that she was right about this as well.

Pillad pressed his fingertips together. "Have you given any more thought to the king's message, my lord?"

"Yes, though I haven't yet decided on any course of action."

"You still believe he may be lying."

"Possibly." The duke narrowed his eyes. "Is that what you think?"

"Actually it is. I've given the matter a good deal of thought, and I find it hard to imagine a member of the conspiracy admitting so much to any Eandi noble. I'd advise you to put little stock in that letter."

Renald nodded, though he suddenly felt cold. Perhaps the duchess was right about him after all. The one thing the duke and his wife agreed on was that Kearney wouldn't have lied about such a thing. Yet here was the minister arguing that the king had done just that.

"It's a fair point, Minister. I'll consider it. For now, however, I'd like to speak with the swordmaster in private."

It was clumsily done—Elspeth would have handled it far better. But Renald could barely keep his hands steady. He just wanted the man out of his chamber.

Pillad merely stared back at him, his face expressionless, his yellow eyes wide, so that he looked like a great owl. "My lord?"

"I wish to speak with Ewan of the men and of their training. I see no need to keep you here for a discussion that could consume the rest of the morning. I'll call for you later."

The minister glanced at Ewan, then stood and sketched a small bow. "Of course, my lord."

Still he stood there, as if confused. He opened his mouth, then closed it again.

After another moment he walked to the door and slipped out of the room, saying nothing more.

"Damn," the duke muttered, closing his eyes and shaking his head.

"You've lost faith in him."

"It's that apparent, is it?"

"I'm afraid so. Can you tell me why?"

"Something the duchess said about the dangers of trusting any Qirsi in these times. And then his suggestion that Kearney's letter was a deception."

Ewan raised an eyebrow. "Actually, I agree with him."

Renald felt his stomach heave. *Damn the woman!* "You do?"

"From what I've heard of these Qirsi traitors, it seems they'd rather die than betray their cause. You remember what happened in Thorald?"

Indeed he did, not merely because it had been only a few turns before but also because the tidings had left him badly shaken. Faced with accusations that she was a traitor, Tobbar's first minister admitted as much, but then took her own life before the duke and his men could question her.

"But would the king lie about such a thing, knowing how easy it would be for one of us to challenge his word?"

Ewan shrugged. "Perhaps it wouldn't be so easy. He might have convinced a Qirsi loyal to his house to play the part of traitor."

Renald sat forward. "Of course!" he whispered. It had never occurred to him to consider this. He felt certain that it had never occurred to Elspeth either. He actually thought it unlikely that Kearney could be so devious, but that was beside the point. Here was the excuse he needed to continue supporting Aindreas.

"Do you think that's what he's done?" Ewan asked.

"Tell me, swordmaster, how many men would we need to pose a threat to the king?"

"Far more than we have, my lord."

"Even with the minor houses that support us? Even with Kentigern?"

"Kentigern is still recovering from the siege, and the armies of four minor houses don't add up to much. Kearney has Glyndwr and Curgh, Tremain and Heneagh, as well as the royal army. Even if Thorald joined us it wouldn't be enough."

"I'm not asking you what we need to defeat the king. Only what we might need to convince him that a civil war would be too destructive to consider."

"To what end, my lord?"

Renald briefly considered telling the swordmaster of his hope that Kearney might abdicate. In the end, however, he decided against it. In the light of day, the notion struck him as too farfetched to repeat. At least for now.

"I fear that the king might attempt to crush Kentigern's rebellion before Aindreas can strike at him. Until we know for certain that Kearney is telling the truth about this Qirsi, I want to do all we can to prevent that."

Ewan's mouth twisted so that he looked, despite his beard and brawn, like a boy grappling with a question from his tutors. "I'm not even certain we're strong enough to do that much. If the king is determined to destroy the threat now, there's little we can do to stop him."

"But he couldn't do this without some cost," the duke said, desperate now for any encouraging response.

"Indeed, my lord. He'd pay dearly for the effort. We can't defeat him, but we can inflict heavy losses."

"And he must know this. Isn't that correct?"

"He should know it, my lord. If he doesn't, Gershon Trasker will tell him as much."

Renald rapped his knuckles on the table and stood, throwing open the shutters and staring out at the grey skies hanging over Galdasten. "That's what I wanted to hear. Thank you, swordmaster."

"But, my lord, you must realize that whatever losses the king suffers will be nothing compared to our own."

"I know that, Ewan. Rest assured, I have no intention of leading our men to a slaughter. I merely need time, and so long as Kearney knows that he can't defeat us without a bloodletting, I have it."

"Time for what, my lord?"

A fine question. One to which Renald had no answer. He needed for something to happen, though he couldn't even give a name to what that might be. He'd know it when it came, and he guessed that he wouldn't have to wait too long for whatever it was. Events in the Forelands had become as changeable and difficult to predict as the planting weather on the shores of Amon's Ocean. One couldn't guess the direction of the winds from one hour to the next. But there could be little doubt that a storm would be blowing in soon.

Pillad hadn't been sitting at his table for more than a few moments when he saw Uestem enter the tavern. He groaned inwardly and lowered his gaze, hoping that the merchant wouldn't notice him, knowing how foolish that was. The man was here because he had seen Pillad come in. The minister was certain of it. And as much as he dreaded speaking with him, he was surprised to find himself trembling with anticipation.

"First Minister, I'm surprised to see you here so early in the day."

Pillad looked up from his ale, frowned at the man, and looked away. "I'd like to be alone, thank you."

"Then why come to a tavern?" He lowered himself into the seat across from Pillad, resting his hands lightly on the table. "Why come to this tavern in particular? How many times have we met here now? Three? Four?"

"Three." The minister kept glancing toward the door, fearing that someone from the castle might enter the tavern at any moment. He had no cause to worry, of course. Only Qirsi came to this inn, and few were likely to do so before the ringing of the midday bells. Indeed, they were the only two people in the tavern aside from the barkeep and a pair of serving women. Besides, Uestem was known throughout Galdasten and the surrounding countryside as a successful and well-respected merchant. No one would have thought it strange that so wealthy a man might know the first minister. Few would have guessed that he was also a leader in the Qirsi conspiracy. But still Pillad watched the entrance. Anything to avoid looking this man in the eye.

"Three then. Nevertheless, you must have known I'd find you. I believe that's why you came."

"What? Don't be ridiculous! I came here—"

"Yes, I know: to be alone." He smiled. "Tell me, Minister, why is it that you've never had me imprisoned?"

"What?"

"You know I'm with the conspiracy—I've been trying to convince you to join us for more than a turn. Yet in all that time, even as you've refused, even as you've called me a traitor, you've never summoned the castle guard. Why?"

Pillad's heart was beating so hard that it hurt. He knew the answer, just as Uestem did. There was so much about himself that he had kept hidden away, that he had been afraid to admit, even to himself. Yet speaking with this man, he felt that all of it was laid bare for the world to see.

"Never mind that for now," the merchant said. "Tell me this: what drove you from the castle today?"

Pillad shook his head, eyes on the door again. "It doesn't matter."

"I think it does. I think your duke drove you here."

The minister met the man's gaze. "If I didn't know better, Uestem, I'd say that you had a spy in the duke's castle."

The merchant grinned. "Who's to say I don't?" He leaned forward. "Tell me what happened."

"You're the one with the spies. You tell me."

"All right," he said. He appeared to consider the matter for several moments, his brow furrowing. "I'd imagine you went to your duke's chambers as you do each morning, to speak with him of Kentigern and the king and whatever else concerns those of you living in the courts. The Eandi may not always know what to do with the authority they wield, but they do seem to enjoy talking about it. In any case, this morning something was different. Your duke seemed more distant than usual, more wary of you. And before you could even get comfortable in his spacious chambers, he asked you to leave. He didn't tell you why, he certainly didn't say that he had lost faith in you, but you knew. And so you came here." He sat back again. "Is that about right?"

Perhaps he really did have a spy. "It's close enough," the minister conceded. He sipped his ale, lowering his gaze once more. He felt humiliated, though Uestem was merely watching him, a look of sympathy on his lean face.

"The same thing is happening all over the Forelands, Minister. The Eandi speak of the faithlessness of the Qirsi, but they're the ones who reward years of loyal service with suspicion and contempt."

"Perhaps. But they do so because of your movement. They're frightened, and rightly so."

The man smiled again. "That's the first time in any of our conversations that you've referred to it as a movement rather than as a conspiracy."

Pillad felt his cheeks redden. "Don't think too much of it."

"Minister, why do you still resist? Your duke has lost faith in you. How long do you think it will be before he banishes you from the castle entirely?"

"It won't come to that."

"Can you be certain? I'm sure you never thought it would come to this." He paused watching Pillad, his light eyes fixed on the minister's face. "Actually, you're probably right. It won't come to that, though not for the reason you think. He won't send you from the castle because he won't have time. Renald isn't a bold man. It would take him several turns, maybe close to a year before he could muster the nerve to send you away. My allies and I will have already struck at the Eandi courts by then. For all we know, Renald will be dead before the end of the growing turns, as will any Qirsi who still serve him."

Pillad looked up at that.

"Is he worth dying for, Minister? After what he's done to you today, can you honestly say that you're still willing to give your life for this man and his house?"

Was it possible that he had come here knowing that Uestem would find him? Had he intended to pledge himself to the movement all along? Listening to the merchant speak, grappling with this last question he had asked, Pillad couldn't help but wonder. For abruptly, the answer seemed all too plain.

"No, I can't."

Uestem smiled, his expression free of irony. "You mean that? You're ready to join us?"

"What would be expected of me?"

"I don't know yet. To be honest, I haven't been confident enough in my ability to persuade you to inquire. But I will now."

"Yes, do." He drained his ale and placed it on the table a bit too sharply. The noise startled him. "So what will happen now?"

"Someone will contact you in the next few days. You'll—"

"Someone? You mean it won't be you?"

The man placed his hand on Pillad's. His skin felt warm and smooth. "It will be all right. Much of what you do in service to the movement will be through me. But not all."

The minister nodded.

"You'll be given a bit of gold—I don't know how much—and you'll be asked to perform some task on our behalf. When you've completed it, you'll be contacted again. What happens after that will depend upon many things, so I can't tell you much more."

The minister pulled his hand away and stood. "I should return to the castle. I'll be missed before long."

"You'll be missed here."

Pillad felt his face grow hot again, but he smiled. He started to walk away, but then halted, facing the merchant again. "What would you have done if I had refused you again?"

"I would have kept trying, for a while at least. Eventually, I would have had to kill you."

As quickly as the smile had come to his lips he felt it flee, along with much of the blood from his face. "You jest."

"No. I like you, Minister. Very much. But I serve a great cause. I'd gladly die for our people, and if I had to, I'd kill for them as well. I'm glad you've made that unnecessary."

Pillad swallowed, nodded once more. He could still feel where the man had touched his hand, though it wasn't merely warm anymore. Rather, it burned like an open wound.

Chapter
Eighteen

City of Kings, Eibithar, Osya's Moon waning

The first of the Eibitharian dukes was to arrive at Audun's Castle before nightfall, meaning that this was Cresenne's last day of freedom. Keziah had explained as much to her the day before, but Cresenne knew that the king would be coming to tell her so himself. It was his way, she had come to realize. She wasn't yet ready to say that she had been wrong about Eandi nobles and the Qirsi who served them. But she did have to admit that Kearney and Keziah were different somehow. Even Lord Tavis was not quite as she had expected.

After speaking with the archminister that first day, Cresenne had answered all of Grinsa's questions, at least all that she could. She had even told them of the Weaver, though she had begged the king not to reveal this to anyone other than his nobles. And to her surprise he granted her request. She expected the Curgh boy to exult in his exoneration, but though Cresenne sensed his relief when she told the others of her role in Lady Brienne's murder, Tavis offered no outward response.

She had spoken with Keziah a number of times since that day, and, most surprising of all, she actually felt that they were becoming friends. They were far more alike than Cresenne ever would have guessed, and after her initial discomfort around Bryntelle, Keziah had taken an interest in the child. Best of all, Grinsa seemed genuinely disturbed by their growing bond. Cresenne would have befriended the emperor of Braedon had she been certain that it would irk the gleaner.

After their first conversation, when Keziah convinced Cresenne to speak to Kearney openly of her involvement in the movement, the two women had not spoken of the Weaver again. Indeed, they had hardly mentioned the movement, or the threat of civil war, or even the messages Kearney had sent, summoning the other dukes to the City of Kings. Mostly they talked of their childhoods, of their families and their loves. Cresenne still sensed that the archminister wasn't telling her all, particularly when the topic turned to Grinsa or the king, and she guessed that one or both of the men had been her lover. But she didn't push the woman on these matters. For the first time in memory, she had a friend, and she was content simply to enjoy their friendship and to accept the limits placed upon it by the minister.

Which was why the previous day's conversation had come as such a blow.

They were in the gardens, enjoying the first clear day in what felt like ages. Keziah had carried Bryntelle for a time, cooing at the girl and playing with her until the baby began to fuss for her mother. But after handing the child back to Cresenne, she grew quiet, her eyes fixed stubbornly on the path before her. At first Cresenne thought nothing of it, but as the silence between them stretched on, she grew wary. For all the laughter and easy conversation she had shared with Keziah, Cresenne had never forgotten that she was, when all was said and done, a prisoner of the king and a renegade in the eyes of all around her.

The baby had fallen asleep, and Cresenne held her in the crook of her arm, gazing down at her and turning her body to keep the sun off Bryntelle's face.

"If you've something to say, you'd best get it over with," she told the minister. "Bryntelle will wake soon, and she'll need to eat."

"All right," Keziah said quietly. But for a long while she said nothing, each moment of silence heightening Cresenne's apprehension. "The king asked me to talk with you," the minister began at last, still staring at the ground. "I'm speaking as archminister now, rather than as your friend." She glanced over briefly. "And I am your friend, Cresenne. It's important to me that you know that."

"I understand." Really she didn't. Her stomach was balling itself into a fist, and she wasn't even certain why.

"Javan of Curgh arrives here tomorrow, and possibly Lathrop of Tremain as well."

"Yes, I've heard."

"In the next few days, the king expects Marston of Shanstead to arrive from Thorald, and also the duke of Heneagh. He's even hoping that some of those who have pledged themselves to Aindreas's cause, will come. Domnall perhaps, and Eardley."

"What's your point, Keziah?"

"The king trusts you, and he's been willing to allow you to remain free in the wake of your confession. But the dukes are not likely to be so generous. Javan in particular will want to know why Kearney grants these liberties to the woman responsible for his son's suffering."

She should have expected it. They thought her a traitor, she had admitted being party to an assassination. Cresenne supposed that she should have been grateful for the freedom she had enjoyed until now. Yet she couldn't help feeling that they had betrayed her. Keziah called herself Cresenne's friend. Kearney had promised that she had nothing to fear from him. And now they wished to lock her away, so as to avoid offending a handful of dukes.

"You must understand," the minister continued. "With Aindreas threatening rebellion, the king can't take for granted the support of any duke. Thorald and Curgh, the major houses, are especially important. If Galdasten—"

"So he wants me in the dungeon?"

"No!" Keziah sounded horrified. "He wouldn't do that!"

"Then what?"

"The prison tower. With the days growing warmer, it should be quite comfortable, and of course Bryntelle will remain with you. The dukes will be here for some time, but when they finally leave, you'll be free to leave the tower."

It was more than she should have expected, but still she trembled at the thought of being locked away. Was this how she would spend the rest of her life? A prisoner in the king's castle? They wouldn't execute her. She felt fairly certain of that. But they couldn't let her go free. Ever. Bryntelle would grow up with iron bars on her windows and guards at her doors. Or she would grow up in the home of another, knowing that the world considered her mother a traitor and murderer.

"What if I refuse?"

Keziah halted and faced her, her expression bleak. "Don't."

Cresenne took a breath, nodded. "I should return to my quarters, then. I don't have a lot, but I should probably gather the few things I carried with me from Aneira."

"Can I help?"

"No." She couldn't help but be moved by the stricken look on Keziah's face. Clearly this conversation had pained the archminister. "I'll be all right," she added, trying to smile.

"May I stop by later?"

"Why don't you walk me to the tower tomorrow? I'd be grateful."

The minister smiled, her relief palpable. "Of course."

Cresenne and Bryntelle passed the rest of the day in their chamber. It took Cresenne but a few moments to gather her possessions, but after speaking with the archminister, she had no desire to be seen by anyone else. Solitude promised to be something she would have in abundance for the rest of her days, but privacy was another matter. There were no bars on the door to this room, and though there were guards posted just outside in the corridor, she didn't have to see them or hear them or endure their stares. For one last day, she savored the basic comforts of the room she was in as she would have the luxuries of being queen.

She slept fitfully and had awakened early this morning, unable to get back to sleep after hearing the peal of the dawn bells. Keziah hadn't told her what time of day she was to be taken to the tower and Cresenne thought it best to be ready whenever the minister and Kearney's guards arrived. She sat with Bryntelle asleep in her lap. She had pulled the tapestry away from the chamber's lone narrow window so that she could watch the sky brighten and listen to the crack of wooden swords and the shouted commands of the king's swordmaster as he trained the royal army in the ward below.

A knock at the door startled her so that Bryntelle awoke and began to cry.

"Come in!" she called, cradling the girl to her chest.

The door opened, revealing the king. Cresenne stood and bowed as well as she could with the baby in her arms. "Your Majesty."

"Good morning," he said, sounding unsure of himself.

"Please come in, Your Majesty."

He hesitated still, eyeing Bryntelle. "Perhaps I should return another time."

"There's no need. She just woke up. She'll be fine in a moment."

The king nodded, then entered the room, still looking uneasy. "The archminister spoke with you?"

It seemed there was a hand squeezing her heart. "Yes, Your Majesty."

He had begun to walk a slow circle around the room, but he stopped now and faced her. "I am sorry. I want you to believe that."

"Of course, Your Majesty." She tried to keep her voice even, but failed.

"You doubt me." Before she could respond, Kearney shook his head. "I don't blame you, though it is the truth. I do this because the dukes will expect no less. As it is, I'll have to answer to those who will wonder why I haven't had you executed."

"I'm grateful for your mercy, Your Majesty."

"And I'm grateful for all you've told us. When the dukes leave the City of Kings, as they must eventually, you'll be free once again."

"Free to roam the castle, Your Majesty? Or free to leave, to take my child and make a life for myself elsewhere in the Forelands?"

Seeing him struggle with the question, she knew.

"We can offer you a fine life here in the castle, Cresenne. Your child will grow up with the sons and daughters of those who serve me. She will be taught with them, she'll enjoy all the freedoms and privileges they enjoy."

"But I'll remain a prisoner, not in the tower perhaps, but in the castle."

"Yes."

"And whenever your dukes journey here, and whenever you welcome nobles from the other kingdoms, I'll return to the tower."

"I would think so, yes."

"Forgive me, Your Majesty, but that isn't freedom."

"No," he said. "I don't suppose it is. Though you've helped us a good deal in the past turn, you're still guilty of crimes against this realm. You made some poor decisions long ago, and now you must live with the consequences of those choices."

I chose to fight for my people! What else could I have done? She knew she couldn't say this. She wasn't even certain she still believed it entirely. And yet she felt that she could barely contain her rage. Not for the first time, she wondered if she had been wrong to turn against the Weaver, even knowing that Kearney and Grinsa would have taken Bryntelle from her.

"There is another way," he said after a lengthy silence. "I can offer you asylum in Glyndwr, just as I did for Lord Tavis after his escape from Kentigern. You would be confined to the castle there, just as you are here, and there are far fewer children in Glyndwr Castle than there are in the royal palace; your daughter might be lonely at times. But Glyndwr receives few visitors, so you'd spend little or no time in the prison tower there."

He was offering her exile. He made it sound inviting, at least when compared with the life that awaited her here, but there could be no other name for it. Eibithar's king was asking her to choose between banishment and imprisonment.

"You don't have to decide today."

"How soon would I leave, were I to agree to this?"

"As soon as the dukes have departed. I'd send a sizable group of men with you—you and your daughter would be safe. The snows linger a bit longer in the highlands, but the journey wouldn't be difficult this time of year."

She looked down at Bryntelle. At least she wouldn't have to see her mother in a prison every second turn. "I'll consider it," she said.

"Good. Personally, I think it a far better place for you than Audun's Castle. That doesn't mean that you're not welcome to remain here. But I believe Glyndwr would be easier. For both of you."

And for you as well. "Thank you, Your Majesty."

He took a breath, his eyes falling on the baby. "She's well, I take it."

"Yes, thank you."

"I'm glad." He stood there a moment longer, then crossed to the door. "I'll leave you. Keziah should be along shortly to take you to . . . to where you'll be staying."

"Yes, Your Majesty. Thank you."

He left her, closing the door softly behind him. Once more Cresenne found herself thinking that there was more to him than she had thought. True, he had angered her—who was this Eandi king to question her choices?—but clearly he had been disturbed at having to imprison her, despite what she had done, despite the consternation his generosity was sure to evoke from his dukes. When she asked herself if the Weaver would do the same for an Eandi in her position, she had to admit that he wouldn't. No doubt others in the movement would take Kearney's compassion as a sign of weakness, but Cresenne saw it differently. It seemed to her that if all Eandi were like Kearney of Glyndwr, there might never have been a conspiracy.

Keziah came for them a short time after Cresenne's encounter with the king. Two soldiers stood with her in the corridor, but otherwise she was alone.

"I have a key to the tower chambers," she said. "The king and I thought it best that we involve as few others as possible."

Yet another kind gesture from the king and his minister. And in that moment an odd thought struck her: what must Tavis of Curgh have thought of all Kearney had done for her? He would have had every right to be offended, even appalled. But for some reason Cresenne doubted that he was. Forced to reconsider her opinion of the king and his archminister, she had begun to question her perceptions of all Eandi, as well as the Qirsi who served them.

The archminister glanced at the soldiers for a moment. "Stay here," she said. "We'll be out in a moment." Without waiting for a reply, she stepped into the chamber and shut the door.

Cresenne gave a puzzled look.

"I need to examine your things before I allow you to take them to the tower. Kearney made me promise that I would, at Gershon's urging no doubt." She smiled, as if at a great joke. "I didn't think you'd want the soldiers watching."

Cresenne made herself smile as well, but her stomach was knotting again. It seemed each time she decided that she had misjudged the Eandi, something new happened to make her question that decision.

"You have a weapon in here, don't you?"

She nodded. "Yes, a dagger."

"I'll have to take that of course."

"Of course."

"And you have gold?"

The minister was pretending to serve the movement. She would have been paid by the Weaver, just as Cresenne had.

"You know I do," she said, her voice flat. "You have to take that as well?"

"Not all the men who serve the king are immune to bribery. A prisoner with gold is halfway to freedom."

It was an old saying, but it did nothing to cushion the blow.

"I'll keep it for you," Keziah told her, misreading her silence as she pulled the blade and leather pouch from Cresenne's satchel. "The dagger as well. Both will be returned to you."

"You told me my imprisonment was for appearances only, that I would be freed after the dukes left."

"Yes, that's right."

"Then why is any of this necessary?"

Keziah straightened, her eyes meeting Cresenne's. "I also told you that the dukes would likely be here for some time. Imprisonment does strange things to people. Even knowing that you're to be released eventually, you may find yourself desperate to win that freedom before we can offer it."

Cresenne wanted to argue, but looking down at Bryntelle, she knew that the minister was right. It would take all of her strength just to endure a few days in the tower. What if the dukes remained in Audun's Castle for half a turn, or more?

"This is your life now, Cresenne. Freedom as you've known it is no longer yours. It pains me to say this, but it is the truth."

Cresenne felt tears on her face, but she didn't bother to wipe them away. Hadn't she said much the same thing to Kearney just moments before? Why would hearing it from this women affect her so?

"Surely you've thought of this yourself," Keziah said, sounding nearly as forlorn as Cresenne felt.

"Yes," she said through her tears. "And I've spoken with the king of going to Glyndwr, of accepting asylum there to escape the confines of this castle."

The minister appeared to consider the idea for a moment. Then she nodded. "I think you should."

Cresenne agreed. She knew in that moment that she and Bryntelle would be making the journey to the highlands as soon as the last of the dukes left the city of Kings. But she kept this to herself for now.

"I told the king I'd think about it," was all she said.

Keziah nodded a second time. "Good." For several moments she continued to watch Cresenne, holding the dagger in one hand and the pouch of gold in the other. "We should go," she said at last. "Javan arrives within the hour. Preparations have already begun."

Holding Bryntelle tightly in her arms, she followed the woman out of the room and then down the stone corridor as the two guards fell in step just behind her. It would have been a far shorter walk had Keziah crossed through the inner ward, but the minister kept to the shadowed hallways, sparing her the humiliation of walking past Gershon Trasker's soldiers; one more kindness among so many.

Despite their roundabout route, they reached the prison tower far too soon. Cresenne had hoped that the anticipation of her captivity would prove to be worse than the reality, but upon stepping foot in the sparse chamber, she began to tremble so violently that she had to sit for fear of collapsing. There was a single straw bed against the wall opposite the door, and she lowered herself onto it, still clutching her child. A simple wooden cradle had been placed by the bed, and a clean woolen blanket laid within it.

"Are you all right?" the minister asked.

"I will be," she managed, her voice shaking.

"Shall I stay?"

"No. We'll be fine."

Keziah started to say something, then stopped herself. "Very well. The next few days promise to be quite full, but I'll do my best to come see you."

"Thank you."

The minister stepped out of the chamber and one of the guards pushed the door shut, the clang of iron on iron making Cresenne jump. She heard him lock the door, his keys jangling like gold coins, but she didn't look up. She didn't want him seeing the tears on her cheeks.

"I don't want her mistreated in any way," the minister said, her voice barely audible through the small iron grate on the door. "If she needs anything, or if her child is in any distress at all, I want you to come to me immediately, no matter the time, day or night. Do you understand?"

"Yes, Archminister."

Even as Keziah's footsteps retreated down the stairway, Bryntelle awoke and began to cry.

"Are you hungry, little one?" she asked, swiping at her own tears and unbuttoning her shirt.

Lifting the baby to her breast, she happened to glance toward the door, only to find one of the guards leering at her through the iron bars.

Didn't you hear the archminister? she wanted to scream at the man. *Don't you think that mistreatment includes gaping at me as I feed my baby?* She glared at him, but he didn't look away. At last, she lay down on the bed, her back to the door, and fed Bryntelle that way.

She heard his boot scrape on the floor as he finally turned away, heard him mutter, "Qirsi whore."

After a time, Bryntelle tired of eating, but she remained awake, cooing at Cresenne and gazing around their new surroundings with wide eyes. Eventually Cresenne refastened the buttons on her shirt and sat up, casting a dark look toward the door. The guards were ignoring her.

From the city, she could hear horns blowing and people cheering. It seemed Javan of Curgh had arrived. She stood and carried the baby to the lone window, but could see nothing from there save the spires of Morna's Sanctuary, and the ridge of the Caerissan Steppe rising beyond the great walls of the city.

Still she remained by the window for a long while, listening as the cheers grew nearer and finally faded. Javan was in the castle.

Only a short time later, she heard voices from the corridor and then footsteps just outside her chamber. She had known the duke of Curgh would come to her eventually, but she didn't expect him so soon, nor had she thought that he would bring his son and wife, as well as Grinsa and a second Qirsi who must have been his first minister.

"This is her?" the duke asked, stopping before her door, his lean, bearded face framed in the small grate.

"Yes, my lord." Grinsa.

Javan stared at her, his eyes boring into hers. Bryntelle gave a small cry, and his gaze flicked to her for just an instant before returning to Cresenne.

She shifted Bryntelle to the other side, feeling uncomfortable under the duke's glare.

"I assumed you were helping the king so that you might avoid the gallows." Javan glanced at the baby again. "I see now that you had other reasons."

Cresenne could think of nothing to say.

"If it were up to me, you'd hang anyway. I suppose you know that."

He watched her, as if awaiting a response. She gave none. A part of her wished that Grinsa would say something in her defense, but she knew that he wouldn't. And they had the gall to call her a traitor.

"You have nothing to say to me?" the duke demanded.

"No, my lord. I don't."

His lip curled up, as if he were snarling at her. "Kearney is wrong to show you mercy. You're a beast and I pity your child."

She shouldn't have cared what this noble thought of her. She should have kept her silence. But his words stung, and Cresenne found that she couldn't just let him leave.

"I cost you the throne, my lord, and little more. If your ambitions had been the only casualties of my actions, I would feel no remorse at all. As it is, I feel that I owe an apology only to your son, and to the family of Lady Brienne."

"Now I truly feel sorry for the babe you hold in your arms. For if you believe that my son's imprisonment and torture cost me nothing, then you don't know what it is to be a parent."

He might as well have slapped her. She felt tears fall from her eyes, and a tightness in her chest that almost stopped her breathing. Before she could answer him, Javan stepped away from her door. A moment later another face replaced his. The duchess. She had golden hair and bright green eyes, and she looked at Cresenne with an odd mix of distaste and sympathy, as if she couldn't quite bring herself to hate the woman she saw, though she knew she should.

"I'm sorry," Cresenne whispered, tears now coursing freely down her cheeks.

The duchess offered no reply, and a moment later was gone.

Tavis appeared in the door's window next, his face truly a blend of his mother's and father's, though he was forever marked by the rage and grief of Kentigern's duke. Strangely, he seemed to hate her least of the three of them. He didn't say anything, however. And having just apologized to the boy's mother, Cresenne couldn't bring herself to say the words a second time. She and Tavis merely held each other's gaze until finally the boy stepped away from the door.

She heard someone speak in the corridor, but couldn't make out what was said. For a few moments it seemed that all of them were leaving the tower. Then another face loomed in the small opening. Grinsa's.

"The others have returned to the king's chamber," he said.

"You should have gone as well."

"I was concerned for you."

She gave a harsh laugh. "Of course you were."

"I should have known that you wouldn't believe me."

"Yes, you should have. You should have known it, and so you should have gone away with your Eandi friends."

He whirled away from the door, and once more she thought he would leave her. Instead he called for one of the guards.

Almost immediately, Cresenne heard the familiar sound of boot on stone.

"Open the door," Grinsa said.

The man did as he was told.

"Now go."

The guard stared at him briefly. "I don't take orders from you. And I'm not going to leave two white-hairs alone, not when one of them is a traitor."

"I'm the baby's father."

"All the more reason for me to stay."

"I'm also a friend of the king."

"So you claim."

Grinsa gritted his teeth. Then he turned to look at one of the torches, and an instant later it exploded like shattered glass, sending embers and fragments of wood in all directions.

"I could do the same to this door any time I wish. I could also do it to your sword. Or your skull. If I wanted to help her escape, I could do so any time I wished, and there would be nothing you and your friends could do to stop me. But that's not my intention. Now leave us."

The guard looked frightened, but still he hesitated.

"Leave!"

At last, the man hurried to the tower stairs, and with one last backward glance, started down them to the floor below.

The gleaner entered the chamber.

"I don't want you here," Cresenne said. "I have nothing to say to you."

"What is it you think I've done to you, Cresenne? I'm the one who's been wronged, not you. You lied to me. You used me to get information about Tavis and his gleaning. You sent an assassin to kill me. All I did was love you."

"That's not true, and you know it. We both lied. I didn't tell you I was with the movement, and you didn't tell me you were a Weaver."

He cast a quick look toward the door, as if fearing that one of the guards had heard. But no one was there.

"You can't possibly equate the two. I kept my powers hidden to protect myself and . . . and others as well. I even wanted to protect you. That's how much I cared for you. I thought that there was a chance we might remain together forever. And you know as well as I what the Eandi do to the wives of Weavers."

"And still you serve them."

"I serve no one. I seek only to prevent war."

She laughed. "You really believe that, don't you? With one breath you speak of saving yourself and the people you love from Eandi executioners, and in the next you claim to be your own master. You're a fool, Grinsa."

He looked as though he might say more, but then he heaved a sigh, shaking his head. "Yes," he said. "I suppose I am."

Without waiting for her reply, he turned and stepped from the chamber, pulling the door closed behind him.

Bryntelle started at the sound, then began to cry.

"Grinsa, wait."

Cresenne crossed to the door, fearing that he would leave the corridor. But reaching the grate, she saw that he was standing at the entrance to the stairway, looking back at her, his face pale in what remained of the torchlight.

She wasn't certain what she wanted to say to him. She just knew that she didn't want him to go after all. At least not like this.

"When I told you before that I didn't love you, that I'd never loved you . . ." She looked away. "That wasn't true."

"I know," he said, and left her.

The rest of her day seemed to stretch on for an eternity. Mercifully, no one else came to see her, her solitude interrupted only by the arrival of her evening meal as the sky outside her window began to darken. But even then, too sickened by her encounters with Javan and the gleaner to eat, she merely sat on the bed, feeding Bryntelle when the child cried, and waiting for the day to end so that she could just sleep.

Still, when sleep finally came, it caught her unaware, like an army advancing through a mist-laden wood. One moment she was sitting beside Bryntelle on the bed. The next she was on the broad plain she had come to know so well, the Weaver before her, framed by the harsh white sun he always conjured for these dreams, his hair looking as black as the sky and even more wild than usual.

Cresenne didn't have any time to feel fright or surprise, or to think that this would be the dream of her death, the one she had dreaded for so long. She merely opened her eyes to the unfathomable sky, the brilliant light, the Weaver, and was staggered by a blow to the temple.

"*You whore!*" the Weaver roared, striking her again, so that she fell to the ground.

She knew she was going to die, that somehow he had learned of her betrayal. But all she could think as she began to weep was that it wasn't right for so many people to be calling her whore.

"*Did you think I wouldn't know? Did you think you could hide from me?*"

Somehow she was hoisted roughly to her feet, though the Weaver hadn't moved. An instant later he struck her a third time, the invisible fist landing on her cheek. She crumpled to the grass once more, her vision blurring and a sound like crashing waves buffeting her mind.

"It's the gleaner, isn't it?"

She lay still, her eyes closed, waiting for the pain to recede.

"*Tell me!*" This time he didn't bother to lift her. Instead, it seemed to be the hard toe of his boot gouging viciously into her side, causing her to gasp and then retch.

"Is he there with you? Is he in Audun's Castle? Is he in your bed?"

He kicked her again. The stomach. Or did he? He hadn't moved. It was so hard to keep her thoughts clear.

An instant later she was thrust to her feet again, like a child's doll.

"He is there, isn't he?"

She should have answered him. She was going to die anyway. Why not give him what he wanted and be done with it? It was only Grinsa he wanted. Grinsa, whom she hated.

Except that she didn't, couldn't. As much as she wanted to despise the gleaner, to curse his name and rid herself of him forever, she couldn't bring herself to tell the Weaver what he already seemed to know. It was a useless act of defiance and she was a fool. He would hurt her until she told him, though he had guessed it already. He wanted to hurt her before ending her life, and this would serve well as his excuse.

But more than that, she thought that she could hear Bryntelle crying. She couldn't say for certain whether it was a trick of her mind, or truly her child wailing in the prison tower of Audun's Castle, the sound reaching across the boundary between her dream and the waking world. It made little difference. What mattered was that Cresenne was going to die, leaving Bryntelle no one in the world but the gleaner. She couldn't betray Grinsa to the Weaver without making an orphan of their daughter. And that she refused to do.

Something touched her face in a strange sort of caress. It took a moment for the pain to reach her, but then abruptly she was in agony. She clutched at her cheek, recoiled at what she felt. Staring at her hands, she saw blood. So much blood. He slashed her a second time, along her jaw.

"You protect him? You dare choose him over me?"

Another gash opened on her brow, blood pouring into her eyes, blinding her, stinging like lye.

A sob escaped her, and she fell back to the ground, not from a blow, but simply from the weight of all he had done to her.

"This is but the beginning," he said with relish. "This will be the longest night of your life, and the last. You betrayed me. You betray me even now, protecting the gleaner. But I'll break you before you die. And I'll find a way to make an example of you, so that any others who might turn against me will know how you suffered and will think better of it."

Bryntelle's crying grew louder in her mind, and Cresenne did all she could to shelter the sound from the Weaver. She didn't know if he could reach the baby from wherever he was—Bryntelle hadn't come into her power yet, of course, and Cresenne didn't know if a child so young could dream lucidly. But she wasn't taking any chances.

Then another thought. The sound of her child was a message of sorts. It was telling her something. If only she could think of what it was.

Before she could consider it further, something crashed down on her hand. The Weaver's heel. A hammer. A stone. She felt bone shatter, screamed out in pain.

A hand touched the top of her head and she flinched away.

"It's all right," Grinsa's voice whispered. "It's me. You need to wake up, Cresenne. Open your eyes and end this."

"I can't."

"Whose voice is that?" the Weaver asked.

"Wake up, Cresenne. Now. Bryntelle needs you."

"I see you!" the Weaver said, his voice a mix of fear and triumph. "I see you, Grinsa jal Arriet."

Cresenne looked up at the gleaner, his face bathed in the Weaver's light. His lips were pressed thin, the look in his eyes hard and dangerous. He wasn't looking at her, but rather at the wild-haired figure standing before them.

"Wake up, Cresenne," he said again, his gaze never straying from the Weaver.

Cresenne knew she should do what he said, but she didn't know how. All she could do was stare at Grinsa, and listen to the Weaver's threats.

"I see you," the Weaver repeated once more. "I know you. I can reach you now."

Grinsa bared his teeth in a baleful grin. "I'll be waiting for you. But just to make matters even . . ."

He raised his hand and brilliant flame leaped from his palm, golden as early morning sunlight and a match for the Weaver's white radiance.

Cresenne heard the Weaver cry out, heard Grinsa say, "Now we know you, too."

She turned to look at the man who had walked in her dreams for so long, and for just an instant caught sight of him. He was tall, lean, muscular. His jaw was square, his eyes the color of gold rounds, and his hair like the mane of some great white lion. She had time to think that he looked just as a Qirsi king should, and then he was gone.

She was in her chamber again, the prison tower of Kearney's castle. Keziah was there, holding Bryntelle in her arms, her eyes wide and her face damp with tears. Kearney was there as well, and Gershon Trasker. Cresenne knew that she should have been trying to take Bryntelle. Her baby was crying. But all she could do was lie on her bed, marveling at the fact that she was still alive.

Grinsa cupped her face in a tender hand—his were the most gentle hands she had ever known—and forced her to meet his gaze.

"Where did he hurt you?" the gleaner asked, looking like he might cry as well.

"My face. My hand." She moved her uninjured hand to the place on her side where the Weaver had kicked her. "Here."

Grinsa nodded. "I'll heal you. You're going to be all right."

She wanted to hold Bryntelle. And sleep. She needed to sleep. She was so very tired. But instead she looked at the gleaner and shook her head.

"Healing me will do no good. Don't you see, Grinsa? He's going to kill me. He failed tonight, but it's just a matter of time. He can reach me anywhere."

"We'll find a way to protect you."

She shook her head, though it hurt to move. "There is no way. You should take Bryntelle and leave here. Now. Tonight. You heard what he said. He knows you now. He'll find you. He'll find her."

"Bryntelle isn't going anywhere without you. And the Weaver isn't going to find me until I decide the time is right."

She started to argue, but he touched a hand to her bloodied brow and said a single word, "Sleep."

Helpless, in pain, fearing for her life and her child, she fell back into darkness.

Chapter
Nineteen

U nlike the wounds on Tavis's face that had been allowed to fester in Kentigern's dungeon for several days before they could be healed, Cresenne's gashes were clean and easily mended. Dark lines would remain on her face for several turns, but eventually they would fade to white and vanish almost entirely. The same could be said of the bruises on her face and body. Her hand, however, proved more difficult. It took Grinsa some time to ease her pain and much of the night to set the bones properly and begin the healing. Cresenne awoke once while he was setting the bones, whimpering like a child, tears rolling slowly down her face. Not wishing to expend any more of his strength than was necessary, the gleaner called for the herbmaster, who prepared for her a powerful sleeping tonic of sweetwort and hemlock. When she had fallen asleep once more, Grinsa resumed his efforts, finally finishing as the first hint of daylight touched the eastern sky. Sitting back in his chair, he instructed the castle's healers to bind the hand with a wrap of dampened bandages and pulped comfrey root.

"You've much skill as a healer," the master healer said, looking approvingly at Cresenne's hand and face. "Is it your profession?"

Grinsa shook his head, rubbing his eyes with a weary hand. "No, though it seems I've done quite a bit of it in the past few turns."

"Well, if you grow tired of whatever it is you do now, come and speak with me. I can always use men with such talent."

"My thanks, sir."

"A word please, gleaner."

Grinsa opened his eyes once more. Kearney and Keziah had remained with him throughout the night, helping when they could and watching as he worked his magic. Now, however, the king fixed him with an icy glare.

"Your Majesty?"

"In my chambers." He glanced at Keziah. "I'd like you there as well, Archminister."

Keziah and Grinsa shared a quick glance. Keziah, with Grinsa's approval, gave Bryntelle to one of the older serving woman, who grinned at the babe and began to coo at her. Then the two Qirsi followed the king from Cresenne's quarters, through the dark corridors, and finally into his presence chamber.

"What happened to her?" the king demanded, as Keziah closed the door. "She was attacked in my castle. I want to know who is responsible."

"She was attacked," Grinsa said slowly, "but not as you think."

"Damn you, gleaner! I don't want riddles! Answer me: who did this?"

"When Cresenne confessed her crimes against the land, she spoke to you of a Weaver who leads the Qirsi conspiracy."

Kearney's eyes widened. "He did this? He's here?"

"No, he's not here. But he is the one who hurt Cresenne."

"How is that possible?"

Grinsa took a breath. He knew where this conversation would lead, but there seemed nothing he could do about that now. The king had been more than merciful in his dealings with Cresenne, as well as with Tavis and Grinsa. He deserved honest answers.

"Do you know what a Weaver does, Your Majesty?"

"A Weaver has the ability to bind together the powers of many Qirsi, to wield their magic as a single weapon."

Grinsa nodded. It was more than most Eandi understood. "Yes. And in order to do that, a Weaver must have the ability to read the thoughts of others, to . . . enter their minds and communicate with them without speaking. We Qirsi wield and control our magic with thought, and so a Weaver must have access to the thoughts of those whose power he seeks to weave. With training, a Weaver can even enter the thoughts of others from a great distance. This is most readily accomplished when the Qirsi is sleeping."

"He enters their dreams."

"Precisely."

It took Kearney a moment. "You mean to say the Weaver has been communicating with her all this time?"

"Not necessarily. But he has had the ability to do so."

The king shook his head. "Demons and fire!" he muttered. "How does one fight such an enemy?" He stared at Grinsa again. "Entering her dreams is one thing. But that doesn't explain her injuries."

"I assure you, Your Majesty, it does. To be honest, I don't know how he did this. Since he's probably communicating with Cresenne from a great distance, I would have thought that he could only attack her with those powers she possesses, bending her mind so that she would wield her magic against herself. But Cresenne has only gleaning, fire, and healing magic. She would have needed shaping power to do such things to herself."

"Maybe not," Keziah said. "Healing might do it."

Grinsa narrowed his eyes. "Healing?"

"A healer has the power to shape flesh and bone, to make the body mend itself. Perhaps the Weaver found a way to corrupt that power, to make it wound rather than heal."

He rubbed a hand over his mouth. "I hadn't even thought of that."

His sister smiled. "Of course not. That's not how your mind works."

"You seem to know a good deal about Weavers, gleaner," the king said, drawing their gazes again. "Why is that?"

Keziah cast a quick look at Grinsa. "Your Majesty—"

Kearney raised a single finger, silencing her. "I watched you in the prison tower. You spoke to Cresenne once or twice before she awoke, but mostly you sat silently, holding her. I didn't think much of it at the time, but now it occurs to me that you could have been communicating with her all that time, sharing her thoughts." He had been pacing the floor of his chamber and now he stopped in front of Grinsa. "I also noticed that you put her to sleep with a word, or rather, with a thought."

"Yes, Your Majesty."

"So I'll ask you again. How is it that you know so much about Weavers?"

He could count on one hand the number of people who knew the extent of his powers. Keziah; Tavis; Fotir jal Salene, Curgh's first minister, who helped Grinsa free Tavis from the dungeon of Kentigern Castle; and now Cresenne, as well. Shurik jal Marcine had known, but Grinsa had seen to it that the traitorous minister died in Mertesse, though at great cost to Tavis. Others had known once—his wife, and the Qirsi master who trained him in the use of his magic—but they, too, were dead now. His parents never knew. He had gone to great lengths to guard his secret, to avoid endangering his own life and Keziah's. And now he found that he had little choice but to reveal the truth to Eibithar's king, the one man in all the realm who had the authority to put him to death, as all known Weavers in the Forelands had been put to death over the past nine hundred years.

"It's just as you suspect, Your Majesty," he said, his eyes meeting those of the king. "I know of Weavers because I am one myself."

"Oh, Grinsa," Keziah said, her voice breaking.

Kearney glared at her. "I take it you've known all along."

"She has, Your Majesty. Keziah is my sister."

He blinked, looked at the minister. "Your sister?"

"She said nothing to you about my powers because I asked her not to, and because under Eandi law, not only are all Weavers to be put to death but their families as well."

Kearney's eyes never strayed from Keziah's face. "Damn," he whispered.

"You have a choice to make, Your Majesty. If you follow Eandi law, you must have me executed along with your archminister, Cresenne, and our child. If you listen to your heart, however, I think you'll realize how cruel and arbitrary your laws are on this matter."

"My heart has nothing to do with it. You've just told me of a man who can walk in the dreams of others, who can reach out across the land and use healing power to tear gashes in a woman's face, who can turn an army of Qirsi into a weapon so powerful I can scarcely comprehend it." He shook his head and stepped behind his writing table, as if eager to place something substantial between the gleaner and himself. "If you wish to convince me that Weavers are not to be feared, you've failed. If anything, I have more sympathy now for the practices begun by our forebears."

"You can't mean that," Keziah said, looking appalled.

"I do."

"Grinsa is nothing like the Weaver who did this to Cresenne. The Weaver is driven by spite and envy and hatred. He despises the Eandi with a passion that borders on frenzy. Grinsa could never be like that."

The king narrowed his eyes. "How is it that you know so much about this other Weaver?"

Grinsa wondered if his sister would tell Kearney of her efforts to learn about the conspiracy, about her dreams of the Weaver. This, it seemed, was a day for revealing hard truths, and though she had not borne her secret for as long as Grinsa had borne his, hers was no less burdensome. She appeared to consider this, but only for an instant. Then her expression hardened, and she stared back at her king.

"One need only look at what this man has done—not only to Cresenne but also to Tavis, to Lady Brienne, and to countless others—to know that he has little in common with my brother. If you can't see this as well, Your Majesty, then I weep for Eibithar."

Kearney's face reddened, and Grinsa feared that Keziah had pushed him too far. A moment dragged by in silence, and another.

At last the king gave a small nod. "You make a good point, Archminister. But you must realize as well that I'm bound by the laws of the land. I can no more embrace a Weaver as my ally than I can the Aneiran king."

"And you must realize, Your Majesty," Grinsa said, "that in order to defeat the conspiracy you may have to do both. The realms of the Forelands can't stand against this enemy without uniting, and you would do well to consider the advantages of having a Weaver by your side in the coming conflict."

"Come now, Grinsa. The people of the Forelands defeated a Qirsi army led by several Weavers nine centuries ago. This new Weaver may be clever, but he's only one man."

"He's one man with followers in every corner of the land, Your Majesty. And he's already succeeded in dividing kingdoms against themselves, in pushing neighboring realms to the brink of war."

Kearney appeared to falter, his doubts written on his face. "Do you have any idea who he is?"

"No. But I know what he looks like now."

Keziah gripped his arm. "You saw him? You didn't tell me that."

"It was just a glimpse, enough to give me an impression of the man. Nothing more. Really, I'm no closer to knowing his name or his whereabouts than I was before. But he knows that I saw him, and clearly he didn't want that."

"Who else knows that you're a Weaver?" the king asked, drawing Grinsa's gaze once more.

"Keziah, Tavis, Cresenne, and one other who I won't name. I assure you, though, this person can be trusted."

Kearney nodded. "I see." He sat, leaning back in his chair and passing a hand through his silver hair. "I have no desire to see you executed, Grinsa. I hope you know that."

"I do, Your Majesty."

"Truth be told, I would feel better going to war against a Weaver with you by my side."

"My sword and my magic are yours, to use as you will."

"I thank you for that. But you understand that others won't be so welcoming. There is more fear of the Qirsi in the courts today than I've ever seen—I daresay matters are worse now than they've been in centuries. If the dukes learn that you're a Weaver, they'll demand that I move against you. My hold on the crown is already precarious. I'd have no choice but to heed their wishes."

"Neither of us wants that, Your Majesty. I don't want you as an enemy, and I assure you, you don't want me as one either."

Kearney eyed him as a soldier might study his next opponent in a battle tournament. "Are you threatening me, gleaner?"

"Not at all. But I'm not certain you appreciate fully the power wielded by a Weaver. It's not just that we can wield the magic of others as if it were our own. We're far more powerful in our own right than are other Qirsi. Your dungeon couldn't hold me, and your executioner wouldn't survive his attempt to carry out my sentence. I offer this not as a threat or a boast but simply as a statement of fact."

"Where does that leave us?"

"I'd say that lies mostly with you, Your Majesty. You asked me how I had come to understand the Weaver so well. I answered truthfully. I've lived my entire life without revealing the extent of my powers to the wrong person. And now I must ask you: is my secret safe, or must I leave here, taking Keziah, Cresenne, and my child with me?"

"I've no intention of betraying your confidence. As I've already said, it would greatly complicate matters for me." He glanced at Keziah, his expression softening for just an instant. "It would also deny me the services of a minister I value more than I can say."

Seeing how his sister blushed, Grinsa allowed himself a small smile. "Then I'd say our discussion is over."

"Not quite. If at some point others learn of . . . what you are, we'll have to revisit this matter. The laws of the land are clear."

"I understand."

"Very well," the king said, standing. "I expect a number of nobles to arrive here today. Javan was but the first. If you'll excuse me, I have much to do."

Grinsa bowed. "Of course, Your Majesty." He started to turn away.

"Gleaner," the king said, stopping him.

Grinsa faced Kearney once more.

"Your daughter . . . will she be a Weaver as well?"

"It's far too early to say, Your Majesty. But her chances are better than those of most Qirsi children."

"Because you're a Weaver."

"Yes, and because her mother is powerful as well."

"And yet you fight to preserve our courts, though they would condemn her to a life of secrecy and fear. Why?"

"Because Eibithar is my home. And because the alternative is a kingdom ruled by the Weaver, and I've seen what kind of man he is." With that he left. Cresenne would not be awake again for hours, and though he knew he was being foolish, that the Weaver couldn't reach them in Audun's Castle, at least not yet, he didn't want Bryntelle to be out of his sight for too long.

For some time after Grinsa left, Kearney simply stood in the middle of his presence chamber, saying nothing. Keziah knew that he had told her brother the truth. With Eibithar's nobles converging on the City of Kings, he did have much to do. But it seemed he could only stare at the door, struggling with his thoughts and his fears.

"You should have told me," he said at last. "I know we don't speak much anymore, but there was a time when we told each other everything." He glanced at her. "Or so I thought."

"It wasn't my secret to tell," she said.

"No, I don't suppose it was." He paused, then, "Did you keep much else from me?"

"No, just this."

"And now?"

She shivered, crossing her arms over her chest. "Your Majesty?"

"What are you keeping from me now?"

For a second time this morning, Keziah had the opportunity to tell Kearney of her attempts to win the Weaver's trust. She had longed to do just that for several turns, since the first night she conceived her plan. In trying to convince those around them that she had been embittered by the end of their love, that she could be turned to the Weaver's cause, she had done terrible damage to what remained of their friendship. She had very nearly succeeded in having herself banished from the castle. Now she could tell him why she had done it. She could make him see that she hadn't meant to hurt him, that she had done all this for him and his kingdom. But once more, she couldn't bring herself to speak the words.

Watching Cresenne writhe in her sleep, hearing her cry out, seeing the gashes open on her face as if she were being attacked by some unseen taloned demon from the Underrealm, Keziah had felt fear of the Weaver grip her heart. But she had also felt rage. The Weaver claimed to love his people; he claimed as his goal a glorious future for all Qirsi and their children. Yet he tortured this woman as her babe lay beside her, crying in the darkness. Keziah wanted to destroy him. And if she admitted to Kearney that she was trying to do just that, despite the danger to herself and his kingdom, he would find some way to stop her. So instead she lied. Again, though it pained her to do so.

"I'm keeping nothing from you, Your Majesty. I swear it."

Even as she spoke the words, however, Keziah was struck at last by the full import of what had happened the night before. She felt her stomach heave and took a step forward, bracing herself on the table to keep from falling to her knees.

Kearney was by her side instantly, an arm around her shoulders, and a look of deepest concern in his green eyes. "Are you all right?"

She barely managed to weather another wave of nausea. "I will be," she whispered. "Just weary. I think the night has finally caught up with me."

"You should sleep."

"No, not with the dukes coming."

Kearney shook his head. "It's only Shanstead and Tremain arriving today. Perhaps Domnall as well. Wenda can stand for you, or Dyre."

"I'll be fine. I just need to . . . I'll get some air, perhaps have something to eat." Actually she didn't think she could keep any food down. "I'll be fine," she said again.

"You're certain?"

She nodded, forcing herself to stand straight. Her head spun, but she managed a smile and the king stepped away from her. "When do you expect Marston?"

"By midday," he said. "Are you sure you're all right?"

"Yes. Thank you, Your Majesty." She stepped slowly to the door, squeezing her eyes shut against the dizziness and biting back the bile rising in her throat.

The air in the corridor was cooler, which helped a bit. She smiled her way past the guards and hurried to find Grinsa.

She found him in the corridor that ran between the prison tower and the stables, walking slowly with Bryntelle in his arms, singing to her in a low voice.

He turned at her approach, smiling a greeting.

"I've almost gotten her to fall asleep," he whispered.

"We have to talk."

His smile vanished. "What's happened now?"

She glanced up and down the hallway to be certain that they were alone. "Have you stopped to wonder what the Weaver will do when he realizes that you're both here, with me?"

Clearly he hadn't. He just stared at her. But a moment later, Bryntelle began to cry, as if she sensed his alarm.

"He'll order me to kill you both."

Grinsa shook his head. "No, he won't. He knows better than to send you after me. He'll have you kill Cresenne, perhaps Bryntelle also, though that would complicate things greatly." He twisted his mouth, gazing down the corridor as if he could see the Weaver standing in the shadows. "He'll tell you to befriend me," he said after a brief pause. "He'll want you to win my trust so that you can find out where I'm going next. He can't have both of us killed here, and given how much she knows about him and his movement, he'll still consider Cresenne the greater threat."

Keziah was trembling now. The nausea had passed, though her stomach felt hard and cold, like a stone on the moors. "So what do I do? If I don't kill Cresenne, he'll know that I've been lying to him. And if he speaks to me of arranging your murder, I may not be able to keep from him that you're my brother."

"You have to, Kezi."

"You make it all sound as if it's just that easy."

"I know it's not. But you'll have to find a way. The hardest part will be finding a way to maintain his trust without killing Cresenne. She'll be guarded, of course, even more heavily now that he's made one attempt on her life. Finding an opportunity to get close enough to kill her will be difficult. That should allow you to put him off for several days. Perhaps more. In the meantime, we'll have to think of some way to keep both of you alive."

"And what about you?"

"As I said, he won't have you kill me. He knows for certain now that I'm a Weaver. If I'm right, and he does want you to win my confidence, you'll do just that. And when the time comes, you can tell him precisely where I'm going. You won't have to lie, at least not about that."

Keziah desperately wanted to believe him. But she couldn't keep the image of Cresenne's agony from her mind. She couldn't forget the sight of Paegar, Kearney's traitorous minister, lying dead in his chamber, his head resting in a pool of blood. That had been the Weaver's doing as well. She felt certain of it. Just as she was certain that whatever Paegar had done to earn his death paled next to her own deception. And she couldn't help wondering how the Weaver would exact his vengeance on her.

When Tavis awoke midway through the morning, Grinsa still had not returned to the chamber he and the young lord shared. The boy knew that there had been something wrong with Cresenne—the guard who came to find the gleaner had told them that much—but he could be certain of nothing more. And for the moment at least, he didn't care. Out of respect for the gleaner, he would spare the Qirsi woman the tongue lashing his father had given her, and the icy indifference shown by his mother. But after what she had done to him, he wasn't about to run to her offering comfort. Besides, there was another he wished to see.

His parents had arrived from Curgh the previous day with a small contingent of soldiers and Hagan MarCullet, his father's swordmaster. The king wished to speak of the Qirsi conspiracy and how best to defeat it, and Tavis's father wouldn't have engaged in such a discussion without Hagan by his side. And knowing that Tavis would be in Audun's Castle, Hagan wouldn't have made the journey from the north coast without Xaver, his son, who also was Tavis's pledged liege man.

The two young friends had seen each other the day before, though only briefly. Almost immediately upon their arrival in the City of Kings, Javan insisted on seeing Cresenne, and Tavis, not yet ready to face Xaver and the questions he knew the young man would ask, had followed obediently. There had been a feast the previous night, the first of many, no doubt, as Eibithar's dukes converged on the castle, but again, Tavis managed to avoid his friend, sitting between his mother and father and enduring their questions as best he could. Did you find the assassin? Yes, but he slipped away. Has the gleaner been kind to you? Very. You've proved your innocence; are you ready to come home with us? No, not yet.

It was easier with his parents. They feared pushing him too hard, challenging his easy answers. Xaver would be different, his questions more difficult, his ability to hear the truth behind Tavis's words more finely honed. Even after all this time, no one knew him as Xaver did, though Grinsa came close.

He would have liked to put off this encounter for several more days, but he knew that he wouldn't. It wasn't just that he didn't wish to hurt his friend. Though he feared Xaver's questions, he also longed for the young man's companionship. Despite all they had been through, all that Tavis had done to hurt him, Xaver remained his most valued friend. So he searched the castle, soon finding Xaver at the edge of the inner courtyard, watching Gershon Trasker work the royal guard.

He wasn't certain that Xaver saw him approach—the young man never turned his gaze from the soldiers—and Tavis stopped a few strides from him, uncertain as to what to say.

"I didn't think you wanted to see me." Xaver glanced at him for just a moment, as if looking for changes in his appearance.

"Of course I do."

The ghost of a smile touched his lips, and a soft wind stirred his light curls. He looked just as Tavis remembered. Broader in the shoulders perhaps, his face a bit more square. But it was still Xaver. Youthful and handsome and a little bit sad, just as he had been every day since his mother's death nearly nine years before.

"Then why have you been avoiding me?"

Tavis looked away, his gaze traveling the courtyard, seeking a safe place to land and settling at last on Gershon. "Who says I've been avoiding you?" But he couldn't help grinning.

"You look . . . you look well, Tavis."

He let out a small laugh. "No, I don't. I'll never look well again. Aindreas saw to that."

"I'm not talking about the scars. You seem older, like you have purpose, like maybe you've found peace."

Tavis shook his head. "I haven't. I had the assassin, Xaver. I had my blade at his throat, and I let him go."

Xaver gaped at him. "Why?"

"Grinsa made me do it. The assassin had been hired to kill a member of the conspiracy—Aindreas's former first minister, actually. If the assassin hadn't killed him, Grinsa would have had to, at considerable risk to both of us."

"I'm not sure I understand," his friend said, frowning.

"It doesn't matter. I had him and I let him go. The rest isn't important."

They stood in silence for a moment, watching the soldiers, Gershon's commands echoing off the castle walls.

"You've managed to prove to the king that you're innocent of Brienne's murder," Xaver said, as if searching for any good tidings. "Surely that's brought you some peace."

"I think Kearney has believed in my innocence for some time now. But if we can convince the other dukes—or at least most of them—I'd be pleased."

"That's all? Just pleased?"

Tavis looked away again. "I don't expect more than that anymore."

Xaver said nothing.

"You think I pity myself too much."

His friend hesitated. "I think you've been through a terrible ordeal."

"It's not over."

"It can be, if you only allow it."

"You want me to surrender? Do you think I can just return to Curgh and resume my life there, knowing that Brienne's killer still walks the land?"

"The conspiracy killed her, Tavis. You know that as well as anyone. The man you're after is a hired blade and nothing more. You said yourself that he killed Aindreas's minister. He doesn't care about the conspiracy or the courts. He cares only for gold."

"You sound like Grinsa."

"Then maybe it's time you started listening."

"The assassin killed Brienne, and I've sworn to avenge her."

"Sworn to who?" Xaver demanded, his voice rising.

"To myself."

Xaver seemed to know better than to question this. "So where will you go?" he asked, his voice dropping once more.

"I don't know. Something happened to Cresenne last night. At this point I might not be able to get Grinsa to go anywhere."

His friend gave a puzzled look. "Who's Cresenne?"

It had been a long time since they last spoke. Too long. Tavis told Xaver what little he understood of Grinsa's love affair with Cresenne, and explained as well the woman's role in Brienne's death.

"I don't know if he still loves her," he said. "I suppose he does. But I'm certain that he won't leave here unless he's convinced that Cresenne and their baby are both safe."

Another long silence, which was broken at last by something Tavis never would have expected.

Xaver cleared his throat, then said, "I'll go with you if the gleaner can't."

It was more than Tavis could have asked; more, in fact, than he was willing to accept. But still, he was moved beyond words by the offer. His gaze fell to the dark thin scar on Xaver's right forearm, a scar Tavis himself had given the boy in a drunken rage.

"Your father would have my head, Stinger."

"He'd have both our heads, but in the end he'd understand."

"I'm grateful. Truly I am. But I can't let you do this."

"I'm your liege man—I've sworn my life to you. Under the customs governing such things, I'm not sure that you can refuse me."

Tavis smiled. "And yet, I have. You said yourself the first time we spoke of my desire for vengeance that I was mad to go after the man. You said he'd kill me. Do you really think that two boys would fare any better against him than one?"

"I'd wager that I'm as good with a blade as the gleaner," Xaver shot back, sounding young.

"I have no doubt that you are. But Grinsa is more than just a gleaner."

"What do you mean? He has other powers?"

"Yes. Mists and winds, shaping, healing." He didn't dare tell his friend more than that. As it was, he had probably said more than Grinsa would have liked, though he wasn't telling Xaver any more than the gleaner himself had revealed during their escape from Solkara several turns back, and during Cresenne's difficult labor in Glyndwr.

Xaver lowered his gaze, chewing his lip as he so often did. After some time he nodded, as if convinced at last that Grinsa was a worthy travel companion for Tavis.

"How's your arm, Stinger?"

Xaver put his hand to the scar, rubbing it slowly, as if the question itself had rekindled his pain. "It's fine. I rarely even think about it anymore."

Tavis wasn't certain he believed that, but it wasn't a matter he wished to pursue.

"And I trust my father's treating you well?"

"Yes, very."

Tavis wanted to ask more, but he didn't have to. It seemed that his friend still knew him better than anyone else.

"He misses you, Tavis. He doesn't say so, but I can tell. Whenever he asks my father to join him for a meal or a ride, he asks me as well. It's as if having me with him is the next best thing to having you."

The young lord wanted to believe this, but he and his father had been at odds for too many years. "He probably just knows that your father wants you there. After Kentigern, Hagan hardly let you out of sight."

Xaver smiled at the memory. Hagan MarCullet had been in Curgh when Brienne died, and had ridden with the duchess to face Aindreas's army, knowing that if Curgh's army was defeated, Xaver, Javan, and Fotir would probably be executed.

"That's true," he admitted. "But the duke isn't doing all this for my father. He often asks me if I've had word from you, or if I have any idea of where in the Forelands you might be."

Tavis could think of a thousand reasons for this—maybe it was a way for his father to make conversation with Xaver; perhaps he sought information to mollify Tavis's mother, who would have asked similar questions of the duke with some frequency; or perhaps he was merely curious. "Does he speak much of the crown?" he asked, eager to change the subject.

"Tavis—"

"It's all right, Stinger. I'm just asking. I expect he wishes every day that he were king."

"He's never said anything about it in front of me, not that he would. But I think you're wrong about him, Tavis. He always speaks well of Kearney, of the need to protect Glyndwr's hold on the throne. I think he's made peace with all that happened in Kentigern."

"You didn't see the way he looked at Cresenne yesterday."

Xaver shrugged. "So he blames her, and the conspiracy. But that doesn't mean that he blames you as well. You were as much a victim of her actions as he. More, really. I'm amazed that you don't hate her."

"Who says I don't?"

"You've hardly spoken of her, except to tell me what she did and that she was Grinsa's lover."

"That's all that matters now," Tavis said, surprised by how little rage he felt. "Even if I did hate her, even if I wanted to exact a measure of revenge, I couldn't. Grinsa wouldn't allow it." He kicked at the grass, squinting in the early morning sun. "To be honest, I can't bring myself to be angry with her. I know that she hired the man who killed Brienne, but I also know that she's confessed her crimes to the king. Without her, Kearney would still have his doubts about my innocence. For all I know, my father would as well."

Xaver started to object, but Tavis raised a hand stopping him. "Forget I said it. The point is, she's trying to mend some of the damage she's done. I'm grateful to her."

"Well, you're more forgiving than I would be."

"If Qirsi and Eandi can't forgive each other, we're doomed," he said, surprising himself a second time. It was something the gleaner might have told him.

Xaver looked at him for a long time, a slight smile on his lips. "You have changed, Tavis. I can see it. I think you'll make a fine duke someday."

He merely nodded. The young lord had been thinking for some time now that his life was on an unknown path, one that neither he nor even the gleaner had anticipated. He couldn't say where it was leading, but he no longer believed that he'd ever be duke of Curgh.

Bells began to toll in the distance, beginning at the north gate, the Moorlands gate as it was known in the City of Kings. Soon all the bells in the city were pealing, as if presaging the beginning of a siege. In the center of the courtyard, Gershon Trasker shouted a command, and the king's soldiers began to line up by the far gate.

Tavis looked at Xaver, who was already watching him, seeming to gauge the young lord's reaction.

"That's probably Shanstead," Xaver said. "Your father thought he would be the first to arrive."

"How many are supposed to arrive today?"

"In addition to the thane? Only one or two. Lathrop, and possibly Shamus."

Only two. That was more than enough. Tavis still remembered how the other dukes had looked at him during Kearney's investiture. Aindreas had convinced all of them that he was a butcher, a demon more deserving of torture and death than the mercy of exile.

"You can prove your innocence now, Tavis. You've been waiting for this since the last growing."

"I'm not convinced that they'll believe her, Stinger. She's a Qirsi traitor. Aindreas will say that she'd confess to anything to save herself and her child. He'll say that Kearney is so desperate to justify his actions on my behalf that he'd gladly believe her lies. And many of them will agree. Galdasten, Sussyn, Rennach. Before this turn is over, a majority of the dukes may be calling for both Cresenne and me to be hanged."

"I think you give the dukes too little credit."

"I hope so," Tavis said. "I've never been so eager to be wrong."

"We should go to the gate. Your father will want us there. From what I gather, Marston is already convinced that the Qirsi killed Brienne. He's an ally."

Tavis tried to smile. Failed. "You go. I'll wait for him in the castle."

Xaver frowned, but then nodded and, gripping Tavis's arm briefly, walked away.

Watching Xaver leave, Tavis wished that he could have shared his friend's faith in the judgement of Eibithar's dukes. He knew he should have been pleased. If Shanstead really was with them, and could convince his father, the duke of Thorald, of Tavis's innocence, there was indeed cause for hope.

Yet as he listened to the city bells, Tavis heard in their ringing not the promise of salvation or the herald of peace but rather the stubborn insistence of a call to arms, and the grim repetition of a dirge.

Chapter
Twenty

ershon's father, a fine soldier in his own right, had often said that a man could grow old and die watching nobles say hello. Standing in the shadow of Audun's Castle, watching Kearney greet Marston of Shanstead, the swordmaster had to agree. The ceremony welcoming the thane to the royal city seemed to drag on for an eternity, until, unable to stand it any longer, Gershon muttered a bit too loudly, "Imagine if the duke himself had come."

One of his soldiers snickered and the king gave them a look that would have melted steel.

It was nearly time for the ringing of the prior's bells before Marston's company was in the castle and the thane and king were able to talk. Still Gershon sensed that the younger man was reluctant to speak freely, as if he feared that their conversation would be overheard by enemies of the realm, though the only ones in the chamber with them were the archminister, Marston's minister, Gershon, and a pair of servants. For some time, Marston and Kearney continued to trade pleasantries, discussing the severity of the snows that had just ended and their hopes for a mild growing season.

Only when the king asked after Marston's father did the swordmaster have the impression that they were approaching matters that truly concerned the thane.

"My father sends his respects, my liege," the young man said, looking grave. "He would have liked to make the journey himself, and he instructed me to thank you for your invitation and to apologize for his absence." The man gave a wan smile. "It seems my father thinks me a poor substitute."

The king shook his head, offering a sympathetic grin. "I doubt that. But I hope you'll tell him that he was missed, and that we look forward to making him a guest at Audun's Castle when he can make the journey."

"I will, my liege." But there was a catch in Marston's voice, the briefest of hesitations when he spoke, which told Gershon that Tobbar of Thorald would never again set foot in the City of Kings.

Apparently Kearney heard it as well. "He shows no improvement?"

Marston sat straighter, as if gathering himself. Gershon had only met Tobbar once or twice, most recently at Kearney's investiture, when he had already begun to grow thin and weak with the illness that had kept him from this journey. He could see so much of the duke in his son's ruddy face. The penetrating grey eyes and noble straight nose, the kindness that seemed to linger in even the saddest of smiles. Aside from the years, there was little to separate father from son.

"Forgive me for being blunt, my liege, but my father is dying. The healers have told us for some time now that his illness lurks too deep for their magic and their herbs. They ease his pain as much as they can, but they've long since given up on trying to cure him."

Kearney looked pained. "I'm sorry, Lord Shanstead. Your father is a fine man who has led his house with wisdom and compassion under the most difficult of circumstances. Bian, it is said, has a jealous heart, and he steals the brightest jewels so that his realm will glitter. Our world will be darker for his passing."

Marston looked away, his jaw tightening. "Yes, my liege. Thank you."

"You sent a message during the snows, in which you wrote of the treachery of your father's first minister."

The thane faced Kearney again, though not before casting a wary look at Keziah. "I did, my liege."

"It's all right, Lord Shanstead. I've already spoken of your message with all my ministers as well as with Gershon."

Marston didn't look pleased, but he nodded. "Of course, my liege."

"Perhaps you should tell me more about what happened."

Still appearing uncomfortable, Shanstead told them how his suspicions of Enid ja Kovar had grown over the preceding year, and of how his own minister agreed to act the part of an embittered servant who wished to join the Qirsi conspiracy. After listening to the man rail against the thane, Enid offered to help him join her cause, at which point Marston's minister left her, related to the thane all that had been said, and accompanied Marston to Tobbar's chamber, where he repeated his account.

"As you might expect," Marston said, "my father was reluctant to believe him at first. Enid had served the House of Thorald for more than six years, and the duke had never thought to question her loyalty. When we summoned her to his chambers, she denied it, accusing Xiv here of fabricating the tale."

Gershon looked for a moment at the thane's minister, who was sitting quietly in the far corner of the chamber, his gaze fixed on his lord. Unlike most Qirsi, he wore his white hair short, so that at first glance he appeared to have none at all.

"I proposed that we search her chamber for gold, knowing that the conspiracy pays its servants well. She refused, of course. That was when my father knew she had to be lying. When the duke said as much to Enid, she admitted everything, calling him the foulest names and making it clear to all that her charm and wit had only served to conceal a black heart."

"Did you learn anything from her?"

"No, my liege. She took her own life before we could question her. She remained loyal to her cause to the very end."

"This must have come as a blow to your father."

Marston nodded. "It did, my liege, in more ways than you may think. Enid came to Thorald shortly after the death of Filib the Elder. For years we assumed that the murder of Filib the Younger was the work of thieves who had come to Thorald with the Revel. My father and I now believe that his death may actually have been the work of assassins hired by the first minister."

Gershon sat forward. "Demons and fire! Do you have evidence of this?"

"No, not yet."

"It makes a good deal of sense, Your Majesty," Keziah said. "Galdasten had been removed from the Order of Ascension several years before, and Filib's death removed Thorald, thus making Curgh and Kentigern the two leading houses in the land."

Kearney looked incredulous. "Are you suggesting that the conspiracy was already planning Brienne's murder when Filib died?"

"Not exactly. I doubt they could have foreseen all the circumstances that led to Brienne's death. But if they wished to use the Rules of Ascension to push the land toward civil war, it would have made sense for them to eliminate as many of the major houses as possible from the order. They would find it far easier to turn events to their purposes if they only had to concern themselves with two or three houses rather than four or five."

"My pardon, my liege," Marston said, looking from Kearney to Keziah. "But you speak of Brienne's murder being the work of the Qirsi with such certainty. Are you convinced that this woman you hold in your dungeon is telling the truth?"

"I am, Lord Shanstead, though you should know that she's in the prison tower, not the dungeon."

"But why, my liege?"

"She has a newborn babe and despite what she's done in the past, she's cooperating with us now. I saw fit to show her a measure of mercy."

Marston didn't look at all pleased, but he seemed to know better than to argue the point further. "She can offer proof that the conspiracy had Kentigern's daughter killed?"

"She claims to be the one who planned the murder and hired the assassin."

Marston's eyebrows went up. "Then you can prove Lord Tavis's innocence."

"We can."

"Does Lord Kentigern know of this? Is he coming here?"

Kearney glanced at Gershon, who couldn't keep the frown from his face. "Lord Kentigern has yet to reply to my summons," the king said at last. "I don't hold out much hope that he will."

"But surely the others . . ." The younger man trailed off, a plea on his face.

"We haven't yet heard from Galdasten, Sussyn, or Eardley."

"Damn," Marston said, shaking his head.

"Javan arrived yesterday," the king told him, as if this were consolation, "and we expect Lathrop before nightfall."

"Yes, but they were allies already. We need the other houses."

Kearney gave a wan smile. "I know."

"Forgive me, my liege. I didn't mean to imply—"

"No apology is necessary, Marston. I share your frustration."

Marston glanced at his minister, who stared back at him for a moment, then nodded.

"Archminister," the Qirsi said. "May I have a word with you?"

Keziah faltered, looking toward the king.

"It's all right," he said.

She forced a smile and led Shanstead's minister from the chamber, leaving the king, with Gershon and Marston.

"You wish to speak without the ministers present?" Gershon asked, eyes narrowing.

The thane looked weary and young in the dim light of the chamber, and though he was eyeing the swordmaster, he addressed himself to the king. "Again, my liege, forgive my presumption. I've found, in discussing such matters with my father, that it's easier to speak freely when there are no Qirsi listening to the conversation."

"Do you doubt your minister, Lord Shanstead?"

Marston took a breath. "No, my liege."

"So it's my archminister whose loyalty you question."

The thane winced and Gershon had to keep himself from smiling, even as he sympathized with the man. It was one thing to speak so with one's father, even when he was duke of a major house. But it was quite another to raise the matter with a king.

"I'm afraid I haven't handled this very well, my liege."

"It's all right, Marston. You may speak, though you should understand that I've known Keziah for a long time. I daresay I know her as well as any man in the realm. She's no traitor."

"Of course, my liege. In that case I'll say no more, save to ask you if you've noticed anything unusual in her behavior."

This time it was Kearney's turn to falter, and abruptly there was no longer anything amusing about their conversation.

The king looked at Gershon, who had little choice but to say, "She has been acting oddly since Paegar's death."

"Paegar?" the thane asked.

"One of my underministers. He fell in his chamber, striking his head on the edge of the hearth. He and the archminister were close, and after his death she . . . changed. She grew defiant and embittered. I finally had to threaten to have her removed from the castle permanently. Since then, she's been more like herself."

"If I may ask, my liege, were she and this Paegar lovers?"

"No," Kearney said, a bit too quickly.

"I see. You say that he fell in his chamber."

"I know how it sounds, Lord Shanstead, but the door was locked from within. It was an accident, albeit a strange one."

Gershon wanted desperately to leave it at that, but he knew that he couldn't, that the archminister would have been the first to tell him so. The swordmaster had long questioned the wisdom of what she was doing and he feared for her life, but he had also sworn to help her in this endeavor. To keep silent now, after she had worked so hard to draw the attention of the conspiracy's Weaver, made no sense at all.

He cleared his throat, shifting uncomfortably in his chair.

"Gershon?"

"It's probably nothing, Your Majesty. Merely something the surgeon said the day we found Paegar's body. I gave it little thought at the time. As you say, the door was locked from within. But after what happened last night to the woman . . ." He shrugged.

"Go on."

Both men were watching him intently.

"He said that he had rarely seen a simple fall result in such a severe wound. He went on to say that he still thought the fall had killed the minister—the way the blood had stained the floor made him all but certain. But now, after seeing what can be done to a person in their sleep, I have to wonder if the Weaver found some way to make him fall."

"The Weaver?" Marston repeated, looking truly frightened.

The king nodded. "That's one of the things we've learned from the Qirsi woman. It seems the conspiracy is led by a Weaver who can communicate through the dreams of those who serve him."

"Gods save us all!"

"Indeed," Kearney said. "We learned last night that this Weaver not only can communicate across great distances with his underlings but can attack them as well. It seems he learned somehow that the woman is helping us and sought to silence her. She's lucky to have survived the encounter." He turned to Gershon. "And now you believe he may have attacked Paegar as well?"

"It's possible, Your Majesty."

"Do you have reason to believe that Paegar was working with the conspiracy?"

He did. There had been a good deal of gold in the man's chamber, far more than there should have been. But Gershon had promised Keziah that he wouldn't reveal this to anyone, not just for fear of endangering her life but also because she didn't want to see her friend disgraced. Already he regretted having said anything to the king and thane, but there was no turning back now.

"No, Your Majesty. But it seems that no court in the Forelands has been completely immune to Qirsi treachery. I find myself wondering if perhaps Paegar was the traitor here."

Kearney walked to the window and stared out at the courtyard below. "I don't like to impugn a man who can't protest his innocence. Paegar served me well for the few turns we were in this castle together, and he was with Aylyn for eleven years before that. He deserves better than to be branded a traitor without cause."

Gershon lowered his gaze. "Yes, Your Majesty."

The three men were silent for some time.

"Tell me more about your archminister, my liege," the thane finally said. "You said she was behaving strangely."

The king shot Marston a dark look, but then nodded, his mouth twitching. "Yes, she was. She grew impudent, she questioned my judgement, she even insulted one of our guests, a noble from Wethyrn."

"Did she continue to offer sound counsel?"

"Actually, no," Kearney said. "Her counsel suffered as well, until I found myself relying more on my high minister and underministers than on her."

The thane glanced at Gershon, raising an eyebrow.

"It does give one pause, Your Majesty," the swordmaster said. "All this time we thought that the archminister merely grieved for a lost friend. Perhaps there was more to it than that. Perhaps they were both in league with the Weaver."

"No!" the king said, stepping away from the window. "Keziah wouldn't betray me that way."

"My father said the same thing about Enid, my liege."

"This is different! She's different!"

Clearly Marston didn't believe this, but it seemed the young noble knew when to retreat. "Of course, my liege."

"Leave me now," the king said, refusing to look at either of them. "Both of you. I wish to be alone."

Gershon rose and stepped to the door, gesturing for the thane to follow. "Shall I send word when Lathrop arrives, Your Majesty?"

"Yes. That will be fine."

The swordmaster led Marston out of the chamber, closing the door softly behind them.

Once in the corridor, the thane closed his eyes and leaned back against the cool stone wall. "That didn't go as I had hoped."

"No, I don't suppose it did."

"I didn't realize that he still felt so strongly for her."

Gershon frowned. "What do you mean by that?"

"Come now, swordmaster," Marston said, opening his eyes. "Shanstead may not be the seat of the dukedom, but it's more than a farming village, and it lies in the heart of Thorald. We hear what others hear."

"And what have you heard?"

"That the king and his archminister were once lovers."

It was an irony more bitter than tansy that word of Kearney's love affair with Keziah had spread through the land only after he became king, and their love ended. It was forbidden under the laws of every realm in the Forelands for an Eandi man to lie with a Qirsi woman. Qirsi and Eandi alike called such unions the sin of the moons, for Panya and Ilias, a Qirsi woman and Eandi man who defied the laws of men and the commands of their gods for a love that ended in tragedy. Over the past several turns these rumors had become one more arrow in the quiver of those who refused to acknowledge the legitimacy of Kearney's claim to the throne.

Gershon didn't know that he had reached for hilt of his sword until the blade was halfway out of its sheath.

"Stand down, swordmaster," Marston said sharply. The younger man's hands trembled, but his voice was steady. A pair of guards standing a short distance from them had paused in their conversation to watch the two men. "I meant no offense to you or your king," Marston began again, dropping his voice. "You must realize by now that I'm loyal to the throne. If I could speak for Thorald, I would throw the weight of our house behind the king and end this conflict before it begins."

The swordmaster slowly slid his sword back into place.

"The rumors are true, then," the thane said.

"You'll never have that from me."

"All right. But do you think the woman could have turned? Would her bitterness at losing him have run that deep?"

"As I said, you'll never get me to say anything about this."

"Damn it, man! We're speaking of the future of Eibithar! Don't you understand? If the archminister has betrayed him, then the rest of this means nothing! It won't matter that this Qirsi woman has confessed, or that Lord Tavis has been vindicated, or even that you might be able to end the threat from Kentigern! She can destroy everything."

Gershon didn't know what to say. He couldn't very well defend Keziah, not without raising suspicions of a different sort. But neither could he bring himself to impugn her further. She was in too much danger already, and though he had never cared for her, he had in the past few turns, come to respect her courage and accept that in her own way she served Kearney as faithfully as anyone in the realm, including himself.

"You heard the king," he finally told Marston. "He believes that she's loyal, and he knows her better than anyone. That's good enough for me."

"It shouldn't be. He's blinded by his passion for the woman. Surely you can see that."

This time Gershon did draw his sword, holding it loosely before him, its tip lowered.

"You're a good man, Lord Shanstead. Young yet, but wise beyond your years and brave. Some might say too brave for your own good. Be that as it may, if you speak thus about my lord and king again, I'll have no choice but to kill you where you stand."

Marston eyed him for a long time, his hands hanging at his sides though he wore a blade on his belt as well. The guards were staring at them again, the silence in the corridor as thick and dark as smoke from damp firewood.

When at last the thane spoke, it was in a voice scraped bare by fear and anger. "Watch her," he said. "Believe what you will. Make your threats against me if you must. But watch her as you would a beggar in your marketplace."

Gershon said nothing, but he nodded and after a moment sheathed his sword once more.

Their eyes met briefly, but before either man could speak, the city bells began to toll for a second time.

"Tremain arrives," Marston said, looking toward the narrow window at the end of the corridor. "What do you know about his Qirsi?"

Keziah and Shanstead's minister walked wordlessly to the nearest of the towers, descending the steps to the inner courtyard and then making their way toward the gardens, which were just beginning to blossom after the harsh cold of the snows. Even after putting some distance between themselves and the guards standing watch in the ward, neither of them spoke. Keziah couldn't help noticing that the minister was quite handsome. She usually liked Qirsi men to wear their hair long, as did Grinsa and so many of the other ministers. But though his hair was as short as the duke of Curgh's beard, she found herself drawn to him; the pale eyes and angular features reminding her of a boy she had known years ago, when she and Grinsa still lived in Eardley. Shanstead's minister was only slightly taller than she, but broad and muscular for a Qirsi.

Walking in the sun now, she also noticed the glint of a gold band on his finger, and she gave an inward smile. *Always the joined ones. Just once, why can't I find a man who wears no ring?*

She knew why they had left Kearney's chamber. The thane wished to speak to the king of the conspiracy, and he didn't want any Qirsi present. And no doubt he had instructed his minister to try to learn whether Keziah had betrayed the king.

"Isn't this where you ask me if I can help you join the Qirsi movement?"

The man glanced at her, a slight smile on his lips. "In Shanstead we call it the conspiracy."

Keziah grinned. So handsome. "Xivled, isn't it?"

"Yes. My friends call me Xiv."

"Does that mean that I can?"

He laughed. "Yes."

"Thank you. Tell me, Xiv, does your thane believe me to be a traitor?"

"My thane knows little more about you than I do, Archminister. He makes no judgements as to your loyalty to the king, or lack thereof."

"But he wonders."

"Shouldn't he? Shouldn't we all?"

"Not necessarily," Keziah said, shaking her head. "You think you serve the realm by questioning the loyalty of every Qirsi in every court. But all you're doing is fueling the doubts of our lords, widening the chasm that already divides Eandi from Qirsi. You're making matters worse, and you're not learning anything new. I congratulate you for unmasking the traitor in Tobbar's court, but I fear that your success has made you too bold."

"You're wrong." He halted, faced her, looking earnest and young. "We didn't create the chasm of which you speak, nor are we responsible for the deepening mistrust between the races. But the conspiracy is real. There are traitors in nearly every court in the Forelands. That's the reason the conspiracy is so strong, so dangerous. I was once a trusting person, as was Lord Shanstead. I wish I could be still.

I don't enjoy questioning the motives of every Qirsi I meet, or assuming the worst about a person until she can prove to me that she deserves my trust. But that's the world in which we now live. The conspiracy has done this, and so long as we continue to trust without question, we enhance its strength."

"I don't believe that. Allowing the treachery of a few to destroy our ability to trust one another—that enhances their strength. They seek to divide us, and you're making it easier for them."

"We're never going to agree," he said. "We could argue this way until nightfall, and we'd still be just where we are now."

"Probably." Keziah began to walk again, and he with her. She had met a great number of Qirsi ministers over the years, particularly in the turns she had spent in Audun's Castle. Many of them—most, really—had struck her as well-meaning, faithful servants to their lords. That was one reason she took exception to Xivled's suspicions. But Xiv was the first she had met about whose loyalty she had no doubts at all. Perhaps it was because he questioned her fealty to the king, as he seemed to question the fealty of all ministers. Perhaps he had thought up the perfect way to hide his treachery. She smiled at the notion. This man was no traitor. Indeed, she found herself thinking that she could tell him of her attempt to win the Weaver's trust. If anyone could see the merit in her plan, he could. She didn't dare, of course. But she thought it a measure of the minister's charm that she would even consider it. "So have you decided yet if I can be trusted?" she asked instead.

"Not yet, no."

"There are many in this castle who'll tell you that I've been defiant of my king, that I've behaved strangely. Some, I'm sure, think me a traitor."

"Are you?"

Keziah smiled again. "Either way, you know that I can only give you one answer."

"That's not true. You could simply confess and be done with it."

"Must you argue with everything I say?"

He looked down, smiling once more, but looking embarrassed. "Forgive me, Archminister."

"Let me ask you a question," she said, pressing her advantage.

"Of course."

"Now that we can prove Tavis's innocence, do you believe Tobbar will ally himself with the king and Javan?"

The minister creased his brow and inclined his head slightly. "I can't say. Lord Tavis's guilt or innocence was always but one consideration among many in the duke's decision to withhold support from both sides in this conflict. He fears that adding Thorald's might to either side will tip the balance so greatly in that duke's favor that he'll feel emboldened and will attack the other. Nothing has happened to allay that concern."

"And your lord is of the same mind?"

"Lord Shanstead would never presume to challenge his father on a matter of such importance."

"At least not openly."

"What are you suggesting, Archminister?"

"That Marston strikes me as a sensible but passionate man. I find it hard to believe that he would do anything to weaken the Rules of Ascension, particularly with his sons in line for the throne. But by the same token, I also have difficulty believing that he enjoys watching Thorald stand idly as the other houses line up against one another. He seems to understand that the kingdom must unite if it's to face the Qirsi challenge, and with Tavis absolved of Brienne's murder, he'll be eager to throw Thorald's support to Javan and end the threat from Kentigern."

"You gathered all of this from the discussion we observed today?" Xiv asked, sounding impressed.

"And from what I've heard of him from others."

The man nodded, his brow furrowing again. "You understand, I can only say so much. But I do believe that if my lord were duke . . . matters might stand somewhat differently."

"Thank you, Minister," Keziah said, not bothering to mask her surprise. "I appreciate your candor."

"I'd ask you not to repeat what I've said to anyone, Archminister. Not even the king, at least not yet."

"Of course. I'll merely tell him that these are my impressions of the thane."

"Thank you."

She considered asking the minister how much longer he thought the duke of Thorald would live, but some questions lay beyond the bounds of propriety, even for the highest-ranking Qirsi in the land.

Rather, she sensed that he was eager to rejoin his lord, so that they might share what they had learned from the king and from Keziah. "Was there more you wished to ask me, Minister?" she said. "Or am I free to return to the king?"

Before Xiv could answer, the city bells began to echo through the castle ward. Keziah glanced up at the sun. It was too early for the prior's bells. "It seems the duke of Tremain has come," she told him. "I should be at the gate to greet him." She smiled. "Thank you for a most interesting conversation."

She started to walk away, but Xivled called to her, making her face him again.

"I asked you before if you were a traitor," he said. "You never answered me." He wore a smile, but the archminister could see that he was keenly interested in her response, or more precisely, how she offered it.

"You're right," she answered, turning away once more. "I never did."

With the arrival of the two lords, and the welcoming ceremonies and the grand feast planned for that evening, Audun's Castle fairly hummed with activity. The royal guard marched to and from the city gates, accompanying the nobles and their ministers. Even in the prison tower, which was on the other side of the inner keep from the kitchen, Grinsa could hear the shouts of the kitchenmaster and smell the faint, appealing aromas of roasting meat and baking bread. And through it all, Cresenne slept, looking small and frail against the dingy linens on her bed. She flailed at times, crying out and raising her hands as if to ward off a blow, but she didn't wake. The wounds on her ashen face, dark and ugly in the dim light of the chamber, seemed to scream at him, an accusation. *How could you allow this to happen? You said you'd protect her. If only she told all she knew, you would do everything in your power to keep her safe, and the baby too.* He spoke bravely of keeping the Weaver from hurting her again, but he knew that if the man was determined to harm her, even kill her, there was little anyone could do to stop him.

The gleaner would have liked to meet with Marston of Shanstead and Lathrop of Tremain himself, to hear how the king and Keziah presented all they had learned from Cresenne. But he refused to leave her side, or to trust care of Bryntelle to anyone else.

A turn before, hoping to compel Cresenne to tell all she knew about Brienne's murder, he had threatened to take the child from her, to find a wet nurse in the city who might feed the babe. This day, he had been forced to do just that, not to punish Cresenne but to let her rest through Bryntelle's feedings. The wet nurse came and went, answering Grinsa's summons, suckling the child, then retreating to some unseen chamber to await word once more. It might have made more sense to let her remain in the tower—she was Qirsi as well, young and quiet and harmless— but Grinsa wanted to be alone with his family, just this once, while he still could.

After Bryntelle's previous feeding, he had held her, walking slow circles around the chamber, whispering stories of his parents and his own childhood until she finally dropped off to sleep. During the past few days she had fallen asleep in his arms several times, but it still thrilled him. He continued to hold her and walk, watching the daylight fade and the chamber darken. He lost all sense of the time, but as the first stars appeared in the sky above Audun's castle, barely visible through the narrow window in the prison chamber, the baby awoke again and began to cry.

Grinsa stepped to the chamber door and called softly to one of the guards. "Have the wet nurse brought again," he whispered.

"It's all right, Grinsa," Cresenne said from behind him, her voice barely carrying across the empty chamber.

Bryntelle stopped crying at the sound.

Grinsa turned from the door and lit a torch with the merest thought. She was sitting up, squinting at the firelight. After a moment, she passed a hand through her tangled hair, pushing it back from her face.

He sat beside her on the bed and let her take Bryntelle. She began to pull off her shirt, then hesitated, looking at him uncomfortably.

"I'm sorry," he said, standing and turning away. He wandered to the door. The guards were by the stairway, talking in hushed voices. "How do you feel?" he asked.

"Sore."

"Where?"

"All over. My hand and face especially."

"They should get better with time."

Silence. Then, "Do I look awful?"

"I'm not sure you could."

"You know what I mean." But there was a softness to her voice that he hadn't heard in so long.

"No, not awful. The scars are still dark, so you may be taken aback when you first see your image in a looking glass. But they should fade to white eventually."

She made a strange, choked sound. "Thank you," she said, the words coming out as a sob.

He turned to see her crying.

"For what?"

"Saving me. He would have killed me, Grinsa. He would have tortured me for as long as he could keep me alive, but then he intended to kill me. He told me so."

He walked back to the bed and sat once more. "You should thank the guards. And Keziah. They summoned her and she sent for me. If it hadn't been for them, I wouldn't have gotten here in time."

She nodded, wiping away her tears. Grinsa sat with her for a moment longer, then stood, intending to return to the door.

"It's all right," Cresenne said. "You're her father. You should be able to watch her eat."

The gleaner smiled, though he still looked away.

"You found a wet nurse."

He looked back quickly, fearing she might be angry. "Yes. I'm sorry. I just thought—"

"I understand, Grinsa. I was going to thank you for letting me sleep."

He exhaled, and they both laughed. "We've been angry with each other for so long, we've forgotten what it's like to be civil."

"We owe it to her to remember," she said, looking down at Bryntelle. "Perhaps we owe it to each other as well."

Before it's too late. She didn't have to say the words. They hung over the chamber like a storm cloud, making the air heavy and carrying the promise of violence and uncertainty.

"I do believe we can protect you, Cresenne. It won't be easy, but we can do it."

She was still gazing at the baby she held to her breast, her tears falling anew. "How? You see what he did to me last night." She looked up at him. "Are you that powerful? Could you do that to him?"

"I am that powerful, but to do it to the Weaver I'd first have to know who he is and where he can be found. The time will come when I can fight him, but for now I'm concerned with protecting you. And as to how, you've already made a good start today."

She frowned.

"You're going to have to change your sleep habits. You can't sleep at night any-more—that's when he'll look for you. From now on, until the Weaver is dead, you sleep by day and remain awake at night."

"And Bryntelle?"

"Her, too, of course. You'll have to change the way you feed her. It will take a bit of time, and you won't be getting as much sleep as—"

"Wait," she said, her puzzlement giving way to fright. "This is your plan for keeping me alive? Sleep in the day, stay awake at night? That's it?"

"At least for now, yes."

Cresenne gave a chilling laugh. "That will work for about a day, and then he'll figure it out, and he'll kill me anyway." She shook her head. "No, the only thing that will keep me alive, is if you're here with me whenever I go to sleep, so that you can enter my dreams and drive him off before he hurts me again."

He couldn't keep the smile from his face. "Are you suggesting that we share a bed again?"

"This isn't funny, Grinsa."

"No, it's not. I understand that you're afraid, but sleeping during the day will do more than you think to stop him." She started to object again, but he raised a hand, silencing her. "We don't know who the Weaver is yet, but I've an idea of what he is."

"What do you mean?"

"He's ambitious and he's accustomed to having people follow his commands. He also goes to great lengths to hide his identity. Even those who serve him don't see his face, or the place he conjures for your dreams, right?"

She nodded.

"That tells me that he's a man of some influence, someone who fears being recognized."

"But if you had been in his position wouldn't you have feared recognition, even posing as a Revel gleaner?"

"Perhaps, but I wouldn't have gone so far as to conceal the terrain. He seems to believe that to know where he is, is to know who he is. That leads me to believe that he's a minister somewhere, perhaps an important one, in the court of a duke, maybe a sovereign."

"I suppose it's possible," Cresenne said. "But what does that have to do with the time I sleep?"

"A man of such importance has demands on his time, things he has to do, a lord to whom he answers. As with most ministers, his nights are his own to do with as he pleases. But his days belong to the court. You're right, he may reason out very quickly how you're avoiding him, but there may not be anything he can do about it, at least not immediately."

She still looked doubtful.

"Contacting another through their dreams requires a considerable effort." He looked back at the door for an instant. "I know," he went on, lowering his voice, "because that's how I communicate with Keziah. I can only imagine what it is to hurt someone using the same magic. Just touching Keziah, or kissing her cheek, takes a good deal of power, far more than just speaking."

"What is she to you?" Cresenne asked abruptly. "Were you lovers? Is that how she knows you so well?"

Grinsa shook his head, smiling. "No, we weren't lovers. We're just close—I've known Keziah nearly all my life."

The woman shook her head. "She says nearly the exact same thing whenever I ask her about you."

"And yet you persist in looking for more. Accept it as the truth, and stop asking."

"I'm sorry. I interrupted you."

"My point was simply this: it takes a great effort to contact another through her dreams. It's not something the Weaver can do in a spare moment as he waits for his lord to finish a meal. He needs time to prepare himself and more time still to rest afterward. Sleeping during the day won't keep you safe forever, but it will protect you for a time, and perhaps that will be enough."

Cresenne pushed her hair back again and wiped her eyes. "I don't want Bryntelle being raised as if she were an owl."

He grinned. "Neither do I. But we're not talking about years. I intend to find the Weaver long before her first birthday. It's just for a few turns."

"All right," she said, nodding and taking a breath. "I'll try."

"Good." He looked toward the door. "I should go soon. Tavis and I have been asked to the feast. But before I leave, is there anything else you can tell me about the Weaver, anything at all? Something you haven't mentioned before, maybe because you didn't think it was important?"

She seemed to consider the question for a moment, then she shook her head.

"What did you call him?"

"What?"

"When you spoke in your dreams, what did you call him?"

Cresenne gave a small shrug. "Weaver. I made the mistake of calling him 'my lord' once, many years ago, and he grew angry. He didn't want me to address him as I would an Eandi lord."

"What did he call you?"

"He used my name most of the time."

"Most of the time?"

"Well, eventually, as I gained more influence in the movement, he gave me a title. He didn't use it much, but others did."

Grinsa felt his heart begin to race. "What title?"

"He made me one of his chancellors."

"His chancellors," the gleaner said breathlessly, repeating the words as if they were the name of his first love.

"Does that tell you something?" Cresenne asked, frowning once more.

"Maybe. Most of the kings and queens in the Forelands call their Qirsi ministers. The suzerain of Uulrann refers to all Qirsi as enchanters, but he gives no formal title to those who serve him. The emperor of Braedon, however, has chancellors as well as ministers. His chancellors are those who have been with him the longest, who have the most authority among his advisors."

"That's what we were," Cresenne said. "There were only a few of us—the others in the movement answered to us, rather than to him directly."

"Braedon," he whispered. He had seen the Weaver's face the night before, but he hadn't noticed much about the moor on which they had been standing. It could have been anywhere in the Forelands.

He stood and walked to the door, calling for a guard.

"Are you going to the feast?"

"Yes," he answered, as the guard unlocked the door. "I wish to ask the king what he knows about Braedon's high chancellor."

Chapter
Twenty-one

Curtell, Braedon

He didn't sleep for the rest of the night, nor did he leave his chambers come morning. Even when the midmorning bells tolled in the city, the echoes drifting through the palace corridors like whispering wraiths, he remained in the chair by his long-dead fire, staring at the blackened remnants of wood, his hands, white knuckled and stiff, gripping the arms of his chair. There was a knock, a timid voice explaining that the emperor was asking for him. But he sent the servant away without bothering to open the door.

"I'm not well today. Offer my apologies to the emperor." He called these things to the boy, motionless in his chair.

The truth. For he wasn't well.

He had known that this day would come. No man leading so great a movement could shroud himself in shadows forever. But he had not thought to have his identity exposed so soon, and never had he dreamed that Grinsa jal Arriet would be the first man in the Forelands to see his face and live to speak of it. Just a few turns before he had killed one of his servants, a man in Audun's Castle, simply to preserve his secret. Paegar jal Berget had been neither the most powerful Qirsi working for his cause nor the most intelligent. But the man had served him loyally for more than two years. His had been a crueler fate by far than what he deserved.

Unlike Cresenne, who by her treachery had earned the painful death he had in mind for her. Instead, the gleaner had saved her, that golden fire in his palm a declaration of sorts, a warning to the Weaver that Grinsa intended to oppose him.

Dusaan couldn't be certain how much the gleaner had seen—he had severed his contact with Cresenne as quickly as possible in a vain attempt to keep the man from seeing too much. Their eyes had met, so surely Grinsa saw the Weaver's face. But had he seen Ayvencalde Moor as well? Had he recognized it?

"Damn her!" he muttered through clenched teeth.

He would go to her again this night. He would kill her, painfully to be sure, but quickly as well, so that the gleaner would be powerless to stop him.

It means nothing if Grinsa knows who you are.

The golden light had been on his face for less than a heartbeat, no more than a flicker of lightning on a warm night during the growing. Surely he hadn't seen enough.

Dusaan spat a curse. He had been leading this movement for too long to allow himself to believe that. He had no choice but to assume that Grinsa had seen everything, that already the gleaner knew where he could be found. So what would the gleaner do next?

He couldn't leave Cresenne, not if he wanted to keep her alive. As far as Dusaan knew, there wasn't another Qirsi in the Forelands who could protect her. And as the father of her child, a man who had loved her, he wouldn't just leave her to die.

The high chancellor felt his grip on the chair begin to relax.

Grinsa couldn't send anyone to Braedon either. He couldn't even tell the Eandi nobles with whom he had allied himself what he knew, not without revealing to all that he was a Weaver as well. Even if Grinsa knew his name and his title, he could do nothing.

Dusaan should have been pleased. He had seen Grinsa's face as plainly as the gleaner had seen his, and for far longer. He didn't have to rely on Cresenne anymore. Not only did he know the gleaner's name and face, he even knew where the man was. Audun's Castle. He could send assassins. Or he could enter the man's dreams himself and test his strength against the gleaner's. Surely he could prevail in such a battle, and even if he couldn't, so long as their encounter took place in Grinsa's mind, the gleaner could do no worse than drive him away.

Dusaan had lost nothing the previous night. At least this is what he told himself again and again, fighting an urge to scream out in frustration. The truth was, he had lost his first battle. Grinsa might still prove to be no match for him when next they faced each other. But for this one night, the gleaner had bested him. And the chancellor had no one to blame but himself. It had never occurred to him that Grinsa was with the woman, though of course it should have. Who else could have convinced her to defy him, to risk certain death by betraying the movement? She had been searching for Grinsa since the growing turns. Was it so strange that she should have found him in Audun's Castle? The Weaver should have known, and he should have made certain that she died. Above all else, he needed her dead, so that she could do no more damage to the movement. Instead, he had allowed his thirst for revenge and his lust for her pain to cloud his mind. He had been a fool, a difficult admission for a man who did not willingly suffer fools.

He stayed in his chamber for the entire morning and well past midday. Servants came to his door with food, or with inquiries from the emperor after his health, but he did not move from his chair, and he gave none of them leave to enter. Late in the day, however, when yet another of the emperor's pages came calling, he roused himself from his brooding and opened the door.

Clearly the boy hadn't expected this. For several moments he just stared up at the high chancellor, his dark eyes wide and his mouth hanging open.

"What is it you want, boy?"

"The emperor, sir!" he blurted out. "He asks for you. He . . . he sounded angry."

"Tell him I'll be there shortly."

The boy bowed, managing to say, "Yes, High Chancellor," before hurrying away.

Dusaan wasn't certain that he trusted himself to speak civilly with the emperor just now, but he had little choice. If he passed much more of the day in his chamber, the emperor himself might come looking for him. Better to face the fat fool in the imperial hall, whence he could excuse himself after a time.

Reaching the emperor's hall, he thrust open the door and strode in, only remembering to pause when he heard the guard by the door call out his name and title. Harel sat on the marble throne, his fleshy face red, his mouth set in a thin line.

"High Chancellor," he said archly, as if a parent speaking to a tardy child.

Dusaan dropped to one knee, lowering his gaze. When the time came, he would enjoy killing this man. "Your Eminence."

"I summoned you a number of times. There are matters I've wished to discuss."

"Yes, Your Eminence," the high chancellor said, still kneeling. "I sent word in return that I wasn't well."

"You seem well enough now."

"The rest you allowed me did much good, Your Eminence. I'm most grateful."

Harel frowned, then made a vague gesture with a meaty hand, his gemmed rings sparkling. "Rise."

Dusaan stood. "Thank you, Your Eminence."

"What was the matter with you?" He flinched away, pressing himself against the back of his throne. "It wasn't something contagious was it?"

"No, Your Eminence. I had a difficult night and feared that I might be succumbing to a fever. But I'm well now. You needn't be concerned." *Not that you cared a whit for me, you coward.*

The emperor straightened. "Well, good. As I said, there are matters I've been waiting to discuss with you."

It was almost comical. One might have thought that the high chancellor had been in his bedchamber for half the year. "I'm here now, Your Eminence. How can I be of service?"

"I hardly know where to begin." He toyed with the jeweled scepter that lay across his lap. "This business in the south has only gotten worse."

"The land dispute in Grensyn, Your Eminence?"

"Yes. The lord there was quite disturbed by the message we sent last turn. He's refusing to abide by my decision."

It was more than Dusaan could have expected. Manyus of Grensyn had never struck him as being particularly bold, nor had he ever seemed inclined to oppose any decree coming from Curtell. Granted, he and his people had long been at odds with the lordship of Muelry, with whom the emperor had ordered them to share the farming lands west of the Grensyn River. But to defy the emperor in this way invited a harsh response.

"Have you had word from the lord of Muelry, Your Eminence?"

Harel waved his hand again, as if dismissing the question. "Patrin sent the letter informing me of what Manyus had done. You know as well as I that the man is too weak minded and timid to act on his own. He begs me to intervene, no doubt hoping that I'll send the imperial guard to take a corner of the plain and protect his farmers."

Dusaan had to agree with Harel's opinion of Patrin of Muelry, and also with his guess as to what the lord wanted him to do.

"Then you've heard nothing from Manyus directly?"

"Not yet, no."

"It may be wisest to await his response before taking any action, Your Eminence. Grensyn may intend to comply, but only after making Muelry wait for a time."

"It's almost Amon's turn," the emperor said. "If he delays too long, the harvest will suffer."

"Perhaps it would be appropriate to send a second message stating as much, and making it clear how displeased Your Eminence would be were he to doom Muelry's crops to failure."

Harel nodded. "Yes. A fine idea. See to it, won't you, High Chancellor?"

"Of course, Your Eminence." He continued to stand there, waiting. "Is there more, Your Eminence?"

"Yes, there's more!" the emperor said, sounding like a peevish child. "We've had word from Lachmas as well. They still have no proof that the lord's death was anything more than an accident."

Actually this message had arrived the day before. Dusaan had brought it to the imperial hall and waited there as the emperor read it. But clearly Harel wished to impress upon Dusaan that he was to be by the emperor's side at all times. The "matters" he claimed to have wanted to discuss with Dusaan were a pretense, nothing more.

"Yes, Your Eminence," he said. "I recall from yesterday."

"Well, what do you make of this?"

He had to answer with care. Lachmas's death had frightened the emperor, and while Dusaan anticipated that Harel's fear might prove useful at some point, he couldn't risk having the man grow so afraid of the movement that he lost faith in all his Qirsi.

"They may well be correct, Your Eminence. Hunting mishaps are said to be quite common. In all likelihood, Lord Lachmas's death was nothing more or less than a tragic accident."

"I'd like to believe that."

"As would I, Your Eminence. But we should remain wary nevertheless. The leaders of this conspiracy have shown themselves to be cunning and dangerous. Just because the soldiers of Lachmas have found no evidence of a murder, we can't assume that there was none."

"If you wish to put my mind at ease, you've done a damned poor job of it."

Good. "Forgive me, Your Eminence. Perhaps I should leave you."

"No. Tell me of the fleet."

Dusaan shrugged. "From all I hear, the ships are in place off Wantrae and Mistborne Islands. They await only your word to begin their assault. Eibithar's fleet has been active as well, perhaps in response to our own maneuvers, but this could hardly be avoided."

"Maybe we should begin the invasion earlier than planned."

"If Your Eminence wishes it. But I believe we'll fare better if we wait for the lords of Aneira to ready their army. Eibithar's fleet is no match for our own. They can take whatever positions they wish off the north coast; they still won't withstand our attack." He paused, watching the emperor's face. Harel didn't look pleased. "Do you wish to alter our plans, Your Eminence?"

"No. I'd just like to get on with them."

"Of course, Your Eminence. I believe, however, that your patience will be rewarded. There can be no question of the brilliance of the strategy you've devised." Actually, Dusaan and the master of arms had done most of the planning for the war, but he knew that Harel would gladly take credit for it.

"Very well," Harel said.

He heard weariness in the emperor's voice, and once more he thought to excuse himself. "I'll leave you now, Your Eminence. Again, you have my apologies for my failure to answer your earlier summons."

"I expect the master of arms shortly," Harel said, as if he hadn't heard. "He'll be reporting on the day's training. I think you should remain for that. Afterwards you may join us for dinner."

It was almost as if the emperor were punishing him for his absence that morning. All the Weaver wanted was to return to his chamber and await nightfall, so that he could be done with Cresenne and turn his attention fully to the gleaner.

"Tell me about the treasury."

"What about it, Your Eminence?" trying to keep his tone light.

"We've a war to wage. My father always used to say that no weapon was more essential to a successful war than gold."

"Quite true, Your Eminence. Your father was a great man."

"I take it we have enough gold to wage and win this war."

He should have known better, but he couldn't resist giving voice to the first response that came to him. "You've enough gold in your treasury to fund two wars, Your Eminence."

"Ean forbid it should come to that."

Dusaan suppressed a smile. "Ean forbid."

The master of arms arrived a few moments later, and as he and the emperor spoke of the training of soldiers and the poor fighting skills of the latest probationers, Dusaan had little choice but to stand and listen. Eventually, the three men walked to the palace's great hall where they were joined by Harel's wives for the evening meal. The emperor said little to Dusaan; once again the chancellor sensed that this was intended as punishment and nothing more.

The Weaver should have been able to endure the evening without effort, but knowing that Harel sought to teach him a lesson, he found himself suffering as if he were on a torture table. Every foolish statement the emperor made, every attempt at wisdom that came out as the trite truism of a child, every fawning compliment paid to the man by the master of arms grated on him until he thought he would shatter his teeth for the clenching of his jaw. The dinner lasted an eternity—it almost seemed that the emperor lingered over the meal, hoping to prolong Dusaan's misery.

When at last it ended, the emperor returning to his sleeping chamber with the youngest of his wives, Dusaan nearly ran back to his own chamber. A freshly fed fire awaited him there, as did a basin filled with steaming water. He splashed his face repeatedly, as if to wash the ignominy of the evening from his skin, before settling into the large chair by his hearth. It was already well past the ringing of the gate closing bell. No doubt Cresenne was asleep.

Or so he thought. When he cast his mind eastward toward Audun's Castle, he found that though he still sensed her presence there, he couldn't reach into her mind. She was awake still, tending to her child perhaps, or making love with the gleaner. He recoiled from the image, opening his eyes to the firelight in his chamber, and clamping his mouth shut against a sudden wave of nausea.

"She's a traitor and a whore," he said aloud. "She's nothing."

Yet he knew better. He had tried to kill her, and would do so again this night. But he could not deny that he still wanted her as his own. Never had he felt this way about a woman before, not even Jastanne ja Triln, the merchant who slept naked so that she might offer herself as a gift to the Weaver each time he walked in her dreams. Yes, Cresenne was beautiful, but there were others who were as well; it was more than that. It was the child she had borne, it was all that she had once given to the movement despite her love for the gleaner. He had intended to make her his queen when the time came. And though he knew now that he could not, that dream would prove far harder to kill than the woman herself.

He allowed himself to sleep for a time, waking again when he heard the midnight bells ringing in the city. He stirred the fire and added a log. Then he reached for Cresenne a second time.

Once more, he found that she was awake, and he had to struggle with a second vision of her and the gleaner, their legs entwined, a candle casting dark, terrible shadows on the wall beside them. But even as he pushed the vision away he realized that it was false, a product of his own jealousy and his lingering feelings for the woman. She wasn't with Grinsa, and she wasn't nursing her baby. She was merely awake, avoiding him. She had no intention of sleeping during the night. The gleaner would have seen to that, for he was a Weaver as well and so understood the effort it took for Dusaan to reach across the Forelands and into her mind.

"Demons and fire!" the high chancellor murmured, opening his eyes again.

He should have anticipated this. Instead, he had wasted the day wallowing in his fear of the gleaner and his regret at having failed to kill Cresenne. He would have to find time during the day to kill her—she had to sleep sometime—though, having angered the emperor with his absence this day, he'd have little choice but to wait several days before making the attempt.

In the next moment, however, cursing his stupidity a second time, he realized that he might not have to wait at all. He closed his eyes once more and reached out toward Eibithar's royal city a third time, this time seeking not Cresenne but the king's archminister. He didn't bother to make her climb the rise, though he took extra care in raising the brilliant white light behind him, as if expecting Grinsa to jump out from the shadows of the plain at any moment.

"Weaver," she said. "I expected you."

She had said something like this to him before, the night she opened her mind to him and fully bound herself to the movement. It had pleased him then. Tonight it did not. He had only thought to reach for her in the past few moments—that she had known he would need to do so before he did only served to make him more aware of how foolish he had been. Cresenne did this to him. It was even her fault that Paegar was dead. The sooner she died, the better.

"Then you know why I've come," he said, his voice thick.

"I believe I do. It's the woman, isn't it? The one who betrayed you?"

"Yes. How long has she been there?"

"More than a turn, Weaver."

More than a turn! He nearly struck the archminister, though he knew it wasn't her fault. He should have contacted her sooner. Not long from now, the invasion would begin and Dusaan would begin in earnest his campaign to take the Forelands from the Eandi. Now was a time for vigilance, and instead he had grown dangerously lax.

"She's told your king much about our movement?"

"She has, Weaver. Forgive me for not stopping her, but I didn't know how. I didn't even know if you wanted me to, or if perhaps this was a ruse of some sort. Only last night did I realize for certain that it wasn't."

"You needn't apologize. What did your king have to say about what happened last night?"

"He was frightened, Weaver. The woman had told him that the movement is led by a Weaver, but until he saw what . . . what you can do, I don't believe he grasped what it means to face a Weaver in war."

Dusaan nodded. "I suppose there's some value in that."

"Yes, Weaver."

"She sleeps now during the day?"

"That's her intention, yes."

"And she was instructed to do this by the gleaner, the father of her child?"

He sensed some hesitation on her part, as if she didn't wish to speak of Grinsa. There was fear in her mind as well, though of what he couldn't be certain.

"Yes, Weaver."

"You don't wish to speak of this man. Why?"

"He frightens me, Weaver. He claims to be a Revel gleaner and nothing more. Yet he found a way to save the woman, and then he healed her wounds."

"Trust your instincts where this man is concerned. They serve you well. He's more than he claims to be. That's all you need to know right now."

"Yes, Weaver."

Again, he felt that she was holding something back, as if there might have been more to her feelings for the gleaner than she was admitting. It occurred to him then that she might have been attracted to the man. Cresenne had fallen in love with him; wasn't it possible that the archminister had as well. If she had, he didn't want to know it. The gleaner had caused him enough trouble already.

"Can you get close to the woman?"

"I've befriended her, Weaver. When I heard that she had been with the movement and now intended to betray it, I thought it wise to convince her that I was a friend. After last night, she's guarded throughout the day and night, and the gleaner is never far from her side. But I believe I can still see her. Why?"

"Because I want you to kill her."

Keziah blanched and her hands began to tremble. "I don't know that I can, Weaver."

"Do you mean that the guards and gleaner will stop you, or that you might not be capable of killing her?"

She lowered her gaze. "Both."

"You may need to befriend the gleaner as well. Win his trust and he may see fit to leave you alone with the woman. That will be your chance. As to your misgivings about killing, others in this movement have had to make similar sacrifices in the name of our cause. When the time comes, I'm certain you'll find the strength to do as I command. If you fail, you'll suffer as the woman has."

"Yes, Weaver."

"I want her death to appear to be my doing."

"Your doing?"

"Yes. Give her a sleeping tonic and then smother her. The gleaner will blame me, just as he should. I want her death to be a warning to other Qirsi who would turn against our movement. And I want our enemies to know that I can reach them no matter where in the Forelands they might try to hide."

"Yes, Weaver. Very well."

Yet there it was again. Her fear, her reluctance . . .

"What of her child, Weaver?"

And then he understood.

There was risk here as well. The child might well grow up to be a Weaver, and she would have cause to hate him, to want him dead and to oppose all that he would have built by then. But even Weavers didn't live forever, and by the time Cresenne's baby grew into her power, Dusaan would probably be dead already. Still, that wasn't the true reason he would allow the child to live. Since learning of Cresenne's pregnancy, he had seen this baby as the embodiment of the Qirsi future.

She was the heir to all that he sought to build here in the Forelands, if not in name, then at least in spirit. He had wanted the woman to be his queen, not only because she was lovely but also because she seemed to carry the destiny of all their people within her body. Cresenne had forsaken the movement, and would die because of it. But Dusaan couldn't bring himself to kill the child as well.

"The child can live," he said.

Keziah's relief was palpable. "That would make this easier."

He nodded. "Good. Do you understand what I expect of you?"

"I do, Weaver."

"Then the next time we speak, I expect to hear that she's dead."

"It will take me some time, Weaver. If I'm to win the gleaner's trust—"

"You've already befriended the woman, and she trusts the gleaner. That should make it much easier for you, and quicker as well. I'll allow you some time, but every day she lives, she further weakens the movement, endangering all of our lives and the cause for which we're fighting. I won't tolerate much delay."

She took a breath, nodded. "I understand, Weaver."

"Don't disappoint me."

Dusaan opened his eyes to the dim golden light of his chamber. The fire had burned low again, but he didn't bother to add more wood. Instead, he rose from the chair, stretched, and crossed the chamber to his bed. Dawn was still a few hours off, and after all that had happened the previous night he needed at least some sleep.

Before he could lie down, however, someone knocked at his door. For just a moment he had an urge to reach for his dagger, though his powers were all the protection he needed. The knock came a second time.

"Who's there?" he called.

"Nitara."

The underminister. Why would she come to his bedchamber at this hour?

He pulled open the door. She stood before him in a sleeping shift, torch fire reflected in her pale eyes, her hair hanging loose to her shoulders.

"What do you want?" he asked.

The woman faltered, as if unsure of why she had come to his chamber. "I—I wish to speak with you."

"Now?"

She swallowed, then, "I know who you are, what you are."

He should have known what to say to this. He should have had some response. But he could only stare back at her, wondering whether to be alarmed or relieved.

More than a turn had passed since Nitara and Kayiv had spoken with the high chancellor about the Qirsi movement. As the chancellor promised, they had each received a payment of gold several days later: one hundred imperial qinde apiece, left on their beds in small leather pouches. The following day, she and Kayiv spoke in private with the high chancellor a second time, though their conversation lasted only long enough for Dusaan to confirm that they had been paid and to promise them that they would soon be called upon to complete some small task. Neither of the ministers had heard anything since.

Kayiv seemed relieved by this—his doubts about the conspiracy and the high chancellor had only grown with the passage of time, forcing Nitara to wonder if he was truly the man she had once believed him to be. He spoke now of the need to find a path to peace, of the dangers the conspiracy presented to all Qirsi in the Forelands. He never said such things in front of the chancellor, of course. He was no fool. Still, she found herself losing patience with his misgivings and his cowardice.

For her part, Nitara was eager to take action on the movement's behalf. She almost didn't care what it was, so long as she had the opportunity to do something. She had been waiting for so long to strike at the courts. Listening to Kayiv fret like an old man, she felt her own fervor for the movement growing, until it seemed that every word he spoke against the conspiracy fueled her own hatred of the Eandi and their allies among her people.

She remained fond of him, and she thought him a skilled lover, but had there been other men of interest to her in the emperor's palace, she would already have turned him from her bed.

This at least is what she told herself. For as it happened, there was one man with whom she had become fascinated in the past turn. The high chancellor himself.

She had never seen a Qirsi who looked as he did: tall as a king, broad in the chest and shoulders, like an Eandi warrior, with wild white hair and eyes as golden as the coins she had hidden beneath her bed. A part of her was ashamed that she should find herself drawn to a man in part because he possessed physical strength more characteristic of the Eandi than the Qirsi. But she saw in his formidable presence and regal features the future of her people, the promise of victory in the coming war. She could no more keep herself from imagining his face as she lay with Kayiv than she could stop counting the gold each night before she slept, running her fingers over the smooth edges of the coins as if they were a lover's lips.

Even before he revealed to them his involvement in the movement, she had thought him handsome. But she had not allowed herself more than that. He was high chancellor, she had told herself. He had no time for her, no inclination to look at her as anything more than another of his underlings. And back then she had been satisfied to pass her nights in Kayiv's arms.

As she grew more consumed with her desire for the man, other thoughts began to intrude on her as well, so that it seemed the high chancellor haunted her dreams at night and occupied every waking moment. These thoughts were more dangerous than mere passion, and more intriguing as well.

The movement was led by a Weaver, he had told them, a man who could walk in the dreams of those who served him. All of them answered to this Weaver, and it was this man, not the high chancellor, who would lead them to the glorious future they had envisioned. Except that Nitara couldn't imagine the high chancellor answering to anyone, not even a Weaver. Indeed, the more she considered the matter, the more she wondered if Dusaan himself were the movement's leader. He was the highest-ranking Qirsi in the most powerful realm in the Forelands. Who better to lead a movement that would strike at the Eandi courts? More to the point, how many other Qirsi, regardless of his or her powers, would have the resources and knowledge necessary to create such a movement, to pay those who joined it, and to direct others to strike at the weaknesses of the other realms? It had to be Dusaan. He had access to the emperor's treasury, and he knew more about Braedon's rivals than any man in the empire, including Harel. Such a man wouldn't have taken orders from some festival Qirsi, even if that person were a Weaver, nor would he have allowed himself to be ordered about by a court Qirsi from a lesser realm. He was too proud, too convinced of his own superiority. And why not? He was brilliant and strong and he looked like a king.

Nitara had considered all of this for some time now, and she no longer doubted that Dusaan, despite all that he had told her and Kayiv, was the movement's leader. But that left her to question whether he had invented for their benefit this Weaver of whom he spoke. He would have good reason for doing so. By telling them that a Weaver led the movement, he not only convinced them that he was a mere soldier in a greater cause but he also fueled their belief that the movement could prevail against the armies of the courts.

Reflecting on all the high chancellor had told them that day, however, Nitara couldn't bring herself to believe this. She had sensed through much of their conversation that Dusaan was not telling them everything. Kayiv had the same impression and had feared ever since that Dusaan had lied to them, hoping to expose them as traitors. She knew he was wrong, but only when she recalled how he had spoken of the Weaver did she begin to sense how wrong he had been.

"None of those who serve him know his name or where he can be found," Dusaan had said. *None of those.* Not, *none of us.*

It could have been nothing. But the high chancellor was not a man to choose his words carelessly, particularly on a matter of such importance.

She knew little of Weavers beyond what the legends told of their magic. They were the most powerful of all Qirsi, sorcerers who could meld the power of many into a single weapon. This was why they had been chosen to lead the Qirsi invasion nine centuries before, and this was why the Eandi, upon defeating the Qirsi army, had vowed to kill all Weavers in the Forelands, a practice that continued to this day. She knew no more than that. But didn't it make sense that Qirsi who wielded such magic should be strong in other ways as well? Wasn't it possible that when she told herself that Dusaan looked like a king, she meant to say that he looked like a Weaver?

She had made the mistake of giving voice to these questions the previous night, as she and Kayiv lay together in the moonlight and tangled bed linens, sated and breathless.

"Have you wondered if Dusaan is the Weaver?" she asked, staring at the fire as her pulse slowed.

"The high chancellor?"

Nitara winced. She rarely used the high chancellor's name when speaking of him with anyone, especially Kayiv. She hadn't meant to just then.

"Yes."

Kayiv gave a small, sharp laugh, rolling off her and stretching out on the bed so that white Panya illuminated his skin.

"He's no Weaver," the minister said. He laughed again, though it sounded forced. "Two turns ago you thought he was little more than the emperor's fool. You even said that his betrayal was worse than that of the other chancellors and ministers because he was intelligent enough to know better. Now you think he's a Weaver?"

She shook her head and sighed, still gazing at the hearth. "Forget that I asked."

They both were silent for some time, neither of them moving. Eventually Nitara began to wonder if Kayiv had fallen asleep. She would have liked to wake him, and tell him to leave. She didn't really want to be alone, but neither did she wish to spend the night with him.

As it happened, he wasn't asleep at all.

"Don't you think it strange that nothing's happened since we received the gold?" he asked suddenly. "Didn't you expect that we would have been contacted by now?"

"I suppose."

He said nothing, as if waiting for her to continue. When she didn't, he sat up. "That's it? Just, 'I suppose'?"

Nitara turned to face him. "What do you expect me to say, Kayiv? That I think the high chancellor was lying to us? That I expect at any moment to hear the emperor's guards trying to break down my door so that they can carry us off to the dungeon?" She shrugged. "I don't."

"Then why haven't we been asked to do anything? That's what he said would happen next."

"I don't know. Maybe the Weaver has yet to think of any tasks for us. Maybe he has more important concerns than what to do with a pair of underministers in Curtell. I just don't know. But if Du—" She looked away. "If the high chancellor was trying to betray us, he could have done it without the gold. If anything, I think our payments prove he was telling us the truth."

"Have you spoken with him again since our last meeting?"

"You mean alone?"

He nodded.

"No. I don't think he'd speak to one of us without the other." She didn't have to ask, but she knew that he'd expect it. "Have you?"

"No. But I'm not the one who keeps calling him Dusaan."

"Meaning what?"

"Nothing." He lay down once more, staring up at the stone ceiling.

She sensed his jealousy as if it were an odor. He reeked of it.

Once again, they lay still for several minutes, saying nothing, and once again Kayiv broke the silence, this time just as she was gathering the courage to tell him to leave.

"What makes you think he's the Weaver?"

Nitara shrugged, no longer wishing to discuss the matter. "I don't know. I was thinking aloud. I shouldn't have said it."

"But you did."

"He's the most powerful Qirsi in the largest, strongest realm in the Forelands. Who else would lead the movement?"

"A Weaver; any Weaver no matter his standing in the Eandi courts."

Look at him, she wanted to say. *How could he not be a Weaver?* But instead she shrugged a second time. "You're right. I was foolish to think it." Anything to end their conversation, to end this night.

"I'm tired," she said. "We should sleep."

He leaned over to kiss her and she barely brushed his cheek with her lips. She didn't so much as glance at him again, but she could feel him staring at her, no doubt looking hurt and angry.

"Maybe I should go."

No doubt he wanted her to argue, to plead with him to stay.

"All right. I'll see you in the morning when we meet with the high chancellor."

He sat unmoving for another moment, then threw himself off the bed, dressed with wordless fury, and left her chamber, closing the door sharply behind him.

She felt a pang of regret, but it passed quickly. Soon she was asleep.

Nitara awoke to the sound of Harel's soldiers training in the palace courtyard. She dressed slowly, enjoying her solitude and realizing with some surprise that she didn't miss Kayiv at all. She heard the tolling of the midmorning bells and left her chamber, intending to make her way to the high chancellor's ministerial chamber for the daily gathering of the chancellors and ministers. She hadn't gone very far, however, when she met Kayiv in the corridor. Seeing her, he faltered in midstride, then continued past her, his eyes lowered and his jaw set.

"Where are you going?" she asked.

He halted, though he wouldn't face her. "Apparently the high chancellor isn't well," he said, his voice flat. "We're gathering in Stavel's chamber instead." He began to walk away.

"What's the matter with the high chancellor?"

"I don't know."

Is he ill? she wanted to ask. *Is he going to be all right?* But by now several of the emperor's other Qirsi had entered the corridor, following Kayiv. Nitara had little choice but to do the same.

Without the high chancellor to lead them, their discussion foundered as might a ship in a blinding storm. They drifted from topic to topic, revisiting old, pointless arguments and accomplishing nothing at all. Stavel tried at first to keep the debate civil, but was soon bickering with the rest of them. Kayiv said nothing, sulking in the corner of the chamber farthest from where Nitara sat, his gaze occasionally flicking in her direction. She held her tongue as well, and when the discussion ended at last, she slipped from the chamber and returned to her own, wishing there were some way for her to learn what ailed the high chancellor.

Too restless to sit still, unwilling to risk a chance encounter with Kayiv or remain a prisoner in her chamber, she left the palace for the marketplace in Curtell city. There she passed much of the day wandering among the peddler's carts and the stalls of the food vendors. It was a fair day, the sky bright blue and a warm breeze blowing down from the Crying Hills, but Nitara could think only of Dusaan. If he were a Weaver, he couldn't truly be ill, could he? Surely a Weaver didn't succumb to fevers as an Eandi or a common Qirsi might. He could heal himself. She wanted to believe this, but everywhere she walked, it seemed that a shadow followed. What if he died? What would happen to the movement? What would happen to her?

The minister finally returned to the palace just as night began to fall, and seeing a pair of guards in the corridor near her chamber, she approached them.

"How fares the high chancellor?" she asked.

Both men looked at her as though puzzled.

"He's fine, so far as I know," one of them said. "He's with the emperor right now."

Relief overwhelmed her, and she felt her face flush. Grateful for the dim light in the corridor, she thanked the men and hurried to her chamber.

She would go to him this night, she told herself. Having feared that she might lose him, she could no longer bear to keep from him her true feelings. But as the night went on, marked by the ringing of the twilight bells, and then the gate close, Nitara lost her nerve. She wanted to go to him, but she feared that he would turn her away, that he might think her foolish, or worse, weak. And too, she feared him. He was a Weaver, and so the most powerful Qirsi she had ever known.

Eventually she undressed, pulled on her sleeping gown, and crawled into bed, trembling with her fright and her disgust at what she had become.

Unable to fall asleep, she merely stared at the fire, much as she had the previous night. The midnight bell tolled and still she lay awake. She longed to ask him if it were true that he was a Weaver, to ask him if he thought he could love her. Yet she cringed at the idea of doing so. Perhaps he already had a woman. She had never seen him with anyone, but the palace was vast, and she really knew so little about him.

Look at you, a voice said within her mind. Kayiv's voice. *You're a child with an infatuation, nothing more. He might pity you, he might laugh at you. But he won't love you.*

That of all things roused her from her bed. It wasn't weakness to want him, she told herself. It was only weakness if she allowed herself to be mastered by her fears. She resolved to go to him then. She started to reach for her clothes, but already she felt herself beginning to waver once more. So she fled the chamber, dressed only in her shift, and made her way to Dusaan's door.

She knocked quickly, as soon as she reached the high chancellor's chamber, thus forcing herself to remain there. At first there was no response and she had to resist the urge to hurry away. She made herself knock a second time.

"Who's there?"

She shivered at the sound of his voice. "Nitara."

The door opened. He was still dressed. He hadn't been sleeping.

"What do you want?"

"I—I wish to speak with you."

His eyes narrowed. "Now?"

She suddenly found that she didn't know what to say, and so she spoke the first words that came to her. "I know who you are, what you are."

He glanced to both sides and she did as well, belatedly. The corridor was empty save for her.

"I don't know what you're talking about," he said. "You should return to your chamber."

"Yes, you do." She stepped forward gazing up into his eyes. "I don't intend to tell anyone. I just want to be with you."

He stared at her a moment longer, then pulled her into his chamber and closed the door.

"What is it you think you know?" he asked, turning to face her, his expression deadly serious.

"I believe you lead the movement," she said, surprised to hear that her voice remained steady. She took a breath. "I believe that you're the Weaver."

For a long time he said nothing, his face revealing little more. "You came to me in your sleeping gown to tell me that?"

She felt her cheeks reddening once more, and she looked away. "Yes."

"What of Kayiv?"

"He and I are no longer . . . I don't love him. I don't think I ever did."

"I meant, does he also believe that I'm the Weaver?"

Her eyes flew to his face. He was actually smiling, kindly, with none of the mockery she had feared seeing in his golden eyes.

"No, High Chancellor. He thinks me a fool."

"Is this why you're not with him tonight?"

"No. As I said, I don't love him."

He nodded, turning away and walking to his writing table. "When you first thought of coming here, to say what you have, how did you think I would respond?"

"I don't know. I hoped . . ." She stopped, shaking her head. "I don't know," she said again, her heart aching.

"I can't love you, Minister. At least not now. It would be dangerous for us both. The emperor demands that I devote my days to his service, and my nights belong to the movement. Someday, perhaps. But for now, you should go back to Kayiv."

She fought to keep from crying, feeling like a chastised child, hearing Kayiv's laughter in her mind. "I can't."

He turned to her. Tall, regal, powerful. How could she ever go back to any other man?

"Very well. But you understand why I have to turn you away, regardless of my desires."

"Yes, High Chancellor."

He paused, then, "Call me Weaver."

Her breath caught in her throat. "Then it's true," she whispered, breathless and awed.

Dusaan returned to where she stood, grasping her shoulders firmly. "You can speak of this with no one. Do you understand? If Kayiv raises the matter, tell him that you were wrong. Make him think that you feel a fool for even raising the possibility. My life depends upon it, and so yours does, too."

"Yes. Weaver."

The smile touched his lips again. Would that she could touch them as well.

"I'm . . . pleased that you know. I didn't think I would be, but I am."

"Thank you, Weaver."

"Go now. In the morning, you must act as if none of this ever happened. If you can't do that, I'll have no choice but to kill you."

She knew that she should have been afraid, but for some reason she wasn't. "Good night, Weaver." She turned, reached for the door.

"How did you know?" he asked.

Nitara glanced back at him over her shoulder. "You have the look of a king," she said, and left him.

Chapter
Twenty-two

City of Kings, Eibithar

ith the arrival in the royal city of the thane of Shanstead and the duke of Tremain, the king seemed eager to begin discussions of the Qirsi threat and all that he had learned from the woman being held in his prison tower. Not surprisingly, therefore, Javan of Curgh and the others were summoned to the king's presence chamber early the following morning. What did come as a great surprise to Fotir jal Salene and the other ministers was the king's request that all Qirsi be excluded from the conversation. The guard who came to Javan's chamber didn't phrase the request quite that way. Rather, the minister received a separate invitation to meet with the king's archminister and the other visiting Qirsi. But there could be no mistaking the king's intent.

"You're angry," the duke said, after the guard had gone.

Fotir didn't wish to lie to Javan, but neither did he think it appropriate to say anything critical of the king. So he gave a vague shrug, his gaze fixed on the floor. A year ago, he felt certain that his duke wouldn't have even thought to speak of this. But the time they had spent together in Kentigern, struggling to win Tavis's freedom and then fighting side by side against the invaders from Mertesse had strengthened their friendship. There may have been a time when Javan questioned Fotir's loyalty, but in the wake of all they had shared those doubts had long since been laid to rest.

"I probably would be, were I in your place," he went on a moment later. "But this is obviously a precaution he's taking with all the ministers—it has nothing to do with you personally."

"Of course, my lord."

"And yet that makes no difference to you."

Fotir looked up. The duke was watching him closely, a troubled look in his blue eyes.

"May I speak frankly, my lord?"

"By all means."

"Every time we divide ourselves it weakens us. It doesn't matter if the divisions lie between realms, between houses, or even between a lord and his ministers. No doubt the king believes that he's merely being prudent. But to what end? If what we hear of the attack on the woman is true, the leaders of the conspiracy already know that she's helping us. And assuming that no duke would bring to the royal city a minister he didn't trust, I would think it likely that all of us will hear eventually of what's said in your discussion, despite our absence. On the other hand, if by some chance one of the Qirsi in this castle is wavering in his loyalty to the courts, this is only likely to drive him or her closer to the conspiracy."

"All that you say may be true, First Minister," the duke said, his expression still grave. "But the king obviously feels that in light of recent events we cannot risk any more betrayals. He's convinced that the conspiracy is real, that it was responsible for Brienne's death. The time has come for the courts to plot a response to this threat. And it behooves us to keep the nature of that response a secret, even at the risk of offending our ministers." He opened his hands. "I'm sorry."

"Of course, my lord. Thank you." He did his best to keep the hurt from his voice, but knew that he had failed.

They stepped into the corridor and walked much of the distance to the presence chamber in silence. At the door, Fotir bowed to the duke before continuing on toward the great hall, where the ministers were to meet.

"First Minister," the duke called to him, forcing Fotir to stop and turn. "You do understand that I'll tell you all I can of what's discussed here today."

The minister had to smile. Again, it was a kindness the duke would not have shown him a year ago. "Yes, my lord. Thank you."

Javan entered the chamber, and Fotir turned once more and resumed his walk to the hall. For a second time, however, he stopped. With the nobles speaking among themselves, the ministers were left with certain freedoms they might not have enjoyed otherwise. And if the court Qirsi were to develop their own strategy for combatting the conspiracy, they would be well served by consulting all who would be aiding them in the coming struggle. Taking the nearest stairway down to the castle's inner ward, the minister crossed to the prison tower, where he knew he would find the gleaner, Grinsa jal Arriet.

There was a good deal Fotir wished to ask Grinsa—about the man's journey with Lord Tavis, about Shurik's death and the strange remarks Tavis had made to Javan about all that happened in Mertesse, and about this woman who had confessed to arranging Brienne's murder, and with whom Grinsa had apparently once been in love. But knowing what he did of the gleaner's powers, Fotir realized that these questions would have to wait. He had aided the gleaner in his efforts to win Tavis's freedom from the dungeon of Kentigern Castle, and so knew that the man was a Weaver. And he knew as well that there was no one in the Forelands he was more eager to have on his side in the coming war.

As the minister expected, Grinsa was there, holding the child he had fathered and walking slowly around the corridor just outside the woman's chamber.

"Good morning," Fotir said, emerging from the stairway.

Grinsa held a finger to his lips, then whispered, "Good morning," in return.

Fotir approached him, eyeing the baby. "Is she asleep?" he asked, lowering his voice.

The gleaner nodded toward the chamber door. "They both are."

Glancing through the iron grate at the top of the door, Fotir saw the woman sleeping peacefully on the small bed against the opposite wall. There were livid scars on her face that seemed eerily similar to those borne by Lord Tavis.

"They'll fade eventually," Grinsa said, standing beside him, "though they won't disappear entirely."

Fotir nodded, unable to tear his gaze from her. Even marked so, she was beautiful. "You healed her?" he asked.

"Yes."

The minister looked back at the guards, who would have been close enough to hear, had the two Qirsi been speaking in normal voices. "It seems," he said, his voice even softer than it had been a moment before, "that you've revealed a good deal of yourself in recent turns."

Grinsa nodded. "And it hasn't gone unnoticed by the king."

Fotir raised an eyebrow. It was one thing for him to know that Grinsa was a Weaver. He was Qirsi himself, and though loyal to the courts, he had no intention of betraying the man's confidence; not after all Grinsa had done for Tavis. Not after he had seen to it that Shurik jal Marcine paid for his betrayal. It was quite another matter, however, for an Eandi noble, particularly the king, to learn of Grinsa's true powers. "Do you think he knows?"

"I'm certain of it. I told him."

"What?"

"I had little choice, and there are . . . other matters to consider, other secrets that must be preserved. Believe me when I tell you that Kearney is the least of my concerns."

"I do believe it. In a way, that's why I've come."

The gleaner eyed him sidelong. "What do you mean?"

"Shanstead, Tremain, and my duke are meeting right now with the king. The ministers are meeting separately in the great hall. We all intend to discuss the conspiracy and what we've learned from . . ." He gestured toward the woman.

"Her name's Cresenne." Grinsa exhaled. "You want me to join your discussion."

"Yes. I think you'd have much to offer."

The gleaner gave a small smile. "I'm not certain the others would even sit in the same chamber with me. You know who I am. The others will see only a Revel gleaner, one who's tied to both Cresenne and Lord Tavis. I can hardly claim to be impartial in this matter."

"Some may see that as a weakness. I don't. And I believe the rest are reasonable enough to consider that your opinions might be of value."

"I'd rather not leave her alone."

"You can bring her with you if you'd like."

"I mean Cresenne. I'm afraid the Weaver will try to kill her again. I don't know that anyone else can protect her."

"I understand," Fotir said. "I certainly wouldn't want you to do anything that might endanger her life." He turned to leave. "We can speak again later. I'll tell you what was said."

"Wait." Grinsa beckoned one of the guards to the door and had him open it. Entering the chamber, he sat on the bed and laid the baby beside the woman. Cresenne stirred, opening her eyes.

"Is everything all right?" she asked, her gaze straying to the open door and Fotir.

"Yes, everything's fine," he told her. "I need to go for just a short while. I won't be long, but I think it best that you remain awake until I return."

She nodded, sitting up and passing a hand through her tangled hair. She glanced at the baby, then looked at Grinsa once more, smiling. "You got her to sleep."

The gleaner grinned, looking embarrassed. "I told you I could." His eyes flicked to Fotir, then back to her. "I'll return soon."

The woman crossed her arms over her chest, the smile slipping from her face. Abruptly she looked frightened and very young. "I'll be all right." She sounded as if she were trying to convince herself as well as the gleaner.

"I know."

He stooped to kiss her cheek, then left the chamber, stopping just in front of the guard. "If there's any trouble—any at all—you come and find me. I'll be in the great hall. Understand?"

"Yes," the man said.

Grinsa looked back at her one last time before gesturing for Fotir to lead him to the hall.

Once they were away from the guards, Grinsa asked, "Whose idea was it for the nobles and ministers to gather separately?"

"I'm not certain. Word of the arrangement came from the king, but others may have suggested it."

"I don't like it."

"Nor do I. I said as much to my duke, but he seemed to feel the king's caution was justified."

"So Javan believes there's a traitor among the ministers?"

"He must think it's a possibility," Fotir said.

"Do you agree with him?"

The minister considered this for a moment as they walked through the ward and into the tower nearest the king's hall. "Shanstead's Qirsi is the one who deceived Thorald's first minister into revealing her involvement with the conspiracy. I trust him. I've never met Tremain's minister, but I have no reason to doubt her loyalty either. And the only one of the king's ministers who has given any sign of being capable of such betrayal is the archminister. I had little opportunity to meet her before Kearney's investiture, but from what I observed, I'm not convinced that she's a traitor either."

Grinsa seemed to falter briefly at the mention of the archminister, but otherwise he said nothing.

"You've been in the castle for some time now," Fotir said. "Do you suspect her?"

"No," the gleaner said quietly. "But I didn't suspect Cresenne either. And she and I shared a bed."

They stepped into the great hall a few moments later. The other ministers had already arrived and they turned toward the doorway when Fotir and Grinsa entered, several of them eyeing the gleaner warily.

"What's he doing here?" asked Dyre jal Frinval, one of the king's high ministers.

"This is Grinsa jal Arriet," Fotir said. "He knows the Qirsi woman being held in your prison tower, and he's spent the last several turns traveling with Lord Tavis, guarding the boy's life. I asked him to join us."

"This isn't Curgh, cousin. I don't care who he is or what he's done, you had no right to bring him, or anyone else, for that matter."

"It's all right, High Minister," the archminster broke in. "I see no reason why the gleaner shouldn't join us."

"You can't be serious," Dyre said. "As the First Minister just said, this man has ties to both Tavis, who may be a murderer, and this woman who bore his child, who admits to being a traitor. Isn't that reason enough?"

Fotir couldn't believe what he was hearing. "You still think Tavis is a murderer? Even after hearing of the woman's confession?"

"I don't know what to believe. Your friend there brought the woman to us, perhaps hoping that the king would take pity on her because of her child. This could all be a Curgh trick, intended to establish Tavis's innocence."

The others were watching Dyre, looking uncomfortable. But none of them disputed anything he had said.

Fotir chanced a look at Grinsa, expecting the gleaner to be beside himself with rage, just as Fotir would have been had the minister said such things about him. Instead, Grinsa wore a small smile, as if all of this amused him.

"And what of the attack on the woman two nights ago?" the archminster asked. "Was that a trick as well?"

Dyre shifted in his chair. "I don't know what that was."

"Then let me tell you," Grinsa said. "It was an attempt to silence her by the conspiracy's leader. He wanted her to suffer first, before he killed her, so he entered her dreams and used her own magic to shatter her hand and carve gashes in her face."

"How can you know this?" Dyre demanded.

"Cresenne told me so," the gleaner answered. "And it's the only explanation that makes any sense. The guards saw the wounds open on her face—there was no blade, there was no intruder. Only the woman and her dreams."

"So the movement is led by a Weaver."

They all turned to look at Tremain's first minister, Evetta ja Rudek. She had paled noticeably, her fear written plainly on her soft features.

Keziah nodded. "It is. We learned this from Cresenne as well."

"Do we know the name of this Weaver?" Xivled asked. "Or where he can be found?"

"Not yet."

"She hasn't told you?"

"She doesn't know," Grinsa said.

Dyre looked skeptical. "Or so she claims."

The gleaner glared at him. "Don't be a fool. You honestly believe that she would still defend this man after what he did to her? She's forced now to sleep by day, because she fears that if the Weaver comes to her again he'll kill her. And because her child needs to be nursed and cared for, she's forced to have the baby sleep during the day as well. She wants us to find him. She wants him dead. And if a minister of Eibithar's king is too blinded by suspicion to see that then I fear for the realm."

"How dare you speak to me so! You, a Revel gleaner—"

"Stop it," the archminister said, her voice flat, as if she were too tired to grow angry with them. "Both of you." She cast a reproachful look at Grinsa before facing the high minister. "I don't believe she's lying about this, Dyre. Grinsa's right. She's frightened. If she knew anything that could help us defeat the Weaver, she'd gladly tell us so."

The high minister didn't look convinced, but he nodded, conceding the point.

Keziah turned to Xivled. "Minister, it's because of you that we're here. Perhaps you'd like to lead our discussion."

"It was your idea to meet separately from our lords?" Fotir asked.

"Actually it was Lord Shanstead's idea."

Dyre sat forward, grinning darkly. "Doesn't he trust you, cousin?"

"Like so many of us today, High Minister, my lord isn't certain whom he can trust. Recent events in Thorald have left him . . . troubled. He thought it best not to risk giving any more information to the conspiracy than was necessary." He faced Keziah again. "As to leading our discussion, Archminister, I'd first like to know all that you can tell us about this woman who sits in your prison tower and what you've learned from her of the conspiracy."

Keziah nodded, taking a long breath. Then she began to speak, and for some time, the other ministers merely listened as she told them of Cresenne's role in the killing of Lady Brienne, and her description of the Qirsi movement, its network of couriers for delivering gold, and the Weaver who led it. Long after she finished, the Qirsi continued to sit in silence, as if trying to absorb all she had said.

"Forgive me for asking this," Evetta said at last, her eyes on Grinsa, "but you believe all that she's told you? Don't you think it's possible that she's making up some of these details in the hope that it will give the king reason to keep her alive?"

"I do believe her," Grinsa said. "Even had I not before the attack on her, I would now. The Weaver wants her dead, which tells me that he fears her, that he doesn't want her telling us more than she already has."

Evetta nodded, seeming satisfied with his reply.

Xivled sat back, pressing his fingertips together. "When my father's first minister died, she had over two hundred qinde hidden in her chamber. Because of this,

Lord Shanstead and I came to the conclusion that if we can find the source of the Qirsi gold we'll be able to find the people who lead the movement. What you've told us of the couriers only serves to make me that much more certain of this."

"I've thought much the same thing," the archminister said.

Wenda ja Baul, another of Kearney's high ministers, looked from one of them to the other "How would we do that?"

"By joining the conspiracy ourselves," Xivled said. He and Fotir shared a brief look. They had spoken of this before, during Qirsar's turn, when Fotir and his duke journeyed to Thorald to speak with Tobbar and Marston. They had agreed then that if one of them could join the movement, it would allow them to learn a great deal about its leaders and its weaknesses. Xivled had raised this possibility with the thane only to have Marston reject the idea as too dangerous.

Evetta shook her head. "You can't be serious."

"It makes a good deal of sense to me," Grinsa said. "There are risks, to be sure, but think of how much we could learn."

"There isn't a lord in the Forelands who would allow such a thing."

"Sometimes," the archminister said, staring at her hands, "we have to defy our lords in order to do what's best for them."

"Meaning what?" Evetta demanded. "You actually think this is a good idea?"

"I believe it's worth considering."

But Fotir thought the archminister meant even more than that. It occurred to him in that moment that she had already made up her mind to try this, that perhaps she had already succeeded in contacting the movement. His first response to the notion was to wonder how she could have been so foolish. Had it been Xivled, he wouldn't have felt so; Xivled, if he failed, brought danger only to the court of Shanstead. If Keziah failed, she endangered the royal court of Eibithar. Still, he could not help but be impressed as well by her bravery. She was small and slight, with a face so youthful that he found it hard to imagine her in the court of a king, much less as archminister. And yet, it seemed possible that she had taken it upon herself to challenge a Weaver.

Evetta looked imploringly at the other ministers. "Please tell me that I'm not the only one who believes this to be sheer folly."

"Our lords have chosen to gather apart from us," Fotir found himself saying. "We may take this to mean that they don't trust us, that they only wish to keep us occupied as they speak of fighting the conspiracy. Or we may take it to mean that they expect us to devise our own strategy for defeating the Weaver and his movement. I choose to believe the latter, and I think this as promising an approach as any."

"Do you believe Javan would approve of such a plan?"

"Perhaps not," Fotir said. "But as the archminister says, the time may have come when we must act on behalf of our lords without their approval."

He glanced at the archminister, only to find that she was already staring at him, as if seeing him for the first time.

"One need only look at Cresenne to know how steep the price of failure will be," Grinsa said.

"Does that mean you think it a bad idea?" Keziah asked.

"Not at all. Just perilous."

Keziah regarded him another moment before eyeing the others. "What of the rest of you?"

"I agree with the first minister," Wenda said, nodding toward Evetta. "I don't think it's worth the risk."

Dyre shook his head. "Nor do I."

Two of the king's underministers, who had said nothing up until now, voiced their opposition as well.

"It seems we're outnumbered," the archminister said with a small shrug. "I feel certain that before this conflict is over, we'll have to take risks that seem unfathomable today, but for now we'll honor the wishes of those who argue for prudence."

Once more Fotir had the sense that there was more to what she was saying than she let on. Despite her words, the archminister seemed relieved to be in the minority, which made sense only if she were concealing something. Perhaps she was a traitor after all. But Fotir didn't think so.

Dyre looked quite pleased, but Xivled continued to gaze at Keziah, as if he, too, were trying to gauge what lay behind her words.

"Isn't it possible, Archminister," he asked, "that as more nobles arrive in the royal city, and with them more ministers, a similar discussion might yield a different judgment?"

"Would that it were, Minister," she said. "But the king doesn't expect many more nobles to answer his summons. Kentigern won't come, and neither, it seems, will Galdasten. And with both of them refusing to make the journey, Eardley, Sussyn, and Domnall have declined as well. Rennach has made no reply at all. We expect the dukes of Labruinn and Heneagh to arrive in the next few days, but even if both first ministers support our position, that leaves us with only a split vote." She looked at the gleaner. "Forgive me, Grinsa. But in deciding matters of the court, I can't allow you to have a formal voice."

He inclined his head. "Of course, Archminister. I understand."

"But with a split vote—"

"No, Minister. I don't think it wise to take such a momentous step with the ministers so deeply divided. As I say, in time, I believe we'll have little choice but to reconsider this question. But for now we'll have to find another way to strike at the conspiracy."

Shanstead's minister continued to stare at her, tight-lipped and silent. And though Fotir couldn't be certain, he could only assume from the man's expression that Xivled thought the archminister a renegade.

"I'm not certain it's our place to strike at the conspiracy at all," Dyre said. "We serve the courts, and when our lords are ready to fight the traitors in earnest they will. My objection to what the minister proposed," he went on, gesturing toward Xivled, "had little to do with it being dangerous, though surely it is that. Rather, I opposed it because the king would oppose it, as would the dukes, I imagine."

"So we're to do nothing, then?" Evetta asked. "Even I don't believe that."

"I'm not suggesting that we do nothing. But we can only do so much. We can remain loyal to our dukes and vigilant in looking for those who might betray them. We can recommend courses of action that the nobles might not consider, but then it becomes their choice as to whether to follow our advice or ignore it."

"You've a narrow view of a minister's role, cousin," Fotir said.

"As is appropriate. Perhaps if the dukes of Thorald and Kentigern had kept their ministers on a tighter rein, the realm wouldn't have suffered as it has over the past half year."

Fotir saw Xivled bristle, but before the younger man could respond, the archminister stood, shaking her head.

"No," she said. "We're not going to do this. We're not going to blame anyone for the actions of a few traitors and a Weaver we don't even know. This conspiracy reaches across all the realms of the Forelands. It's been claiming lives in the courts for far longer than any of us realized until recently. Either all of us are to blame for its success thus far, or none of us are. We can disagree as to what actions to take, but I will not allow this discussion to descend into a fight over which houses have failed the realm."

She paused, staring at each of the Qirsi in turn, as if daring them to argue with her. "Now, given that we've decided not follow the minister's suggestion, at least for now, what other options can we offer the king and his dukes?"

For a long time, no one spoke, and when finally the discussion did resume, the ministers could think of few suggestions to pass on to the nobles. When the midday bells rang in the city, Keziah reluctantly ended their discussion.

The king's underministers left the hall immediately, speaking quietly among themselves. The others remained for a few moments until Grinsa stood and excused himself, explaining that he wished to return to Cresenne's chamber in the prison tower. Fotir stood as well and the two men walked from the hall together.

"I had hoped our discussion would yield more than it did," the minister said, as they descended the tower stairs to the inner ward.

Grinsa gave a wan smile. "I'm sure all of us did. But though I'm disappointed, I can't say that I'm surprised."

"You think we should have allowed Xivled to join the movement?"

The gleaner glanced at him, but didn't answer.

"I actually had the sense listening to the archminister speak that she had already considered doing so herself. I even wonder if she's done more than just consider it."

Still Grinsa kept his silence, and they walked the rest of the way to the prison tower without a word passing between them.

When they arrived at her chamber, Cresenne was awake, walking a slow circle with her baby in her arms. Seeing her, it finally occurred to Fotir that the gleaner might not want him there, that Grinsa's silence had not been a response to what the minister said, but rather to his presumption that he could accompany the man back to the tower.

"My apologies, gleaner," he said, abruptly feeling a fool. "I should leave the two of you—" He smiled sheepishly. "I mean, the three of you."

"Not at all, Minister. I'm glad you're here. Cresenne needs to sleep, and I'd enjoy your company."

One of the guards unlocked Cresenne's door, and the two men stepped past him into the chamber. It was warm within, the air too still.

"I'm sorry I had to leave," Grinsa said, taking the child from Cresenne.

She walked to the bed and sat. "It's all right." Her eyes strayed to the minister briefly before returning to Grinsa. She looked as if she were eager just to sleep, but felt that she needed to talk to them, at least briefly. "Did you decide anything important?"

"No," the gleaner said. "But one of the ministers suggested that it might be useful to have a Qirsi loyal to the courts join the conspiracy."

Cresenne's eyes widened, and once more her gaze flicked toward Fotir. "Did you? . . ." She stopped, shaking her head, as if unsure of how to finish the thought.

Grinsa shook his head. "No. Most of the ministers thought it too dangerous and the archminister ruled it out for now."

The woman nodded, but still seemed uncertain of what to say. For a third time, Fotir found himself thinking that there was more to what was being said than either speaker was letting on. Before he could give voice to his suspicions, however, he heard footsteps on the stairs. He turned toward the door, as did Cresenne and the gleaner.

A moment later, Keziah stepped into the corridor.

"Open the door," she said to the nearest of the guards without even looking in the chamber. "Then I want both of you to leave the corridor. I'll tell you when you can return."

"Yes, Archminister."

The door opened again and Keziah entered the chamber. Seeing Fotir, she faltered, glancing quickly at Grinsa. But she said nothing until the guards had gone.

"I had hoped we could speak in private," she said to the gleaner.

Fotir started toward the door, which remained open. "I'll leave you, Archminister."

"No, don't." Grinsa. "He knows about me, Keziah. I've told you that before."

"Yes, but—"

"He holds my life in his hands. He might as well hold yours as well."

A strange look came into the archminister's eyes. There was so much more passing between them than Fotir could possibly understand. But he was certain now that the archminister served the king loyally.

Keziah faced him, eyeing him appraisingly. "Even before we met in Kentigern, I had heard a good deal about you, Fotir jal Salene. I wonder if you're prepared to match your reputation."

"And what is my reputation, Archminister?" He knew that some thought him arrogant, disdainful of his own people, and more attached to his duke than to any Qirsi in the land. But he sensed that she referred to something else.

"I've heard it said that you're the most brilliant minister in the land, and one who is less likely than most to be lured into the conspiracy. It's said that this is why your duke places such faith in your counsel."

"I'm flattered."

"Did you mean what you said in front of the other ministers? Are you prepared to accept that there are times when, in order to serve the courts, we must keep truths from those nobles who trust us most?"

"I think you already know the answer to that, Archminister. As Grinsa said, I know who and what he is, and I know what he did for Lord Tavis."

Keziah nodded, although her expression didn't change. For some time, she merely continued to stare at him. Then she took a breath. "Very well. It should have been obvious to you that I support the idea of having a loyal Qirsi attempt to join the conspiracy. As it happens, I've done more than just consider the notion. I've acted on it. I've spoken with the Weaver, and I've begun to win his trust."

"I suspected as much, Archminister."

Keziah's face whitened so that it was nearly a match for her hair. "You what?"

"Please don't be afraid. I don't think any of the others would have drawn the same conclusion. Indeed, I believe Xivled thinks you a traitor."

That brought a smile to her lips, though she still looked frightened. "I'm sure he does. He as much as told me so the last time we spoke."

"You have nothing to fear from me, Archminister. I'll tell no one what I've heard here, and I'll do everything in my power to help you. You have my word."

"And you my thanks, First Minister."

"You wished to speak with us, Kezi," Grinsa said. "What's happened?"

"He's instructed me to kill Cresenne."

The other woman blanched, much as the archminister had done moments before.

"What about Bryntelle?" she asked, her voice unsteady.

"He told me to spare the child."

"Gods be praised."

"And me?" Grinsa asked.

"As you guessed yesterday, I'm to win your trust, so that I can get close enough to Cresenne to kill her, and so I can help the Weaver find you when he decides it's your turn to die."

For the first time that day, Fotir truly felt afraid. "He knows about you?" he asked the gleaner.

"Yes. In order to save Cresenne's life, I had to enter her dream. He saw my face. And I saw his."

Fotir gaped at him, fear giving way to hope. "Did you know him?"

"No." But even as Grinsa said this, he appeared to be thinking of something else. "I had hoped to speak with the king last night, but I never had the opportunity." He looked first at Keziah, and then at Fotir. "I suppose I could ask the two of you, though. What do you know of Braedon's high chancellor?"

"Almost nothing," Keziah answered. "We've never met, and with the king preoccupied with Kentigern and his allies, he's had little opportunity to look beyond Eibithar's borders."

Fotir shook his head. "I know very little, as well, beyond his reputation."

"Even that would be more than I know," Grinsa said.

The minister shrugged. "His name is Dusaan jal Kania. From what I hear, he's intelligent, powerful, and ambitious, just as one might expect of the most influential Qirsi in the empire."

"Do you know what he looks like?"

"No. I've heard that he's tall, that he's built more like a warrior than a minister. But that could be said of you as well."

"Precisely."

"You think he's the Weaver?"

"When I was with the movement," Cresenne said, answering for the gleaner, "I was one of the Weaver's highest-ranking servants. He called us his chancellors."

"It doesn't prove anything," Grinsa said. "But it's worth considering."

Fotir thought so as well. "With Aylyn the Second and Filib the Elder of Thorald dead, I can think of no one in Eibithar who has met the emperor or the high chancellor."

"What about elsewhere?"

"Perhaps Sanbira's queen. Certainly the Archduke of Wethyrn."

"I'll have the king send a message to them both," Keziah said. "Perhaps one of them can offer a better description of the chancellor."

"That's fine," Cresenne said, her cheeks still drained of color. "But in the meantime, Keziah is supposed to kill me. And when she doesn't, the Weaver won't only come after me, he'll start to question her loyalty to the movement as well."

Grinsa took her hand. "We have some time, Cresenne. You heard what she said. She's supposed to win my trust first. He can't think that will happen immediately. And as long as the Weaver expects her to kill you, he won't try it himself."

"So I can sleep at night again?"

"I wouldn't go that far. But at least you can rest during the days assured that he's not determined to kill you himself."

She grimaced. "That's hardly comforting."

Fotir had to agree.

The audience with Eibithar's king lasted throughout the morning and well past the ringing of the midday bells. Kearney informed the dukes of what he and his advisors had learned from the traitor, and Marston spoke in greater detail of Enid's betrayal and what little he and his father had managed to learn from the woman before she took her own life. It was a sobering discussion, one that clearly left Lathrop of Tremain disturbed. The others in the presence chamber—the king, Javan, Marston himself—had known something of these tidings prior to this day's gathering. Lathrop had not.

"Filib the Younger," the duke said softly, still sitting though the others had stood, intending to leave the chamber. "Lady Brienne." He glanced at Javan. "It seems your son is a victim of their treachery as well, Lord Curgh, albeit a living one. They strike at our youth, our children, because they know that's where we're most vulnerable."

"All the more reason for us to be watchful," Marston said. "We can't trust the Qirsi as we once did. We have to be willing to see them all, even those we consider our friends, through critical eyes, searching for signs of treachery where we never would have thought to look before." He spoke to the duke, but he intended the words for Kearney.

The king, he believed, was incapable of seeing his archminister in this way. Perhaps he still loved her. Perhaps she had served him for so long that he had come to take her loyalty for granted. Whatever the reason, Marston thought the woman Eibithar's greatest weakness. He couldn't be certain that she was a traitor, though he hoped that Xivled might discover the truth about her before long, but he certainly wouldn't have been surprised to learn that she had cast her lot with the renegades. All that Gershon Trasker had told him of her recent behavior had left the thane truly frightened.

"Have you come to question the loyalty of your minister, Lord Shanstead," the king asked, his tone making it clear that he knew just what Marston had meant to imply.

"No, my liege. I've known Xivled since we were children, and he's never given me cause to doubt that my faith in him is misplaced."

"As my archminister has."

Marston hesitated, then nodded. "Yes, my liege."

"And what is it you'd have me do? Shall I imprison her simply on the basis of your suspicions? Shall I torture her until she confesses to crimes she hasn't committed?"

"No, my liege," the thane answered, with as much asperity as he dared allow to creep into his voice. "I don't hate the Qirsi, no matter what you may think. Nor do I think it just to imprison or torture anyone without cause. But I fear the archminister is a threat to you and this realm, and I believe she should be sent away from the castle."

Kearney shook his head. "I won't do that."

"With all respect, my liege, I think that you offer more loyalty to this woman than she deserves."

"I disagree."

Marston wanted to say more, but Javan caught his eye and gave a slight shake of his head.

"Very well, my liege," the thane said instead. He bowed to the king and left the chamber, his jaw clenched so tightly that his temples ached.

Xiv was waiting for him in the corridor outside the chamber, leaning against the stone wall. Seeing Marston, he straightened and fell in step beside him as they walked to the nearest tower.

"What happened?" the minister asked. "You look as if the king branded you a traitor."

"It didn't go quite that badly. But if Thorald's standing in the realm turned on my friendship with Kearney, we'd be in a good deal of trouble right now." He waited to say more until they were out of the stairway and in the castle ward. "The king remains convinced that his archminister can be trusted," he finally said, squinting in the sunlight, "though from all I hear, she's behaved erratically for the past several turns." He glanced at the minister. "Have you learned anything from your conversations with her?"

"Very little. If she is a traitor, she's far more clever about hiding it than Enid was. She denies nothing, but neither does she say anything that suggests she's with the conspiracy. At least not when questioned directly about it."

"What do you mean by that?"

Xiv raked a hand through his short hair. "There was something strange about our discussion today. We were speaking of the need to find the source of the conspiracy's gold, and I suggested that we might be well served to have a loyal Qirsi join the movement. I had the impression that she agreed with me, but when the king's other Qirsi opposed the idea, she seemed to go out of her way to give in to their point of view. She almost seemed relieved when the vote went their way."

"As if she feared that your plan would reveal her betrayal?"

"Perhaps," the minister said, frowning. "Or else . . ."

"Or else what?"

For several moments Xiv just walked, silent and pensive. At last, he shook his head. "I don't know. It's probably nothing."

"It sounds to me as if she's hiding something, which merely confirms what I've known since we arrived here. This woman is dangerous; I'm certain of it. And the king is too blinded by the love they once shared to see it. It's up to us, Xiv. We need to do everything in our power to make Kearney see her for what she really is. We have to convince him to banish her from the castle."

Xiv nodded, though there was an uneasy look in his yellow eyes that Marston couldn't quite explain.

Chapter
Twenty-three

H e could see them fighting, both men crouched low, their blades held ready as they circled one another, looking for any opening to attack. It seemed that Tavis bled from a wound on his forearm and another on the side of his neck, but Grinsa couldn't be certain. The distance was too great, and though he was moving as swiftly as he could, the terrain was difficult. He picked his way across the great boulders with an eye toward the combatants, glancing down only occasionally to check his footing. Twice he nearly fell, for the stone was slick. He could feel sea spray on his face, he could smell brine and a coming storm riding the wind. Gulls cried overhead.

I'm on the Crown, he thought to himself. He paused, looking around, suddenly more aware of his surroundings than of the battle before him. He could see the dark mass of Enwyl Island in the distance, and to the west of that, the cliffs of Eibithar's eastern shore. *This is the Wethy Crown.*

He heard laughter and looked ahead once more. The two figures before him continued to circle, the other man, dark haired and tall, just as the gleaner remembered from Mertesse, switching his dagger from one hand to the other, the motion so fluid he seemed a dancer rather than a musician. He was smiling now, his confidence written in his expression, his stance, his pale blue eyes. The singer made a feint with his blade hand, and Tavis flinched. The man laughed a second time. Grinsa was nearly close enough now, though for what he couldn't be certain. He wanted to cry out to Tavis, to warn the young lord away from this man, from this fight, but he kept his silence, fearing that if he distracted Tavis for even a moment, it would mean the boy's death. He sensed that he was supposed to do something, that Tavis expected him to use magic against the singer, but for some reason he couldn't bring himself to do anything more than watch.

Again the singer pretended to lunge, and when Tavis moved to protect himself—a desperate, clumsy movement with his blade hand—the singer launched himself at the boy. They struggled briefly, a tangle of arms and legs and flashing steel. Then they fell to the stone, rolling to the side. Tavis cried out the gleaner's name, then shouted something else. Grinsa couldn't make out what he said, and in the next instant the two figures rolled again, reaching the crest of the boulder on which they fought and dropping out of view. Grinsa hurried toward them, calling to the young lord even as he stumbled again. To his left a wave crashed, sending a towering fountain of foam and spray over the huge rocks. Lightning carved across the purple sky, seeming to plunge into the Gulf of Kreanna like a dagger into flesh. Thunder followed a moment later, the clap so sudden and fierce that it staggered him, as if a blow. In an instant it was raining. But this was not the soft rain that presages a storm during the growing turns, building gradually as the storm grows near. Rather, this rain came like a hail of arrows during a siege. Abrupt and merciless, and so thick he could barely see what was before him. He cried out for Tavis, but the torrent drowned out his voice and swallowed the light. Thunder crashed again, and a voice beside him made the gleaner jump.

"It's raining."

Grinsa opened his eyes. Lightning flickered like a flame in the narrow window near his bed. He could hear rain slapping against the stone walls of Audun's Castle.

Tavis was sitting up in his bed, gazing toward the window as well. Grinsa rubbed a hand over his face, trying to clear his mind. They were in Audun's Castle still; they weren't in Wethyrn at all. It had been several days since the arrival of Marston of Shanstead and the discussion among the Qirsi to which he had been party. Little had happened in the intervening days, though the dukes of Heneagh and Labruinn had reached the castle the previous morning.

"You called out my name," Tavis said after some time. "Were you dreaming?"

Grinsa nodded. Then, when the boy didn't look his way, he managed to say, "Yes," in a hoarse voice.

"What about?"

He didn't want to say. This hadn't been just another dream. He felt drained, weak, as if he had been healing wounds for the better part of a day, just as he always felt after a vision. As much as he would have liked to believe otherwise, the gleaner knew that what he had seen would happen someday, probably soon. Tavis and the singer would meet on the Wethy Crown. They would fight their next battle—perhaps their last battle—in that storm Grinsa had seen. And, it seemed, Grinsa would be unable to stop them or, for that matter, to do anything more than watch helpless and useless. How was he to explain any of this to Tavis?

"It's hard to say," he answered. "I need a chance to sort through what I saw."

"It was a vision, then."

The boy was too damn clever. "Yes," he admitted. "It was a vision."

"Of me?"

"Give me some time, Tavis."

The young lord gave a nod, staring at him another moment before turning back to the window and the storm.

"It's early for a storm like this," the boy said quietly, as lightning brightened the window again.

"Osya's turn will be over in another two days. It's not that early."

"In Curgh, this would be early. Maybe it's not down here. I'm not used to spending the planting away from the north coast."

"You could probably go home now if you wanted. The king believes in your innocence, and though others might not, you no longer need Glyndwr's protection."

"I'm not ready to go home."

I still have to kill the singer. He didn't have to say it. If by some chance Grinsa thought that Cresenne's confession had made the young lord any less determined to avenge Brienne, his vision would have been enough to dispel the notion.

"Perhaps you should anyway," Grinsa said, his voice barely carrying over a rumble of thunder.

"What did you see, gleaner?"

Tavis had turned to face him again, forcing Grinsa to look away.

"Nothing." He lay back down. "Go to sleep."

For several moments Tavis continued to sit there, saying nothing. Then he lowered himself to his pillow, pulling his blankets up around his neck.

It seemed that Grinsa fell asleep immediately, for when he awoke once more, the silver light of day lit the chamber and Tavis's bed was empty. Several turns ago he might have been concerned for the boy's safety, even with Aindreas of Kentigern and his soldiers fifty leagues away. He had learned during their travels, however, that Tavis could take care of himself. *Usually,* he amended, recalling his vision.

He dressed and started toward the prison tower. No doubt Cresenne would be weary and ready for sleep.

But as he crossed the ward he saw two men dueling on the grass, the sharp crack of wood echoing off the castle walls as their swords met. Training weapons rather than steel. It took him a moment to recognize one of the men as Tavis. Hagan MarCullet stood nearby, and Grinsa soon realized that the man fighting Tavis was the swordmaster's son, Xaver. He hesitated a moment, glancing toward Cresenne's tower. Then he walked over to Hagan, who was shouting encouragement to both lord and liege man.

"Are you to be training the king's men as well, swordmaster?" he asked.

Hagan regarded him briefly, then gave a short laugh. "Trasker would never allow that, and you know it." He nodded his head toward the two young men. "Actually it was the boy's idea."

"Tavis's?"

He nodded a second time. "Sword up, Tavis! You can't defend yourself with the tip held too low!

"His footwork has gotten a bit careless," he went on a moment later, lowering his voice once more. "And his attacks aren't quite as precise as I remember. But he still wields a quick blade. He's nearly a match for his father." He glanced at the gleaner. "Have you been working him?"

"Not at all. I don't know much about swordplay."

"I guess some are just born to it. Was you that healed him though, wasn't it? After Kentigern?"

Grinsa had long denied this, fearing that if he revealed his ability to heal, some might begin to question what other powers he possessed. But most in the castle knew by now that he had healed Cresenne's injuries, and though he felt certain that the king would not betray his secret, he sensed that it wouldn't be long before others learned that he was a Weaver.

"Yes," he said. "It was me."

"You did well. Xaver tells me the boy was in a bad way when last he saw him in the dungeon."

"Thank you."

Grinsa and Hagan watched them fight for another few moments, before the swordmaster called to them, "That's enough for now, lads!"

The two boys stopped, stepped back from one another, and bowed, first to each other, and then to Hagan. Their faces were as red as Sanbiri wine and their hair was damp with sweat. But both of them were grinning, Tavis looking happier than Grinsa had ever seen him. Whatever his reason for requesting the training, clearly it had done him some good.

Seeing the gleaner, Tavis's smile began to fade.

"Has something happened?" he asked, wiping the sweat from his face with his sleeve.

"No. I was on my way to the prison tower and saw you here. I just stopped to watch." He faltered. After all this time, he still found it hard to pay the boy compliments. "You're very good," he made himself say.

Tavis shrugged, looked off to the side. "I used to be."

"You still are," Xaver said.

"As are you, Master MarCullet."

An uneasy silence fell over them, until Grinsa cleared his throat, forcing a smile. "Well, as I say, I was on my way to the tower. I didn't mean to interrupt."

"Not at all," the swordmaster said. "I shouldn't work him too hard if he hasn't been training."

But Tavis didn't say a word. It seemed he was eager for Grinsa to leave.

"If you need me, I'll be with Cresenne," he told the boy.

Tavis nodded once, his lips pressed thin.

Grinsa tipped his head to Xaver and Hagan in turn, then walked away, making his way to Cresenne's chamber, all the while wondering if he should insist that Tavis return to Curgh. Javan and the duchess would support him, he knew. They wished only for their son's safety; neither of them cared anything for revenge. And Grinsa wasn't convinced that Tavis's thirst for the assassin's blood was something to be encouraged. If his vision the previous night was to be believed, it might be the death of the boy.

For his part, Grinsa would have been glad to end their journeying here, in the City of Kings. He had come to like Tavis despite the boy's many faults. But Cresenne and Bryntelle needed him, and though he had resisted it for a time, he could no longer keep himself from thinking of them as his family. He still loved Cresenne, even after all she had done, and while he couldn't be certain that she would ever love him, he wasn't certain that mattered. Because of him, the Weaver wanted her dead. How could he leave her, knowing the danger she faced every time she closed her eyes to sleep? How could he leave Bryntelle?

More to the point, there was a war to be fought, and though few of the Eandi realized it now, it would fall to Grinsa to lead them, whether to victory or defeat. He had to remain here, so that when the time came, he would be ready to fight the Weaver. Certainly that's what Keziah would have told him, and Cresenne, too, and perhaps the king himself.

Then why did Oirsar send the vision?

He faltered in midstride, as if suddenly stricken by some unseen pain. The vision. It was a warning. It had to be. Tavis should stay far from the Wethy Crown. He should break off this pointless and perilous pursuit of the assassin. That's what it had to be saying. Except that visions didn't always work that way. Long ago, before he left Cresenne to go to Kentigern, before he'd even met Tavis in the Revel gleaning tent in Curgh city, he had a vision of himself journeying with the boy, fighting beside him against the conspiracy. And though it seemed that what he had glimpsed in that vision had already come to pass, he couldn't be certain that his path didn't still lie with the boy. He had yet to have that moment of recognition, the one that came a turn or a year or ten years after a vision, when he realized that he was living the prophecy. He couldn't be certain that he ever would—with some visions it never came. This didn't mean the vision wasn't true; it most cases it meant nothing. In this case, because of his dream the night before, it meant everything.

If that vision from so long ago had yet to be realized, then perhaps Tavis had nothing to fear from the singer. If, on the other hand, that moment had passed . . .

Except that visions didn't always work that way, either.

Grinsa spat a curse.

Of all his powers, gleaning was the one he liked least. The glimpses it offered of the future carried burdens he didn't wish to bear and uncertainties that often left him frustrated and fearful. Even this latest dream, the meaning of which seemed so clear at first, had become muddied in his mind over the past few hours. If he chose to remain with Cresenne and Bryntelle, would it make a difference? Tavis might resume his pursuit of the assassin without him. Certainly the boy was stubborn enough to do so. And though the gleaner had seen the events on the Wethy shore as if he were there, Tavis and the assassin had paid him no heed. Even when he called out to the young lord, Tavis didn't appear to hear him. Had his voice been overwhelmed by the sea and the storm? Or was it that he wasn't even there? Had Qirsar, the god of the Qirsi, merely offered a glimpse of what awaited the boy if Grinsa did not accompany him on his coming journey eastward? The god had done such things before, many times.

Yes, it was a warning. But of what? If you go with the boy to the Wethy Crown, he may die; if you don't go with the boy, he may die. Either was possible. Keeping Tavis in Eibithar seemed the only way to ensure his safety. And so long as the young lord didn't learn that the assassin had gone east, Grinsa thought he could do that much.

He continued on across the ward, reaching the base of the prison tower a few moments later. He climbed the stairs quickly and upon emerging into the corridor outside Cresenne's chamber, heard Bryntelle cry out. Hurrying to the chamber door, the gleaner saw Cresenne sitting on her bed, with the baby lying in her lap.

"Is she all right?" he asked.

Cresenne looked up, a brilliant smile lighting her face. "She laughed!"

"Really?"

"Yes. Come and see."

One of the guards opened the door for him, and he stepped quickly to the bed to sit beside them.

"Watch." Cresenne lowered her face to the baby's belly and kissed it loudly, shaking her head as she did. Bryntelle let out a delighted squeal, her mouth opening in a wide, toothless grin. Cresenne did it a second time, drawing the same response.

"You see?" she said, straightening. "You try it."

Grinsa smiled, but shook his head. "I don't think she's ready to laugh for me."

"You don't know that."

He shrugged, staring at his daughter, unwilling at that moment to risk a look at the woman beside him.

"At least take her. She's in a wonderful mood."

"All right."

He allowed Cresenne to place Bryntelle in his arms, grinning when the child continued to smile and coo. Cresenne laid her hand gently on his arm, leaning closer so that she could look at the baby as well. It almost seemed that his skin was aflame where she was touching him.

"You see?" she said, glancing at him.

He merely nodded, still not looking at her.

"What's the matter?"

"Nothing. I'm just enjoying her." *Both of you, really.*

"Something's troubling you. I can tell."

As quickly as it had begun, the moment passed. Briefly, as they sat there together, they truly had been a family. But this was a prison, and even as they spoke, the land moved inexorably toward war.

"It's nothing. I had a vision, that's all."

"Of what?" He could hear fear tightening her voice, and he regretted saying even this much.

He shook his head. "It doesn't matter."

"Of course it does. What did you see?"

"I saw Tavis fighting the assassin."

"Did you see the outcome?"

"No."

She nodded, removing her hand from his arm and shifting on the bed so that there was more distance between them. "Where?"

"The Crown."

"Is that where you're going next?"

"I don't intend to go anywhere, Cresenne." He made himself meet her gaze. "I don't know yet what this vision means. I'm not even certain that I'm to be there with them."

"Of course you are. You're tied to the boy in some way. You told me that long ago, in Galdasten."

The gleaner remembered, of course. There had been a storm that night, much like the one to which he had wakened out of this most recent vision. Was there meaning in that as well?

"You must be tired," he said. "You should get some rest. Bryntelle will be fine with me."

Cresenne leaned forward and kissed the baby on the forehead. Then she stretched out on the bed, closing her eyes.

"If it means anything," she said, already sounding sleepy, "I know that you don't want to leave us, that it will pain you to go."

"I'm not going anywhere."

"I think you are. In the end I think you'll decide that you have no choice. You've pledged yourself to protecting both Tavis and me, but you can only be with one of us at a time. And you feel somehow responsible for the boy."

"Don't you think I feel the same way about you, about Bryntelle?"

"Bryntelle isn't in danger. Keziah told us so. And whatever danger I'm in is of my own making. That's what you'll decide." She opened her eyes for just a moment. "And you'll be right."

She closed her eyes once more and rolled away from him. After a few moments he stood and began walking around the chamber with Bryntelle, rocking her gently and singing an Eibitharian folk song in a near whisper. Soon both the baby and her mother were asleep.

The day passed slowly. Grinsa couldn't keep the vision from his mind, nor could he help but think that in the end, Cresenne's words would prove as prescient as any gleaning. It seemed that Bryntelle was beginning to adjust to the strange hours she and her mother were keeping. She slept for the rest of the morning and well past midday before waking, hungry and wet. Grinsa changed her swaddling, then woke Cresenne so that the baby could nurse.

As Bryntelle ate, the city bells began to toll. It was far too early for the prior's bell.

Cresenne frowned, looking from the window to Grinsa.

"Has another duke arrived?"

"None were expected after Labruinn and Heneagh. The rest have refused to come."

"Then what?" She sounded alarmed, and Grinsa silently cursed the Weaver once more. Cresenne had lied to him when they were still lovers and the gleaner couldn't be certain that he had known her as well as he believed at the time. But she hadn't struck him then as the type of person who was easily frightened. Only now, bearing scars from the Weaver's assault, did her face turn the color of ash at the merest hint of danger.

"It's probably just a messenger," he said. "From one of the other dukes, I'd guess." He made himself smile. "I'm sure it's nothing to be afraid of."

But he could feel his own pulse pounding too hard in his temples, and though he tried to appear calm, he found himself looking repeatedly toward the window on the chamber's steel door, as if expecting at any moment to see Keziah's face, or the king's.

Eventually the pealing of the bells ceased, and though he could hear voices rising to the narrow window from the castle ward, none of what he heard gave him cause for concern. Still, he wasn't entirely surprised when at last he heard the scrape of a boot in the corridor and a low voice speaking to the guards.

A moment later a face loomed at the door's steel grate. It wasn't the king or Keziah. Rather, it was Tavis.

"Forgive me," the young lord said, his dark eyes flicking briefly toward Cresenne, who covered herself with a corner of the bed linens.

"What is it, Tavis?"

"A message. I think you should hear it."

"Can it wait?"

"It's all right," Cresenne said, her voice low and tense. "I won't be able to sleep anyway."

He looked at her and whispered, "I'm sorry."

She shook her head, swiping at a tear that had appeared suddenly on her cheek. "It's not your fault. I knew this would come. Actually I dreamed it. I just didn't expect it would happen so soon."

Grinsa and Lord Tavis entered Kearney's presence chamber together but quickly separated, Tavis going to where his father stood near the window, and the gleaner sitting on the arm of Keziah's chair. The other dukes were there as well, as were the thane of Shanstead and Gershon Trasker. All of the nobles had brought their ministers, so that the chamber felt crowded and warm.

When Tavis and Grinsa arrived, the king had just asked the older dukes—Javan, Lathrop, and Welfyl, the duke of Heneagh—about the realm's past relations with the matriarchy in Sanbira. Now Welfyl, bent and frail looking in his chair by the dormant hearth, began a rambling reply, telling of his one visit to Sanbira in 853, when the queen at that time, Meleanna the Ninth, had honored him with an invitation to Castle Yserne.

"What's happened?" Grinsa asked, his voice so low Keziah could barely hear him.

"Didn't Tavis tell you?"

Welfyl paused long enough to frown at the two of them before continuing his tale.

"Only that a message had come," Grinsa went on, lowering his voice even further. "I gather it's from the queen."

"Yes."

"My pardon, Lord Heneagh," Marston said, interrupting the old duke before Keziah could tell her brother more, "but I'd be interested in knowing if the queen ever spoke to you of an alliance between our two realms."

"I was getting to that," Welfyl said crossly. "Meleanna told me at dinner that night that the Matriarchy wished to avoid alliances with any of the northern realms. She said that the Sanbiris valued their friendship with Eibithar, but that they didn't wish to risk offending the lords of Aneira and Braedon. 'We have no wish to be party to your quarrels,' is how she put it." His brow furrowed. "Or something to that effect."

"It seems Olesya is more willing than were her grandmother and mother to take such risks," the thane said, turning to the king. "I believe this is a fine opportunity, my liege. We'd be wise to accept her offer as quickly as we can."

Grinsa was watching the king as well. "Forgive me, Your Majesty. But am I to understand that the queen of Sanbira has proposed an alliance?"

"Yes, she has. I assumed that Lord Tavis had informed you on your way here."

"No, Your Majesty. He merely said that a message had come. I believe he thought it more appropriate that you inform me, since the message was clearly intended for you."

Keziah knew better. The tension between the young lord and her brother had been thick as a coastal fog when they entered the chamber. She could imagine the two of them walking in complete silence all the way from the prison tower. But Grinsa would conclude properly that the state of their friendship was no concern of Kearney's or the other nobles. The message was what mattered.

"I've already read it to the other lords," Kearney said, "so I won't waste time with it again. Briefly, the queen writes of an attempt on the life of one of her duchesses, Diani of Curlinte. Diani is young—her mother just passed to Bian's realm a few turns ago—and she survived the attempt. But House Curlinte is closely tied to the royal house, and it seems Diani's first minister was behind the assassination attempt. The queen fears the conspiracy will strike at her again, and she proposes an alliance to fight the Qirsi threat."

Grinsa's gaze had shifted to the boy, who was staring back at him, his face pale, so that the scars he bore appeared even more livid than usual. Keziah couldn't say what passed between them in those few moments, but within the span of a single heartbeat, Grinsa looked as troubled as the boy.

"I must disagree with the thane, Your Majesty," Fotir said from where he stood, near his duke and the young lord.

"How so, First Minister?"

"I don't believe this message represents a change in the Sanbiri attitude toward alliances. The queen doesn't suggest that we join forces with her against any other realms, but rather only against the conspiracy. I can't know for certain, of course, but I would guess that she sent similar messages to every sovereign in the Forelands."

Grinsa nodded, his mouth still set in a thin line. "That sounds likely to me, as well."

"This isn't to say that we shouldn't pursue the alliance anyway," Fotir went on. "But you should recognize her offer for what it is."

"The queen's letter also proves beyond doubt what we've thought for some time now." Javan. "The conspiracy is a threat to every realm and every court. From this day forward, any time we hear of a noble's death, we must question the circumstances surrounding it. We can't assume that anything is as it seems. Not until this threat has passed and the Qirsi have been defeated."

Marston nodded. "I agree with Lord Curgh. And though it saddens me to say it, I'd add that we can no longer simply trust the counsel of our Qirsi without question. It seems there are more traitors in the Forelands than we feared. Blind trust can only lead to disaster."

"So we're to assume then that all of them have betrayed us?" Lathrop shook his head. "That's nonsense."

Keziah felt as if an arrow had buried itself in her chest. Several of the other ministers looked angry. She thought Evetta might cry. Even Xivled, who had appeared unfazed by the decision of the king to exclude Qirsi from his discussion with the dukes a few days before now seemed disturbed by what his lord had said. But Keziah's pain had far less to do with Shanstead's words than with the way Kearney was looking at her. She had worked hard to make him doubt her. But more recently, since the Weaver instructed her to begin winning back the king's trust, she had tried as best she could to do just that. It had seemed a gift, a spar of light in the shadows she had woven about herself. She had known it wouldn't last, but for just a short while she had thought to continue her deception of the Weaver while also repairing some of the damage she had done to what remained of the love she and Kearney once shared.

Seeing how he regarded her now, however, she understood that it was too late. She saw fear in his green eyes, and so much suspicion. There might have been love there as well, a residue of the passion she remembered from their time in Glyndwr. But it had been twisted and defiled by all that had come since. Marston might find it hard to convince the other nobles to stop trusting the Qirsi who served them, but he had already swayed the king.

Caius of Labruinn glanced at his first minister, the oldest of the Qirsi in the king's chamber. "Forgive me, Ottah," he said, "but I'm not ready to dismiss the thane's suggestion so quickly. No doubt the duchess of Curlinte trusted her minister, just as Lord Shanstead's father trusted his."

Caius was a young man in comparison to the other dukes. Not as young as Marston, but close. The young ones, it seemed, would lead this battle. Perhaps they hadn't grown as close to their ministers, having only led their houses for a few years. Perhaps, having come into their birthrights at a time when the conspiracy was already beginning to spread across the land, they found it easier to question the loyalty of those who served them. Whatever the reason, Keziah found herself hating this man, and the thane as well.

Caius had risen from his chair and was pacing the floor now. "It seems there's something in the Qirsi heart that breeds treachery. It runs like a river through the history of your people."

Fotir bristled. "With all respect, Lord Labruinn, I find what you've said offensive."

"As do I."

Everyone in the chamber turned to look at Tavis.

"If it wasn't for the Qirsi I never would have escaped from Kentigern. In all likelihood I'd be dead by now."

Marston gave a small laugh. "My Lord Curgh," he said, as if speaking to a child. "If it wasn't for the Qirsi, you might never have been in Kentigern's dungeon in the first place. Lady Brienne would still be alive and you would be in line behind your father for the throne."

"That's true, Lord Shanstead. Not all the Qirsi can be trusted. But neither can they all be dismissed as traitors. Even I can see that, though I have more cause than any of you to hate them."

"The boy makes a good point," Gershon said from the far corner of the chamber. Then his face reddened. "I mean Lord Curgh. Forgive me, my lord."

Tavis actually smiled. "Apology accepted, swordmaster."

The king stood, compelling the rest of them to their feet. "I'll consider a response to the queen of Sanbira," he said. "As to the rest . . ." He faltered, his eyes straying to Keziah for just an instant. "We'll speak of it again tomorrow."

The nobles and ministers bowed to him and began to file out of the chamber. Keziah lingered a moment, and Grinsa with her. She hoped that Kearney would call her back. Perhaps if she could talk to him, she might allay whatever fears Marston had planted in the king's mind. But Kearney kept silent and soon she and Grinsa were in the corridor.

Tavis was waiting for them. It struck her as strange that this young lord, whom she still thought of as spoiled and undisciplined, should be the most vocal defender of the Qirsi among all the gathered nobles. Even stranger, Gershon Trasker had been the only person to agree with him.

"You think it was him," Grinsa said to the boy without preamble.

"I think he was behind it, yes. According to the message, the assassins are all dead. But I find it difficult to believe that the singer would have allowed himself to be killed."

"You almost managed it in Mertesse."

Tavis's eyes narrowed, as if he thought Grinsa were mocking him. "I was fortunate, and you know it."

Grinsa looked away, twisting his mouth sourly. There was more to this than Keziah could possibly have understood. "So, you think we should go to Sanbira," he said.

"If we're going to look for him, we should start there."

If we're going to look for him. . . . The words hung between them like a lofted arrow between two armies. A challenge.

"You can't go," Keziah said. She watched Grinsa, searching for some response. When he offered none, she turned her glare on the boy. "You know that he can't. Without him, Cresenne will die." She realized there were guards nearby and she started down the corridor away from them, drawing Tavis and Grinsa after her as if by the sheer force of her will. She didn't stop until they had reached her chamber and she had sent away the servants and closed the door. "Cresenne needs Grinsa here," she began once more, keeping her voice as low as her emotions allowed. "It's just a matter of time before the Weaver tries again to kill her. We all know it, just as we all know that Grinsa is the only one who can protect her, the only one who can pull her from the dreams."

"Keziah—"

"I know that you want vengeance," she said to the boy, ignoring her brother. "I can even understand why you might need it. But it's more important that he remain here."

"Then, I'll go alone."

"No," Grinsa said, "you won't."

"I don't answer to you, gleaner."

"I know you don't. That's not what I meant."

The boy said nothing, looking more astonished than relieved.

Keziah could think of nothing to say. Grinsa couldn't leave the castle; it was as obvious to her as the scars on Cresenne's face, as clear as the sound of Bryntelle's cries. Whatever he owed this young lord, whatever they had shared during their travels through Aneira, none of it could mean as much to Grinsa as his family. Surely he knew that.

"You can't mean that you intend to leave with him," she finally managed in a quavering voice.

"I do."

"But—"

He held up a hand, silencing her. "There's more at work here than my wishes, more to this than any of us can understand."

"Your dream."

She looked at Tavis, then turned back to Grinsa. "What dream?"

He was eyeing the boy. "I had a vision last night. I saw Tavis fighting the assassin on the shores of the Wethy Crown. I don't know the outcome; I'm not entirely certain what it meant. But it seems the gods are telling me to go."

"You can't know that."

At last he met her gaze. "Cresenne dreamed that I'd be leaving."

Keziah opened her mouth to argue, closed it again. She couldn't begin to guess what it might mean. She wished she could deny that it meant anything at all, but she knew better, possessing gleaning magic herself.

"But who'll protect her?" she asked, tears stinging her eyes. "Who'll protect me?"

Grinsa stepped past the boy and gathered her in his arms. "You're the answer to both questions, Kezi," he whispered.

"I can't protect her from a Weaver."

"He expects you to kill her. He won't do anything himself so long as he believes he can count on you. You told me yourself that he intends this as a test of your commitment to the movement. He'll give you every opportunity to succeed, because he has ample reason to want you to."

She clung to him, laying her cheek against his broad chest. "But I can't put him off forever. Eventually he'll lose patience with me, and then we'll both die."

"Tavis and I won't be gone that long."

"You're going to the Crown, Grinsa, and then you'll be searching for a single man. This could take you half the year."

"It won't. Can you prevail upon Kearney to give us two mounts?"

The familiar twisting in her chest nearly made her wince. "I don't think I can convince him to do anything anymore."

"I can," Tavis said. "Or more precisely, my father can."

"But will he?" Grinsa asked. "He won't want you to leave. Certainly not for this."

"He won't want me to, but he'll let me."

"All right," Grinsa said. He looked down at Keziah. "Tavis and I will ride to Rennach, which shouldn't take us more than five or six days, if we push the horses a bit. From there we'll find passage on a merchant ship to the Crown."

"A ship?" Tavis asked.

"Yes, of course. Riding all the way around the gulf and up the peninsula would take far too long." He eyed the young lord. "Is that a problem?"

Tavis looked away. "I don't fare well on ships. I never have."

"If the weather's reasonably fair, the crossing should take less than a day. It's not like crossing the Scabbard during the snows. This time of year the Gulf of Kreanna is actually rather pleasant."

Tavis nodded, clearly unconvinced.

Grinsa looked at Keziah once more. "My point is, we can be in Helke in seven or eight days."

"But then you have to find the assassin."

"I dreamed of him, Keziah. I know where to look."

She wanted to say more, to argue the point until he changed his mind. But that wasn't Grinsa's way. He knew just as she did what he was risking. No doubt he realized as well that the journey he was about to undertake wouldn't be as easy as he made it sound.

For several moments she and her brother stared at one another, until finally, his eyes still locked on hers, Grinsa said, "Tavis, you should tell your parents that we're planning to leave. See if you can get those horses."

"When will we be going?"

"Tomorrow morning, at first light."

"All right." He regarded them both for a moment, then let himself out of the chamber, leaving Keziah and Grinsa alone.

"Does he survive the encounter you saw?" she asked.

"I don't know, but I think his chances are better with me there."

Back in the growing turns, when Grinsa had risked so much to save Tavis from the dungeon of Kentigern, Keziah had asked him if the boy was worth the possible costs. She nearly asked him again now.

"I don't know how you can bring yourself to leave them," she said instead. "It would kill me."

He closed his eyes briefly, taking a long breath. "I'm not sure that I can explain it. He has a role to play in this war before it ends. Killing the assassin isn't it—to be honest, I'm not certain what it is—but I sense that he can't do the rest if he's still consumed with his need for vengeance. And if he dies, and his destiny remains un-fulfilled, we'll all suffer for the loss."

"And what of Cresenne? Doesn't she have a part to play in this as well?"

"Yes, of course she does. But I fear that . . . that I love her too much to see clearly what it might be." He swallowed, looking more unsure of himself than Keziah could remember. "For all I know, she did her part by having Brienne killed and betraying me."

Keziah shook her head. "I think there's more to it than that. She's not the same person she was then."

"I know."

She felt his weariness as if it were her own. Much as she wanted to convince him to remain, she understood that she could help him best by not trying to do so.

"If the Weaver comes for her again, you'll have to find a way to wake her," he said. "He can't make her remain asleep, although it may seem that way at times. This is something you need to learn as well." He held his face close to hers, his yellow eyes fixed on her own, as if he could will her to comprehend what he was saying. "When he hurts you, when he closes a hand round your throat, it's all an illusion. His magic only allows him to reach into your dreams. After that, he's using your magic and your mind to hurt you. So you have to train your mind to resist him. You can't panic, you can't give in to fear of what he seems to be doing to you. He can't kill you with-out your complicity. If you keep your thoughts clear, you should be able to wake yourself before he can harm you. Explain this to Cresenne. Work on it together."

Keziah nodded, feeling tears on her face again. "We'll try."

He started to say something, then stopped himself. *Trying isn't enough, Kezi.* He had said this to her before and no doubt he was thinking it now. But he merely kissed her and wiped away her tears with a gentle hand. "I know you will," he whispered. And left her.

The light in her chamber was just as she had envisioned it, soft and golden, deep orange from the sunset seeping through the small window to mingle with the bright yellow of the torches. She had bathed earlier in the day, rousing herself from her tears and her fright to clean the stale smell from her limbs and hair. Then she had bathed Bryntelle as well, so that they would both be clean for him on this last night.

He entered the chamber with food from the kitchens and a small carafe of wine. After the guard closed the door, Grinsa asked that he and his comrade leave the corridor so that the three of them might have some privacy. Just to the bottom of the tower, he pleaded. When the men refused, he pulled two daggers from his belt, stuck them in the wooden door just above its steel grate, and draped his over-shirt from them so that it hung in front of the small window. This, too, was just as she had seen.

They ate, he sang to Bryntelle until she slept. And as night settled over the castle, moonless and cool, Grinsa took Cresenne in his arms and began to remove her clothes, gently and silently.

She hadn't been with any other man since their time together, and the memory of his touch seemed to awaken her passion as from a long sleep. His lips on her neck and breasts, his hands traveling her body, deft and sure. There was something familiar about it, and yet something new as well. Moving above him, her back arched, her hair falling loose, she finally found it within herself to admit what she had known for so long. She loved this man, and somehow, a gift of the gods, an offer of forgiveness beyond any she had imagined possible, he loved her as well.

She felt it in the rhythm of their movements on the small bed, in the way he gazed up at her, watching her love him.

A part of her wanted to hate herself for all that she had done to him, to the world in which their daughter would live. But his touch wouldn't allow it. *If I can forgive you,* he seemed to say with his kisses, his caresses, *if I can love you, you must do the same for yourself.*

And as she arced over him one last time, biting back a soft cry, her body seeming to burn with what he had done to her, what they had done together, she realized that she could do this much, for him, for herself, for Bryntelle.

Afterward, drained and sated, happier than she had been in many turns, and more afraid as well, she watched him sleep, touching his white hair, studying his face by the faint light that the window allowed into the chamber.

When the sky began to brighten with morning, he awoke, dressed quickly, and stooped to kiss her where she lay.

"I'll come back to you," he whispered. "To both of you. I promise."

He kissed Bryntelle, brushed her cheek with a slender finger. Then he straightened, and left the chamber, tears glistening on his cheeks.

It was all just as she had dreamed it would be.

She had seen much else in her vision as well, things that made her tremble for herself and for her child. She hadn't seen enough, however, to know if Grinsa could keep this last promise he had made.

Chapter
Twenty-four

Curtell, Braedon, Amon's Moon waxing

T he high chancellor didn't have to look at Nitara to know that she was watching him, following his every movement with her ghostly pale eyes. He felt her stares as he might the breath of a lover, stirring his hair, touching the nape of his neck, the harbinger of a kiss. He had regretted turning her away from his bed every night since their encounter in his chamber, though he knew he had been right to do so. For years he had dreamed of finding a woman with whom he could lead the Forelands when at last his plans bore fruit. He had thought to make Cresenne his queen, and when he realized that she had betrayed him, he had turned such thoughts to Jastanne. Certainly it had never occurred to him to look for his queen within Harel's court.

There could be no denying that Nitara was beautiful and intelligent. When Dusaan first thought to turn Kayiv and her to his cause, he had considered the man the more promising of the two. Only as he spoke to them of the movement and its needs did he begin to see just how wrong he had been. She was brilliant, and Kayiv proved far more limited than the Weaver had hoped.

That she knew who and what he was only served to deepen Dusaan's fascination with the woman. It was one thing to touch Jastanne with his mind as she stood naked before him, her hair dancing in the wind on the plain he had conjured for her dreams. It would have been quite another to lie with a woman who knew his face and his name, as well as the extent of his power. He realized, however, that there were dangers as well, and thus far, his caution had overmatched his need and his passion.

The greatest risk, he felt certain, came not from Nitara herself but rather from Kayiv, who had been her lover until recently. Dusaan didn't know what she had told him, or how she had explained her decision to end their love affair. The Weaver had made her swear that she wouldn't tell anyone what she knew about him, and he had urged her to go back to Kayiv and repair their relationship. But though she had promised to keep his secret, she had made it clear that she couldn't love the minister anymore. And judging from the way Kayiv was glaring at the high chancellor, as the other Qirsi in the ministerial chamber argued some arcane point of Braedon law, Dusaan could only assume that the man had guessed where her affections were now directed. He might even have concluded that Nitara was already sharing the chancellor's bed.

Dusaan didn't fear the man. He had far more pressing matters with which to concern himself than the pique of a spurned lover. But the chancellor knew from what Nitara had told him that when she first began to consider that he might be the Weaver, she voiced these suspicions to Kayiv. If Kayiv's resentment ran deep enough, he might repeat what he heard to other ministers, perhaps even to the emperor.

He thought he could ease Kayiv's anger, and with it the danger that the man might act against Dusaan, if he could manage to speak with him in private. The mere need to arrange such a conversation, however, pointed to a far greater problem. Kayiv had cause to hate him, and therefore to spread rumors that he had betrayed the emperor, that he might in fact be far more than he admitted. Nitara, who knew for certain that he was the Weaver and did lead the movement, was in love with him. And though she seemed satisfied for now to love him from a distance, it was possible, even likely, that she would grow restive with time, coming to resent him for refusing to return her love.

Cresenne had betrayed him. Grinsa had seen his face. Yaella ja Banvel, first minister to the duke of Mertesse, had thought to blame him for the death of Shurik jal Marcine, her lover. In the past half year, the movement had lost, in addition to Shurik, Enid ja Kovar, first minister in Thorald, Paegar jal Berget, high minister to the king of Eibithar, and Peshkal jal Boerd, first minister to the duke of Bistari. Their deaths had little in common—one had died at the hands of a drunken musician, another succumbed to the poison of a ruthlessly ambitious Eandi noble, and yet another died at the hands of the Weaver himself, who had been forced to kill Paegar to guard the secret of his identity. Only Enid had died as a direct result of her duke learning that she served the Weaver's cause. Yet it seemed to Dusaan that for the first time, his movement was in danger of being exposed to too much scrutiny. From what he had been told by his chancellor in Yserne, he gathered that the recent assassination attempt in Curlinte had fooled no one. The movement hadn't suffered for this failure. A minister loyal to the courts had been killed in such a way as to convince the duchess and Sanbira's queen that he was the traitor responsible for the assault. But they had been fortunate in this instance. A similar failure elsewhere might be disastrous.

Which brought him to the crux of the matter. He wasn't ready to reveal himself and challenge the courts directly; the Eandi weren't sufficiently weakened yet. But perhaps the time had come to push the emperor into a war with Eibithar. Such a conflict, if it succeeded in drawing Aneira, Caerisse, and Wethyrn into battle as well, might succeed where more subtle machinations no longer could. Even if the emperor gave the order to begin preparations for the invasion now, it would take another turn or two before the fighting began in earnest. Enough time, Dusaan believed, for the final pieces of his plan to be put in place.

Yes, the time had come at last. Perhaps this was a bit earlier than he had intended originally, but a skilled leader knew when to hold true to his initial designs, and when to change them to meet the exigencies of circumstance.

"Wouldn't you agree with that, High Chancellor?"

He stared blankly at Stavel. He had completely lost the thread of their discussion. "I'm sorry, Chancellor. My mind must have wandered."

The older man frowned. "I was saying that we may be able to satisfy both Muelry and Grensyn by making whatever solution we propose temporary."

The high chancellor shook his head, finding it nearly impossible to believe that they were still discussing this foolish dispute among the southern houses. The matter should have been settled days ago. "No wonder my attention drifted," he muttered.

A few of the ministers laughed, Nitara a bit too loudly. Kayiv didn't even smile, nor, for that matter, did Stavel.

Dusaan laughed with the others, though inwardly he berated himself for his carelessness. He didn't usually allow himself to be so thoroughly distracted. There could be no doubt: the time had come to move forward with his plans.

"Yes, Chancellor," he said. "That does strike me as an equitable solution to the problem. I'll mention it to the emperor, and I'll be sure to tell him that it was your idea."

Stavel nodded, obviously trying not to appear too pleased.

Dusaan stood. "Perhaps we should adjourn for the day."

The others stood as well, Nitara lingering as if she wished to speak with him privately. The Weaver, however, was watching Kayiv, who strode past the older chancellors toward the door.

"Minister," Dusaan called.

The man stopped, casting a dark look his way.

"A word, please."

Kayiv looked at the door once more, seeming to consider leaving anyway. His mouth was set in a thin line, his hands flexed restlessly, but he remained by the door, allowing the other Qirsi to file past him.

Nitara stared at the high chancellor for several moments, until it occurred to Dusaan that she was awaiting an invitation to remain as well.

"Was there something you wished to discuss, Minister?" he asked.

She furrowed her brow. "No, I . . . I merely thought . . ."

"I won't keep the minister long," he said, indicating Kayiv with an open hand. "Perhaps you can wait for him in the corridor."

Her face colored, her eyes straying to Kayiv briefly. An instant later she left the chamber, as if suddenly eager to get away. Dusaan closed the door.

"I hope you didn't think to fool me with that little deceit."

The Weaver gave a small frown. "I'm afraid I don't know what you mean."

"Please don't play games with me, High Chancellor. You know as well as I that Nitara wasn't interested in speaking with me. It's you she wants." He looked away, his gaze flitting about the chamber as if searching for an escape. "For all I know, she already has you."

"She doesn't."

Their eyes met. Kayiv appeared to be trying to gauge whether Dusaan was telling the truth.

"Please," the chancellor said, gesturing toward a pair of chairs in the center of the chamber.

After a moment, Kayiv stepped to one of them and sat. Dusaan did the same.

"You're right. I do know that she wasn't waiting for you. I said what I did to make her leave." He paused. If he was to keep Kayiv from turning on him, he'd have to allay the man's jealousy. And that meant being completely honest with him where the woman was concerned. "I'll also grant that you're right about Nitara. She has admitted that she harbors some . . . affection for me. But nothing has come of it, and nothing will. I have more important matters with which to occupy my time."

"I'm not certain I believe you."

"That's your heart talking, not your mind. Think about it for a moment. Given what I've told you—both of you—about my role in the movement, would I risk an affair with her, knowing that it would anger you, that if it ended badly, it would anger her as well? She's an attractive woman, and under different circumstances I wouldn't worry about bruising your feelings. But I'm not about to risk my life and the movement merely to bed her."

"Is this why you asked me to stay? To tell me that she's not your lover?"

"Not entirely, no. I did sense your jealousy, however. It concerns me that you conceal your emotions so poorly. Others in the movement, myself included, are depending upon you to be more subtle."

"You have nothing to worry about." He gripped the arms of his chair, as if waiting for the high chancellor to give him leave to stand.

"I'd like to believe that." Dusaan regarded the man for a moment. "Nitara told you that she believes I'm the Weaver."

"Yes." His eyes narrowed. "Are you?"

The Weaver gave an easy laugh. "What do you think?"

"I think she's so taken with you that she sees far more than is there."

He made certain that the smile remained on his lips, but he allowed just a hint of anger to shade his voice when he said, "Careful, Minister. I may not be a Weaver, but I'm still high chancellor, and I do have some influence with the leaders of the movement."

"Forgive me, High Chancellor. I forget myself."

"Don't give the matter a second thought." Dusaan stared out the window, watching a raven circle over the palace walls. "Tell me, Kayiv, are you comfortable with your decision to join the movement?"

Even without looking at the man, the Weaver sensed his unease.

"Of course I am, High Chancellor. Don't I appear to be?"

"I can't say for certain. You were reluctant the first day I spoke to you of ally-ing yourself with our cause. I seem to remember you saying that you didn't trust me. At the time I assumed that Nitara would be able to convince you where I could not, and that the gold you were to be paid would do the rest, and I've continued to hope this would be the case in the days since. Now . . ." He opened his hands and shrugged. "I worry that perhaps your anger at Nitara will effect your relationship with us."

"I hated the Eandi before I met Nitara, and I hate them still, though I'm no longer with her. One has nothing to do with the other."

"Good. I'm pleased to hear that. But you haven't really answered my question. Hating the Eandi is one thing, working with the movement to end Eandi rule in the Forelands is quite another."

Kayiv nodded. "I know that. I'm with you, High Chancellor. You have my word."

"Thank you, Minister. That's what I wanted to hear."

They sat a moment in silence.

"You're free to go."

The minister stood, though it seemed he wished to say more.

"There may come a time when I'll need to speak with both you and Nitara to-gether. I hope that won't be a problem."

"It won't be, High Chancellor." He started toward the door, then halted, fac-ing Dusaan again.

"What is it, Minister?"

He opened his mouth, closed it again, shaking his head. At last he smiled, though clearly it was forced. "It's nothing. Thank you, High Chancellor."

A moment later the minister was gone and Dusaan stood, intending to make his way to the emperor's hall. Harel would be expecting him. Before he could leave, however, there came a knock at the door. He knew who it was even before he opened it. He hadn't time for this.

Pulling the door open, he found Nitara standing before him, an odd mix of fright and pique in her sand-colored eyes. Two guards stood nearby.

"Have I displeased you?" she asked.

He took her arm and pulled her into the chamber, closing the door and whirling on her. "Are you mad?" he demanded, struggling to keep his voice low. "Asking me a question like that in front of the emperor's men? I should kill you where you stand!"

"I . . . I'm sorry. But after you sent me away like that—"

"I wished to speak with Kayiv in private. He thought that we're lovers and I wanted to disabuse him of the notion before his jealousy overmastered his judgment."

"Did he believe you when you told him that we weren't? . . ." She faltered, swallowed. "That there was nothing between us?"

"I think he did. I can't be certain." He glowered at her. "You coming here so soon after he left doesn't help matters."

She lowered her gaze. "Forgive me, W—"

He stopped her with a raised finger. "Not here," he whispered. "Not when there are guards outside the door."

Nitara nodded, eyes wide.

"You must remember, Minister, that we're not lovers, and that as far as anyone else knows, we have nothing more in common than our service to the emperor. Every time you come here like this, you draw attention to both of us. When I need to speak with you of matters pertaining to the movement, I'll let you know. Otherwise, we're to have no contact beyond our daily ministerial discussions. Do you understand?"

"Yes, High Chancellor."

"Then go. No doubt the emperor is wondering where I am."

She let herself out of the chamber, glancing back at him just once, looking young and lovely and dangerous. He followed her into the corridor, relieved to see that she had the sense to walk in the direction opposite his path to the emperor's hall. The guards eyed him briefly, but kept their silence.

He had been eager to begin turning some of Harel's Qirsi to his cause, he recalled, as he strode through the palace hallways. But he could no longer remember why. Between Kayiv's suspicion and jealousy, and Nitara's infatuation, he feared it was only a matter of time before one or both of them betrayed him, or, more likely, tried to take a blade to his throat themselves. All the more reason to push the emperor toward war.

Harel was eating when Dusaan reached the imperial chamber, his mouth full and a cup of honey wine in one hand. He waved the high chancellor into the hall, and once he had swallowed, offered Dusaan some food.

"Thank you, Your Eminence. I'll eat later."

"Nonsense, High Chancellor. Sit." He turned in his chair, and beckoned to the servants standing nearby. "Bring the high chancellor some wine." Facing Dusaan again and taking a bite of fowl, he pushed a bowl toward the chancellor. "Try the pheasant," he said, still chewing. "It's superb."

"Your Eminence is most kind."

He began to eat, and had to admit, in response to Harel's expectant gaze, that the food was indeed excellent.

"You've just come from your audience with the other Qirsi?" the emperor asked, after they had eaten for some time.

"Yes, Your Eminence."

"And you gave further consideration to the dispute in the south?"

"Yes. It was agreed that you might wish to ease the concerns of Lord Grensyn by making whatever arrangement you decide upon temporary."

Harel nodded slowly, as if weighing this. "A fine idea, High Chancellor. I may do just that."

"It was Stavel's idea, Your Eminence. He'll be most pleased to know that you took his counsel to heart."

"Stavel," he repeated, frowning. "He's one of the older ones, isn't he?"

"Yes, Your Eminence."

The emperor smiled, looking for just an instant like a boy who is praised by his tutors for a correct answer. "What else did you discuss?"

Despite the question, Harel already looked bored. If Dusaan didn't raise the matter now, the emperor would turn their conversation back to food and it would be another day before the high chancellor could speak to him of the invasion.

"It was suggested by some, Your Eminence, that we might wish to begin the invasion sooner than we had planned." There was some risk in lying about such a thing, but not much. Harel almost never spoke with his other ministers, and in this case he would see no need to. He had been eager for this invasion to begin since Dusaan first suggested the idea to him. He had begrudged every delay, and would probably have been willing to send his fleet into battle without any planning at all had the high chancellor and master of arms allowed it.

Harel had been about to take another bite, but he paused now, the pheasant leg hovering just in front of his face, his small green eyes fixed on Dusaan. "Sooner, you say?"

"Yes, Your Eminence. We've assumed for some time now that the longer we had to prepare, the better our chances of success. But some have begun to question whether by waiting we give our enemies time to strengthen their forces in the north."

The emperor set the food on his plate, straightening in his chair, a strange expression on his face, as if he were trying not to smile.

"Are you one of those arguing so, High Chancellor?"

"Yes, Your Eminence, I am."

"What of the Aneirans? Since Carden's death you've counseled patience. You've said that the new regent will need time to consolidate his authority with the dukes and his army before committing to an alliance with the empire."

"In recent days I've found myself rethinking this as well. Had power in Aneira fallen to another house, such a delay might be necessary. But House Solkara still holds the throne, and while the other dukes may not be familiar with the regent, they're unlikely to oppose him on a matter of such gravity, particularly if it means war with the hated Eibitharians. Besides, even if we send word to the fleet commanders today, instructing them to begin their assault on Eibithar, it will take better than half a turn for the invasion to begin. The messengers need time to reach them and the commanders will need time to make their final preparations. You can send word to the regent, informing him of your intention to attack. That still leaves him a bit longer to speak with his dukes."

"Your reasoning seems quite sound, High Chancellor. To be honest, I've thought all along that you were being a bit too cautious with respect to this war. I'm glad to see that you've come around to my point of view."

Dusaan had to grit his teeth. "Yes. Thank you, Your Eminence."

"Still, I think it wise to speak of this with Uriad before making my decision. Don't you agree?"

Dusaan winced inwardly, but said only, "By all means, Your Eminence. I have no doubt that the master of arms will have much to say about this."

Uriad Ganjer, the emperor's master of arms, was one of the most intelligent and formidable Eandi the Weaver had ever met. Dusaan actually liked the man, though he knew that when the time came to wrest control of the empire from Harel, Uriad would have to be the first man to die. The master of arms was also a talented military strategist who weighed risks carefully and cared a good deal about the men under his command. Dusaan fully expected Uriad to oppose any attempt to hurry the invasion along. He felt equally sure, however, that when faced with conflicting advice from the chancellor and the master of arms, the emperor would side with Dusaan, not because he trusted the Qirsi more but rather because he wanted to invade now.

The emperor called to one of his guards and instructed the man to have Uriad summoned to the chamber at once.

"Do you have evidence that the Eibitharians are building up their forces?" the emperor asked, as he began to eat again.

"Nothing certain, no. But they will have noticed our ships in the Scabbard and the Strait of Wantrae. They'd have to be fools not to see this as a threat to their fleet and their northern shores. In addition, we have some reports of discussions between Eibithar's new king and dukes from Wethyrn and Caerisse. Kearney may be hoping to gather allies in preparation for a war."

Harel nodded, chewing vigorously. "No doubt he is. We can't allow that to happen."

"Quite so, Your Eminence."

Uriad arrived a few moments later, his face flushed and damp with sweat. He was a tall man, and lanky. His hair and eyes were black, making it clear to all who saw him that while he now served the empire, he had been born elsewhere. As Dusaan understood his family history, the man's father had been a merchant from Tounstrel in southern Aneira who took his family from that realm when the wharfages imposed by the Solkaran king became too onerous. Uriad had been but a boy at the time and he spoke without a trace of an Aneiran accent.

He dropped to one knee just inside the doorway, bowing his head to the emperor.

"Rise, Uriad," the Emperor said, waving him toward the table. "Join us."

"Thank you, Your Eminence," the armsman said, standing and walking to where they sat. He nodded to Dusaan. "High Chancellor."

"Good day, Commander."

"Forgive my appearance, Your Eminence. I was working the men when you summoned me."

"Of course. Please sit. I've called you here to discuss the invasion. The high chancellor has informed me that he and the other Qirsi believe we should begin the assault on Eibithar sooner than we had planned."

Again the chancellor winced. Harel might not have any inclination to speak with the other ministers and chancellors about this, but if the master of arms was angry enough, he surely would.

Uriad frowned, turning to Dusaan. "Why would we do such a thing?"

Harel answered before the chancellor could speak. "We fear that by delaying, we give the Eibitharians time to prepare."

"I've heard of no troop movements along the northern coast. Most of Kearney's army is still guarding the Aneiran border." He looked from the emperor to Dusaan. "There's no need for this."

"Kearney has been speaking with dukes from Wethyrn and Caerisse."

"Yes, Your Eminence, I imagine he has. But again, I believe he does this because he expects to be at the war with the Aneirans, not with us. Our plans for the invasion are sound, but they require additional preparation. If we act too quickly, this opportunity will be wasted." He looked at Dusaan again, as if pleading with the chancellor for his support.

Harel toyed with his wine goblet, clearly displeased. "I thought our fleet was ready."

"It is, Your Eminence, but the Aneiran army is not. The failed siege in Kentigern weakened the army of Mertesse, and though the new duke has begun to fill his ranks once more, his army is not yet at full strength and many of the men are poorly trained."

"Aneira has other dukes, Commander."

"Of course it does, Your Eminence. But the men of Mertesse will lead any attack across the Tarbin. And even if they don't, there are new dukes not only in Mertesse but also in Bistari, Tounstrel, and Noltierre, not to mention the new regent. It's simply too soon to ask the Aneirans to join us in this war. In six turns perhaps, or better yet ten, they should be ready, but—"

Harel looked horrified. "*Ten turns?* Now you want me to wait the better part of a year for this war? I've already waited too long."

"We might only have to wait six, Your Eminence. I was merely saying that ten—"

"Even six is too many! I'm tired of waiting. You've had ample time to prepare the fleet and the army, Commander. It's time this invasion began. Send word to your captains that they're to begin their assault on Eibithar as soon as possible."

Uriad held himself still, his jaw clenched, and for just an instant Dusaan thought he might argue the point further, or even refuse to carry out the emperor's order. In the end however, he wisely chose to comply. Harel might have been a fool, but he had little tolerance for dissent and often dealt cruelly with those who showed the least defiance.

Uriad bowed a second time, murmured, "Of course, Your Eminence," and turned on his heel to leave the chamber, casting a dark look at Dusaan as he did.

After watching the master of arms leave, Dusaan took a last sip of wine and stood. "Perhaps I should leave you as well, Your Eminence."

"Yes, very well," Harel said peevishly. "Have word sent to me as soon as the orders are dispatched to my fleet."

Dusaan bowed. "Yes, Your Eminence."

As he had expected, the master of arms was waiting for him outside the chamber.

"How could you let him do that?" Uriad demanded, heedless of the soldiers standing nearby. "How could you and the other Qirsi even suggest such a thing?"

"It was my idea, Commander. I honestly feel that further delay might keep us from victory."

"You can't possibly be that foolish, High Chancellor. I know you too well."

Dusaan made himself smile. "Is it foolishness merely because you say so?"

"When it comes to matters of war, yes. I'm more qualified than any man in this palace to make judgments pertaining to our fleet and army."

"Including the emperor himself?"

Uriad faltered, his eyes darting in the direction of the guards. "The emperor depends upon my counsel at times like these, and I, in turn, expect others to defer to my knowledge of military planning."

"In this case I couldn't do that. I'm sorry, Uriad. Truly I am. But I believe I've done the right thing."

"You've doomed our invasion to failure is what you've done."

Exactly. "I hope that's not true, for your sake as well as mine."

The man stared at him another moment, shaking his head. Then he walked away, leaving Dusaan to hope that he wouldn't see fit to speak of this with any of the other Qirsi.

Stavel ate his midday meal alone in the kitchen as he did each day, reflecting with satisfaction on the morning's discussion. He knew that the high chancellor didn't particularly like him, and that the younger ministers thought him too cautious. But he knew as well that voices of reason were needed in a court like this one, that at times it was more important that a chancellor be respected than liked.

This matter in the south was a perfect example. It would have been too easy to advise the emperor to capitulate to the demands made by Lord Muelry. No one wanted to see the people in Muelry starve, Stavel least of all. He had been born in the city of Muelry. Even after his mother and father journeyed to Hanyck so that his father could become a minister in the court there, his mother continued to refer to Muelry as their home. Few in the palace knew this about him. He had told the emperor once, many years ago, but no doubt Harel had forgotten. None of the other Qirsi had ever bothered to ask.

Nevertheless, his loyalties to Muelry were of little importance, and though he didn't wish to see the people there suffer, he also didn't believe that customs were to be abandoned lightly. The people of Grensyn had long laid claim to the lands in question, and they deserved consideration as well. That was why he had been so pleased when he thought of the compromise he presented that morning, and why he had been even more delighted when the high chancellor agreed with him. Serving in the emperor's court was a great honor, but it could be disheartening at times. Harel had so many Qirsi advisors that a man like Stavel, who lacked the ambition of others, could find himself ignored more often than not. All of which made what had happened that morning so gratifying.

There had been a time when Stavel thought he might become high chancellor. He had been here longer than most, and when the former high chancellor died, many expected that the emperor would choose Stavel to replace her. But around that time Dusaan came to the court, and though he was young, even Stavel could see that he was not like other Qirsi. He carried himself with the confidence of a warrior and made no secret of the fact that he wielded four magics, more than most Qirsi. Harel, who had long taken pride in the number of powerful Qirsi he attracted to his court, saw this new minister as a prize, and immediately offered to make him high chancellor. Dusaan, of course, accepted, as any Qirsi would have done. Stavel's friends in the court were outraged, though naturally they kept their anger to themselves, fearing the emperor's wrath. For his part, Stavel accepted the emperor's decision with equanimity. He thought himself a formidable man—intelligent, passionate when passion was warranted, and powerful in his own right, possessing gleaning, fire, and shaping magic. But he couldn't compete with a man who wielded four magics, and so he didn't even think to try. Whatever disappointment he felt was tempered by his knowledge of how difficult was the life of a high chancellor. He didn't envy the man, at least not much.

He had hoped to build a friendship with the new high chancellor, just as he had with Dusaan's predecessor, but it soon became apparent that Dusaan and the emperor meant to change the high chancellor's responsibilities from what they had been. What little contact Stavel and the other Qirsi had with the emperor diminished even further. Dusaan became a conduit of sorts, meeting first with the emperor and then with the other ministers and chancellors, carrying orders from one and counsel from the other. Stavel could see where the new arrangement might be attractive to Harel, keeping his audiences brief and simple, but it left many of the Qirsi feeling superfluous, even resentful. For his part, Stavel accepted this new state of affairs, realizing that there was little he could do to change it. "All that matters," he told himself and any others who would listen, "is that we continue to offer sound advice to the emperor."

He viewed days like this one as a vindication of his forbearance.

When he had finished his meal, he returned to his chamber, as he did each day, to write out the minutes of the day's discussion. No one had ever asked him to do it; he had taken on the task himself. But Dusaan had once mentioned that he found the documents helpful, and so Stavel had continued the practice. Once he completed his work, he walked to the gardens, enjoying the late-day sunshine and the warm breezes blowing down from the hills.

It was there, wandering among the swelling buds of the roses, blackthorns, and woodbine, that he encountered the emperor. Harel was with the youngest of his wives, and several guards walked before them and behind. Stavel stood to the side and allowed them to pass, bowing as the emperor and empress stepped by him.

The emperor nodded to him, then hesitated.

"You're Stavel, aren't you?" he asked.

The chancellor could not help but smile as he said, "Yes, Your Eminence, I am."

"The high chancellor told me it was your idea to make our solution in the south a temporary one, as a way of appeasing Lord Grensyn."

"Yes, Your Eminence."

"A fine idea, Chancellor. Well done."

Stavel bowed again, his heart racing. "Thank you, Your Eminence."

"I was also pleased to hear that the rest of you thought it wise to begin the invasion early. It's good to see all the gold I pay you Qirsi being put to good use."

Harel started to walk on

"Yes, Your Eminence," the chancellor called after him, abruptly confused. "Thank you."

They hadn't even discussed the invasion. Not at all. They hadn't spoken of it in days. Certainly the ministers and chancellors as a group had reached no decision at all regarding the timing of the assault on Eibithar. Stavel doubted that they would decide anything of the sort without hearing first from the master of arms. And even then, he didn't see how rushing the invasion could serve any purpose. For a moment he considered following the emperor to ask just what Dusaan had told him, but he quickly thought better of it. Harel had honored him by speaking to him at all. For Stavel to ask any more of him, and in particular to ask him about a conversation he and the high chancellor had in private, would have been utterly inappropriate. There was no telling how the emperor would respond.

Instead he chose to find Dusaan, hoping that the high chancellor might be able to explain the emperor's comment. Before he reached the man's chamber, however, he remembered hearing Dusaan ask the young minister, Kayiv, to remain behind so that they could speak. Perhaps the two of them had discussed the invasion and the emperor had merely confused Kayiv for Stavel.

He stopped at Kayiv's door and knocked. He heard no reply from within, and was about to leave in search of Dusaan when the door opened, revealing the minister, his bright yellow eyes bleary with sleep, his hair disheveled.

"Forgive me, Minister. I didn't mean to disturb you."

Kayiv peered into the corridor as if to reassure himself that Stavel was alone. "What can I do for you, Chancellor?"

Now that he was standing before the man, Stavel wasn't certain how to ask the question. The two of them had never gotten along very well, in part because they invariably found themselves on the opposite sides of every argument. Stavel thought the minister ill-mannered, and no doubt Kayiv saw him as weak and narrow-minded.

"I couldn't help but notice that you remained with the high chancellor after our discussion today."

Kayiv narrowed his eyes. "Yes. What of it?"

"Did you and he speak of commencing the invasion earlier than we had planned?"

The man's brow furrowed. "The invasion?"

"Yes. I've just come from the gardens, where I saw the emperor. He complimented me on the compromise I proposed for the dispute in Grensyn, and then said that he had been pleased to hear that we were in favor of beginning the invasion early. I thought perhaps you would know what he meant."

For several moments Kayiv said nothing. He was staring past the chancellor, chewing his lip.

"Did you speak of this with the high chancellor?" Stavel asked after a time, the silence making him uncomfortable. "I thought perhaps that you and he had talked about the invasion after the rest of us left, and that the emperor had simply mistaken me for you."

"Did the emperor say anything else?"

Stavel shook his head. "No. Just that he was pleased that the rest of us liked the idea—and by 'the rest,' I gathered that he meant the other ministers and chancellors aside from Dusaan. Then he said he was pleased that all the gold he paid us was doing him some good, or some such thing. And that was all." He watched Kayiv for a moment. "Do you know what he meant?"

Again, it took the man some time to reply. But finally he gave a disarming smile, and said, "Yes, Chancellor, I believe I do. This is all a misunderstanding, just as you thought."

"Well, I suppose I'm relieved. Though I must say that if the high chancellor wishes to offer counsel to the emperor on matters of such importance, he should speak with all of us, not just a select few."

"Yes. Perhaps you should mention this to him during tomorrow's discussion."

Stavel felt the blood drain from his face. He had no more desire to anger the high chancellor that he did the emperor, especially in front of the other Qirsi. "I'm certain he had good reason for offering this counsel the way he did. It's not my place to question him."

"Of course, Chancellor. I understand."

Stavel couldn't tell whether the man was mocking him or being sincere, but he didn't care to find out. "Thank you, Minister," he said, turning away.

"You're welcome. Good day, Chancellor."

Stavel turned and walked away, and, a few seconds later, heard the door close gently behind him. He made his way back to his chamber, wondering if he had been wise to raise the matter with Kayiv or if he would have been better off keeping it to himself. Palace politics could be a perilous game, the rules of which he had once known, the subtleties of which he had once taken the time to master. But that had been long ago and much of what he had known was lost to the years. At this point in his life, he was far too old to begin learning these things anew.

He waited until he heard Stavel's door open and close before leaving his chamber silently and stepping carefully to another door. He knocked once, just loud enough for her to hear. Belatedly he remembered that his hair probably looked a mess and that his clothes were rumpled. *It doesn't matter. She loves another now.*

He didn't have to wait long. She pulled open the door, revealing a chamber bright with lampfire. Her hair was down and her eyes seemed to glow like the stars. Kayiv felt his stomach tighten and he cursed himself for being so weak.

"What do you want?" she asked, crossing her arms over her chest.

"To talk. It will only take a moment."

She hesitated, then turned away, stepping farther into her chamber but leaving the door open. An invitation.

He closed the door, watching her pace.

"You don't look well," she said. "Are you sleeping?"

"I'm well enough."

She shrugged, said nothing.

"You were right about him, weren't you?"

Nitara halted, stared at him. "What do you mean?" she asked, though clearly she already knew.

"Dusaan. He is the Weaver, isn't he?"

"I thought you said I was a fool for even thinking it."

"I did. I was wrong."

"No, you weren't. I was a fool. He's just another Qirsi. That's all."

"I don't believe you, Nitara. He leads the movement, and it seems he's just convinced the emperor to begin the invasion of Eibithar early."

"What? How do you know this?"

"Stavel told me. Apparently Dusaan presented it to the emperor as counsel recommended by all of us."

"Then it's begun," she whispered.

"So it would seem. We're about to go to war, and Dusaan is poised to make himself ruler of all the Forelands."

"I already told you. He's not—"

"Yes, I know." Kayiv smiled, though his chest ached. There could be no question as to her loyalty to the high chancellor. "He's just another Qirsi." He walked to the door, pulled it open. "I'm sorry to have disturbed you."

He thought briefly about returning to his chamber, but he suddenly felt the need to leave the castle. Perhaps a walk in the city marketplace would do him good.

But Kayiv knew better. Dusaan was the Weaver, the man who would lead the Forelands if the Qirsi movement succeeded. And though the minister no longer had any doubts as to the truth in all the high chancellor had told him about the movement, he still couldn't bring himself to trust the man. Quite the opposite. He was more afraid of him now than ever.

Chapter
Twenty-five

or the better part of a turn, all talk in Castle Yserne, home of Sanbira's queen Olesya centered on the death of Kreazur jal Sylbe, Diani's first minister. After some initial confusion, there could no longer be any doubt as to the meaning of his murder. He had been found in a part of Yserne city known for attracting thieves and assassins. There had been an empty pouch beside him and two stray gold pieces under his shattered body. And though many of the nobles gathered in Castle Yserne were still reluctant to speak of the matter, most now believed that he had gone to the northwest corner of the city in search of a new blade to hire with his Qirsi gold. Perhaps he intended to have Diani killed, hoping to succeed where he had failed before. Or maybe he had some other victim in mind, another duchess, or, Ean forbid, the queen. Whatever his purpose, the gods had chosen to mete out their own justice. Some speculated that he had offered too little gold to the men he wished to hire, or had sought to impose conditions that weren't to their liking. In either case, they took exception and, it seemed, threw him from the roof of one of the many ramshackle buildings lining the lane where he was found.

Many of the duchesses had expressed their sympathy to Diani, as if she had lost a dear friend. Even the dukes of Brugaosa and Norinde offered condolences for her loss, and seemed sincere in doing so. Diani, however, felt no grief. Her mother would have been aggrieved, she knew, just as was her father. Kreazur, Sertio kept reminding his daughter, had served House Curlinte for nine years and whatever he had become, he had once been a loyal counselor to the old duchess. But as far as Diani was concerned, the first minister's betrayal negated all that he had done for her mother. No, she felt no sadness at his death. None at all. What she felt was vindication.

Her father had scolded her for imprisoning the first minister and her other Qirsi, telling her that she had allowed her fears to cloud her judgment, as if she were still a child. The queen had done much the same, seeming to imply that she had been guided by her need for vengeance and her inexperience with the courts.

Kreazur himself had tried to tell her that he had earned better treatment by serving the old duchess for so many years, as if he sought to use her guilt, and her grief at losing her mother, to win his freedom. Eventually Diani had given in to all of them. Now she knew—they all knew—that she had been right from the beginning.

The white-hairs could not be trusted. If Kreazur was a traitor, how many other ministers might be as well? Olesya began to meet with her duchesses and dukes in closed audiences, with none of the Qirsi ministers present. Even Abeni ja Krenta, the queen's own archminister, was excluded from these discussions, for in the wake of Kreazur's death, even the most powerful Qirsi were suspect in the eyes of Sanbira's Eandi nobles.

Much else had changed as well. When Edamo of Brugaosa and Alao of Norinde first arrived in Yserne they were unwilling to concede that the conspiracy was behind the assassination attempts against Diani. Both men had been loath to cede any more authority to the Matriarchy, and since at the time Diani could offer no proof of Qirsi involvement in the attacks, the dukes were able to convince the other nobles that it was too early to do so.

Now, though, with Kreazur dead and his treachery revealed, there could be no denying that the conspiracy had struck at the realm. It seemed obvious to Diani that the dukes still would have preferred to find some other way to meet the Qirsi threat, but with the other houses solidly behind the queen, they had little choice but to acquiesce. Within only a day or two of the first minister's death, the nobles gave Olesya leave to conscript more men, to raise the levies necessary for waging a war, and to forge alliances with any realm that would join Sanbira in its fight against this so-called movement.

Diani, who remained the youngest leader of any of Sanbira's houses, and the least experienced, had seen her standing in the realm altered as well. Where she had once been made to feel ashamed of her decision to imprison all of Castle Curlinte's Qirsi, she was now complimented for it. A turn before, Edamo had made her feel a fool for arguing so forcefully that Sanbira should be preparing for war with the renegade sorcerers. Now every noble in the land spoke as she had. Once there might have been some shame in leading the house that harbored Sanbira's first known traitor. But by leading the call for action against the conspiracy, even in the face of opposition from other nobles, she had turned Curlinte's disgrace into a triumph. Indeed, the assassination attempt itself had only added to her newfound stature. As word spread of all that had happened that day on the Curlinte coast—of the injuries she had suffered, of the three arrows that had pierced her flesh, and of her desperate escape and ride back to the castle—she became a hero of sorts. Soldiers from other houses cheered when they caught sight of her. In their audiences with Olesya, duchesses who had ruled their houses for years deferred to her, though she had only ruled Curlinte for a few turns. Even the queen was not immune, turning to Diani for counsel when, only a short time before, she would have gone first to Rashel of Trescarri of Ary of Kinsarta.

Curlinte's standing in the realm hadn't reached such levels since the end of the Curlinte Dynasty more than five hundred years before, and Diani had every intention of taking advantage of her influence. She didn't covet power; she remained loyal to the queen and had no desire to rule the land herself. But she was determined that no other houses in Sanbira would suffer as she had at the hands of white-haired traitors. She didn't expect Olesya to order the imprisonment of all the Qirsi in the realm, or even of all the ministers currently in Castle Yserne. The queen lacked the will to go so far, and even had she not, the duchess realized now that such an approach carried risks as well. Rather, Diani wished to see the Qirsi remain free, but under constant watch from afar, so that when the next traitor tried to strike at the realm, the nobles would be ready. At Diani's urging, Olesya had sent spies into the city to watch the Qirsi taverns and the marketplace. They were instructed to look not only for Qirsi who strayed from the castle at odd hours but also for any white-hairs, including the queen's ministers and healers, who spent too freely at the peddler's stalls or tavern bars.

Of all the nobles in Castle Yserne, only her father continued to argue against the measures they had taken, and, not by coincidence, only her father still maintained that Kreazur could not have been a traitor. Diani knew what lay behind his intransigence. To admit that the first minister was a traitor was to admit that his beloved Dalvia had erred in choosing Kreazur to serve House Curlinte so many years ago. Still, though the duchess found it hard to blame Sertio for his devotion to her mother, she did find her father's repeated defenses of the first minister embarrassing. And earlier this day, the second of the new waxing, she had made the mistake of telling him so.

They had been in the marketplace, strolling among the peddlers' carts and stalls, enjoying the first clear day since the middle of the previous waning. A soft breeze ruffled the heavy cloth with which so many of the sellers covered their carts, and the air smelled clean and sweet, as from the blossoms that had begun to appear on the hills above the castle and city. Even with the guards walking ahead of them and behind, it would have been easy on a day such as this to forget about the Qirsi and their conspiracy, but Sertio wouldn't allow it, staring glumly at the wares displayed by each vender, and saying little.

"You should buy something, Father," Diani said, hoping to pull him from his dolor. "A new blade perhaps, or at least a new sheath for the old one."

"I have no need of a new blade, or a new sheath."

She looked at the sheath hanging on his belt, raising an eyebrow. "Have you looked recently at the one you have?"

"The one I have was given to me by your mother."

"During which dynasty?"

He grinned at that, though only briefly. "It just needs a bit of oil, that's all. I'll take care of it when we return to the castle."

"Well, a new blade, then."

"I told you, I have no need of one. This dagger was a gift from your mother as well."

"Oh, Father," she said, throwing up her hands and shaking her head. "So what if it was from Mother? Do you think that she'd expect you to keep all the gifts she gave you for the rest of time, even after they had outlived their usefulness?"

"I expect that I would do so," he said severely. "And I'd expect you to as well."

Diani closed her eyes for a moment, realizing that she had spoken rashly. "I would never throw away anything that was hers," she said quietly. "You know that. But neither would I keep using a blade of hers if it no longer served its purpose. I might put it away, so that my children could see it, and their children in turn, but I wouldn't hesitate to replace it with a better one when need demanded."

Sertio stared past her, looking back toward the walls of the castle. "It seems you and I differ in this."

"You can't keep on like this, Father. She's gone. We loved her, and we miss her, but she's gone."

His entire face seemed to turn to stone, his dark eyes still fixed on the queen's fortress. "Don't you think I know this?"

"You know it, but you make no attempt to ease your own grief. How long will you mourn her, Father? How much longer will you allow yourself to suffer?"

"I'll mourn her as long as I live."

"She wouldn't want that. She'd want you to find happiness, even if that meant finding a new love."

His eyes snapped to her face. "I could never love another! I'm appalled that you'd even suggest such a thing! You would have me forget her, forget the years we spent together?"

"I don't expect you to forget anything. But you can't live the rest of your years in the company of wraiths, nor can you cling to every token that reminds you of Mother. Some things need to be discarded, no matter the sentiments you attach to them."

She could see the muscles in his jaw bunching as he turned on his heel and began to walk away. "I won't listen to this," he said.

"You must!" She strode after him, grabbing his arm and forcing him to turn toward her. "I loved her, too. You know I did. But I also know that she wasn't perfect. She was wise and strong and beautiful, but she made mistakes, just as all of us do."

"Perhaps," he said, his color high, so that his lean face appeared even more austere than usual. "But when she erred, it was on the side of kindness and trust and justice."

Diani felt her cheeks burning as well. Somehow their argument had moved from daggers and sheaths to Kreazur and the other Qirsi.

"Hers was a simpler world than mine," Diani said. "I face dangers today that Mother couldn't have fathomed."

Sertio shook his head, looking so sad. "Do you know how foolish you sound, Diani? You're not the first duchess to be betrayed, nor even the first to have attempts made on her life. But a leader doesn't surrender all to suspicion and fear simply for having been deceived once. Your mother understood that. I hope someday that you will as well."

"You dare call me a fool? You're the fool, arguing for Kreazur's innocence when we all know that he was a traitor. You act like an old man who has lost all sense to his dotage. You shame our house with your simplicity."

He stared at her another moment, looking sad and old. And in that instant, she wished that she could take the words back. No matter how blind his devotion to the first minister, she should never have spoken to him thus. But she couldn't bring herself to apologize, or take back what she had said. A moment later, it was too late. Sertio was walking back toward the castle, and the soldiers who had accompanied them were looking at each other in confusion, wondering who among them should follow the duke, and who should remain with Diani.

She returned to the castle sometime later, searching halfheartedly for her father, and fearing that she might find him. Eventually she gave up, knowing that she'd see Sertio again when he wished to be found. She started back toward her own chamber, but before she had gone far, she saw the dukes of Brugaosa and Norinde. She had no desire to speak with them—though they now claimed to agree with Diani and the other duchesses on how best to face the conspiracy, Diani hardly considered either man a friend.

Before she could duck into another corridor, however, Edamo spotted her and raised a hand in greeting.

"A word please, Lady Curlinte."

What choice did she have but to halt and wait for them? This, too, her father would have seen as a betrayal of her mother and their house. Diani was more convinced than ever that the Qirsi were responsible for Cyro's murder. In a sense, House Curlinte and House Brugaosa were bound to each other by the tragedy, both of them victims of Qirsi treachery. Still, Sertio continued to blame the Brugaosans for the loss of his son, just as the white-hairs had intended. It almost seemed that the duke chose to be ensnared by the white-hairs' deceptions, as if he found some perverse comfort in believing what the traitors wanted him to believe.

Edamo and Alao stopped before her, the older man smiling, the younger man merely watching her, without his usual sneer, but without much warmth either.

"Is there something you wish of me, Lord Brugaosa?"

"Lord Norinde and I were on our way to speak with the queen, and we thought it might help if you joined us."

"What did you intend to discuss with her?"

"In light of the dangers facing all of Sanbira's houses, and the preparations necessary—"

"We wish to return to our castles," Alao broke in, glancing impatiently at the older man. "If we're to wage a war against the Qirsi, we should be in command of our own armies. We can't do that from here."

"I gather," Diani said, "that the queen wishes us to remain here until we've heard from the sovereigns of the other realms."

"Clearly," the younger duke said, sounding as brusque with her as he had with

Edamo. "I fail to see the point, however. She can send messages to all of us when word comes from the other realms. But if we leave now, we can be ready to march to battle immediately, and we can be certain that we'll be leading our own men to war."

"And what if some of the kings refuse to march with us?" she asked. "What if Eibithar and Caerisse choose to ally themselves with us, but Wethyrn and Aneira don't?"

Edamo's eyebrows went up. "Surely you don't expect that to happen."

"I believe it's possible. Some are less willing than others to believe that the Qirsi would challenge the might of the courts."

If the two men knew that she spoke of her father, they had the good sense to remain silent.

"The queen might need us here," she went on, "so that we can decide upon a response when word arrives from those who would be our allies."

"So you won't support us," Alao said, his voice flat.

"No, Lord Norinde, I won't. Please understand, I—"

He started to walk away. "Good day, Lady Curlinte."

Edamo stared at her another moment before following the younger man.

"Why are you in such a rush to begin this war?" she called after them.

Alao stopped, faced her. "You of all people have to ask?"

"Yes, I do. We don't know yet where this war will be fought, or how. There is no Qirsi army, at least none of which we know. You speak of marching to war as quickly as possible, but I see no battle plain. What is it you really want?"

"I won't listen to this."

"You're still worried about the queen strengthening her hold on the throne, aren't you?"

Norinde said nothing, but after a moment, Edamo gave a harsh grin.

"Shouldn't we be?"

"No. Sanbira faces an enemy more dangerous than any we've faced in nine centuries. You should be concerned only with guarding the realm and defeating those who would destroy us."

"I wouldn't expect you to understand, Duchess. You lead a house that has been allied with the throne for centuries. You have nothing to fear from this power Olesya is accumulating. We do."

"But the Qirsi—"

The duke opened his arms wide. "Where are the Qirsi, Duchess? As you yourself just said, there is no Qirsi army, there is no battle plain."

"But there will be."

He let his arms drop to his side once more. "Yes. I'm sure you're right. And while we wait for the enemy to show himself, we cede all authority to the queen. Well, there are limits to just how much Alao and I are willing to give her. We'll pay her tribute, and we'll send men to the royal army. But we will not allow Olesya to command all of our soldiers as if they were hers to do with as she pleases. Without an army of its own, Brugaosa would have been destroyed by the Matriarchy long ago. You see the Qirsi as the only threat, but I know better, and even with the white-hairs massing on our borders, I will not give my forces over to Yserne."

With that they left her, their footsteps echoing through the corridor. Diani still wished to find her father, but after this encounter with the dukes, she thought it best to speak first with the queen.

When she reached Olesya's presence chamber, however, she heard voices from within. She knocked on the door and after a moment, the queen called for her to enter. Olesya sat on her throne, looking toward the door. And there at the window, his lean frame shadowed against the light, stood Diani's father.

The duchess barely managed to bow to the queen before whirling toward him. "What are you doing here?" she asked, her conversation with Edamo and Alao forgotten for the moment.

"We were speaking of the Qirsi," Olesya answered. "Sertio is concerned that we've been too quick to dismiss all of our ministers, that perhaps some of them can be of help in this fight. He also fears that we've been wrong to assume that Kreazur was a traitor"

"Forgive me for saying so, Your Highness, but my father does not speak for House Curlinte. I do."

"He doesn't claim to speak for your house, Lady Curlinte. He came to me as a friend and that is the spirit in which I've considered his words."

Diani glanced at her father, not bothering to mask her anger. But then she nodded to the queen. "Yes, Your Highness."

Olesya was eyeing the duke as well. "Perhaps you'd like to tell her what you've told me."

The duke shifted uncomfortably, saying nothing.

"She has a right to know, Sertio."

"Know what?" Diani narrowed her eyes, glaring at her father. "What is this about?"

He cleared his throat, casting a quick glance at the queen. "You know that I've had my doubts about Kreazur's guilt all along. Shortly after his death, I sent word to Curlinte that his quarters were to be searched."

"You what?"

"I reasoned that if he was with the conspiracy, there would be gold hidden somewhere in his chamber. That's the one thing we know about the Qirsi who lead this movement: they have a good deal of gold and they pay those who serve them quite well."

"How dare you do such a thing!" Diani said, her voice quavering with rage. "I lead our house, not you! You should have discussed it with me first! You should have asked my permission!"

"Would you have let me do it?"

She started to reply, then closed her mouth again, looking away.

"That's why I didn't discuss it with you."

Diani felt her face redden. She didn't want to have this conversation in front of the queen. "You had no right," she muttered.

"I received word from Curlinte today. Don't you want to know what they found?"

She looked at him. Of course she wanted to know, but she couldn't bring herself to ask.

"Nothing," he said. "Nothing at all. Kreazur had twenty qinde to his name, about what you'd expect for a man living on a minister's wage."

"That doesn't mean anything. He might have spent it all."

"On what? He had no jewelry, no riches of any sort. He wore simple clothes beneath his ministerial robes. He carried a blade with a wooden hilt."

"Maybe he gave his gold to someone else. Perhaps he had a woman in Curlinte. Or maybe he brought all his gold with him to Yserne and it was taken by the brigands who killed him. This tells us nothing."

"I'm afraid I must disagree, Diani," the queen said. "It may not establish his innocence, but in my mind it certainly casts some doubt on his guilt."

"Who was it searched his chamber?" the duchess demanded, glowering at Sertio again. "Another white-hair?"

"Actually it was your master of arms."

She felt her mouth twitch.

"Isn't it possible that we were wrong about him, Diani? Isn't it possible that there's some other explanation for the way he died?"

"Like what? If he wasn't a traitor, what was he doing in the city? Why did he come to Yserne at all? There's no other explanation that makes any sense."

Sertio looked at the queen, abruptly seeming unsure of himself. "Perhaps we were intended to think that he was a traitor."

"To what end?" the queen asked. "His death certainly didn't help the Qirsi in this castle. It's only served to deepen our suspicions."

"Maybe whoever was responsible didn't have any choice. Maybe Kreazur had learned that this person was the traitor, but he died before he could tell anyone else."

"I don't believe any of this," Diani said, shaking her head. "We found Kreazur in the city, not someone else. It was his body that was covering those gold pieces and lying next to an empty money pouch. What you learned from the master of arms changes nothing." Even as she spoke the words, however, Diani felt doubt seeping into her mind. She couldn't countenance what her father had done—certainly he never would have sent instructions to anyone in Castle Curlinte while her mother was duchess—but neither could she ignore what he had learned. There should have been gold in the man's chamber, or failing that, some evidence of the riches that would have accrued from his service to the movement. What if she had been wrong about Kreazur? What if his denials had been true, his devotion to Curlinte genuine? Wasn't this one instance where it was preferable to be mistaken?

"In a way she's right," Sertio was saying to the queen. "This message from Curlinte doesn't change a thing. In fact, it makes it more likely that one of the other ministers is a traitor."

"You're certain it would be one of the ministers?"

"If we're right about Kreazur, it would almost have to be. They're the only

Qirsi with whom he had any contact after his arrival. If he went to the city because he overheard something—"

"Or if he followed someone there," Diani broke in, the words seeming to come to her unbidden.

Sertio and the queen looked at her.

"Now you agree with us?" her father asked.

"I'm willing to admit that it's possible." Seeing the smile on her father's face, the relief, she felt much of her anger at him sluice away. "You may not believe this, Father, but I never wanted to believe that he was a traitor. I know how much Mother cared for him."

Sertio gazed at her another moment before facing the queen once more. "As I was saying, if he overheard a conversation among traitors or followed someone to the city, it would have meant that he first encountered them here in the castle. In which case, the traitor is still here, and we need to figure out who it is."

"There could be more than one," Diani said. "That's why I still believe we need to keep all of the ministers at a distance."

"For a time perhaps," Sertio said. "Until we can winnow out those who have betrayed us. But eventually we need to begin trusting the Qirsi again. Even in those realms that have suffered the most for the betrayals of their Qirsi, only a few of the ministers have proven to be traitors. It would be folly for us to assume that all of our Qirsi have abandoned Sanbira for this conspiracy of theirs."

"But how are we to know who we can trust and who we can't?" Diani asked, looking from her father to the queen. "All it takes is one traitor to endanger the queen's life or—" She stopped abruptly, the realization coming to her with such force that for a moment she couldn't draw breath.

"Diani?" her father said, taking a step toward her, his eyes wide with concern.

"Your Highness," she began, finding her voice, "do I remember correctly that you questioned the gate guards who were on duty the night Kreazur died?"

"Yes, and all of them said the same thing. They saw no one leave the castle, not even your first minister."

The duchess nodded, her mouth suddenly dry. "Then I regret to say that our search for the traitors must begin with those Qirsi who serve House Yserne."

Olesya's brow furrowed. "Why would—?" She lifted a slender hand to our mouth, the color draining from her face. "Ean save us all! You're right, of course."

Sertio shook his head. "I don't understand."

"Kreazur didn't know this castle well enough to find a way out that would allow him to avoid all of the queen's guards. Regardless of whether he was accompanying someone else or merely following, the other person had to be one of Yserne's Qirsi."

"How many Qirsi live in the castle, Your Highness?" the duke asked.

"I have six ministers in all, and many healers—I'm not certain of the number."

"We should question them."

Diani brushed the hair from her face with an impatient hand. "I disagree. We need more information first. If we make it known that we've narrowed our suspicions to the queen's Qirsi, we'll give them time to escape, or at least to prepare their lies. Best we reveal nothing for now."

"You're right," the queen said. "I believe it would be a mistake even to inform the other nobles." She gave a small smile. "It seems the two of you have a bit of work to do."

Diani frowned. "Your Highness?"

"As you just said, Lady Curlinte, we need more information. And it seems I have little choice but to leave it to the two of you to find it for me." She stood, as if to signal an end to their audience. "You're to start immediately, and work as quickly as possible. I agree that loyal Qirsi will be invaluable to us in the coming war. The sooner we can begin to win back their trust and offer them ours, the better."

"But, Your Highness," Diani began. "How—"

"You can begin by searching the quarters of all the Qirsi who live in Castle Yserne," the queen told her. "It worked in Curlinte, perhaps it will work here as well."

"Very well, Your Highness." Diani met her father's gaze and held it briefly. After a moment, they both started toward the door.

"Lady Curlinte," the queen said, stopping her. "I assume that you came to my chamber looking for me. Was there another matter you wished to discuss?"

She had forgotten. "Yes, Your Highness. I just had a conversation with Lord Brugaosa and Lord Norinde. They're eager to return to their duchies, fearing that if they remain here you'll take command of their armies. They intend to request that you give them leave to go, and they tried to convince me to support them in this. I refused, but I thought you should know what they have in mind. They may go to the other duchesses."

"No doubt they will," the queen said, looking pensive. "Thank you, Diani. I'll deal with the dukes. You just find the traitors in my castle."

"Yes, Your Highness," she said, pulling the door open. "It will be my pleasure."

Abeni had known it would come to this, that in making it appear that Kreazur was a traitor and thus confirming in the minds of all the worst suspicions of Diani of Curlinte, she would deny herself the one asset that made her most valuable to the Weaver: her access to the queen. Given some time, she felt reasonably certain that she could regain Olesya's trust, but until that happened, she lived in constant fear of her next encounter with the movement's leader.

She actually believed some good might come of the queen's refusal to confide in her, though she knew that explaining this to the weaver might prove difficult. Among the Qirsi who had come to Castle Yserne with their ladies and lords, two were already pledged to the movement—the first ministers of Macharzo and Norinde. The rest remained loyal to the courts. For now. But with each day that passed, the queen and her nobles made it easier for Abeni to draw others to the

Weaver's cause. She sensed the growing resentment of the loyal Qirsi. Olesya and Diani may have believed that they were guarding themselves from further treachery by keeping the ministers from their discussions, but in fact they were making it more likely that others would turn against them.

At the same time they were also allowing Abeni to win the ministers' trust. During the past turn, she had begun to convene discussions of her own. She claimed that these audiences, like those of the queen, were intended to find some way to combat the movement. "If we can help our lords and ladies," she told the others at their first gathering, "perhaps we can prove to them that we deserve their faith."

In fact, she hoped to determine which ministers were most angered by the way they had been treated, and to begin forging deeper friendships with these few. And she wished to remind all of them as frequently as possible that she was no better off than they were, that she had been shut out by the queen, just as they had been by their lords and ladies. She was one of them, a victim of Eandi suspicion and prejudice. Perhaps, when the time came for the Weaver to reveal himself and for his followers to strike at the courts, she would be able to deliver to him not one or two ministers but many.

She also knew, however, that she could not allow her ties to Olesya to become too tenuous. To that end, every few days, she requested and was granted an audience with the queen. On this day, Olesya did not see her until after the ringing of the prior's bell, as the sun began its descent toward the western horizon, its golden light reflected in the still waters of Lake Yserne.

"Good day, Your Highness," the archminster said, stepping past the guards into the queen's presence chamber and bowing before the throne.

"Archminister."

"I trust you're well?"

"Yes, quite." As an afterthought, the queen added, "And you?"

Olesya seemed particularly distant this day. Abeni wondered if something more had happened, if perhaps word had come from one of the other realms of another betrayal.

"I wish I could say that I was well, Your Highness."

The queen glanced at her, her expression unreadable. "Does something ail you?"

"Of course. The same thing that ails all the ministers in your castle. I'm concerned, not only for myself and for the other Qirsi but for you and the nobles as well. The Qirsi in this realm seek only to serve the courts, and you must know that you're stronger for the counsel we offer. This rift between us must end."

"I agree, Archminister. But until I know who among you can be trusted and who among you can't, I fear that your service to the courts is more dangerous than it is valuable." There was something strange in the queen's manner. It almost seemed that she knew of Abeni's ties to the movement.

"But perhaps we can help you in that regard, Your Highness," she said, searching the queen's face.

Olesya smiled, though the expression in her dark eyes didn't change. "Can you see into the hearts of others, Abeni? Is that one of the powers you wield?"

"No, Your Highness. I think you know it's not."

"Then how can you possibly help me? How can you even ask me to let you try, when you can't prove beyond doubt your own fealty to House Yserne."

"Haven't I served you well for all these years, Your Highness? Isn't that proof enough?"

"Yes, you have, and no, it's not." Olesya hesitated, as if considering something. But then the thought seemed to pass and she said, "After Kreazur, I don't know if I can ever trust a Qirsi again."

Even Abeni could see the irony. She had killed the man and made him seem a traitor to conceal her own treachery, and yet by doing so, she had made herself suspect in the queen's eyes. Somewhere in the Underrealm, the first minister was laughing at her.

They held each other's gaze for several moments, Olesya's face grim but composed. At last, Abeni looked away, wondering what she would tell the Weaver if he came to her that night.

"It seems there's nothing more to say."

"No, I don't suppose there is." The queen continued to watch her, as if she expected the minister to attack her at any moment. Something definitely was wrong.

"Thank you, Your Highness." Abeni bowed, then stepped to the door.

"If you were to help me," the queen said, forcing her to turn once more, "what would you do?"

"Your Highness?"

"Just now you offered to help us determine which Qirsi are loyal and which are not. Is there a way to do that?"

She briefly considered lying, telling the queen that there was. But she knew that eventually Olesya would learn the truth, and when she did, Abeni's life would be forfeit.

"None that I know of, Your Highness. At least none short of torture. That's what makes this movement so . . . insidious."

Olesya nodded. "I thought as much. Thank you, Archminister."

Abeni bowed a second time and left the queen's, chamber, making her way back to her own. Was it possible that Olesya knew something? she wondered, winding through the corridors. Kreazur had been dead for more than a turn. Surely if his death had raised the queen's suspicions, Abeni would have known it long before now. And nothing had happened since that would give Olesya cause to question Abeni's loyalty in particular. Yet, there could be no mistaking the change in the queen's manner.

The archminister was so preoccupied with her thoughts of the queen that she was nearly to her chamber before she noticed that someone was there in the corridor, leaning against the stone wall beside her door. Craeffe, Macharzo's first minister.

Abeni glanced behind her, fearing that there might be guards nearby. There were none. Still, she was hardly in the mood to speak with anyone right now, even another member of the movement.

"Archminister," the woman said, straightening as Abeni approached and sketching a quick bow. "I assumed you were meeting with the queen." She pitched her voice to carry, in case there were others nearby. "I was hoping that you had managed to convince her that she and the nobles had been wrong to doubt us."

"Not yet," Abeni said.

"May I have a word with you, Archminister? In private."

Abeni took a breath, scanning the corridor a second time. "Briefly," she said at last.

She unlocked her door and pushed it open, waving the woman inside, then following.

"Is everything all right, cousin?" Craeffe asked, once the door was closed.

"I'm not certain. I just had a strange conversation with the queen. She seemed more guarded than usual."

The woman shrugged. "Isn't that to be expected? I know that you've served her a long time, but with every other noble in the castle afraid of their Qirsi, it's only natural that her suspicions should grow as well."

It was a fair point. "You may be right."

"Then again, it was your rapport with the queen that first drew the Weaver's attention, wasn't it? I don't suppose he'd be pleased to hear that she's growing more wary of you."

Abeni regarded her for some time, a small smile on her lips. Craeffe had always been a bit too ambitious for Abeni's taste. Though they had long been tied to each other by their service to the Weaver, Abeni had never fully trusted the woman. She didn't look formidable. Like so many of their people, she was slight, almost frail. She had a long, narrow face and overlarge yellow eyes that made her look like some strange white owl from the northlands. But the archminister knew that she was quite clever, and she gathered from what she knew of other men and women recruited by the Weaver that she must also be a rather powerful sorcerer.

"I don't expect that the Weaver will hear anything of the sort, cousin," Abeni said. "I have no intention of telling him, and I'm sure you don't either."

Craeffe raised her eyebrows, feigning innocence. "Of course not."

The archminister was already tiring of the woman's company. "You came to me," she said. "Why?"

"I've just had an interesting conversation of my own, and I thought you'd want to hear about it."

"With whom?" Abeni asked, hoping that she sounded bored.

"The first minister of Prentarlo. I believe she could be convinced to join us."

"What did you say to her?" the archminister asked, bored no longer. "You know that I'm the only one the Weaver wants speaking to newcomers."

Craeffe grinned, showing sharp white teeth, like some crazed demon of Bian's realm. "Don't worry, cousin. I didn't tell her anything; I just listened. And given what I heard, I believe she's hurt and angry enough to turn against her duchess."

Abeni nodded, though she wasn't pleased. She should have been. This was what she wanted. This was how she would convince the Weaver that the queen's distrust hadn't lessened her value to the movement. But she didn't like feeling beholden to Craeffe, not even in this small way.

"That's good news," she managed. "I'll be certain to speak with her as soon as the opportunity presents itself."

"Or you could let me do it for you."

"I just told you—"

"Yes, I know. The Weaver wants you to handle these matters. But he needn't know. I've already won her trust. Wouldn't it be easier to let me do the rest?"

Easier perhaps, but Abeni had little doubt that Craeffe would tell the Weaver as soon as she possibly could, presenting what had happened in such a way as to make herself appear a genius, and Abeni a liability to the Weaver's cause.

"Thank you, cousin. I know that you wish only to serve the movement as best you can. But the Weaver has been quite clear on this point."

The forced smile again. "Of course, cousin. I understand."

They stood in silence for several moments before Craeffe finally returned to the door. "I suppose I should be going."

"So soon, cousin?"

The woman didn't even bother looking at her. "I hope that this rift between you and your queen doesn't widen, Archminister. Now more than ever, the Weaver needs Qirsi who serve the major courts."

A moment later she was gone, and Abeni was left to wonder who was the greater threat to her standing in the movement: the queen or Macharzo's first minister.

Chapter
Twenty-six

Kentigern, Eibithar

A indreas stared at the words scrawled on the outside of the scroll, unwilling to remove the ribbon that held it and read what was written inside. The ribbon was white. Of course. He would have known from whom the message had come even without the "*White Erne*" penned in a neat, bold hand for all to see. No doubt the time had finally come for the duke to fulfill his promise to the conspiracy—there could be no other reason for her to contact him. They wanted him to act on their behalf. And he was too frightened to unroll the scroll and see what it was they expected of him.

"Father."

He looked up, seeing Brienne in the doorway, her golden hair gleaming in the torchlight.

"Not now, my love," he said, his voice low.

"But Mother is asking for you. There are men riding toward the gate."

As she spoke, Aindreas realized that the city bells were ringing, that in fact they had been for some time.

He frowned. "Tell her I'll be along shortly."

"She said I should bring you to her immediately."

The duke exhaled through his teeth. "Very well. I'll be there in just a moment."

"But—"

"I told you, I'll be along soon. Now leave me, Brienne!"

The girl winced, looking as if she might cry. "But I'm Affery."

Aindreas stared at her, his vision swimming. He squeezed his eyes shut, rubbing them with a meaty hand. Opening them again, he saw that it was indeed his younger daughter standing before him, golden haired and pretty as her sister had been at this age, but not yet grown to womanhood.

"Affery," he said, the name coming out as a whisper. He rose and stepped around his writing table to where she stood. She looked afraid, and he knelt before her, taking her in his arms. "I'm sorry, my love. Of course I knew it was you."

She nodded, but said nothing. When he released her, he saw that there were tears on her cheeks. "Do you miss her, Father?"

"Very much," he said, his voice suddenly rough.

"So do I. I think Mother does, too."

"We all do. But your mother is better now than she was, and . . . and so am I."

Again the girl nodded.

"You said there are men approaching the castle?"

"Yes."

"And where is your mother?"

"She's atop the tower, watching the city gates."

"Very well. Tell her I'll be there very soon. Have her instruct the men not to allow anyone into the castle before I arrive."

"All right." Still she didn't move. "Are they coming to attack us again?"

For a moment, he wasn't certain what to say. By ignoring Kearney's summons to the City of Kings, Aindreas had made himself a renegade in the king's eyes. Glyndwr would have been justified in sending the royal army to Kentigern. But Aindreas had known Kearney a long time. The man didn't want a war, and would go to great lengths to avoid one. He wouldn't have sent his army, at least not yet.

"No one's going to attack us," he told her, making himself smile. "They probably just want to talk to me."

Affery smiled in return, looking relieved.

"Go now. I'll be along in a moment."

She kissed his cheek, then turned and ran from the chamber.

Aindreas returned to his writing table, lowered himself into his chair and picked up the scroll again, his hand beginning to tremble. For a moment he was tempted to throw it on the flames dancing in his hearth, as if by burning the parchment he might rid himself of the Qirsi. Instead, he pulled off the ribbon and unrolled the scroll.

Lord Kentigern:

> Events have begun to unfold more swiftly than we had anticipated. We can no longer wait for you to convince other houses to oppose the king. You must break with Kearney now, and hope that others will follow. We will be watching to see that you do as we expect. Do not disappoint us.

Jastanne ja Triln
Captain, the *White Erne*

Perhaps he should have been surprised. Certainly he had a right to be angry. Yet he couldn't bring himself to feel anything at all. Somehow the Qirsi felt that they could order him about as he himself might a servant, or a foot soldier in his army. And though he was appalled by the mere notion of it, he also knew that he had only himself to blame.

"What will you do?"

He looked up to find Brienne standing beside him, looking lovely and so very young. No wonder he had confused Affery for her.

"I don't know."

"You should go to the king. You should tell him what you've done and beg for his mercy."

"He'll have me hanged as a traitor."

"He might. But perhaps if you can show honor and courage at the end, it will save our house from disgrace. Don't Affery and Ennis deserve that? Doesn't Mother?"

The city bells continued to toll and Aindreas glanced toward the window. "There are men coming. I have to—"

Turning to Brienne once more, he saw that she was gone. He took a long shuddering breath and stood, walking slowly from his presence chamber to the nearest set of stairs, and then up to the ramparts of the tower. He found Ioanna there, wrapped in a woolen cloak, though it wasn't particularly cold. A stiff wind made her golden hair dance wildly, and she gazed eastward, squinting in the sun, though she had both hands lifted to her brow to shade her eyes. Ennis and Affery were with her. Seeing Aindreas, she pointed toward the road, a dark band of brown dirt that wound past tawny fields and small farmhouses to the city's easternmost gate. It was a long way off, but following the line of her gaze, Aindreas could see riders approaching the tor, bearing the purple and gold of Eibithar. The king's men.

"I sent Villyd to the gate," the duchess told him, her eyes never leaving the horsemen. "I hope that's all right."

"Yes. I would have done the same."

She glanced at him. "Will you go as well?"

He had yet to decide. Had it not been for the missive from the Qirsi, he probably would have. After Kearney's last message, with its tidings of the Qirsi woman being held in the prison tower of Audun's Castle, the duke had been searching for any path to reconciliation with the Crown. This was a time to end his conflict with Glyndwr and Curgh, to accept that he had been wrong, and unite the realm so that it might face the conspiracy united and strong.

His alliance with the Qirsi would not allow this, however. He had cast his lot with the white-hairs, and he had little choice but to fulfill his pledge to them. To do less was to invite disgrace, not only in the eyes of Eibithar's other nobles but also in those of his wife and children. Had it been only his life hanging in the balance, he would have gladly humbled himself before the king rather than help the white-hairs. But he could not bear the thought of bringing such humiliation to Ioanna or damning Ennis to lead a shamed house.

"Aindreas?"

"I'll go," he said. "If for no other reason than to send them away myself."

"Do you know why they've come?"

He shrugged, looking at her. "I refused the king's summons to a parley. And I've yet to pay Kearney his tribute for the last three turns." He gave a wan smile. "I'd think that has something to do with it."

She nodded, her lips pressed in a tight line.

Aindreas turned to go.

"Can I come, Father?" Ennis asked.

"Not this time, son." The duke mussed the boy's red hair, drawing a grin. Then he left them, stopping in his chamber to retrieve his sword, which he strapped to his belt. Though the riders would reach the gate before he did, he still took his time. *Let them wait,* he told himself, the pounding of his heart giving the lie to his bravado.

Sheftam, his horse, awaited him at the castle gate, though he hadn't ordered the beast saddled. Villyd, no doubt. It would speed his arrival at the city gate, and make him look even more formidable than he already was. The Tor atop the Tor, they called him, and with reason. Even before Sanbiri wine and the fine food in his kitchens made him fat, he had been a large man, broad and powerfully built. This messenger from the king would be merely the latest to quail before him.

He stroked the animal's nose for a moment, then climbed into his saddle and rode out of the castle toward the eastern gate. The lanes leading through Kentigern city were choked with people who paused now in what they were doing to watch the duke ride past. They didn't cheer. They only stared after him, their apprehension manifest in widened eyes and pallid faces. All of them could hear the bells echoing through the narrow streets, and by now word would have spread through the marketplace that the riders bore the king's colors.

One didn't have to be a minister in a noble's court to understand that Aindreas's defiance of the king had pushed Eibithar to the brink of civil war. And though the duke's people would not have dared give voice to any doubts they harbored as to his judgement, they could not hide their fear. Nor could Aindreas blame them. His own hands remained unsteady, and he was thankful for the castle that loomed behind him, ponderous and grey, like some great beast called forth by the clerics in Bian's Sanctuary.

When at last he reached the city walls and steered his mount through the massive gate, the duke found Villyd Temsten, his swordmaster, standing in front of more than half the army of Kentigern. Villyd had his arms crossed over his broad chest and his stout legs spread wide, so that he looked almost as unassailable as the castle itself. Before him, mounted still, their banners snapping in the wind, were nine men, all of them wearing chain mail and bearing short swords on their belts and bastard swords in baldrics on their backs. One of the men, who was clearly older than the others, wore a surcoat of silver, black, and red over his mail, the colors matching those of the baldrics. These were men of Glyndwr then, whom Kearney had brought with him to Audun's Castle upon taking the throne.

The city bells ceased their tolling, the last peals echoing off the city walls and dying away. A moment later, the older man rode forward a short distance, his hand raised in greeting. When he reined his mount to a halt again, the horse nickered, cantering sideways nervously.

"My lord duke," the man said, his voice ringing clearly over the wind, "I bring greetings from King Kearney the First, who commands me to ask that you shelter us and name us guestfriends."

The duke gave dark grin. "And why would your king ask that, Glyndwr? Does he fear for your safety?"

"Yes, my lord, I believe he does."

The smile fled Aindreas's face, and he felt his color rising. "Is there more to your message?"

The man's eyes darted past the duke to Villyd and the soldiers. "There is, my lord. But perhaps the rest should wait until we can speak in private."

The duke briefly considered forcing the man to say his piece here, in front of all. A moment later, however, he thought better of it. His men knew that their duke and the king were at odds, but few of them understood how far the conflict had progressed. He didn't want them to learn in this way that the duke was already considered a renegade in the City of Kings. By the same token, he wasn't willing to name them guestfriends and allow them to stay in his castle. If there were Qirsi spies about, he didn't want them to see that he had welcomed the king's men onto the tor. He couldn't very well make the men guestfriends if he intended to continue his defiance of the Crown.

"Very well," the duke said. "You and your men may make your camp in the shadow of these walls."

The man frowned. "My lord—"

"Make certain they're properly provisioned," Aindreas said to Villyd, ignoring Kearney's man.

"Yes, my lord."

Kearney faced the soldier once more. "I assure you, no harm will come to you here. My guards stand at this gate day and night." He grinned again. "And I have little doubt that men trained by Gershon Trasker can defend themselves from brigands and wolves, should any approach the city."

"Yes, my lord," the man said, clearly displeased.

"I'll send for you when I'm ready to hear the rest of Kearney's message." He turned his mount and started back through the gate. "Don't keep me waiting," he called over his shoulder.

Crossing through the gate and emerging once more into the city, Aindreas thought he heard a voice call to him. Turning, he saw Brienne again, standing amid the vendors and their customers, gazing back at him sadly. She shook her head slowly and mouthed the words, "End this."

Aindreas reined his mount to a halt, wondering if she meant for him to go back to the soldiers and welcome them into the castle.

"Brienne!" he called.

She began to walk away, drifting in and out of view as she passed the others in the marketplace. The people around the duke were staring at him, looking fright-ened and uncertain, but Aindreas was too intent on watching his daughter to speak to them. She glanced back at him once last time, then stepped deeper into the crowd around her and was gone.

He shouted her name again, but he couldn't see her anymore, and with all the people and peddler's carts lining the lane, he couldn't follow.

He raised himself up, standing in his stirrups, but still couldn't spot her.

"Are you well, my lord?"

He whirled toward the voice, nearly losing his balance. Villyd stood beside his mount, eyeing him with obvious concern.

"I'm fine," Aindreas said, sitting in his saddle once more. He looked for Bri-enne one last time, then stared down at the swordmaster. "Shouldn't you be taking care of the provisions?" he demanded.

"I have a man seeing to it, my lord. I wanted to make certain that you were quite yourself."

"I just told you: I'm fine."

"Yes, my lord. But I heard you call out. . . ." He swallowed. "I heard you ask-ing for Lady Brienne."

"Yes. I was . . ." He had raised his hand to point in the direction she had gone, but then let it drop to his side. Brienne was dead. Of course he knew that. But then who had he seen? "I think of her often, Villyd," he said quietly.

The man lowered his gaze. "Yes, my lord."

"I should get back to the castle. Ioanna will want to know about the riders."

"My lord, shouldn't we allow them to stay in the castle? Perhaps a gesture of friendship on our part will ease tensions with the Crown."

"I have no interest in easing tensions, swordmaster. If it turns out that the king's men have brought word of Kearney's willingness to address our grievances, I can al-ways welcome them onto the tor later. But until I have proof that they've come suing for peace, I'll give no indication of any willingness on our part to surrender."

"Yes, my lord."

Aindreas could hear the disapproval in Villyd's tone, but he chose to ignore it. He flicked the reins, and his horse started toward the castle once more.

"My lord!" the swordmaster called after him.

"Tell Kearney's man I'll speak with him tomorrow," Aindreas answered, not even bothering to look back. "I trust he and the others will be comfortable until then."

He rode the rest of the way up the tor as quickly as he dared. He didn't allow the horse to break into a gallop, not wishing to appear afraid or too eager to be back within the walls of his fortress. But he felt himself trembling again, and he had to resist the urge to search for Brienne's face among those he passed along the way.

As he ascended the winding road toward the castle gate, he saw Ioanna gazing down at him from same tower on which he had left her. She vanished from view be-fore he reached the barbican, and Aindreas knew that she would be waiting for him by his presence chamber, anxious to hear what Kearney's men had said to him. He would gladly have postponed the encounter until later, but he knew better than to try. Villyd and the others were afraid of him and easily put off; his wife was neither.

He left his mount at the stable and returned to his chamber. Ioanna stood in the corridor just outside the door.

"What did they want?" she asked, as he opened the door and gestured for her to enter the chamber.

He closed the door before facing her. "I don't know yet. Their captain wishes to speak with me in private. I'll grant him an audience tomorrow and hear what he has to say."

"Why didn't they come back with you to the castle?"

He looked away, stepping past her to stand behind his writing table.

"I didn't offer to quarter them in the castle."

If she thought him a fool, she did a fine job of concealing it.

"Do you think that's wise?" was all she said, her voice even.

Of course I do, he wanted to say. *Would I have done it otherwise?* Instead he shrugged. "I don't know. I couldn't bring myself to welcome them within these walls. I've ordered Villyd to give them whatever provisions they require." He gazed out the window, watching a flock of doves circle one of the towers. "If the weather holds, they'll have no cause to complain."

"They'd have no cause in any case," she said. "Not after what Glyndwr and Curgh have done to us."

Aindreas closed his eyes, rubbing a hand over his face. There was so much he hadn't told her, so much that she deserved to know. Yet he was afraid to reveal any of it, lest he see the shame he felt at all he had done reflected in her eyes.

"You must tell her." Brienne's voice.

Opening his eyes again, he saw the girl standing behind her mother, their hair the same shade of gold, their faces so similar that he nearly wept at the sight.

"What is it Aindreas?" Ioanna asked, a frown creasing her brow.

"Tell her, Father."

"There's something you should know," he said, wishing Brienne would leave them alone. He paused, searching for the right way to begin. *There's something you should know.* He nearly laughed aloud at his choice of words. The truth was he had so much he needed to tell her that he didn't know where to begin. *I spent the better part of the harvest torturing Qirsi in the castle dungeon, looking for someone who could lead me to the leaders of the white-hair conspiracy. Having finally found her, I proceeded to ally our house with the Qirsi traitors, all so that I could strike at Kearney and Javan and the others I believed at the time to be our enemies. I've since become convinced that it was the Qirsi and not Tavis who were to blame for Brienne's death. I've betrayed our land and shamed our house for generations, all for nothing. I'm sorry.*

That's what he should have said. But even knowing this, he couldn't bring himself to speak the words. He looked past Ioanna once more, gazing at Brienne, hoping she could read the apology in his eyes. She shook her head, tears on her face, and then began to fade, as if swallowed by a sorcerer's mist.

"Aindreas?"

"Yes," he said, facing his wife again. "You remember the message that came from Kearney about a turn ago?"

"Of course."

He took a breath. "In it, the king claimed to have imprisoned a Qirsi woman who had confessed to being with the conspiracy. This woman, according to Kearney's message, had admitted arranging Brienne's murder."

Ioanna shook her head. "That's impossible. Tavis of Curgh killed Brienne. We know that."

"We know what we saw, Ioanna. But this woman—"

"No!" she said, shaking her head again, so that tears flew from her face. "There was blood on his hands! Her blood! His dagger—"

She choked on the word, gagging and struggling to breathe until Aindreas thought that she might be ill. He reached for her, but she backed away from him, her entire body shaking, her trembling hands raised to her face, her eyes wide and wild like those of a feral cat, cornered and afraid. "You believe them!" she whispered. "You think this woman might be telling the truth!"

"I don't know what I—"

"Don't say it!" She leveled a quaking finger at him. "Don't you dare say it! He killed her! You know he did! They're lying to protect themselves, because they're afraid now! They know what they did to her, all of them! And they're afraid!"

"Ioanna—"

"If you give in to them," she said, her voice dropping low, the finger still aimed at his heart, like a blade, "if you surrender and let them do this, I'll hate you for the rest of my days. I swear it to you on Brienne's memory. We know what happened. They're trying to change it, to confuse us and fool everybody else in the realm, but *we know*. Don't let them do this, Aindreas. Do you understand? Don't let them."

What could he say to her? For so long he had been pouring his venom into her mind, telling her what he believed was true, and what he wanted her to believe as well. That she should spew the poison back at him with such fury was just one irony among too many. He took a step toward her, and this time she didn't back away. A moment later she was pressing her face to his chest, sobbing like a babe, clutching his shirt with both hands. "Don't let them," she said again and again as he held her, stroking her head.

"I won't," he murmured at last. "I promise you I won't."

Eventually her tears began to slow, her sobbing to subside. Aindreas gestured to one of the servants skulking by the door.

"Summon the duchess's ladies," he told the boy quietly. "Tell them the duchess needs to rest."

"Yes, my lord."

Still Aindreas held her, until two of Ioanna's servants came. Only then did he release her, kissing her forehead as she pulled away. She seemed dazed, only vaguely aware of where she was and who was with her. It was much the way she had been in the turns immediately following Brienne's murder.

"Put her to bed," he said to the women. "I'll be in to see her later. If the children need anything, send them to me."

They both curtsied, and one of them whispered, "Yes, my lord," before they led Ioanna from the chamber.

The duke stood in the center of his presence chamber for several moments after they had gone, cursing himself for having said anything to her at all, and cursing the Qirsi for their treachery and the ease with which they had ensnared him.

"Wine!" he bellowed at last, returning to his chair by the writing table.

He picked up Jastanne's message again. *You must break with Kearney now, and hope that others will follow.* They were asking him to knot his own rope and slip it around his own neck. They might as well have commanded him to lead Kentigern's army to the City of Kings and lay siege to Audun's Castle. None of the other dukes would stand with Kentigern now. Those who were inclined to side with the king would have been convinced by word of the Qirsi woman's confession. And those who had sided with Aindreas thus far weren't yet ready to stand in open defiance of the crown. Perhaps they would be eventually, when they knew for certain that they could stand together against an attack from the King's Guard and Kearney's allies, but not until then.

"They wish to make a traitor of me," he muttered.

To which a voice in his head replied, *You're a traitor already, made so by your own actions.*

"Where is my wine?" he called again, his voice echoing in the corridor like thunder.

A moment later a boy peered into the chamber like a frightened dog.

"You have my wine?" the duke demanded.

The boy nodded, stepping warily into the chamber. He carried a flagon and cup.

"Quickly, boy!" he said, waving the servant forward.

The boy set the cup on Aindreas's table and began to pour. But the duke grabbed the flagon from his hand, spilling Sanbiri red on the table and floor.

"Go get more," the duke said. "I've a mighty thirst today."

The boy fled the chamber, eager to obey.

The rest of that day and the entire night were lost to him in a fog of wine and grief and rage. It was only the following morning, when Aindreas awoke to a hard rain and keening winds, that he even remembered that the king's men had come and had made camp outside the walls of his city. Dressing quickly, he left his bedchamber in search of Villyd, only to find that the swordmaster was waiting for him outside his presence chamber.

"My lord," the man said, bowing to him.

"Swordmaster." He opened the door to the chamber and entered, with Villyd close behind. Now that he had found the man, he was reluctant to reveal his concern for the king's soldiers. Had Villyd had his way, the men would have been sheltered for the night. "I've been looking for you," he finally said. "When I saw that it had been raining I . . ." He trailed off, glancing toward his writing table, hoping that perhaps there would still be wine there. He would have given his sword for a drink just then.

"I had tarpaulin and poles taken to the men last night, my lord, as the storm moved in. I knew that you'd want them to be sheltered, even if they did come here as agents of the king."

Aindreas tried to keep himself from looking too relieved. "My thanks, swordmaster. As you say, we have no quarrel with these men, only with those who sent them."

"Quite so, my lord." Villyd hesitated, eyeing the duke closely. "Shall I send for their captain, my lord? He awaits word from you."

"Not yet, Villyd. Later, when I've had a chance to consider what message I want to convey to the king."

The man pursed his lips briefly, then nodded, "Very well, my lord." Still he lingered, seeming to muster the courage to say more.

"Is there something else you wish to discuss, swordmaster?"

"Forgive me for saying so, my lord, but I wonder if you've considered the consequences of further angering the king."

Aindreas glowered at the man. It was one thing for the duke to question his own judgment. It was quite another for one of his underlings to do so, even one as trusted and intelligent as Villyd. "To be honest with you, swordmaster, I haven't given the matter any thought at all. I don't give a damn if I anger the king, nor do I care if his men rot in their little camp outside my walls. Kearney offered protection to Tavis of Curgh when I was certain that the boy had killed my daughter, and he embraced Javan as his ally though Curgh and Kentigern were on the verge of war. He has shown no consideration whatsoever for the House of Kentigern. Why should I care a whit if I anger him?"

Villyd stared at the floor, his color high. "Of course, my lord. Forgive me."

"Now get out."

Villyd started to leave, turned once as if to say more, then shook his head and walked out of the chamber.

Aindreas didn't see the swordmaster for the rest of the day. Twice guards came to his chamber, asking if the duke was ready to speak with Kearney's man, and both times the duke sent them away, telling them that he would summon the captain when he was ready. The truth was, however, he feared this audience with the king's soldier. The duke didn't know what the man had been instructed to say to him, but he felt certain that the captain would expect Aindreas to reaffirm his loyalty to the realm or declare his intention to stand against the Crown. The duke wasn't prepared to do either. He needed more time, but it seemed clear that neither the conspiracy nor the king was willing to give it to him.

An hour or so after the ringing of the prior's bells, as Aindreas sipped from yet another cup of wine, someone knocked at his door again. Squeezing his eyes closed and rubbing them with his thumb and forefinger until they hurt, he called for whoever had come to enter.

The door opened and a soldier stepped into the chamber.

"My lord—"

"No," Aindreas said angrily, "I'm not yet ready to speak with him."

"I'm sorry, my lord, but that's not why I've disturbed you."

He narrowed his eyes. "Then what do you want?"

"There's a Qirsi woman at the gate, my lord. She's asking to speak with you."

Somehow Aindreas was on his feet. "Which gate?"

"My lord?"

"From which gate did she come?"

The man shook his head, a puzzled look on his blunt features. "She's at the east castle gate, my lord."

"No, I mean the gate through which she entered the city."

"I believe it was the north gate, my lord."

Of course. That was the gate nearest the quays. The king's men never would have seen her from their camp. He let out a breath, steadying himself with a hand on his table.

"Shall I bring her to you, my lord?"

This wasn't a discussion he wished to have tonight either, but he couldn't very well refuse her. It struck him as a measure of the Qirsi threat that he should fear this white-haired merchant so much more than he did his own king.

"Yes. I'll speak with her now."

The man bowed and withdrew. Aindreas drained his cup of wine, but when his servant lifted the flagon to pour more, the duke shook his head. "Leave me," he told the boy. "I don't wish to be disturbed."

The boy nodded and all but ran from the chamber. Aindreas stepped around his table and began to pace, wishing now that he had let the boy fill his cup before leaving. He was about to call the servant back when he heard a knock on the oaken door.

"Enter!" he said, a flutter in his voice.

The door swung opened, revealing Jastanne, slight and pale, like a candle flame, standing between two guards who towered over her.

Aindreas eyed her for a moment, then nodded to the men. "We'll speak alone," he told them.

Jastanne gave a wry grin and sauntered into the chamber, leaving it to the guards to close the door.

"I thought you didn't want to risk any more meetings," Aindreas said, trying to keep his tone light. "Only written messages, you said."

"Yes, I remember." She dropped herself into a chair. "But I thought a visit to your castle was warranted. The movement's leaders wanted me to make certain that you appreciated fully the importance of our last message." She opened her hands. "What better way to do so than to come here myself?"

"I only received your message yesterday. That's hardly time enough to give it the consideration it deserves."

"I realize that. But I also know that the king's men arrived yesterday as well." She tilted her head to the side. "Such a strange coincidence." The woman continued to watch him, as if searching his face for some response. When he offered none, she gave a small shrug. "In any case, I didn't want the arrival of Kearney's men to serve as a distraction."

It shouldn't have surprised him that she would know about the soldiers. No doubt the Qirsi had spies in every major city in the Forelands by now. But he found it disturbing nonetheless. Even had he been ready to make peace with the king and find a way to extricate himself from this alliance with the white-hairs, even had Ioanna allowed it, Jastanne and her underlings would have found a way to stop him.

"It hasn't distracted me at all," he said sourly, "and it won't. If you know they're here, then you also know that I refused even to shelter them in the castle."

"I'd noticed that. Your treatment of these men has been quite interesting, Lord Kentigern. You refuse to quarter them, but you offer them provisions and when the storms come, you give them material to build shelters. One might get the impression from all this that you're of two minds about this king you claim to hate."

"Nothing could be further from the truth. But I couldn't merely send them away, not without provoking the king."

She raised an eyebrow, a cold smile on her lips. "You don't seem to understand, Lord Kentigern. That's precisely what we want you to do. I would have thought that my message had made that clear."

He stared at her, as if seeing her for the first time, his stomach turning to stone. "You knew they were coming," he said hoarsely. "It was no coincidence at all that your message arrived just before they did. You were instructing me to turn them away."

"I prefer to think that we were offering you an opportunity to fulfill the oath you swore to us several turns ago. I must say that I'm disappointed you chose not to."

"You gave me no time."

"Nonsense! You've had since Qirsar's turn."

Aindreas shook his head. "That's not what I mean."

"I know it's not. But you entered into our agreement thinking that you would use us as a weapon in your dispute with the king. You gave little thought to what we would ask of you, because you believed that our movement could be turned to your purposes. Only now, with the arrival of my message and this visit from the king's men, do you begin to see how wrong you were. No doubt this is difficult for you, but to be honest, I don't care. You've pledged yourself to our cause, and we expect you to honor that pledge. You wanted to strike at your king; now is the time."

The duke stood dumb, like a man who had just been cozened out of his wage by one of the tricksters who followed the Revel from city to city. He could think of no words with which to counter what she had said, because all of it was true. He had thought to use them only to find himself a tool in their hands.

"I've yet to speak with the king's captain," he said at last, surrender in his voice. "Shall I send them away without granting him an audience?"

"I'm not certain that's enough anymore."

He swallowed. "What do you mean?"

Before she could answer, there came yet another knock, this one loud and insistent. Aindreas's eyes flew to the door, his chest tightening. "In a moment!" he called. He turned to the Qirsi woman and in a whisper said, "No one must see you here."

For a moment she stared at him, as if daring him to try to make her leave. After what seemed an eternity, with the pounding at his door resuming, she stood and walked to a second door, which led to the duke's private antechamber. Only when she was hidden within the smaller chamber did Aindreas go to the first door and pull it open. As he had expected, Kearney's captain was there, standing between two of the duke's guards.

"I'm sorry, my lord," said one of the guards. "We tried to stop him, but . . ." He shrugged sheepishly, leaving the rest unspoken. *But he's the king's man.*

The duke resisted the impulse to point out that two of his guards should have been able to stop one man no matter whose colors he wore. Instead he motioned the captain into the chamber, glaring at the guards. "Return to your posts," he said. "Make certain that none of the king's other men find their way into my castle."

The soldier looked at the floor. "Yes, my lord."

Aindreas closed the door smartly and turned toward Kearney's man.

"You have no right entering my castle unbidden."

"On the contrary, my lord. I have every right. I was sent by the king himself, who is sovereign of all lands in the realm. I awaited word from you for as long as I felt I could, but I refuse to allow you to put me off for another day."

Any other day he might have argued with the man, but with Jastanne in the adjacent chamber he thought it better just to hear what the captain had to say and be done with it.

"You bring word from the king," he said, prompting the man.

"I bring a warning, my lord. Your payments to the Crown are in arrears, you have yet to respond to the king's message summoning you to the City of Kings, and the king knows that you speak openly of rebellion. The king has been tolerant of these lapses thus far, knowing how you and your family have suffered in the last year. But his patience wears thin. Soon he'll have little choice but to send men to Kentigern in far greater numbers than he has this time."

Such arrogance! Aindreas wanted to slap the man, to watch the outline of his hand appear, livid and red on the captain's cheek. He knew, however, that these were Kearney's words, not the soldier's, and he found his old hatred of the king returning. This was why he couldn't accept Glyndwr as his ruler. This was why he had turned to the Qirsi.

"And does your liege speak only of threats and war?" the duke asked, his voice like a drawn blade. "Does he offer no apology for the injustices heaped upon my house? Has it even occurred to him to hear our grievances?"

"He will gladly hear your grievances, Lord Kentigern, just as he does those of all his loyal subjects. But you must first demonstrate your good faith by submitting to his authority and swearing an oath of fealty to the Crown."

Aindreas heard a light footfall behind him, his breath catching in his throat.

"Splendid!" Jastanne said, clapping her hands with clear disdain as she stepped to the center of the chamber. "Do you hear how he speaks to you, Lord Kentigern? He speaks of submission to the king's authority and oaths of fealty. But in return he offers only threats. How typical of you Eandi."

The captain's hand strayed to the hilt of his sword. "Who is this woman, my lord?"

"Don't you see, Lord Kentigern?" she went on, ignoring the man. "Your loyalty is wasted on such a sovereign. You owe nothing to Kearney, because he offers nothing to you."

"What is this?" the man demanded, the expression on his face almost comical. "What is she talking about, my lord?"

"I think you should go," Aindreas said, not entirely certain to which of the two he was speaking.

Jastanne smiled. "Now? When things are getting so interesting?"

"My lord—"

"This is my new first minister, Captain. And as you can see, she has little regard for what your king has to say. Frankly, I don't either."

Jastanne gave a small laugh. "Your new first minister?"

"I think you should leave," Aindreas said again, clearly speaking to the soldier this time.

The captain regarded them both in silence, shaking his head.

Finally, he started toward the door. "Very well."

"No," Jastanne said, stopping him. "This has gone on long enough."

"What?" the duke said, staring at her.

But she was intent on the captain.

It all happened so fast that Aindreas was helpless to do more than watch.

The muffled crack, so much like the splintering of wood, was followed an instant later by a choked cry of pain as the soldier collapsed to the floor, grabbing at his leg. A random thought: *she's a shaper.* Jastanne strode to where the man lay writhing, his face contorted with anguish. Candlelight glinted off something in her hand. A dagger; Aindreas hadn't seen her pull it from her belt. The Qirsi grabbed Kearney's man by the hair, lifting his head off the floor, dragging the edge of her blade across his throat. Blood pulsed from the gaping wound, a pool of red that spread across the chamber floor like fire across parchment.

He gaped at her, his head spinning as if he were fevered. *"Are you mad?"* He dropped to his knees beside the man, but already he could see the life fading in the soldier's dark eyes. There wasn't even time to call for a healer.

"No, Lord Kentigern. I'm merely doing what's necessary, what you couldn't bring yourself to do."

"Surely you didn't expect me to do this!"

"I expected you to honor your agreement with us. Now you have no choice but to do so."

"You are mad."

She wiped her blade on her trousers and returned it to the sheath on her belt.

"You'd best send Kearney's other men back to the City of Kings, Lord Kentigern. And then I'd suggest that you prepare for war." She glanced at the dead man one last time, then let herself out of the chamber.

Aindreas should have gone after her. He should have killed her for what she had done, though he wasn't certain how to go about killing a shaper. Instead, he just knelt there.

And the king's man stared sightlessly at the ceiling.

Chapter
Twenty-seven

Duvenry, Wethyrn, Amon's Moon waning

heir ride from the City of Kings to Rennach took two days longer than Grinsa had told Keziah it would. Two days. And though the gleaner and Tavis quickly found a Wethy merchant who agreed to give them passage across the Gulf of Kreanna, they had to wait a full day before he and his crew were ready to set sail. The man's price was reasonable, but they would be sailing to Duvenry rather than Helke, which would add more time to their travels. Still, Grinsa and Tavis were not in a position to be particular. Even the passage itself would have cost them a day had it not been for Grinsa's magic. The weather was clear, the winds calm, as he had hoped they would be for Tavis's sake. Indeed, the day proved so mild that the ship nearly was becalmed in the first hours of their journey.

The captain, a dour, black-haired Eandi, with a barrel chest and thick forearms that were tanned and marked with pale scars, had his men lower the mainsail and go belowdecks to row. Grinsa thought about offering to raise a wind, but judging from the way the captain eyed him, he knew the man would refuse. He and Tavis had been fortunate just to gain passage—clearly this Eandi captain didn't care for Qirsi. Still, their speed on oar was intolerably slow, and even with the waters of the gulf as tranquil as Grinsa had ever seen them, Tavis was leaning over the edge of the top deck, his face so ashen that his scars looked black.

With nothing to lose and time to be gained, Grinsa stood beside the young lord, using his magic to raise a soft breeze. He did it so gradually, with so little visible effort, that neither the captain nor his crew seemed to suspect anything. He even went to far as to draw the wind from the southwest, so that they couldn't steer a direct course to Duvenry, fearing that a more favorable wind might have raised the captain's suspicions.

Feeling the wind freshen, the crew raised the mainsail again, and the small ship began to carve a crooked course across the gulf. After a time Tavis raised his head, eyeing the gleaner.

"Are you doing this?" he asked, his voice low.

"Yes. I'm sorry, Tavis, but already this is taking more time than I would have liked."

The lord shook his head, the mere motion seeming to make his stomach turn. "It's all right. The sooner I'm off this damned ship the better."

They sailed around the north shore of Brigands' Island, a small mass of trees and rock whose narrow coves and difficult landings had once been a haven for privateers. Then they turned south, away from the promontory of the lower Crown and toward the port of Duvenry. The shore appeared close, as if they could reach it in just moments if they simply turned due west, but the passage took the better part of the day.

Tavis said little, though after emptying his stomach early in the journey, he did seem to adjust to the gentle rhythm of the ship. The captain's men ignored them, as if ordered to do so, leaving Grinsa to his thoughts and the subtle, constant demands of the wind he had conjured. Eventually, as the day went on, a natural breeze began to rise, and he was able to drop his wind, a good thing, since they encountered more ships as they drew nearer to Wethyrn, and it would have raised eyebrows had theirs been the only ship under sail.

As he watched gulls wheeling over the ship, and murres floating lazily on the gentle swells of the gulf, Grinsa's thoughts turned again and again to Cresenne and Bryntelle. For just that one last night in Audun's Castle, they had been a family, tied to one another by love and the shared sense that this was the future awaiting them, if only they could survive the coming war. He had long dreamed of again sharing his life with another, of knowing such passion and intimacy and—dare he think it?—joy. Years before, when he had been too young to appreciate fully what it meant to be tied to someone in this way, he had thought to share his life with Pheba, his Eandi wife, who died from the pestilence shortly after their joining. Now, it seemed, he had it with Cresenne. In the night they passed together, there had been the promise of a lifetime together. Yet there had been something else as well, an aching sadness, as if they both understood that the future they foresaw was but a dream. So many obstacles stood before them, so many paths to pain and grief and loss. Grinsa felt as though he were standing at the mouth of a great labyrinth, knowing that Cresenne and Bryntelle stood waiting on the other side, but unable to discern any pattern to the twists and turns in between that might lead him to them.

"Is that Duvenry?"

The gleaner looked up from the dark waters. Tavis was pointing toward a great walled city before them on the shore, bathed in the golden light of late day. Beyond the rocky coast and the formidable wall of the city, stood a great fortress, solid and implacable, grey as smoke save for the yellow and black banners rippling in the light wind above its towers. Grinsa had only been to Wethyrn's royal city once before, and that had been many years ago. But Duvenry Castle was unmistakable and there was no other city in the realm that compared with this one.

"Yes. That's Duvenry." The gleaner straightened, and glanced about the ship. Already the captain was calling for his men to lower the mainsail and return to their sweeps. They would be docking shortly.

"How long will it take us to reach Helke?"

Hearing the tightness in Tavis's voice, Grinsa regarded him for a moment before responding. His color had returned, leading the gleaner to hope that their return voyage across the gulf wouldn't take such a toll on the boy. But still the young lord looked anxious.

"We can still turn back, Tavis. There'd be no shame in it, despite what you might think. Certainly I would never question the wisdom of doing so, nor would your parents."

"I don't want to go back. I'm just asking how long the journey north will take."

Grinsa shrugged, staring at Duvenry Castle. "Five or six days, perhaps four, if we can manage to purchase mounts."

Tavis's father had given them more gold for the journey, though he had made no effort to conceal his disapproval. They could afford horses, and they would have no reason not to stay at whatever inns would have them. They would have little choice, though, but to stay in Duvenry this night before setting out for the northern city in the morning, and Grinsa begrudged even this delay. Every day he spent away from the City of Kings placed Cresenne, Bryntelle, and Keziah in greater danger, for each passing day increased the likelihood that the Weaver would grow impatient with Keziah's failure to kill Cresenne and would make another attempt on her life himself. The gleaner would gladly have traded all the gold in their pockets for a quick return to Audun's Castle.

"And you're certain he's in Helke?"

"Not entirely, no. In my vision the two of you were fighting at the northern end of the Crown, but I couldn't tell the time of year. We'll find him near Helke eventually, but I can't say for certain when. I can only hope that it's soon."

Tavis said nothing, and for some time they stood in silence, gazing at the city and its port as the merchant ship approached the shore, the rhythmic cries of the rowmaster and the splash of the sweeps marking their progress. Whatever else Grinsa might have thought of the vessel's captain, he could only admire the skill with which the man and his crew steered the ship to the broad wooden dock. In a few moments, the ship had been moored and the plank lowered. Grinsa and Tavis crossed the deck to where the captain stood, the young lord counting out gold coins to pay the man the balance of what they owed.

"W' made fine time," the captain said as Tavis handed him the gold, his accent so thick Grinsa barely understood him.

The gleaner nodded. "Yes, we did, Captain. Thank you."

"I didn' 'spect w' would when w' started out." He gave Grinsa a sly look. "Yer a good'un to have 'round, aren't ye?"

"I'm not certain I know what you mean."

"Aye, ye do." He started to walk away. "If ye need passage back, ye c'n 'ave it. Nex' time, though, give us a more d'rect wind. Crossin's slow 'nough as 'tis."

The gleaner could only smile. After a moment he touched Tavis lightly on the shoulder and gestured for him to lead the way off the ship.

It was a short walk from the pier to the city gates and before long they had found an inn at which to stay the night. Relations between Eibithar and Wethyrn had been good for centuries, and so they were able to eschew most of the precautions they had taken while traveling through Aneira. Still, because of Brienne's murder, the name Tavis of Curgh was now known throughout the Forelands, and the two companions agreed that it would be safer if the young lord went by Xaver's name instead of his own, just as he had while traveling through the southern realm.

At Tavis's suggestion, they spent much of the evening walking the streets of the city, searching for musicians in Duvenry's taverns. They asked about the assassin in several of the inns, describing his appearance and claiming that he was a friend who they were supposed to meet here in the royal city, but none of the musicians or innkeepers with whom they spoke seemed to know the man.

As they left the fifth or sixth tavern—Grinsa had lost count—the gleaner cleared his throat, intending to suggest that they return to their inn and go to sleep. They had a good deal of travel ahead of them, and he was eager to be on the road with first light.

Before he could say any of this, however, he heard a light footfall behind them. Apparently Tavis heard it as well, for they turned at the same time, both of them drawing their blades.

A woman stood before them, her face illuminated by a nearby torch. She had long hair, pale blue eyes, and a round, attractive face. In the dim light, Grinsa couldn't tell how old she was, but he wouldn't have thought her much past her middle twenties.

She eyed their daggers briefly, raising an eyebrow. "For men who claim to be searching for a friend, you're rather quick to draw your blades." She glanced at the short sword hanging from Tavis's belt. "You're well armed, too."

The sword had been Tavis's idea, and Grinsa hadn't approved at first, fearing that the weapon would only serve to draw attention to them. Few outside the courts traveled with such arms. It bothered him as well that he hadn't seen the blade in his vision, though perhaps he should have been heartened by Tavis's insistence that he bring it along. Didn't its presence here at least raise the possibility that his vision no longer carried the weight of prophecy? No matter his feelings on the matter, he did understand why the boy would want the weapon with him. He had seen Tavis training with Xaver MarCullet in the courtyard of Audun's Castle. Whatever the young lord's limitations with a dagger, he had some skill with the longer blade. And, as it turned out, this sword belonged to Xaver; no doubt Tavis took some comfort in carrying it with them on this journey.

"Forgive us, my lady," Grinsa said, relaxing his stance and returning his weapon to the sheath on his belt. From the corner of his eye, he saw Tavis do the same. "We've only just arrived in Wethyrn today and our previous travels have taken us places that are somewhat less hospitable."

"I see," she answered, sounding unconvinced.

"Can we be of service in some way?"

She seemed to consider this for several moments, her eyes flicking from one of them to the other and finally coming to rest on Tavis's face. "I don't think so," she said, shaking her head. "Forgive me for disturbing you."

She turned to go.

"You heard us asking about the singer," Grinsa said.

The woman halted, though she kept her back to them.

"You know him?" A moment later, he answered his own question. "Of course you do. Why else would you have stopped us?"

"I just want to go," she said softly, her voice trembling. "I don't want any trouble."

It was the last thing Grinsa had expected, though it shouldn't have been. They were tracking an assassin. "I assure you, my lady, we have no intention of harming you." He paused. "But you do know him, don't you?"

She nodded, turning slowly to face them once more. "I heard you say that you were his friends and that you were looking for him. And since I'm looking for him, too, I thought that perhaps we could help each other."

"Perhaps we can."

Their eyes met, and in that moment Grinsa knew: she and the singer had been lovers.

"I don't think so," she told him. She nodded toward Tavis. "I see his scars, and I see the way both of you draw blades at the least hint of danger. You're no friend of his."

The gleaner considered denying this, but he didn't bother. She wouldn't have believed him.

"It's important that we find him, my lady."

"Did he give those scars to the boy?"

"He didn't wield the blade, but he's as responsible for them as anyone. Does that surprise you?"

She shrugged, looking off to the side. "Not really. But it tells me that the boy must have wronged him in some way."

"I didn't," Tavis said, his voice hard and low. "I did nothing to him, and he killed the one—"

Grinsa laid a hand on his arm, stopping him. "It's all right," he whispered.

"Who did he kill?" she asked, her eyes wide.

"My lady—"

"Tell me."

"He killed someone dear to my friend here. That's all you need to know."

"But he would have had a reason. He doesn't kill for the sake of killing. I know him better than that."

"You're right," Tavis said savagely. "He doesn't do it for the sake of killing. He murders for gold."

Abruptly, she lifted a hand to her mouth, taking a sharp breath. "Gods!" she whispered, recognition in her eyes. "I had thought he might be a mercenary, or perhaps a thief. But it never occurred to me. . . . He's an assassin."

"What can you tell us of your time with him?" Grinsa asked.

"I'm not certain I want to tell you anything."

Tavis glared at her. "He kills for money. And still you protect him?"

"I didn't know him as a killer. I knew him as a musician, and as . . . as a friend."

Grinsa gestured toward the tavern door. "Can we sit together and speak of this, my lady? My friend can be a bit too direct, but he does make a point. You may care for this man, you may even love him, but that doesn't change who and what he is. You say that you know him as a singer; you may have known him to be kind as well. But I assure you that in time, he'll kill again."

"I saw him fight," she said, making no move toward the tavern. "We were returning to Ailwyck from Fanshyre, and we were attacked by road brigands. He was going to let them take the gold." She let out a small laugh. "If he was an assassin, the gold would have meant nothing to him. But when the men started to threaten my sister and me, he stopped them." She swallowed, shaking her head. "There were five of them, and he bested them all without any help from the rest of us. I'd never seen anything like it. He seemed almost . . . crazed, as if once he began to kill them, he couldn't stop himself. I knew then that he had to be so much more than just a singer."

Grinsa and Tavis exchanged a look, the lord looking pallid and terribly young.

"What name did he use?" the gleaner asked.

"Corbin." She narrowed her eyes. "Isn't that his real name?"

"It's not the name by which we know him."

"Maybe we're speaking of different men," she said, clearly wanting to believe this.

"No. It's the same man."

She seemed to shiver. A moment later she crossed her arms over her chest.

"Are you sure you wouldn't like to go inside, my lady?"

"What name did he give you?"

The gleaner hesitated, uncertain of whether he should tell her, though he couldn't say why. "Cadel," he told her at last.

"Cadel," she repeated, giving a slight shake of her head.

"How did you meet him? Was it in Ailwyck?"

"No. We met them several years ago. In Thorald."

"Them?" But even as Grinsa asked, he knew the answer. The other assassin, the man Cresenne had sent after him, the man he had killed in Kentigern Wood.

"Yes. Corbin and his friend, Honok." She had been looking off again, but now her eyes snapped back to his. "Did Honok lie about his name, too?"

The gleaner was certain that he had, but the man had given him the same alias, and he sensed that she needed to hear this. "I knew him as Honok as well."

"Honok wasn't with him anymore when he came to Ailwyck. Corbin said that they had parted ways some time back, though he told me they were still friends."

He saw no reason to tell her what had really happened to Honok. "So, was it mere chance that brought you both to Ailwyck, or? . . ." He stopped, the full import of what she had said finally reaching him. "You met him in Thorald?"

"Yes. My sister and I were traveling with the Revel, and—"

"When?"

"I told you, several years ago."

"What year exactly?"

Her brow furrowed. "I guess it would be three years ago." She nodded. "Yes, that's right. Three years."

Grinsa turned to Tavis, who was already watching him.

"Filib," the young lord said.

The woman nodded. "Yes. It was the year Filib the Younger . . ." The color fled from her cheeks and she reached out to steady herself against the wall of the tavern. "Demons and fire! He killed Filib, didn't he?"

"We don't know that," Grinsa told her, though there was little doubt in his mind. Marston of Shanstead was right. The conspiracy had been striking at the Eandi courts for years now, though the nobles and their Qirsi allies had been painfully slow to realize it.

"But that's what you think."

"You see now why we have to find him," Tavis said, his voice surprisingly gentle. "Whatever he was to you, he's also a killer. I lost the woman I was to marry. Thorald lost its duke and Eibithar its future king. We have to find him before he murders again."

"So you intend to kill him."

Grinsa winced, fearing that now she would refuse to help them. But the woman surprised him.

"You'd better have more than mists and winds, Qirsi," she said, eyeing the gleaner. "Because blade to blade, the two of you won't stand a chance against him."

"You followed him here from Ailwyck," Grinsa said. "Do you think he might have gone farther north?"

"I don't know where he went. I came north because there's little in Wethyrn's southern cities to attract a musician. Krasthem is a minor city, with few good taverns, and Olfan is little more than that. Ailwyck, Duvenry, Jistingham—those are the places I'd go, were I looking to find taverns in which to sing."

"What about Strempfar, or Helke?"

"Helke, maybe," she said. "It's smaller than some of the other cities, but the port is always busy, and seamen tend to like music when they put in to land."

Grinsa nodded. "Thank you, my lady. You've told us more than we had any right to expect."

She said nothing and after a lengthy silence, Tavis and Grinsa shared a look and turned to go.

"You were right before," she said. "He could be kind when he wasn't killing. And he sang with a voice that came from Adriel herself."

"Did the brigands hurt you?" Tavis asked.

"No, nor did they hurt my sister. But her husband is still recovering from the beating they gave him."

"I'm sorry. I hope he heals quickly."

"From the looks of your face, it seems that you suffered mightily for what Corbin did to you. You must hate him very much."

"More than I can say."

Grinsa sensed that they were now straying into dangerous terrain, and he thought it time to end their conversation. "Again, my lady, you have our thanks."

"Will you continue to search for him?" Tavis asked her.

The woman shook her head. "I've already been away from my sister for too long, and I've nearly run out of gold. Even if he is in Helke, I haven't the means to get there. And I'm not certain I want to be anywhere near the two of you when next you meet."

"No," Tavis said. "I don't believe you do."

She glanced at the gleaner, her expression grim, her cheeks still pale. Then she left them, walking quickly down the narrow lane that led back to Duvenry's marketplace.

"You were right," Tavis said softly, as they watched her go. "We do want to be in Helke."

Grinsa wasn't so certain. He had no doubt that they would find the assassin there. Even had the vision that came to him in the City of Kings not been enough to convince him, this conversation with the woman would have been. But after listening to her description of the singer's fight with the road thieves, he was more certain than ever that Tavis had been fortunate to survive his first encounter with the man. Chances were that he wouldn't fare so well the second time they met.

"You heard what she said about the brigands."

The boy nodded, still gazing down the lane.

"And still you're sure that you want to pursue this matter?"

"You said yourself that he'll kill again, given time."

"Maybe he will. But the last time he killed, he struck at the conspiracy."

"I need to do this, Grinsa. I need to clear my name."

Grinsa turned to face him. "Stop saying that. Your name has been cleared, at least to the extent that it ever will be. Cresenne saw to that when she admitted to the king what she'd done. Aindreas may refuse to believe it, and the lords of Galdasten as well. But for any reasonable person, her confession should be enough."

"So you think I should just let Brienne's killer go free?"

"I think you should admit that this is all about vengeance, nothing more, nothing less. The singer killed your betrothed, and because of that you suffered greatly, not only from grief but also from her father's thirst for revenge. I, of all people, know how much pain you've had to endure. I healed you, and I've journeyed the land with you for the better part of a year. I have no sympathy for Cadel, and I understand why you want him dead. But that doesn't change the fact that you only pursue him to exact a measure of revenge. No good will come of his death, should you manage to kill him. And chances are, you'll die in the attempt. All for nothing. You can tell me that you want to clear your name, to reclaim your place in the Order of Ascension, but in the end, you're driven solely by your need for retribution. You're no different than Aindreas."

As soon as he spoke these last words, the gleaner knew that he had gone too far. But rather than railing at him, the young lord simply stood there for a moment, his lips pressed thin, before stalking past Grinsa and entering the tavern once more.

"I'm an idiot," the gleaner muttered to himself. He would have liked to return to the inn at which they had taken their room. Tavis needed some time to himself before he would be ready to listen to an apology. But he wasn't sure that the young lord could find his way back to the inn, this being his first night in Duvenry. Grinsa waited a short while, though he knew it wouldn't be enough time to cool the boy's rage at what he had said. Finally, reluctantly, he stepped into the tavern.

He spotted Tavis immediately, sitting alone at a small table by the side wall, his back to the door as he sipped an ale. Grinsa walked to the table and sat.

"I'm sorry," he said.

The young lord stared at the dark ale in his tankard. "I'm not like Aindreas."

"Tavis—"

"I'm not. Aindreas assumed that I had killed Brienne, and so he tortured me. He enjoyed seeing me suffer, and it never occurred to him to wonder if he might be wrong." He looked up. "We know that the singer killed her, and I'm not interested in torturing him. I want to kill him and be done with it. This may be a quest born of vengeance, but at least it's justified."

"You're right. I was wrong to say what I did."

Tavis regarded him briefly, as he often did when the gleaner agreed with him. It almost seemed that the young lord expected Grinsa to argue with him, that he was surprised when the gleaner paid him any compliment or acquiesced to anything he said.

"What is it you saw in your vision, gleaner?"

Grinsa shifted in his chair. "I've told you. I saw you fighting with the singer on the north coast of the Crown."

"Did you see him kill me?"

"No. I didn't see the ending at all."

"But you saw enough to convince you that I don't survive the encounter."

He shook his head. "I swear to you I didn't."

"Then why is it that ever since that dream, you've been trying to warn me off this pursuit?"

"It's precisely because I don't know how it all turns out. If I knew he was going to kill you, I'd do everything in my power to keep you away from the Crown. And if I knew that you were going to prevail, I wouldn't be so frightened. But I have no idea what's going to happen, and that's a very difficult thing for a gleaner."

Tavis grinned. "We Eandi live with such uncertainty every day."

"Yes. And at times I don't know how you do it." They sat in silence, Tavis staring at his ale again, Grinsa watching him. "There will be a storm," he said at last.

Tavis looked up, his eyes widening slightly.

"And the singer will have cut you at least twice, though neither wound looked too serious. You'll be right on the coast, on rocks that are slick with sea spray and rain. But that can actually work to your advantage if you let it. On even footing, you're no match for him. You know that. But anything can happen when the terrain is uncertain. Try to use that."

The young lord nodded. "Where does he cut me?"

"Your neck and your right forearm. But as I said, neither wound looked too deep."

"Had I marked him?"

Grinsa hesitated, shook his head.

Tavis forced a smile. "Of course not."

"You can defeat him, Tavis. You have to believe that, or you're doomed to fail."

"I thought you didn't approve of all this, that you didn't want me to face him."

"I don't."

"Then why offer the advice?"

A barmaid approached the table, but Grinsa waved her away. He was in no mood for another ale. "If I were to command you to leave the Crown without facing this man, would you do it?"

"You know I wouldn't."

"Well, there's your answer. You intend to do this no matter what I say or do. And even if I were willing to kill him for you, I don't think you'd want that either. This is your battle, for better or for worse. I believe you have a role to play in the coming war, an important one, though I don't know what it is. I know you well enough to understand that you won't be able to fulfill that role until you've faced the assassin one final time." He gave a small shrug, opening his hands. "Your chances of surviving this encounter will be better if you know what to expect."

Tavis nodded, taking a long breath. "Thank you."

The gleaner stood. "Come on. We've a long journey ahead of us, and the sooner we get to Helke the better. We need sleep."

Tavis dropped two silvers on the table and they left the tavern, making their way back to the inn.

"Did you notice anything else in your vision?" Tavis asked as they walked.

Grinsa faltered, but only for an instant. Best to tell him all, the good and the bad.

"The singer seemed quite confident. He's not afraid of you, even after what happened in Mertesse." Then, to soften it, he added. "But that too could work to your advantage. Too much confidence can be a dangerous thing."

The young lord gave a wry grin. "Then I have nothing to worry about."

Tihod jal Brossa watched from his table in the back corner of the tavern as they left, keeping his face in the shadows, and his head lowered so that it would seem to all who saw him that he was just another drunk Qirsi, intent on his ale.

He felt reasonably certain that they would be heading back to their inn, and so he made no effort to follow them. He knew where they were staying the night, and he had every intention of following them come morning. For now it seemed most prudent to remain here until the Qirsi gleaner and his Eandi companion had time enough to put some distance between themselves and the tavern. Then he would return to his ship.

He had been fortunate to find them at all. Dusaan had sent him to Wethyrn in pursuit of different quarry, an assassin who had done a good deal of work on behalf of the movement and to whom Tihod had paid large amounts of the Weaver's gold. But late this day, as he left his ship, the *Silver Flame,* intending to return to the city marketplace, he saw a strange pair disembarking from a nearby Eandi vessel.

They would have caught his eye under any circumstances, but in his most recent conversation with the Weaver, Dusaan had told him of another Weaver living in the Forelands, a man named Grinsa jal Arriet. Dusaan had described this man briefly, but it was the Qirsi's companion who made him so easy to spot. He had never seen Tavis of Curgh before, but he couldn't imagine that any other young Eandi of noble bearing carried such scars on his face.

Usually Dusaan asked little of him. He knew that Tihod would gladly have done more for the movement, but he had made it clear long ago that he dared not risk Tihod's life on matters that could be handled by others.

"I need you to distribute my gold," he had once said. "And to do so in a way that makes it untraceable. No one else can do this for me." Tihod knew that he was right. The payments he made to Dusaan's other followers were not terribly complicated; any merchant with a bit of sense could have set up a similar network of couriers. But not all of them were so successful that they could absorb all of the imperial qinde Dusaan sent to him and exchange it for common currency, and fewer still had such extensive knowledge of all the major ports in the Forelands. And of these few, only Tihod had known Dusaan since childhood; only he could be trusted with the knowledge that the man was a Weaver in command of a great cause. It was no exaggeration to state that after the Weaver himself, Tihod was the most important man in the movement. This was why Dusaan sought to protect him. This was how Tihod knew just how much the Weaver wanted Grinsa jal Arriet dead.

Because when Dusaan spoke to him of this second Weaver, in a dream less than a turn before, he didn't hesitate to tell Tihod to kill the man if he had the opportunity.

"Remember that he's a Weaver," Dusaan told him that night. "Take great care in approaching him. But he's seen my face and so must die, and as much as I'd enjoy killing him myself, I can't risk waiting that long."

Tihod may not have been a Weaver, but he was not without formidable powers of his own. He was a gleaner and a shaper, and he also possessed the power of mists and winds, a valuable asset for any sea captain. He had some skill with both sword and dagger as well, and one did not brave the storms of the Scabbard and the unpredictable currents and winds of the Narrows without growing strong and agile. Watching Grinsa and the boy make their way from the pier toward Duvenry's marketplace, he had every intention of following them and making an attempt on their lives this very night.

But Dusaan had also told him to find the assassin. The man had not plied his trade on behalf of the movement in some time, though Dusaan's servants had sought to hire him for the past several turns. Few even knew where he was, and so when word reached Tihod that a man matching the assassin's description had been seen in southern Wethyrn two turns before, he steered his ship southward, past the Crown, to Grinnyd. He soon learned that the singer had been there only a half turn before, but had moved on. Rumor at the time placed him in Ailwyck, too far inland for a sea merchant to venture without calling attention to himself, but near enough to send a courier. Once again, however, the assassin resumed his journeying before the movement's gold reached him, and for much of Amon's waxing Tihod was at a loss as where to search next for the man.

But just a few nights before the Night of Two Moons, word reached him of another singer, a woman named Kalida Betzel who had sung with the assassin in Ailwyck and who, it was said, might even have been his lover. This woman had left Ailwyck shortly after the assassin did, journeying north to Duvenry. Having no other clues as to the man's whereabouts, Tihod came to the royal city as well, and soon found Kalida. He kept his distance, not wishing to raise her suspicions, but he gathered that she was inquiring after the singer, and the merchant guessed that if he waited long enough, she would lead him to the man.

It seemed to Tihod that more than coincidence and good fortune had brought Grinsa and this woman to the same city and, ultimately on this night, to the same tavern. But only when he heard the gleaner asking the barman about the very singer she had been seeking, did he finally understand. He remembered now that the assassin had been paid to kill Lady Brienne of Kentigern, and that Tavis had been blamed for her murder. Thus, it didn't surprise him when Kalida followed Grinsa and the boy outside, or when creeping to the doorway himself, he saw the three of them speaking in the lane just beyond the tavern door. He didn't step into the street himself, though he would have given a good deal of gold to hear their conversation. He merely watched, noting Kalida's shock at what they told her— was she just learning now of the singer's true profession?—and when the Curgh boy raised his voice in anger, hearing snatches of conversation. From what he observed, he could only assume that the Qirsi and the lord intended to continue their search for the man.

It seemed he wouldn't be killing Grinsa jal Arriet here in Duvenry after all. Clearly, the gleaner still had to die—Dusaan had left no question of that and Tihod was more than happy to strike the killing blow. But first, Grinsa and his companion were going to lead Tihod to the assassin, Cadel Nistaad.

Chapter
Twenty-eight

"H e's a good 'un, tha' singer at the Grey Seal. Best I've heard in some time."

The peddler took another long pull on his ale and wiped the foam from his mouth with the back of his hand. He had been talking to Grinsa and Tavis for the better part of an hour, drinking ales bought with Curgh gold and regaling them with tales of all the taverns in Helke.

"If it's music yer lookin' fer—good music, mind ye—tha's where I'd begin."

It had been Grinsa's idea, and Tavis had to admit that it had worked quite well.

"The closer we get to Helke," the gleaner had said a few days before, "the more likely it becomes that we'll run across people who know of Cadel. So rather than asking about him in particular, and possibly drawing attention to ourselves, I'd like to try just asking about the musicians in the city. From what we've heard, this man can sing. If he's there, we'll hear of him."

At the time, Tavis hadn't been convinced that the strategy would work, but on this night the peddler had given them all the information they would need to find the singer. And then some.

"Now, if ye like the pipes," he went on, draining his tankard and beckoning to the serving girl with his free hand, "then I'd send ye t' the Mainmast, over on the south end o' the city. Tha's a rougher place, though." He grinned at Tavis, revealing broken yellow teeth. "From the looks o' the boy, I'd say he's had enough o' tha' kind o' tavern. Better t' stick wi' the Grey Seal."

"Well, friend," Grinsa said, digging into his pocket for coins to pay for all the ale the man had drunk, "we thank you for your advice. When we're in Helke, listening to all this fine music you've told us about, we'll raise an ale and drink to your good health."

Tavis and the gleaner pushed back their chairs.

"But wait!" the peddler said with widened eyes, no doubt fearing the loss of his free drink. "I've told ye nothin' o' the taverns in Strempfar. The musicians there aren' as fine as those in Helke, but there are a few worth mentionin'."

Grinsa stood and motioned for Tavis to do the same.

"Perhaps another night, friend."

The peddler's face fell. "Very well. I thank ye fer the ale."

They left him there, sipping this last ale far more slowly than he had the previous ones and looking around for his next patron.

Tavis and the gleaner didn't speak as they wound their way through the crowded tavern to the door. Once they were in the street, however, Grinsa smiled, looking pleased with himself.

"I told you it would work."

"If you were half as clever as you think you are, you would have thought of this while we were still in Aneira, asking questions of barkeeps who refused to speak with us."

"I'm not certain it would have worked as well in Aneira. We didn't know what city he'd be in, and I wouldn't have wanted to listen to tales of every tavern singer in the realm."

Tavis nodded, conceding the point.

It was a warm night, the air heavy with a light mist and the faint scent of the sea. They were already in the dukedom of Helke, though they still had another two leagues to travel before they reached the ducal city. The sky flickered briefly—lightning from a distant storm—but they heard no answering rumble of thunder. It had been like this for several nights now, the pale glimmering of the sky holding out the promise of rain, but as of yet none had fallen.

"So now we know where to find him," the young lord said.

"Yes, I suppose we do."

Something in the gleaner's voice made Tavis falter briefly in midstride. It almost seemed that he didn't believe what the peddler had told them. Or perhaps he hoped that they wouldn't find the singer, fearing—knowing?—that Tavis wouldn't survive their encounter.

Tavis regretted having said anything.

They had hardly spoken since leaving Duvenry, though not because of any conflict between them. Tavis simply didn't feel like talking, and the gleaner seemed to understand this. The young lord could think of nothing but his coming confrontation with the assassin and what Grinsa had told him of his vision of their battle. He had bested the man once, in Mertesse, when Grinsa forced him to let the singer go, and he should have been able to draw some confidence from that memory. But if anything, it merely served to make him more afraid of their next meeting. Tavis had no illusions as to his skills as a fighter. He had brought along Xaver's short sword, hoping that it might improve his chances somewhat. Thanks in large part to his training under the keen eyes of Hagan MarCullet, he had always been good with a sword, far better than he was with daggers. But even so armed, against a man like Cadel Tavis could expect to prevail once in a hundred fights. And he had already claimed his one victory, hollow though it was. Chances were the assassin would prevail the next time they fought.

It's not too late to turn back. Grinsa had spoken the words so many times that Tavis now heard them in his dreams. And sometimes, late at night, when Grinsa was asleep and Tavis should have been as well, he considered returning to Eibithar without facing Brienne's killer. He wanted to avenge her. Ean knew he did. But he also wanted to live, to reclaim his place in the court of his forefathers and pass his years as a noble, as he once had thought to do. Certainly Grinsa would have leaped at the chance to leave Wethyrn. Even traveling in silence, Tavis sensed how much Grinsa longed to be with Cresenne and their daughter. He was equally certain that if he returned to Curgh without facing the assassin, his parents would welcome him back without question, as would Xaver and Hagan MarCullet and anyone else whose opinion mattered to him.

A few days before, Grinsa had said that Tavis pursued the man out of vengeance and nothing more. But in the days since the young lord had come to realize that he wasn't doing this for revenge, or for pride, or even for love of his lost queen. He did it for himself, because he knew that if he turned away now, and never faced the assassin, he would curse himself as a coward for the rest of his days. Was it better to die a fool's death than to live a long life hating oneself? The question had kept him up the last four nights running, and probably would again tonight.

"It shouldn't be hard to find the Grey Seal," Grinsa said after some time. "Chances are Cadel will be staying there—musicians often take a free room as part of their compensation. Perhaps we can find some way to gain access to his chamber—"

"You know that's not going to happen," Tavis said in a low voice. "We fight on the seashore. You've already seen it."

"I've told you before, Tavis. When I have a vision of someone's fate, be it in a dream or during a gleaning, I'm merely seeing one possible future among many."

"Then why tell me all that you did about my fight with the singer?"

Grinsa gave a small shrug, his mouth twisting. "Because if what I saw turns out to be real, I want you to know what to expect." He started to say more, then appeared to stop himself.

"You don't want that vision to be real, do you? You've said all along that you never saw the end of our battle, but you don't like what you did see, isn't that right?"

"When it comes right down to it, I don't like the whole idea of you fighting this man. But yes, given the choice, I'd rather you fought him elsewhere, somewhere a bit less—"

He halted abruptly, falling silent and turning his head slightly, as if listening for something behind them.

"Did you hear that?" he whispered.

"Hear what?"

"Footsteps."

Tavis looked back down the lane they had been following. They were near the inn at which they had taken a room and the street seemed to be empty. Actually the entire town, the name of which he had already forgotten, struck him as rather desolate.

"I didn't hear anything."

"This isn't the first time I've had this feeling."

"What feeling?"

"That we're being followed, watched. I even had it in the tavern just now, while we were sitting with the peddler. It seemed that someone else was listening to our conversation."

Had it been any other man, Tavis wouldn't have been alarmed. Even coming from the gleaner, it sounded like little more than irrational fear born of too many days worrying about assassins and conspiracies. But he had never known Grinsa to speak of such things without cause, and though he wasn't certain that a Weaver's powers of perception were any stronger than those of other Qirsi, he felt certain that they were more finely honed than his own.

"What do you want to do?" he asked.

Grinsa continued to stare down the street. Finally he shook his head. "I don't think there's anything we can do. If we were being followed, whoever it was will have seen us stop and will be ever more cautious." He started walking again, a bit more quickly than before, and the young lord hurried to follow him. "I should have been more careful," he murmured, more to himself than to Tavis. "Next time I won't turn until I'm certain that I can catch him."

Tihod watched them from a shadowy alleyway between a smithy and a wheel-wright's shop, cursing his own foolishness and fearing that at any moment the gleaner might start back up the lane toward where he was hiding. He had already determined to his own satisfaction that Grinsa and the Curgh boy were returning to their inn. After their conversation with the drunken peddler, he was certain that they would be eager to retire for the night, so as to begin the final leg of their journey to Helke with first light. Once he realized the direction in which they were walking from the pub, he should have stopped following and gone back to his own room. Instead, he had continued after them, ignoring the risk.

It had been no more than the scuff of his boot on the dirt lane that made Grinsa stop, a slight misstep that other men would have missed. Certainly Tavis hadn't noticed it. Dusaan would have, but the Weaver was not like other men—it seemed he and Grinsa had more in common than just the extent of their powers.

Perhaps wielding such magic—knowing that if the extent of their power were discovered by the Eandi they would be executed—made men like Dusaan and Grinsa more cautious than others, and thus more aware of their surroundings. Or maybe possessing so many magics that were linked to the land and the elements—fire, mists and winds, language of beasts—also served to heighten a Weaver's perceptions of the world in which he lived. Whatever the explanation, Tihod knew that he would have to be more careful if he were to make an attempt on Grinsa's life without getting killed himself.

He couldn't hear what the gleaner and Tavis said to each other, but after a few moments they started walking again. Without leaving the alley, Tihod watched them enter the inn. Still he didn't move, lest Grinsa was watching for him from within the tavern. Only after he had waited for some time did he finally step warily into the lane and make his way back to his inn and the small, dingy room he had rented for the night.

He missed his ship. For a man accustomed to sleeping in the comfortable cabin of his own vessel, being carried into his slumber each night by the gentle rise and fall of the sea, a tavern bed was a terrible place to pass the night. He hadn't slept well since leaving Duvenry, nor did he have much of an appetite. He knew that many found the sea unsettling to the stomach, but he, of course, did not. He didn't understand how anyone could live and sleep and eat on this dead rock they called land. On the ocean Tihod felt that he was riding the back of some great living beast, moving as she did, living by her rhythms and off her bounty. The pitch and roll of his ship on the ocean waves, the taste of sea spray on his lips, the scent of brine in the wind—these gave him more than a livelihood, they gave him life. They fed his appetite and his thirst, they told him when to sleep and when to wake, they gave life and color to his dreams at night. They even enhanced the act of love. He had once lain with a woman on land, in some tavern bedchamber in Aneira, and the experience only confirmed for him what he had already known. Women, like food and wine, like storms and sunsets, were best enjoyed on the sea.

Dusaan, who had never traveled well by ship himself, had nevertheless come to appreciate Tihod's passion for the sea, and so had been deeply surprised three nights before when he entered the merchant's dreams.

"You're not on your ship," the Weaver had said immediately, a look of concern in his golden eyes. "Why?"

They were standing together on Ayvencalde Moor, as they always did during these encounters, the stones and grasses bathed in bright sunlight, a soft wind stirring Dusaan's wild white hair.

Tihod told him of finding Grinsa and Tavis in Duvenry and of his decision to follow the two of them north to Helke, where he hoped they would lead him to the assassin. He had expected Dusaan to be pleased by these tidings, perhaps even to compliment him on his decision to follow the gleaner over land. Instead, he warned Tihod to be careful and vowed that they would speak again before the merchant and his quarry reached Helke.

Thus, Tihod knew even as he drifted toward sleep that Dusaan would walk in his dreams again this night. In fact, it seemed the Weaver had been waiting for him, for as soon as he fell asleep he found himself on the moor again, wading through the tall grasses. Dusaan stood some distance away, the still waters of the Scabbard at his back.

"What news?" he demanded, as Tihod halted before him.

"I'm in Krilde, less than a day's walk from Helke."

"Grinsa and the boy are there as well?"

"Yes. They spoke with a peddler tonight, a man who had heard Cadel singing in Helke just a few days ago. He gave them the name of a tavern. If all goes as I expect, this matter will be settled by this time tomorrow."

"This isn't something that can or should be rushed," Dusaan said, his face grim.

"I know that. I was only saying—"

"I want you to find the assassin before they do. Get to Helke first—leave tonight if you have to. Pay him the usual and have him kill both men. I don't want you fighting Grinsa."

"You're going to send an Eandi assassin to kill a Weaver?"

"He's killed Qirsi before."

"Never a Qirsi like this."

"And you have?"

"That's not the point, and you know it," Tihod said. "I'm sure that Cadel is very good at what he does—"

"He's the best in the Forelands."

"But skill with a blade or a garrote isn't enough in this case. No matter how good he is with a weapon, without any magic at his disposal, he stands no chance against Grinsa."

"Believe me when I tell you that you don't either."

"Then neither of us should make the attempt."

Dusaan narrowed his eyes, as if trying to gauge whether Tihod was merely arguing the point to anger him.

"This is a task for an assassin," he said slowly. "And should Cadel die trying to kill Grinsa, then I'll find another assassin. If necessary, I'll send a dozen. Assassins can be replaced. You can't."

Tihod grinned. "True. But I've left my ship, and come a long way. I refuse to allow this effort to be in vain. I may not be a Weaver, but I have powers and I know how to use them."

"Any power you have Grinsa can turn to his purposes. You think that because you can shape, and raise a mist, that you're powerful enough to fight him?" Dusaan gave a short, sharp laugh. "You're not."

"Perhaps you're right, but surely he'll be expecting Cadel to attack him. There's no chance at all that the assassin will surprise him. Both he and the boy know what Cadel looks like. They know he's in Helke. But they know nothing of me. If I strike fast enough, Grinsa won't have time to turn my powers against me."

Dusaan glared at him, the look on his face as cold and hard as ice in the northern reaches. Tihod had pushed him far, perhaps too far. Dusaan was not a man accustomed to having others argue with him, either in his capacity as Harel's high chancellor or as leader of the movement. No one else in all the Forelands would have dared speak to him this way, and though Tihod did not think that Dusaan would harm him, he did realize that one way or another, this discussion was nearing its end.

"You'll work with Cadel," the Weaver said at last. "There are two of them, there should be two of you as well. I still want you to get to Helke ahead of the gleaner. Find Cadel and tell him what's happening. I've heard that he doesn't particularly like taking our gold—apparently he has little more regard for our people than do the nobles he kills—but one would hope that he'd see the benefit of working with you in this instance."

"And if he doesn't?"

"Offer him more money. That always seems to work with the Eandi."

"And if after Grinsa is dead, he's still reluctant to take on this new job?"

"We have other inducements that should convince him to do as we ask. They always have in the past."

The merchant nodded. "Very well."

"I still don't like this, Tihod. I've made no secret of the fact that I want this man dead, but losing you would be too high a price to pay for his life. If it seems that your encounter is going badly, get away from him as quickly as you can. I won't think ill of you for doing so."

"Don't worry," Tihod told him. "I don't want him killing me any more than you do."

"No," the Weaver said, "I don't suppose you do."

Tihod awoke with a start to a room still dark with night. He had no idea of the time, though he couldn't imagine that it was much past midnight. Still, he didn't feel tired, and while he wasn't one of Dusaan's servants, to drop all that he was doing and follow the Weaver's commands, he did recognize sound advice when he heard it. Best he start for Helke now and find Cadel before Grinsa and the boy did. Had he been in a larger city—Duvenry, for instance, or Strempfar—he would have had to contend with a locked gate and guards who saw in every Qirsi a possible threat to their realm. But Krilde was too small a town for walls and guards. He could come and go as he chose. The innkeeper might think it strange that he was leaving at such an hour, but an extra five qinde would buy his silence.

In a few moments, he had dressed and was making his way down the tavern stairs and out into the warm night air. He didn't like being abroad at night, but the moons were still up, peering dully through the mist, shedding some light on the village and the surrounding country. And if his powers were enough to let him face a Weaver with confidence, certainly they were more than a match for any road brigands he might meet.

Soon Tihod was out of the village, following a winding, rutted mud road through the moors of the Wethy Crown. Under the red and white moons, the jumbled boulders and swaying grasses took on a ghostly quality, as if wraiths lurked behind each stone. The sky to the north flashed again and again with lightning, but the night remained silent save for the soft wind and the intermittent call of a distant owl.

He walked for several hours, pausing at dawn to pull a piece of dried meat from his travel sack and drink from a small spring by the road. With first light, he caught sight of Helke Castle, an austere ash-colored fortress that towered above the city of Helke. To the west he could see the waters of the Gulf of Kreanna, dark as a scar and dotted with whitecaps. The wind had begun to freshen, and Tihod smelled a storm brewing. It would rain later in the day. A sea captain knew such things.

By the time he reached the city walls, the gates had been opened, and though the guards at the south gate eyed him with the suspicion and contempt such men seemed to reserve for Qirsi travelers, they let him pass into the city without question. He went first to the marketplace, where he found a Qirsi peddler and asked about the Grey Seal.

"I hear it's a fine tavern," the man said, spreading his wares on the ground and pausing occasionally to examine his work with a critical eye. "Good food, excellent ale, and, as o' late, decent music as well. The cost is a bit dear, but tha' doesn't seem to stop them tha' goes there from fillin' themselves." He looked up, meeting Tihod's gaze. "It's no' one o' ours, though, cousin, despite the name."

Qirsi taverns and inns often bore names such as the White Dragon, or the Grey Falcon, as a way of letting Qirsi patrons know that they would be welcomed. They were, of course, free to spend their gold in any tavern, regardless of whether it was run by a Qirsi or an Eandi, but most Qirsi tended to limit themselves to those establishments run by others of their race.

"Yes, I had heard that," Tihod said. "I need to find someone there." Then, as an afterthought, he asked, "Is there an inn within the city walls where I might take a room?"

" 'Course there is. The Silver Whale, on the west side o' the city. Not far really from the Seal. Go t' the west end o' the marketplace, then follow the prior's lane toward the sanctuary. There'll be three narrow alleys on yer right—the first will take ye t' the Seal, the second t' the Whale."

"Thank you, cousin." He began to fish into his pocket for a coin to give the man, but the peddler shook his head.

"It's bad luck t' take free coin before the first sale o' the day. Me father always said so." He grinned. "Now, if ye'd like t' buy somethin' . . ."

Tihod laughed, quickly picked out a Sanbiri blade that looked to be worth perhaps half the price the peddler was asking, and paid him five qinde extra for it.

"A wise purchase, cousin."

"Thank you," Tihod said. "With what I've paid, I expect you'll tell no one of our conversation."

The peddler began once more to arrange his goods. "I recall no conversation, cousin," he said absently.

Smiling, Tihod left the man and followed his directions to the Grey Seal.

The inn looked much as he had imagined it would: well tended, with polished wooden tables within and a fine bar made of oak and brass. The barkeep was an older man, grey-haired and stout, with thick arms and a full beard. He eyed Tihod warily as the merchant stood in the doorway, searching the tavern for Cadel. When Tihod didn't see the assassin, he stepped to the bar, placing a five-qinde piece on the smooth wood.

The barkeep glanced at the coin, but remained where he was. "I think perhaps you're in the wrong place, friend," he said, the word *friend* devoid of any warmth.

"The Silver Whale is down the next lane from here. I believe you'd be more comfortable there."

"Thank you, friend," Tihod answered in the same tone. "I intend to take a room at the Whale. But I've heard that you serve a fine ale here, and I've heard as well that you have a singer who's worth hearing. I was hoping to speak with him."

"I haven't seen him today."

"That's all right. I've nowhere in particular I need to be. Why don't we start with that ale, then?" He sat, placing his travel sack on the stool beside him and making it clear that he had no intention of leaving the tavern anytime soon.

"It's a bit early for ale, isn't it?"

"I had a long night."

The barkeep stared at him for several moments before finally taking the five-qinde piece and filling a tankard. He started to make change from the gold piece, but Tihod stopped him.

"There's no telling how long I'll be here. We'll consider that payment for the next few ales."

The man frowned, then nodded and turned his back on the merchant, perhaps hoping to convince himself that Tihod wasn't actually there.

Tihod was still sipping this first ale—he had to admit that it was quite good—when he heard voices coming from the top of the tavern stairs. Glancing back, he saw three men, two of them were clearly brothers. They both had yellow hair, fair skin, and the same lean build. The third man, however, was tall and dark, broad in the shoulders, with long black hair, sharp pale eyes, and a beard. Looking closer, the merchant saw a scar on the side of the man's face. Judging from the descriptions he had heard of the assassin, he knew that this had to be Cadel.

He turned fully so that he was facing the men. Still, none of them appeared to notice him until they had reached the bottom of the stairway. Even then, the brothers gave him no more than a passing glance. But Cadel faltered when he saw him, the smile fleeing his lips, leaving a look as deadly as any blade the man might have carried.

The brothers halted as well.

"You all right, Corbin?" one of the brothers asked, looking from the singer to Tihod.

"Yes, fine," the singer said, never taking his eyes off the merchant.

"Why don't the two of you go ahead and eat? I'll be along shortly." The other men hesitated and Cadel looked at them at last, flashing a quick smile. "It's all right."

The two men moved off toward the back of the tavern, and Cadel approached Tihod, his hand resting on the hilt of his dagger.

"What is it you want?"

"We need to talk. Perhaps we should go somewhere more private."

"No. Here is fine."

"I disagree, Corbin." He put just the faintest emphasis on the name, but it was enough to make the assassin's eyes flick toward the brothers.

"Where?" Cadel asked, his voice thick.

"You tell me."

The singer exhaled through his teeth before walking back to where his friends were sitting and speaking with them briefly. Striding back toward the stairs, he cast a dark look at Tihod, and said simply, "Upstairs."

Tihod followed him to a small room with a single bed and a large chair. Cadel closed the door behind them, then whirled toward Tihod so suddenly that the merchant backed away.

"Now, who are you?" the assassin demanded. "And what do you want with me?"

"You may not believe this, Cadel, but I'm a friend. As to who I am, I won't give you a name, but I think you know already that I'm with the movement."

"I have no friends in the movement."

"I'm sorry to hear you say so. And here I came all this way, just to warn you that Lord Tavis of Curgh is on his way to Helke to kill you, along with a Qirsi companion who is a somewhat more formidable foe than the boy."

Cadel's eyes had widened slightly at the mention of Tavis. "How far are they from here?"

"They passed the night in Krilde."

The man shook his head. "I don't know Wethyrn very well."

"It's a small village about two leagues south of here. They should be reaching Helke today."

"Demons and fire."

"As it happens, I'm here to kill the Qirsi, so if you can take care of the boy, we should be able to eliminate this threat without too much difficulty."

Cadel regarded him with obvious mistrust. "And after that?"

"As it happens, I do have a small task that lends itself to your particular talents."

"No," he said shaking his head. "I don't work for you or your movement."

"You've taken our gold in the past."

"That doesn't mean anything."

"It does to us."

"I'm a hired blade. I've taken gold from many people, but that doesn't mean that I work for them."

"We're willing to pay you a good deal for this, Cadel, more than we have for any previous work you've done on our behalf."

"That's not—"

"Three hundred qinde."

The assassin gaped at him. "Just who is it you want dead?"

"The king of Eibithar."

"You can't be serious," Cadel said with a small nervous laugh. "I'd have to be a fool to make an attempt on the king's life. Audun's Castle—"

"He won't be in the castle. He'll be riding to battle within the next turn. We aren't certain yet exactly where he'll be, but I would assume it will be the north coast of Eibithar, near Galdasten."

"He'll be surrounded by his army. He might as well still be in the castle."

"We didn't expect that this would be easy, Cadel. That's why we're paying you so handsomely."

He shook his head again. "No. I'm not doing this."

Tihod said nothing for several moments. He could tell that Cadel meant what he was saying—this wasn't some ploy intended to increase his pay. "Very well." He stepped past Cadel to the door. "I wonder how your friends downstairs will react to the news that you're not really a musician, but rather an assassin who's been killing nobles throughout the Forelands for the past eighteen years."

"I'll kill you if you go anywhere near them."

"No, I don't think you will. Have you ever seen what a shaper can do to a blade, or human bone for that matter?"

For a long time neither of them spoke. Tihod kept his back to the man, but he could sense Cadel's frustration, his rage, and, at last, his surrender.

"I'll help you kill the boy and his Qirsi friend."

Tihod released the door handle and turned. "That's a start."

"That's the end of it. We'll kill them, then part ways. Shaper or not, if you come near me again, I'll kill you."

"This isn't a matter for us to discuss right now. Let's just start by dealing with Grinsa and the boy."

Cadel stared at him, clearly unwilling to concede even this much. After a some time, however, he nodded. "Do they know to look for me here, as you did?"

"Yes."

"How is that possible? Have I been that careless?"

"They learned that you were at the Grey Seal from a peddler in Krilde who spoke highly of your singing."

"But how did they track me to Helke?"

"From a woman you knew in Ailwyck, who was looking for you as well."

"Kalida," he said, his voice as soft as a planting breeze. "She betrayed me?"

"I don't think she did so knowingly."

"Does she know . . . what I do?"

"I believe she does now."

He closed his eyes briefly, shaking his head. "I'm a fool. It will follow me everywhere, won't it?"

"You mean the movement?"

The assassin shook his head. "Never mind. We'll take care of this matter, and then perhaps I'll take your gold after all. I seem to have little choice in the matter."

Tihod smiled at that. "Splendid!"

Bells began to ring from the city gates.

"Midday," the assassin said.

"Yes. They'll be here soon. We should prepare for their arrival."

Tavis and Grinsa entered the city of Helke an hour or two before the ringing of the prior's bells. The gleaner had made certain throughout the day's travel that no one followed them from Krilde, but at the same time he sensed that there had been no need for such caution. The feeling of being watched, even hunted, that had haunted him for the past several days had vanished completely. Rather than easing his mind, however, this only served to deepened his apprehension, as did the dark sky looming before him, and the distant, but unmistakable growl of thunder that now rode the wind.

Tavis was even more withdrawn than usual, his silence as ominous as the freshening wind and the smell of rain.

They walked through the marketplace, asking a Sanbiri trader there where they might find the Grey Seal. From there, they made their way to the western end of the city. Tavis was walking quickly and as they drew near the alley leading to the singer's tavern, Grinsa laid a hand on his shoulder.

"Slow down," he said, keeping his voice low. "This doesn't seem right."

"You mean because we're not at the shore?"

Grinsa shook his head, scanning the lane, searching for something—anything—that might explain this feeling of foreboding that had taken hold of him.

"Do you think that we're being followed again?"

And abruptly he did.

"Watched, yes."

Tavis drew his dagger from the sheath on his belt. "Do you think it's been Cadel all along?"

"Possibly."

"What should we do?"

"I'm not certain. I suppose we should find the tavern. But be watchful, Tavis. We may not be at the shore, but I think this is the day that I saw in my vision."

As if to prove the point, the sky brightened for an instant, and a few seconds later thunder rumbled through the city, louder than Grinsa had expected. The two companions shared a look and walked on.

They found the alley described by the trader and entered it warily. Grinsa had his weapon in hand as well, and he kept a loose hold on his magic, so that he might draw upon it at any moment. They hadn't gone very far when the gleaner felt a sudden, brief gust of wind brush past him, like a wraith. He faltered in midstride, struck by an odd sensation. *That was magic,* he had time to think. Before he could give voice to the thought, however, he saw a dark form emerge from a doorway and hurry off in the opposite direction.

"That was him!" Tavis said, as if scarcely believing his good fortune.

He started forward.

Grinsa grabbed for his arm, but wasn't fast enough.

"Tavis, wait!"

The boy spun. "No!" he shouted. "You're not going to keep me from doing it this time!"

"I don't mean to. But this is a trap."

"You don't know that."

"Did you feel that wind a moment ago?"

But the young lord was already looking over his shoulder in the direction the shadow had gone. "He's getting away! Are you coming or not?"

Cursing the boy, cursing himself for having allowed matters to come this far,

Grinsa followed. Tavis was running now, heedless of whatever danger awaited them in the alley, and the gleaner had little choice but to do the same. At any moment he expected to come face-to-face with the assassin, or perhaps the Weaver. He wasn't certain anymore who it was they were hunting, or who in turn was stalking them.

As it happened, though, there was no ambush, at least not in the alley. They ran for some time, following the twists and turns of the narrow byway until it suddenly opened up onto a far broader lane just a short distance from the city's western gate. Stopping in the middle of the lane, Tavis turned a quick circle, desperation on his face.

"Where is he?" the boy shouted. *"Where is he?"*

Grinsa scanned the street as well, though not for the assassin. He was certain now that someone was following them, even as they chased Cadel.

"There!"

Tavis was pointing beyond the gate. A moment later Grinsa saw it as well: a man with long dark hair, dressed in black and running from the gate, toward the water. Of course.

Immediately the boy took off after him, and again, as if swept up in his wake, the gleaner ran with him. Lightning arced through the sky, followed quickly by a tremendous clap of thunder.

They were through the gate in seconds and running across the moor, stumbling on dense tufts of grass and hidden rocks. The waters of the gulf looked angry and dark, and the waves pounding the rocky coast sent plumes of spray high into the air.

His vision. It was all coming to pass.

Except that in the next instant his entire world shifted in ways for which that dream couldn't have prepared him.

He could still see the assassin making his way toward the shore, and Tavis running after him, not losing ground, but not gaining any either. But he also realized that someone was behind him again, far closer than before.

He halted, started to turn, glimpsing a white beard and pale eyes. Still, he didn't understand the nature of this threat until it was too late. He felt the pulse of magic as only a Weaver could, and so had a split second to ward himself, though it wasn't nearly enough. He couldn't take hold of the other man's power—he had no hope of turning it back on his attacker. It was all he could do to recognize the magic—shaping—and to deflect it with his weaving magic. Had he not done that much, the man would have succeeded in crushing his skull before Grinsa could even see his face.

As it was, the magic missed its target by just a single span. Pain exploded in the gleaner's shoulder, searing and unbearable, as the bones there splintered like dry wood. Grinsa fell to the ground, a cry torn from his chest. He knew the second attack would be immediate, and he forced himself into motion, rolling over his good shoulder, gritting his teeth against the agony. Even as he scrambled to his feet, trying a second time to reach for the man's power, he felt the bone in his leg shatter, driving him to the ground a second time.

He couldn't see for the fire in his limbs, the pulsing anguish screaming in his mind. Magic could save him; he knew that. He could heal his mangled limbs. He could turn his attacker's power back on itself. He could shatter bones and burn flesh. He was a Weaver, and all of these magics were his. But pain held him like iron shackles, denying him his strength and his will.

"I've bested a Weaver," a voice said, seeming to come from a great distance.

And as the words echoed in his head, like the tolling of far-off bells, Grinsa sensed the man gathering his power one last time to strike the killing blow.

Chapter

Twenty-nine

 voice in his mind—Brienne's perhaps, or his mother's—screamed at him that this was folly, that he was racing headlong to his death. But still Tavis ran, his eyes fixed on the assassin. He was vaguely aware that Grinsa was no longer with him and he felt certain that this was important somehow. But he didn't stop to think it all through. The singer fled, and Tavis pursued.

The heavy clouds over the Gulf of Kreanna continued to darken, breakers hammered at the rocky shore, and lightning sliced across the sky, seeming to pierce the water's surface like a blade. Wind clawed at Tavis's clothing and thunder roared like some great beast from Bian's realm, but still no rain fell.

As Cadel drew nearer to the shore and the great rocks that withstood the gulf's assault, he glanced back, as if marking Tavis's progress. Whatever he saw must have pleased him, for he stopped abruptly, a slight smile on his lips, and turned to face the young lord. Tavis noticed that he had a dagger in his hand.

The boy stopped as well, pulling his blade free and glancing about quickly. He saw no sign of Grinsa. Was that what the singer had been hoping to see? Had he been trying to separate Tavis from the gleaner? If so, it meant that all this had been a trap, just as Grinsa feared.

Tavis started forward again, far more slowly this time.

"Come on, then, Lord Tavis," the singer said, his voice barely carrying over the wind and the pounding of the surf. "You've followed me this far. Don't tell me that you intend to stop now."

Tavis said nothing, but neither did he break stride.

After a moment, the singer's grin broadened and he began to nod. "Good. You've got some courage. I'll give you that much."

Approaching the man, Tavis pulled his sword free as well. He knew the footing wasn't right for the longer blade, but he thought it likely that Cadel had been preparing himself for a knife fight, and it occurred to him that anything he could do to upset the assassin's plans would work to his advantage. And indeed, seeing the sword, Cadel's smile vanished and he began to back away, seeming to search with each step for more favorable terrain. Soon they were off the grasses and on the slick rocks that fronted the gulf.

Tavis closed the distance between them quickly and while still in motion leveled a blow at the assassin's head. Cadel danced away easily, waving his dagger at the young lord, but doing no damage. Tavis swung his sword a second time to the same effect, then tried chopping down at the assassin's shoulder. This time, however, rather than backing away, Cadel turned quickly to the side, switching his blade to his left hand in a blur of flesh and steel, and slashing at Tavis's arm.

The boy knew immediately that he'd been cut, and he took a step back, allowing himself a quick look at his forearm. Blood was soaking into his torn sleeve, but he could still move his hand freely. Cadel was eyeing him closely, crouched low, his blade ready and the grin on his lips once more. Tavis raised the sword again and crept forward, searching for an opening. He feinted with the sword, hoping to strike with the dagger he held in his left hand, but the assassin gave him no opening. They circled each other, wind whipping around them, waves crashing against the rocks and dousing them with spray and foam.

Tavis swung the sword, missed, saw Cadel lash out with his front foot. He tried to jump away, but he wasn't fast enough. The toe of the assassin's boot caught him in the side, ripping the breath from his chest. He stumbled. Cadel's blade flashed, turning a swift arc toward his face, but he managed to duck under the attack before stumbling a second time, backwards this time as luck would have it, and out of harm's way.

Or so he thought. Seeing him off-balance, Cadel lunged at him. Tavis tried to block the blow with his left arm and strike back with his sword, but it seemed the assassin was expecting this. Moving so quickly that Tavis could do no more than watch, Cadel switched his blade hand a second time, striking the boy's sword arm with an open hand and stabbing at Tavis's neck with his dagger. Tavis tried to wrench himself to the side, but he felt the edge of Cadel's knife slice into his neck. He backed away again, raising a hand to the wound and seeing blood on his fingers.

The singer will have cut you, Grinsa had warned him in Duvenry. *Your neck and your right forearm . . . Neither wound looked too deep.* He should have expected this. So why was he shaking so?

Cadel was stalking him now, circling ever closer, as if he knew that he had nothing to fear from the boy, despite his sword and his thirst for vengeance. Tavis pretended to back away, then leaped at him, swinging the sword again. But as with all his other attacks, Cadel responded as if he had known all along what the young lord would do. Holding his ground, the assassin swung his free arm at Tavis's wrist, catching him with the full force of the blow so that the sword flew from Tavis's hand, clattering on the rocks before being swallowed by the waters of the Gulf.

Tavis quickly switched his dagger to his right hand, expecting Cadel to press his advantage. But the assassin didn't lunge at him again. It seemed he was content to have denied Tavis the use of the long blade.

"I'd say we're a bit more even now. Wouldn't you, my lord?"

Hardly, Tavis wanted to say. But he kept his silence. The assassin laughed, and the two combatants resumed their circling. Cadel passed his blade deftly from hand to hand, a confident grin on his face. He made a sudden move with his blade hand, and Tavis flinched, raising his arm to defend himself. But the attack never came, and Cadel laughed again.

"You should have stayed in Eibithar, boy. I would have kept away and we both could have lived out our days in peace."

He feinted again and for a second time, Tavis raised his blade hand. Rather than merely laughing, however, the assassin used this as an opening for a sudden attack. Launching himself at Tavis, his blade abruptly in the other hand, he slashed at the boy's chest. Somehow Tavis managed to catch hold of the assassin's wrist, fighting with all his strength to keep the blade from plunging into his heart. And he wasn't strong enough. Not nearly.

Tasting his own death, desperate to do anything that might forestall the fatal blow, Tavis allowed his leg to buckle. He fell to the rock, Cadel on top of him, but both of them fell awkwardly, and at least for the moment, the assassin's blade was no longer aimed at his chest. They rolled first to one side, then to the other, each struggling to free his blade to strike at the other. Out of the corner of his eye, Tavis spotted a figure hurrying across the rocks in their direction. Grinsa. It had to be the gleaner, though he couldn't see well enough to be certain.

"Grinsa!" he shouted. "Shatter his blade! Quickly!"

Nothing happened. They continued to roll, toward the raging surf now, the uneven stone digging into his back and legs. He could feel the assassin's hot breath on his face, he could smell the stale sweat in his clothes. They rolled again, and for just an instant Tavis found himself above Cadel. He fought to pull his arm free, but before he could raise his blade the assassin pushed off with his foot and they were turning again.

This time, however, as Tavis was forced down once more, he realized that he had reached the edge of the boulder. He let out a panicked gasp, trying with all his strength to halt their momentum. Cadel seemed to sense the danger as well, for he grunted a curse. For just a second, they tottered on the edge, both now fighting as one to keep their balance. But to no avail. A moment later they dropped off the boulder, releasing each other to try to break their fall.

Tavis landed hard on his side and shoulder, his head snapping down onto the wet stone. He sensed that Cadel had fallen beside him, but he was too dazed to strike at the man or flee. He saw a flash of light, almost immediately felt the thunder clap, as if it were a war hammer.

And then the rain began, instant and harsh, filling his mouth and nostrils as if he had been submerged in the gulf. He started to sit up, realized that he still held his dagger. Clawing the rain from his eyes, he tried to find the assassin.

He saw movement—the rain was too thick to see more—and raised his blade to stab at the man. He felt something crash into his temple—white pain blinded him as if lightning. Before he could recover, a fist crashed into his cheek and he sprawled onto the rock. The assassin was on him immediately, hitting him a third time, this blow to his jaw leaving him addled. He felt himself being heaved off the rock, but he couldn't seem to fight back.

Then Cadel released him and he fell, his chest smashing into the stone, but his head finding water. Shockingly cold. Salt stung the wound on his neck and another on his cheek. He tried to push himself up, but the assassin was on him again, his knee on Tavis's back, one hand like a vise, clamped on his neck, and the other holding Tavis's face in the water.

Fear seized his heart like a clawed demon. Tavis fought with all his strength to throw off the assassin, thrashing wildly, flailing with his arms and legs. But Cadel had him. He could hit the man, but not hard enough. He twisted his neck from side to side and managed for just an instant to lift his mouth out of the water. He gasped at the precious air, taking in some, but swallowing a mouthful of briny water as well. And before he could try again, or cough the water out of his lungs, Cadel had pushed him under again, tightening his grip on the young lord's neck and grasping a handful of Tavis's hair.

He whipped his limbs about, desperate now, his chest starting to burn, his head spinning. Something in the water gleamed and Tavis tried to reach for it, but it was too far. He groped around in the pool, searching for a rock or anything else he might use as a weapon. Nothing. His lungs screaming, consciousness starting to slip away, he reached for Cadel one last time. To no avail. He thought he heard laughter. The assassin's, or perhaps Bian's.

"I've bested a Weaver."

Grinsa heard the words. He felt the gathering magic. And so even without opening his eyes, even through the miasma of pain, he knew just where to direct his power. He would only have the one chance. If he failed here, he would die. He didn't need gleaning magic to tell him that.

He reached out with his mind, fighting off agony and fear, thoughts of Tavis and Keziah, Cresenne and Bryntelle. At his first touch, the man tried to resist him, and because Grinsa was so weakened, his attacker nearly succeeded. But the gleaner held fast to the magic he found, as if it were a scrap of wood and he adrift in a violent sea. Shaping, gleaning, mists and winds. The shaping magic was the only real threat, and once Grinsa had control of it, even this couldn't hurt him.

But he had forgotten how close the man was. Just as he opened his eyes to see his assailant's face, the man kicked his maimed shoulder. A wave of pain crashed down upon him, stealing his breath, nearly making him retch. For a moment he feared that he might lose his hold on the man's magic, but he clung to it, desperate and enraged.

Before the man could hurt him again, Grinsa hammered at his leg with shaping power. He heard the muffled crack of bone, a wail of pain from his attacker, and, a moment later, the sound of the man's body hitting the ground. Somehow the man kicked at Grinsa a second time, his boot missing the gleaner's shoulder, but striking him in the side of the head. Still drawing upon the man's shaping power, he broke the other leg as well. Hearing him cry out, Grinsa smiled grimly.

The gleaner wanted to shatter every bone in the man's body. He wanted to kill. But he needed answers first. Forcing his eyes open, fighting through his pain to sit up, he crawled to where the man lay.

The attacker was powerfully built for a Qirsi, lean, but broad in the chest and shoulders, with muscled arms. His face was ruddy, even tanned, at least compared to the skin of most Qirsi. His beard was full and he wore his long white hair tied back.

As Grinsa came closer, the man attempted to crawl away, his eyes fixed on the gleaner's face. With barely a thought, Grinsa shattered his wrist. The man collapsed to the ground once more, swearing through clenched teeth.

"Who are you?" the gleaner rasped. "Do you work with Cadel?"

The man reached for the blade strapped to his belt. Drawing on his own magic, Grinsa conjured a flame, which he held to the man's arm.

"Damn you, Weaver! Kill me already, and be done with it!"

"Not until—" Grinsa stopped, gaping at the man. "Weaver," he repeated. "You knew from the start that I was a Weaver—I sensed no surprise from you when I reached for your magic. In fact, you were prepared for it. You were warding yourself. You're with the conspiracy, aren't you? You were sent by the other Weaver."

He felt the man struggling to use his magic, not as a weapon, Grinsa realized, but against himself.

"You'd rather die that talk?"

"You wouldn't understand."

"Then explain it to me." And speaking the words, Grinsa pressed hard on the man's mind.

Usually Qirsi with mind-bending magic only used it on the Eandi. It worked best when the person at whom it was directed didn't suspect that any magic was being used, and most Qirsi could tell immediately when the power of another touched their minds. But the practice of this particular magic was predicated on two notions. One was that the Qirsi wielding the power didn't want his victim to perceive that any magic had been used. And the other was that he didn't wish to do any lasting damage to the victim's mind. In this instance, neither was true.

The man cried out in pain, his head cradled against his good hand.

"The other Weaver sent you," Grinsa said again. "Isn't that right?"

"Yes." It came out as a sob.

"Who are you?"

"Tihod jal Brossa, a merchant."

"How long have you been with the conspiracy?"

"Since the beginning."

The gleaner squeezed his eyes shut for a moment, trying to clear his vision. Then he looked at the man more closely. "Since the beginning," he repeated. "When was the beginning? When did all this start?"

"Long ago. The Weaver spoke to me of taking the Forelands from the Eandi before Galdasten."

"You mean before that madman brought the pestilence to Galdasten Castle?"

"Yes."

"Was the conspiracy responsible for that?"

"No. But we saw in it the opportunity for which we'd been waiting."

"So the Qirsi did kill Filib of Thorald."

"Filib the Younger, yes."

Grinsa exhaled though his teeth. Eight years the Weaver had been planning this. Every noble who had died since Galdasten might well have been a victim of his movement.

"I take it you're one of the Weaver's chancellors?"

The man stared at him. "You aren't supposed to know about the chancellors."

Grinsa lashed at the man's mind with his power until he screamed in anguish. "Are you one of them?"

"No. I'm more. I take his gold and pay his couriers."

The gleaner gaped at him. "What?"

"He can't pay them directly. He needs me to do it for him, so that no one can trace the gold back to him."

"So you know where the gold comes from!"

The merchant clamped his mouth shut. Grinsa felt him struggle once more to take control of his own power.

He tightened his grip on the man's magic and pounded his mind with mind-bending power.

"Tell me where it comes from! Is it Braedon? Is that where the Weaver is?"

The merchant screamed again, his head lolling from side to side.

A clap of thunder made the ground tremble and a moment later it began to rain in torrents.

Tavis! The gleaner had forgotten for a moment that the young lord was fighting the assassin. For all Grinsa knew, he was dead already.

"Tell me!" he shouted at the man. He pushed ever harder with his magic, heedless of the man's suffering. "Tell me, and I'll end this!"

Tihod said nothing, his mouth open in a silent wail. A trickle of blood seeped from his nose and was washed away by the rain.

"It's Braedon, isn't it?" Grinsa demanded, thinking it through. "That's why he needs a merchant, so that he can convert imperial qinde to common coin." He grabbed the man by the throat with his good hand and shook him. *"Answer!"*

A strange smile touched the merchant's lips, as blood suddenly gushed from his nostrils. "Never," he whispered.

Grinsa let go of his neck and forced open the man's eyes. The whites of his eyes were shot through with blood. One pupil was far larger than the other, and neither changed when the eyes were opened.

"Damn you!" the gleaner roared. "Tell me where he is!"

Even as he berated the merchant, however, Grinsa knew that the man was gone. His chest still rose and fell, though slowly and with great effort. But the gleaner still held his mind and his magic, and so could feel Tihod's life draining away.

"Damn you," he muttered.

He released the man and sat back, even that slight movement bringing another rush of pain. He needed to find Tavis and the singer, but first he had injuries to heal. His shoulder pained him more than the broken leg, but he could walk with a shattered shoulder. He placed his good hand on his leg and closing his eyes, probed the flesh and bone with his mind. He was weary beyond words, and the break wasn't a clean one, but he poured what power he still had into setting and mending the bone, grinding his teeth together as he fought the pain. It grew so bad that he had to stop once and vomit. But at last, as the bone fragments began to knit together, his torment eased, as did the nausea.

Soon he could stand and, though his leg still ached, and a fire burned in his shoulder, he found that he could walk as well. He gazed out toward the shore and the gulf waters beyond, straining to see through the rain that still pelted the coastline.

At first he saw nothing, but then he realized that there were figures standing on the rocks. Two of them. Neither appeared to be moving, although the distance was great and the storm still obscured his view. Were they both still alive, then? Was that possible?

He quickened his pace, shielding his eyes from the rain. But only when a third figure suddenly appeared, seeming to rise from the rocks and the water like some beast from Amon's deep, did the gleaner break into a hobbled run.

He held the boy fast, forcing his head down into the dark water and trying to keep the rest of his body still. Tavis was stronger than he looked, but he was no threat to Cadel, at least not anymore. He could thrash his arms and legs all he liked—it would only steal his breath. A few moments and it would all be over.

"Corbin."

He started at the voice, recognizing it immediately. He shouldn't have been surprised.

"Go away," he said, over the rain and the keening wind. "You don't want to be here for this."

Tavis twisted his head suddenly and managed to get his mouth out of the water for just an instant before Cadel strengthened his grip once more. He couldn't allow himself to be distracted. Not now.

"Let him go."

"I can't do that. He's as intent on killing me as I am on killing him."

"Why? Because you killed Lady Brienne?"

Cadel turned at that, keeping a firm grip on the boy, whose struggles grew more frenzied by the moment.

Kalida's hair and clothes were soaked, and rain ran down her face in rivulets. But her blue eyes were fixed on his, her brow furrowed.

"Yes," he said at last. "Because I killed Brienne."

"You're an assassin."

He turned his back on her. "You should leave."

"I followed you from Ailwyck because I wanted to be with you, regardless of what you are. I still do. But you have to let him go."

"This isn't some innocent boy I'm murdering for no reason, Kalida. He came here to kill me. He nearly succeeded in killing me a few turns back. If I let him go, he'll just try again."

Tavis's movements were becoming slower, weaker. A few seconds more and the boy would lose consciousness. It wouldn't be long after that before he was dead.

"In Ailwyck, when we were together, you were trying to change. I know that now. You didn't want to do this anymore."

"And you saw how that turned out."

"At some point you just have to stop. You can find an excuse for each new murder, be it gold, or revenge, or the need to defend yourself. But when does it end? Do you want to keep doing this for the rest of your life?"

He said nothing.

"Please, Corbin." A pause, and then, "Cadel."

It was his true name that reached him, that finally convinced him to relent. He did so knowing precisely what would happen, how all of this would end. But still, he didn't do it for love. He didn't even do it for Kalida, though he wasn't foolish enough to think that he would have released the boy had she not been there. He did it because he knew that none of this would ever end. Already he had told Tihod that he would take this newest job. They wanted him to kill the king of Eibithar, on a battlefield, surrounded by thousands of armed men. And he had said yes. He did it because of the brigands he had been forced to kill on the road leading from Fanshyre to Ailwyck, and because of the questions that had followed. He did it because of Brienne's ghost, whom he had encountered in the Sanctuary of Bian at Solkara.

"By this time next year, I expect you'll be dead," she had told him on the Deceiver's Night, her words carrying the weight of prophecy. After Mertesse, and his narrow escape in the tavern corridor, he had allowed himself to believe that the girl's wraith had been wrong. But no.

In a sense he did it because of all his wraiths. How many spirits could one man face on the Night of the Dead? How many kills was too many? He felt no sympathy for the boy, but he didn't want to stand before Brienne and Tavis together, not after what he had endured this past year.

Slowly, he eased his grip on the young lord, pushing himself off the boy's back until he was kneeling on the rock rather than on Tavis. The boy made no move to leave the water and so Cadel grabbed him by the collar and hoisted him out of the pool and onto the slick stone. Immediately Tavis began to cough and sputter, and his eyes fluttered open briefly before closing again.

"Thank you," Kalida said.

Cadel looked up at her. Perhaps he had been wrong a moment before. Perhaps he did do this for her. Their time together had been brief, but it had been the longest romance of his life. Such was the life of an assassin, the life he had tried so hard to leave, the life that had clung to him as Kalida's wet hair clung to her forehead.

"I'm sorry I lied to you," he said. "About my name, about who and what I was. As you say, I had hoped to change."

"I understand."

She smiled at him, and his chest began to ache.

"I have gold," he said, standing. "I've made a good deal over the years. I carry a bit of it with me, but there's far more of it hidden away."

He glanced down at Tavis. The boy was coughing less and had opened his eyes again, although he still looked dazed.

"I don't care about your gold, Cor—" She stopped, looking embarrassed. "I'm not sure what to call you."

"It doesn't matter, Kalida. Just listen a moment. The gold is in Cestaar's Hills, near Noltierre."

"All right, we can go there."

He shook his head. "No, listen to me. There's a pass just north of the city that leads into a narrow, grassy valley. A river flows through it, and there are a few trees, though it's fairly open. At the south end of the ravine there's a pair of oak trees— they're the tallest by far in the entire valley and easy to spot. The gold is there, buried between them."

She frowned. "I don't understand. Why are you telling me this?"

"Do you understand what I just told you?"

"Yes, but I—"

"Repeat it to me." Out of the corner of his eye, he saw Tavis staring up at him. His color had returned and he seemed far more aware of his surroundings. In another moment, he would remember the thing he'd seen, the thing Cadel had seen as well, but had ignored.

"The . . . the pass north of Noltierre," she said, her brow creased. "A narrow valley with two tall oaks at the south end. The gold is between them."

He nodded. "Yes. That's right."

"But surely you want the gold, too. It's for both of us."

Only someone who had never killed for hire could think as she did. She was strong-willed, and she possessed a fire, a passion, that her sister lacked. But she was far more innocent than she could ever know. That was the only way to explain the hope he heard in her voice, the belief that they might actually have a life together. Had she spent the last several turns as he had, trying to escape from all he had done over the past eighteen years, she would have known better.

"I'm sorry," he said again, seeing Tavis plunge his hand into the icy water.

Kalida said nothing. By this time she too had taken notice of the young lord. But she seemed unable to do more than just stare, her mouth falling open, her eyes widening in horror, as Tavis retrieved his lost sword from the water.

Even knowing the attack would come, even having resigned himself to his own death, Cadel was caught off guard by the speed with which the boy struck at him, the grace with which Tavis stood and spun. He held himself perfectly still, wondering that he should feel so calm, noting the way water ran off the gleaming steel, like small rivers flowing off the steppe. He saw rage and hate and bloodlust in Tavis's eyes, in the fierce, feral grin on his face. And he watched the blade accelerate until it became little more than an arc of silver light, like a ghost sweeping through the rain.

Only then, marking the trajectory of the young lord's sword, knowing where it would meet his flesh, did Cadel Nistaad close his eyes. At the end, he was aware only of the storm around him, and of Kalida's anguished cry.

The first blow sliced into the assassin's neck, nearly severing his head. Blood spouted from the wound, darkening Tavis's blade and pouring down Cadel's shirt. The assassin toppled to the rock, landing on his side and then rolling lifelessly onto his back.

Cadel made no sound, no movement, but still Tavis didn't hesitate. Drawing back his weapon a second time, he drove the point of his steel into the man's heart. Lifting his arm to strike again, he heard the woman cry out, saw her rush at him, her fists raised, her face contorted with fury and grief.

"Stop, you bastard! Stop it! Stop it!"

He dropped the sword rather than level a blow at her, and as she started to beat at his face and chest, he caught her wrists in his hands.

"Let me go!" she said wrenching herself from his grasp and falling to her knees.

For a moment he thought she might take up the sword, but instead she crawled to where the assassin lay, his blood flowing over the rock and mingling with the sea foam. She was sobbing, one trembling hand held to her mouth, the other reaching for Cadel's cheek.

"Why did you do that?" she demanded.

At first Tavis couldn't tell if she had asked the question of him or of the dead man. But a moment later, she turned to glare at him over her shoulder. "Why?"

"Because he killed Brienne, and too many others to count. Because he destroyed my life."

"He didn't want to kill anymore."

"I don't believe that," Tavis said. He was starting to shake, whether from the cold or the memory of how close he had come to dying, or the realization of what he had done, he couldn't say. "You know what he was. Even if you didn't believe us, you heard him admit it himself."

"He let you live. He didn't have to—a moment more and you would have died. But he gave you your life. And then when you attacked him, he didn't even try to defend himself."

The young lord looked away, rubbing his hands together. It was so damned cold. "That was his choice."

She didn't answer, but still Tavis felt her eyes upon him. After a moment he stooped to retrieve his sword. Xaver's sword. Returning it to its sheath, he glanced about, looking for his dagger. Spotting it near Cadel's body, he hesitated, then picked it up as well.

"You're a coward," she said. "You butchered a man who spared your life and allowed himself to be killed. You may have avenged Lady Brienne, and rid the Forelands of a hired blade, but that doesn't change the fact that you're a coward."

He made himself face her. "I know."

She stared back at him, as if unsure of how to respond.

He glanced at the assassin one last time, then started back toward the moor.

Before he had gone far, Tavis spotted Grinsa hurrying in his direction. He moved awkwardly, favoring one leg, and he held his left arm to his chest, as though it pained him. His face was the color of ash.

"Tavis!" the gleaner called, sounding relieved.

"You're hurt! What happened?"

"I was attacked by a Qirsi, a man working with Cadel. I'm all right."

"No, you're not," Tavis said, reaching him at last and immediately draping the gleaner's good arm over his shoulder so that he could help him walk. "You need a healer. We'll go to the castle."

"Cadel?" Grinsa asked, as they began to make their way across the grasses.

"He's dead."

"How . . . How did you manage it?"

Tavis shook his head. "Not now. I'll tell you eventually, but I need time."

"Of course," Grinsa said, concern written on his face. After a few moments he said, "I saw a third person with you."

"Yes. The woman from Duvenry."

Grinsa glanced at him. "Did you? . . ."

"Of course not," Tavis said with a frown. "She chose to remain behind. It seems she loved him more than she let on."

The gleaner nodded, and they walked for a time in silence, rain soaking them, wind whipping their clothes and faces.

"So you've done it, then," Grinsa finally said. "You've gotten your revenge."

Tavis swallowed, staring straight ahead. "Yes."

"How do you feel?"

He shrugged, uncertain of how to answer.

How long had he hungered for the assassin's blood? How many nights had he lain awake, tormented by the memory of waking to find his dead queen lying beside him on the bed? One needed only look at his face and body to see how he had suffered for Cadel's crime.

He should have been pleased. The weight he had been carrying for nearly a year had been lifted from his shoulders. Or at least it should have been. But still he felt the world pressing down upon him. He should have been thinking of how it would feel to face Brienne's spirit once more, to tell her that her murderer was dead, killed by Tavis's own hand. He should have been looking forward to the day when he could relate to his mother and father how he had struck back at the conspiracy, repaying the Qirsi in small measure for all they had stolen from the House of Curgh.

Instead, he found himself remembering a trivial incident that occurred in the ward of Curgh Castle. It had been a bright, warm day—the day of his Fating, as it happened. The day when all of this first began. He had been training, testing his skills with a wooden sword against a trio of probationers. And in the midst of their mock battle, he had used his weapon on a defenseless man, nearly killing him.

You're a coward, the woman told him this day, kneeling beside the man he had killed. And he had agreed. It seemed he had always been a coward, and always would be.

What kind of man raised his sword against helpless foes? What kind of noble allowed pride and vengeance to guide his actions?

"Tavis? Are you all right?"

"I feel nothing, Grinsa. And I don't know why." He looked at the gleaner, feeling tears on his face, hoping his friend would think them drops of rain. "I should be pleased, shouldn't I? What's wrong with me?"

"You killed a man, Tavis. If you were pleased, I'd be concerned for you."

He knew Grinsa was right, but still he had to fight to keep from bawling like a child. "At least it's over," he whispered.

"No, it's not," the gleaner said. "It's only just begun. We've a war to fight and you've drawn your first blood. But I fear we'll need your sword again before long."

What kind of man, indeed?

Chapter
Thirty

Glyndwr, Eibithar

he healers in Helke Castle had mended his shoulder and eased what remained of the pain in his leg. They healed the cuts on Tavis's arm, neck, and face as well, though the boy seemed to have suffered other wounds that lay beyond the reach of any healer. The duke of Helke clearly was not pleased to have Tavis of Curgh as a guest in his castle, but, perhaps as a way of honoring Wethyrn's longstanding friendship with Eibithar, he offered to let them remain for as long as they wished. They stayed only for the one night.

Grinsa was desperate to return to the City of Kings. He wanted to see his daughter once more, to hold Cresenne in his arms and protect her from the Weaver. He could tell that Tavis was nearly as eager as he to be leaving, though he sensed that the young lord's urgency had little to do with a desire to be back in Eibithar. He simply wished to put as much distance as possible between himself and the Crown.

The morning following their encounter with Cadel and the Qirsi who had attacked Grinsa, they secured passage on a merchant ship bound for Rennach. By the time darkness fell they were back in Eibithar. They slept that night outside the city, knowing that the duke of Rennach had allied himself with Aindreas of Kentigern, and would imprison Tavis if given the chance. Half a turn earlier, before leaving for Wethyrn, they had left their mounts with a farrier in a small village just north of Rennach. They reclaimed them the next morning, paying the man handsomely for his care of the beasts, and began the long journey back to the City of Kings.

Tavis had yet to tell Grinsa about his battle with the assassin, and the gleaner didn't feel that it was his place to ask questions. He could see that killing the man had left its mark on the boy. He was at once both more at peace than Grinsa had ever seen him, and more withdrawn. During their brief stay in Helke Castle, he had carried himself with the confidence and purpose of a noble, calling for healers immediately upon their arrival and insisting that they attend to Grinsa's injuries before allowing them even to look at his own gashes. When the duke asked why they had come to the Crown and who had inflicted their wounds, Tavis explained that they had killed two men who had been party to the Qirsi conspiracy, and cautioned the older noble to be wary lest he believe that Wethyrn was too remote to be of interest to the renegades and their movement.

It seemed to Grinsa that with Cadel dead, Tavis had been released at last from the haunting memory of his captivity in Kentigern and whatever guilt he felt for Lady Brienne's death. He no longer flinched when people stared at his scars, and except for the few hours they spent in and around Rennach, he made no effort to conceal his identity. But while he seemed to have matured five years in the span of a few days, he remained somber and distant. Indeed, if anything, killing the assassin had only served to deepen the darkness that had lurked within him for so long.

On the second night after their departure from Rennach, as they sat beside a low burning fire near Silver Falls, where the Thorald River flowed off the Caerissan Steppe, Grinsa asked the young lord whether he intended to ride with the gleaner back to the City of Kings.

"If you wish to return to Curgh instead, I'll understand," he said, eyeing the boy across the fire. "No doubt you wish to tell your mother and father that the assassin is dead."

"If I tell them that," Tavis answered, his voice low, "they'll want to know how I killed him. At least my father will. And I've no stomach for that conversation just now."

Grinsa nearly asked him then, but seeing the pained expression in Tavis's eyes, he decided against it. As it was, this was the closest the boy had come to telling Grinsa anything about what had happened on the Wethy coast. He doubted that Tavis would tell him more.

Three days after their conversation near the falls, the two riders reached Glyndwr Castle, where they thought to rest their mounts and enjoy for one night the comfort of real beds. Immediately upon riding into the city, however, Grinsa sensed that something was amiss. The marketplace was nearly empty of peddlers and buyers alike, and the few people they did see eyed the two riders warily, as if thinking them the vanguard of some invading force. On the other hand, soldiers were everywhere. The city bristled with them.

"Does this seem strange to you?" Grinsa asked quietly as they steered their mounts toward the gates of Glyndwr Castle.

"The guards, you mean?"

"The guards, the fact that there's no one in the marketplace. It's as if . . ."

"As if they're expecting a war?" Tavis said.

Grinsa stared at him, knowing instantly that this was precisely what he had meant to say. He felt an icy hand take hold of his heart.

The young duke of Glyndwr, Kearney's son, stood waiting for them just inside the castle gates. He looked small and lonely, as might a child whose playfellows had all abandoned him.

Tavis dismounted and bowed to the boy, as did the gleaner.

"Rise, Lord Curgh, and be welcome."

"Thank you, my lord duke," Tavis said, straightening.

"You bring tidings from the City of Kings?"

"No, my lord. We've been . . . elsewhere. You await word from the king?"

"Yes. I received word not long ago that I was to have the men prepare to march. We've been gathering weapons and provisioning for several days.

"Are we at war, then?"

"Not yet, but we will be soon. It's simply a matter of where the men will be sent."

Something in the way he said it caught the gleaner's attention. It seemed the duke wouldn't be riding with his men, and so wouldn't be fighting alongside his father. Kearney was still two years shy of his Fating, younger than any soldier in his army. Nevertheless, it couldn't be easy for him to watch his men prepare for war, knowing that he wouldn't be fighting by his father's side.

"Won't they go north?" Tavis asked.

"It's hard to say. The empire's fleet menaces us from the north, but the Aneirans are massing on the Tarbin. That's the shorter march. My father may send Glyndwr's men there."

"Do you know yet where the king will be going?" Grinsa asked.

"Not for certain, no. But I should think he'll go north."

Tavis glanced at the gleaner, his scarred face grim. "That's where Curgh's men will go, as well."

Grinsa nodded. Of course. The empire was the greater threat. No doubt Keziah would ride with Kearney, which meant that Cresenne and Bryntelle would be left alone in the City of Kings, with no one there to guard them from the Weaver's next assault. He could barely swallow for the tightness in his throat.

Tavis shook his head. "Aneira to the south and Braedon to the north. They've succeeded in dividing us."

"More than you know, Lord Curgh," the duke said. "My father expects that several of the houses will refuse to join the fight."

"What?"

"Yes. Galdasten, Rennach, Eardley, Domnall, and Sussyn. And of course Kentigern, as well."

"Surely they wouldn't just stand by while the empire and the Aneirans carved up the realm."

"He fears they'll do just that."

"Damn them!" Tavis said. "They're fools."

It all seemed to be coming together, like some terrible, fragmented dream. Even the little Grinsa had learned from the Qirsi he killed in Helke had convinced him that the Weaver was in Braedon. Why else would he have needed to send gold to his underlings through a merchant? "He can't pay them directly," the man had said. It had to be because he only had access to imperial qinde. Now the empire's fleet was poised to attack Eibithar's northern shores, and all the land teetered on the precipice of war.

"This is what the conspiracy has been waiting for," he said. Both of the young nobles looked at him. "The Weaver will wait until the slaughter begins, and the armies begin to weaken one another. Then he'll strike."

"Where should we go, Grinsa?" Tavis asked.

"If it's at all possible, we should be with the king when he rides." He saw Kearney the Younger wince, as if the mere thought of accompanying his father pained him. "I think we should leave for Audun's Castle immediately." *I want to see Cresenne. I want to hold my daughter.*

Tavis nodded and faced the duke again. "We had thought to pass the night in your castle, Lord Glyndwr, to enjoy your hospitality and your company. It seems, though, that the time for such pleasures is past. If we can impose upon you for some food to take with us, and for water and grain for our mounts, we'll be most grateful."

Once more the gleaner was struck by the changes he saw in Tavis. A turn ago, he would have left it to Grinsa to speak for them both and make such requests, lacking the self-possession to do so himself.

"Of course, Lord Curgh. Come, and we'll see to it immediately."

The two young men started to walk away, but Grinsa lingered in the ward.

"Is something wrong?" Tavis asked.

"No, I . . ." His eyes flicked toward the duke for just an instant. "I'd like some time alone."

Tavis seemed to understand immediately. "We'll find you shortly, then," he said, and walked away with Kearney.

Crossing to the far corner of the ward, where no one could see him, Grinsa closed his eyes and sent his mind soaring north and west, down off the steppe and into Audun's Castle. He quickly found Cresenne, sleeping of course, though it was the middle of the day.

As soon as she appeared before him, whirling around in the middle of the plain, her pale eyes wide with fright, he called to her.

"It's all right," he said. "It's only me."

Seeing him, she ran to where he stood, falling into his arms. He kissed her forehead, and, when she turned her face up to his, kissed her deeply on the lips.

"Where are you?" she whispered.

"Glyndwr."

"Are you coming here?"

He smiled. "Yes. We should be there in a few days."

"Gods be praised," she said, resting her head against his chest. After a moment she looked at him again.

"There's talk of war."

Grinsa nodded. "I know. Tavis and I won't be able to stay long. When Kearney rides, we'll go with him."

She swallowed, dropping her gaze. "Of course."

He looked down at her, pushed a strand of hair back from her brow. Her scars were fading, and she looked less weary than she had when he left for Wethyrn. "Tell me about Bryntelle."

Cresenne fairly beamed. "She's beautiful. She's getting big, and she smiles all the time." She lifted a slender hand to his cheek. "I think she misses her father, though."

He gave a small laugh, looking away. "I doubt that."

She touched him again, making him meet her gaze. She stood on her toes and kissed him. "I miss her father."

"And I miss you." He should have been happy; he was going to see them both in a matter of days. Yet already the thought of leaving them again made his chest ache, as if the Weaver had struck at his heart. "You know that I want to stay with you, that if all this—"

She held a finger to his lips and smiled, though suddenly there were tears on her face. "I know."

"This is what he's been waiting for, isn't it? This war is his doing."

"I think so. I don't know for certain, but it fits with all that's come before."

"I agree."

"If we're right, then he must believe that he's strong enough to prevail. He won't allow the war to begin if he has any doubt."

He saw so much fear in her eyes, as if she had foreseen in these final steps toward war the inevitability of her own death. "Maybe," Grinsa said. "Or maybe knowing of me, knowing how much we've learned from you, he feels that he can't afford to wait any longer. He couldn't have anticipated all of this, Cresenne. He escaped our notice for a long time—too long—and he did great damage to so many of the courts. But we've hurt him, too. He hasn't won yet. You see in this move toward war the confidence of a man who thinks himself on the verge of victory. I see in it the desperation of a man who sees success slipping through his hands."

"I want to believe you."

"Then do."

She took a long breath, finally nodding and forcing a smile. "I'll try."

"How's Keziah?"

"I don't see her much. With war coming, she's busier than ever. But I think she's all right."

"Good." He touched her silken hair. "You should sleep," he said. "And I have preparations to make. We'll be leaving here soon."

He kissed her once more, and was about to break his link to her mind, when she stopped him.

"The assassin?" she asked.

"Tavis killed him."

Her eyebrows went up. "Tavis did?"

"Yes."

She looked relieved.

"I love you, Cresenne. Kiss Bryntelle for me."

"I will. I love you, too."

The gleaner opened his eyes, blinked against the brightness of the day. Their conversation had tired him, but as he hurried to find Tavis and the duke of Glyndwr, that seemed the least of his concerns.

Within an hour, he and Tavis sat astride their mounts once more and were riding forth from the Glyndwr gates bearing two large leather pouches filled with cheeses, breads, smoked meats, dried fruits, and several skins of wine. The sun already hung low in the west. They wouldn't get far this day before having to stop and sleep, but Grinsa was glad to be riding again, closing the distance between himself and his family.

"I think he wanted to come with us," Tavis said after some time.

"Who?"

"Kearney. He fears for his father, and he wishes to have some role in this war."

"Did he say as much?"

Tavis shrugged. "I could tell. He and I aren't so different."

Grinsa considered this, remembering how sad and lost and terribly young the boy had looked as they bid him farewell at the castle gate. He shuddered to think of how quickly the young duke would have been killed in battle.

"You make it sound as though you're eager to fight."

Tavis glanced his way, perhaps thinking that the gleaner was baiting him. After a moment he faced forward again.

"I suppose I am."

Grinsa said nothing, and they rode in silence for several moments.

"The assassin had me, Grinsa," Tavis said abruptly. "He was on the verge of killing me. He'd knocked my sword away and was holding my head underwater. I tried to get free, but he was too strong. All he had to do was keep me there for a few seconds more, and I would have died."

Grinsa stared at him, not knowing what to say.

"Somehow the woman convinced him to let me go. And while they were talking, I retrieved my sword and killed him." He grimaced, looking like he might cry. But then he merely exhaled and went on. "He didn't even try to defend himself. He just let me do it."

"You couldn't know that he wouldn't fight back."

"But I did. I sensed it from what he was telling her. And I killed him anyway."

"Tavis—"

"It's all right. Given the chance, I'd do the same thing again. I wanted him dead—I believe he deserved to die." He looked at the gleaner. "But there was nothing heroic about it. I want you to know that."

"Why?"

He shrugged. "I'm not sure. You said a moment ago that I was eager to fight. I suppose I want you to understand the reason."

"Wars and battles have nothing to do with heroism, Tavis. If that's what you hope to find—"

"No, that's not it either. I just want to prove to myself that I'm not a coward. I thought I could do that by avenging Brienne, but I was wrong."

Grinsa smiled, which, judging from the look on Tavis's face, was the last thing the boy had expected.

"You're no coward, Tavis. That's been clear to me since Kentigern. You shouldn't need a war to make you believe it yourself."

"Maybe I shouldn't, but I do."

"You can't think that way, Tavis!" he said, surprising himself with his vehemence. "You have to see this conflict for what it is! When the time comes, we won't be riding to Galdasten simply to kill the emperor's soldiers, or even to repel his invasion, though we will do that. This war is a deception; it's a feint. You must remember that. Harel isn't the real foe and neither are the Aneirans. I know that you hate them, and I know better than to try to convince you that they could ever be friends of your realm. But you must put that hatred aside, for the good of all the Forelands. Our enemy is the Weaver and his conspiracy. Every arrow we aim at the soldiers of Braedon, every sword thrust that we level at the men of Aneira, strengthens the Qirsi. If I can prevent this war, I will. Failing that, we have to end the fighting as quickly as possible. The Weaver wants war, so we have to seek peace. He wants the Eandi courts divided, so we have to find some way to unite the armies of the seven realms against him. That's our best hope of defeating him."

"I thought you were our best hope."

Grinsa nodded. He remembered saying as much to the young lord during the snows, as they made their way from Mertesse back into Eibithar. "My time is coming," he said. He thought of Bryntelle; he pictured Cresenne in his mind, seeing once more the scars the Weaver had left upon her face. "I'm going to destroy the Weaver. I promise you that. But he'll have an army, and it will fall to the rest of you to defeat them."

"You're asking a lot of the courts. You realize that, don't you? None of these conflicts is new. Most of them date back a thousand years, to the time of the clan wars."

"I know. But the clans managed to overcome their differences once before, during the war against the Qirsi." Grinsa shivered. "The first one."

Tavis eyed him for another moment, but offered no reply.

They rode on in silence, nearing the edge of the steppe just as the sun dipped toward the western horizon. And all the while, Grinsa turned over in his mind what he had said to the boy. The realms of the Forelands could unite. He was certain of it. What choice did they have?

But another matter occupied his thoughts. Without intending to, he had, in effect, compared the coming war with the Qirsi Wars fought in the Forelands nine centuries ago. And having done so, he couldn't help wondering at his own role in the conflict. Hundreds of years before, when the clans faced invaders from the Southlands, there had been no Qirsi fighting alongside the Eandi, for there had been no Qirsi living in the Forelands. Ean's children had fought Qirsar's children; one could distinguish friend from foe by the color of their eyes. That is, until Carthach betrayed his people and helped the clans defeat the Qirsi army.

In this war, Grinsa's war, there was no such clarity. Or was there? He had just told the boy that the Weaver and his movement were the real enemy. By standing against the Weaver, Grinsa allied himself with the Eandi. Was he Carthach, then? Was he the betrayer of his people, the white-hair whose heart was more Eandi than Qirsi? He wanted to believe that this looming conflict had no precedent in the history of the Forelands. Never before had Weavers waged war against each other.

Never before had the nobles of the seven realms had so much difficulty discerning their enemies.

Still, try as he might, the gleaner could not rid himself of the feeling that history had turned back on itself, that the Forelands were crumbling under the weight of conflicts as ancient as the land itself. And though he had resolved long ago to vanquish the Weaver and his movement or die in the attempt, he wondered if his people would judge him as cruelly as they had the traitor Carthach.

"Was everything all right in the City of Kings?"

Grinsa looked at Tavis. "What?"

"With Cresenne and your daughter."

He nodded, trying with little success to thrust thoughts of Carthach from his mind. "Yes, fine. Thank you."

"You're looking forward to seeing them."

"Of course." Grinsa smiled, though he felt as if his heart were being cleaved in two. *How will I ever find the strength to leave them again?*

"Then why do you sound like a man in mourning?"

The gleaner shook his head. "It's hard to explain."

Tavis regarded him for a moment before facing forward again. "Actually," he said, "you don't have to." And Grinsa believed him.

"We owe you a great debt, Grinsa," the young lord went on after a brief pause. "Few realize it, but they will before all of this is over. I'll make certain of it."

"That's not necessary."

"But it is. You could easily have decided to stay with Cresenne, and no one would have thought any the worse of you for it. Instead you're risking your life and your family in defense of the Forelands. I know of few men who would make the same choice."

He shrugged. "There are a good many among my people who wouldn't see it as you do."

Tavis frowned. "Like who? The Weaver? The man you killed in Helke?"

"Not just them. I'm a Weaver who fights to preserve the Eandi courts. Some would see that as a betrayal."

The boy reined his mount to a halt and stared at Grinsa, forcing the gleaner to stop as well.

"I'm not sure which is more ridiculous: the suggestion that you're doing all this to preserve the courts or the idea that you should care what such people might think of you."

Grinsa looked away. "You wouldn't understand."

"What wouldn't I understand, Grinsa? The pain of being judged unfairly? The shame of being hated by one's own people? Who could understand those things better than I?"

Grinsa opened his mouth to argue, but somehow he couldn't bring himself to give voice to the doubts with which he'd been grappling for much of the day. Tavis was right—if he couldn't understand, no one in the Forelands could. Perhaps that was the point. Tavis would think him a fool for comparing himself to Carthach, and just maybe he'd be right about that, too.

"You're not fighting for the courts, Grinsa, and neither am I. We're fighting to keep the Weaver from ruling the land. We're fighting because, as flawed as some Eandi nobles may be, he's worse. He's arbitrary, and cruel, and given the chance, he'll prove himself the most brutal despot the Forelands have ever known."

"You and I know that. But others . . ." The gleaner shook his head.

"Do you remember Kearney's investiture? You tried to tell me that I had to learn to live without the acceptance of the other nobles, that it was enough for me to believe in my own innocence, regardless of what they thought."

"I remember."

"This isn't that different. You haven't betrayed anyone. The Weaver claims to fight for all Qirsi, yet he hurt your sister when she defied him, and he threatened to kill her if she failed to do as he commanded. He tortured Cresenne, and would have killed her if you hadn't stopped him. That's treachery, the worst kind. Even if no one else sees it that way, you know it to be true. That's why you fight him, and that's why you have to prevail." The young lord turned his head, gazing northward, as if he could see the army of Braedon massing on the Moorlands. "You're as honorable and as wise a man as I've ever known, Grinsa. For the last year you've been telling me that nothing matters more than defeating the conspiracy. And I've believed you, at first because I didn't know any better, but more recently because I've seen the evil of this Weaver. I've seen how he treats those who serve him, and I've seen the lengths to which he'll go to feed his ambition." Tavis faced him again. "But I shouldn't have to tell you any of this. You healed my wounds in Kentigern, and you healed Cresenne's in Audun's Castle. You shouldn't need me to tell you that you're fighting a worthy battle."

Grinsa looked at the young noble for several moments, saying nothing, trying to discern in the man he saw before him some sign of the spoiled boy he met in the gleaning tent in Curgh city just over a year ago. "Thank you, Tavis," he said at last. "I needed to hear that."

The young lord's eyebrows went up in surprise. "Really? I expected you to be angry with me."

The gleaner smiled and shook his head. "No. If you haven't earned the right to speak to me so, I don't know who has." He glanced to the west. The sun stood balanced on the horizon, bathing the highlands in its golden glow. "We should ride. We haven't much light left."

They started northward once more, their shadows stretching across the grasses. His doubts lingered still, but perhaps that was as it should be. Only a fool rode to war without misgivings. He knew, though, that he was meant to fight this war, to stand against the Weaver, regardless of how history might remember him. And for better or worse, it was Tavis's fate to fight beside him.

About the Author

DAVID B. COE has published five other fantasy novels. His first series, *The Lon-Tobyn Chronicle* received the William L. Crawford Memorial Fantasy Award. He lives in Tennessee with his wife, their two daughters, and, of course, Buddy, the wonder dog. *Bonds of Vengeance* is the third volume of *Winds of the Forelands*. Two more volumes are planned for the series: *Shapers of Darkness* and *Weavers of War*.